BLACKBEARD'S BLOOD

THE VOYAGES OF QUEEN ANNE'S REVENGE COLLECTION TWO

JEREMY MCLEAN

POINTS OF SAIL
PUBLISHING

Points of Sail Publishing
P.O. Box 30083 Prospect Plaza
FREDERICTON, New Brunswick
E3B 0H8, Canada

Edited by Ethan James Clarke

and

Edited by Vicky Brewster
https://vickybrewstereditor.com/

This is a work of fiction. Any similarity to persons, living or dead, is purely coincidental... Or is it?

ACKNOWLEDGEMENTS

As the next compilation of four books, I wanted to challenge myself with my writing. I tried to send Blackbeard beyond the trappings of the first two books' search for the keys, and hopefully create characters worthy of a reader's interest. It took many years to get there, more than the first two books, but I feel I accomplished my goal.

Throughout it all I've been supported by loyal fans sending encouraging emails, a loving wife who supports me when I'm in over my head trying to meet a self-imposed deadline, and my parents who give constant feedback on my writing even when it's mainly praise (As parents are wont to do. At least aside from the one time my father, after reading a very early draft, wondered if I was going to fix all the spelling mistakes.)

I hope you'll all stick with me as I try to finish the series.

PREFACE

Hello! I want to first thank you for your purchase of this collection of novels. If you're not familiar with them, this is the second compilation which contains the third and fourth novels in a series about the origins of the dreaded pirate Blackbeard with a fantasy spin on things, and the third and fourth novellas in a series about the pirate Bartholomew Roberts in a straight historical fiction setting.

If you haven't gotten the first compilation or read the first two books in their respective series, I highly recommend you do so. It being a series should make it understandable, but these books contain characters who were not who they were in books one and two and it builds on the story that came before. Enemies met in passing, shared bonds and old wounds come to haunt the crew in these books, and it won't feel the same without reading them in order.

I will warn you that the first two books are a little rough (they are my first two books I've ever written), but, unless I'm being too biased, they do get better the more you read.

And of course, I just hope you enjoy them however you try to chart the waters of Blackbeard and Bartholomew Roberts' voyages.

Don't forget to let me know what you think of them as well by dropping a review and sharing it with friends and family. It helps more than you'll ever know.

TABLE OF CONTENTS

BLACKBEARD'S JUSTICE

BLACKBEARD'S FAMILY

BARTHOLOMEW ROBERTS' MERCY

BARTHOLOMEW ROBERTS' SPIRIT

BOOK THREE OF
THE VOYAGES OF QUEEN ANNE'S REVENGE

BLACKBEARD'S JUSTICE

1. I'M COMING FOR HIM

William's forehead was slick with sweat. The sun was approaching high noon above the clear skies of Bodden Town, and the heat had been rising steadily all day. It didn't help that he had been digging up dirt all morning.

He held a sharp spade in his hands, his exposed muscles taut from work. He slammed the spade into the ground and ran his fingers through his wet hair away from his eyes. The men he was working with were slowing down, and even he was tiring.

"What say we break for noon, men?" William asked.

The men let out sighs and some even dropped their spades and bodies to the ground, taking great heaves of air to regain their strength. Keeping at William's pace since early morning had taken its toll on them.

William turned to one of the Boddens' attendants. "Fetch us some food and drink, would you?"

The young man nodded and then ran off towards the Boddens' home not far from where they were.

William sat down on a pile of wood which was standing by for use after they'd laid the foundation. His eyes gravitated towards the harbour where ships of all sizes were entering and leaving. He couldn't see the bustle created by the ships, but he could imagine the multitude of characters arriving and leaving as the locals did business with them. He imagined the smell of the glistening fruit, the rich vegetables, and the various cured and cooked meats on display in the market. Though William was not one for fine dining—food was for sustenance, not pleasure—he could not help but enjoy the scents dancing from his nose to his palate, and often enjoyed walking the market for that reason alone.

"When's the captain due to return?" one of the men asked.

William turned his attention back to the men with him.

They were breathing heavily and wiping the sweat from their brows as they talked. Some of them looked at William, anticipating his answer.

"Our captain is set to dock in a few days' time, should their prospects hold true," William replied.

"I wonder what the captain'll bring back this time," the same crewman said.

"I pray for some spices. Old Liz from the Boar's Hat says spices have been too expensive for them to buy, and the food's bad enough as it is without something to mask the taste," another of the *Queen Anne's Revenge* men commented.

"It's yer own fault if ye keep eatin' there when ye hate the food."

"Boys, it's simple: he ain't there for the food and drink. He wants to wet his other whistle." A ripple of chuckles went around.

"Hey now, Elizabeth is warming up to me. Only a matter of time a'fore I bed her."

"Not if the owner has anything ta say about it!"

William let the voices of the men fade from his consciousness as he began meditating. He tried to clear his mind, but his thoughts lingered on his captain, Edward Thatch, and his charge, Anne Bonney, whom he'd promised to protect. William had volunteered to stay and help build new houses for Bodden Town while the majority of the crew left to secure a cargo ship, but he couldn't help but think he'd made the wrong decision. As the days turned to weeks of them out to sea, William couldn't shake the feeling of foreboding, as if there was a lasting gooseflesh in his mind.

The captain will protect her. There is nothing to worry about.

The sound of footsteps approaching forced William's eyes open. The Boddens' attendant rounded the bend with a tray of food—light sandwiches, dried meat, and cheese—and a pitcher of water in his hands.

William allowed the other men to dine first, then approached the young man and took the tray and pitcher from him. "Thank you. That will be all for now, so you may rest." The young man thanked William, then ran off back to the Boddens'.

2

William set the tray down on some timber nearby, and, despite their protests, proceeded to fill everyone's cups. With the other men looked after, William took some of the food for himself and sat back down to eat.

The men continued to talk about various affairs: when they would sail again, how long they would be working for, what tavern they would attend in the eve, and which women they would court from the local brothel and elsewhere. The steadfast William was not the type to engage in such talk, so he stayed to the side as he ate, not paying them any heed until one topic caught his attention.

"What do you think that ship is doin' out there?" one of the men commented.

William peered to the harbour as he chewed on a tough piece of spiced meat and soft cheese. He spotted the ship the other crewman was talking about. The vessel seemed to be circling the edge of the harbour, and, if William's memory served, he recalled seeing it earlier.

The ship piqued William's curiosity. "Perchance is anyone carrying a spyglass?" he asked.

"Here you are, William," one man said, removing the tool from his belt and handing it to his mate.

William took the instrument and studied the harbour through magnified gaze. He could see the ship was a lighter class with no gun deck, but a complement of thirteen cannons on its main deck. Perhaps it was the foreboding feeling William had been having, or boredom, but he could not take his eyes off the ship despite seeing nothing out of the ordinary. He continued to watch the ship and the men manning it as he chewed his leathery meat, until his men were ready to return to work.

William tore the spyglass away from his eye and rose to his feet. As he turned to present the glass back to its owner, he had to do a double take.

He'd noticed two other ships join with the first out of the corner of his eye. William turned back around to review the harbour again, and it was unmistakable that the three ships were approaching Bodden Town.

He put the spyglass up to his eye once more, and he could

see the crews of each of the ships hailing the other as they prepared their cannons. At the same time, each ship raised another sail—or rather, a flag: black with a red trim, and in the middle there was a large skull with crossed cutlasses beneath it.

"Warn the citizens. Prepare for battle!" William shouted over his shoulder.

The men's jaws dropped and some snorted a nervous laugh before questioning William's statement.

"Pirates are attacking. We must evacuate everyone we can and prepare for a counterattack."

William's words stunned them still, but when their eyes took in the harbour and the ships approaching, they were swift to move.

William began running towards the Boddens' to warn them and rally the militia, but the roar of cannon fire hit his ears. There was just enough time for him to glance down the hill and see the wave of destruction sweeping towards them.

The walls of the houses near him exploded as cannonballs tore through the wood and stone. William jumped and landed on his stomach in a nearby alley with his hands covering the back of his head, as wood and stone rained on him from above. Chunks of cobbled stone hit his arms and legs, and jagged pieces of wood struck his back.

When the hail of wood and stone subsided, William uncurled his body and rose to his feet. He surveyed the area to see his crewmates in varied states of turmoil amidst the wreckage of recently built homes, upturned earth, and billowing dirt.

William closed his eyes and took a breath. "Move, men!" he shouted. "Someone get to the Boddens' and ensure their safety. The rest of you, gather weapons. We won't take this assault lying down."

One of the men headed up towards the Boddens', and some moved in the other direction to the militia's barracks, while a few stayed behind for a brief moment.

"Where are you heading, William?" one of the men asked.

"I'm taking the fight to them," he replied.

William exited the alley and rushed down the dirt street.

All around him, the houses had been blown open from the cannon fire, and men and women of all ages were running in the opposite direction. He had to push past them and weave his way through the crowd trying to escape the mayhem.

Wide-eyed and frightened parents carried screaming and crying children, and the elderly tried to keep pace with the young. Some had minor injuries like cuts and scrapes, and many were covered in dirt and debris from the cannonballs' upheaval.

William could hear the faint sound of battle above the din of screams and frightened shouting around him. The smell of gunpowder hit his nose and reminded him of bitter, cruel days of fighting aboard the *Queen Anne's Revenge*. Despite his loathing for bloodshed, his body knew the sensation and reacted by invigorating him, readying him for what was to come.

Another wave of cannon fire swept over the town as the sound of the cannons met William's ears mere seconds before the carnage began. The crowd around him ducked in response to the sound, an automatic response that only the battle-hardened could prevent. William had the sense to stand his ground this time, and he watched as the cannonballs ripped the feeble houses to shreds. Pieces of the former shelters were flung at those it had previously protected.

Dust and dirt and debris forced William to cover his face with his arm as he pushed through the cowering crowds. After passing through the dense throng he could run more freely.

As William ran he could see some stragglers in a slow advance up the town's street. The closer he got to the harbour the more injured the people. He couldn't stop to help them; he would be more use at the coast.

"Help! Help please!" a voice in a nearby home cried.

William's paced slowed, but he didn't stop.

"Please, someone help my baby!" the voice called to any brave soul that would listen.

He glanced in the direction of the voice, then to the harbour where he could see rising smoke and hear the clang of metal clashing. He gritted his teeth in frustration, but headed to the poor woman begging for help.

William followed the screams to a half-demolished home. The building was falling apart before his eyes, as cannonballs had sheared off some of the support beams. Another blast and the whole house could come toppling down.

He entered the house and made haste to the back where a woman was trying to lift pieces of wood from a fallen corner. When she noticed William out of the corner of her eye, she flew to him as though he were a lifeline during a storm. She was on the verge of tears and her eyes filled to the brim with fright. Her hands gripped his arms in a desperate vice, as if she felt he would leave and she had to keep him there.

"Please, please, my son, my boy, he's trapped beneath the rubble. You must save him, sir, I beg of you."

William nodded before moving closer to the collapsed area of the home. He could see the young child, possibly no more than two years of age, crying in the middle of pieces of timber and stone with a few gashes on his forehead and arms. One of the support beams for the side of the house was leaning almost on top of him, holding up parts of the roof just over the boy's head. There was no way to grab the boy from where he was.

"I'll lift the beam, and you must grab your son. You must move quickly, I don't know how long I can hold it."

The woman nodded and thanked William profusely while holding back tears.

William stepped over jagged pieces of wood and rough stones, cautious as he made his way to where he could lift the beam. He positioned his legs as best he could to give himself the support he needed when lifting, then wrapped his arms around the fractured beam. He looked over to the mother, and she nodded to him with a determined yet still anxious look in her eyes.

William lifted up with his legs, and forced his already strained muscles to work. The beam and bits of roof were heavier than he'd expected. He grunted as he pushed with his legs and pulled with his arms. His muscles bulged with the effort. He panted in short breaths as sweat beaded down his face, cheek, and chin. With each breath, the beam inched upwards, and it became both easier and harder to continue lifting—easier because momentum was helping him, harder because the grip he had on the beam became awkward.

William fixed his eyes on the child, and his only thought was on saving the life of the innocent in front of him. The thought gave him strength, and helped him maintain his shaky grip on the beam.

When the beam and bits of roof were high enough off the remaining rubble, the mother crawled her way over to her child and grabbed him in her arms. The sobbing boy wrapped his tiny arms tight around his mother's neck. She crawled back out and back to safety, allowing William to gradually let the beam down.

"Thank you, thank you so much, sir." The woman repeated her thanks over and over, the tears she'd been holding back now streaming down her powdered cheeks.

"We must take our leave of this place before it comes down upon us," William warned. "Once free, run inland and do not look back until you can no longer hear the sound of the cannons."

The woman nodded with a renewed look of urgency on her face, and the two headed outside.

The sounds of battle rang on all sides, closer inland than it had been before. William glanced down both ends of the side street, and could see more people running from the harbour, but this time there were people with weapons chasing after them.

"You must move, quickly," William urged. He guided her away from the centre of town.

Before they could make it to another street leading inland, one of the pirates attacking the city turned around one of the bends. The man stopped on his heels when he noticed William and the woman and her child.

"Well, whut do we have 'ere? A precious family too slow on their feet, eh?" the pirate mocked.

"Get behind me," William commanded.

The woman shielded her son as she cowered behind William's back.

"Aww, ain't that sweet. Too bad it'll do ye no good, missa.

First, I'll have my way with ye, then I'll have my way with yer missus." The pirate brandished his cutlass and licked his foul lips in sick anticipation.

William, though he held no weapon, raised his fists and steeled himself for the fight.

The pirate howled a ghoulish laugh as he rushed towards William. He slashed with his cutlass, aiming for William's shoulder. William punched the pirate's wrist, and the cutlass fell to the stone street with a clang that echoed around them. William punched at the rogue's throat, but he deftly dodged and darted out of the way before jumping back.

"Hoo, yer better than I thought," the pirate said with a toothy smirk.

William's thoughts echoed the pirate. He tensed as he got a glimpse of the man's skill. He was no normal pirate.

"All right, les' have a friendly fist fight then." The pirate raised his hands in the air and balled them into fists.

William hunched down and readied himself for the next assault. Just as he was about to go on the offensive, he felt something hard touch his hip. He instinctively glanced down, leaving himself open.

The pirate didn't miss his opportunity and barreled towards William, throwing a punch his way. Before the fist made contact, the pirate stopped in his tracks. The meaty thunk of a cutlass hitting flesh sounded in William's ears.

"Sorry, I've no time for a fist fight," William said.

The pirate looked down to see his own cutlass embedded in his stomach. He lurched back a few steps with his hands on the blade, looked at William and chuckled as blood gushed out of his mouth, then fell to the ground with a thud.

William turned around to ensure the woman was well. "Thank you for passing me that sword. It made that fight easier."

"I should be thanking you, you save us once again."

"It's not over yet. You must get to safety. Will you be able to make it on your own now?"

"I hope so, sir," The woman said as she tip-toed her way past the dead pirate. "Thank you again, sir." She took a brief moment to wave back to William with a smile.

For the third time, the sound of cannons firing washed over the island. The sound was quicker than the doom it ushered, but not by much.

William's eyes went wide. He shouted "Run!" just as another wave of cannonballs peppered the houses.

The woman didn't have William's reflexes, and she could only pull her son in tighter and squeeze her eyes closed as the speeding iron cracked the corner beam of a house at the foundation. The house gave way, and the roof fell to the side towards the woman and her child. She opened her eyes just as the roof collapsed on top of her.

"No!" William screamed.

He ran over to the wreckage, but it was no use. There was no doubt that the woman and child were dead. Blood pooled around her rubble-covered body, trickling towards the harbour like dark red treacle.

William's hot, heavy breaths made his cheeks flush as he watched the pool make its way through the cracks of the stone. His fist tightened and his shaking fingers dug into his palm near to the point of drawing blood. He pulled the cutlass from the pirate's dead body and turned around in one swift motion. He stalked towards the main street where most of the pirates were invading.

On the main street, William could see men and women still running from the continued onslaught, and no organized militia as there should have been to drive the devils out. Farther down the street he thought he could see pirates carrying women slung over their shoulders to shore, or attacking those not quick enough to run.

The town was in shambles. The new town square was torn to bits, the fresh cobblestone ripped apart by the rolling cannonballs, and the square's shops and architecture destroyed. Homes and businesses along the main street were halfway demolished, and throughout the town smoke and dirt wafted and swirled in the wake of the pirates' attacks.

William was able to see one man fighting against the horde, and he rushed to join his comrade-in-arms. He ran over to a group of pirates set upon his friend, slicing one in the back, and another in the gut. After another second, his mate dispatched the others with two mighty thrusts of his spear.

Pukuh, the Mayan warrior, turned around to face William, ready to strike, but when he saw the face of his friend and crewmate he smiled. "You join the hunt, brother?"

"Yes, and by the looks of it we're on our own for now," William said, glancing down the main street with pirates running towards them.

Pukuh grinned. "Too bad for them," he said as he spun his spear between his fingers.

William couldn't help but smirk before he readied himself for the next wave of enemies.

Five pirates stormed at them with various sharp blades in hand, their one-time-use gunpowder weapons evidently spent closer to the harbour. Three charged the one-armed Mayan, while the remaining two went after William.

The two after William attacked at the same time in coordinated strikes. One man swung his blade horizontally, while the other thrust forward in case William decided to jump backwards. William kicked the second man's hand, knocking his blade away and at the first man mid-swing. The blade spun and nicked the first man in the leg, forcing him to stop and take a step back. William stabbed the pirate with no weapon in the chest as the other swung at him again. He clashed blades before grabbing the pirate's arm and pulling him forward to slice his neck open. The pirates were no amateurs, but William was the superior fighter.

Just as William was about to head to help Pukuh finish off his remaining two enemies, the glint of another sword caught his eye. He pulled his head back just in time to see the blade flash in front of his face. He jumped away and slapped the blade with his own before he took sight of his opponent.

The man in front of him had two inches on his five foot eleven, and easily twice William's bulk. He wore cotton-print clothing, and his face was clean-shaven. There was a scar that went from his right eye down to his mouth.

Calico Jack! William thought as he took in the giant before him.

"Where is Blackbeard?" the pirate asked in a calm yet

forceful voice.

William's answer was to slash at the pirate captain in front of him. Jack Rackham, better known as Calico Jack, swung his blade to counter William's. There was a brief clash where the sound of metal ringing echoed off the buildings before William felt no resistance on his end.

William looked down to see his cheap blade split in two. It was then that he noticed Rackham had a blade made of a golden metal. It reminded him of Edward, his captain, and the golden cutlass he owned, which was made of a mysterious and unbelievably sharp alloy.

Before William could recover from his shock, a large hand gripped his throat. Rackham picked William up off the ground, and slammed him onto the cobblestone on his back. There was a loud snap as several of his ribs broke, and the blow knocked the wind out of his lungs. It felt like a hand was gripping him on the inside, not allowing him to breathe. As he struggled on the ground, Rackham rose up to his full height.

William could hear Pukuh running towards them, but he stopped short. William looked over, and Pukuh's eyes were wide with what he thought was fear. It looked like Pukuh had seen a ghost.

Calico Jack scowled, looking down on the two in front of him with unmatched contempt. "Tell Blackbeard I'm coming for him."

2. (IN)JUSTICE

Edward waited on the quarterdeck with Herbert, the quartermaster, as the crew of the *Queen Anne's Revenge* secured their vessel to a merchant ship. He stroked his long beard as he watched the crew of the *Fortune* do the same on the other side of the merchant ship.

After a month of travel, bribes, and biding their time, the dual pirate crews had found the ship they had been searching for.

Armed to the teeth, the two ships were ready to take on the merchantman and secure its cargo by force, but it was unnecessary. There was no great battle, no bravado, no clash of swords with a mast at one's back as the wind whipped the sails. No, mere moments after dropping the black, their mark had raised the white and furled their sails.

Now, after half an hour of suspense as the ships slowed to match speed with each other, the cowards were aboard the main deck. The men threw the pirates curious and fearful glances as they assisted their transgressors in their task.

The noonday sun shining above them was blistering. Invisible steam rose up from the sea water sprayed on deck during sailing, and it created small mirages when looked at from certain angles. The smell of brine and seaweed and fish was strong in the air due in no small part to the steam. Edward didn't mind the heat, nor the smell. He was used to all the features and forms of the sea from years of experience working on a ship. He might even go as far as to say that he loved the smell if only his companions would not use it as ammunition for some form of jesting. Although, anything served that purpose for Bartholomew Roberts, the captain of the *Fortune*.

After the crew secured the ships, one of the mates approached and informed Edward. "Ensure the crew holds no weapons, and keep them in line. Move the captain to the stern. I will be over presently." The crewmate nodded and issued orders to other men aboard the *Revenge*.

"How's the weather looking, Quartermaster?" Edward asked, looking at Herbert. "Are the waves going to give us any trouble?"

Herbert leaned over in his wheelchair to look off the bow at the sky. "Should be clear, Captain."

"How are you adjusting to your new position?"

Herbert smirked. "Well, I was already working the helm, so now it's essentially just more responsibility on my hands."

Edward patted Herbert on the back. "I'm sure John would be proud of you. You've been doing a fine job."

"God rest his soul," Herbert said, and Edward copied the chant.

Anne Thatch, a fiery redhead and Edward's wife, approached him on the quarterdeck. She held one hand firm on the hilt of a cutlass, ready for anything. "They're acting rather cooperative, wouldn't you say?" she said with a smirk.

"Aye, I would say. Very cooperative," Edward replied. "Do you believe it to be a ruse?" he said with a sarcastic tone.

Anne frowned in thought, then looked over her shoulder at the merchant ship. The crew was searching the men's belongings and rounding them up, being more than a touch rough with them as they did so.

"Hard to say, truly. They did fly the white rather quickly."

Edward eyed the ship and the two pirate crews as he leaned on the quarterdeck's railing. He fiddled with the gold ring on his finger for a moment before he rose. He sauntered down the quarterdeck ladder and over to a gangplank connecting the ships, with Anne following behind him. He crossed to the merchant ship and Bartholomew Roberts approached him.

"You'll handle the search below?" Edward asked.

"Aye, and, God willing, I and my men will find what we've been looking for," Roberts replied.

"You sound confident."

"So far, your first mate hasn't steered us wrong," Roberts said, patting Anne on the side of her arm with a grin.

Anne smiled and bowed her head to the Pirate Priest.

Roberts returned to the bow, and then he and a few of his mates descended into the belly of the merchant ship to search for their treasure.

Edward and Anne walked to the stern of the ship to where the merchant's captain was. "He's right, you know. You're the best person for the job, and you can't keep ignoring the crew's vote like you have been."

Anne's mouth became a line. "I know, it's just..." She trailed off with a pensive look on her face.

Edward stopped walking. "What is it? If you have some misgivings, I'd like to know. I am your partner in more ways than one," he coaxed.

Anne nodded. "It's big shoes to fill. Henry was an age-old friend and confidant long before I came into your life."

Edward nodded, thinking back on his friend and the terrible night when he'd left. Henry couldn't handle life as a pirate, and had decided to leave the crew. Edward had run after him alone, and pointed a gun at him in desperation, trying to convince him to return. He hadn't meant to hurt Henry—would *never* have harmed a hair on his head!—but when the local authorities had intervened, things had gotten out of hand quickly, and Edward had shot his friend in the back, killing him. He still hadn't told anyone of the incident.

Edward shook his head to shake off the memory of that night, and didn't touch on what Anne had said. "The crew trusts you with their welfare, and I know they would have no one else in charge of their battle training. You've proven yourself time and time again."

Anne smiled. "I suppose that's true. I've already been training many of them since day one. Especially you, husband."

"Yes, and I recall that you led them into battle against three enemy ships that time I was kidnapped."

Anne frowned. "Well, the actual number was two. Roberts and his crew took care of the third."

"Still, that's not something I could have done, nor many others aboard this ship."

Anne smiled again, but changed the subject. "Come, we've work to do."

"Right," Edward replied.

Edward walked over to where the captain of the merchant ship waited. One of Roberts' men had a pistol trained on the captain, and another was lazily holding a cutlass in his hand, pointed in the merchant's general direction.

"How do you do, Captain? What may I call you by?"

The older gentleman scoffed. "What does it matter? Just take what ye came for and be gone. I do not wish to prolong this injustice."

Edward chuckled. "Injustice?"

"You believe what you are doing is just? I never knew pirates to think so highly of their own integrity."

Edward rubbed his chin as he glanced at the ship's deck, and then he moved to the merchant ship's stern railing. He leaned his back against the railing and folded his arms.

"You know, my father used to tell me these stories of a man named Robin Hood. I don't remember all the details, as I'm sure any can say of stories from childhood, but his actions always stuck with me," Edward said while gesturing with his finger. "Robin Hood stole from the corrupt rich to give to the poor, and he was the hero."

The merchant settled his thumbs between his belt, and looked annoyed. "What does this have to do with anything?" he spat.

"You are rich, we are poor."

The merchant gritted his teeth. "You believe yourself to be the hero, boy? I may be the owner of this ship, but these men are the ones who will pay for your theft," he said, pointing to his crew. "Though your attack stings, I have savings. Most of the men here are not so lucky. In a month's time they'll have to return to their wives and tell them how a *hero* stole their cargo, so I couldn't pay them. Then, their children who are sick with fever will die because they couldn't afford the medicine, or they'll starve because food is too expensive." The merchant's voice grew louder and louder as he spoke until his entire crew could hear him. "Why do you think I flew the white so fast? Did you think me a coward? I did it because men like you would kill men like us. At least this way these men keep their lives and have another chance to right

15

your wrong. Steal what you want, take it all, but don't you dare hide behind some twisted morality that affords you sleep at night."

Edward was quiet during the captain's speech, but within a moment of it ending, he burst out laughing. His unrestrained and lengthy howl was boisterous to the point that many in the merchant crew thought him mad by the time he ceased.

"You're good. I'll give you that." Edward got to his feet and raised his voice to ensure the whole crew could hear him. "There's just one thing though: Who said that we're here to steal your cargo?"

The captain eyed Edward suspiciously, but before he could question him Roberts returned from below deck with a notebook in his hands. Edward walked over to Roberts.

"Does it have what we were looking for?"

Roberts nodded. "Just as expected."

Edward smiled. "Good." He took the notebook in hand.

"Who are you?" The captain had a confused look on his face as he eyed Edward up and down.

Edward grinned. "I'm Blackbeard." He began thumbing through the notebook.

"Stop! Stop, I say," the merchant commanded, reaching for Edward.

Roberts' crew stepped forward, but it was Edward's massive hand on the merchant captain's throat that stopped him. "No," he stated simply.

Edward, at his height of six feet four inches, lifted the merchant captain up in the air by the throat with ease. He walked over to the crew amidships and tossed the captain unceremoniously to the deck.

"Crew of the *Tabernacle*, you may see me as nothing more than a common rogue, but I am here to right a wrong that was going to be committed on you. I am here to avenge those that had this wrong committed on them in the past."

"Don't listen to him, men! He's nothing but a liar and a thief," the captain shouted.

Edward called to some of his men to bind the captain and gag him, which they carried out with no amount of gentleness. Once complete, and sure that the captain could no longer interrupt, Edward continued.

"Your captain was so fervent to denounce us as thieves, as you no doubt overheard earlier, and while that may be true we are not the only ones. As is often true, the most vocal detractors of a sin are those most guilty of it." Edward pulled up the notebook and showed the pages to the crew. "Your captain recently purchased rather large insurance precisely two weeks before your journey. Should pirates attack this ship and steal the cargo, he would stand to make a small fortune. But you wouldn't know anything about that, would you, Captain?"

The merchant captain tried to yell through the gag in his mouth, but only muffled expletives filtered through.

The crew, understandably confused, called Edward a liar at best and variations of what the captain was saying at worst. One thing stood out from the rest: apathy. An insurance policy wasn't proof of guilt.

"I hear what you are saying, but I can assure you that your captain was going to let this happen. In fact, he hired another pirate crew to attack the vessel and steal the cargo. We intercepted them on our way here to stop them."

The merchant crew were less enthusiastic with their objections, but still not entirely convinced from what he could tell.

Edward shook his head. "Of course, you don't have to trust in my word. After all, I am a dirty pirate," he said while shrugging his shoulders. "James!"

A man, not of Edward's crew, came from the *Queen Anne's Revenge* over to the *Tabernacle*. He was plain, and every bit the normal-looking sailor. As he came into view, the captain's eyes widened further, and his muffled screams ceased, to the notice of the other crewmates.

Edward backed up a few paces to allow James some room, and he sat down on top of a barrel near the mast.

James pointed to the merchant captain. "This man was once my captain."

At the declaration, the current crew of the *Tabernacle* glanced from James to their captain and back.

Blackbeard's Blood

"I was hired as a gunner a month before departure on a shipping contract going from Jamaica up north. One thing the captain told me was odd, but it wasn't what he said, it was the way he said it. He told me that if everything went according to plan then there shouldn't be any need to use the cannons, but he was smiling like a man ready for a payday."

James looked at the captain with contempt as the other crewmates continued glancing at the two as he told his story.

"After we departed, it wasn't long until we were beset by pirates. It was a small sloop with fewer guns than we had, so I thought it was a given that we would attack and I readied the cannon I was in charge of, but we were told to surrender. Our entire cargo shipment was stolen, and we were never paid because the captain said he couldn't afford it. We went back to Jamaica, but he didn't hire us again. I later found that the captain had purchased a new, larger ship. It never sat well with me what happened, and so I followed the captain around to find him hiring the pirate crew to attack his new ship. Unfortunately, or fortunately, the pirates found me out and attacked me, but Edward Thatch saved my life," James said, pointing at Edward. "I told him my story, and he promised me and my former crew revenge."

Edward stood up from the barrel and went over to stand next to James. "If you won't believe my word, then believe this man's." Edward pulled out a pistol from his belt, and pointed it at the merchant captain. Despite all the evidence presented, and the testimony from a former crewmate, the crew still protested to the violence. He ignored them, and a few nudges from Roberts' crew silenced them. "I would ask what kind of twisted morality allows you to sleep at night, but what does it matter? I do not wish to prolong this injustice." Edward flashed a devilish grin, cocked the pistol, and fired it at the captain's chest.

The bullet hit the captain in his heart, and he slumped over, hitting the deck with a thump.

Another smell emanated from the pistol and overtook the aroma of the sea. Edward also loved this scent, though for a different reason, and he would never admit it even to himself.

As blood drained from the slumped-over captain, his crew watched on in a mix of horror, indifference, and praise over justice being done. Quite a number were nodding as they looked at the body and whispered various versions of "serves him right."

"Now," Edward said, the pistol in his hand still trailing smoke, "there is the matter of your cargo. Who is first mate aboard this ship?"

After a moment, a man raised his hand and stepped forward to answer Edward's call. "I am, sir. Y-you're not going to kill me, are ye? I tell you true, I had no part in this plot," he said while wringing a cap in his hands.

Edward chuckled. "No, no, the captain was our only target today. What I wish now is to buy your stock, and seeing as the position of captain is left wanting, you will have to fill that role. You have many spices, which will fetch a good price where I hail from. Of course, I will not pay anywhere close to the market price, but if you divide it amongst the crew it will be more than your standard wages. Does this appeal to you?"

The man glanced from Edward to the dead captain, then over his shoulder to all the armed pirates surrounding them. After a moment he nodded, accepting the deal.

Anne came over and pulled the first mate aside. "Let us discuss the particulars in private, Captain," she said sweetly as she took him to the captain's cabin.

"Men, let's get this cargo moved!" Edward commanded.

Over the course of an hour, the crews of the *Queen Anne's Revenge* and *Fortune* moved several tonnes of various spices to their respective holds. The merchant crew stood around, watching the pirates with wary glances. They never seemed comfortable with the idea of pirates taking their precious cargo, even if it was technically paid for.

James, the former sailor on the merchant ship, thanked Edward for his service, and decided to stay with the merchant ship to return to fairer shores, as he was not a Bodden Town native.

After they'd secured the cargo, and Anne had issued payment, Edward met with the new captain for the last time.

"Good day to you, Captain," he said, holding out his hand.

The man glanced from Edward's eyes to his hand, and then gave it a shake with an expressionless face. "I hope you do not take offence to my saying this, but I hope we never meet again."

Edward grinned, and without a word he returned to his ship, then addressed his crew. "Let's return home. Our business here is done!"

3. SCARS

Edward watched the horizon as Bodden Town came into view. It would still be some time before they would land, but he could already see the small edge of the Caymans as it grew larger.

The sun was close to setting, but it would still be light out when they arrived. Edward could see the sun, resolute in its arc, off to his left when he stood at the bow. It was bright, but not harsh as it was during the day. Its soft glow shimmered on the water as the sea danced endlessly to the east and west.

The light heat helped the sea's stench subside, taking on an overall pleasant tone, and helped productivity and morale.

The men seemed excited to see their home close, and they worked all the harder to coax more wind into the sails. Sweat glistened off many of their faces as they pulled rigging lines, but they wore small smiles as they did so.

To Edward's right, off the starboard bow, the *Fortune* was well ahead of them. Being the smaller ship, the *Fortune* had the advantage in speed, and Bartholomew Roberts enjoyed rubbing it in whenever he beat Edward to port.

Edward chuckled to himself, remembering the last time Roberts had made a glib comment, and Edward had threatened to sabotage Roberts' sails if he kept it up. The serious look on Roberts' face after Edward's comment still made him laugh.

Tala, a wolf with reddish-grey fur, jumped up beside Edward and placed its front paws on top of the bow railing. The suddenness of Tala's arrival startled him, but he quickly recovered and patted the wolf's back. Tala was panting and glanced from him to the approaching island before barking.

Edward grinned. "That's right, you'll have solid ground under your feet soon enough."

"There you are, Tala! Don't run off like that," Christina,

Tala's owner—if a wolf could be said to have an owner—came running up after the animal. "Hello, Captain," she said with a wave.

"Sometimes I wonder just who the real owner is between you two. She has you running around more often than not some days."

Christina grinned as she brushed some of her strawberry-blond hair out of her face. "Some days I'm not so sure myself." Christina patted Tala, and the three watched the island as the ship bobbed up and down on the waves. "She seems to know when we're approaching land."

Edward glanced at the wolf. "Perhaps it can hear when the crow's nest calls down that they see land."

"She."

"Pardon?" Edward questioned with a raised brow.

"Perhaps *she* can hear," Christina corrected.

Edward stroked his beard. "Yes, my apologies. She."

"Perhaps you are right. She is a smart one. Yes you are, aren't you Tala?"

Tala answered with a loud bark, then moved down from the railing and lay down at Christina's feet.

"So, my eyes and ears, how are the crewmen faring?" Edward asked affectionately.

"They're doing well. They groan about the usual matters: taste of the food, seasickness, when they'll next be on land and at the brothel. Morale is high, though. They've been through much on this voyage, and so it will take much more than tedium to break their spirits."

"Good, good." Edward nodded.

"There is one thing, the same thing actually." Christina leaned her side against the railing and folded her arms. "The men are wondering, what with all this revenge business, when we're going to go and rescue Sam and kill Kenneth Locke for what he did."

Edward gripped the railing and cast his eyes to the deep abyss of the sea. "And I suppose you wish to know this as well?"

Christina gave a short, derisive laugh. "Of course I do," she answered in a harsh whisper. "We have had this conversation three times already, and you never give me an answer. I know for a fact I'm not the only one either."

Edward let out a sigh; even now the name Kenneth Locke caused his hands to tremble inexplicably. The only thing he could do to mask the tremors was to grip the ship's railing. He wasn't afraid of Locke, but the thought of him brought back painful memories. Memories of John's death flashed in Edward's head, and after them the remembered wounds of torture ached all over his body.

"We're just concerned, Ed, that's all," Christina said as she touched his arm. "And the sooner we settle things with Locke, the sooner we can move on to Herbert's revenge and mine, like you promised."

Edward peered at Christina suspiciously. "Yours and Herbert's?"

Christina removed her hand. "Yes. I want the same as my brother, and why should I not? Calico Jack deserves to die for crippling him. He deserves much more than that, actually."

"Well, you'll have to have some patience. The Boddens are looking into Locke's whereabouts. Sam will be able to take care of himself until then."

"Yes, but it's been four months. Perhaps the Bodden Brothers aren't qualified to handle the task if they still haven't found anything."

Edward held the railing so tight his knuckles turned white. "Drop it," he said.

Tala opened her eyes and looked up at Edward, no doubt sensing his anger. Christina was taken aback and blurted out, "Excuse me?"

"I said, drop it," Edward seethed.

Christina stood there for another moment, her mouth a line. "Fine. I guess that's what I get for trying to help. *Venir*, Tala," Christina called, and the two left, one of them in a huff.

Edward closed his eyes and took a few deep breaths. John's dead eyes kept appearing, and the blood pouring from the poor old man's neck felt like it was filling his lungs and choking him. All over his body he could feel sharp pain in specific spots, each one a reminder he would carry for the rest of his life.

He could feel a cold sweat on his forehead despite the cool breeze. He wiped his forehead and took a few more deep breaths as he stared at the ring on his finger. After another moment, his heartbeat slowed, and his chest no longer felt constricted. He could breathe normally again.

When Edward was sure that the feeling had passed, he turned around to leave the bow. He went down to the main deck, where he noticed Jack Christian, the musician, and boatswain in William's absence.

"Jack," he called. Jack walked over to Edward. "I'm retiring to my chambers. Keep the crew busy and send someone to fetch me when we're closer to land."

Jack nodded, a definite note of concern in his eyes, but he didn't address Edward's obvious pallor. "Aye, Captain."

Edward descended to the gun deck and headed to the stern where the captain's cabin was. He noticed Anne talking to the ship's surgeon, Alexandre, but Edward was in no mood to talk so he tried his best to avoid being seen. He entered the captain's cabin and closed the door behind him.

He went to his bed and flopped down in it, clothes and all still on him. He lay there, staring at the wooden boards of the ceiling as he held his head in an attempt to prevent a headache.

What's wrong with me?

Edward awoke with a start as a crewmate jostled his shoulder. He grabbed the man by the scruff of the neck before he recalled where he was. When his senses came to him he let the man go.

"Sorry, you startled me."

The crewmate adjusted his clothes. "My apologies, Captain. I only meant to wake you as we're approaching land. Jack says there's something you need to see."

Edward raised his brow as he stretched his legs and got

up from his bed. "What is it?"

The crewmate shrugged his shoulders. "A group'a the men gathered at the bow, but before I knew what the general commotion was about I was sent to fetch ye."

Edward nodded, but he felt it could mean only one thing: Something bad had happened to Bodden Town. He rushed out of his cabin and up to the weather deck.

The sun was a thumb above the edge of the horizon now, giving off a reddish glow to the darkened sky. There were few clouds in the deep blue above them, and in a few hours it would be a dark night.

Edward could see crewmates hanging onto the rigging while standing on the side railings or leaning on the rope ladders as they looked towards Bodden Town. Some peered through spyglasses with their mouths agape, before a neighbour slapped their shoulder to steal the opportunity to look through its magnified scope. There were also many crowding around the bow doing the same. They stood on their toes, leaning to the left and right as they tried to see over their the heads of others.

Edward approached the crowd and began pushing people aside. "Make way for your captain," he instructed.

He weaved his way forward as he stared ahead to the enthralling scene. At first he didn't notice anything off, but as his eyes focussed and he took note of the state of the homes and ships, it dawned on him.

"Someone hand me a spyglass," he said as soon as he reached the front of the crowd.

"Here, Captain," Jack offered.

Edward took the magnifying device and peered through it to take in the state of Bodden Town, the town he partially owned, in its entirety.

The majority of the homes and businesses nearest the shore were completely destroyed, mere husks of their former selves. The palms and grass and flowers in front of the harbour market were torn, disturbed, or outright obliterated. In the harbour, there were several boats and ships which were also decimated from what looked like cannon-fire. The place was more wreck than town.

Blackbeard's Blood

When Edward had last seen Bodden Town, it was the polar opposite. The sun had been shining, birds chirping, and people bustling. It used to be a lively, thriving, and growing town that he'd taken pride in helping build up. Now he nearly couldn't bear to look upon it.

Edward handed the spyglass back to Jack, and gripped the bow railing. As the ship closed in on Bodden Town, Edward grew more and more enraged. He gritted his teeth as his thoughts shifted to his crewmates whom he'd had stay behind to assist in building homes, and he wondered whether they were still alive. William, Pukuh, and Nassir, his ship's carpenter, were all among those who'd agreed to stay in town—each one of them an irreplaceable friend to Edward.

"Who or what do you believe is responsible?" Jack asked.

"Pirates," Edward guessed.

"Pirates?"

"If it were the British Navy, or any navy for that matter, they wouldn't have left. We would still see them in the harbour. If pirates attacked, they took what they wanted and left. And there is no chance of a storm causing this type of destruction. I struggle to think of another explanation."

"Why would pirates attack Bodden Town?"

Edward scoffed. "Why indeed. It's not as if we've made any enemies," he said grimly, his tone dripping with sarcasm.

Jack nodded. "Yes, I see your meaning. The question is then: which of our past transgressions comes back to haunt us today?"

Edward caressed his beard. "I can only think of one pirate with the power and the gall to do this," he replied.

Jack raised his brow. "Oh?"

Edward glanced over his shoulder at Herbert sitting in his wheelchair, manning the helm with Christina beside him, and Tala the wolf beside her. Jack followed his gaze to the brother and sister, and nodded when he understood.

Edward leaned close to Jack. "Best to not mention him by name. I could be wrong," he said in a low whisper.

"I see," Jack said, glancing around. "I fear you may be right. I am surprised it took this long. It's been, what, two or three years since we killed one of the captains in his squadron?"

Edward glanced down at his sword, the weapon made of a mysterious alloy that was the last remnant of the captain that Herbert had killed. Given that some called Calico Jack the King of the Caribbean, such an offence would require an equal and opposite response, lest Calico Jack be considered weak.

"Whoever it was, they will pay for what they've done."

The crews of the *Queen Anne's Revenge* and *Fortune* eased into the far end of the harbour and dropped anchor before securing themselves to the dock. The dock was also damaged and in need of repair closer to the main road, but it was not as dire as the rest of town.

Edward didn't wait for a gangplank to be dropped, and instead opted to jump off the side of the ship to the pier.

"Edward!" Anne called before following him.

Edward scanned the wharf until he saw people on a nearby boat cleaning debris and removing the small mainsail. He sprinted over to them, and they turned to look at him when his heavy footsteps met their ears.

"What happened here?" he asked.

Some of the sailors eyed him and Anne and their ship. One of the ones more focussed on his work answered. "What, ye just arrived, did ye?"

"Yes. Did pirates attack?"

"Aye, must have been. Though, don't ask us who they was. We was too busy running to ask them their particulars," the man said with a laugh.

Edward turned to Anne. She had a concerned look on her face, no doubt thinking on William, her friend and protector. "It is as I feared. Tell the crew to stay on alert and remain on the ship." Edward began walking off without another word.

"Wait, where are you going, Edward?"

Edward turned around and walked backwards a few paces. "I need to speak with the Boddens and learn more of this attack. They will know."

"Hold, hold, I wish to join you. I need to know what happened to our crewmates."

Blackbeard's Blood

"Wait a minute, you're that Blackbeard fellow, ain't ye?" the sailor from the boat asked. Edward and Anne both turned their attention back to the man, but neither answered. "This is all yer fault!" he shouted.

Edward and Anne both looked at each other, confused. "I believe you are mistaken, sir. I have not been here in near abouts a month. I had no part in this, I assure you."

"Yea, ye may not 'ave shot the guns, but you brought them here."

Edward stepped forward, his brows furrowed. "What do you mean?"

The sailor pointed to the harbour street. "I was about when those bastards rained iron down on us, and before I could get me and mine out I saw clear as I see you a man calling for your head. They came here for you, and you weren't here."

The man was becoming agitated, and it was then that Edward noticed that the men in the boat had various bandages and visible injuries. He also saw them picking up tools or thick pieces of wood and holding them menacingly.

"Edward, perhaps it's time we leave," Anne whispered as she placed her hand on his chest and pushed him back, all while keeping her eye on the sailors.

"Yes, I believe you are right." Edward turned around and the two stepped away at a quick pace.

"Oh no, you can't just walk away from this, you dirty pirate," the man yelled.

The sound of boots hitting wood echoed across the pier, and it soon turned into sprinting. Edward and Anne had no choice but to face their aggressors, or they would be attacked from behind.

"We want no part of this, hear? No part!" Edward said with a swipe of his hand.

"You should'a thought of that before ye brought this to our shores."

The men all stood in front of Edward and Anne, seven in total, ready to strike with their makeshift weapons.

"I don't believe we can reason with them, Edward," Anne said.

28

Edward glanced at her, knowing she was right but wishing the opposite. These people were rightfully angry, but their anger was misdirected.

Edward slowly placed his hand at the hilt of his cutlass. He glared at the men, looking down on them with all the fury he could muster. "Are you sure you want to do this?"

The men wavered at Edward's look and his stature, glancing at each other. The original man who had started the conflict seemed undeterred, and he lunged forward, aiming a metal tool at Edward's head.

Edward didn't draw his sword, and instead grabbed the sailor's weapon mid-air and punched him in the stomach. The man doubled over, clutching his belly.

With their mate's display of courage, four of the men went to attack as well, while two ran away because of Edward's display of power. The attackers all came after Edward and ignored Anne, possibly thinking she wouldn't fight.

Anne twisted her hip, leapt into the air, and kicked one of the men in the side of the head. The man sprawled the ground, unconscious.

Edward ducked under another man's attack and swept his leg. He fell to the pier, hitting his head violently on the wood.

Anne punched another man in the back of the head, and when he turned around to face her she kicked him in the stomach and face in rapid succession.

The last sailor rushed at Edward with a wooden beam raised high in the air. Edward slammed his body into the man's chest, grabbed his legs, and used his momentum to flip him onto his back. After he landed, Edward punched him in the face for good measure and rose to his feet.

Edward and Anne were not winded in the least. Their attackers were simple fishermen from what Edward could tell, and no match for trained fighters.

A moment after their battle, Jack, Christina, Roberts, and Roberts' first mate, Hank Abbot, came running up to them. "What happened?" Roberts asked, glancing at the bodies lying on the pier.

Edward noticed that their commotion had caught the attention of others on the pier and around the harbour. Many eyes were on them, interested in what was happening. Edward could hear some people calling for the militia.

"It seems some are under the impression that we are the cause of the attack. The pirates who attacked town were after me," Edward explained. "We need to hurry to the Boddens' before anything else happens. Roberts, would you join Anne and me?" Roberts nodded. "Jack, Christina, keep the crew on the ship for now. I don't want any further trouble in town until we have this situation sorted."

"We're on it," she replied before she and Jack ran back to the *Revenge*.

"Hank, it might be wise if you do the same," Roberts said.

Hank nodded. "I reckon that's wise. I'll inform the men."

After Hank set off to the *Fortune*, Roberts, Anne, and Edward went farther down the pier to the main street. Luckily, those who had seen the scuffle didn't recognise Edward, and none pursued them so they were free to move.

The three of them did their best not to bring attention to themselves as they walked up the damaged cobblestone. Most of the people in the street were working at cleaning or repairing the broken homes and businesses, too busy to notice them.

Now that Edward had a closer look, the town was even worse off than he had thought. It looked as if some of the buildings had also been burned during the attack, and like the fire had spread throughout the area before it could be stopped. The smell of burnt wood, fresh dirt, and spent gunpowder lingered in the air, but there was another smell Edward couldn't pinpoint until he looked at his feet.

There were spots and pools of dried blood that had yet to be washed away, all along the main street. It wasn't fresh, but the faint smell lingered in the air.

"The attack could not have been more than two days ago," Anne speculated as the three walked along the street.

"We just missed it," Edward said.

"It is good providence that we were so fortunate." At Roberts' comment, Edward and Anne glanced at him with pursed lips. "Had we been here, we would not have been able to help." Roberts pointed to the destruction around them.

"This was not done with one ship, unless it was a galleon. If this pirate was after you, there was not much we could have done to stop them."

"I suppose you're right," Edward conceded.

The three of them quickened their pace. They passed by the many different citizens, a multitude of whom had a bevy of wounds all over them. Despite this they continued work to fix their broken town.

They made their way quietly to the Boddens' mansion, and met no resistance along the way. At the Boddens' gate there were more guards than usual, and Edward could tell that they were from his crew.

As Edward approached, his crew recognised him. Before they could do anything to alert passersby, Edward placed his finger over his lips. "Where is William?" he asked.

"He's bedridden in the Boddens' estate. Good to see you, Captain. It's been pretty bad here the past few days."

Edward glanced over his shoulder "Yes, I've come to see that firsthand. Let us in, would you?"

The crewman nodded and opened the lock on the gate before swinging it open.

"Was there always a lock?" Roberts asked.

Edward shook his head. "Things must be truly bad, and I'm afraid once word spreads of our arrival it will only get worse."

"We must be quick about this then," Anne suggested.

The three walked up to the front door of the mansion, waving to the crewmates keeping watch. Edward went to open the door, but it too was locked. He glanced at his companions with a frown before knocking on the door.

Another crewman holding a musket opened the door, and his eyes opened wide when he noticed his captain standing in front of him. "Captain!" he shouted.

"In the flesh." Edward bowed his head. "Care to allow us entry?"

The man looked flustered and stepped aside. "Sorry, Captain. It's just surprising to see you."

"Yes, well, under the circumstances it almost feels as if we shouldn't have returned."

The man chuckled. "The people are on edge. They'll calm themselves soon enough."

Edward nodded. "Where are William and the Bodden brothers?"

"William is in the balcony room on the left side with the Mayan—"

"Pukuh," Edward interjected.

The crewmate nodded. "And the Boddens are in their study working on construction plans with the negro."

"Nassir," Edward said, giving the crewmate a foul look. Edward looked at Anne. "You'll be seeing William first, I imagine?"

Anne nodded. "You don't think you'll need me with the Boddens?"

"I'll manage. I'm not completely useless without you," Edward said with a grin.

Anne smirked. "Not completely." She gave him a kiss and headed up the wide stairs to the second floor to see William.

Edward and Roberts headed up the stairs just behind Anne and through double doors into the Boddens' study. The Bodden twins, Neil, who was wearing a red jacket, and Malcolm, wearing a blue jacket, were working at a desk near the back. They were looking over what appeared to be plans with Nassir, Edward's dark-complexioned shipwright.

They looked up when Edward entered. "Mr Thatch," Niel said.

"We were expecting you back soon, but not this soon," the other brother, Malcolm added.

"Our business went smoother than expected."

"Welcome back, Captain," Nassir said in his heavy accent, flashing a smile.

"Nassir, I'm glad to see you safe and unharmed."

"I was one of the lucky few."

Edward looked at the brothers. "Can you tell me what has happened here?"

The brothers looked at each other and then sighed. "It is one of our greatest fears realised. The pirate, Calico Jack, attacked us three days ago while you were away."

"There were three ships, and thankfully we and the

majority of the houses this far inland were spared the brunt of the attack."

"And how are repairs going?" Edward said, looking at Nassir.

"Everyone in town is helping in rebuilding what was lost. Much of the work we did in the past few months and before was undone. Some have left for better shores, as they lost their homes, but those that remain are committed to the work."

Edward nodded at his friend's assessment, then turned his attention to the Boddens. "You are putting some money towards this, I hope?"

The immaculate and lavishly clothed brothers nodded as they said "Of course!" in unison.

"We sent one of the unharmed ships to hire workers from other towns to assist in our repair efforts."

Edward nodded. "Good, use my funds at your discretion. We can't stay long, as the townspeople seem to be against us. Gather any information you can on Calico Jack and his crew's whereabouts so we can prepare a counterattack. Nassir, would you be opposed to remaining here to continue repairs?" Edward asked.

Nassir shook his head. "I will gladly stay and help for now. But I ask that I join you again before fighting Calico Jack. Christina is like a daughter to me, and I would help her and her brother with their vengeance."

Nassir's eyes were fiery, and Edward recalled that Christina had had a relationship with his son before he passed away. Edward knew that if Nassir wasn't there and something happened to Christina, he would never forgive him.

Edward nodded. "I won't leave for that battle without you," he said before he turned around to leave and visit William.

The brothers' brows raised and they glanced at each other. "You plan to fight the King of the Caribbean? That is madness!" Niel said.

"He attacked our town. If we back down now, what does that tell other pirates? Besides, we planned on going after him someday. There's only one king, and I'll be the one to take that title." Edward started for the doors again, but Malcolm stopped him.

"How will we get you the information?"

"We'll return once this all blows over." Edward paused just shy of the doors leading back to rest of the mansion. "When the citizens have calmed, paint part of your mansion red so we'll know it's safe to land."

The Boddens looked dumbfounded by the quickness of the meeting with their partner. Edward didn't wait around for them to regain their composure.

Outside the Boddens' room, Roberts grabbed Edward's arm. "Edward, you never mentioned to me that you angered Calico Jack."

Edward glanced at Roberts' hand, and he removed it. "I suppose I did not. I'm sorry, it never came up. Is it a problem?"

Roberts chuckled. "No, not in the slightest. I'm simply curious what it was you did to provoke his wrath."

"You're familiar with Herbert, our quartermaster?" Roberts nodded. "When he was a young man, he was working on Calico Jack's ship. There was an accident involving gunpowder, and it left him crippled."

Roberts shook his head. "Powder-monkeys. As I learned more about running a pirate ship, and the ease with which misfortunes such as that occur, I banned the practice. I believe I mentioned that to you already, when we created the Pirate Commandments."

Edward nodded. "I remember. I can assure you, from Rackham's treatment of Herbert he has no qualms about using powder-monkeys. Instead of taking care of Herbert after the accident, and raising him to a different role, he left him in Port Royal with nothing. Herbert and his sister had nothing but hardships after that, and they asked me to help them exact vengeance upon Rackham. As we searched for the keys to my ship, we came across one of his commanders and battled him. The man is no longer of this world, and I have this sword as a reminder," Edward said as motioned to the golden cutlass at his side.

Roberts gave a hearty laugh. "You always know how to

pick them, don't you, my boy?"

Edward joined in the laughter, but didn't quite know how to respond. The two of them moved on to find William.

Edward and Roberts went to the left side of the Boddens' mansion to the room in which William was staying. The door was open, and when Edward entered he saw Anne and Pukuh sitting on stools near the bed, and William lying down with dressings wrapped around his entire chest. He looked sick with fever, and there was an odour that could only be from William being bedridden for days, and the application of foul medicines. His eyes were baggy, his lips chapped, and his face as pale as the white sheets under which he lay.

"Dear Father, William, what happened to you?" Edward exclaimed as he rushed over to William's bedside.

William flopped his head over to the side to better see Edward, and gave a listless salute. "Hello, Captain. I apologise for what has happened. I take full responsibility for not mounting an effective defence."

"Nonsense. I will hear no more of this. There was nothing you could have done. I heard from the Boddens that there were three ships. No matter what happened it would have turned out the same with that kind of firepower. You did what you could and that's all that matters," Edward said, folding his arms. "Though I do wish to know how you became so injured. Did you fight against Calico Jack himself?" Edward asked with a chuckle. An awkward silence came over the room, and when Edward eyed William, Anne, and Pukuh, they all looked sheepish.

"Good God, man!" Roberts blurted out.

William turned his head and stared at the ceiling. "He is a fearsome man indeed. He broke my ribs like they were nothing. His men kill, maim, and rape without regard for innocent life. He is every bit the reason common men fear pirates, because he encourages violence. I could see the anger and hate in his eyes, as a storm hurtling waves forty feet tall." There was no fear in William's voice. All Edward could hear was the same anger that he had spoken of, and a desire for vengeance that wasn't typical of him. William looked at Edward. "If you were here, I do not doubt that he would have killed every man, woman, and child in this town."

Edward glanced at Roberts. "Perhaps it is as you said—it was better that we were not here."

"There is more," William said.

"More?"

"Rackham seems to have a sword similar to the one you have. It is made from the same strange metal you recovered from one of his officers, and it was sharp enough to break a cutlass I was using in two."

Edward glanced at the cutlass at his side, curious over how Rackham had come upon such an abundance of the strange metal which made their swords.

William continued his story. "Before Rackham left, he pulled a dull golden hunting horn off his belt and used it to issue their retreat."

Golden Horn? But that's... Edward looked at each person in the room, finally settling on Pukuh, who had been silent throughout William's story. He looked angry and confused.

"Calico Jack is Benjamin Hornigold," Pukuh declared.

4. TRAPPED

"That's impossible," Edward said.

Pukuh's expression was as stone. "It is true. I saw him with my eyes. I am telling you, the man who attacked us was Benjamin Hornigold."

"How can you be sure?"

"I remember him from my childhood. I will never forget his face, and the man I saw had the same face but older. It was him."

Edward was going to object again, but Pukuh's eyes brooked no further argument. He'd seen what he'd seen. Benjamin Hornigold, the man who'd given his ship to Edward one fateful, black-out drunk night, the man whose clues had sent them on deadly quests for the keys to that same ship, and the man who had been friends with the Mayan warrior's father—that man was now called Jack Rackham.

Edward ran his hand through his hair. "Why would he do such a thing as this? Why change his name? Why... why?" was all he could think to add.

"Men change," Anne said. "From what I understand of the timeline, Benjamin Hornigold was only with Pukuh's father for a few years at most, and that was over ten years ago." Pukuh nodded in agreement. "Much can happen in ten years, much to change a man. Think about the past three years or so since *you* started sailing as a pirate."

Edward thought back on his adventures of life and death against Benjamin's game for the keys, his year of imprisonment for his crimes, his torture at the hands of Kenneth Locke, and the many friends he'd lost, and the one he'd killed. He was no longer the whaler he had been three years ago, and no longer the naive boy he once was.

"You have a point," Edward conceded.

"He could have changed his name for any reason. He was famous as Benjamin Hornigold; he could have wanted to turn over the hourglass. A new name, a new identity, and a new personality completely different from the Benjamin Hornigold who loved riddles and playing games." Anne glanced over to Pukuh with her last comment, and he looked down at the floor.

"But why give me the ship and then attack me? Where is the sense in that?"

Roberts spoke up this time. "Perhaps the man knows not who you are." Edward eyed his friend and raised his brow, intrigued. "You call yourself Blackbeard now, as you did with the man in his crew you killed, going by what you told me. He sold that ship to an Edward Thatch, not Blackbeard. Not to mention that the ship used to be called *Freedom*. Now it has a new name, one he wouldn't recognise."

Edward nodded. "That seems possible, though hard to believe." He stroked his beard in thought for a moment, all eyes watching him. After a moment he let out a sigh. "I suppose this doesn't change what we were going to do, unless you have a problem with killing him now, Pukuh."

Pukuh shook his head. "No... He's not the Benjamin my father sailed with. Not anymore."

"Now the question is how we get William and the rest of our men back to the ship without being seen?"

Anne stood up. "What? No, William cannot be moved, he needs to rest."

"The longer we stay here the more dangerous it is for us. As we speak the men who attacked us could be rallying others to find us or go after the ship. There's between six hundred and a thousand people living here, and only a little over two hundred of us."

Anne furrowed her brows in anger. "He'll die."

"I can make it," William croaked as he tried to sit up, but his arms were trembling under his own weight and he eventually collapsed back in a heap as he struggled for air.

Anne pulled Edward aside and whispered to him. "He is safe here with the Boddens. You can leave. I will stay with him and Roberts here until he is healed, and in the meantime I will attempt to bring order back to the town. If we cannot, we shall meet you again at sea."

Edward looked into Anne's sea green eyes filled with concern, and then at William's sweat-drenched face and clothes as he tried to catch his breath. He let out a sigh. "I suppose that is for the best... Roberts," Edward called.

"Yes, my boy?" the giant Roberts said as he came over.

"Anne has elected to stay here with William as he heals and attempt calming the citizens. Would you and your crew stay with her to try to keep the peace, and then meet up with us at Montego Bay?"

"Aye, I'll stay and ensure the princess isn't bored to tears," Roberts said with a grin.

Edward gripped Roberts' shoulder. "Thank you, friend. I know we've been neglecting your desire for vengeance for some time, and I'm sorry for that. Once we find out where Walter Kennedy is, and settled this business, we'll go after him."

Roberts shook his head. "The Lord will deliver Walter Kennedy when it is his time, and no sooner. Do not worry about me. You find the man who did this and bring him justice."

"We will," Edward replied. "Together," he said as he squeezed his friend's shoulder.

Roberts smiled and put out his hand to shake, and the two laughed as each gripped the other's hand as hard as they could a show of strength. After a moment they released their hands and Roberts pulled Edward in for a bear hug.

After Roberts released him, he gave Anne a goodbye kiss and then looked at Pukuh. "Pukuh, let's get back to the ship so we can find the man who destroyed our town, whatever you want to call him."

Pukuh rose to his feet and grabbed a spear resting against the wall in his one hand. "I am with you, brother. Benjamin has much to answer for, and I wish to question him before I shove my spear through his heart," he said with a menacing look on his face.

Edward grinned. "Well said." He went over next to William's bed. "William, we've decided to let you stay here and be the lazy sod you have been for a bit longer. Use your vacation well, as I'll have you working double-time to make up for it when you're back with us."

William stared at Edward with a stoic expression on his face. "I wouldn't have it any other way," he replied. "Godspeed, Captain. Give him hell for me."

Edward could now see the anger he heard in William's voice reflected in his eyes. "You have my word," Edward said.

Edward and Pukuh gave their final goodbyes to William, Roberts, and Anne, and exited the room. They headed down the stairs and to the front door of the Bodden mansion, quickly telling the crew serving as guards that they were leaving and that Anne was in charge.

Upon exiting the mansion, Edward noticed that it was close to dark out. The red glow from the sun was nearly gone, and he could see long bands of light stretching across the sky. They rushed to the front gate, but as they got a better view of the main street they slowed their pace to a stop.

There was a large crowd of people walking up the street, led by a man that, at least from as far away as he was, looked like one of the men Edward had fought on the pier. Many in the crowd held makeshift weapons like hammers meant for construction, timber, and farming tools.

"This isn't good," Edward said. "Men, get inside," he said to the men guarding the gates.

The crewmates jumped at the sound of his voice, and glanced over their shoulders at him and then back at the advancing crowd. One of them fumbled with a set of keys in his hand to open the lock as he kept peering at the angry mob headed straight for him. He shoved the key in the lock and twisted it open. Edward pushed the gate open and pulled his men in, then slammed it shut again.

"Lock it! Lock it!" he shouted, eyeing the mass of people marching towards them.

The crewmate nervously wrapped the lock around the bars of the gate and closed the clasp just as the crowd reached the mansion.

Men, women, and children from across Bodden Town made up the crowd. Edward had seen many of them before, either in their businesses, walking around town, or today cleaning the main street. They were so different than before, with their anger directed at him. Wrinkled foreheads, furrowed brows, and clenched teeth plastered many faces in front of him. The people were calling for blood. Blackbeard's blood.

The man at the front, the sailor who had attacked Edward before, stepped up to the gate.

"Goin' somewhere, Blackbeard?" he said with a smirk.

Edward gritted his teeth. "End this, sir, before any further blood is shed. I want vengeance as much as you, but you are asking for it from the wrong man. End this and I will bring you Calico Jack's head."

"Oh, you'll bring us his head, will you? Just so his men can come back to attack us for yer murder? What about when another pirate comes because of something ye did? Or what about when the Brits come after you and charge us for treason because we helped ye?" The man shook his head. "The only way this ends is if you never sail again."

Edward backed up a few paces, but kept his eyes on the crowd. They were hitting the gate with their homemade weapons, and the metal clanged with each blow. They attacked the surrounding stone walls as well, and it all mixed with the din of the mob. It wouldn't be long before the throng brought ladders in to scale the barrier.

Edward turned his head towards his men, but kept his eyes on the crowd. "Is there a way out back?" he asked.

"Yes, Captain. There is a door at the back of the mansion leading outside the wall."

"Let's hurry," he replied.

The four of them ran to the side of the mansion and to the back. They could hear the sound of the angry voices behind them, but before long they could hear footsteps on the other side of the wall following them. When they reached the small door near the corner of the mansion's perimeter, it moved. The men on the other side were testing the door, but thankfully it was locked.

"Get something from the house, we must barricade the door," Edward said.

Edward and Pukuh stayed behind as the other men

41

rushed into the Bodden mansion from the back door.

The simple pushes from outside the door quickly turned into full-blown attacks meant to break the door down. Edward and Pukuh bolted to the exit and pressed their bodies against the wood. The door was the weakest link in their defence, and it buckled under the strength of the adversaries behind it. With each hit, the door jolted forward with a crash, and it pushed Edward and Pukuh back with it.

The crewmates came back with chairs, and a few others carried a lavish floral-patterned couch. They put the couch up vertically and after Pukuh moved aside they jammed it against one side of the door. Edward kept his shoulder on the door as the other crewmates wedged one chair up against the knob and the other in some fashion between the first chair and the couch. Edward and Pukuh continued to hold onto the furniture until more, heavier items were added to the collection. When Edward felt that the door was secure, he stood up.

Edward was sweating. "Hopefully that will hold. Keep an eye on it just in case."

"Aye, Captain."

Edward and Pukuh entered the Boddens' mansion and went to the main hall. Anne, Roberts, Nassir, the Boddens, the rest of Edward's men, and some of the Boddens' men were standing in the middle of the hall talking amongst themselves with looks of concern on their faces.

When Anne saw Edward her face lit up. "Edward!" She ran over and hugged him. "When we saw the crowd and no sign of you we thought the worst. What's happening out there?"

"The citizens have revolted, they're after my head, and we're trapped in here."

5. SNARE

"How much food do you have in your storehouses?" Edward asked the Boddens.

"Edward, you cannot be thinking about defending this place, can you?"

"What other choice do we have? We're trapped."

Anne looked at the Boddens. "Is there any other way to escape here?"

"I'm afraid not," Niel Bodden said.

"We only have a defensible basement, which you're familiar with already, with enough food to last a month."

Edward nodded. He pointed his crew and the Boddens' men. "I want you to go on the second floor or to the roof, take all the bullets and gunpowder you can, and shoot at anyone who tries to climb the wall. Don't kill anyone unless you have to, and try to stick to warning shots."

The men nodded and ran off to fulfill their orders.

"Have you tried talking with them?" Roberts asked.

"I tried talking with their supposed leader. It's the same man who attacked us on the pier. He won't listen to reason, and the rest are too riled up."

"What will we do then? Eventually we're going to run out of bullets, and they outnumber us ten to one," Anne said, folding her arms.

"We'll have to take everything as it comes. I can't see them trying to breach the walls this late at night. If we take shifts we can keep watch to make sure no one sneaks over the wall, and in the morning we'll see if they'll be more willing to listen to reason."

Anne sighed. "I see no other way around this, so we'll go with your plan. Nassir, why don't you and I start boarding up the windows?"

Nassir nodded. "I know where the supplies are. I'll lead the way."

Before Anne and Nassir could get far, they heard loud pops coming from outside and reverberating through the house. Not long afterwards, the shouts from outside became louder.

Edward and the rest of them glanced at each other, and were about to head outside when the glass of the main hall windows shattered open. A large rock had been thrown in from outside and crashed on the floor of the mansion.

Edward looked at the rock, pursed his lips, and ran up to the second floor and to William's room. William was sitting up now, and had a concerned look on his face. On the balcony was one of Edward's crew with a musket in hand. He was aiming at the front gate, preparing to fire.

Edward gave a cursory glance over at William and dashed over to the other crewmate. Outside, someone was already climbing up the front wall with a ladder.

"How many shots have you fired already?" he asked the crewman.

"Only one, but there must be other people trying to breach the wall, because I heard shots on the other side of the house."

"Stop this," Edward shouted at the horde of people pressing against the gates. "There's no need for anyone to lose their lives!"

A cacophony of responses flooded in from the crowd, but Edward caught the general gist of it. He noticed Anne and Roberts come into view on the balcony on the other side of the mansion.

Edward's crewman fired a shot at the stone of the wall, causing the man climbing to duck down and then give them a dirty look, but he didn't stop. He pulled himself up to the top of the wall.

Edward pulled out a pistol from his belt, and fired. The bullet hit the climber in the leg. He clutched his leg and fell forward into the grounds of the mansion.

There was a collective gasp from the crowd. Edward jumped over the balcony and rolled when he hit the ground. He went over to the man he had shot and picked him up by the scruff of his neck. He dragged the man over to the fence, where the crowd watched in relative silence.

"This is what will happen to each of you who tries to breach the wall," he yelled. "We also have cannons. Do not test us. There has been enough bloodshed here over the past days. There is no need for more. Take the night. Be with your family, your brothers, your sisters, your sons and daughters, and come back with clearer heads so that you can think on who the real enemy is, and what the best course of action for this town is."

The crowd murmured amongst themselves as the cold of night took over the town. The orange glow of lanterns shone between several members of the mob. It illuminated the faces, allowing Edward to see their confused and tired eyes clearly.

The leader was also looking at the crowd as they whispered to each other. Eventually, he spoke up. "Some of you go home, and whoever wants to volunteer to stay watch, stay here," he said. "Come back tomorrow and we'll settle this."

After another moment, the majority of the crowd dispersed, their lanterns bobbing in the distance as they moved. Within five minutes only twenty people remained.

"Step back so I can give this man to you," Edward said. "His wound needs to be dressed."

The sailor leading the charge nodded and waved to the others to move away from the gate. Edward called for someone to open the gate, and soon one of the Boddens' men tentatively exited the mansion with keys in hand. He opened the gate and Edward pushed the injured man outside where he fell to the ground, still clutching his leg. Edward locked the gate once again as someone helped the injured man up to take him away.

The twenty men still left stared at Edward as he backed away and into the Bodden mansion. Soon Anne and Roberts returned to the first floor of the main hall to join Edward with Pukuh and Nassir already there.

"Well," Roberts began, "that went well." He gave a hearty laugh.

Edward ignored Roberts' comment; he was in no mood for jesting. "There are still people watching us, so we won't be able to leave, but at least now they're not trying to tear down the gate to get at us."

"That bought us more time, but what are we going to do with it?" Anne asked.

"We'll keep an eye on the people outside the gates, and make sure that they don't try anything. I'm hoping tomorrow the rest of the townsfolk will have clearer heads and stop this."

Anne had one hand on her hip. "And if not?"

"If not," Edward sighed, "perhaps I can convince them of who the true enemy is."

Anne, Roberts, Nassir and Pukuh all looked at Edward with confidence shining through. They believed in him, and the look in their eyes showed it. The Boddens looked less than enthused, but Edward didn't blame them given that their home was under siege.

"We can take shifts for watch. Any volunteers for first watch?"

Anne stepped forward. "I'll take first watch, if there are no objections."

"I will as well," Pukuh said.

"Good… Boddens, could you work with my men and yours to create a rotation so we have all sides of the perimeter covered?"

The Bodden brothers nodded. "It will be done."

"Nassir, you get some rest. You've been working hard enough here all day already."

"Thank you, Captain," Nassir replied.

Anne and Pukuh both went up to the second floor and went to watch from each of the balcony rooms. Edward, Roberts, and Nassir stayed on the first floor and went to sleep in one of the guest rooms.

All three of them lay awake, trying to sleep against the backdrop of the night. Birds, crickets, and the faint rustling of trees filtered in through an open window along with fresh, clean air devoid of gunpowder, saltwater, and, most importantly, blood.

Despite the siege, Edward's mind was clear. He could think of only a few outcomes to this scenario, and he was prepared for any of them.

"So, what happens if you cannot coax the townsfolk back to your side? I'm well aware of your charisma, my boy, but nothing is certain even where the Lord is concerned."

Edward stared at the whitewashed wood of the ceiling for a moment. "Then we'll have to kill them."

"Edward, wake up," Anne's voice called.

Edward's eyes opened a crack, finding the blurry orange glow of a lantern directly in front of him. He turned over and blinked a few times, and the orange glow turned into red curls, sparkling green eyes, and freckled cheeks.

He pulled himself up out of bed, his bare chest exposed to the cold night. He glanced outside and could see the stars but not the moon, so he had no idea what the hour was. He sluggishly placed his feet over the side of the bed and donned his boots and clothes and weapons.

"Any movement?" he asked.

"None," Anne replied. "They are keeping watch and rotating shifts, just as we are."

"Good, let us hope it stays that way."

Edward and Roberts sleepily made their way to the balcony rooms to keep watch from there. They left Nassir alone to sleep, as he needed it more than they. Edward headed to the left with William, and Roberts headed to the right with another crewmate keeping watch.

As Edward entered the room he yawned and stretched, feeling the call of the captain's cabin. The pitching and rolling of the waves was soothing in a way, and he wasn't able to sleep as well without it, despite the ship's bed not being anywhere near as comfortable as the Boddens'.

William was awake, and welcomed Edward. "Captain," he said with a shaky salute.

"William, you should be resting," Edward replied.

Edward went to the balcony and sat down in a chair already stationed outside. Near the chair, on top of a table, he saw a musket which appeared to be fully loaded and ready to fire. He pulled it closer to where he was sitting for ease, and then rested his feet on the balcony railing.

"Sleep comes and goes. I slept the day away, and so the night welcomes me instead."

"I suppose when one is sick day and night are meaningless," Edward said.

"Most times," William replied. "Tell me, how does it look?"

Edward scanned the town and the wall and gate protecting them at the moment. Lanterns moved in the night, carried by men with heavy clothes on. The faint glow cast angry shadows on their faces, faces which didn't need more anger. It was quiet, save for the creak of the swinging lanterns and the *clack clack clack* of hard leather on stone. The night animals had quieted, and the wind lost its howl as it stopped moving.

"It's calm, but the men outside carry tension on their faces. Lost sleep will not help their mood, I'm afraid."

"I didn't mean out there. I meant how does it look for us? Will we make it out of this?"

Edward looked at William, but aside from his sick, tired eyes, he carried no expression. "I never knew you to be afraid, William."

"I don't care what happens to me, only Anne."

Edward chuckled, and then went back to watching the wall. "We've been in worse situations."

There was a short pause before William said, "That wasn't an answer."

"Go to sleep, William," Edward said with a smile on his face.

Behind Edward, he could hear William shuffle around with his bed sheets, and then he went silent.

Over the next hour, Edward kept a diligent watch, though it was quite boring work. One of the Boddens' housekeepers brought him coffee, which he sipped on, and it helped keep him awake. It would still be several hours before morning, and he needed it.

Edward was looking down the main street when he

thought he noticed movement. At first, he thought his eyes were playing tricks on him, but when he saw movement again, this time closer to the Boddens', he decided to investigate. He rose to his feet and pulled out a spyglass from his belt. He scanned the street for what he had seen, and at first he couldn't see anything more, but after another moment he noticed two cloaked figures running towards the mansion.

Edward stopped looking through the glass and knocked on the wooden railing of the balcony to draw Roberts' attention. After a few raps on the hardwood Roberts looked over. Edward motioned with his spyglass and then pointed to the street. Roberts caught the message and pulled out his own spyglass to peer through.

The two of them watched the street and the approaching figures. While they were being cautious, it seemed they were trying to hide from the men standing watch outside the wall, not from Edward and crew.

When they were fifty feet away from the gate, Edward put down the spyglass and picked up his musket. Roberts noticed the noise, and went to do the same, but Edward motioned for him to stop. He wasn't sure who it was, and it could be one of his crew. If someone was going to have the blood of his crew on their hands over a mistake, it was going to be him.

The two cloaked shadows continued their advance, careful to avoid the light of the homes and standing still when the townsfolk made their rounds. Edward wasn't able to tell who they were, or if they carried any weapons, but he could tell that they were skilled in stealth.

Could it be Calico Jack's men here to finish me off?

Edward looked upon the figures in a new light, and he gripped the musket tighter. He leaned his head up against the barrel, and he could smell the gunpowder resting on the weapon's pan. He traced the movement of the figures with the gun barrel until they came up to the last houses before the Bodden mansion. The two paused as a man passed in front of them, his lantern swaying in his hand. Edward pulled back the hammer and lowered the frizzen over the pan, then fully cocked his gun. The hammer snapped as it locked into place.

That distinctive noise was not loud in the least, but in the dead of night it was easy to hear. For those not familiar with the sound, it could be brushed off as an animal or someone dropping something, but for those who recognised it, it was undeniable.

The two cloaked figures knew the sound of the gun cocking, and instantly looked at Edward. He swore to himself, and moved his index finger to fire before it was too late. The front cloaked figure unmasked himself.

Standing there was Alexandre, the surgeon aboard the *Queen Anne's Revenge*, in all his baggy-eyed glory. He waved to Edward with a smile on his face before he motioned to keep quiet.

Edward let out a sigh and released the cocking of the musket. He gave an exasperated look over to Roberts, and Roberts shrugged his shoulders.

The ever-eccentric Frenchman Alexandre and his companion eyed the men keeping watch on the mansion for a few moments as they whispered amongst themselves. After a moment, the one at the back ran—while being inexplicably silent—over to the gate and knelt down while holding a shield above his shoulder. Alexandre followed soon after and jumped on top of the shield, then the other figure vaulted Alexandre up the side of the gate. He placed his hand on the top of the gate, swung his legs over, and landed on the other side with a roll. The other figure then ran to the edge of the gate where it met the stone wall and jumped off the side of the gate to the stone and back where it gave him enough height to vault over the side of the gate.

Edward's jaw dropped at the sight of it all. The event only took a matter of seconds, but the ease with which it happened was almost a thing of beauty. He hadn't thought that Alexandre was that dexterous, and had he not seen it with his own eyes he wouldn't have believed it.

Edward dashed back inside and to the second floor's main hall. "Open the door," he commanded his men.

They obeyed and let Alexandre and the other crewmate in.

Alexandre peered at his surroundings with squinted eyes. "I do not believe I've been in here," he said nonchalantly. His eyes opened wide and he raised his finger. "*Non, non*, that is not true. I have been here… perhaps."

Edward rubbed his eyes with his thumb and forefinger. "Alexandre, what are you doing here?"

"*Le plaisir* to see you as well, Captain. We came for a few reasons. First, we wanted to know if you needed help escaping, or if you wanted us to have the crew come to the rescue."

Edward thought on it for a moment. If they escaped, or attacked, then there was no chance to keep the town as their home base. The townsfolk wouldn't accept him as their leader if they couldn't trust him. Even then, the chances of them escaping were slim with all their numbers. Not all were as agile as Alexandre was.

"We can't take the risk. Our only chance is to convince the townspeople to stand down. The situation's not as dire as it once was, so I'm hoping tomorrow they'll listen to reason. Tell the crew to stand by in the harbour, captain's orders. We may still need to use force, but for now we're safe."

Alexandre bowed his head. "We thought that you might say something like that. We are also here because one of your crewmates has something to tell you," he replied, looking at the crewmate who'd come with him.

The crewmate pushed the cloak back, but it was a woman Edward didn't recognise. His jaw dropped open. *A woman, one of my crewmates? But, only Christina and Anne are…* He stared at the woman's face, and she stared at him. After a few seconds, it finally dawned on him. "Victor!"

The crewmates around them were just as astonished and voiced their amazement with several expletives.

Alexandre smiled, but the woman remained was expressionless. "Her true name is Victoria, but yes, *Capitaine*, you knew this person as Victor, my assistant." Victor punched Alexandre in the arm, eliciting a glare. "My partner," he corrected, although begrudgingly.

The news stunned Edward. Victor had been aboard his ship almost from the beginning, as far back as he could remember, and he had never seen anything out of the ordinary.

"Don't trouble yourself, *Capitaine*. She's good at hiding her identity. It even took me some time to figure it out."

Edward took a moment to review all of his and Victoria's interactions up until that point, and then he shook his head. "Why, why… why now? Couldn't this have waited for a better time?"

"No, Captain, it couldn't," Victoria said, the hint of an unfamiliar accent present in her voice.

Victoria's sober face and serious tone spoke to the gravity of what she needed to discuss. Edward nodded; there was evidently more to this than just revealing her true self.

Edward pointed to one of the guards on the door. "You, take my post. You two," he said, pointing at Alexandre and Victoria, "come with me."

Edward went into the Boddens' study and Alexandre and Victoria followed in behind him soon after. Alexandre closed the door behind him.

"This had better be good. Truly, I couldn't care less that you're a woman aboard my ship, and you should know that already. Why did you hide your identity from the crew?"

Alexandre was leaning against an alcove bookshelf, wearing a smug smile. Victoria, on the other hand, was as stone-faced as William.

"I hid it because of the crew I was with before this. I knew that if anyone found out, especially the young navigator and his sister…"

Edward clenched his fist. "You were on Calico Jack's crew?"

"A long time ago, yes."

"So I assume the crew has found out about who attacked the town?" Victoria nodded. Edward gritted his teeth. "Damn. I was hoping we could have this resolved before Herbert found out."

"Oh, the boy knows," Alexandre said. "Do not worry yourself, he is sleeping right now on the ship."

Edward nodded. "So, what was so urgent about your previous captain that you needed to tell me now?"

"It's regarding the way he operates. I was with him for many years, and I've seen similar occurrences as what happened here. Jack Rackham is a calculating man, and he would not have left, and allowed the townspeople to live, if he didn't expect this to happen," she said, motioning towards the town. "He knew that this was your town, so he sowed the seeds of discontent to ensure the people turned on you. There could even be some people he paid to see that things progressed this way. This is his snare, his trap, but so far you've managed to save yourself from the noose. His goal is to make it so you no longer have your safe haven, and will run in fear."

"What would he have done if I was in town?"

Victoria looked at him as if he were the village idiot and folded her arms. "He would have killed you, of course," she said. "This was his backup plan."

Edward scratched his face sheepishly. "Yes. I should have known that."

"Now, what you do with the information I've provided is up to you, but you may be able to convince the townspeople of Calico's plot and stop the riot." Victoria pulled her cloak up over her head, and made her way to the door to leave the study.

"Wait, where are you going?" Edward asked.

Victoria turned around, the same look plastered on her face. "I'm going back to the ship. I don't want to be here should you fail," she said before turning around and leaving. She muttered some further things under her breath Edward couldn't make out.

Victoria's candor had caught Edward off-guard, and left him speechless. Before she got too far, he said, "We're going to have to talk more on this later." She waved the back of her hand to him without turning around. Edward glanced from her to Alexandre, who still wore a grin.

"Yes, Captain. She's always like that," Alexandre said before pushing himself off the bookshelf and walking to the door.

"You seemed to enjoy that, didn't you?"

Alexandre turned around and walked backwards, still with the wide smirk on his face. "Of course. She's entertaining, and a bit challenging. I like that in a woman."

"I know the feeling," Edward said, mimicking the grin. Before Alexandre was out the door, Edward grew serious. "Keep an eye on Herbert for me."

"*Oui*, Captain."

Edward went back to his post and relieved the crewmate. He watched as Alexandre and Victoria went back the same way they'd come, jumping over the wall and sneaking off into the shadows.

Victoria's comments about Jack Rackham helped Edward plan what he would say to the townspeople if they were still incensed about the attack. He would have to discuss Victoria's allegiances, and broach the subject with Herbert, but that would be for another time.

As night turned to day, Edward and the others had no more disturbances. The sun gently poked up from the horizon and illuminated the town in a clear light. The birds of the morning sang their songs, and the sound of footsteps and various voices drifted up from outside.

The townspeople, just waking from their slumber, were returning to the mansion in droves. Many yawned and stretched as they walked alone and in groups up the small hill. Despite the many that were gathering, no children were attending, and with good reason. Edward was glad for that at least. If it came down to shedding blood, he didn't want children in the way.

Anne, Pukuh, Nassir, and the rest of the crew also rose from their slumber to join those who had taken second watch. Anne and Pukuh joined Edward, while Nassir and the other crewmates joined Roberts. Edward called Roberts and his crewmates over to his side.

"Did you sleep well?" Edward asked Anne.

"Yes, despite how little of it I managed, it was pleasant to be on solid ground again," she said.

"After all this time you're not used to sleeping on a ship?" Edward said with a smirk.

Anne folded her arms. "It's not that I am not used to sleeping on a ship, it's just that I'm accustomed to certain… luxuries from my former life. I claim no responsibility for the things my mother gave me. I was simply privileged, and it will take me more time to become accustomed to the constant waves, and... and... shut it, you big brute," she finished with a pout.

Edward laughed at the look on Anne's face, and she smiled back.

Roberts, Nassir and Edward's crewmates joined him on their side of the balcony. "Have some of the Boddens' men—" Edward started, but stopped when two of the Boddens' men walked onto the other balcony. "Forget that. Prepare William for transport. I want him ready to leave on a stretcher at a moment's notice."

Two of the crewmates nodded and went to find a stretcher for William.

"Do you think it will be necessary, brother?" Pukuh asked, glancing at William and then the crowd.

"I don't want to take any chances," he replied. "To that end, perhaps it would be best to arm yourselves."

The group nodded, and everyone save Pukuh and Nassir left to retrieve weapons. Nassir prepared William for transport, and helped clear some of the sweat from his brow as Pukuh, with his spear in his hands, walked over to the balcony edge.

"The gods laugh at you, Edward. They have given you the gift of making everyone hate you."

Edward chuckled. "At least that would give me some peace of mind. Then I would know the reason why we can't seem to have it easy for longer than a month at a time." Pukuh laughed with his friend. "I'm glad to see you in better spirits."

"Sleep is a friend to a weary mind and a troubled heart."

"That it is," Edward concurred.

Pukuh took on a sombre look as the crowds were almost finished gathering. "Something your mate said helped." Edward looked at Pukuh, eager to hear what he had to say. "When we were discussing it, she said that the seas could have changed him from the time with my father... You know, in the Maya, we have no god for the sea?"

Edward grinned. "No?"

"We have a god for rain, lightning, those things, but not

the sea. Maybe one of the lesser tribes had one, I do not know. If there was to be a god of the sea, I would imagine him to be great serpent. A serpent that loves to create and ride the waves, but also enjoys the calm, still waters of sleep. When it strikes its fancy, I would imagine he would jump from the sea to the heavens, perhaps angering his brother, Kukulkna, the god of the wind. When the serpent lands back in the sea, he causes great waves in his wake, and his brother sends winds of anger his way so that together they create the storms."

Edward laughed with a wide smile. "Did you come up with that just now? It sounds like it could be real."

Pukuh shrugged. "Perhaps it is, who knows?" he said. "The sea is like this fickle serpent, and those who ride in its wake are forced to withstand the storms, or be broken by it. I feel that Benjamin was too kind a soul, and those storms broke him. Now, he is Calico Jack, a broken man desperate to withstand the next storm."

Edward stared at the sea, and at the *Queen Anne's Revenge* with his precious family aboard it. "I wonder if we will be able to withstand that storm."

Pukuh chuckled and slapped Edward's back, then looked at him with wide eyes. "Brother, you *are* the storm."

I am the storm? Edward was speechless as he stared at Pukuh, the Mayan warrior prince. *I am the storm.*

Edward turned towards the gathering crowd. It appeared that all that had been present the day before had returned, and brought more with them. They watched him, waiting to see what he would say or do.

"People of Bodden Town," Edward began. "You know me as Blackbeard. Perhaps you may think of me as a pirate, a scoundrel, scum who steals from others so he may gain. What you may not know is that my name is Edward Thatch, and many years ago my dream was to own a whaling boat, as my father did before me."

The crew returned with a stretcher, and Anne and Roberts with weapons. Nassir quickly and gently placed William in the stretcher. Anne and Roberts stayed back, out of view of the townsfolk so they wouldn't see their weapons.

"My dream was stolen from me before I could even sell my first catch, and soon I found myself on the run. As I ran from men trying to steal my freedom from me, I found a new dream with the family I created aboard that ship you see in the harbour." Edward pointed to the *Queen Anne's Revenge*. "I found a new dream here, in this town. A dream where men and women could be free to pursue their passions without oppression and tyranny."

As Edward gazed upon the faces in the crowd, he could tell that many were responding to his message. Men nodded, and women listened with perked ears. Some whispered to their neighbours, and in those whispered to theirs. It appeared that he was winning them over.

"Calico Jack now threatens not just my new dream, but yours as well. He wants to tear down what we've built. He wants us to fight amongst ourselves. He wants us to rip ourselves apart so he doesn't have to. Do. Not. Let. Him."

The crowd seemed to be more riled up now. They were talking along excitedly, shouting words of agreement. Some still had their arms folded, but their heads nodded in agreement.

"You have lost sons, daughters, lovers, parents. For mercy's sake, do not lose yourself to the true pirate who seeks to steal your dream you've built so hard to protect. I vow to be your sword on the sea. I vow to be your veng—"

The sound of gunfire ripped the sound from Edward's voice, and he and the others instinctively ducked down and covered themselves. The men and women of the crowd gasped, and Edward heard the sound of many footsteps running away from the mansion.

Edward checked himself for injury, and when he felt no pain and saw no blood he rose back to his full height. His heart was beating like a drum in his chest. "Is everyone well?" he asked his crew. Everyone responded with various affirmations.

Edward looked over to the balcony, and noticed two smoking muskets lying on the table. *Those were the Boddens' men over there,* he thought.

A scream let out in the gathered crowd again, this time

more focussed, more high-pitched, and more terror-filled than the first. Edward turned his attention to the crowd, and he could see two men, dead, pools of blood already forming beneath their bodies.

"Edward, look!" Anne shouted as she pointed to the harbour.

Edward followed Anne's finger, and saw the *Queen Anne's Revenge* in full sail, leaving the harbour.

Edward clenched his teeth and his fists. "Herbert."

6. LURE

Yesterday

A crewmate came running up to the quarterdeck, where Herbert and Christina stood. "Herbert, you'd better look at this," he said, handing him a spyglass and pointing towards town.

Through the magnified gaze, he could see all the way up the main street of Bodden Town. A group of about a hundred people were heading towards the Bodden mansion. They appeared to have weapons on them.

"Oh Father, this isn't good," Herbert said as he peered through the spyglass.

"What is it?" Christina asked.

Herbert wheeled himself over next to Christina and handed her the spyglass. Tala glanced back and forth between the two of them, panting and unsure of what was going on, but riled up by the excitement. "The townspeople are trying to overtake the Boddens."

Christina looked through the spyglass. "First Edward is attacked, now they move on the Boddens? Why? Is it something to do with the attack? We had nothing to do with that."

"The townspeople might not see it like that. Whatever happened, they seem to hold either us or the Boddens responsible."

Christina gasped. "I think Edward is trapped inside."

"What?" Herbert looked at his sister with one brow cocked.

"Edward came to the gate just as the crowd closed in, and they had to lock the gate from the inside." Christina took her eye away from the spyglass and gave her brother a concerned look.

Herbert clenched his teeth and moved his wheelchair around so he could look over the quarterdeck railing. "Someone fetch Jack, and get our men ready for battle. Our captain is in trouble."

Two crewmates nodded and went to task. The others on the weather deck, near abouts twenty out of the crew, retrieved some muskets and proceeded to load them.

Christina started to leave the quarterdeck with Tala following behind her. "Where are you going?" Herbert asked.

"I'm going to load a weapon and grab a cutlass," she replied with a quizzical look.

"I need you to stay with me. We're going to need people to defend the ship in case some of the townsfolk decide to attack us, and I want you by my side."

"But—"

"Please, Christina," Herbert pleaded, "I need you here. I'm not fit to fight in my state, you should know that."

Christina stared at her brother for a few seconds before letting out a sigh. "Well, when you put it *that* way," she said. "Just so we're clear, forcing guilt on your sister isn't fair."

Herbert smirked. "It worked though, didn't it?"

Christina lightly punched Herbert in the arm, but with a smile on her face.

A few minutes later, Jack and almost the entire crew of the *Queen Anne's Revenge*, a little over two hundred of them, came to the weather deck. Some gathered weapons, while others went to the bow or clambered up the rigging ropes to catch a glimpse of the scene unfolding. There was a buzz amongst the men itching for a fight.

"Listen up, men," Herbert shouted. The crew turned their attention to the quartermaster. "It looks like our captain needs us up there, but I don't think I have to tell some of you that the townspeople are not to be harmed. Some of you hail from this town, so you know their feelings. To everyone else, keep your pistols at the ready, but you are to be no more than a threat. These people have been through enough already, and they're only doing this because they're scared. Get the captain, and get out of there without bloodshed. Understood?" The crew agreed loudly. "Move ou—"

"Herbert, look!" Christina called out, pointing to the pier.

Herbert lifted himself up with his hands on the wheelchair to see properly. A group of fifty or so people were coming from all directions to their ship. They were running towards them with crude excuses for weapons and angered looks plastering their faces.

"Bring the gangplank up!" Herbert commanded. The crewmen were watching the approaching townspeople. "The gangplank! The gangplank!" he shouted.

A few crewmates heard the order and pulled up the temporary bridge. Just as they finished, the townsfolk rounded the bend to their dock.

Herbert wheeled himself over to the port side of the ship. His wooden apparatus creaked and groaned as it moved, complaining of its age and closeness to sea water.

Jack was also on the port side, and he leaned his elbows on the railing. "Hello gentlemen, what might we do for you?" he called down to the approaching men.

Herbert looked over the group, and they were all the epitome of normal. He could tell some were sailors, with their rugged hands and weathered faces, and others, with their tanned forearms and hair lightened from the sun, were farmers. None of them were fighters, and they were a far cry from pirates.

They wouldn't last five minutes, the lot of them, even if they had the same weapons as us.

"Would ye mind droppin' yer plank for us? We have something we need to discuss with ye," one of the farmers said.

Jack cast his gaze on the many people gathered, then shrugged his shoulders. "I'm sorry, gentlemen, I simply cannot in good conscience have my men lower our gangplank. You see, I'm not generally a violent man, but these men here?" He motioned to the crew. "These men are quick to violence because they are generally used to life-or-death situations. If I lower that gangplank, and you board, I cannot say what would happen. My captain wouldn't like it if any of you were injured."

The men gathered around the ship seemed to calm down at the threat. They took in how many crewmates there were, and how many carried actual weapons.

The farmer pointed a sharp hoe in Jack's direction. "Your

captain is the reason I lost my brother!" The man's words seemed to rile up the crowd and give them renewed courage in the face of overwhelming odds.

Jack scratched his face. "That's strange, because up until today we had been out to sea. If you're referring to what happened to the town, we were not responsible. Trust me, sir, I know your plight. I have lost loved ones in the past, but I would not put the blame for their murder on someone not at all involved in it."

The farmer did not seem convinced, though he paused for a moment to consider his words. "The pirates who attacked us kept shouting to bring them Blackbeard. We don't want any further trouble, so we're going to bring your captain's head to Calico Jack and be done with it."

Herbert's heart stopped, and it felt as if the icy hand of the Devil had gripped hold of it. Calico Jack, the pirate he used to work for, who left him with nothing after he was crippled, was the one who'd attacked Bodden Town. He froze in place, and he could no longer hear the words exchanged between the farmer and Jack.

"Herbert!" Christina called. "Herbert, are you well?" she said as she knelt down and gripped his arm. Tala barked excitedly, mimicking her master's concern.

Herbert shook his head. "I'm here, I'm here," he replied.

"I can't believe it… Calico Jack was the one to attack. Why?"

Herbert was still reeling from the mention of that name. It took him a moment to answer his sister's question. "We killed one of his subordinates. Of course he would want vengeance. The real question is… where is he right now?"

Herbert could feel a great surge of anger welling up inside him. He too desired vengeance. Vengeance for what Jack Rackham put him through. Edward had promised to help him in his quest, but now he was stuck in the Boddens' mansion. The more time they wasted here, the farther Rackham got away from them.

The sound of gunshots rang out from up the hill of the town. Several sharp pops caused all eyes to turn in its direction.

Herbert grabbed the spyglass that Christina still held and looked through it. He could see the crowd at the mansion had placed a ladder in front of the stone wall, and someone was climbing up it. On the balcony of the second floor, one of their crewmates was re-loading a musket as Edward stepped out. He had a concerned look on his face as he questioned the mate, his massive beard moving as he talked.

One of the rioters climbed the ladder, and the mate shot at him, but missed on purpose from what it looked like. The rioter ducked down, but after another moment he resumed his climb. When he reached the peak of the wall and stood atop it, Edward shot a pistol at him, hitting him in the leg. The man fell inside the mansion grounds before the sound even reached the ship.

Edward jumped down and out of sight, but soon reappeared in front of the gate with the injured man held by the scruff of his neck. After some words from Edward, and a long pause, the crowd dispersed. Twenty or so of the townspeople remained, and the worst of it seemed to be over, but the twenty weren't allowing Edward to leave.

Jack and several other crewmates had also been watching the event as it unfolded. Afterwards, he turned back to the townsfolk at their ship. "It seems as though we no longer have an issue. Most of your neighbours have gone home," he said with a smile.

The farmer looked confused. "What?" he said. He looked at those gathered, then towards town, and at Jack. From their position on the dock, they weren't able to see the Boddens' house. After another moment of internal debate, the lead farmer stormed off in a huff with everyone else following soon after.

"Well, it seems as though the captain managed to calm most of the people down," Jack said to the crew.

"So now we storm the rest of 'em, right?" a crewmate asked.

Jack laughed. "No, no, that won't be necessary, unless the captain wants us to. We need to speak with him first and see what he wants us to do. Although I doubt the townsfolk will let us get close. Someone needs to sneak inside the Boddens' to talk with him. Any volunteers?"

Immediately, a lone crewman spoke up. "I will."

Jack nodded. "Victor, thank you for volunteering. Anyone wish to help Victor?"

"That's not—" Victor began before being interrupted.

"I will go," Alexandre said, placing a hand on Victor's shoulder.

Jack raised his brow. "Truly? Well, I suppose you can see if there are any injured. Thank you, Alexandre."

"*Pas de problème*. We will watch how they patrol and sneak in later in the *nuit*."

Jack nodded before fielding a flurry of questions and objections from the crew on what they should do next.

"We should leave," Christina said.

Herbert cocked his brow. "What?"

Christina began whispering. "Think about it, Herbert. These people were just attacked. Wherever Calico Jack went, he can't have gotten far. We can catch up to him if we hurry."

Herbert paused for a moment. It was as if his own thoughts and desires had been spoken aloud. He badly wanted to chase after Calico Jack, but his concern for Edward overpowered it, even if only just.

"We can't, the captain needs us."

Christina glanced at the Boddens' house. "He's going to be fine. Most of the crowd has left. He just needs to convince those left over to stand down. Besides, we'll just be the advance party. Once Edward's out he can ride on the *Fortune* to join us."

Herbert scratched his chin. His sister made a good point. Splitting up might be the better option if they wanted to find Calico Jack quickly.

"The crew would never accept it," Herbert said.

"They would, if we convinced them," Christina replied. "They trust me. I can tell them how it's a good idea, making it seem as if it's what we should be doing, and soon enough everyone will be saying it. Then, by tomorrow, all you have to do is say a few words and they'll follow."

Herbert looked at the sole of the deck. "I don't know."

Christina pulled his neck up. "This is our best course.

You want revenge, don't you?" she asked.

"Yes, of course I do."

"If we don't move soon, we won't catch up to Calico Jack, we won't have the upper hand, and you won't have your revenge."

Hebert had no rebuttal. He was caught between an uncontrollable urge to do as his sister suggested, and staying to ensure his captain—his *friend*—was safe. He sat there in silence for a moment as his sister's gaze bore into him.

"Very well, you don't have to decide. The crew can decide."

"What?"

"We'll put it to a vote tomorrow, after Alexandre and Victor return with Edward's orders. If he doesn't order us to attack, then we'll propose a vote on whether to stay or leave."

"But how? The captain is the one who has the final say."

Christina sprouted a devilish grin. "Only in battle, and only if he's here. The quartermaster is next in line—that's you. The crew voted you into the position after John passed, and you gained all the privileges that comes with the rank. You are the authority now."

Herbert peered at his sister with newfound respect and terror. He knew she was intelligent, but he didn't know when she'd become so devious.

"Mr Christian," Christina called in a sweet voice.

The crew seemed to have calmed down, and that allowed Jack to see them. "Yes, what is it, my dear?"

"I was just thinking that it might do us well if we raised the anchor. We may need to depart rather quickly," she said with a smile.

"You may be right. Good thinking," Jack replied. He issued an order to raise the anchor, and several crewmates hopped to complete the hours-long task. Jack glanced at the brother and sister with concern written on his face. "How are you two holding up? Trust me, I know how I would be feeling if…" Jack paused a moment and took a breath. "If the man I wanted revenge on was just here."

"I am well," Herbert replied. "I just want this business concluded so we may move on and catch Rackham before he does any more harm."

Jack nodded as he scrutinized Herbert. He appeared unconvinced. He was about to say something else, but a voice from the pier stopped him.

"Oi, is everything well over here?"

Herbert looked over the railing as Christina and Jack turned around to see who was hailing them. Hank Abbot, Bartholomew Roberts' first mate, was at the pier with a few armed crewmates.

"We are well, thank you Hank. Come, Christina, help me with the gangplank."

"Tala, *rester*," Christina commanded, causing her wolf to sit patiently beside Herbert.

Christina and Jack went to the weather deck, and, with the help of some other crewmates, they restored the wood and rope gangplank so that Hank and the crew of the *Fortune* could board.

As they worked, Herbert watched them and petted the reddish fur of the wolf. "What do you think I should do, girl?" he asked the wolf. Tala looked at him when he spoke, but soon went back to watching her mistress, providing Herbert no insight on his dilemma.

Hank boarded and shook Jack's hand, and then he, Jack, and Christina walked up to the quarterdeck. Hank, a shorter but well-built man, looked distraught despite the brave front he seemed to be trying to maintain.

"It seems that we have a slight problem on our hands," Hank said.

"Indeed," Jack replied.

"At least most of them have backed down," Herbert added.

Hank nodded. "Yes, that is fortunate. It looked as if you were planning on heading up to the mansion with your forces until the townsfolk showed up. What will you be doing now?"

"We thought it best to wait, as the immediate threat is over." Jack motioned to the crewmates pulling on the rope of the anchor. "We've decided to raise anchor in case we need to make a quick getaway. Perhaps you should as well."

"Wouldn't want our trousers stuck around our ankles, now would we?" Hank said with a laugh.

"Most certainly not."

Hank told one of his crewmates to go back to the ship and get the others working on the anchor. "Did the townsfolk let slip anything on our captains or any more information on the attack?"

"All we were able to find out was that it was Calico Jack who attacked the town, and they were here for Edward."

Hank unfolded his arms in shock, and several of his mates' jaws dropped. "Now, you wouldn't be tellin' me you had a run-in with this Calico Jack before, would you?" he asked, his face reddening and on the verge of sweat.

"We killed one of his men..." Jack glanced Herbert's way, and Herbert nodded to the silent question. "Our quartermaster here also has some business with Calico Jack."

Hank eyed Herbert, but then focussed on Jack. "He's a dangerous man. Does Roberts know about your involvement with him?"

"I'm sure he does now," Christina replied with a chuckle.

"This won't sour our relationship, will it?" Jack asked.

"No, we have nothing to do with the man, but everyone's heard the stories of Mad Jack Rackham. I reckon any one of us would steer clear of him if we had the choice."

"We don't have a choice, not with him," Herbert said.

Hank stared at Herbert, and nodded after a moment. Hank was afraid, and he had every right to be. If the stories were true, Calico Jack was the truest of villains, and not someone to be trifled with.

"We need to find out where he went."

All eyes were on Herbert after his statement. Hank had a look of concern, but Jack appeared resolved, and Christina smiled. Even Tala seemed to sense the mood and let out an eager bark.

Hank spoke up. "My men and I can go to the local tavern and discreetly ask around. They don't know us like they do you, so we shouldn't have to worry about getting into fights."

Jack chuckled and looked at the broken town. "You think there's still a tavern left?"

Hank joined in the laugh. "With the state the town is in, there's somewhere selling ale, I guarantee it."

"Stay safe Hank, and get some sleep, yea?"

"You as well, friends. I have a feeling we won't have much over the next while."

Hank and the crewmates of the *Fortune* left the ship and walked towards town to gather information. Through all the excitement, Herbert only just now noticed that the sun had descended fully below the horizon. The town was dark, and the cold of the sea wind came in full force.

In an instant, Herbert's upper body was shivering. He looked down at his legs and placed a hand on the thin, frail thing that was half his body. He could feel through his hand that his legs were freezing. The feeling in his legs had been stolen from him by a pirate who probably didn't care. Though the feeling would never return, he wanted revenge regardless.

Herbert told himself that it wasn't just for him. He told himself that he was going to get revenge for everyone else... but he didn't feel grief, or sadness, or any shred of empathy for those who'd lost something because of Calico Jack. He felt only anger. A single-minded, self-serving anger which consumed him the more he thought on it. If he hadn't have heard that name, he could have gone through another day not even thinking on the fateful day when his ability to walk was stolen from him, but that was all it took. Two words, and a flood of memories gripped him and wouldn't let go.

"Herbert, are you well?" Christina asked.

Herbert looked up at his sister's face. Her sweet, caring face that he knew and loved was now grown, and slightly weathered from hard work aboard the ship. He hoped that she would never feel the cold that he felt deep inside, but he feared that it was already too late. She, too, had lost something that had crippled her, but she had been able to build herself back up again. She still carried the weight. He could see it in her face, and in a memento from the past: a carved wooden rose hanging from her neck. He wondered if she was as fragile as he, and if, like him, two words could take her legs from her as well. Whatever the case, he resolved to protect her from that ever happening.

Herbert smiled. "I am well," he said. "Let's leave, shall we?"

Herbert hoped that his words were not lost on Christina, and from the look on her face it didn't seem like they were. She smiled, and the two of them went to the crew cabin to eat, sleep, and wait for word to get back from Alexandre.

"Herbert, wake up," Christina's voice called.

Herbert opened his eyes, blinking to help him focus. It was pitch black inside the ship, as it usually was, so he had no sense of what time it was. Christina held a lantern at her side, and she was fully dressed.

Herbert pulled himself up and moved his legs so they were dangling off the side of his hammock. "What's the hour?"

"Before dawn. It's time for us to make our move. Hank informed us of the direction Calico Jack went, and I've prepped some of the crew's more influential members. Should we put it to a vote, I'm confident they will vote in our favour."

"What of Edward? What of the townsfolk?"

"They haven't awakened, but they will soon. As for our captain... Alexandre said that he's going to stay behind and try to convince the townsfolk that he's on their side." Christina picked up Herbert's clothes from his pack tied to his hammock and tossed them to him. "And," she added, taking a breath, "he's going to stay and help with the repairs."

Herbert eyed his sister. Something about the way she said it made him question her sincerity. "He is?"

"Yes, so we don't have to worry if we leave anyway. Edward will stay as a sign of goodwill, and we can pursue Calico Jack. Then, once they're ready, the *Fortune* can catch up with us. If need be we can leave letters at each port to inform them of where we've gone."

Herbert nodded. He wanted to believe his sister, and that

desire made him convince himself that what she said was true.

He moved from his hammock to his wheelchair with a plop, and after he adjusted himself for comfort he wheeled over to the ladder leading up.

Along the way he noticed Tala sleeping on the sole of the deck. She looked at the two of them as they made their way to the ladder, but went back to sleep a moment later. Their dealings didn't excite her at this hour. Herbert felt the complete opposite. He could feel the blood rushing through him, invigorating him in the moment.

At the foot of the ladder there was a rope specifically for him to climb, and he used it to go to the gun deck while his sister carried his wheelchair up for him. They did the same for the next ladder, and then they were on the weather deck.

It was still dark out, but the fringe rays of the sun peeking from beyond the horizon added some light to their surroundings. Christina placed her lantern on a notch above the main mast's fife rail. The wind swirling around the ship caused the lantern to sway and creak.

"Which way did Calico Jack go?" Herbert asked.

"South, south west. Possibly to Panama."

Herbert scanned the skies, shifting in his seat and looking out to sea as far as he could. "The wind is in our favour, and the sky is clear."

"All the more reason to leave now."

Herbert noticed that there were quite a few crewmates on deck, more than usual at this hour. They glanced at Herbert and Christina as they talked to each other, clearly waiting for something. Herbert could also tell that the sails were prepared and ready to be released and secured at a moment's notice.

"Someone bring Jack here," Herbert commanded.

One of the crewmates said they would, and descended to the crew cabin to wake Jack up. During that time, Herbert and Christina went up to the quarterdeck. Herbert used a platform attached to a pulley created by Nassir to raise himself up to the helms level rather than having to crawl up the steps. Once there, they waited for Jack to come up.

After a few minutes, Jack appeared on the weather deck. When he noticed the multitude of crewmates already there, he looked confused for a moment. He saw Herbert and Christina and went to join them on the quarterdeck.

"Herbert, has something happened at the mansion? Why is the crew gathered?"

"They are gathered because I... they feel we should be pursuing Calico Jack instead of waiting around."

Jack chuckled, believing it to be in jest, but his smile faded as he glanced at Herbert and his sister. "You're being true with me?" Herbert gave a slight nod, but kept his face expressionless to ensure Jack didn't think this driven by emotion. "Our captain is in danger right now, and you want to leave? He gave orders to stand by in case we're needed." Jack looked to be straining to keep his voice low.

"The captain can handle himself, and if anything goes wrong then the *Fortune* can help. We know where Calico Jack went, as does Hank, so the captain can join us when he's ready by travelling with them. In the event that we pick up the trail and have to leave another port, we can leave letters for them so they know where we've gone," Christina's words echoed from Herbert's mouth.

Jack's jaw was open and he was speechless. He uttered a few single laughs, then shook his head and covered his mouth with his hand. "This is madness," he said. "Not that it amounts to much, since no one here has the authority to make such a decision."

"The crew does," Herbert replied. "Article one of the Commandments, which I shall remind you were created by Edward and Roberts, states that each crewman may vote on current affairs. I would wager that this is considered a current affair, would you not, sir?" Herbert, though sitting, did his best to cast his gaze down upon Jack. "Or shall we put that to a vote as well?"

"Those Commandments were meant for outside of battle," Jack retorted.

Herbert glanced around, then raised his brow. "I don't see a battle happening currently... do you?"

Jack simply stared at Herbert for a moment, still

speechless, but this time his good humour was spent. He closed his eyes after a moment, let out a sigh, and knelt down. "Herbert, trust me when I say I know how you're feeling, but this isn't going to help things. It is best if we wait for the captain to be done with his business, and then we leave these shores together. Don't let your anger cloud your mind."

"Tell me then, Jack, if you have such intimate knowledge of how I feel, what would you do in this situation?"

Jack paused for a moment, then his gaze hit the deck. "That should have no—"

"As I recall, there was once a time when you pulled a musket on the man on whom you want revenge," Herbert said.

"I was—"

"You were endangering the crew, because at the time we were surrounded by enemies, and you were provoking them. And then, after that incident, you did what?" Herbert said, his words harsh and biting. "You drowned yourself in bottle after bottle for a year, trying to swallow your sorrows in drink." Jack had no more words, and despite the mournful look on him, Herbert pressed on. "I have looked upon this situation from all angles, and weighed the options. This is the best course of action, and it doesn't affect Edward's situation in the least. Perhaps it is your mind that is clouded."

Herbert wheeled himself forward to the quarterdeck railing, leaving Jack there, still knelt down. After a few seconds, he heard Jack pick himself up off the sole and leave to go below deck. If he was not so caught up in the moment, he might have felt remorse for what he had said to Jack, but he was numb to pity right now.

"Men, right now we have an opportunity to catch the bastard that destroyed Bodden Town. This ship was renamed in the spirit of vengeance upon our enemies, and if we wait any longer we risk losing out on vengeance for you, and for the people of this town," Herbert shouted. "All those in favour of setting sail and finding Calico Jack to put him to death, say aye!"

The crew responded with a resounding "Aye" which echoed from the ship out onto the great wide sea behind

Herbert. They looked at Herbert with more respect than they ever had in the past.

"Hop to it, then. I want this ship moving immediately," Herbert commanded.

"You heard the man," Christina added. "Clear the mooring lines, shove us off, and jump those halyards!" she shouted.

The crew shouted another "aye" and went to work. The men ran this way and that, removing the ship's ropes from the pier, pushing it away from the dock with spars, and unfurling the sails.

Christina looked over to Herbert and smiled at him. He smiled back to her, excited at the prospect of finally getting his revenge.

As the *Queen Anne's Revenge* turned itself around with the wind, Herbert thought he might have heard the sound of gunshots in Bodden Town. With all the noise of the crew and the wind beating the sails, however, he couldn't be sure, and so he paid it no heed.

7. BODDEN TOWN'S END

Edward's ship diminished in size as it got farther and farther away from Bodden Town's port, heading south-southeast to God-knows-where. The *Fortune*, on the other hand, stayed where it was, moored to the pier.

The sounds of angered screams told Edward to focus on the immediate issue at hand. The townsfolk believed that he was the one who'd shot the muskets and became enraged by the death of more of their people. They had been incensed the other day, but mostly tired and desiring an end to the bloodshed. Now, against an enemy they knew they could defeat, and with fresh wounds, they were rioting outside the gates.

Edward ran out of the room and jumped over the second-floor railing to the main hall. He landed on the hard wooden floor and rolled before jumping to his feet. Just as he expected, he noticed two of the Boddens' men heading towards the secret basement entrance beneath the stairs to the second floor.

Edward drew his cutlass, and the golden blade sang. The two men heard the beautiful tone, and their heads flashed to the side, their eyes wide with fear. Edward took two steps forward, reared back, and threw his blade at the man closest to the basement entrance. The first man was able to jump through the door, but the second man moved into the path. The sword hit him through the chest with such force that it knocked him against the wall and pinned him there.

Edward flew over to the corpse and yanked his sword from it. The other man was running down the winding staircase, his footsteps echoing through the corridor. Edward pursued the man down the steps, jumping down two at a time like the lion that he was. He would have his prey; it was only a matter of time.

He caught up at the bottom of the steps where he leapt at the man with his cutlass poised overhead. He swung it down with both hands at the man's skull, and nearly cleaved him in two with the blow. Blood splattered across Edward's face and clothes, dyeing his hair and beard reddish-black as it dripped from one strand to the next.

The anger of the townspeople was as a child's tantrum compared to Edward's fury. He'd trusted the Boddens, and they had betrayed him. They didn't even have the decency to do the work themselves, and used one of their men to do it for them. Whatever reason they betrayed him for—money, power, or their own version of revenge—they would not live to see it to fruition. Edward would make sure of that.

He went down a hallway into a small square room with man-made cover of stacked wood and sandbags. At the back of the room was an iron vault, the door of which was halfway opened. He peeked around the corner to check for traps, but the vault was empty.

He had first seen the vault when he'd fought the Boddens for control of the town, and when he entered it again he saw a familiar scene. There were lanterns on the walls, loaded cannons on wheels, and stacks of cannonballs and many barrels of gunpowder in the vault, but there was something new: A door leading out the back.

There is an escape route. Those bastards will pay for this!

Edward dashed forward, but stopped after a few steps. The door leading out was open a bit, and he could hear voices from behind it.

"Light it, quickly!"

It was one of the brothers, and they were just on the other side of the door.

An idea struck Edward. He pulled one of the cannons in front of the door, and lit a linstock in one of the lanterns, then opened the door.

Standing there in a long, dark hallway which seemed to go back for miles, were the Bodden brothers, Neil and Malcolm. One of them was doing something on the floor, but Edward's wasn't able to see what it was.

Edward didn't say a word; he allowed the brothers to re-alise for themselves their fate. After a few seconds they turned around to see the cannon facing them. Edward waited just long enough to see the fear and shock in their faces before he lowered the linstock into the cannon.

The cannonball exploded from the cannon towards the brothers. The angle wasn't quite as straight as Edward would have wanted, and it caused the cannonball to strike only one of the brothers in the chest. The power of the blow knocked the brother back as it crushed in his ribs and killed him instantly. The ball then missed the other brother and flew off down the corridor.

The second brother had covered his face and ducked down during the blast. He glanced around in his crouched position when it was over. When he noticed the dead body of his brother beside him, he called out to him, tears streaming down his cheeks.

Edward stalked forward, ready to finish the job, until he noticed what the Boddens had been doing before he interrupted. There was a large set of gunpowder kegs with fuses bunched together, and the fuse was lit.

Edward jumped backwards, slammed the door shut, rolled to the side, and covered his head with his hands. A few seconds passed before the gunpowder ignited and exploded. The door blasted off its hinges and into oblivion, and sent chips of wood flying everywhere. The explosion shook the entire home, as far as he could tell, and it didn't end immediately. The shaking and rumbling noise lingered for a few moments past what Edward would have thought was normal.

When the shaking subsided, Edward removed his hands from his head and examined his surroundings. Dirt swirled and flowed into the vault from the Boddens' escape route. He stepped over to the opening, and looked at the hallway. He waved his hand to try to disperse the fragments of earth in the air, and after a few seconds it settled and he was able to see the corridor.

The corridor was no longer a corridor; the earth above

and below had been blasted away, causing a cave-in. Mounds of dirt and rock blocked the escape route, and Edward could not see how far the rubble extended. On the ground and the sides of the walls he noticed great splashes of blood, and the remains of unrecognizable body parts. The corridor had become the final resting place of the Bodden brothers, and the end of their era.

Footsteps came from behind Edward and several people entered the vault. He turned around to see Anne, Roberts, Nassir, and Pukuh there. Anne had a sword drawn, and she raced to his side and clutched his arm.

"Edward, are you unharmed? What happened?"

Edward took a few quick breaths. "I'm well. I caught the Boddens as they were making their escape. They had planned to explode this tunnel, and they succeeded, but not before I stalled them enough to have them caught in the explosion as well."

"You are certain they are dead?" Roberts asked.

Edward nodded. "I am certain. Their blood stains the walls of this place now, and this will be their grave."

"Now we have no escape, and the people are soon to breach the walls. Will we fight?" Pukuh asked, holding his spear at his side.

"We will never win if we fight. They have the numbers, while we have an injured man to worry about, and we have no way to signal our..." Edward paused for a second, looking away. He shook his head and looked at Roberts. "Your crew," he finished. "We have no way to signal your crew to help us."

"Then what will we do if we cannot fight?" Nassir asked, concern written on his face.

Edward glanced around the room, thinking on their options. "I only see one way out of this, and it will be dangerous."

"I doubt there is an option that wouldn't be," Anne said.

"Point taken," Edward replied. "Anne, I want you to take some of the men to remove the furniture from the back door. Nassir, you and another mate bring William down to the main floor and be ready to leave." Anne and Nassir nodded and ran out of the vault together. "Roberts, help me remove this cannon from its mount."

Edward and Roberts went on either end of the six-pounder and gripped it as best they could. "One, two, three," Edward said.

He and Roberts lifted the cannon off the mount. The cannon was easily over three hundred pounds, but the two were able to manage. They gently dropped the cannon to the floor, and it rolled off to the side of the room.

"Now we need to take the mount upstairs. While Roberts and I handle this, Pukuh, I need you to take some of these gunpowder barrels upstairs as well. Make sure to bring some of the fuse wire as well."

Roberts laughed deep from his gut. "Edward, you can bring some barrels yourself. This is nothing for me," Roberts said as he slapped Edward on the shoulder.

Roberts, a giant even by Edward's standards, bent down and grabbed hold of the cannon's mount. He then lifted with his legs, and brought the wooden apparatus over his shoulder and above his head in a monstrous feat of strength.

Edward gazed in wonder at the teetering mass of wood which must have weighed over one hundred pounds, possibly even two. "Are you sure you're fit to carry that?"

"It's just a tad awkward, is all, but I will manage. I once had to carry Hank through the jungle for three days as we were chased by—" Roberts paused mid-sentence, his mouth open, but he closed it and waved his hand. "Perhaps this is a story for another time," Roberts said before he slowly moved from the vault to the other part of the basement.

Edward shook his head at the sight, and at Roberts' carefree attitude despite all that had happened. He didn't know how Roberts managed to keep so positive in the face of imminent death. *Perhaps some of it comes from his Welsh accent. It nearly sounds as if he'll start singing with each sentence.*

Edward helped Pukuh place one of the gunpowder barrels over his shoulder, and then took one for himself after storing some fuses in his trouser pocket. They left the vault and walked up to the main floor while staying mindful of their cargo. Once on the main floor, they placed the barrels near the door leading outside.

Edward could hear the townsfolk outside, still rioting and presumably acquiring the tools to scale the wall. They were lucky that it seemed none had the foresight to bring any equipment back in the morning. *If it hadn't been for those fools the Boddens, I could have convinced them to lay down their arms.*

Edward rushed back towards the basement. "Come, we need at least two more," he said.

Edward and Pukuh went back down the spiral staircase. They met with Roberts halfway down, still carrying the cannon mount. They were cautious as they bent down and walked underneath the wood and metal device.

Once it was safe, they rushed to procure another barrel of gunpowder each. By the time they were back upstairs, Roberts was in the main hall, bending down to drop the mount.

Nassir and another crewmate were also there, with William strapped into a stretcher between them. "What do you want us to do, Edward?"

"Stay here, we're going to leave soon. Be ready to move."

Nassir nodded, his strong arms taut and ready for work. He would have no trouble carrying his end of the stretcher.

Edward set his barrel down and helped Roberts drop the mount. Once it stood on solid ground, he glanced from it to the door leading outside. *It looks to be just the right size. Perfect.*

"So, what now?" Roberts asked as he caught his breath and rubbed his arms.

"Now we tie the gunpowder on the cannon mount, and move it to the front gate," he said before picking up one of the barrels again.

"You don't mean to…?" Roberts asked, looking at Edward with a stern expression.

Edward placed his barrel on top of the mount and held it there for a moment. "It's just a distraction. There should be enough time for the townsfolk to run away, and then we'll escape out the back and into the woods."

Roberts nodded at Edward's explanation and helped the other two place the other three barrels onto the cannon mount. They used rope from a nearby storage closet to tie everything down, and Edward placed fuses in each of the barrels. He took the fuses and tied them together beneath the centre of the mount so it was dangling on the ground.

After they finished, Anne and one of Edward's mates returned. They were sweating and breathing heavily.

"The back door is clear, Edward," Anne said. She looked between the three men at what no doubt looked like an odd contraption. "What is that?"

"It's what's going to get us out of here," Edward replied.

"Well, whatever you have planned, it must be done soon. They are about to clear the walls."

Edward walked over to the front door of the Bodden mansion and grabbed two lanterns. He turned one off and emptied the oil all over the mount. "Now, when I open the door, you must push that out as hard as you can. It needs to reach the gates."

Roberts nodded, and positioned himself behind their powder kegs on wheels. Edward placed his hand on the doorknob. Roberts bent his knees and put his shoulder on the mount.

"One, two... three!" Edward shouted as he opened the door.

Roberts pushed the cart forward with all his strength. The hundred-and-some pound bomb stood no match against the seven-foot-tall bear of a man. As he and the cart approached the door opening, he picked up speed. When he reached the opening the cart jumped over the threshold and bounced down to the stone walkway below. At the last second, he gave the cart one last shove with his shoulder. The cart tumbled down the walkway and smashed into the iron gate with a loud clang.

Edward took the burning lantern in one hand, reared back, and threw it as he had his sword not ten minutes ago. The lantern arched through the air, the tiny flame protected by glass. It landed just beneath the cart, and the glass shattered on impact. The oil spilled out from the lantern, and the tiny flame ignited it into a fair-sized blaze. The oiled wood of the cart attracted the fire, and before long it enveloped the mount.

The townsfolk saw the mount and the kegs and the flames and feared what would happen next. They ran away from the gate and the mansion, some trampling over each other to get farther away.

Edward waited until he saw the fuse ignite, and then closed the door. "Run!" he shouted.

His men, and his wife, ran through the Boddens' mansion to the back. Nassir and the other crewman carrying William did their best to keep up.

When they reached the back of the mansion, the thunderous roar of an explosion shook the walls. Screams, louder than before, filtered through from the outside.

Edward and the others left the mansion and continued their mad dash to escape. He kicked the back door open and held it for the rest of his friends. They ran through as quick as their tired legs would carry them. After Nassir and his helper were through with William, he rejoined them in their flight.

In front of them was a long stretch of cleared field, then grass followed by waist-high bushes, and only then did the forest start. Two hundred metres separated them from freedom, and it was the farthest two hundred metres Edward had ever had to travel in his life.

When he reached the grass, his legs were already burning. Halfway through the grass he was breathing heavily and his lungs were calling for more air than he could manage at such a pace. As they approached the waist-high bushes and shrubs, his body was pushing against him, telling him to stop. He couldn't help but slow down and look behind him, and when he did he noticed townspeople pointing in their direction.

"They've spotted us," he yelled between deep breaths.

Edward's group entered the woods and continued advancing as best they could amidst the branches, bushes, and roots. The dew of the morning wasn't helping either, adding slickness over the roots.

Nassir's foot caught on a spindly root, and he stumbled, nearly dropping William, but he held his grip firm. Edward helped Nassir up and they kept pressing onward, every so often glancing backwards. William, though still sleeping, didn't look well, and the travel was not helping.

Sweat beaded on Edward's forehead and cheeks. It slid down into his brows and beard, mixing with the blood and keeping it wet in his hair. He could feel the clingy moisture all over him, making his body heavy and his tongue thirst for water.

Edward could hear the townspeople behind them in the forest, but he couldn't see them when he glanced back, which was good. It meant they were also hidden.

Anne was leading the charge, taking them in a random route to best hide them. Edward could tell she was favouring the west to keep them in the woods yet still not far from Bodden Town. She was thinking ahead to when they would need to return to the *Fortune* once free of their pursuers.

William hindered their escape, and, if their angered shouts were any indication, the townspeople were catching up.

After they had been running for over an hour, there was a small rise of a hill which sloped to the south. Anne took them up it and travelled near the edge to give them a vantage point over their pursuers. When they reached the peak, Anne called a halt.

She motioned for everyone to kneel down, and she creeped over to the edge of the cliff. She went down on her stomach and crawled forward to get as close as she could.

Edward joined her cliffside. "What is it?" he whispered.

Anne pointed down to the forest below them, and Edward noticed some of the townspeople, this time with guns in hand. He recognised them as former militia-men. They were searching the area below. Now that Edward wasn't running, he was able to hear.

One of the men came upon the cliff, and let out a sigh.

"Dammit all, we've been at this for hours and they keep getting away from us."

"It hasn't been hours," another replied. "They're around here somewhere, and they're bound to be tired. We'll catch them soon, you'll see."

"That's what you said twenty minutes ago."

The two men bickered for a moment until someone else came running through the trees to them. The two pointed their weapons at the newcomer until they noticed it was another townsperson.

"Need you... back in town..." the man sputtered through ragged breaths.

"We can't leave now, we've almost caught that bastard Blackbeard," the first man said. When his friend gave him a look he shrugged his shoulders.

The third man choked down air. "We need everyone back... some of the houses caught fire after that explosion."

"Fire?" the two men said, and then they started running back with the third.

Anne and Edward rose to their feet. "I suppose that explosion you caused was an even greater boon than we thought," Anne said.

"Yes, I suppose it is. I pray none were injured."

Edward said the words, but even as he said them he could tell he didn't feel it in his heart. He had been betrayed by the Boddens, yes, but he was also betrayed by his people. If they hadn't stormed the mansion the first time, or if they hadn't come back in the morning, this wouldn't have happened. He didn't feel any remorse for any loss of life that he caused; perhaps it was just for their betrayal.

Now that they didn't have to worry about being chased, they were able to rest and take their time heading back to shore. Edward was eager to see whether Roberts' crew knew what happened with the *Queen Anne's Revenge*. At the very least he hoped that they knew where it went.

As they walked, Edward wiped the sweat from his brow and tried to dry his hair. The trees gave them no respite from the heat, and with it came flies. There was no end to the mosquitoes attacking him, despite his furious swatting. The buggers got everywhere, and he knew that soon he would itch all over.

Anne stayed back with William and did her best to feed him water while on the move. She kept his blanket and body secure in the stretcher, and even wiped the cold sweat off him. After happening upon a natural stream, she wet a cloth and placed it on his forehead.

After they had walked for an hour, heading southeast in a roundabout way back to Bodden Town, Edward and Roberts switched with Nassir and the other crewmen in carrying William. Edward was at the back, and Roberts at the front.

"He's gotten worse," Anne said.

"He has to get worse before he'll get better," Edward replied.

Anne stared daggers at him. "Does it not concern you in the slightest when one of your crewmates is on the verge of death?"

Edward scoffed. "Don't be so dramatic, woman," he said. She clenched her fist, and looked about to strike him. "I'm sorry," he said quickly. "All I mean is that William is the strongest among us. He will make it through this. He's been through worse. Trust me, we shared a prison for almost a year."

Anne took a deep breath and unclenched her fist. "I hope you're right."

Everyone was quick to tire of walking. The flies were making a meal out of them all, and there was no end to them. The heat was oppressive, and seemed to be trapped beneath the forest's canopy. It was never this hot aboard the ship, at least not while on the weather deck. Perhaps in one of the lower decks from time to time, but Edward could escape from that. Here, he was stuck, and it was wearing on him.

Mercifully, after another hour, they were able to leave the forest. They were a mile out from Bodden Town on the lower west end, and quite near the harbour. When they reached open air, the sea breeze cooled them and renewed their spirits. Soon they would be on the *Fortune*; all they had to do was sneak into town and down to the harbour.

Edward and Roberts switched William back to Nassir and the other crewmate as they reached the edge of the forest. Upon stepping out from under the canopy, Edward's gaze first went to the harbour. He could see *Fortune* still docked, which lifted his spirits.

"Oh Father," Anne cursed.

Edward glanced at her, then followed her gaze. What he saw knocked him back a few steps as if he had been punched in the gut.

Towering flames reaching twenty or thirty feet high engulfed half of Bodden Town. The red and yellow inferno was taking over the town, and showed no signs of slowing. From Edward's small blaze, the entire town was being burned away.

Edward was stunned into silence. Despite his feelings on their betrayal, this was too much harm for retribution. The townspeople didn't deserve this. Not after they had already lost so much.

He also felt mourning over the work that he and his crew had put into the town. They had made it their own over the years, and it was all being destroyed in front of his eyes.

Roberts placed his hand on Edward's shoulder. "Come, there is nothing we can do to help them now," he said, pushing him forward.

Edward's steps became listless, and his gaze centred on the fire in the middle of town. The buildings soon covered his view, but they could hear the crackling and breaking of wood as the fire consumed the houses. It even felt hotter in town than outside, as if the heat from the blaze was able to reach them where they were.

No one was in the streets, so they were able to reach the pier in no time. In the centre of the pier, people had lined up in a human chain, passing buckets of seawater to each other in a futile effort to douse the flames. Others watched as their homes burned, either wide-eyed in shock or broken down in tears. More still were running around with their belongings in hand, boarding the only undamaged boats and ships to flee the devastation.

At the *Fortune*, a throng of people were pleading with the crew to let them aboard. Men, women, and children all tried to get aboard the ship, but the armed pirates kept them at bay. Hank was on the bow, looking at the people with sorrow clear in his eyes.

Roberts gave a loud whistle a few times to get Hank's attention. When Hank noticed and looked their way, he almost couldn't contain his excitement. He whispered orders to the crew, and twenty of them left the ship with muskets raised. Those twenty forced the begging crowd back. At the same time, men pulled in the mooring lines. Edward noticed the anchor had been raised already, so the lines were the only thing keeping the ship in dock.

As the crew pushed the citizens back, some fell off the pier and into the water. After a few minutes, they had moved back enough to allow Edward and the others to enter the pier and board. As quick as they could, Edward and his friends ran from their spot between the houses and up the pier and onto the ship. The twenty men with muskets followed them onto the ship.

After they were all aboard, the crew pulled the mooring lines in, and the ship floated away. Other crewmates tried to push the *Fortune* back with spars, but the townsfolk grabbed them and pulled on them.

Roberts motioned for Nassir to head below deck to get William looked at by their surgeon.

Hank walked over. "Glad to have you back, Captain," he said.

"Let's save the pleasantries for later. Right now, let's get this ship moving."

Roberts' crew responded with a loud "Aye, Captain!" and got to work turning the ship around.

Some of the townsfolk jumped into the water and swam over to the ship as it was trying to leave. They clung to the sides, and tried to climb aboard. The crew pointed muskets at them to deter them, but some didn't stop. They had to throw a few families overboard, and kicked some men right off the side as they all screamed for their lives.

It took them twenty-some minutes to get the ship oriented and the sails to the wind, all the while dealing with desperate townspeople trying to board them to seek safer shores.

When it was over, Edward, Roberts, Anne, and Pukuh all flopped down on the deck, exhausted. Behind them, they could see in full the burning town they once knew as home. Somehow, distance made it appear not as bad it was, but Edward knew better. The town was gone forever. On the other hand, it had been gone well before the blaze took it. It was already gone the day Calico Jack attacked, and the day the Boddens betrayed him. They no longer had their safe haven, and now they too had to seek safer shores.

"What now?" Roberts asked.

"Now, we go after Herbert," Edward said. "I've lost my town. I will not lose my ship."

8. INFLUENCE

"All I'm asking is that you set aside some of your men to work during the night," Edward said. "I'll join them as well. I'm not asking them to do something for me that I wouldn't do for them."

"I am sorry, Edward. I will not have my crew run ragged to increase our speed by a whisker or two," Roberts replied.

Edward and Roberts were sitting in his cabin on opposite ends of a table. Roberts was drinking tea, holding the cup in his hands to stop it from spilling with the waves. The ship rocked up and down with the small ocean swells. Edward held his cup as well, but he was not yet interested in partaking of his host's hospitality.

"We lost hours in Bodden Town, and if we do not do this we will lose days. Herbert will be running my crew in shifts to keep the ship at top speed, and you don't know him as I do. His madness will drive him to coax more wind out of the sails than any other."

"I understand your desire, Edward, and I know what will happen, but this is all that we can do. We have a small crew, unlike yours. We can afford a few crewmates to watch the sails and warn of impending storms, but that is all."

"It doesn't have to be many more than that. I can—"

Roberts held up his hand, and Edward stopped his plea. "Let us move on to other business," he said. The look in Roberts' eyes told Edward to not say another word. He was slow to anger, but Edward could tell that he had pushed past what was acceptable. "I am not one to be troubled over such things, but the crew has a right to know what you will do about their lost money. We, too, had invested in the town, and that was lost when you burned it to the ground."

"I will repay you all in full at a later date. There is some money aboard the *Revenge*, and we have yet to sell the plunder from our previous exploit. You may have all the profit from it instead of the half we agreed upon. That should put a dent in what we owe you."

Roberts nodded. "Aye, that it would. What say we call that even? I know the crew would not blame you for what happened, so I'm sure they will accept that as payment."

Edward leaned forward and finally sipped on his tea. "Thank you, Roberts. You are a true friend."

Roberts laughed. "You honour me. Truthfully, you have also done much for us. We are only returning the favour."

Edward shook his head. "No, it is more than that. You honor yourself by your actions. You could have left at any time, heading off to complete your revenge, but you didn't."

"Justice, Edward. Heading off for justice," Roberts said, lifting his cup.

"Yes, justice," Edward replied, lifting his cup as well.

Roberts took another sip of his tea, and then set it on the table with one hand holding the side. "I have to say, you have shit for luck."

Edward chuckled. "Perhaps," he said.

He glanced off to the bright interior of Roberts' quarter-deck cabin. The large windows and lanterns provided much light in the generous space. He could see the sea from the stern, churning and swirling in their wake.

"I cannot fathom what Herbert was thinking, nor how he convinced the crew to join him."

Roberts smirked. "He may have a bit of that Edward Thatch magic in him. A stirring speech and off they went," he said with the wave of his hand. "Something like that, perhaps?"

"Perhaps. I can't help but feel responsible somehow."

Roberts raised his brow. "How so?"

"I built my crew on one thought," he said, lifting his finger. "Freedom. Freedom to choose how we want to live our lives. Freedom from oppression. As you no doubt recall, as soon as we had our freedom, I called on my men to change that focus to revenge. Herbert's always wanted revenge on Calico Jack and his men, and gone to great lengths to get it. My shift in focus could have emboldened him to do this. He knew that your crew was still ashore, and that if anything happened you could come to our aid, and then follow after them. He's gone to such lengths just to gain a few days' head start on finding Calico Jack. For revenge. And, in a way, I taught him it was a good idea."

For a moment, the two were silent. Edward hunched over in his chair, staring at the tea as it gently rocked in his cup.

" Ezekiel eighteen-twenty: *The son shall not bear the iniquity of the father, neither shall the father bear the iniquity of the son*," Roberts recited.

Edward looked up from his cup at Roberts, pausing for a moment to consider the words. "So, we're responsible for our own actions?"

Roberts smiled. "Yes, that is the core of it."

"I'll be sure to tell him that when I sock him in the face," Edward said with a smirk.

Roberts grinned with his friend and raised his cup. Edward returned the gesture, and the two took swigs of their drink.

There was a knock at the cabin door. "Enter," Roberts said. Anne opened the door, stepped inside, and closed it behind her. Roberts rose to his feet, and Edward joined him. "Ah, join us, princess. Come, come, we were just having a bit of tea." He put his empty cup down and filled another with some fresh tea, holding it out for Anne.

"Thank you, Mr Roberts. I should quite like the refreshment."

Anne took her cup and sat down next to Edward. The men sat again, and Roberts poured himself some more of the drink.

"How is William?" Edward asked.

"Better now that he's stationary, but he is still in the grips of a fever. He was badly injured in his fight, so it will take some time for him to recover."

"What did my surgeon say? He might not be as skilled as your Frenchman, but he gets the job done."

"He said that there was nothing we could do save making him comfortable. Since then, he's been feeding William rum by wringing a soaked rag over his mouth, to dull the pain," Anne said.

Roberts grinned. "That gets the job done too," he said with a wink.

Anne held back laughter and looked away. "So, what were you gents musing about?"

"Fathers and sons, my dear," Roberts answered. "Fathers and sons."

Anne raised her brow and looked at Edward. He shifted in his seat to better see Anne. "We were discussing whether I am responsible for Hebert absconding with my ship."

"Ah," Anne murmured with a knowing look on her face as she glanced at Roberts. "Ezekiel eighteen-twenty."

"Spot on, my dear," Roberts said, pointing at her.

"Well, as much as I would enjoy having a dissenting opinion, I have to say Herbert is responsible for his own actions. He is an adult."

"That's what I said," Roberts added with a hearty laugh. "You see, Edward? Even your wife agrees with me. You should listen to her, she's a smart woman."

"That she is," Edward said.

"Not to diminish your compliment, Mr Roberts—thank you as well for that— but if I were to play Devil's advocate for a moment I would say that it's not entirely one way or the other. We cannot deny that you have enabled Herbert in many ways. He wouldn't be seeking out revenge if not for your intervention."

Edward gestured towards his wife, but peered at Roberts. "See? She can see what I am thinking."

"Of course, he is responsible for taking the ship, and should be punished for it."

"Of course," Edward repeated.

"But to deny that we are influenced by our surroundings, or the company we keep... well, that isn't right, now is it?"

"Yes, but to be influenced we must allow ourselves to be influenced. Even if that influence goes by unheeded, it is due to our looking the other way or choosing not to be bothered by it."

Anne's mouth was a line. "So, you believe that we are who we are from birth?"

"We are as God shaped us, and from there, we grow into

that mould by our decisions."

Anne shook her head vehemently. "No, no. There is simply no truth to that. We certainly make choices, and I do believe that inaction is choosing not to act, but there are many things outside our control which affect our perception of the world."

"Tell me then," Roberts said.

"Tell you what? Tell you of something outside our control?" Roberts nodded. "As babes we are told certain truths by our parents, but who is to say whether they are truths? We are not in control of what our parents tell us is the truth."

"Yes, but when one grows and becomes an adult, there is no longer an excuse to be blind to the real truth of the world. Blindness is a choice as well."

Anne let out an angry sigh. "Sometimes you can be so bull-headed," she said, but her anger was only on the surface. Edward chuckled aloud, and Anne glanced his way. "You've been silent this whole time, Edward. What's on your mind?"

"Nothing," he replied. "I'm simply enjoying this bit of theatre between you two."

Anne grinned and finally took a sip of her tea. Her eyes widened. "Is there rum in this tea?"

Roberts put his finger over his smiling lips. "Shh, it's my secret brew."

Edward grinned and raised his glass to Anne before downing the last of his cup and filling it again.

Anne chuckled and she too drank of the Pirate Priest's special brew. The three of them drank well into the afternoon, discussing all manner of topics. And, for a brief time, they forgot their troubles.

Edward stared at the protruding hump of one of Roberts' crewmen's backside as it swung in the hammock above him. He couldn't sleep in this unfamiliar place, with a mostly unfamiliar crew. Even the smell was different. The smell of sweet, slight Caribbean pine on the *Queen Anne's Revenge* was gone, and in its place that of red cedar. He could tell because the scent was almost foul in the sort of way that tickled your nose, and, as he wasn't used to it, it lingered in the space around him. The only blessing was that it was so powerful in the closed-off area of the ship that he had trouble smelling the normal odours emanating from men who had been working all day.

As if to repeal Edward's thought, the man above him expelled gas right on top of him. The hammock was poor protection from the flatulence, and Edward had to cover his face. He jumped from his hammock and walked away to escape the stench.

Edward donned his coat, boots, and a cap, and decided to visit the weather deck. As he poked his head out above the boards, a gust of cold wind hit him and nearly took his cap with it. He kept one hand on his cap as he stepped onto the deck proper.

The *Fortune* was a rare three-masted sloop-of-war with a solid gun deck and a small stern quarterdeck cabin, but no bow cabin. It was lighter and faster than Edward's frigate, and even had enough cannons to be a threat to ships like his. The superior speed was the key, and meant that it could do swooping arcs to fire broadside and right itself before it was left open to attack.

Something Edward only noticed now, being on board for one of the only times where the ship was moving, was that having no forecastle made it easier for the quartermaster to see their direction. It also offered a smaller profile to the wind, which no doubt contributed to *Fortune*'s speed.

I wonder if we'd be able to beat Roberts if we rid ourselves of the forecastle and aftcastle. It could certainly help in battle to have a bit of extra speed. Perhaps I should talk to Nassir about it.

Edward glanced around the ship, and noticed several crewmates walking about, checking the rigging and keeping watch, some enjoying the night air, and some playing cards.

Speak of the Devil.

He noticed Nassir conversing with one of Roberts' crewmates at the bow. He walked over to them, and waved as he approached. Nassir and the crewmate waved back, then

Roberts' man finished talking and went back to his watch.

"Couldn't sleep either, Captain?" Nassir asked as Edward joined him at the bow railing.

He shook his head. "No. I've always been a light sleeper, but put me on an unfamiliar ship and it seems I'm even worse."

Nassir grinned. "It's the smell, no?"

Edward smirked and raised his brow. "You noticed it too? Is that keeping you up as well?"

"Cedar lingers. Much too strong for my tastes."

"Exactly my thoughts."

Edward faced the bow and leaned his elbows on the railing, letting the chill air of the night sea cool his face and body. The smell of the cedar washed away, and a more pleasant aroma replaced it. He closed his eyes.

Nassir chuckled. "Better?"

Edward nodded and opened his eyes. "Much," he said. "I was just thinking about something I should discuss with you."

"Oh?"

"I notice on this ship there is no forecastle, and the aftcastle is not as large as our own. Roberts' cabin is barely tall enough for him to stand upright in," he said with a grin. "So, would we be able to remove our forecastle and perhaps lower the aftcastle to give us more speed?"

Nassir stroked his chin in thought. "I'd need to see the ship to be certain, but I don't see a reason why we couldn't."

"Good, good. That could help us out in the future. Perhaps when this business is over we can look into it."

Edward went back to staring at the sea water as it crashed against the ship. The sails were low to avoid dangerous conditions should the weather change without warning and send the ship too far off course. There was little bounce in the *Fortune* as it crashed against the water, but he could still feel the slight dampness of spray against his pant leg. He knelt down and placed his hand on the bow, and the ocean's cold water splashed against his hand.

"Was there something else keeping you up, Edward? Something on your mind?"

Edward dried his hand on his chest and stood up again. "Anne, Roberts, and I were discussing whether someone is responsible for their own actions, or if another can influence them and is also responsible. Anne took the middle way in saying it's not wholly one side or the other, as both are correct, but Roberts believes that someone's choice is ever-present, and they cannot be influenced without their choice."

Nassir raised his brow. "How did you come upon such a topic as this?"

"I feel as though, because of my enabling Herbert in his madness for revenge, I am partially to blame for him taking the ship."

Nassir pondered the situation for a moment. "When our quartermaster first joined to run the helm, was it a choice, or did you force him to come aboard?"

"It was a choice."

"And I recall hearing he wanted revenge even then, no?"

"That's correct. He wanted me to promise that we would help him with his revenge."

"Then you are not to blame. There is no question in this."

"How can you be sure?"

"He had already desired revenge before boarding your ship. You did not create that desire. It would be the difference between him asking 'do you think I should get revenge for this?' and 'I'm going to get revenge for this, will you help me?' If it was the first question, then yes, you influenced him, but it was not. It was the second question, and you agreed to help him. If you hadn't agreed, he wouldn't have boarded, and might have sought help elsewhere."

"I suppose I had not thought of it that way. Thank you, Nassir."

"You are welcome," he said. "I believe I would have to side with your beloved on the topic. Perhaps thinking of it as a ship is best. Herbert has chosen the course, and he has asked you to adjust his sails. By helping him, he will reach his destination faster, and there is no doubt of that influence as he has no control over what you do, but he decides what his destination is."

"So, our friends are the crew of each of our ships,"

Edward said, a slight smile on his face. "I like that."

The wind seemed to have picked up since Edward and Nassir first started their conversation. It was chillier than before, and he was not dressed for the weather as he should be if he was to be working on deck.

One of Roberts' men approached them. "Could ye help us with the sails? The wind's changed, so we need to beam reach if we want to stay on course and keep our speed."

"Come, Nassir, let's show these men how it's done," Edward said with a grin.

Nassir smiled as well. "Yes, Captain."

⚓ ⚓ ⚓

"So, you're sure that this is where Herbert will have gone?" Edward asked.

"If he's not gone completely mad, then yes," Hank Abbot replied. "Porto Bello, and in fact the entirety of the Spanish Main, is a popular spot for pirates to raid, from what I hear, so it makes sense that Calico Jack would frequent the area."

Edward, Hank, Anne, and Roberts were on the quarterdeck. They watched the ever-expanding mass of land stretching across the horizon. They headed towards a small inlet with natural, grassy hills, and several ships either anchored in the water or leaving the inlet.

"Why would Calico Jack head here after Bodden Town? He already raided it, so why attack another immediately afterwards? Why not head to a familiar port to sell and spend their spoils?" Anne asked.

"I'm sorry, miss, I wish I had the answer. This is just what the people in town said they overheard during the attack."

"Could it be his base of operations?" Bartholomew pondered.

"I don't believe Calico Jack or his crew would let slip where his home port was located to their enemies," Edward said as he pulled out a spyglass.

"Then that begs the question of why his men would say where they were heading either."

"You think it could be a trap?"

"Perhaps, but not for us," Bartholomew said, then he pointed at Edward. "For you."

Edward gritted his teeth as he looked through the spyglass. *Damn it! Herbert, you'd better not have gotten into trouble.*

He scanned the approaching inlet with his magnifier, searching for his ship or signs of battle. They had a full view of the inlet, and he wasn't able to see any ships the size of the *Queen Anne's Revenge*. He could see several three-masted ships, and a few had a gun deck, but they were not as long as his.

Edward let out a sigh. "Well, unless it capsized, *Revenge* isn't here," he said.

"Let's hope it's because Herbert left, and not the alternative," Anne said.

Edward smashed his fist on the quarterdeck railing. The sound of the blow placed all eyes on him. "This wouldn't have happened had we been more active during the night." He let out a sigh, then glanced over at Roberts and the rest. "Sorry, this is all a bit frustrating."

"As long as you don't break my ship I do not mind the occasional outburst," Roberts said.

"Rather than acting a fool, why not pray that Herbert left a message for us at the very least?" Anne said.

After entering the inlet, Roberts and crew manoeuvred *Fortune* into an empty side of the harbour and dropped anchor. There were other larger ships stationed around the harbour, and they didn't want to attract any unwanted attention by allowing their ship and name to be examined.

Even should they have wanted to, there was no way Roberts' ship would be able to dock, as Porto Bello's pier was only meant for small fishing ships.

The tropical Porto Bello was covered in lush green trees on its tall rolling hills above and on the sides of the small town. Edward could see mixed palms and cedars and even some trees with blooming flowers on them which he couldn't recognise. They swayed and bowed in the wind, welcoming the newcomers to their home with gleeful dances.

Less welcoming were the many cannons lining the sides

of the harbour, and the watchtowers dotting the landscape. The whitewashed stone battlements were well maintained, and he could see many men keeping a watchful eye on the ships in the harbour. No doubt those cannons were ready to fire at a moment's notice.

Edward recalled that Hank said Panama was a hunting ground for pirates, and it showed in the defences Porto Bello had installed.

"Let's head ashore and see what we can find out," Edward said.

Edward, Anne, and Roberts entered a longboat with a few other crewmates, and rowed to the dock. As they rowed, several men on the ships anchored in the harbour stared at them. They had wary looks in their eyes, and seemed to be trying to size up the new arrivals.

Though there was plenty of noise, birds off in the distance, wind rustling the trees, people chattering, and the oars beating the water, it felt silent in the middle of all those ships. Distrust was in the air, and soured the otherwise beautiful surroundings.

Anne chose to stare straight ahead, towards their destination, while Roberts was gazing at the scenery and didn't seem to notice those staring at them. Edward chose to return the glares in kind, despite being outnumbered.

They docked the boat at the harbour, and Edward helped his wife up to the pier. Roberts jumped over, dipping part of the boat into the water as he did so.

Edward looked at the other crewmates. "We shouldn't be long, so stay alert and be ready to leave soon." The crewmates nodded and continued mooring the long boat to the pier.

Edward did a quick scan of the harbour to find the harbour officials. There was a building just before heading into town which seemed to be what he was looking for, so Edward headed there with Anne and Roberts following behind.

Edward entered the building, and noticed an older, dark-complexioned gentleman at a desk. On his desk, which spanned most of the length of the small building, there were a multitude of papers of various shapes, sizes, and discolourations. The gentleman was busy scrawling on a piece of paper with a short quill.

The man said something in a foreign language, which Edward presumed to be Spanish, seeing as how this was a territory controlled by Spain.

"I am sorry, I do not speak the language. Do you speak English?"

The man peered at Edward, nodded and asked, "How may I help you, sir?" in near-perfect English, and then he went back to writing on his paper.

"I am looking for a ship that may have been here in the past few days," Edward said.

The gentleman looked up from the paper he was writing on. "You're the second Englishman in just so many days that has been asking for the same thing. You wouldn't happen to be from a ship called *Fortune*, would you?"

Edward glanced to his fellows. "By chance, we are," he replied.

The gentleman did a double-take, then cocked his brow. "Truly?" Edward nodded. "That is interesting," he said before opening one of his cabinets and pulling out a sealed letter. "Here, this was left for you. I presume you know who it's from? They did not give any names, only the ship name *Fortune*."

"Yes, I believe I know who wrote the letter. Thank you," Edward said. He tore off the seal and walked away from the desk as he read it.

"What does it say, Edward?" Anne asked.

"It's from Herbert... We're heading to Panama City."

9. HOW TO MEASURE A MAN

A few days ago

"You lied to me," Herbert said.

Christina and Herbert were in the quarterdeck cabin, a small war room with an ornate table and lavish chairs. Light from the stern windows poured in, and, coupled with the lanterns, illuminated the room. It also made the room hot and humid, despite some of the windows being open.

Christina had a distraught look on her face, and her wolf, Tala, was looking at her with concern. "I know, and I'm sorry. I thought the only way you would leave was if you thought Edward was going to stay behind and delay things."

Herbert cast his hot gaze on his sister, but he had a hard time being angry at her. After all, he had allowed himself to be deceived by not questioning her—or anyone else, for that matter—on Edward's supposed decision. He'd wanted to leave to pursue Rackham, and any excuse would have pushed him over the edge of reason.

Herbert sighed. "I heard gunshots," he said.

Christina raised her brow before glancing out the window and then back at him. "When?"

"As we were leaving Bodden Town," he said, his eyes on the floorboards. He was looking at the pinewood, but his focus wasn't there. He was days ago, reliving a memory he'd pushed away. "I know I heard them from the quarterdeck when we were heading out. God, Edward might have perished and we would not know it." Herbert held his hand over one side of his face, pressing on his temple.

Christina knelt down next to her brother and gripped the side of his wheelchair and his other hand. "Hey, hey, you don't know that." She said the words, but her eyes spoke to a fear even she didn't want to admit. "Edward's been through worse than that. If what happened to him with Cache-Hand didn't kill him, then it's going to take a lot more than a silly riot to do it."

Herbert recalled the incident where one of Edward's former crewmates came back for revenge, and kidnapped him and John. Edward was the only one who came back, and it wasn't the story that Edward told that spoke to his resilience. Herbert remembered a day a few months back when the men were at a bathhouse, and Edward joined in. The memory of all the bullet wounds, knife wounds, and white scars ten inches long across his body still made him cringe.

"Yes, perhaps you're right."

There was a knock on the door to the war room, and Christina stood up before calling the person in. The crewmate poked his head around the corner. "We're dropping anchor in the harbour now, Herbert."

"Thank you, we'll be out in a moment," Herbert replied.

"If he is just a few days behind us, we must keep moving forward, so when he does join us we'll be able to show him something for our actions. If we're lucky we'll find Calico Jack somewhere here in Panama and we'll take him down together," Christina said with a smile.

Herbert wore no smile, his bravado and joy of chasing after a prey lost to the ether. He knew that Edward would see it as his crew abandoning him, and could only pray that Edward would forgive him.

Herbert and Christina left the stern cabin with Tala at Christina's side. Many who were not normally on duty were talking with each other while pointing towards the town beyond the docks, Porto Bello.

Herbert scanned the ships in the harbour, seeing a few that might have been the ships that attacked Bodden Town. None matched the description of Calico Jack's ship, and none flew black flags either, so there was no telling if they were pirates or common merchants. Their one advantage would be the distinct style of Calico Jack's ship. He rode a French-style man-of-war with three gun decks, and it was nearly as big as a galleon, though not quite as long.

As we've only been under the name Queen Anne's Revenge *for a few months now, it's doubtful that Calico Jack has heard of the change. I suppose we have more than one advantage in that case.*

Herbert wheeled himself over to the edge of the railing, and looked at some of the crew talking. "You there, prepare a longboat so we may dock," he said.

"Aye, Captain," one of the men replied.

Herbert opened his mouth to object, and managed to say "I'm…" before the crewmates were gone. In that moment, he felt unworthy of the title, because not only was he not truly the captain, but he felt he was a lousy one. Even so, deep down, some part of him liked being called by that title.

"I'll go and help them," Christina said, walking to the quarterdeck ladder. "*Rester*, Tala," she commanded the wolf, and it lay down to wait at Herbert's side.

As Christina went down the ladder, Alexandre was coming up them. "Quartermaster," Alexandre called. "Or, is it captain now? It is so hard to recall names and titles aboard this ship, as they seem to change so often," he said with a grin.

Herbert frowned. "Quartermaster is my title, and you may call me Herbert. What is it you need, Alexandre?"

"Victor and I wish to go ashore. Victor knows some from the area, and they may be able to *aider* us, if the harbour watch cannot."

Herbert nodded. "I wasn't aware Victor was from here. He doesn't seem to have the complexion."

Alexandre grinned and shook his finger as if speaking to a child. "*Non*, I did not say he is from here, I said he knows some from the area."

"True, I misheard you," Herbert said. "I apologise."

"You would do well to listen carefully, *mon ami*. People always tell more than they wish to. You need but to listen." Alexandre pointed to his ear before he made his way down the quarterdeck to where Victor was waiting.

Why did he say that? Herbert tried to make sense of what the French surgeon was trying to say as he scratched Tala's ears, but eventually he ceased and shook his head. *No wonder the crew dislikes him so.*

Christina walked back up to the quarterdeck. "Shall we go?"

Herbert nodded, hopped off of his wheelchair, and crawled to the longboat. Christina picked up the wooden chair and carried it down. With the help of a few other mates, they managed to get the chair aboard the longboat without issue. With the cargo secure, Christina, Alexandre, Victor, and a few others boarded, and then the crew lowered the longboat into the water.

Tala jumped up, placing her front paws on the railing near the boat. "*Rester*, Tala," Christina said once again, producing a whine from the red wolf.

The longboat fell into the water with a small splash, and bobbed up and down with the movement of the waves as it settled. After the bouncing subsided, the crew placed oars into the water and paddled towards shore.

As they passed by the multitude of ships anchored in the harbour, Herbert felt as though he was being watched. He looked at the ships they were passing, and could see the sailors casually glancing their way or even outright staring at them. Having such a large ship was a threat, even if they weren't here to fight. The sailors were no doubt studying them to measure their mettle in the off chance there was a battle.

Herbert decided to pay them no heed, and instead focussed on the task at hand. He scanned the dock and found a building which could be where the port authorities were stationed. He glanced over to see Christina staring at the various ships and men looking back at them.

"Christina!" he called in a harsh whisper.

Christina looked his way with one brow cocked. "What?"

"Don't antagonize them. We can't get into a fight here, not with all these guns on us."

Christina sighed and turned her attention to the water at the side of the boat. She dipped her hand into the water and made lazy circles on the surface.

They moored the boat to the pier before departing from the vessel. The boat was close enough to the pier that Herbert could climb over, and then the crew helped him with his wheelchair.

Once he was sitting in his mobile seat, he told the men to

come in close. They formed a wall of people around Herbert to contain the sound from their voices. "The air around here feels off. It's almost as if the ships in the harbour are expecting a fight," he said.

"Do you think they're Calico Jack's people?" Christina asked.

"It's hard to say, but I don't want to take any chances. We'll get the information we need and leave immediately. Christina and I will talk with the port authorities and see if they're aware of any ships matching Calico Jack's, and you two," Herbert said, pointing at Alexandre and Victor, "find out what you can from your friend and then head back to the ship. If you aren't back by the time we've raised anchor, head northeast to shore. I noticed some small islands off the coast which could hide our ship from those approaching from the sea. We'll stay there for the rest of our time here in Panama."

The men nodded, agreeing to the plan, and Alexandre and Victor headed straight for town. The other crewmates stayed with the longboat so they were ready for departure. Christina and Herbert went into the port authorities building.

Inside, there were a few sailors standing around who appeared to be swapping stories. They were all speaking Spanish though, so Herbert couldn't tell exactly what they were talking about.

He realised there was a problem. "Do you know Spanish, Christina?"

Christina gave him a look back that answered the question before she even opened her mouth. "Maybe a few phrases."

"We're in the same boat then, it seems. Well, we'll see if we can manage, and if we need to we can come back."

At the back of the building, there was an older gentleman sitting behind a desk while working on some papers. Herbert and Christina approached the man and he greeted them in Spanish.

"Hola, la búsqueda de información," Herbert said in a broken accent.

The man behind the counter chuckled and said, "I know English, but that was a good attempt. You almost had it."

Herbert grinned sheepishly and glanced at Christina. "Thank you. We're looking for a ship that might have passed by here in the past few days, or possibly even today."

"What does the ship look like?" Herbert described Calico Jack's tallship to the man, but he shook his head. "No, no ship like that recently. Often, we do have galleons arriving, but no French ships. We do have the occasional French ship, but none of that size."

Herbert nodded. "Thank you for your time," he said before turning his wheelchair around and heading outside.

The disappointment hit Herbert immediately. This was one of the only developed towns in Panama on this side of the coast, so there weren't many places Calico Jack could have gone if this wasn't where he'd headed.

"So, if he wasn't here, where did he go?" Christina asked.

Herbert rubbed his chin. "I'm unsure. This was where he was headed, but he could have changed direction once out of Bodden Town's sight."

Christina sighed. "What do we do now?"

"Well, we have to hope that Victor comes through with some information we can use," he said. "Let's head back to the ship and have the crew raise the anchor. I don't want us in this harbour for any longer than we have to be."

Christina and Herbert both went back to the longboat, and they paddled back to the *Queen Anne's Revenge*. Back on the ship, Herbert let the crew know that they were still seeking information on Calico Jack's whereabouts. He had some crewmates return to shore with the longboat for Alexandre and Victor, and ordered the anchor raised so they could leave at a moment's notice.

Herbert noticed Jack on the bow of the ship, playing a tune on his fiddle. Herbert had tried to apologise for his harshness over the days of travel to Porto Bello, but hadn't been able to find the words. Now that he knew of Christina's deception, he had somewhere to start.

Herbert pulled on the rope to lift the platform so he could approach the bow. As soon as he reached the top, Jack was beginning to leave. "Hold, Jack, hold a moment!" he said.

Jack kept walking. "I do not wish to speak with you, Mr

Blackwood. You said your piece days ago."

"Please, Jack, hear me out."

Jack stopped and placed his instrument at his side. "Yes?" he said, his mouth a line and his eyes full of daggers.

"I want to apologise. I'm sorry for what I said, and what I've done. I… was misinformed of the situation in Bodden Town, and if I had known the truth… well, we wouldn't be having this conversation."

"And yet you still pursue your quarry?" Jack said, glancing at the longboat and then back at Herbert.

"Yes, what's done is done and we are here now. What would you propose we do?"

Jack looked away and chuckled. "I would propose we return to our home and retrieve our captain. Though, I suppose we would have to determine his wellbeing first. Considering we left him for dead," Jack said loudly, "we don't quite know how he'll be when next we see him. From the look of things it doesn't seem as if you care." Jack motioned towards Herbert before moving towards the ladder again.

Herbert was struck by Jack's words, at first hurt, but soon angered. "I care deeply about our captain," Herbert said. "I've apologised for my actions… what more must I do to right this offence?"

Jack glared at Herbert, his brows furrowed. "There's the rub, isn't it? You may offer your sincerest apologies time and time again, and while the other party may accept it, it does not mean they will offer forgiveness. You may have been deceived into acting, and our situations have been similar in the past, but no one held your hand while you acted cruelly. I've always believed you can tell the measure of a man moreso by how he treats his allies than his enemies. To answer your question: to right this offence, and to receive my forgiveness, you will have to show me how you treat your allies, especially when faced with situations like this." Jack walked down the ladder. "I'll be watching," he said over his shoulder.

Herbert had no rebuttal. All Jack said was true. There had been no reason for him to be vicious when talking with Jack before, other than his anger. He would do better, but for now he needed to keep moving forward.

Edward is alive, and he will join us soon. I'll show him that this was the right thing to do.

The crew worked hard to bring the anchor back onto the ship for when they left. Raising the heavy iron piece was a laborious process, and in truth they probably should not have dropped it in the first place, but Herbert hadn't been sure how long they would have been on land.

Two hours into the middle of raising the anchor, Alexandre and Victor returned to the pier. They used the longboat to return to the ship.

Once they were on the weather deck, Herbert went up to them. "So, did you find any information?" he asked Victor.

Alexandre responded for him. "Victor's contact wants to meet with you, and discuss what we have to do for his *aide*."

Herbert glanced back and forth between Alexandre and Victor. "I thought this person was your friend? What kind of a friend will only help you with a favour?"

Alexandre wagged his finger. "I did not say he was Victor's friend, only that he knew them."

Herbert let out an angry sigh. "What does it matter?" he said, to which Alexandre shrugged with a smirk. "Does he truly know where Calico Jack is? What does he want us to do?"

"He will not say. He wants to speak with you first."

Herbert scoffed, and wheeled over to the side of the ship. "Let's get on with it then," he said before lifting himself from his wheelchair onto the railing.

As he entered the longboat, Alexandre, Victor, and Christina joined him. "Wait, Christina, I need you to stay behind to move the ship if we're not back by the time the anchor is secured."

Christina's jaw dropped for but a moment. "No, I'm coming with you." Herbert opened his mouth to object, but she held up her hand. "Would it be possible to not go through this dance right now? You know you'll just give in eventually, so let's save some time and move straight to that. Yes?"

Herbert's mouth slowly closed, and he motioned for her to join them. When he glanced at Alexandre and Victor, this time they both had grins on their faces.

They brought Herbert's wheelchair aboard, and then went back to the Porto Bello shore and onto the pier. Alexandre and Victor guided Christina and him through the town towards Victor's contact.

The town was lively enough, but seemed quite dull for having so many ships in the harbour. There were few food vendors out, despite it being early in the afternoon, and only one merchant selling general goods from what Herbert could see. Men and women with sun-tinged skin were talking with each other in the street, but the main bustle was coming from a small tavern near the harbour, and no doubt those were sailors, not locals.

As if somehow reading his mind, Alexandre said, "Most of the townspeople work in silver mines. It is… how do you say… lively, at night after the mine closes."

Herbert glanced around at the small town. Most of the buildings were one storey, drab, and made of poor quality wood and stone. There were also many beggars in the street, holding dirty caps out, listlessly asking for spare coin. "For having a silver mine, the town doesn't seem to have benefitted much."

"Spain strips much of its wealth. They send ships to collect the silver and bring it back to the homeland, leaving little for the townspeople."

Herbert shook his head. Spain and England were currently at war, so it made sense that they would want all the money they could have for the war effort, but to leave a town like this in shambles from it was a poor way to run a country. He supposed there were quite a few cities like this one, and no doubt on both sides.

Victor took them to a larger, more affluent home located next to a brothel. A fat Spaniard with a patchy beard mainly consisting of a mustache and chin whiskers guarded the front door. He was smoking and didn't move as Victor and the others entered.

Herbert looked down to see steps, which would be a problem for him. "Christina," he called.

Christina turned around and gasped. "Sorry, Herbert," she said as she ran behind him to push him over the stairs.

The fat guard didn't help her, and was content to watch the two of them trying to enter the building. He blew great puffs of pungent smoke into the air as he watched them from the corner of his eye. Herbert got the same feeling from him as those watching from the boats when they went ashore. He was being measured, weighed, and, as usual, found wanting.

I'll show them. Whatever task they want me to complete, I'll finish it.

Once Christina pushed Herbert inside, he was able to take over and wheeled himself forward to meet with Alexandre and Victor. Inside, there were other men waiting, watching, and smoking. They sat at tables or sprawled out on patterned blankets and rugs and pillows as they filled the air with smoke. Hebert could see many of them either had weapons directly on their person, or lying on the table in front of them.

"Where to now?" Herbert asked, ignoring the many eyes on him. Victor pointed up, and Herbert groaned. "You must be joking," he said with a sigh.

Victor walked to the right wall of the room, and pulled aside a blanket to reveal a set of stairs. Herbert wheeled himself into the small opening to examine his next struggle. Stone steps, two dozen of them, led to the second floor.

Christina leaned into the alcove and looked up the steps. "I can push you up," she offered.

"No, no," he said. "It's easier if I climb myself."

Herbert pulled himself from his wheelchair and flopped down on the stone floor below. He climbed up the steps, dragging his dead legs behind him as he did so. Though the day was hot, the stone was cold on his hands, as cold as his legs had been a few nights ago. His strong arms pulled him up each step with ease, and before long he was at the top.

Victor followed behind, carrying Herbert's wheelchair. At the top of the steps he set the contraption down, and Herbert was able to return to his seat.

Victor walked ahead of Herbert into the room on the second floor. Inside, directly in view of the stairs' opening, was a man sitting in a chair next to a table. He had been watching with a smirk on his face the entire time.

"This is who's looking for Calico Jack?" the man said, incredulous. He had a Spanish accent, but spoke English easily.

Herbert wheeled into the room to better see who was insulting him, and Christina and Alexandre followed right behind him. The man was a skinny Spaniard, who nonetheless looked lithe and agile. He was clean-shaven, and his hair was slicked back. He had a pistol on the table next to him, and beside that a plate of half-eaten food. On the other side of the table were two men, no doubt his personal guards. Their hands were hidden underneath the table, probably holding weapons at the ready. To the right side of the room, there was an open set of double doors, and two naked woman lying on a bed. Herbert did a double take upon seeing them, but once the shock of the sight was over, he stared at Victor's contact.

"Hello, sir. I am Herbert Blackwood, and this is my sister, Christina. I understand you have information on where Calico Jack is."

The man had a wide grin on his face. He glanced to the women in his bed, then back at Herbert. "You like 'em, do ya?" he said. "Give them a couple pieces of eight and I'm sure they'd have those legs of yours workin' in no time." The men at the table laughed.

Herbert ignored the comment. "It is customary to give one's name after receiving one."

"I was waitin' for this one to introduce me," he said, pointing to Victor. "But I suppose that's not possible at the moment, is it?"

The man and Victor exchanged glances, but Herbert was unable to decipher the significance of what he was saying.

"The name's Luis Delgado. So, you fancy yourself chasing down the King of the Caribbean, do you now?"

Herbert gritted his teeth. "Yes. I was told that you had information for us."

"Aye, I do, but not for you," he said.

Herbert's jaw dropped. "What is your meaning? Are you not a man of your word?"

"Oh, I am. I told… Victor here, that there would be a hefty price for the information I'm selling. I wanted to see who it was I was dealing with before then, because when you go against the King of the Caribbean you want assurances. You can't pay the price, boy, so piss off." The man turned around and went back to eating his food.

"What is it you want, exactly? Gold? We have that. Weapons? We have those too. Whatever price we have to pay, we'll pay it," Herbert said.

"It's nothing so simple as money or weapons, boy. You would need to kill someone for me. That task is too much for a crippled boy to handle. Go home before my men here throw you on the street."

Herbert's blood boiled. He didn't come this far to leave empty-handed. "I've been a cripple since I was young, and I can handle a bit. Want me to show you how I handle a gun?" Herbert said.

Delgado looked at Herbert with a smirk on his face, and then got up and walked over to him. "Cheeky one, are you?" he said. "I like that." He backhanded Herbert hard in the face, knocking his wheelchair over and spilling him on the floor.

Christina and Victor started to draw weapons, but Herbert held up his hand. "Stop!" he commanded. The two stopped before things escalated, but both gritted their teeth and furrowed their brows in anger at Delgado.

Herbert turned himself over and crawled back to his wheelchair. Delgado stood in the exact spot where he had hit him, watching Herbert as he lifted the wheelchair back upright. Herbert carefully pulled himself halfway up the chair, and then punched Delgado in the nether regions. He doubled over, and then Herbert smashed his head into Delgado's. He was sent back and landed on his ass, clutching his head with one hand, and his groin with his other.

Herbert mounted his wheelchair, ready to protect himself or get out of the room, but Delgado's men were just sitting there at the table, laughing and pointing at their leader. They were saying things in Spanish that Herbert wasn't totally able to pick up. He was able to understand a few words, such as "knocked," "beaten" and "balls."

Delgado sat on the floor, in pain and rubbing both ends of himself for a bit. "Now, that's what I was looking for!" he yelled, but immediately he winced from the pain again. "Are you going to help me up or what?" he said, looking at Herbert.

Herbert extended his hand, and Delgado grabbed it and pulled himself up. "I need a drink after that one," he said in a lively tone.

Herbert's brow was now permanently cocked in confusion. He looked at Victor for an answer, but Victor just shrugged.

Delgado sat down at his seat and downed whatever was in his cup in one drink. Then he let out a great belch.

"I'm sorry, so now you're going to help us?"

Delgado nodded with a smile on his face. "You can always tell who a man is by how he reacts to an insult. If I needed a negotiator, and you had convinced me, I would have helped. If I needed a dog, and you left here with your tail between your legs, I would have helped. Today, I needed a fighter, and you didn't disappoint," he said while pouring himself another drink. "You didn't have to go for my manhood, though." Delgado once more rubbed himself as he took another long swig of his drink.

"So, you'll tell us where Calico Jack is?"

Delgado shook his head. "Not quite. Calico Jack never sailed here, and I've no idea where he is."

Herbert glanced at Christina. She had a disappointed look on her face, but it seemed to be more for him than her own sake. He wasn't going to be able to have his revenge as he'd wanted. In some way, deep beneath the surface, the news relieved him.

"But I know where one of his subordinates is going to be. From there, you should be able to do the rest."

Herbert's eyes lit up. Being able to find one of Calico Jack's men was good enough for now, and would go a long way towards repairing things with Edward when he arrived.

"So," Herbert said, "where is he?"

Delgado held up his finger. "Not so fast. The deal, if you'll recall, is that you'll need to kill someone for me. Only then will I give you the information."

Herbert glanced over at Christina, and she nodded. "Who is it?"

Delgado lost the smile he had been wearing since agreeing to help Herbert. "I need you to kill my brother," he said.

Herbert was shocked. "Your brother?" he blurted out. "Why do you want your brother dead?"

"I prefer to keep such business in the family. Just know that he is heavily guarded, and it won't be easy. None can know it was me, or I stand to lose much. That's why I'm fortunate to have you all fall into my lap," he said while motioning to Herbert and the others.

"Where is your brother?"

Delgado got up, went over to a dresser on one side of the room, and pulled out a piece of paper along with a quill and ink. He began writing something. "My brother lives in Panama City. He is owner of a large brothel, and you will find him there surrounded by many armed men who work for him. Take care when you kill him. I wouldn't want you dying on me," he said with a smile over his shoulder.

Delgado handed the paper to Herbert, and it had the name of the brothel written on it: *Las Tetas*. Herbert didn't know exactly what it meant, but he could guess. Underneath that, the name 'Marco Delgado' was written.

Herbert blew on the ink to dry it, then folded the paper and placed it in his pocket. "We'll be back soon," he said, turning around and heading to the stairs.

"I cannot wait for your return," Delgado replied.

With the others' help, Herbert descended the stairs and left Luis Delgado's house. Herbert had a wide smile on his face. Though he wasn't going to get Calico Jack, he was closer than ever to one of his men, and it was only a matter of time before they found the rest.

Herbert turned around to face his comrades and his sister. "Let's head to Panama City."

10. PANAMA CITY

"Steady, now," Christina said while holding Herbert's wheel-chair place.

"I know." Herbert carefully gripped his chair and one end of the stagecoach they had been travelling on. After his grasp was secure, he moved from the coach to the wheelchair in one swift motion. Once seated, he wiped his brow of sweat and gazed at the sun, which was now lowering below the horizon. "There, that wasn't so bad," he said.

Christina smiled at her brother, then glanced around as the stagecoach sped off down the road. Surrounding Herbert and Christina were five crewmates who had also just left the stagecoach, and Tala. A short distance the road Alexandre, Victor, and five more crewmates emptied out of another stagecoach.

After hiding the *Queen Anne's Revenge* northeast of Porto Bello, Herbert and some crewmates had taken stagecoaches to Panama City the next morning. The trip had been slow and bumpy, the day was nearly spent, and they were all the more sore for it.

Herbert sighed and glanced down. *If not for these legs and that wheelchair, we could have ridden horses and been here hours ago.*

"Now, to find the brothel," Christina said as she absently scratched Tala's fur.

"First we should find an inn. We're not going to rush this," Herbert said. "We need to find the nearest inn from here, otherwise Edward won't know where to find us."

"That's assuming he even gets the letter you left," Christina said, eyeing her brother.

"He'll check for it, I'm sure," Herbert said, hoping his words would come true. He turned around to head down the road. "Come, let's move." Christina nodded, and they joined the other crewmates to enter the city.

Unlike Porto Bello, Panama City was bustling with

activity. They'd had the coach leave them at the edge of the city where they could see the winding road leading to the centre of town. Dozens of people walked in all different directions, and another dozen stood around talking. The smell of fresh dirt, food, sweat, and the sea all found their way to the group as they took in the sights and sounds.

Travelling through the dirt road brought them through the heart of the city, and they were quick to find an inn in which they could stay.

Christina helped push Herbert up the stairs, and the crew all entered the establishment. Inside the inn there was a small area for receiving guests, a set of stairs to the right, and a large first floor for eating and drinking. The inn smelled of spilled ale, piss, and the collective odour of those in the room as well as those who had long since departed. It overpowered the smell coming from the food, but it was not unlike the smell in lower decks of the *Revenge*, so Herbert found it tolerable.

"Oh! Pets stay outside, miss," the innkeeper said, pointing to Tala.

Christina smiled and apologised as she pulled Tala outside and ordered her to stay.

They paid for some rooms, and sat at the tables to have something to eat other than the travel rations they'd had on the ride over. Herbert, Christina, Alexandre, and Victor sat with a few crewmates, while the rest of the men sat at another table nearby. They made sure to occupy the corner so that none could overhear them while they discussed their plans.

"Victor, you seem to have been in this area before," Herbert said. "Do you know anything of the brothel Luis mentioned, or of his brother?" Victor shook his head. "So we wouldn't be able to request an audience under the pretense of you catching up, would we?" Herbert's question was rhetorical, but Victor still shook his head once more. "I suppose the first step is finding it. After that, we can inspect it to see what we should do next."

"Why don't we just burn the whole thing down?" Christina suggested.

Herbert looked at her as if she were mad. "No! That's a

horrifying thing to say. Why would you even think of that?"

Christina shrugged her shoulders. "Edward would do it," she said.

"No, he wouldn't."

"To have a second opinion," Alexandre began, "*la fille* has a point. It would be the safest... for us at least."

Herbert glared at Alexandre. "No fire." He took a drink from his cup. "I want this to be clean. We only have to kill Marco, so we should only kill Marco. There's no need to have anyone else involved unless we have to."

Alexandre bowed his head. "By your command, Captain," he said, producing some laughter from the other crewmates.

Herbert sighed. There was no point in telling the Frenchman to stop. He knew what he was saying and was just trying to get a rise out of Herbert. "We need to find out who Marco is before we can kill him, so I'll go to the brothel tonight and investigate. Perhaps I will bring some other crewmates with me as well, just in case." Herbert was looking at the men at his table and the one next to theirs.

"I'll go with you," Christina said.

Herbert gave her a similar look as before. "A brothel is no place for a young woman... well, not unless you're— no, absolutely not."

"What of it? I know what goes on there. You don't have to be afraid of me participating, if that's the problem."

Herbert was taken aback at first, but quickly regained his composure. "That's not the... The men might try to take advantage of you."

The anger was clear on Christina's face. "I can take care of myself, and besides, that's why the rest of the crew is there, is it not? We'll be watching out for each other."

Herbert stopped looking at his sister and instead stared straight ahead. "I've said all I'll say on the matter."

"You're treating me like a—"

"Enough!" Herbert yelled. His voice cut through the din of the inn, and caused a slight hush. All eyes were on their table, staring at him and his sister.

Christina's tan cheeks reddened a touch, and her mouth was stone. She didn't say another word as she left the table and headed for the second floor. On her way she pointed at the open doorway. "Venir," she commanded Tala, and the wolf raced to her side. She rushed up the steps before the innkeeper could say a word to her about the beast, and slammed the door to their room behind her.

Alexandre had a smirk on his face, and his dark, sullen eyes showed a hint of amusement. "That went well," he said.

Herbert looked at the crewmates sitting with them. "After we eat, we head out to the brothel. Choose five amongst yourselves to join me, and tell them to stay alert and find out any information they can on Marco. One way or the other, tomorrow Marco dies."

Herbert wheeled himself up to the front of the brothel names Las Tetas. It was late into the night, almost time for people to be sleeping, and yet lantern light poured from all the rooms inside the brothel. Judging from the noise alone one would think it were the middle of the day in a busy street.

The brothel was located in a secluded part of the city with few houses nearby, so they didn't have to worry as much about noise as others might. It was a large, three-storey house with many rooms, and many of them overlooking the sea.

Herbert looked at the shallow steps leading to a small patio and an open doorway. *I might be able to...* He pushed himself forward and leaned to one side, lifting the right side of the wheelchair up. He moved forward on the left wheel and dropped the right end down on the top step, then with another push over the side of the steps he was on the patio. The wooden machine creaked and groaned with the movement, but stayed together throughout the affair.

Someone nearby whistled and clapped. "Where'd you learn to do that?"

Herbert looked over to see a few men standing around, looking at him. The one who spoke was eating an apple. He was shirtless, and looked to be a local patron, with his tanned complexion and short, dark curls. He had several tattoos adorning his body in various patterns Herbert didn't recognise. Around his neck he also wore necklaces that clinked against each other as he moved.

Herbert chuckled. "You spend enough time in this contraption and you learn a few things," he replied. "Where did you learn how to speak English so well?"

"You spend enough time around you Brits and you learn a few things," the man said with a wink.

Herbert held out his hand. "Herbert Blackwood."

The man looked Herbert over for a moment as he took a bite of his apple. After a few chomps, he threw away the core and shook Herbert's hand. "Fernando." After shaking his hand, Fernando walked up to the door. "Care to join us inside?" he asked.

Herbert grinned. "I would enjoy some company, lads, but of a different persuasion. You flatter me with the offer."

Fernando laughed, and his friends joined in. "Cheeky. I like that."

"I'd be glad to join you for some ale," he said.

Fernando waved him in. "After you."

Hebert went into the brothel, followed by Fernando and his comrades. The first floor was filled with rooms, with a small area for dining and drinking. There were five tables strewn about, and Edward could see men and scantily clad women sitting at all of them. At one end was a stocked bar with what seemed to be one of the few men working at it.

He noticed and made eye contact with several of the patrons, all of whom were his crewmates. They nodded back to him subtly.

Some of the men cleared away from one of the tables, the women they were with leading them by the hand to different rooms. Herbert, Fernando, and his friends went to the now empty table.

A server came over to their table, a young woman and possibly the only one not working as a woman of the night. She was a local, and greeted them in Spanish, but when she noticed Herbert she spoke in English. "What can I get for you—?"

"Just fetch us some ale, dear," Fernando interrupted.

The girl's mouth went agape, and she glanced from Fernando to Herbert before she nodded and went to the bar to complete the order.

"So," Fernando said, "what brings you to Panama City?"

"I'm with a merchant ship, looking to make some deals between here and Porto Bello. We just arrived in the city after a day's travel, so I'm here to rest before business begins."

Fernando's eyes widened. "A day's travel?" he said. Herbert nodded. Fernando shook his head. "It must be hard with those legs of yours."

The server returned with the ale and passed a mug to each man. Herbert took his in hand and took a long sip from it.

"Yes, travel is rather difficult."

Fernando smirked. "What about your downstairs business? That work, or does it just hang low?" he said, pointing in Herbert's direction as he took a swig of his ale.

Herbert chuckled. "Oh, he works just fine." He didn't elaborate and hoped that the men would move on so he could try to find out more about this place. "This is quite the establishment," he said. "I don't think I've seen one quite so big."

"She's the biggest one in Panama City. All the men from the shore to the centre come here for a night with our girls."

"Must make a pretty pence." Herbert took another drink of his alcohol and peered over the edge of the cup at Fernando. The ale tasted like the inn smelled, but he didn't let on about his thoughts, lest his guests not take kindly to the comment.

Fernando nodded. "That it does," he replied.

"I wonder if the owner would want some of what I sell? Do you know him?"

"I know him. What is it that you sell exactly?"

"This and that. My crew and I were seeing where the need was, and whether we could fill it," Herbert leaned forward in his wheelchair, "not unlike these girls," he finished with a forced grin.

Fernando laughed heartily at the joke. After a moment he pointed at Herbert, his cup of ale still in hand. "I like you," he said, and then he downed the rest of his drink. "Come, I'll introduce you to him." Fernando rose from his seat and walked away from the table.

Herbert's face lit up. "Ah, thank you, sir. You do me a kindness." He set down his cup and followed Fernando.

"Don't thank me yet. The owner is a fickle man."

Herbert glanced to the other tables, and noticed his crewmates were still there, but distracted by the women tempting them to their beds. He continued following Fernando into a room in the corner on the first floor.

Upon entering the room, Fernando's men followed in behind and closed the door. Fernando walked over to a desk at the back of the room, turned around, and half-sat on it.

"So, where's the owner?" Herbert asked, suddenly feeling nervous.

Fernando motioned to himself. "You're looking at him," he said.

Either he's lying, or I've been set up. "Oh, sneaky. Why didn't you say so to begin with?" *If I can just fire my pistol, the others will rush over here.* Herbert slowly moved his hands closer to his waist, where a pistol sat on his lap, covered by a blanket.

"I already know why you're here, Herbert, as do my men," he said.

His comrades grabbed his arms to stop him from grabbing his weapon. "Hel—" he tried to yell, but the third man came up behind and placed his hand over Herbert's mouth while choking him with his large arm.

"I've always told my brother to watch the people he trusts, but he still couldn't see the spy right in front of him."

Herbert couldn't breathe with the muscle wrapped around his windpipe. His body struggled to pull air in, as did his arms to pull away from the men pinning him, but he couldn't win against their strength.

"You, though… I didn't expect him to send someone like you."

Herbert felt pain across his neck, face, and head, as each muscle strained to bring him life-giving air. He could feel the slow, methodical beating of his heart across the skin of his face. Thump, thump, thump, it went in his ears. It was slowing down as each second passed. Thump, thump, thump.

Herbert's vision faded, black spilling into the corners of his eyes, and weakness sapping the strength from his arms. His eyelids sagged, and soon fell to a close.

"Goodnight, Herbert."

Those words from Fernando—or Marco, Herbert supposed—were the last thing he heard before he blacked out.

Christina awoke with a start. She was breathing heavily, and there was a cold sweat across her forehead. She didn't remember if it was a bad dream that had forced her out of her slumber, but if it was, the remnants of it took hold of her heart. A feeling a dread gripped her, and stayed with her even after she caught her breath and wiped her face with a wet cloth.

What is this feeling? Tala was beside Christina, fully awake as well, and whining. She kept glancing from her master to the door and back. "Do you feel it too, girl?" she asked while scratching behind Tala's ear. Tala responded with a loud bark.

Christina clothed herself, told Tala to stay in the room, and went down to the inn's dining area. The room was mostly empty at this hour, and much of the smell from earlier in the day was gone, but some still lingered in the air. The smell of the open cups of ale and the food still coming out of the kitchen was more prominent now.

As it was late at night, most of the crewmates were in their rooms already, but a few were sitting at one of the tables playing a game of cards. She went over to the men.

"Where is Herbert?" she asked.

The men glanced her way before continuing their game. "He's gone with some mates to the whorehouse. They gettin' the skivvy on how to go about it."

"Or gettin' their loins wet," another man said, causing the others to laugh. After a moment they stifled their laughter and glanced at Christina.

Christina ignored the comment and looked at the door to

the inn, now closed, but with shutters open and showing the dark of the night. Lanterns lit the outside of the inn, but beyond that she couldn't see anything. A cold gust tried to penetrate the door, but instead made it bang and crash against the loose lock keeping it in place. The cold still seemed to hit her somehow, and a chill went up her spine.

"How long has he been gone?"

The same man who answered before peered at the ceiling in thought. "Hmm, before the sun fell, wouldn't you say mates?" The others at the table nodded. "Yea, near that time." The crewmate looked at Christina over his shoulder, and he had his brow cocked. From the look on his face, he could tell Christina was worried. "Nothing ta worry yerself over, Miss Blackwood. No one knows who we are."

The mate's words were little comfort to Christina. She absentmindedly touched and tugged at the wooden carved rose around a chain on her neck. She would never admit it to herself, but whenever she was afraid it would show in that nervous tic of playing with the memento around her neck—a constant reminder of one she lost, and could not let go of.

"We should check on him. Something doesn't feel right," she said, the fear she wanted to hide creeping out into her voice.

The men glanced her way again, but this time they stopped playing their game. "No need to trouble yourself. Everything is well, and your brother will be back before you know it." The other men nodded with the comment and joined in reassurances.

Their comfort did little to ease Christina's heart. "I can tell when my brother is in danger. I can always tell," she said, force behind her words this time.

The men looked at each other, some with slight smirks on their faces. The main crewmate who was talking with her walked over to her and began pulling her back to her room. "My dear, do not let your worries send you into hysterics. After a night's sleep you'll feel better."

Christina pulled away from the man, furious. "Enough!" she yelled. "I'm not in hysterics. Something is wrong, and you can either come with me and help my brother, or wait here and let a girl overshadow your valour."

The men were speechless at Christina's burst of anger. They stared at her, unsure of what to do. The room became silent, and even those who weren't in their crew were watching the scene.

"Hmph," Christina said, turning around and going back to her room.

She gathered a cutlass, a pistol, and a musket, and strapped them all to her person. Then she donned a cloak to help with the cold of the night and to cover the weapons up from prying eyes.

"*Venir*, Tala," she called to the wolf, who came running over to her.

She and the wolf went back down to the dining room, which was now empty of the crewmates. Their pride afforded them leave of the embarrassing situation, but did not spur them to prove her wrong, it seemed.

"I guess we're on our own, Tala." The wolf simply looked up at her, not understanding, but staying by her side regardless.

"*Pas nécessairement*," a voice said behind her.

She turned around to see Alexandre and Victor standing there, garbed for battle. They both looked as awake and fresh as always, and Alexandre looked as ready for physical activity as he ever would.

Christina smiled widely, and felt the twinge of tears forming in her eyes. She stifled them before they showed. "You heard what happened?" she asked.

Alexandre glanced at Victor and then grinned. "We rarely sleep much, if at all," he said. "I was itching for something exciting to happen, and this seems just the thing to save me from death by *ennui*."

Christina chuckled. She'd always liked Alexandre and his odd way of doing things. "Let's go then. Marco's not going to kill himself!"

The first thing Herbert noticed when he awoke was pain. Pain around his sore and dry neck, pain in his head, and pain around his arms.

As he blinked, and the focus returned to his eyes, he moved his head around to see where he was. His stupor faded, his memory returned, and he recalled being choked by one of Marco's men. He was lucky to still be alive, but he doubted he was any safer for having survived. He pulled on his arms and discovered they were tied behind his back.

"Finally awake, yes?" Marco asked from his chair in front of Herbert.

Herbert glanced around, still not fully aware of his surroundings. He hadn't been moved to a different location, it seemed, and Marco's allies were nearby.

Herbert tried to talk, but his throat felt raw and he coughed. He hacked several times until his throat seemed warmed up and he was able to talk. "So, your name isn't Fernando, is it?" Herbert asked, his voice hoarse from the punishment from earlier.

Marco laughed. "No, and you already know who I am now. At least I hope so. You look smart."

Herbert didn't see the need to hide his intentions any longer, but wouldn't mention the crew in case that was still a secret. "How did you know about me?"

"You don't remember?" Marco said, getting up from his seat. "Before you fell asleep I mentioned how I have a spy with my brother. He sent word of an English crippled assassin coming for my head." Marco went to the front of the desk and leaned his back against it. "Few of those in these parts, so here we are."

Herbert nodded. "No, I don't imagine there are," he said.

He was fortunate that they had left him in his wheelchair, because it afforded him an opportunity to escape. His hands were tied behind him, not around the back of the chair, so no one could see him fiddling with the knots. *If I can get my hands free, I can take out the knife hidden under my wheelchair.*

"Care to tell me why I'm still alive?"

Marco chuckled. "You do not sound happy."

"Simply confused. I can't think of a reason why you'd

keep me alive."

"Well, I can tell you it's not because of your pretty face, or lack thereof." Marco had a smirk plastered on his face, and he took his time in replying to Herbert. "We know you didn't come alone, my friend."

Herbert cursed in his head, but stifled himself from blurting it out. The momentary shock caused him to halt his progress on the knot. "Is that so? This is new to me. I hope these phantoms didn't go spending my pocket money."

Marco poured himself a drink and took a swig of it. "You came here with four others, but there are more somewhere in town," he said. He pointed at Herbert. "The sooner you stop lying to me, the sooner we can finish this business."

Herbert swore again, and gritted his teeth. The momentary pause to stop himself from cursing before had tipped Marco to the lie, Herbert was sure of it. He continued trying to take the knots apart.

"If you tell me where your people are, I promise it will be quick. I can't promise painless, that I cannot do," Marco said with a wave of his hand.

Herbert wasn't going to let him take his life without a fight. If he'd learned anything on his time aboard the *Queen Anne's Revenge*, it was that no situation was without hope. He could feel the knots around his wrist loosening.

I need to keep him talking. "How about we just forget this whole thing happened and we can all leave here alive?"

Marco howled with laughter. "You think you still have a chance to barter with me?"

"Why not? If you don't, I can guarantee you won't make it through the night," Herbert said. "First off, I'll tell you I won't give up my crewmates, but let's say that I do. What then? You send some of your goons to take care of them? I'm not sure what your spy told you, but we're pirates. We're trained. You might be able to kill a few of us, but any one of my men are worth ten of yours."

Marco listened to Herbert without interrupting him, all the while taking sips of his pungent drink. It was just as Herbert wanted, and he was taking the opportunity to keep working on the tight knot on his wrists.

"Even if you kill me, my crew will still kill you. Trust me when I say we're focussed on revenge, and your brother has information we need. Either way, you're a dead man. But if you let us go, we can handle your brother ourselves and get the information from him by other means."

Marco shook his head back and forth, took another sip of his drink, and pointed at Herbert. "You see, you shouldn't have said that," he said.

Marco reared back and punched Herbert in the stomach, nearly sending him to the floor. The blow knocked the wind out of him, and a similar choking feeling overtook him. The sudden need for air arrested his thoughts. Between the pain of the blow and the dry gagging for air, Herbert couldn't keep untying the knots.

Marco punched Herbert again, this time in the face. His head snapped to the left and pulled his body over with it. His eye started swelling immediately. His cheek felt hot and aching, and he knew that there would be a bruise there later. After a moment he was able to regain his breath, but the pain lingered.

Marco pulled Herbert's face forward with one hand and the other gripped his wheelchair. "My brother may be a little shit, and he may have sent you to kill me, but he's still family," he seethed. "We'll have a talk after this, but no one lays a finger on my family. We'll take our chances with you pirates any day." Marco's men hooted in response. "Now, where is your crew staying?"

Herbert was dizzy from the punches, and his mouth was also swelling by now. He couldn't see straight, and it, as well as the pain in his stomach, was sending waves of nausea through him. He breathed in and out deeply, and soon he was able to see again.

"Fuck you," he spat.

Marco's grip on the wheelchair turned his knuckles white. He punched Herbert in the face again, and in the same spot as before. He kept punching him again and again until Herbert's cheek tore open.

Herbert's head felt like there was an anchor attached to it, pulling it down over the side of his wheelchair. The hot, throbbing, stabbing agony spread all across his face. Debilitating fatigue replaced his nausea. Herbert wanted nothing more than to sleep and be rid of the pain, but he forced himself awake. He needed to remove the knots, or he would die.

"What the hell is that noise?" Marco shouted, his accent coming back with his anger. He yelled something in Spanish to his comrades.

Herbert didn't hear any noise over the ringing in his ears. He was able to hear the screaming Spaniard just fine, but hardly anything else.

He leaned forward and turned his head as best as he could to watch the door leading outside. One of Marco's men was approaching the entrance with a knife drawn. He slowly opened the door and peeked outside, only to have it slam open and hit him in the head.

Christina rushed in and halted just inside the room.

Christina!

The sight of his sister sent a wave of energy into Herbert's body. He needed to get out of the ropes, and he was so close. The energy he gained was just the thing he needed to finish the last bits of the knot.

Behind Christina, Alexandre, Victor and Tala were soon to follow. They each had weapons drawn, Christina with two daggers, Alexandre with a rapier, and Victor with a small sword and shield. And Tala, of course, had her fangs and claws.

Marco and his three comrades also had their weapons drawn. Before a battle could erupt, Marco flung Herbert's wheelchair around and placed a blade at his neck.

"Don't move, or I'll kill him," he growled.

For a moment, no one moved or said a word. It was a stalemate between the two sides. Christina began talking—or rather shouting—at Marco, telling him to let Herbert go. They argued back and forth, but Herbert stopped listening.

He focussed on the image of the knot around his wrists in his mind. He twisted and turned his shoulders, arms, and hands to release its hold on him. With all that was going on, he was able to move more freely without worry of being caught. Through his foggy mind, he could feel the ropes loosening. As the knots loosened, it gave him more room to move, and when he used his newfound space, the rope gave way even more. With one last tug, Herbert's hands were free.

Herbert slid open a secret compartment on the left armrest of his wheelchair, revealing a long dagger. He clutched the dagger tightly in his hand, and arched it over his shoulder. The blade hit Marco's hand, and he lost his grip on his weapon. Herbert pulled out the dagger as Marco staggered back, and then he leaned over to stab Marco in the stomach.

Herbert lost all sense of the others in the room, trusting in their ability to take care of themselves. They were fighters, all of them, and he knew that with their superior numbers and skills they would be fine.

Herbert stabbed Marco again and again in the chest. Blood gushed out with each piercing blow of the dagger, and before long Herbert's face and chest had turned red. He kept thrusting and thrusting, his teeth clenched and bared in anger. He stabbed and stabbed and stabbed until his arms could take no more, and they fell to his sides.

Herbert fell on top of Marco, heaving large, ragged breaths. It was only then that he noticed that Marco had fallen on top of his desk, and Herbert had climbed atop Marco while attacking him.

Marco's eyes reflected his last, painful moments of life. His face, chest, and legs were also covered in his own blood. Marco Delgado, Luis Delgado's brother, was dead, and their task was complete.

Herbert pushed himself off of Marco's dead body and flopped onto his back. As he struggled for air, he thought of the brothers' relationship, and just what had driven them so far apart that only death could reconcile the hate.

Herbert hoped that he and Edward wouldn't end up the same as the brothers, and that, with what they gained, Edward would forgive him for what he'd done.

11. STERLING PROMISE

For the second time upon waking, Herbert first felt pain. His body ached, but it felt especially concentrated around his face and stomach. Even though he had just awoken, he already felt tired.

He couldn't lift his upper body without sending spasms through his stomach, and when he lifted his shirt he noticed a grotesque welt forming. His left eye had swollen shut overnight, and he tried to touch the bruise, but even the slightest pressure was too much to bear.

He pulled himself up—forced himself, really—and every move was agony on his stomach. After a few minutes of struggling he was sitting up, propped on his hands as he arched his back to forestall the pain. He was already sweating from the exertion.

"Painful, is it?"

Herbert's gaze flashed to the source of the voice. "Edward!" he said, and then clutched his stomach.

Edward Thatch, his captain, was sitting in a chair not far from him. His eyes, his expression, and his demeanor were all as stone. He was leaning forward, his elbows resting on his knees, and his hands clasped in front of his face, obscuring his mouth and part of his great beard.

"When did you...?" Herbert paused for a moment and took a deep breath. "I'm sorry."

Edward stared at Herbert for a moment, his blazing gaze worse than the heat from Herbert's wounds. "You've given me a lot of time to think about what to do with you. The first thing I thought I would do was sock you in the face, but seeing as someone has already taken care of that I'll forgo physical punishment... for now," he said. "You and those who joined in your mutiny will be disciplined accordingly."

Herbert moved into his wheelchair, doing his best to avoid the painful areas. Once settled, he took a few deep breaths and wiped his brow. "They are not to blame," he said, taking in more air. "I am the one who told them to leave, and I am the one who should suffer the consequences."

"You and I both know that's not true. You put it to a vote. The crew had just as much a choice as you to leave Bodden Town, and they chose to join with you."

Herbert thought to tell Edward of the false premise which propped up the choice in his favour, but he refused to implicate Christina, so he stayed silent. Even so, it almost seemed as if Edward read his mind.

"Regardless of what influence you had on the men, their decision was still their own. They aren't children, so whatever sway you had on them, it was their choice to be swayed."

Herbert thought back on when Christina had told him the lie about Edward staying in Bodden Town. He wanted it to be true; he wanted it so badly that in his mind it *was* true. He pushed aside his misgivings so he could have the lie to make him feel better about what he did.

"I only ask that you do not punish Jack. He was against us leaving, and tried to convince me not to bring up a vote on the matter. He was more passenger than participant."

Edward nodded. "I'll keep that in mind," he said. "With that out of the way, did you find out any information on Calico Jack?"

Herbert's jaw dropped. "What?" he said.

"Calico Jack. Did you find out where he went?"

"Are—" Herbert stumbled over his words, still in shock. "Aren't you angry? How can you trust me after what I've done? From what it sounds like you aren't taking me off the crew. Why?" he asked, waving his arms with each question.

Edward stared at Herbert for a moment, and then looked off towards one of the open windows pouring light into the room. The sea air, and the scent of the town, flew in from the small frame.

"To be true, up until I entered this room, I was furious with you. At first I blamed myself for pushing you towards vengeance, but as I said before, you are grown and your decisions are your own. Seeing you here now, it's a painful reminder of my own madness, of which I have much.

Freedom, revenge, family... I've fought for these, men have died by my side for these. I killed..." Edward paused and glanced at the floor, seeming to have one word in mind, but choosing another instead. "I've killed many people along the way, and almost died myself on many an occasion."

Edward looked at Herbert again. "When I saw you, lying there, bloody and beaten, I thought: What if I had gotten word about my father? Or what if someone had taken Anne away? I couldn't say how I would react in the moment, but more than likely I would have done the same as you, and probably not as cleanly. You had the decency to give the men a vote. Would I have? If our past is any indication, probably not."

Herbert grinned as best he could. "We're quite the pair, aren't we?"

Edward chuckled. "Yes, yes we are," he said. After a moment, he leaned back in his chair. "So, care to answer my question?"

"Right," Herbert said. "We came here to complete a favour for a friend of Victor's to get information he had."

Before Herbert could continue the story, Edward asked, "Victor?"

"Yes, Victor has a contact here in Porto Bello. That's who we were doing the killing for." Edward nodded, but remained silent. "Sorry, was that not what you were wondering?"

Edward waved his hand and shifted in his seat. "No, no. You reminded me that there's something else we'll need to discuss, but it can wait until later. Continue."

Herbert nodded. "I was going to mention that the only issue we have is that Victor's contact doesn't know where Calico Jack is. He has information on where one of his subordinates will be, and that's what he was offering us."

Edward frowned. "I suppose that will have to do for now. Did he at least say who it was?"

Herbert shook his head. "No, he wouldn't tell us anything until I killed his brother for him."

Edward cocked his brow. "His brother?"

"They seemed to have some sort of ongoing feud. I was

forced to be the end of it, and, well, you can see how that went," Herbert said, pointing at his eye.

Edward grinned. "The ladies won't be fawning over you anytime soon."

Herbert laughed, but stopped when pain lanced through him. "Not that they ever did before."

The two men were back in good spirits, and ready to move forward to find out about their quarry. They headed towards the exit of the inn room, but Herbert stopped just shy, as he was curious of something.

"What happened in Bodden Town? How did you escape?"

Edward lost his smile, and paused a moment. "I burned Bodden Town to the ground."

Herbert let out a nervous laugh, but when Edward didn't change his expression he stopped. "Wait, you're being true right now?" Edward nodded. "Oh, Father," Herbert said, his gaze hitting the floor.

He thought on the people he had come to know from there, some of whom were even part of the crew, and on how many people lost their homes or their lives. He felt it was especially tragic given how they had just survived a pirate attack days before, only to have it burn by the hands of another pirate. He wondered who had done more damage, Edward or Calico Jack.

"Was it... on purpose?"

Edward sighed. "I don't know anymore," he said.

It was a vague answer at best, but the look in Edward's eyes told Herbert of the conflict he was having within himself. If it had been an accident, he didn't seem to feel any remorse, and perhaps that was where his confusion lay.

"What of the Boddens?"

Edward furrowed his brows. "They are dead, and that was on purpose. They had one of their men kill some of the townsfolk as I was trying to talk them down, and then they tried to flee."

"Why would they do that?"

Edward shrugged his shoulders. "We will never know. It could be that Calico Jack or one of his men paid them to betray me and ensure we lost the town." Edward paused for a moment, and then shook his head. "Come, everyone is waiting outside."

Edward opened the door to the inn's first floor, and Herbert could see his crewmates and Bartholomew Roberts' crew sitting at tables and eating. When the two of them left the room, a slight hush fell over the dining area. Edward stood beside Herbert as he scanned the crowd.

"As you were," he said, and the crews went back to eating and talking amongst themselves.

Edward went to a table where most of the senior officers were. Roberts was sitting beside Hank, Anne and Christina were together with Nassir nearby, and Pukuh was sitting more or less on his own. They all had their eyes on Herbert and Edward as they joined the table. Edward sat beside Anne, and Herbert went between Christina and Nassir.

"Let's eat quickly now, so that we may make a swift return to Porto Bello," Edward said.

Christina leaned over and whispered to her brother. "How did it go?"

"We're still part of the crew, so I believe it went as well as can be expected."

Christina smiled. "That's good news, then."

"Yes, now we just have to talk with Luis and ensure he keeps his end of the bargain."

The inn's servers and cooks worked overtime to bring the pirates their meals to break their fast. Before long they placed a plate of sausage, eggs, and local vegetables with exotic spices in front of Herbert.

The server didn't seem to pay his injuries any mind as she handed him his food. Herbert thought it was either to be polite, or she was too busy to notice, or perhaps she served many such customers on a regular basis.

Herbert tried to eat quickly, but the unfamiliar—but delicious—spices forced him to slow down and savour the food. He had never tasted anything quite like the sausage and the spices within, and it was the same for the entire meal. Out of all the random inns they had been in over the years, Herbert felt that this one had the best food. And, judging from the looks on the crew's faces and the time they were taking eating, the others agreed.

While Herbert was scanning the crowd, he noticed two people missing. "Where are Alexandre and Victor?" he asked.

"They are trying to work with the local authorities on obtaining proof of death," Christina replied. "We would have taken Marco's head, but the authorities were already on us so we couldn't very well be seen with a severed human head in our hands."

Herbert uttered a bark of laughter at the thought. "No, I suppose that wouldn't look good," he said. "What were Alexandre and Victor going to tell them to get proof of death?"

"When I asked, Alexandre replied with 'I have my ways.'"

Herbert shook his head. "Ever the ass," he said.

Christina smacked Herbert on the arm, but smirked. "It's not as if he were lying."

"I suppose not."

The crew continued their meal, and Alexandre and Victor returned as they finished and began packing up. In Alexandre's hands he held a sealed letter, and Herbert assumed it was from the authorities detailing how Marco had died. They had somehow managed to convince the authorities that they had the right to an official document, and the curiosity of how they accomplished such a feat maddened Herbert. It maddened him further because he knew if he asked, Alexandre would say "Oh, this and that," and would say it in French even though he knew the English words.

He may be an ass, but I cannot complain about his results.

Edward, upon noticing the duo enter, walked over to them and pulled them aside. He spoke with them about something for a moment, glancing Herbert's way a few times, and then they parted.

"Men, attention please!" Edward shouted to the crew as they were finishing preparations. "I'll be returning with the coaches presently. If anyone wants to take a horse, mine will be free as I will be travelling by coach. If you go by horse you will no doubt arrive sooner than us, so head to the *Queen Anne's Revenge* and we will meet you later tonight.

Understood?" The crew responded with a holler. "Good. Now let's go get the bastard who burned Bodden Town!"

The crew responded with another resounding cheer, which echoed off the walls of the inn and surely woke any who were still asleep at this hour.

Edward's comments confused Herbert, so he wheeled himself over to Anne and bid her to come closer. Anne bent over and leaned close to Herbert. "I thought Edward was the one who burned Bodden Town?" he whispered.

Anne nodded. "It was an accident, but yes, that is true," she replied. Anne glanced to her left and right and leaned in closer. "Edward is telling the crew that it was one of Calico Jack's men who burned the town to further rally them together. If he told you the truth it means he trusts you with the knowledge, but you mustn't tell anyone else," Anne said, squeezing Herbert's arm. "Right now, we need the crew on Edward's side, and trying to explain the… muddied circumstances could cause those from Bodden Town to leave. You understand, yes?"

Herbert looked into Anne's eyes, the eyes of Edward's wife, the one who had the wit, strength, and charisma to protect her love at any cost. He knew Edward wasn't the one who had come up with the plan. His lack of remorse and loose tongue told Herbert that. Anne was the mastermind behind the cover-up, and it was all to protect Edward.

Herbert simply nodded, and Anne smiled. "Good. Once this is all over, we'll tell the crew the truth, don't worry. It's just for now."

"I understand," he said.

After Herbert and Anne had their talk, it was another while before Edward returned with the coaches. He had three for those who wanted to take them, which was enough so that all who wanted to return would be able to. Their caravan was forty strong, and from the looks of it, it was the biggest to travel the road from Panama City to Porto Bello.

Many of the townsfolk couldn't help but stare at the spectacle of so many people in one spot all mounting horses or entering wagons.

Edward approached Herbert. "Herbert, will you ride with

me? I would have your sister join us as well."

"Yes, of course," he replied. He turned around and called to his sister, and the three of them went up to one of the stagecoaches.

Edward said a goodbye to Anne, who was going to travel in another coach, and they kissed before they parted. After-wards, he called Alexandre and Victor over.

Why are they joining us? Could it be what they talked about earlier?

Herbert pushed aside his thoughts for the moment, as he would soon have an answer, and entered the coach. Edward was gracious enough to strap the wheelchair to the top of the coach, and soon they were on the road.

Once they were away from Panama City, Herbert spoke up. "Edward, care to tell us why we're riding as a group?"

Edward, instead of answering, looked over at Victor. Victor stared back at him for a moment, then let out a sigh and removed his cap. After the cap, Victor ran his fingers through his short black hair to let it down more.

Herbert wasn't sure of the purpose of the display, and first glanced at Christina to see if she understood something he didn't, but she shrugged her shoulders. He looked at Edward with his brow cocked. "I'm afraid this doesn't explain much."

Edward opened his mouth again, but paused for a moment and stared at Victor again. "It is better to show than explain first, as I know you wouldn't believe it if we just told you."

Victor glared at Edward as he unbuttoned the heavy coat he always wore, and then he opened it to reveal his white undershirt.

Herbert laughed at first, amused by the nonsensical dis-play, but then he took in what he was seeing. His jaw dropped after a few seconds. "You're a—" he said, pointing at Victor, and then he looked at Edward. "He's a woman!"

"Herbert, this is Victoria. She's rather reserved, for good reason, but you two actually have some things in common."

"Victoria? Amazing," Herbert said. "Simply amazing. Who would have thought another woman was hiding aboard the ship?"

Christina was smiling. "I'm quite glad for another woman," she said. "Lord knows we must stick together."

Victoria smiled at Christina's comment, but it quickly faded.

"I've only known of her since Bodden Town, but Alexandre has known for quite some time now."

Herbert and Christina had trouble containing their excitement and astonishment. They wore wide grins. "Bodden Town? Oh, yes! I recall that you volunteered to breach the Boddens' gate to see if Edward was well."

"Yes, well, there was more to it than that," Edward said, then looked at Victoria.

Herbert's and his sister's smiles faded as they glanced from Edward to Victoria. Victoria had a stoic expression as she waited for Herbert and Christina to calm themselves. After a moment, she began speaking to them for the first time in her normal, undisguised voice.

"I, like you, once worked on Calico Jack's ship."

Herbert needed a moment to process the words. He shook his head in disbelief. "I— In secret? Did he know you were a woman?"

"I don't know how long you were on his crew, but women were not allowed unless they were captives to later be thrown overboard when the crew lost interest in them."

Herbert shuffled in his seat, suddenly uncomfortable and unable to sit still. "So why did you leave his ship?" He clenched his hands into a fist. "Are you still working for him?" His voice rose. "Did he send you here to spy on us?" His lips curled into a snarl. "Captain, you cannot trust this woman. She should be left here, or killed."

Herbert felt his face grow hot, and this time not due to the wound near his eye. His anger nearly overpowered him, but in front of Edward and his sister he contained it.

"We are cut from the same cloth," Victoria said. It was clear from the look of her that the threat angered her, but her voice held a subtle, calm menace. She was slow to show anger, and seemed confident in her abilities should a fight erupt.

Edward nodded. "So, we kill her, and what do I do about

the other former Calico Jack crewmate? You both joined my ship at the same time, served for all its years, and even came back when I was imprisoned to save me. The only difference is, one of you hid your identity as protection, and the other stole my ship. Judging by one's actions, I'd say the more likely spy would be you, Herbert." He cast a pointed glance in Herbert's direction.

Before Herbert could respond, Christina placed her hand on her brother's to stop him. "I want to hear what she has to say," she said. "Please, tell us your relationship with Calico Jack."

Herbert folded his arms and arched his back against the coach.

Victoria bowed her head a touch in Christina's direction. "I shall be brief, but it is best to start at the beginning." After a cursory glance to the other passengers, she started her story. "I joined Calico Jack's ship a few years ago in disguise as a man, as I had done in the past many times. Working with pirates was never an issue for me, and oftentimes a blessing as the money was better, and I was never found out. As you have seen, I do well in disguising myself, and pirates are idiots," she said with a smirk. Edward cleared his throat. Victoria grinned. "Most pirates are idiots," she revised. "After a few times sailing with Jack Rackham, I learned just how cruel a man he was. I decided to leave the crew at the next port, but it was long before port came, and Mad Jack found out about my identity. He kept the secret, but forced me to stay aboard. I will not tell you the horrid things he did to me, but please know that when I say I am no friend of his that I am not lying. Having said that, I was able to use my captivity well, as I learned about his operations and his contacts. I never wanted revenge, I just wanted to run, but being aboard this ship gave me hope that it could be done."

"So why reveal yourself now? Why not months or even years ago?" Herbert asked.

"Before now, it wasn't necessary to tell you my identity. And I didn't know how you or the crew would treat me after you knew the truth," she said, her lips pursed. "Now I don't have the luxury of standing by. If you want to kill Calico Jack,

I can help."

Herbert nodded. "A believable story, I will give you that. However, you'll forgive me if I am still skeptical. If you aren't a spy, then why did you join this ship? Out of all the ships you had a chance of boarding, you approached this one out of what? Coincidence?" Herbert spat. "Pirates are idiots, are they? Spin some lies and they'll believe every—"

"Do you wish me to address your claim, or is this conversation pointless?" Victoria asked. Herbert sighed and waved his hand at her. Victoria looked at Edward. "I joined this ship because of your Anne," she said.

"Anne?" he replied, his brow raised. The others in the coach were also confused. "What does Anne have to do with any of this?"

"Anne was how I escaped Calico Jack," she said. "Before you ask, no, she doesn't know who I am. Anne is smart, and she would have recognised my face had she seen me before." Edward nodded at the comment. "She joined Calico Jack's crew some time after me, and, like me, she didn't know what she was getting into. She was quickly found out by the crew, and killed some of them and cut Calico Jack across the face before jumping overboard. Her distraction allowed me to escape as well, and luckily we were close to shore. I knew she would continue boarding ships for work, and resolved to protect her so she didn't fall into the same situation I did." Victoria looked at Christina. "Lord knows we must stick together," she said, echoing Christina.

"And that's how you ended up on my ship," Edward said at last. "I can't believe she's never mentioned that before."

"I can imagine it was not a pleasant experience, especially as she seemed so unused to killing at the time. I will also say that as you were catching onto Anne's identity, I came close to cutting you down. You should be grateful you are nothing like Calico Jack."

Edward chuckled, but it was a nervous chuckle rather than a humorous one. Victoria wasn't laughing; she looked all too serious.

"Any more questions?" she asked, staring at Herbert.

Herbert, his arms still folded, returned the stare for a

moment as he thought, then glanced at the other passengers. "No, no more questions," he said.

Throughout the remainder of the coach-ride, Herbert remained silent. Victoria also didn't seem too talkative, despite revealing her true self to everyone. She hadn't been talkative as Victor, and Herbert guessed that it hadn't been just to hide her voice.

Christina continued asking Victoria questions like how she'd learned to disguise herself so well, where she came from, why she chose to try to work on ships instead of being a lady, and other menial queries. Herbert didn't listen to anything, and instead tried his best to sleep. All she said was probably full of lies, so why listen to her?

By nightfall, they arrived back in Porto Bello. Victoria donned her cap once more, and buttoned her baggy clothing to hide her identity once again.

"Why are you hiding yourself again?" Christina asked.

"We haven't told the crew yet, and it would be best to address them all together before they start asking questions and spreading falsehoods," Edward said.

"So we're going to spread the falsehood that she's an ally?" Herbert muttered under his breath.

"Something to say, Herbert?" Edward asked, the anger clear in his voice.

He arched his eyebrow and looked at his captain. "Hmm? No, no, nothing to add, sir."

Edward eyed him in the way he usually did to have men cower from him, but Herbert was unaffected. He stared back at Edward, and tried to mimic the same glare back at him. After a short time, they both looked away.

The cold air swept in from the sea and hit them as soon as they opened the door to the coach. It was unusually chilly for a place that had such harsh heat during the day, and the crew had to button their jackets and coats to stave off the sharpness of the wind.

After Edward, Alexandre, and Christina left, Herbert grabbed Victoria's arm and pulled her in close. "Just know that I don't trust you, and I'll be watching you from now on. If you are a spy, I'll know."

Victoria's face was rigid and unreadable. "Then you and I don't have anything to worry about," she said.

"Tch, yea, we'll see about that."

Edward retrieved Herbert's wheelchair from the roof of the coach and brought it down for him. Through some deft maneuvering, Herbert gripped the sides of the open doorway and swung from it to the door, and then into his wheelchair. His legs became twisted in the process, and he had to lift them up to get them aligned just right before he was comfortable.

"Ready?" Edward asked.

Herbert nodded. "Let's go see what I paid for with this eye," he said.

The coaches emptied, and soon Anne and Roberts joined Herbert's group. Herbert wheeled in the direction of Luis Delgado's place of business, leading the others there.

Once they arrived at the whorehouse, they were let inside. Thankfully, Luis was on the first floor this time.

When the group entered, they were met with bitter looks, and more than a few put hands on their weapons. Luis, for his part, grinned from ear to ear, and when he saw Herbert he spread his arms wide.

"My friend! You are back. With good news, I hope?"

"Yes," Herbert replied. "We managed to kill your brother for you."

Victoria stepped forward and handed Delgado the letter she and Alexandre had received from the Panama City authorities. He broke the seal and read through it. After a moment, he nodded his head, seemingly satisfied with its contents.

Delgado picked up a glass which seemed to be filled with rum. "To my brother, may he rot in hell," he said morbidly, and then seemed to repeat it in Spanish for those around him. With a cheer, he downed the drink in one gulp.

"There is something else," Herbert said. "There appears to be a spy in your midst. Your brother knew I was coming. I have that to thank for these injuries."

"Oh, is that so?" Delgado said.

Delgado started to walk around the room, staring into the

eyes of each man while saying something to them in Spanish. As he paced the room, he pushed some of the men, and they answered his questioning. Given that none of them were killed on the spot, they all seemed to deny the accusation.

As time passed, and Delgado's questions became more incensed, the tension rose. Many of his men were sweating despite the cold of the night, and glanced warily at their neighbours.

One of the men darted towards an open window. He was ten feet away, and could jump out without fear of injury, as it was the first floor.

The crack of thunder from a pistol rang in the room, and the spy dropped to the floor. Edward held the weapon, the barrel of the pistol still smoking and releasing a hot metallic scent into the air.

The spy was still alive, bleeding from his back and desperately trying to pull himself closer to the window.

Delgado stalked over, and the wounded man noticed the footsteps. He turned over and pleaded with Delgado to spare his life. He put one of his hands in front of him, and the other held his wound. He continued glancing from Delgado to the window as he shouted and begged. Delgado ignored the pleas and didn't hesitate to execute the man with a swift stab through the neck.

Delgado watched the spy bleed out for a few seconds, and then spun around towards Herbert and the others with a wide grin on his face. "Sorry about that nasty business. Thank you for letting me know, and thank you," he said, pointing to Edward, "for the help. By the way, who are you? I see many new faces today."

"I am Edward Thatch, Herbert's captain."

Delgado furrowed his brows. "I thought *you* were the captain," he said, looking at Herbert. Herbert shook his head. "Well, no matter. So, let's conclude our business. You wanted information on Calico Jack's subordinate, correct?" Delgado walked over to the back of the room and rummaged through some of his drawers.

"Yes, that was what Herbert struck a deal for. Do you know this man's whereabouts?"

Delgado was still searching for something in stacks and stacks of papers lining the drawers of the shelves. "I do indeed. He needed help for his next assignment. He told me that he's doing an initiation of sorts, so he's not one of Calico Jack's subordinates just yet, but should he perform well he will be." Delgado pulled out a piece of paper and said, "Aha, here it is!"

Delgado brought the piece of paper over for Edward to examine. Edward took the paper and glanced over it. Herbert and the others leaned over to see that it was a map of the Caribbean Sea. Several ship routes, showing as dotted lines, crossed this way and that, and at the bottom of the map there was a list of dates, each spanning a week of time.

"What am I looking at?" Edward asked.

"That is the routes of various Spanish galleons, what some of you pirates are calling the Spanish Treasure Fleet. They make various trades to Spanish colonies in the new world, and bring back silver and gold mined from all over back to glorious Spain so that the colonies can rot with nothing but trinkets from the Old World."

Edward still had a confused look on his face, perhaps even disbelief. "So, if I'm to understand you correctly, the trial this man is taking to join Calico Jack's fleet is to steal from one of these galleons?"

Delgado nodded. "More or less. He has to make it a show, so the galleon has to be sunk and the treasure stolen, from what I was told." Delgado shrugged his shoulders. He went over to Edward and pointed on the map to an island northwest of where they were near one of the routes. "Providencia. That is where your man will be right now. He is getting ready to attack the galleon with some other ships."

"How much time do we have?" Edward asked.

"Not much," Delgado replied. "The galleon is due to be here in two days, and then it will stock up and take our silver before heading north. The restocking usually takes a day at most. Five days after that it will arrive there. I'm assuming your ships are smaller, so you can make the trip in three days, maybe four, which is just enough time to figure out a way to stop them."

Edward glanced at Herbert with a smile on his face. Herbert could tell that they were thinking the same thing. If Herbert hadn't left when he did, who knows whether this opportunity would have still been here for them?

"You said it's a fleet. Wouldn't that mean more than just the galleon is arriving?"

Delgado grinned and tapped his finger on his temple. "One would think that, and that's what our beloved motherland wants you to think." Delgado's grin widened. "This one does not have an escort, not for little Porto Bello. The Spanish try to keep it a secret, and most pirates are too busy trying to raid our shores to find that out. This is the one galleon with the least amount of treasure, but also the easiest to take," he said, balling his fist with the last few words.

Edward grinned, and Herbert thought that more than revenge was on his mind. "So, who is it we should be looking for in Providencia?" Edward asked.

"Strange fellow he is, you'll be able to find him with no issues, I imagine. For some reason he has this... treasure chest attached to his right arm," Delgado said, gesturing wildly as he did. "Calls himself some foolish name. What was it? Chest-Hand? No, that couldn't be it. Cask-Hand? No, that wasn't it either."

Edward's eyes were wide. "Cache-Hand."

12. DEBT OF JUSTICE

"Yea, that's the one. Cache-Hand. It's so... what's the word? Obvious. It'd be the same if you up and called yerself Blackbeard, or if Blackwood here called himself Weak Legs," Delgado said with a hearty laugh as he motioned towards Herbert.

"Excuse me for a moment," Edward said, and then he turned around to leave.

Delgado had a smirk on his face. "Don't tell me you're actually called Blackbeard? Sorry mate, I didn't know you were that plain."

"It's nothing you said, sir," Edward replied, then he looked at Roberts. "Roberts, take over for me, would you? Find out what we need to know." Roberts nodded, a look of concern in his eyes.

Edward left the whorehouse, walked a few houses down, and then stepped into an alley. He fell to his side against the wall of the home and was breathing heavily. He could feel the beads of sweat pouring from his forehead despite the cold of the night. His hands were shaking, and he felt nauseated.

Why does it have to be him? The picture of Cache-Hand, of William Locke's face, invaded Edward's mind like a sickness. The name repeated over and over in his head until Edward slammed his heavy fist against the wall. *Why that name? Why?*

The old, healed wounds across Edward's body began to ache again. The fresh pain was like a memory, his body's memory. His body was telling him of the danger, warning him to stay away from the one who did this to him.

Footsteps approached behind him, and he looked over his shoulder to see Anne standing there. Edward pushed himself off the wall and turned around. He wiped the sweat off his brow.

"It was hot," Edward said. "I needed some fresh air."

Anne did not say a word, and instead stepped over to him and embraced him. "My sweet Edward," she said, her gentle voice penetrating the pain.

For a moment he stood there, stock still, his heart beating in his ears, but then he reached his arms around and accepted his wife's love. Her warmth washed over him, as if she were sharing her calm to quell his storm.

"You are here, you are now, you are not then," she chanted.

With each breath they shared, Edward could feel his heartbeat returning to normal. He ignored the thoughts that plagued his mind, and focussed on the moment rather than the past. After a few minutes, he felt relaxed and fresh again.

Edward laughed. "You have a strange power over me," he said.

Anne grinned. "I should hope so, husband. After all, I am your better half."

"This is true," Edward said with a mirrored grin.

"Tell me what you want, and I would see it done," Anne said, a serious look in her eyes.

"You do not need to do anything. We, however, need to kill Cache-Hand. Only then will I be rid of this curse."

Anne looked at him, concern in her eyes. She placed her hand on his cheek. "There is no shame in fear."

Edward shook his head, pushing her hand away. "I'm not afraid," he said.

Before Anne could talk with him further, Edward turned around and left the alley. He head back to Delgado's whorehouse. Anne followed behind him at a distance.

Outside, the crewmates who had joined him, and Roberts, were waiting for Edward to return. They were talking with each other in hushed tones, and had concerned looks in their eyes. When he approached, they ceased talking.

Roberts waved to Edward. "Ho, Edward. Are you well?"

"I am well, friend. I felt close to hitting the floor with the heat in the room, so I had to step out."

Roberts scratched his face. "Yes, of course. It was rather stifling."

"So, was there any other information of use to us?"

Roberts shrugged his shoulders. "I'm afraid not," Roberts said, but then he grinned. "But we did learn that one of the other pirates helping Cache-Hand is Walter Kennedy."

Edward's mouth went agape. "Walter Kennedy? That's…"

Roberts nodded. "That's the man who stole my ship years ago. He's still with Kenneth Locke, it seems. It looks as if we both will have our justice soon enough, isn't that right old friend?"

After a moment, Edward smiled. "Yes, I suppose we will."

"Did you have any plan in mind for how to attack?" Herbert asked. "We only have two ships on our side, and they'll have three."

Edward stroked his beard. "I'll have to think on it some more. For now, we should head back to the ships and let the crew know the particulars of the day."

The crew were in agreement, and they headed back to the harbour to board the *Fortune*. They would need to head just northeast of Porto Bello to where Herbert had anchored the *Queen Anne's Revenge*.

Roberts rushed ahead to walk by Edward's side. He patted his friend on the back to get his attention. "Are you well, truly? You were quick to leave after learning whom we are attacking. I do not believe one among us is not aware of who that man is, and the trial you endured."

Edward gripped Roberts' shoulder and gave it a squeeze. "Trust my words when I tell you I am well. I only want to see this business concluded, and, as you always say, to see justice done."

Roberts nodded. "He also has one of your crewmates, does he not?"

Edward's eyes hit the floor. "Yes, Samuel Bellamy. He may still be hiding aboard their ship under a false name, if he wasn't found out. John, God rest his soul"—and here Roberts repeated the chant with Edward—"and I paid the price to see his cover maintained."

"You were told of the letter he left behind, were you not?"

"Aye," Edward said. "He swore revenge on Kenneth Locke."

"I don't think I have to tell you that, seeing as Kenneth Locke seems to be very much alive, Sam may have failed."

Edward glanced off to the *Fortune* floating in the water under the light of the moon. "I am aware of the significance."

"I shall pray for his safety, but you should prepare yourself and your crew for the worst," Roberts said. "Come, let's return you to your ship."

The crews boarded longboats and returned to the *Fortune*. After the long process of raising the anchor, which was faster with Edward's men helping, they dropped the sails to leave Porto Bello's harbour.

As they travelled north and east along the coast, the moon was approaching its zenith and giving a faint glow to the surrounding sea and trees of the mainland. It didn't take long for them to reach the small islands just off the shore hiding the *Queen Anne's Revenge*.

As they came into the waters between the islands, Edward's crew who were still awake were all watching and waving, hooting and hollering across to their partners. The *Fortune* furled the sails, dropped the anchor, and after half an hour they were able to secure the ships together with rope and lower a gangplank.

Edward held his back straight to keep himself at full height as he marched across the gangplank. He maintained a stern expression as he set his gaze upon his borderline mutinous crew.

Jack stepped forward, a smile on his face despite the look Edward was giving everyone. "Captain, you're back. We weren't expecting you for a few days more."

"The situation in Bodden Town turned dire, so we had to leave," he said. "I must address the crew, please have any men sleeping woken up and bring them here."

Jack nodded. "Aye, Captain," he said before heading below deck.

"Herbert, Victor, join me on the quarterdeck."

Edward, Herbert, and Victoria all joined Edward on the quarterdeck, and waited for the crew to come to the weather deck. The tired men stumbled up to the deck, curious but exasperated. When they noticed the crewmates who'd returned, Roberts' ship, and then Edward on the quarterdeck, their tiredness faded away in an instant.

"Good evening, men," Edward said. "I have a few announcements to make regarding current affairs. Firstly, due to the scoundrel, Calico Jack, and his interference, the Boddens turned on us and caused the town to burn to the ground. Bodden Town… is no more."

Those words alone were enough to send a wave of disbelief through the weary crew, and Edward quickly lost control of the crowd. Most of the men causing a stir were those from the former town.

Edward raised his hands to try to calm the men. "I understand your doubt, but it is true. The only reason I am here today is thanks to the fire distracting the townsfolk. Our only home is now this ship."

The crew who had come from Bodden Town were overtaken by great melancholy in that moment, as well as concern over their family members still in Bodden Town. Many of them had their gazes downcast, and the other crewmates found them inconsolable.

"Do not despair, men," Edward shouted. "For those who hail from Bodden Town, I give you freedom to return there, and you will not have to follow the commandments to pay for your leave. However, for those of you who stay, I promise you we will be pursuing Calico Jack and will bring justice upon him. Calico Jack owes us for what he's done, and we owe it to the people of Bodden Town to return his violence back to him. Do not let your grief take away from your vengeance, for we cannot let him escape a pirate's justice."

Edward was able to bring back most of those crewmates who had been lost in their own thoughts. They looked up at him, this time with a fierceness in their eyes.

"What do you say, then? Do you want to leave, or do you want to kill the bastard who attacked and burned your town?"

The crew hollered in agreement with Edward, the fire in their eyes inspiring those around them into a frenzy.

Edward nodded. "Good, because we have new information on where one of Calico Jack's subordinates will be. We will send a clear message to Calico Jack that he can't make us run and cower." The crew yelled a resounding "Hear, hear" back to Edward. "It is a man some of you may know well. Kenneth Locke, Cache-Hand, who killed our previous quartermaster, John, and who still has one of our crewmates, Sam, hiding in his crew. And he is working with someone you, crew of the *Fortune*, know as well," he said, motioning to the other ship's men. "Walter Kennedy, the man who stole your ship and left you for dead is with Kenneth Locke. These two owe us a debt of justice, and they need to pay for what they've done. We will seek them out and destroy them as repayment."

Both crews now cheered for Edward.

"We wouldn't have been able to get this information if not for the help of a specific crewmate. One who has been with us since the beginning, and helping behind the scenes. You all know this crewmate as Victor, but Victor has been holding onto a secret which we will reveal to you now."

Edward looked at Victoria, and she did the same thing for the crew as she did for Herbert and Christina. She removed her cap, and then unbuttoned her jacket to show off her figure.

"Men, welcome Victoria into the crew."

After a moment of confusion, the crew caught on. Each of them were once again in a state of disbelief, with many whispering to their neighbours or pointing.

"Victoria, like our quartermaster, Herbert, was a former crewmate of Calico Jack's, and was a boon in finding his crew's whereabouts. I cannot say how she will dress aboard the ship any longer, but her clothes and her name should have no bearing on how you treat her."

Many in the crew nodded, but some showed visible signs of anger, though those were in the minority. Most seemed indifferent towards her being a woman, given that they had been working with two already.

"And, finally, the matter of you all voting to leave Bodden Town in its time of need, rather than staying to help,"

Edward said, his level tone taking on a hint of anger. "As I mentioned before, Bodden Town has burned to the ground due to what happened there. Had you all decided to stay, that could have been prevented. Lives and homes wouldn't have been destroyed, and we wouldn't have lost the safety that Bodden Town provided. You all are partially to blame for this happening, and owe a debt just as Calico Jack does."

Before Edward lost the crew again, and they began to object, he continued. "As such, all those who voted to leave Bodden Town in its hour of need will have their shares cut in half for the next haul. Afterwards, it will return to normal." Edward stared daggers at the crew, scanning the crowd and looking into each man's eyes.

The look seemed to quash any thoughts of going against the captain's decision. It might have also helped that the punishment, while severe for the moment, was light when compared to how many ships they raided.

Edward glanced at Herbert, who had been watching the speech, waiting to hear his fate. "Also," he said, looking at the crew again, "Herbert, as he was the one who instigated the vote," Edward paused and took in a silent breath, "will have half shares for the next three hauls. His rank and authority as quartermaster on this ship is hereby stripped. He will still man the helm, and you are to follow his orders as before, but only orders in relation to steering and navigation. He is not permitted to propose or take part in a vote, he will no longer be in charge of supplies and provisions, and any man found conspiring with him will be guilty of mutiny and punished by death or marooning."

Edward could not hold back the crew's objections any longer. They felt the punishment for Herbert was too harsh, and loudly voiced their opinion. Edward was silent as their voices grew louder and louder still. He looked over at Herbert, who was glancing between Edward and the crew shouting their support for the wheelchair-bound man.

Herbert raised his hand. "Please, everyone, stop," he yelled. After a moment, and another call from Herbert, the crew silenced themselves. "I thank you for your protection, but the captain is right and just in his decision. We have wronged, myself most of all, and this is the price I pay. I pay it gladly if I can only achieve forgiveness for my actions, and you too should feel the same... Forget Bodden Town, forget Calico Jack, forget revenge. We owe this man our freedom, and we abandoned him in his time of need. He could have died because of us. I accept my punishment, as should you," he said with a small smile.

Edward was looking at Herbert, and when Herbert glanced over to him, he nodded.

The crew's anger subsided after Herbert's admission and acceptance of the punishment, but one question still remained: Who would be in charge of supplies, and who would represent the crew's wishes as their new quartermaster?

"I elect Anne Bonney as our new quartermaster," Edward said, pointing to his wife. "And with your vote, the position shall be secured."

Anne looked at Edward with her brow raised, and then she glanced at the crew. The crew had been wanting her as the first mate for some time, but she had declined it, despite still serving in some capacity since. The crew watched her as she climbed the steps to the quarterdeck while glancing at Herbert and Edward.

On the quarterdeck, Anne placed her hands on the railing. "I will accept the position of quartermaster, if you will have me. I promise to serve your interests, and if there are any decisions my husband makes which you do not agree with, I will knock some sense into him."

The crew chuckled at her comment, and many nodded and muttered words of agreement with the decision.

"All those in favour?" Edward asked the crowd.

All two hundred of the crew responded with a deafening "Aye."

"I welcome your new quartermaster," Edward said, lifting Anne's hand up in the air.

The crew, in the dead of night, shouted and cheered for their new electee, their morale high despite the lost shares and change. Anne, though at first reluctant, smiled happily to the crew who had just elected her, and soon appeared eager to take on a new experience on a pirate ship.

13. PARLEY PROPOSAL

William stepped up to the weather deck for the first time in the week and some days they had been travelling for. The cool, fresh sea air was a welcome respite from the stale, sweaty interior of the *Fortune*.

It was early morning, the sun just peeking out on the horizon, half-blocked by the island east of them providing them cover. The glow of the rising sun washed over the ship, casting great shadows from the masts over the deck.

The *Fortune* was lashed to *Queen Anne's Revenge*, and the two seemed to be caught in a dance with the waves. Each ship rose and fell independently, but in near synchronous movements. The slight difference caused the wood to creak and groan more than usual from the ropes tying the ships together.

Few men were up this early, but those that were wished William good day and praised his good health. He could see men from both ships mingling on the two decks, relaxing before the inevitable labours of the day began. Some were sitting on the steps leading to the upper decks, others leaned against the railings, and some sat with their backs against the masts.

William crossed the gangplank, holding steady to the railing as he did so. Every movement caused a slight but sharp pain to run through his chest. Though his fever had broken some days before, his ribs were still healing. It would be several weeks yet before he was fully recovered, and longer if he didn't give himself proper rest.

"Good day, William," Jack called on the deck of the *Queen Anne's Revenge*. "It is good to see you returned to your home. Are you well?"

William nodded. "As well as fortune allows me to be, under the circumstances. Bones do not heal so easily, in my experience. How have you found it?"

Jack chuckled. "One time, in my tavern-hopping days, I was involved in a brawl of sorts, and my arm was broken. I was lucky the bone didn't pierce my skin, and I healed after two months, if I recall. It still aches during storms."

"I am not alone in my suffering for eternity then. That brings me small hope."

Jack waved his hand. "With a ripe young body such as yours, you'll be better in no time."

"Thank you, sir. I hope you are correct, as I hear whispers of a battle on the horizon."

Jack leaned against the port railing, his back to the *Fortune*. "Aye, that is true. We may head into a battle soon. I suppose you're not privy to all that has occurred here?"

William shook his head. "I have not had the luxury of my faculties of late."

Jack folded his arms. "Let me attempt to brief you. First, Herbert insulted me when I tried to dissuade him from voting to leave the captain. Then he stole the ship, managed to find out where one of Calico Jack's subordinates will be, and is no longer our quartermaster as punishment." Jack smiled at the last part.

"You seem happy over Herbert's misfortune," William said, more statement than question.

Jack raised his brow. "Misfortune? Misfortune is losing coin making a bad bet. Herbert deserved punishment for what he did. If not for Edward's mercy, and that the crew might riot, his action should have been considered mutiny." Jack's anger took hold of him for a moment, but he soon regained his composure, and glanced warily at the crew on deck. William supposed that there were still those who sided with Herbert, judging from Jack's expression.

William nodded and stroked his chin. "So you would have killed him for mutiny?"

Jack's eyes went wide. "No, no..." He let out a sigh. "I don't know what I would have done differently in Edward's position."

"Perhaps you are simply agitated by Herbert's insults prior to taking the ship?"

"By rights I am agitated. I was trying to convince him not

to propose the vote or leave Edward behind, but he didn't listen."

"And?" William said, his brow raised.

"And..." Jack paused for a moment, searching for the words. "He compared his actions to what I did against George Rooke years ago, and brought up my drinking habits when I've not touched a drop of drink in quite some time."

"So, he compared his actions to your pulling a gun on George Rooke and turning to alcohol in your time of need, and this angered you?" Jack nodded. "Then, and please do not take offence to this, sir, would it be more appropriate to say that the reason you are upset is because his words were true?"

Jack's eyes widened and his jaw dropped, but after a moment he seemed to reflect on what William said. His lips made a line, and his gaze lowered to the sole of the deck, staying there for some time.

"You may be correct," he said after a few moments.

"Do not trouble yourself over the past, friend. You are not the same person you were then. Only worry about who you are now, and work to ensure you do not repeat past mistakes."

Jack nodded. "I struggle with it every day," he said. "I do suppose I should let go of my anger. Herbert accepted his punishment with grace yesterday, and discouraged the crew from mutinying."

Before they could talk any further on the subject, Anne called to him.

William turned around and stepped to the side. "Princess, good day to you."

"And good day to you, but I'm not a princess any longer, as you'll recall."

William bowed his head a touch. "I will do my best to remember."

"A good day to you as well, Mr Christian," she said with a wave.

"How do you do, Mrs Thatch?" Jack asked.

"Better, now that we are home. If I may, sir, I wish to speak with William."

Jack waved his hand. "Certainly," he said as he lifted himself off the railing. He smacked William on the arm. "Good fortune to you, William, and thank you. You've given me a lot to think about."

Jack left Anne and William, and picked up one of his instruments nearby to play. After he left, Anne raised her brow. "What did you give him to think about?"

William shook his head. "A trifle, really. The man was angry with Herbert over some words he said regarding his past aboard the ship. I reminded him that only the present and one's current actions matter, not the past actions they regret."

Anne glanced over her shoulder at Jack, who was now playing a tune on his fiddle. "Sound advice from a friend," she said. "Perhaps you could assist me also?"

"Whatever could I help you with?" William asked.

"Did Jack mention to you about Herbert losing his position?" William nodded. "I was elected to replace him as quartermaster. Herbert will remain the ship's sailing master, but I will be in charge of the crew and supplies, and, of course, represent their wishes to the captain."

William couldn't help but flash a rare smile, as he felt overjoyed by her promotion. "That is excellent news, my la... Quartermaster," he said. "I suppose I answer to you now."

Anne smirked. "Yes, it strains credulity to believe you are up to the task of following my orders. The very thought of having to teach you proper chain of command causes my head to ache already."

"I shall do my best to learn quickly."

Anne and William chuckled together for a moment. William felt happy to see Anne smile, as her smile too seemed to be a rare display these days.

"I was wondering if you would assist me in creating a training regimen. I've already discussed with Alexandre a few considerations, and I should like your opinion as well."

"Certainly," he replied.

As the sun rose, the two discussed various activities and drills which could help improve their prowess in battle, including some manoeuvres which involved the use of more than one ship that they might be able to use in the near future.

Edward sat in the stern cabin's war room, staring at the map showing the Spanish treasure ship's routes. He had been staring at it off and on the night before and all this morning, but the various outlines of islands, land masses, and lines—both dotted and straight—began to blend together. He rubbed his eyes and tried to refocus on the details, but the map was beginning to lose all meaning to him. No matter how many times he looked, he could glean no information that could help him with his dilemma.

How are we to face a galleon and three other ships when we only have two?

After another moment, Edward threw the paper aside. The air of the room caught it, caused it to arc in the middle of its flight, and it swooped back onto the table amongst other miscellaneous papers.

The door to the war room opened, and Roberts stepped inside, closing the door behind him. "Good day, Edward," he said with a wave.

"Good day, Roberts. I trust you are well?"

"Very well, thank you. And you?" Roberts asked, and then he took a look at the table in front of Edward. "Judging from the mess you've made I would wager that a no?"

"You would be correct. I've been attempting to create a suitable battle plan, but the only one I have is too dangerous. Thus why I've called this meeting." Edward glanced to the door. "Were you the only one on the way?"

Roberts nodded and adjusted his tall, bulky frame in the small seat. "Yes." He looked over his shoulder to the door. "I did not see any others approaching, though I am certain they are on the way."

Edward leaned back in his chair. The light from the cabin's windows and a few lanterns dotting the walls gave the room a soft glow. The dancing waves reflected the sun's light and made it dance on the ceiling. The day was warm, but not as blistering as the previous week had been. He still felt the need to pat himself off with a cloth, though, and the rag came back moist to the touch.

"It is a curious feeling, is it not?" Roberts asked.

Edward chuckled. "What?"

Roberts too was leaning back in his chair, his feet pushing against the oval table in the centre of the room. "We are closing in on vengeance years in the making for the two of us. The feeling is... surreal."

Edward mimicked Roberts and pushed his chair into a leaning position with his boots against the table. He gazed at the ceiling as he thought on Kenneth Locke's homely face, but he felt his heart beginning to race and his throat seize, so he shook it away.

"You've been waiting far longer than I," Edward said. He began squeezing his hand tight, the pressure and pain bringing him back to today. *You are here, you are now.* His wife's voice rang in his head.

"Yes, I've been waiting nearly... four years now. Travelled across the globe, and only now that we're upon the edge of this business am I beginning to think on the truth of it all."

Edward eyed his friend curiously. "What do you mean?"

"Well... I suppose over the years it's become quite removed. What I mean to say is..." Roberts pulled his boots away from the table and his chair landed back on the deck with a snap. "Walter Kennedy served as a destination moreso than a prize. As if I moved forward to find him, but I wasn't truly thinking of catching him. It felt as if I never would catch him, I suppose."

"And now he is at your door," Edward said. Roberts nodded and stared at the papers on the table, but he wasn't focussed on them. "What will you do when we catch him?"

Roberts looked at Edward, but his expression was unreadable. "I suppose... I don't know."

Edward also plopped his seat back on the sole. "You're not going to kill him?"

"My friend, not knowing means I could do any number of things. I simply have not chosen my course of action. I've never had to think on it until now."

"Very well, what have you been thinking until now of doing?"

Roberts laughed and sat up straight. "You ask a similar question expecting a different answer," he said, which made Edward chuckle as well.

"A reasonable objection."

"I have been saying since the beginning that I would bring God's justice upon him." Roberts appeared deep in thought for a moment, and then he looked at Edward again. "What will you do to Kenneth Locke?"

The name still had an arresting hold on Edward, but now he had a method to diminish the pain. He repeated his wife's chant over and over in his mind. Thankfully, his pause could pass for contemplation.

"I'm going to do the same thing you should do: Kill him, and remove the curse he's placed on me."

Roberts ran his fingers through his straight chestnut-brown hair. "I wonder if that is God's justice."

"Hmph," Edward scoffed. "No, of course not... It's pirate justice."

The sound of the door opening took their attention away from their conversation. One after the other, Anne, William, Alexandre, Victoria, Pukuh, and Herbert entered the stern cabin.

"Hold a moment, Herbert," Edward said, holding up his hand. I apologise if another summoned you here... but this meeting does not involve you."

Everyone in the room glanced from Edward to Herbert, and he to them. His jaw dropped for a second as his gaze shifted to Alexandre and Victoria, both of whom had no official rank aboard the ship, and one of whom he distrusted. The tension was visible by a slight redness on Herbert's cheeks, aside from the recent injury, which held a perpetual redness.

Edward felt no such tension or embarrassment.

"By your leave, Captain," he said with a modest bow

before turning his wheelchair around.

"Wait, Herbert," Anne said. "I'm vetoing that order. You may stay."

"Veto, Quartermaster?" Herbert asked, his brow cocked.

Anne grinned. "It means I'm denying the captain's order, by my authority as quartermaster. If we are discussing battle plans, it is crucial you be privy to them so you may guide our crew when the time comes."

Herbert smiled. "I see," he said, turning around again. "Thank you."

As Herbert wheeled himself forward, the others in the room took their seats. Each person's mouth was a line, save Alexandre, who was smirking as usual.

Edward eyed his wife, and she stared straight back at him. "Now that everyone is present," he said, glancing at Herbert, "we may begin." Edward cleared his throat. "First, I was wondering if you are well, Victoria? Any of the crew troubling you?"

Victoria shook her head. "I believe from Anne and Christina they are accustomed to women being aboard. I had no issues."

"That pleases me," he said. "Now then, let's discuss why I summoned you all. From what we know, Kenneth Locke will attack a Spanish galleon on its route to Havana after it lands here in Porto Bello for a silver shipment." He picked up the sheet of paper with the shipping routes on it and handed it to Victoria to pass around. "He will be aided by Walter Kennedy, and another unknown pirate, totalling three ships of similar size to our own..." He looked each person in the eyes briefly. "We need to stop them... and not die in the process."

"The only plan I could come up with would be to attack them after their battle with the galleon. If luck aids our cause, they will lose against the galleon and give up, then we pursue them and finish them off."

"And if luck is not on our side?" Roberts asked.

"They defeat the galleon, take the treasure, and still have three ships to attack us with."

"How long until the galleon arrives at Kenneth's point of

attack?" William asked, not having been privy to the conversation with Luis Delgado.

"A week or a fortnight at most," Edward replied. "The galleon will be here in a matter of days, then it restocks for another day, and then it takes four days to reach the island Providencia. If weather is not in their favour, or if a storm comes, it could delay them another few days."

"Then we should go to where they are, and attack them on land," William suggested. "On land they won't be as difficult to defeat, as we may have crews of similar size."

"We cannot rely on that," Victoria said. "We don't know the size of the ships or their crews, only that they are similar to ours. They could have the same number of crew as us for each ship."

William nodded. "That is a risk we may have to take."

"What about if we just attack one crew?" Anne suggested. The others in the room looked at her. "We can... say, land on Providencia, scout the pirates for their weak link, and attack them instead of all the ships."

"You might have the right idea, but we can't simply attack the crew. The others will rush to their aid." Edward stroked his beard.

"Simple, *mon ami*," Alexandre said. "Sabotage one ship, and they will be delayed. If you only damage it slightly... say, enough to warrant a few hours' repairs, the others may leave to their destination and wait for the damaged ship to catch up."

"I think that may be our best option yet," Edward said with a smirk.

Herbert chuckled. "There's a better way," he said.

Edward waved his hand. "Share it then. That is why you're here."

"The simplest way would be to recruit another ship to our cause," Herbert suggested.

"Where would we find someone to help us at this hour?" William asked.

"We could appeal to some of the ships in Porto Bello. I'm sure, at minimum, one of them would be willing to join our cause for the right price."

The talk of having another ship join them caused Edward to jump up from his seat. "I've got it! I know who we can recruit," he exclaimed.

Those in the room looked at him strangely, but they all wanted to know his idea. "What ship did you have in mind?"

"Not just any ship will do," Edward said. "We need *the* ship on our side if we want to win."

"And that ship would be…?" Anne asked.

"The Spanish galleon," Edward said with a wide grin. "We'll convince the Spanish to join forces with us against Kenneth Locke."

14. NEGOTIATIONS

"I believe you will need to explain this to us again, husband," Anne said with furrowed brows. "I'm afraid some of us may think you've gone mad."

"I've not gone mad," Edward replied. "If we have a galleon on our side, it won't matter how many ships they have on their side. We would be able to fight together and crush them, and then we won't have to fear picking at the scraps."

"He *has* gone mad," Roberts said with a raised brow.

Edward sighed. "I'm not mad. If we aren't able to convince the Spanish to join with us, we can simply focus on the other plan," he said with a wave of his hand. "Having the galleon is the safest way to achieve our plans."

"You are aware we're pirates, yes?" Anne said, incredulous.

"I am fully aware of what we are, and also aware of with whom we've been fighting. I don't believe we've had any encounters with Spanish forces, nor have we hit any of their harbours."

"Save Panama City," Anne said.

"Yes…" Edward said, glancing to Herbert, Alexandre, and Victoria. "Save for Panama City, we haven't attacked the Spanish, only the British. None in Panama City know who attacked the whorehouse, so we're safe there. Surely some of our exploits have reached Spanish ears."

Anne tapped her foot on the wooden floorboards of the cabin, and she had her arms crossed. Her mouth was a line, and she seemed to be searching her mind for some further objections, but she seemed unable to come up with more.

"It may work," she conceded.

Edward looked at Bartholomew Roberts. "You may be able to assist in the negotiations as well, Roberts. If my name isn't common knowledge, yours should be well known."

Roberts raised his brow. "How so?"

Edward looked at Anne. "Portugal is in an alliance with England at the moment, is it not?"

Anne nodded. "Yes, it is, but I know not what this adds to the discussion."

"He aims to use my past exploits as proof of our camaraderie, Mrs Quartermaster."

"Your... past exploits?"

"You may recall a time I mentioned when I stole some rather valuable jewels? They were owned by the King of Portugal," he said, motioning with his hand.

"Ah..." Anne said. "And Spain is none too happy with Portugal at the moment, as it sides with the British. Especially so now, as not long ago there was a concentrated attack on Spain's borders from Portugal, from what I've heard."

"And we can use that to our advantage here," Edward said. "We'll hide the fact that we're pirates at first, but if we need to convince them we're on their side we can tell them everything."

"Are you sure this is wise?" Victoria asked. "Pirates have ravaged this country just as much as the British have ravaged Spain in this war. How do you know they will not kill you if and when they discover the truth?"

Edward thought the problem over for a moment. He ran his fingers through his wavy black hair, slicking back some of the sweat that had gathered on his forehead. "We will ask him to parley with us, at a location of our choosing, outside of Porto Bello... We can have men on guard to ensure nothing goes wrong while we discuss the alliance," he said. "We can be smart about this, and even if negotiations sour, we will leave with our heads."

"The next issue is," Anne said, "how do we secure the Spanish captain's attention?"

"I say we be direct and tell them about the attack and how we wish to help," Edward said. "Perhaps... you could draft a letter?" Edward looked at Anne as he said the words.

Anne's brows raised. "Me?"

Edward nodded. "You're far more formal than the lot of us. You would be the most persuasive and... respectful with your words."

Anne glanced to the others in the room. "You have a point, I suppose." She sighed. "My Spanish is a bit rusty, but I shall do my best."

"Thank you," Edward said. "In the meantime, Roberts, would you like to scout out a location with me?"

Roberts smiled. "Yes, that could be a bit of fun."

Edward rose from his chair and looked at all those in the room. "If no one else has anything to add...?"

Herbert shuffled in his seat for a moment, and then spoke up. "I have a question," he said.

Edward's mouth was a line. "Yes?"

"Should we not put this to a vote?"

"I believe I made it clear that you may no longer propose votes."

Herbert stared at Edward, his brows furrowed. "Yes, abundantly," he replied. "I believe the Commandments are clear in that every man shall have a vote on current affairs."

Edward looked down for a moment and clenched his teeth in frustration. "Shall we vote on when we decide to wake, or sleep, or shit, for that matter?"

"Edward!" Anne looked mortified.

Edward ignored his wife. "Votes are a provision only outside of battle. This is something that has always been in effect. This involves battle, and battle plans, so that means my decision on how we go about our attack is not a voting matter," he said, staring daggers at Herbert. "Understood?"

Herbert's face once more reddened around his cheeks. His injured eye still covered most of his embarrassment, but not all. His teeth and jaw locked in place for the briefest of moments as he and Edward stared at each other.

"Understood, Captain," he said eventually.

"Good," Edward replied with a nod. "Roberts? Care to join me?"

Roberts glanced from Edward to Herbert and back. "Uhh... yes, let's be on our way."

Edward walked around the oval table and left the room, with Roberts following behind. He called upon a few crewmates to arm themselves and join him on their expedition, and they gathered supplies for the short trip.

Edward didn't talk as they organized their supplies. His anger was plain to see, and plain to feel on his own face. He felt hot and flushed, and the sun beating down on him did not help.

Edward and company entered one of the *Queen Anne's Revenge*'s longboats and paddled to the shore nearby. The air was hot and humid, as expected this close to shore, and it didn't seem to get any better after they landed and entered the nearby forest.

The tall palms were side by side with thick cottonwood trees, hanging vines, chest-high bushes, and obtrusive roots. As the group moved through the forest, they had to keep an eye on their feet to keep from tripping.

"If we can find a clearing nearby, that should do," Edward said. "No need to stay so close, men. We won't be able to see everything all bunched together like bananas. Keep within sight of each other."

The crew shouted "Aye, Captain," and then split up into a few smaller groups.

Edward pulled out his cutlass and whacked at some low-hanging branches in his way. The closest branch shook with his strike, and the rustling of the leaves travelled up to the top, sending some local birds fluttering from their perches to escape the potential danger below.

Around him, he could hear the sounds of different birds and animals he wasn't familiar with. He thought he might have heard monkeys, but he couldn't be sure. The noise reminded him of the first time he had seen a monkey. It was his first time on a trip with his father. It jumped on the ship when they were docked and stole some food before someone could shoo it away.

"Edward, may I talk with you a moment?" Roberts said behind him.

"Of course you may," Edward replied as he moved aside some long leaves.

"I don't wish to inspire your rage, but… captain to captain, I feel you are being too harsh on the boy."

Edward glanced over his shoulder and took a breath. "Herbert?"

"Yes."

"Nonsense," Edward said. "I spoke my mind, as I always do."

"That may be, but your tone was cavalier. I have seen you act this way before, when you are angered with someone."

Edward stopped and turned around. "And what of it? By rights I should be angry. He stole my ship, Roberts!"

"Aye, and he's paid the price. You've doled out your punishment, and he accepted it with grace." Edward looked away from Roberts' gaze for a moment. "None are telling you to discard your anger—though that is sound advice—but I simply believe you would do well not to punish Mr Blackwood over and over."

Edward furrowed his brows in anger. "You presume too much, and reach too far, if you would think to tell me how to run my ship, Roberts."

Roberts didn't back down, and instead straightened his back and puffed out his massive chest to intensify his countenance. "You may soon find yourself losing your ship if you continue the way you're going."

"Are you with me, Roberts? Because from *your* cavalier tone it sounds like you aren't."

"Being your ally and agreeing with your every action are not one and the same," Roberts said. After a moment, the man took a step back and shook his head. "I do not wish for the same thing as happened to your former first mate, Henry, to happen to Herbert."

Thoughts of his departed best friend bombarded Edward. The sight of Henry falling to his knees with a gunshot at his back, and the smoking pistol in Edward's shaking hand took hold of him. He looked down to his hands now, holding a cutlass instead of a pistol.

Roberts didn't know about Edward's sin; he only knew that Henry decided to leave the crew, not what happened afterwards. Despite that, Edward's frustration and anger intensified.

Edward tightened his grip on his cutlass. "This conversation is over," he said. "Concern yourself with your crew, and leave mine out of it."

Roberts' mouth opened to say something, but Edward turned around and walked away. He went through the forest with leaden feet and a heavy heart. He couldn't tell if Roberts followed after him, and at that moment he didn't care.

What does it matter anyway? Edward thought as he hacked and slashed his way through the bush. *Either they're with me or against me. Why should I spare a second thought for my enemies?*

With no foil to Edward's thoughts, his self-rationalization continued unimpeded. He lost all awareness of his surroundings as he cut branch after branch, vine after vine, and bush after bush. He walked long enough that he forgot where he was going, but kept walking forward and cutting down everything in his path nonetheless.

When Edward noticed a lack of roots beneath his feet and obstructions in front of him, he finally looked up and took note of his surroundings. He had stumbled upon a wide field of grass surrounded by the forest. Somehow an acre of field was devoid of trees, and the local wildlife must have fed on the grass to keep it short.

Edward's chest heaved with each breath he took; the exertion of slashing his way to the field had taken its toll on him. His arm was tired, and sweat covered his face ear to ear.

As he gazed upon the empty field and rested, it was as if the forest had gone silent. He could hear nothing but the rustle of the leaves and grass swaying in the wind.

Edward sheathed his cutlass and searched for the tallest tree he could see. Once he found a suitable one, he climbed up its branches. He took care as he moved from one branch to the next, his feet and hands keeping him steady as he moved up to the peak. As he climbed, the branches became thinner and thinner, and the canopy over the forest receded before his eyes.

Just before reaching the top of the tree, he stopped and stood on the thinnest branch that could still hold his weight. He held onto the trunk and gazed around the forest from his new vantage point.

He was so high up now, he was able to see the ocean to his left, but he could only see a sea of trees on his right. He scanned the horizon out over the ocean until he found what he was looking for: the *Queen Anne's Revenge*.

He wasn't able to see the whole ship, but he could see the tip of the middle mast poking out from the forest canopy. While he wasn't able to see Porto Bello, judging by the location of the ocean in relation to the trees and the ship he could guess where it was. He had travelled far, and he was only ten or twenty minutes' walk to the town at most.

Edward looked below, and began climbing back down the tree. After a few minutes of careful descent, he noticed some of the other crewmates entering the clearing.

"Oi!" he yelled.

The crewmates followed the sound of his voice, and once they noticed him they grouped together at the base of the tree. By the time Edward had reached the bottom branches, they had all entered the field.

Edward jumped down to the ground and rolled before standing up and facing the men. "This is where we will have our meeting with the Spanish," he stated. "I want two of you to scout a path to Porto Bello; try to make it short but easy to walk. The rest of you, come with me. We're going to get this set up properly. We wouldn't want to disappoint our new allies," he added with a smirk.

Edward sat at a table under a fabric canopy in the middle of the clearing they had found the day before. Anne, Roberts, and William accompanied him at the table, and an assortment of men from both crews were scattered around the forest. Pukuh and Hank were leading the defence, and each of them kept a close watch on the proceedings.

Edward got up from his seat, reached over to take a piece of cheese from a plate in the centre, and threw it into his mouth. He barely even had to chew as it had been softened by the heat of the day.

"If you eat any more, there won't be any left for our guests," Anne warned.

Edward shrugged his shoulders. "All this waiting is taking

its toll on my insides."

Anne gave him another look, and he promised her he wouldn't eat another piece.

The air around the table and in the field was hot and oppressive. It was nearing noon, and it was the most torrid it had been since they'd arrived in Porto Bello. The tension wasn't aiding the stifling heat either, as each man was on alert and ready to fire their weapons at a moment's notice. That alertness and nervous energy keeping them on edge was like a sickness that invaded their neighbours, and soon all the men were sweating and jumping at shadows.

The lot of them had already been waiting for three hours, and only ten minutes ago Pukuh had informed them that the guests were on their way. The captain of the Spanish galleon would arrive any minute, but they were later than they had all expected.

"Is everyone clear on our story?" William asked.

Edward grunted and leaned back in his chair. "I believe so, as we recounted it not twenty minutes ago." William stared at him, his cold gaze saying all it needed to say. "I am a merchant by the name of Edward Teach, as is Roberts, who will go by the name of... Benjamin Kinney. We heard about the proposed attack and wish to lend our aid, as it involves pirates who wronged us in the past."

"And the terms?" William pressed.

"The terms..." Edward said, pausing for a moment. "We assist in the attack by ambushing the pirates, and take the fight to their deck while the galleon focusses on the biggest ship. When the battle is concluded, we take the pirates' cargo as payment."

William nodded. "Good," he said.

"I can't fathom why it matters when Anne will be translating," Edward said, gesturing to his wife.

Anne frowned. "We don't know if the captain speaks English as well, or if he has someone who can translate as well. We would do well to not say something regrettable."

The sound of branches crunching underfoot and the heavy rustling of leaves brought everyone's attention to the forest edge. The sounds grew louder, and before long a group of ten armed men broke through the forest and entered the small plain.

Two of the men stood in front of the others, taking in the surroundings and the people whom they were meeting. The other eight had a tight grip on their weapons, and also took in their surroundings, but in a more focussed and defensive way.

One of the two men in front wore a traditional Spanish naval uniform of gold colour with ornate decorative accents and a dozen wooden toggle buttons fastened at the centre. The man had several distinguishing medals on the breast of his uniform.

The other man wore a cloak covering his entire body, with a hood obscuring his face. Edward wasn't able to see inside the cloak, but from the two men's mannerisms, he could tell that it was a person of importance, even when compared to the Spanish captain.

Edward and the others rose from their seats and tried not to stare at their guests. He pulled at his coat and tried to straighten the creases that always seemed to form between his gut and his chest.

After a moment, the cloaked man whispered a few things to the captain, and the two approached the table.

"Thank you for joining us here, gentlemen," Edward said.

Anne translated the message, taking her time to ensure she said what she meant to say. Before she could finish, the captain held up his hand.

"I know your tongue. There is no need to strain yourself," he said.

"Ah, good. I daresay we were a bit worried over that," Edward said, and then he smiled and nodded to Anne.

"Then you may send the girl away now. I want no further delay—"

Edward held up his hand. "The *girl* is my wife and my quartermaster," he said, clenching his teeth afterwards to stop himself from saying something else.

The captain's eyes widened, and he and the other man stared at Anne. "A woman quartermaster?" The captain shook his head. "No matter. She can stay," he said. "Who are you, and how did you come to find out about this supposed attack on my vessel?"

Edward took a few seconds to breathe, and then began. "I am Edward Teach, and this is my associate, Benjamin Kinney. We are merchants who deal in this area, and we heard a rumour of the upcoming attack on your ship... Normally, we wouldn't act on such rumours, but we've had confrontations with the pirates in question, and wish to aid you."

The captain held a stern look on his face as he looked in the eyes of each person at the table, save Anne. The men behind him had their hands on their weapons, wary of the men surrounding them. The tension from before they arrived was only magnified by the arrival of the Spaniards.

Edward tried to mitigate the tension by continuing the conversation. "We have given you our names; it would be good to know how we should address you and your... companion."

"Hmph," the captain scoffed. "I am Miguel García, captain of the..." The man paused for a moment, glancing at those at the table, then shook his head. "I would tell you, but you would not understand the name, nor be able to repeat it," he said. "My companion does not need to give you his name." He seemed to hold much contempt for Edward and company, and Edward could not see why. "Where will the attack happen, how many ships, and of what size?"

"Our contact says it will happen off the coast of Providencia, and they have three ships of frigate class or lower."

"And your ships?"

"We have a frigate and a sloop-of-war. Over sixty guns between us."

Miguel nodded. "And why are they not in the harbour? Why choose to meet out here, and not in town?"

Edward breathed again. The tension was wearing on him, and he was sweating. It was lucky the day was hot, otherwise the sweat could be seen as a sign of duplicity. "They are not in harbour for the same reason we meet here: We don't know who we can trust."

The cloaked man leaned over to Miguel and whispered something in his ear. After a moment Miguel asked, "And what would you have in return for your *protection*?"

Edward nodded. "We wish to have the cargo the pirates have. A simple request, I should think, given the circumstances."

Miguel nodded. "Yes, that does seem reasonable," he said. "But tell me, how am I to trust a *liar*?"

Edward was taken aback, but he was speechless for but a moment. "I'm afraid I don't understand."

Miguel smirked. "We talked with the governor of Porto Bello after receiving your letter. The governor knew of your ship's names, but not their owners. You are pirates."

At the mention of the word, Edward and those spectating placed their hands on their weapons. Muscles were taut, ready to spring at the slightest movement. Eyes darted from one person to the next, waiting and watching for a surprise.

Edward's brows were furrowed, and he stared straight at Miguel. "That is quite the accusation you lay upon one who is trying to help you."

"I accuse you of the truth. Or do you wish to wait until the morrow when I see your ship's names first-hand? I know one of you is Bartholomew Roberts, captain of the *Fortune*. The other ship, *Queen Anne's Revenge*, I'm unfamiliar with, though I doubt a merchant would be working with pirates."

Edward glanced at Roberts and the others, and Roberts and Anne both nodded to him. "If you think us pirates, why come to meet us? Why did you not attack our messenger to draw us out and put us to the sword?"

"Bartholomew Roberts, though a pirate, stole from the traitorous Portugal. I felt we owed him a meeting at the very least."

Edward nodded and tapped his fingers on the table. "I believe re-introductions are in order. I am Edward Thatch, captain of the *Queen Anne's Revenge* and this," Edward said, motioning to Roberts, "is Bartholomew Roberts, captain of the *Fortune*."

"Edward Thatch?" Miguel questioned. "Where have I heard this name?"

Edward shook his head. "My ship was formerly called *Freedom*, if that aids your memory."

Miguel muttered the two names under his breath a few times until his eyes shot open and he looked at Edward in a new light. "You killed the queen's daughter!" he nearly shouted.

For the second time, Edward's jaw dropped. He glanced over to Anne, the living, breathing daughter of Queen Anne, sitting to his right. "I believe you are mistaken, sir. The reports stated that the pirates involved were unknown," Edward said, referencing a newspaper they had come upon over six months before.

The paper said that Edward's Anne had been killed, as a symbolic way of disowning her after her repeated acts of delinquency. The last they had heard, the pirates in the false scandal were never named. News from the Old World was always rather scarce in the New, and unless it pertained to local events they rarely paid attention. Either that, or the Boddens never thought to mention it.

Did the Boddens know about Anne? I can't recall, Edward thought.

"That was revised months ago," Miguel said with a wide grin. "Come, come, no need to be shy of your exploits. You are both friends to Spain."

Edward glanced at his wife, and her gaze was stony as she stared in the direction of Miguel, but not directly at him. The subject was a sore spot with her; despite holding no love for her mother, the implication that one is dead to them does not inspire familial affection.

"I do not wish to brag, lest my ego grow too large. Let us discuss the attack," Edward said, trying to steer the conversation back. "I apologise for the ruse. We couldn't be sure of your trust in us. Pirates seem to have frequented this area."

Miguel waved his hand, then rose from his seat to take some of the cheese and meat off the plate on the table. "You haven't attacked any of Spain's ships or shores, so you have no reason to fear, my friends." Miguel took bites from the cheese. "Though, if you are not trying to deceive us, what do you stand to gain from attacking other pirates? Why not join them and attack us? If we had not of heard of this attack, I cannot say if we would have survived. If your two ships had joined the other pirates, it would have been assured."

Edward, too, took some of the food off the table and mimicked the Spanish captain. "The pirates involved in the attack wronged Roberts and myself. They stole his ship, and killed one of my crewmates. Another of my crewmates may still be in hiding with them as well, but the story of why is, frankly, too long and involved for today," he said.

Miguel shook his head. "Such treachery should not go unpunished. Why do you need our help with this?"

"We felt that if we could gain the help of a Spanish galleon, it would all but guarantee our success."

Miguel smirked and pointed at Edward. "Ah!" he said. "So, you plan to use me, do you?"

Edward chuckled. "Somewhat," he replied. "Consider this a partnership. One where we both benefit."

Miguel nodded. "I believe we can come to an agreement," he said. "We can work out the details on the way to Providencia. For now, let us say that we will sail together at dawn."

Miguel rose from his seat, and the cloaked man did the same. The Spaniard reached forward to shake Edward's hand, and with that their arrangement was sealed.

"On the morrow," Edward said.

After the handshake, Miguel and the rest of the Spaniards left to finish their trades for the day and prepare to sail. The cloaked man and Miguel whispered back and forth as they left.

When they were well and gone, the crews hooted and hollered their cheers. The tension that had permeated the area washed away, and a happy mood spread to each of them instead. Many of the men slapped Edward on the back, congratulating him and commenting on how well he did in the negotiations, despite the fact that everything went wrong. The fears of their covers being seen through and most of the negotiations hinging on their reputations were lost with the deal being struck.

After a few moments of revelry, Edward hushed them. "Back to the ship!" he ordered. "Tomorrow, we set sail."

15. TURNABOUT

Edward pulled in a deep breath as a yawn overtook him. The sun had yet to arise from the threshold of the horizon, and he had already been up for an hour to help prepare the ship. His jaw opened wide, cracking in the pre-dawn light. Other crewmates, a few of whom had been up even longer to secure the anchor, caught his yawn.

Before long, the crew secured the anchor, and they were ready to depart. Herbert was at the helm with Christina, the two of them working out their route. Anne was nearby issuing orders to the crew to get the *Queen Anne's Revenge* seaworthy. William was watching from the starboard railing, ordered by Anne not to work, given that he was still recovering. Pukuh, not just a warrior, was helping the crew with the sails, and despite his missing arm he was proving to be a match even for the seasoned sailors. Meanwhile, Jack was playing an instrument on the bow for all to hear to boost morale, and Nassir was there, talking with him.

To Edward's left, the *Fortune* bobbed up and down with the waves. He could see Roberts near the helm, and Hank, his first mate, shouting at the crew to get moving. They were slightly ahead of the *Queen Anne's Revenge*, and nearly ready to sail.

Anne walked over to Edward. "We can loose the sails on your order, husband."

"Let's let Roberts go on ahead. They'll need to match speed with the galleon moreso than we. We can give them the time they need and then do the same."

Anne nodded. "I am overwhelmed with disbelief over this situation. It's unthinkable that we were able to convince Captain García to side with us."

"Yes, it was surprising. I had expected more resistance, but according to him it's as if we're heroes to Spain."

"From pirate to patriot, it all depends on the country

176

you're backing," Anne said. "Now we have an even number of ships, and possibly a greater number of guns in our arsenal. Any plans for the battle?"

Edward smirked. "I thought that was between my quartermaster and the helmsman?" he said.

Anne grinned. "Oh, but a captain should be intimately involved in all affairs aboard his ship. I wouldn't want to intrude."

"With your new responsibilities, I thought it might be best if the crew became accustomed to taking orders from you, so I'll let you take over for the battle this time."

Anne put up her hand. "No, no, I insist. It is a captain's duty to direct his crew in battle."

Edward couldn't help but chuckle with his wife. There had been precious few exchanges of that nature between them of late, and it warmed his heart.

He could only imagine how she were feeling at the present. He was so focussed on his own personal vengeance, he never stopped to think about how she might feel about the man who'd tortured her love and left him for dead. For a brief time, she'd even thought Edward dead, and the thought of how she had to have felt then sickened him. He never again wanted to see her face like the moment before she realised he was alive.

Edward grew serious, and pulled his wife into an embrace. "It will be over soon," he said softly.

After a few seconds, she pulled away from him and arched her eyebrow. "I know."

Edward leaned in and kissed Anne on the forehead, and she smiled. She stood on her toes and pecked him on the cheek in return.

"You know it's been four months now?" she asked.

Edward glanced away in thought, and scrunched his nose. "Four months... twelve days," he replied.

Anne's eyes widened, twinkling with amusement. "Oh, twelve days, is it? I believe I've forgotten, thank you for the reminder."

Edward pushed his wife playfully, and the two smiled and laughed together once more.

"Captain," Herbert called. "The *Fortune* has raised anchor."

Edward looked over to his companion's ship, and it was moving past them, slicing through the waves. Roberts was on the quarterdeck, and when he noticed Edward watching he tipped his hat to him. Edward returned the gesture.

"Let's get this underway, Herbert. Lay our course."

The helmsman grinned. "Aye, Captain," he said. Herbert leaned over in his chair and shouted, "Lay aloft and loose all sails!" as his first order.

The crew went up the rigging and unfurled the topsails so the wind could fill them, and then moved down to the other sails. The ship lurched forward, swaying back and forth, bobbing up and down, and all the while sounding off its usual groans and creaks.

Edward patted the wood of the railing. *You'll survive, girl. You've been through worse.*

The ship moved with the power of the wind between the two islands they had hid behind, and back into the open ocean. Roberts and the *Fortune* were already out and heading west, back towards Porto Bello to meet with the galleon.

Edward looked at the sails, filled to the brim with wind, trimmed appropriately, and yet something felt off. He turned to look at Herbert. "Herbert, do you find her a little slow today?"

Herbert glanced over at Edward, then at the sails, and then at the sides of the ship towards the churning water. "Perhaps the wind just isn't as strong as we think," he speculated. "I see no cause for concern, Captain."

Edward accepted Herbert's judgement on the matter. "It's not as if we'll need the extra speed regardless. We're escorting a galleon, after all."

Herbert chuckled. "True."

They followed the *Fortune* around the shore of Panama towards Porto Bello. After the near hour-long trip, most of which *Fortune* slowed down for, they neared the Porto Bello inlet. The sun had finally burst from its hiding spot on the horizon, and the glow afforded them better sight of the sea and surrounding area.

"Captain, I believe I see the Spanish galleon," Herbert said, pointing off the bow.

Sure enough, the Spanish vessel was there, sailing out of Porto Bello. It was a behemoth of a ship, with four masts and at least ninety cannons across two gun decks, and swivel cannons on the main deck. The sight of it was awe-inspiring and fearsome.

The two ships approached the galleon heading west as the Spaniards headed north. As they came closer to the massive ship, their own ships' sizes were brought into an inevitable comparison.

The *Fortune* and the *Queen Anne's Revenge* were alike in that they had a single gun deck, but the *Fortune* didn't hold as many cannons. It was shorter in both length and height, but swifter. In the presence of the galleon it looked as a dwarf standing next to a giant such as Roberts.

The *Queen Anne's Revenge* was longer and taller than the *Fortune*, had more guns, larger masts and sails, and was superior to most other pirate ships. Even with all that, Edward's ship—with masts removed—didn't look half as big as the galleon, so tall and wide was its berth.

Edward whistled as they drew closer. "If we had a ship as big as that, none would be able to touch us," he said.

"Don't be fooled by its size, Captain," William said, walking over to him. "True, a galleon's broadside could wreck a ship of smaller size than the *Fortune* with one, clean blast, but they are slow and troublesome vessels. Just as with most things of such a size, the larger they are, the easier they topple over."

Edward leaned against the quarterdeck railing. "Is that so?"

William nodded. "Notice the top half of the ship?" he said, pointing to the galleon as they approached. Edward pulled out his spyglass to get a better look. "It's bowed inward towards the top so the weather deck is more compact. This is to bring more weight to the centre of the ship in an attempt to keep it steady, but it still sways like no other in the water."

Edward scanned the ship with his spyglass, taking note of

the shape it, as well as its movement. He chuckled. "It does sway like a bitch, doesn't it?"

Anne smacked Edward's chest. "Don't be so crude."

Edward looked away from his spyglass for a moment to grin at Anne. When he did, something to the south, towards Porto Bello, caught his eye.

Edward noticed two ships heading out of Porto Bello, itself nothing out of the ordinary. He looked through his spyglass to see two sloops of similar size to the *Fortune* a league behind the galleon.

Strange that they too are heading north.

Edward turned his spyglass back to the galleon, and looked at the crew on the weather deck. He could see them moving back and forth, maintaining the trim of the sails as the wind shifted. A new unease grew in his belly. He could see men running about with what looked to be boxes of something. As if that weren't enough, Edward also noticed fewer men than should be needed on the main deck. There were enough to man the sails, but that was all. There should have been more up top to relieve the others, should the need arise.

On their own, the ships, the movement on the top deck, and the lack of men manning the sails would be nothing. But together, it caused a stir in Edward, and he could not shake the anxious feeling overtaking him.

"Turn us to starboard, Herbert," Edward commanded.

Herbert turned in his seat and raised his brow. "Starboard? But we're almost beside the galleon."

Edward didn't repeat the order, and instead noted to himself that Roberts was just in front of them, and in thirty minutes would come within cannon range.

"Belay that. Get us next to Roberts on his port side. No, no, that won't work."

"Captain, could you please apprise me of the situation?" Herbert asked.

Edward must have had a strange look on his face, as Anne walked over to him. "Husband, is something the matter?"

"Please, everyone, cease your questions! I need to think,"

Edward shouted.

Those around Edward gave him strange looks, but no one asked him any further questions.

Even if we turn now, with the speed we're going and the speed of the galleon, we're still going to be in range of its cannons. If we don't turn now, we'll be dead in the water.

"The galleon is going to attack us, we need to move to starboard now and get out of its path," Edward announced. "Someone, get me a musket."

"What caused this change? Not moments ago you thought them our allies," Anne asked.

Edward pointed to the two ships approaching to their left. "I believe the Spanish hired those ships to aid them against Kenneth Locke, and to attack us. There's some strange movement on board the galleon as well," he said, handing his spyglass to Anne.

Someone brought Edward a musket, and he began loading it.

Anne looked at the approaching ships, and then to the galleon's deck. "There does appear to be some oddities, but why would they act our allies one day, and betray us the next?"

Edward frowned as he finished loading the musket. "I have neither the clairvoyance nor the patience to puzzle out whether I'm right or wrong. If I'm right, we'll escape with minor damage. If I'm wrong, we can laugh with the Spanish about it later," he said. Edward moved to the port side of the ship. "Turn this ship starboard, Herbert!" he shouted.

Herbert sank himself deep into his wheelchair and flung the ship's wheel hard to port. The ship lurched with the sudden change in direction, and the men aboard were not prepared for the shift. Some fell to the deck, others grabbed onto the rigging or the fife rails, and some simply leaned to avoid tumbling.

Christina grabbed hold of Herbert's wheelchair, holding it close like a piece of driftwood in a storm. She also helped him from taking a tumble as well by planting her feet down to secure the both of them.

The ship cried out at the change in direction, the wooden

planks stretching and straining against each other. The force from the wind pushed it in one direction, the rudder in another, and the sea a third, and the ship protested with its wooden voice, as it had many times before.

Edward held fast to the port railing in one hand and his musket in the other, and waited for the moment to pass.

Herbert eased the rudder back to have the ship turning in a looser arc. If they continued to turn at that pace it could rip the ship apart, and he knew that. At least now the worst of it was over.

Now that the ship was moving at ease and Edward had his legs firmly on the deck, he took aim and fired his musket at the stern of the *Fortune*.

The sound of the shot rang off across the sea, its echo bouncing off the water and wood. The men on the *Queen Anne's Revenge*, confused over the change in direction, became alert at the noise of battle, but when no other thunder met their ears they put away their weapons.

The crew on the *Fortune*, however, reacted as Edward had hoped. They first searched for the source of the noise on their ship, then turned to their companions. Roberts, on the quarterdeck, was quick to look Edward's way.

They were too far to shout, but Edward could tell Roberts had his brow cocked in confusion. He motioned towards the sloops approaching, and Roberts took out his spyglass and looked through it. Roberts then turned to the galleon, which was now turning starboard to match the course Edward's ship. Roberts understood immediately, and issued orders to follow the *Queen Anne's Revenge*.

The two ships were now turning as quickly as they could to the north, but they still had to go in a wide arc otherwise it could put too much strain on their hulls. Meanwhile, the three ships were closing in on them from the west and south.

While he waited for the *Fortune* to catch up to them, Edward walked back over to the helm. He tossed the musket back to the crewmate who brought it, and approached the railing.

"Men, I need your attention," Edward said. "If I am right, our Spanish allies set out to deceive us, and would have attacked us had we entered their cannon range."

The crewmates looked at each other, questions hot on their lips. Not a day before, Edward was telling them of the alliance they had with the Spanish galleon. They believed they were heading off to get revenge on Kenneth Locke and strike a blow to Calico Jack's crew, and this called everything into question.

Edward could sense their doubts, and sought to quash them before they grew any further. "We will still head north to pursue Kenneth Locke, however right now we're not out of the range of the galleon. I need you men to bring me more speed to this vessel. I'd say we have a good..." Edward turned to Herbert. "Would you say half hour?"

Herbert checked on the galleon's position and theirs. "That sounds about right."

"We have half an hour before the galleon is on us. We must broad reach the sails, so we're already at a slight disadvantage. William?"

William was promptly by Edward's side. "Yes, Captain?"

"I know you are still injured, but I need you to find us more speed. Can I count on you?"

Without hesitation, William saluted out of habit and shouted "Yes, Captain!" before turning around and yelling orders to the crew to change the positions of the sails. He went to each group of men responsible for each of the sails and attempted to tailor each one to the position of the wind.

"Christina, Anne, could you measure our speed for us?" Edward asked.

The women nodded and went to grab a chip log from the bow cabin. They rushed past the men working on the rigging and pulling the sails over to the bow's portside.

As they worked on the sails, the *Fortune* crept ever closer to their port side. Edward could see Roberts leaning out over the bow, holding onto the rigging to keep him aboard. Edward went to the stern and did the same, and soon the two were close enough to hear each other.

"They were to attack us?" Roberts yelled over the sounds of sails flapping and water pounding into a mist on the bow of his ship.

"I presume," Edward shouted back above the din. "Go on ahead, you can't take the broadside."

"And you can?"

Edward's mouth became a line. He took a breath and adjusted himself on the rope holding him to the ship. He wiped his face of sweat and salt water. "We must," he replied.

Roberts grinned, and then bowed to Edward, holding that sign of respect far longer than necessary. Whatever animosity he might have had from their disagreement seemed to be gone. After his bow, he turned to his crew and issued new orders.

The *Fortune's* sails were trimmed and broad-reached, matching *Queen Anne's Revenge* in position, but vastly outmatching them in speed in the process. It wasn't long before the *Fortune* had already met and surpassed the position of Edward's ship, and they were in front of them once more.

"Eight and a half knots!" Edward heard Anne shout.

Eight and a half! Edward thought. He looked over at Herbert, who also looked astonished. "How in the Lord's name are we only eight and a half knots in a broad reach?"

"I don't know, Captain. Let me think it over. There must be some explanation." Herbert held his head in his hands as he mumbled over calculations in his head. Edward gave him a moment, but listened intently. "The *Fortune* can go sixteen to eighteen knots, fourteen to sixteen in a broad reach if not laden down with cargo. Our top speed in a broad reach is eleven to twelve knots if we're not..." Herbert's eyes shot open. "The cargo!" he shouted.

"What cargo?" Edward said, his brow raised in question.

"We weren't able to sell the cargo we took from the merchant ship. It's still in the hold," Herbert said.

Edward clenched his teeth together, anger washing over him. He cursed and ran down to the weather deck. "I want twenty men with me!" he yelled.

Volunteers jumped to and followed Edward to the crew cabin. Once in the belly of the ship, Edward woke their reserve crewmates still sleeping, some fifty or so men who would normally take over during the night. The men were groggy and irritated by the early wake-up, especially considering they had only just been relieved, not two hours before.

"Men, we need to jettison the cargo in the hold, as much as we can as quick as we can." The crew, still weary, looked confused. "There's no time to explain. Form a line from the hold to the top deck. We're going to dump it over the side of the ship."

The men started to form up and create a line extending from the hatchway to the hold all the way up to the weather deck.

As the crew formed the line, Edward opened the hatchway to the hold and descended a ladder with four other crewmates. He had to bend over to go inside the hold proper. In the hold there was an assortment of pungent barrels, boxes, and bags filled with spices and other miscellaneous cargo. The overpowering smell had permeated the hold. It made his nose sting and his eyes water the instant he sniffed, and he could not smell anything of the sea or the pine of the ship any longer.

Judging from the number of containers filling the hold, Edward estimated that it was several tonnes worth, and they had less than thirty minutes to clear it all.

"Let's get the barrels first, then we'll get the boxes and bags."

Edward went to work and grabbed the first barrel in his hands on his own, hefting the thing over his shoulder. His hands struggled for grip around the large, relatively smooth circumference. He took a few breaths and unbent his knees, then stepped back to the ladder and climbed up the first few rungs.

Once he was high enough, he dropped the barrel on its side, and the first crewmate rolled it over to the second, then on to the next in line until it got to the last mate before the ladder. The mates at the ladder passed it along to each other until it was on the next deck, and then the process continued.

The first few barrels were taxing, and Edward could feel the pressure across his shoulders, chest, hips and back as he worked. Once the rhythm of the work took over, the pain faded and he lost sense of everything else in the monotony.

Lift, walk, climb, drop; lift, walk, climb, drop.

Edward could hear nothing save the sound of his own hot breath, while all thoughts of the fight ahead fell to the ether. The feeling of the wood scraping his hands, the coarse grains grinding against his palm. The metal bilge hoops cool from the chilly hold pressed into his shoulder. His arms and legs stretched and strained with the exercise, growing into an almost stabbing pain as the time passed. Before he knew it, all the barrels were gone, and the raw stench of spices with it.

He glanced around at the other four men, who were carrying two barrels in pairs. His fatigue and pain hit him all at once, and he had to lean against the hull. He caught his breath in deep swells of his chest, panting tiredly. He arched his back and it cracked, sending a wave of relief through him, though it was only temporary. He brought a shaking, aching hand up to wipe the sweat from his forehead. His rough fingers scratched against his skin as the beads of water and salt were pulled together. He flung the sweat to the damp floorboards of the hold.

He pushed himself from the hull and went to the hold ladder. He climbed up it, following the last barrel on its track between the brigade of men. He went up to the gun deck, then back to the weather deck all the way up to see it tossed into the sea.

The sealed barrel fell into the water and floated, bobbing in the water as the *Queen Anne's Revenge* passed it by. Down the port stern, Edward could see a hundred barrels or so in a line extending so far back he wasn't able to see them all.

Off centre of the abandoned cargo, Edward could see the galleon, and he knew they were approaching the vessel's cannon range. The galleon was closing in on them, its presence even more overwhelming than before.

To the bow, on Edward's right, the *Fortune* was already heading north, and well out of the way of danger. He was glad for that fact at least.

"Speed?" he called.

Christina and Anne were on the bow still, and they looked to have been routinely checking the speed. Anne tossed the chip log into the water; the wooden piece fell in and pulled along the rope it was attached to. When it hit the sea, Christina turned over a small hourglass, watching intently as the sand fall through the small opening in the middle. After a half-minute, the last grains fell through.

"Time!" she called.

Anne grabbed the rope which the chip log had been pulling, taking note of each knot that had passed. "Ten knots!" she shouted.

Edward pounded his fist against the railing. *That's not enough!* He turned around to his crew. Many of them were still working, holding the rigging steady, making small adjustments here and there to try to improve their speed. Some looked at their captain, waiting to see what he was going to say.

"Men, secure the halyards. Brace for broadside," he said.

The crew dropping the cargo passed the order down the line so they could finish with what they had. The main sailors tied down the ropes holding the sails onto the fife rails at the masts, or along the sides of the ship to keep the sails in place.

Anne pulled in the chip log, and wrapped the rope up. She went over to Edward. "We did everything we could. If luck is on our side, she'll only be in position for half a broadside."

"And if luck is on their side, even half their broadside is enough to sink us, should it hit below the water-line," he said.

They shared a pensive, wary look. Though their lives were on the line, they had been through many similar situations in the past. They could see in each other the fear buried deep within, the fear that deadens with time and is mixed with anger and tenacity. Edward wasn't about to give up, and from that look in her eyes, Anne wasn't either.

The crew were piling bags filled with sand from the bow storage cabin across the starboard side of the weather deck. With the entire crew working, in a few short minutes they had stacked the bags high enough to crouch behind. They worked to stack more around the ladders leading to the quarterdeck and the stern, as the blast was most likely to hit there.

Edward and Anne checked the rigging to ensure the sails

would hold in place while the crew were busy. They tugged and pulled on the lines, testing the knots and the location of the rope. Once satisfied, they moved behind the line of sandbags and knelt down.

Edward glanced around to the ship and the men huddled together behind the makeshift barrier. These men had the same, weathered fear in their eyes, preparing for the worst but ready to spit in God's eye for letting them die should it happen.

Edward tried to find a vantage point which would provide him sight of the galleon, but at their angle it was impossible. The quarterdeck and stern were blocking his view. Judging from where the ship last was, it was only a matter of minutes now.

He looked at his men once more, their tense bodies and light whispers so vastly different from their normal boisterous and easy-going nature. But there was more to it than this moment in time, and he could tell the mood aboard his ship was shifting. The betrayals, the battles, and the injuries were piling on top of one another, and it wasn't just Edward who'd paid the toll.

The sound of thunder rippled over the ship, shaking the wooden beams and planks in its wake. The tremor ran up Edward's feet, rattling his bones as it passed over him. He braced himself.

"Incoming!" he shouted.

The sound of the cannons was followed by a full two seconds of eerie silence, a moment of pure waiting. The cannonballs came and went in a flash, ripping through the wood and blowing holes through the hull of Edward's ship. The wooden beams and planks broke apart with violent snaps as the iron rained down on them.

As the iron crashed through the stern and the railings and the doors, it carried the pieces of its destruction with it. Wood, glass from the windows, and bits of metal flew in the wake of the cannonballs.

The deadly iron hit the sandbags, and the pieces of the ship followed immediately afterwards. Dozens of sandbags exploded from the impact of the cannonballs, flung away from the blast. Sand joined the other pieces of the *Queen Anne's Revenge* to pepper the crew, once a part of their home, now another weapon against them.

Edward felt sudden pain on his face, shoulder, and chest. As soon as he was able to feel the pain, and the warm blood seeping from his wounds, he noticed the attack was over. It had all happened so quickly he hadn't even had time to think.

He rose on unsteady feet, glancing at the horrors before him. Before he could take it in, movement caught his eye. He looked up to see one of the main mast's halyards loose, pulling away from its belaying pin on the fife rail.

Without thought, Edward jumped on top of the sandbags still intact and leapt into the air. He stretched out his hand to grab the rope, which was rapidly slipping from its confines. The sound of the scraping rope against the wood was the only thing Edward could hear at that moment. If that rope got loose, the mainsail would go loose, they would lose some speed, and it would mean another broadside would be able to reach them. The rope zipped passed the fife rail. Edward pushed his hand out farther, closing his fingers around the rope, and caught the end of it with the last inch to spare.

The force of the rope escaping the fife rail pulled Edward from his mid-jump up into the air. He swung forward on the rope over the port side of the ship. At the top of his arc, he looked over to see the galleon trying to turn back straight to pursue for another broadside. The next moment Edward swung back down towards the ship, but this time with the full tack pulled down from his weight. He slammed into the port side of the ship, and whatever was in his shoulder and chest sent a lancing pain through his body.

Edward took a few breaths, clenched his teeth, and climbed the rope back to the port side railing; he wrapped the rope around his arm, and pulled himself over the top. The pull of the heavy mainsail nearly toppled him as soon as his feet hit the sole, but he stuck his feet in and managed to get to the fife rail without incident. He fastened a halyard hitch around the fife rail and secured the mainsail once more.

He noticed the screams of the injured and the shouts of Herbert and the crew around him. Herbert was already back up to the quarterdeck, his face bloody but otherwise unharmed, and his wheelchair intact. Tala was beside him, barking to accompany his orders. He noticed Christina working the rigging with the other men to fix the sails and straighten their trajectory so they could outrun the three ships in time.

Anne and Pukuh were also uninjured, and helped with the foresails. Anne was shouting, but Edward couldn't hear what she was saying. He was just happy to see her safe.

Jack was diligently playing his music, trying to play above the din to inspire the crew to work faster with the beat he was playing. He could tell Jack had injured his hand, but the man played on regardless.

Edward looked at the destruction around him. Bits of his ship strewn about the deck, holes from the front of the quarterdeck out to the stern, broken railings, chips off the mast. Large iron balls, leftovers that couldn't make it through the whole ship, pitched and rolled with the movement of the *Queen Anne's Revenge*. Heavy, unwieldy things, far larger than could fit in any of their cannons, and a danger even without the speed behind them. This was worse than he had seen from several cannon broadsides in the past.

Crewmates had been struck in the legs, the arms, the chest, and the head. Legs had been torn off, arms split in twain, chests compacted, and heads…

Alexandre and Victoria, previously below deck, were now in the middle of the fray, tending to the injured and patching them up as best they could. Nassir was helping to carry the more severely wounded below for the tough surgery ahead. The three were already covered in the blood of their allies, and the deck around their feet was running red.

Edward ran down below deck, dodging past Nassir and one of the crewmates who had lost his leg, and down to the crew cabin. He checked the stern and noticed a few holes, but nothing low enough to worry about, and then jumped into the hold hatch. It was nearly empty, with half the original number of boxes left, and a few dozen bags.

He scanned the hold, and when he found no cannonball holes in the hull he moved on to the bilge. The stench of the bilge was an order of magnitude worse than the hold had been before they'd removed the spices. Edward had to cover his nose and mouth to stop it from overwhelming him. He lay down and lowered his head into the bilge, not wanting to enter the filth if it wasn't necessary. He couldn't see well, having just come from above deck, so he listened for the sound of gushing water. After a few seconds, and satisfied he could hear nothing resembling a breach, he closed the bilge hatch and took a few deep breaths.

Edward searched for the source of the pain in his shoulder and chest, and found it to be a splinter and a nail embedded in his skin. The splinter was in the side of his chest, but wasn't deep and rather easy to remove. The nail, on the other hand, took some doing. He had to pry at it with sweaty fingers, which soon became slick with blood. He took hold of the tip of the nail, and with a shaky hand yanked the metal piece out. He dropped the bloody metal to the sole of the hold, and it hit the wood with a clang.

His shoulder wound seeped blood, and he had to clamp down his hand over the hole in a weak attempt to stop it up. He could still feel the vestiges of the metal nail in the hole in him, as if something was missing. A piece of him lost for a time, but one that would come back later—yet it still pained him.

Edward pulled himself up and returned to the weather deck. By the time he was up top, the wounded had been given aid, and three dead men were now covered by a sheet and placed at the front of the entrance to the stern cabin.

He went up to the quarterdeck, glancing over the side at the back of the ship. It appeared that the galleon had stopped giving chase, and the two sloops had turned back as well. Normally Edward would have some sense of pride at having escaped, but he only felt anger at the betrayal by the Spanish.

Friends of the Spanish. Edward spat over the side.

Edward walked over to the helm, examining the destruction that had been wrought. Their masts and sails were miraculously unscathed for the most part, but the stern decks were riddled with holes and pieces of the ship lay underfoot at every turn.

He looked out over the bow to see the *Fortune* furling her

sails to slow and join with *Queen Anne's Revenge*. Now that the threat was gone, they could talk about what to do next, but it was clear in Edward's mind what he wanted to do.

As Edward approached the helm, Herbert asked, "No breaches?" Edward shook his head. Herbert seemed to look twice at Edward, then asked, "What now, Captain?" as if he sensed Edward's mood.

"Now…" Edward said, looking Herbert in the eyes. "Now, we burn them all."

16. MEMENTOS OF WEAKNESS

"My boy, I tell you true, I am ever grateful for your insight and perceptiveness. You saved us once again," Roberts said with a boisterous laugh. He raised his cup in the air and then took a long drink from it.

Roberts and Edward were in the stern cabin of the *Queen Anne's Revenge*, talking about the recent events and what to do next. Most of the glass in the room had been shattered, the wood punctured with large holes, and the floor littered with their leftover splinters, but Edward had insisted on having the meeting there.

"If only I had noticed sooner, perhaps we would have escaped unscathed," Edward replied, and then he too took a drink from his cup.

"Nonsense. You acted as swiftly as any could be expected. Who would think we would have been betrayed? The Spanish seemed eager to work with us not a day before. None could spot the lie soon enough, so this was bound to happen."

Edward nodded. "I suppose you are right, but I don't believe he was lying the other day."

Roberts raised his brow. "Oh no?"

"You said yourself, none could spot his lie. Given our collective experience with liars, cheats, and tricksters, we certainly would have known."

"So, you believe Captain García was telling the truth?" Edward nodded. "Then what could have changed his position overnight?"

Edward shook his head. "I don't know," he replied. "But I believe it to have something to do with the hooded man with him."

Roberts leaned back in his chair. "Ah, yes, the mystery man. Strange fellow, to be sure, but you think him to be the mastermind of this deception?"

"It seems the most likely. He was whispering in the captain's ear the entire time, but stopped after we confirmed who we were. He probably thought it best to let the captain tell us what we wanted to hear, and then later told the captain what they would do, or at the least advised him to change his mind."

"You may be correct," Roberts replied, swirling the drink in his hands.

The sea air swept in from outside of the holes in the cabin, preventing the room from becoming stuffy, as it was prone to do. The splash of the waves as the ship crashed against them and the shouts of the men outside came in loud and clear as well.

"I want you to continue ahead of us," Edward said.

Roberts tilted his head, and his lips curled. "Continue on… to what end?"

"To the end of our enemies. I want you to head to Providencia and proceed with our initial plan of sabotaging one of the ships."

Roberts glanced around. "And what will you and your men be doing?"

"We need to repair our ship, so we'll be travelling rather slowly. Also, there are some… renovations I believe need to happen if we are to survive on the sea any longer," Edward took another drink from his cup. "I want you to take some of my crew with you as well. They can help you so you can continue at speed during the night." Edward placed his cup on the broken table in the middle of the room. "If all goes well, we should be able to arrive a day behind you."

Roberts' mouth was a line, and he stared at Edward for a moment before placing his cup on the mangled table as well. "You are sure of this?"

"Currently, this is the best way to proceed. If the two sloops that were with the galleon earlier today join her, it would be an even match for Kenneth Locke. We need to cripple one of his ships, perhaps take it for ourselves, and we may be able to destroy all of them. The galleon, the sloops, and the pirates."

Roberts rose from his seat and extended his hand.

Edward got up and took Roberts' hand, and the two gripped hard, testing each other's strength. After a moment of equal back and forth, they laughed amicably, and Roberts slapped Edward's shoulder.

"Until next we meet, then," he said.

"Until next we meet."

Roberts turned around to leave, and Edward made to follow. "Oh!" Edward blurted out. "Before I forget, the cargo… Herbert didn't have a chance to sell it and—"

Roberts held up his hand. "I watched the scene firsthand, Edward. I know the toll you paid. You will find another means to repay me, I am sure of it. Don't let it trouble you."

Edward smiled and nodded. "Thank you, Roberts. As always, you are a true friend."

Roberts waved his hand. "Do not mention it. You loan us your crew to aid in our revenge. What more could I ask for?"

Edward folded his arms. "Well, you are already asking for coin…"

Roberts burst out laughing. "You have me there."

Edward also chuckled, and the two left the stern cabin. Repairs were already underway the weather deck, and the sounds of hammers hitting nails and wood met their ears. Roberts' crew were working with Nassir and Edward's crew in repairs to the railings and the stern.

Edward and Roberts went up to the quarterdeck of the *Queen Anne's Revenge* to address the crew. After a moment of calling for their attention they ceased repairs, and Edward could explain their plan.

"Firstly, I want to thank the crew of the *Fortune* for your help in repairing the damage we received. With your help, our ship is already beginning to look like its former self." At that, Edward's crew hooted and hollered their agreement and thanks as well. "Roberts and I have conferred, and we think it best if you all move on to ensure our plans come to fruition. You'll be heading to Providencia ahead of us to sabotage one of the enemy ships, and when we meet with you again we will take the fight to Kenneth Locke and Walter Kennedy together!" Both crews shouted their enthusiasm to have this years-long story of revenge over and done with. "To ensure the *Fortune* arrives on time, I want twenty men to join them and help run their ship at night. Do I have any volunteers?"

Many of Edward's crew raised their hands, several of whom glanced at their neighbours and friends from the other ship, nodding and smiling at them.

"Choose amongst yourselves who to send, then pack your things and get on with it. You're to follow Roberts' orders as my own, you hear me?"

The crewmates who volunteered responded, "Aye, Captain!"

"Now, there is one other matter which requires a vote from you all," Edward said, bringing the crew's attention back once more. "In this battle, and those to come, lack of speed will be our disadvantage. We barely survived, and I have no doubts that a few extra knots would have saved us. I propose that we fix that. I propose we tear down the forecastle and the poop deck to give us more speed."

Thankfully, the crew seemed to like the plan, and nodded in approval before voting to pass the ship renovations without a debate. They appeared excited to see the ship in better fighting condition after being hurt by the galleon.

Edward took note of how the *Queen Anne's Revenge* looked in that moment. He tried to ignore the wounds and the battle scars, and instead to focus on how the ship used to look. He wanted to remember his home as it was, and tried to burn that image into his mind.

The three masts with the thick canvas, the decks of carved Caribbean pine, all the way up to the figurehead of Anne at the bow. Over the years, from planks being replaced, Nassir carving the figurehead, and changing sails, many things had changed aboard the ship. This was just one more change to make it their own.

It will still be our home. It will just be more our own that someone else's. More than Benjamin Hornigold's. Edward gritted his teeth. *More than Calico Jack's.*

It would be a fitting tribute to Calico Jack if he realised who Edward was, and that this used to be his ship. It no longer bore the name he gave it, and it would soon look nothing like it had. In both name and appearance it would soon be Edward's ship, his home, in full.

"By your vote, it shall be done," Edward said.

The crew cheered with the decision, excited to see the change and the added speed. Roberts said his goodbye to Edward and went back to the weather deck to instruct his crew and the new volunteers readying to help him.

After the cheers subsided, Edward waved down Nassir. "Nassir, could I speak with you?"

The tall carpenter nodded and climbed up to the quarterdeck. "What do you need, Captain?" he asked in his thick accent.

"I wanted to have your thoughts on the time situation. How long will we need to repair the holes and remove the decks?"

Nassir rubbed his clean-shaven face as he glanced at the damaged stern and then over to the bow. "It will save us some time with the poop deck if we do not repair it..." Nassir trailed off and mulled it over a bit more. "It won't be pretty, and I'll need many men working day and night, but two days and we should be finished."

Edward nodded with a grin. "She doesn't need to be pretty, she just needs to be fast. Mind the figurehead though; a talented carpenter carved that for me, and I think it goes rather nicely with our ship."

Nassir grinned as well, and thanked Edward before heading off to brief the other men.

Edward then noticed Victoria bringing some planks of wood up from the storage to the stern, and walked over to greet her. "Victoria," he called. She nodded to him, saying nothing and continuing with her work. "Do you have a moment?" he continued.

"No," she replied before dropping the planks and walking back to the quarterdeck steps.

Edward stepped forward, trying to catch her. "I wanted to know if you've been having any issues aboard."

"None," she replied without turning around. She went down the steps, heading towards the ladder to the gun deck, her boots snapping against the wood as she moved.

Edward followed her. "I was also wondering if you could provide some insight on Calico Jack. What types of ships he commands, how many allies he has…"

Victoria turned around just before reaching the steps leading into the belly of the ship. "He commands a ship as any other. I know nothing of his other ships or allies, and I was more a prisoner aboard his ship than sailor, so I cannot tell you anything useful," she said curtly. "Any further questions, or may I return to work?"

Edward shook his head, and Victoria went down the steps to the gun deck. He was left speechless and stock still, as if he were lame of body and mind.

"That one spits fire, doesn't she?" Pukuh asked, coming up beside Edward.

"Yes, she does," Edward replied. "I suppose for a woman to have the courage to board a pirate ship, she would have to be of a certain calibre."

Pukuh nodded. "Far more than you or I, that is sure."

"I believe you are right." Edward stopped staring at the ladder and turned towards his friend. "She isn't fond of me, it seems."

Pukuh shook his head. "No, no, in her eyes there is deep respect for you. I know this. She simply doesn't enjoy chattering about nothing as birds do."

Edward raised his brow. "How do you know this?"

Pukuh chuckled. "She told me," he said. "I tried to see if she knew anything of Calico Jack's old moniker of 'Benjamin Hornigold.' She gave me a look that spoke to her confusion and gave a simple answer. As I pressed, she told me as I told you."

Edward joined Pukuh in laughing, a brief but welcome moment of levity. "Speaking of the pirate with two names, do you recall anything your father might have mentioned about why he turned out this way?"

Pukuh shook his head. "Nothing of note. I don't believe my father was with him throughout all his adventures, but all the stories he did tell were joyous and fantastic in nature. Although, those could have been exaggerated stories for a child, to put them to sleep."

Edward's mouth creased as he thought on it for a moment. "Perhaps we'll have to ask him about it when we see him next."

Pukuh's face was stone. "Perhaps we will... Of course, it would have to be after we inform him of how this happened first," he said, looking at where his right arm used to be.

Edward paused for a moment, thinking over whether he should ask what he wanted to ask. "I imagine it's not something you take joy in talking of, but how is your arm?"

Pukuh grinned as he looked at his right shoulder. "I believe you would call this a stump, no? Not much of an arm anymore."

Edward chuckled nervously. "I suppose not."

Pukuh's grin faded as he eyed the scarred and bumpy remnants of his right arm at the base of his shoulder. The skin had covered up the wound from so long ago, and some of the colour had come back to it, but scars from the hasty amputation remained white and jagged, streaking across his shoulder and over to his chest.

"I still feel it, you know," Pukuh said, glancing at Edward. "In the darkness of night, when I first wake, it itches, but when I reach over to scratch it there's nothing there. The itch remains... Do you ever have an itch that you cannot scratch? It is frustrating, is it not?"

Edward shook his head. "The worst," he replied.

Pukuh nodded. "Imagine that, but never the ability to scratch."

"If only there were some way to help you," Edward said with a sigh.

"Do not mistake me," Pukuh said, shaking his finger. "The itch is a useful reminder. It reminds me of my weakness, and pushes me not to slack in my training."

Edward chuckled. "Only you would enjoy such a burden."

"Perhaps," Pukuh replied. "I should return to work, you said you wanted more speed for this ship, did you not?" He punched Edward in the arm, and then joined a group of men receiving instruction for the removal of the cabins.

Edward peered around the ship and noticed that his men were now boarding the *Fortune*, and they seemed to be making final preparations to leave. He walked over to see Roberts still on the *Queen Anne's Revenge*, greeting and thanking the men boarding to help them.

"Departing so soon?" Edward asked with a smirk.

Roberts grinned as well. "Yes, well, a certain captain wishes me to leave, and he's got a rather short fuse from what I've seen."

Edward folded his arms. "Oh, is that so?" After a moment of staring Roberts down, the two burst into laughter. After another moment they ceased laughing, but Edward still carried the smile. "Safe travels, friend. Find Walter Kennedy and give him hell," he said.

"I shall," Roberts said before tipping his hat. "We'll be watching the seas for your return in three days."

"We'll be there," Edward replied.

Roberts crossed the gangplank connecting their ships, and the crews released the bonds tying the vessels together. The two ships drifted apart for a few moments, and when there was enough room the *Fortune*'s sails were loosed and it took off north towards Providencia.

Both crews shouted and waved as they sent off their brethren. The sun shone bright that afternoon as they parted. Before long, the *Fortune* had become a dot on the horizon and soon the light reflecting off the water hid it from view.

Herbert gave the order to loose the sails and the *Queen Anne's Revenge* began crawling towards Providencia as well. Herbert made sure the sails were as full as could be, but not as much as when they had been trying to escape the galleon. Too much pressure on the masts over an extended period of time could wear them down.

After the *Fortune* was out of sight, Edward walked up to the quarterdeck. Some of the men were already working with Nassir on removing the planks from the poop deck. They started with the top planks and worked their way back. Nassir did his best to instruct them in the proper removal to save the wood, but more often than not they were too hasty. Edward hoped that by the time they reached the forecastle the men would have enough experience and patience.

Edward walked over to Herbert, who was at the helm. "Herbert, how much speed do you feel these modifications will gain us?"

Herbert turned to examine the men at work on the poop deck, and then glanced over at the forecastle. "It's tough to say... Perhaps one to two knots at most."

"That would put us only a few knots below Roberts' ship, no?"

Herbert nodded. "It would close the gap a bit, yes."

Edward smirked and stroked his beard. "Perhaps we should challenge them to a race when they're laden down with cargo? Then we may be an even match."

Herbert chuckled. "Perhaps."

There was a moment of silence between the two of them, and the sounds surrounding them filtered back in—the banging of hammers, the grunts and shouts of the men, the gust of wind and the splashes of sea water against the hull.

"We can't keep fighting each other as we have been," Edward said, peering at Herbert from the corner of his eye. "You know that... yes?"

Herbert raised his brow as he looked at Edward. "I know that. Do you?"

Edward stared at Herbert for a moment, the gaze lingering. In Herbert's eyes and tone, he detected a hint of annoyance. After taking his punishment, Herbert was rightfully upset at the way he had been treated. Edward had realised he'd wronged Herbert after Roberts berated him back in Panama, but his pride wouldn't allow him to apologise.

Edward removed his gaze and instead peered towards the bow at the water crashing against the figurehead and spraying onto the deck. "If what Calico Jack did in Bodden Town is any indication, he will try to split us apart more than ever before. We must stand together."

Herbert stopped staring at Edward and he too focussed on the sails and sea and ship in front of them. "I believe in the family you have created, and I believe in you. I know I may not have shown it very well over the past weeks, but I do. I know I have a weakness, but this family is my strength.

You've reminded me of that. You conquered a town, you've gained us an ally beyond compare, and you've brought men together and made them better men by your example. Our family alone is what will help us weather the coming storm, and I will never take that for granted again."

Edward looked at Herbert, and there was no denying the resolve in his eyes. Edward nodded, and then smirked when he recalled something Pukuh had said to him in Bodden Town.

Herbert grinned and turned his head to the side. "What?"

"I trust in what you've said, and I will trust in you, but one of your statements is wrong."

Herbert cocked his brow. "Oh?"

"*We* are the storm."

17. A PERSONAL DECISION

Clouds covered the afternoon sun, blocking most of its light from reaching the sea. The wind became colder and more biting the longer the clouds lingered. Heat never seemed to last on the surface of the sea, and the splashing water only cooled the ship and crew further.

Even Edward, in his thick coat, layered on top of undershirts, and breeches and boots covering every inch of him, shuddered as the mist of the sea touched his face. "How can it never be that we are neither hot nor cold? Why must it be one extreme or the other?"

Christina chuckled daintily. "You would think after many years at sea you would be accustomed to the weather."

"One being accustomed to something and enjoying it are separate matters."

"Should I fetch you a blanket, oh Blackbeard the wicked?" Christina asked with a smirk.

"No, thank you," Edward replied, ignoring her jibe. "Tala will keep me warm, won't you girl?"

Tala's head was resting on her paws. When she heard her name, she glanced at Edward, but then ignored him.

Edward frowned, and Christina laughed. "Well, I suppose not," he said.

He peered out to the bow, towards their destination, Providencia, somewhere off on the northern horizon. Two hours prior, when the weather was fair, though hot, they had passed by the island of San Andrés. From Herbert's estimation they were one hour from seeing Providencia on the horizon, and two from landing.

The *Queen Anne's Revenge* now had no forecastle, and, aside from the masts and the sails, they were better able to see off the bow than ever before. The railing still needed some work, but Nassir had managed a crude implementation for the time being. The stern was another matter. The holes were repaired, and the ceiling for the stern cabin was in place, but there hadn't been enough time to cut or sand the edges. Some of the planks jutted out off the hull as if screaming out about the rushed nature in which they had been put together.

Nassir was still doing his best to fix the appearance, but planing wood by hand was tough work for an already exhausted man, and he was the only one capable. Edward had ordered him to rest for the day, as it could wait for another.

On a positive note, they had been testing their speed since the change, and there was a noticeable difference of a knot or two depending on the wind. Herbert's prediction had been on the nose, and the crew were thankful for it. Most of all, the men were excited to test their new speed in battle.

William had recovered even more over the course of the few days' travel, and had returned to full duty. He used his expertise to guide and instruct the men in maintaining the sails. The men were still getting used to the new speed and the way the wind travelled over the ship, and William helped speed that process up.

After adjustments necessary from the change in weather, William returned to the quarterdeck. "Captain, you'll be happy to note we're travelling close to fourteen knots."

Edward nodded. "I am pleased to hear that. Glad to have you running this crew, William."

William gave a slight bow. "The pleasure is all mine."

"How's your chest? Still giving you trouble?"

William shook his head. "There's still slight pain when exerting myself, but aside from that I cannot feel a thing."

Christina whistled. "You heal quickly. I recall it taking some time for me to heal after Plague attacked me. I was still feeling the pain for weeks after it happened."

Edward recalled the assassin called Plague sent after him long ago, and what had happened to Christina. She had been lucky to survive a dagger to the stomach.

"Nonsense," William said. "You have a youthful, strong body. Had another been attacked in the same place they would not have fared as well as you had."

Christina was taken aback by the compliment at first, but then grew a devilish grin for a brief moment before switching to a shocked expression. "Youthful and strong? My dear William, I've never known you to flirt with a young woman's affections. And in front of my brother, no less." Christina fanned her face with her hand, feigning a swooning fit.

In a rare display, William's jaw went agape and he looked aghast. "I... That is..."

Herbert, nearby at the helm, shook his head. "Shameful, William. Simply shameful."

William stammered an attempt at a reply, but couldn't gather his wits to produce one.

Edward burst out laughing, which sent the other two into a fit as well. William glanced from person to person, and slowly closed his mouth and stood up straight.

William coughed. "That was not amusing."

The laughter of the three subsided into low snickering. Edward grabbed William's shoulder for support. "I'm afraid you'll have to forgive us, William, for we'll have to disagree with you. If only you could have seen your face," he said, grinning widely.

Before William could object any further, a mate shouted "Captain!" down from the crow's nest.

Edward and the rest looked up to the mate near the top of the main mast. "What do you see?"

"Two ships, north north-west. They're engaged in battle."

Edward looked off the bow, but couldn't see anything unaided. "Tell me when you're able to see what class the ships are."

The man in the crow's nest nodded. "Aye, Captain."

"Could it be Roberts?" Christina asked as she tugged at the rose pendant around her neck.

"We can't be sure, but if it is him he may need our help. We can afford a slight detour if necessary. William, Herbert, send us straight in the path of those ships."

"Aye, Captain," the two of them replied in unison. Herbert turned the wheel a few degrees to port, while William instructed the crew in adjusting the sails to maintain their speed. In no time, they were heading north north-west, straight at the two fighting ships.

Anne came running up to the quarterdeck. "Why have we

changed course?" she asked.

"There are two ships fighting ahead of us, and we're heading to intercept."

Anne raised her brow. "Roberts?"

Edward nodded. "Possibly. If it is him, he's fighting against someone from Kenneth Locke's group, no doubt."

"Unless he was caught by authorities in the area."

"Either way, we're going to help him out."

As the *Revenge* moved forward, the ships came into view. At first they were two dots, melded together on the horizon as small as a fly against the meeting of sea and sky. The minutes passed and the dots separated and became more distinct, eventually taking shape. Then, the shape took form, as a piece of clay, being molded before their eyes. They could see the separation of mast to sail, and sail to hull, each minute bringing new details into view.

"Captain, the two ships be sloops," the mate in the crow's nest yelled down.

Edward nodded to the man, and went back to watching from his post. He glanced at Anne. "It seems more and more likely to be Roberts. Prepare the men, Quartermaster. You're about to take control of your first battle."

Anne looked at Edward with a wide grin. "Aye, Captain," she said before stepping forward to the quarterdeck railing. "All hands, prepare for battle!"

The crew looked up at her, registered the order, many giving the briefest of smiles, and then shouted, "Aye, Aye!"

The men charged with manning the small cannons on the top decks prepared their armaments, while others gathered muskets and powder to use. William went below deck, presumably to tell the gunners of the coming battle, and soon returned with weapons of his own.

William stepped up to the quarterdeck and handed muskets to Anne and Edward, then went back to gather one for Christina and Herbert each before finally taking his own. The four held to their weapons, waiting for the ships to get closer.

Now that they were facing a sloop and had two ships instead of one, the mood was distinctly different from the galleon flight. It was no longer a desperate hope and fear, but an itch to destroy the lesser opponent and regain their pride. As if by magic, the mood carried itself to each of the crewmates, though none exchanged words. It manifested in excited laughter, crazed eyes, and jumps in their steps.

The faint sounds of battle sped across the ocean, and grew louder the closer they came—the loud roar of cannons, the sharp crack of guns, and the varied shouts of men's battle cries... or their death wails.

Smoke billowed out from the sides of each ship, lingering for a brief moment before the wind swept it away. No matter how the wind tried, the smoke was replenished with each roar and crack.

The ship closest to *Queen Anne's Revenge* straightened after their latest broadside and headed west south-west to try to flee.

The ship trying to flee had two masts, while the other had three. Provided this wasn't a random battle they'd happened upon, the one fleeing was not the *Fortune*.

"It's trying to escape," Edward commented.

"Intercepting," Herbert said. "Beam reach!" he shouted before he turned the wheel to port so the ship headed northwest.

"Beam reach!" William relayed.

The crew changed the direction of the sails as they were now to be perpendicular to the wind blowing north northeast.

Edward looked at the approach the other ship was taking. Where it was headed, it had to have its sails in a close reach or close-hauled, which was not an ideal position for escape. The enemy ship would try to head north, as long as *Fortune* didn't cut them off. Failing that, if they outran the *Queen Anne's Revenge*, they could try to swoop around, but it would be risky as they would be tacking against the wind, and Edward and Roberts could still follow them.

We've got them, Edward thought.

Over the next thirty minutes, the ships stayed their courses, with the *Fortune* heading west to circumvent their enemy if they tried to head north. The wind stayed mostly true, with some minor trimming needed to maintain a beam reach.

The *Queen Anne's Revenge* was closing in on the enemy ship, on the side of which they could now see the name *Gallant* emblazoned. In a few minutes they would be in range to hit them.

"Fire a warning shot," Anne said. "Let them know we're here for them."

William nodded and shouted, "Chasers! Raking fire!"

A few men manning cannons at the bow, remnants from the forecastle, acknowledged the order, and prepared their cannons to fire. After a moment, the sound of three blasts rang out from the bow, and three puffs of smoke erupted along with cannonballs.

As expected, they landed well short of their mark, making three splashes into the sea far in front of them.

In a fearful response, the *Gallant* changed direction, trying to switch to a northward bearing. They were hard-pressed to switch their heading, however, and lost much speed in the process.

Herbert barely had to touch the wheel to switch them from going north-west to north. The change brought about the need to trim the sails further, putting them in a broad reach, the *Queen Anne's Revenge*'s fastest position.

The *Gallant* seemed to have forgotten about the *Fortune*, which was coming up beside them, and would be in line for a broadside in short order.

After a ten-minute struggle, when they realised in full the situation they were in, the *Gallant* waved the white flag and furled their sails.

Cowards, Edward thought.

"Do not grow complacent, men," Anne shouted. "This could be some ruse."

As the *Gallant* slowed, the *Fortune* made to match its trajectory and speed to board. The *Queen Anne's Revenge* was still behind the two faster ships, and so Herbert didn't give the order to furl the sails right away.

Instead, as the *Fortune* was pulling up beside the *Gallant* on its starboard side, Herbert manoeuvred their ship over to the port side. Then he gave the order to furl the sails so they could slow to a stop beside the *Gallant*.

Now that they were up close, Edward could see damage from battle all around the hull. Holes from cannonballs were scattered here and there, but not much harm had been done before they had arrived.

Roberts wasted no time in having the two ships lashed together. Edward could see them dropping gangplanks and boarding, fully armed and taking the crewmates prisoner. They rounded up the crew to the waist of the ship, but Edward noticed Roberts was talking with the crew and searching for something or someone. After a moment, he called to his crewmates, and two answered by heading below deck.

The *Queen Anne's Revenge* approached and the crew began tying the ships together as the *Fortune* had done. All the while, the gunners had their hands tightly gripped to their linstocks, ready to drop them into their cannons at a moment's notice.

Edward pulled out a pistol from his belt and loaded it. He took his time pouring the black powder into the barrel, placing the cloth and the lead ball on top and ramming it into the shaft. As he finished, he headed over to the starboard side of the ship.

Edward jumped over the railing of the ship over to the weather deck of the *Gallant*. He walked over to Roberts, who was standing off to the side near the quarterdeck.

"Roberts, I'm glad we made it in time," Edward said.

Roberts shook Edward's hand. "Well met, Edward. I too am glad you arrived when you did. It could have been a long, arduous endeavour without your assistance." Roberts glanced at the *Queen Anne's Revenge*. "I see you've completed your modifications to the ship. It looks like a whole new vessel."

Edward glanced over his shoulder at his ship. "Aye, she's faster now as well. We might even be able to challenge you," he said.

Roberts flashed a slight grin, but said nothing. Before Edward could say anything else, Roberts' crewmates returned to the weather deck with someone in tow.

The man they were pushing and prodding along with their muskets was a lithe, average-looking man with light red hair and faded freckles across his cheeks.

Roberts' crewmates dropped the man, whom Edward knew was the Walter Kennedy he had heard so much about, to his knees in front of the captains. He fell on his hands, but quickly righted himself on his knees as he cowered in fear in front of Edward and Roberts.

Edward cocked and primed the pistol in his hands, then turned it over to Roberts. "Time for justice, Roberts."

Roberts looked at the pistol in his hands for a moment, and then pointed it at Kennedy. The look in Roberts' eyes was far more serious than Edward had ever seen before.

Kennedy's eyes, on the other hand, were filled with fear and despair. "Please, Roberts," he said with a trembling voice. "I—"

"Shut your mouth, Walter," Roberts seethed as he took a step forward and pressed the pistol against Kennedy's forehead.

Kennedy sobbed and closed his eyes, letting out a pathetic cry like a mewling babe. His whole body shook, and it looked as if at any moment he might soil himself. His hands clasped together in front of him, tightening in preparation for what was about to happen.

A moment in silence passed, with the three crews waiting for the foregone conclusion to this tale of betrayal. The clouds broke, and the sun of the afternoon shone on them. Even the wind seemed to have silenced itself in the face of this tale's climax.

And yet, the thunder of the pistol never roared into that silence. Instead, Roberts released the cock on the gun and lowered it to his side.

"Roberts," Edward said, a nervous chuckle following his call, "what are you doing?"

Roberts sighed, but then smiled. "You are correct. Now is the time for justice, Edward. My justice." He looked at Walter Kennedy with a strange look in his eyes. "I will grant you mercy this day, old friend. You will live to see another day."

Walter burst into miserable tears and fell to the deck, as if he were bowing before Roberts. "Thank you, Roberts.

Thank you, thank you!" he kept repeating.

"Do not mistake my mercy for weakness," Roberts said. "If I see you after today, I won't hesitate to kill you. Live out the rest of your days as you will, but live them far away from here, someplace where we are sure never to meet."

Kennedy looked up at Roberts, tears still streaming down his face. He wiped his eyes. "I swear to you, I will do as you say."

Edward clenched his teeth and balled his fist. The sight filled him with inexplicable rage. He grabbed the pistol from Roberts' hand, cocked it, pointed it at Kennedy, and pulled the trigger.

Roberts grabbed Edward's hand and pushed it up towards the sky. The pistol fired, its thunder finally releasing, but the bullet flew up in the air, hitting nothing.

"What the hell do you think you're doing, Edward?" Roberts shouted as he pushed Edward back to the quarterdeck bulkhead. His anger turned his Welsh accent into a booming song.

For what Edward believed to be the first true time, he saw anger in Bartholomew Roberts' eyes. A great, deep well of rage billowed forth and pressed in on Edward, and he suddenly felt very small in the face of this giant of a man.

Edward tried to move his hands, but he wasn't able to. "I'm doing what you're not capable of, because you're weak. The only reason you're sparing him is because of a false sense of camaraderie which is long since removed," he said. "You leave him to roam the seas, and he will come back to kill you in the end, not the other way around."

Roberts kept his hands steady on Edward, not letting him go, and boring his gaze into him. "My reasons for sparing him are based solely on what he has done to me. If we are to serve as our own judge, jury, and executioner, we do not have the right to forgo the first two responsibilities." Roberts loosened his grip on Edward.

Edward pulled his hands away, dropped the gun on deck, and pointed a finger in Roberts' face. "I will tell you of mercy and what it brings. I spared the naval captain who falsely accused me of piracy, and he brought a fleet of warships to bear against me, resulting in my jailing. Kenneth Locke was marooned for killing one of my crewmates instead of being killed himself, and he came to torture me nigh to death. Had I done away with them when I had the chance, I would have been spared those atrocities. I do you a favour in attempting to save you future injury, but seeing as you don't desire my help, do yourself a favour and kill him while you have the chance," Edward said, pointing at Kennedy. "As for me, I will correct my mistakes, and kill anyone who crosses me or my crew." Edward pushed past Roberts and headed back to his ship. "You would do well to learn from my mistakes, Roberts."

Edward returned to his ship, leaving Roberts with the silence, and, he hoped, the weight of just what his decision meant.

18. PROVERBS 16:18

"That was not wise," Anne said.

Edward and Anne sat in the war room, now with a slightly lowered ceiling from the renovations, and fewer windows for light to enter. The repairs were complete, with minor, superficial improvements still outstanding.

Edward tapped his finger on the oval table in front of him as he eyed his wife. "As my wife, are you not to stand by my decisions?"

Anne's face was as stone. "You presume much to think I would stand by you as you push everyone away," she said, her words ice. "I choose when and where to stand by you, and when to tell you you're acting the fool."

Edward clenched his jaw and looked away, his tapping increasing in tempo. "What would you have me do? Stand idly by as my friend proceeds to sail into a storm of his own making?"

"As your wife, and your quartermaster, I would have you retract your earlier statements and offer apology to your ally and friend."

"Tch," Edward spat. "You would have me show weakness in the face of my crew?"

"If your pride won't allow you to apologise in public, then offer it in private. I care not how it is done, just have it done and over with."

Edward leaned back in his chair, reliving the event again and again in his head. He saw in Kennedy's eyes the same look as Kenneth Locke and Isaac Smith. He had known then that Roberts would soon find himself on the other end of that pistol if Kennedy were not executed, but Roberts had stopped him.

He stared his wife in the eyes. "If anyone should apologise, it's Roberts. I was saving his life, but he chose to throw it away."

Anne got up from her chair. "You're acting more a fool than I took you for. I take my leave of you before I say something I will regret. Just know that if you don't do the right thing you will lose more than my respect."

Anne walked towards the cabin door, her feet nearly stomping on the planks. Edward thought to say something about respect being for lords and ladies, not pirates, but he thought better.

After she left the room, another entered directly afterwards. Jack Christian walked into the war room and approached the oval table. "May I sit, Captain?"

"You're not attempting to lecture me as well, are you?"

Jack chuckled as he placed his hand on one of the chairs, but stopped short of sitting in it. "If you consider having a conversation a lecture, then I suppose I am."

Edward waved his hand, and Jack sat down across from him. "What did you wish to discuss?"

"I suppose the first order of business I should mention is that Roberts and crew are stripping the *Gallant* of valuables for themselves."

Edward nodded and scratched his chin through his thick beard. "As it should be. We owe them, and after dumping the cargo we have no way to repay that debt."

Jack frowned and leaned forward in his chair. "There is… something else you should know."

Edward raised his brow. "What?"

"The men returned from aboard Roberts' ship after what happened on the *Gallant*, and some overheard Roberts telling his first mate to prepare to leave."

"That doesn't seem odd. We head to battle soon."

Jack nodded. "Yes… but the men claimed they heard him wishing to head east."

"East? But that's…" Edward trailed off.

"He may be planning to leave us and not aid in the fight against Kenneth Locke and the galleon."

Edward gazed at the oval table in shock. He and Roberts had been through so much, and it was hard to think that this small squabble would set them apart. He began thinking on just what it was he had done and said, and whether Anne was correct and he should apologise. After a moment, he shook off the feeling.

"He was here before us; east must be where Kenneth Locke will attack us. That must be why."

Jack's jaw went slack for a few seconds, and he cocked his brow. He seemed at a loss for words. "That could be, Captain, but perhaps you would do well to ask him yourself."

"Would you send for him?" he asked.

Jack nodded, and rose from his chair. "I'll see it done," he said. "And, Captain, I wish to give you the advice I tried to impart upon Herbert before he went chasing after his enemy: Don't let anger cloud your mind. I may not be a shining example, but you can at least learn from my mistakes. Roberts is a friend and ally, and some due kindness may prevent a lasting rift."

Hearing the same thing over again wore on Edward's anger. That Roberts could be so troubled over what had happened that he would leave was a sobering thought. After some silent reflection, the stubbornness returned, and he thought it wasn't possible for Roberts to be so childish.

Edward simply nodded in Jack's direction, and Jack nodded back with a smile before he left the war room.

Roberts wouldn't leave over this. That would be foolish. Edward was more or less certain of that, but he stroked his beard and rethought what he knew about the man.

After a few minutes, a knock came at the door. "Enter," Edward said. The door opened and Roberts walked in. Edward forced a smile. "Roberts, please, come in, sit," he said, motioning towards the seats at the table.

Roberts hesitated for a moment, and then stepped over to the table and took a seat. "You wished to speak with me, Edward?"

"Yes… Did you follow my advice in handling your friend Walter Kennedy?"

Roberts grinned briefly, but it seemed more from surprise. "You still don't understand, do you?"

Edward sat up straight in his chair. "I believe it is you who misunderstands, friend."

Roberts' hand gripped the arm of his chair hard. "You

undermined me, insulted me, and called into question my judgement in front of my crew." The normally sweet tones of his Welsh turned to a harsh melody. "You are lucky that my crew holds the both of us in high regard, or we would be having a very different conversation right now."

Edward could feel his legs and arms tense and itch. He took in a deep breath to calm himself. "I was trying to help you, that is all."

"Hmph," Roberts scoffed. "It is the height of pride when one thinks to offer help to someone who doesn't need it. A high mind comes before a fall," Roberts added.

"And who's to say you aren't the one with the high mind?" Edward spat with a wave of his hand. "You can't even see that you'll just be betrayed again." Edward held up his hand. "My apologies, you only seem to understand when quoting scripture. How does it go…? Ah, yes, you aren't able to see the beam in your own eye, or something along those lines."

"You distort the meaning of the passage, and it just shows your own lack of awareness," Roberts seethed, his eyes wide and full of anger.

Edward rubbed his face, frustrated with the talk. "Could we perhaps move on? We have a battle to sail to, if you'll recall."

Roberts sat up straight in his chair and folded his arms in front of him. He stared at Edward for a moment which seemed like an eternity. Edward felt as if he were being scrutinized, judged, and found wanting.

"So, you will offer no apology for what you've done?"

Edward clenched his teeth once again, then licked his chapped lips. "I tell you again: I was trying to help you. If you don't want that help, that's not my issue. I've done nothing wrong."

Roberts stared at Edward again, his hands still folded, and eventually Edward groaned. "Fine, you want an apology? I apologise for trying to help you do something you should be doing yourself," he said in a mocking tone.

Roberts sighed. "I asked Walter Kennedy where the others were headed, and he said they would wait twenty nautical miles northwest of Providencia for the Spanish galleon. That seems to fall in line with the map Luis provided. You may have the *Gallant* so you are still able to fight in the coming battle." Roberts rose to leave.

Edward bolted from his seat; his chest felt like it had been knocked around. "Hold, hold. You are leaving? Over this?"

Roberts shook his head. "No, not just for this. You've changed, Edward. Or… perhaps I've simply been able to see you for who you are now that we've had some time together," Roberts said, scratching his chin. "There is some sort of darkness within you, and while I do not claim to be a saint, I have lived by a code. It may seem as if I've changed my ways here today, but I have only tempered myself in that code to come out stronger. Walter Kennedy wronged me, yes, but he doesn't deserve death." Roberts placed his hand on the chair, and looked Edward in the eyes. "You seem to live by the whims and changes of the tide. Every person who wrongs you and situation in which you are wronged turns you into a more angry, bitter man… I suppose that is a tempering in its own way, but it is a tempering I want no part of."

Roberts turned around and headed towards the door of the war room, leaving Edward standing speechless. He was reminded of another time a friend of his left him, the scene nearly mimicked in his head with Henry's back flashing into his mind. The same feelings welled inside him as well—confusion, fear, anger, and an overwhelming sense of guilt over what he'd done to Henry.

"I thought we were brothers," Edward said, the words forming without thought.

Roberts turned around. "We were," he said, pulling Edward back to reality and making him realise he had said that out loud. "But, like Cain and Abel, we find our beliefs at a crossroads. Our beliefs in what a pirate is, and what one should do to those who've wronged us. And… before one of us kills the other, we should part ways."

Unwittingly, Roberts struck a dagger in Edward's heart. The guilt of killing his best friend Henry Morgan overwhelmed him in that moment. He was Cain to Henry's Abel, as he could soon be to Bartholomew's.

"Despite this, I wish you and your wife well, Edward. I will hold the memory of marrying you two as precious for all my days," Roberts said, taking a moment to breathe and compose his shaking voice. "I hope this world doesn't sink you into its depths."

Roberts left the war room of the *Queen Anne's Revenge* and closed the door behind him. Edward fell back into his seat, slumping down and pressing on his temples as an ache surfaced on the sides of his head.

I am Cain… am I? Edward thought. He gazed at the door, the lingering thought of Henry's and Roberts' backs in his mind's eye. *So be it.*

19. FORMATIONS

"With the *Gallant* in our possession we have a fighting chance against the Spanish galleon and Kenneth Locke. I want to discuss the battle plan I have in mind," Edward said to his senior crew once they had gathered in the stern cabin.

Edward had summoned Anne, William, Herbert, and Christina to the room after Roberts left and the *Fortune* sailed away. Edward listened from the room as quick and confused goodbyes were given, then had a crewmate gather them for the meeting.

All eyes were on him now, and they all had similar expressions of shock on their faces.

"Are we not to discuss what just happened, Edward?" Anne asked, not bothering to hide her annoyance.

Edward shrugged his shoulders. "What is there to discuss? What's done is done."

"What's done is—" Anne looked away, her jaw rigid from her clenching her teeth. "Our greatest allies simply sail away without so much as an explanation, on the eve of what is sure to be one of our toughest battles, and you think this is nothing to talk about?" she said, annoyance replaced with anger.

Edward looked straight into his wife's eyes, took a silent breath, and tried to maintain a level tone. "Roberts was with us only until we helped him capture Walter Kennedy, as I'm sure you'll recall. Our contract with him is completed, and he's left. He was gracious enough to leave us the *Gallant*, and with the size of our crew we should have no issues manning both ships."

"So..." Christina started, before glancing to those sitting at the oval table, "you're saying he just... left?" She chuckled. "You'll have to do a bit better than that, Edward."

Edward stared daggers at Christina. "Watch your tongue, young lady," he said.

"Do not talk to my sister that way," Herbert warned.

"I will not tolerate disrespect," Edward said. "Tell her that."

"Am I not sitting in front of you?" Christina said. "You may tell me yourself if you have something to say."

The conversation continued to devolve into a slew of back-and-forth passive aggression between the three parties for a brief moment until—

"Enough!" Anne shouted. "As quartermaster I'll have you all thrown in the brig if you do not cease this inane bickering," she said, her arms folded in front of her chest. "Edward, we know Roberts' departure was due to your indiscretion. The crew demands answers, and they will not suffer your lies."

Edward looked at his wife, anger still coursing through him. His heart beat as quick as a storm whipping the waves, and he clenched his hands tighter than a rope knot. "They want answers, do they?" he said. "Fine, I'll give them answers."

Edward rose from his seat and stormed off to the stern cabin door. The four glanced warily at each other before quickly following behind him. They called to him, but he ignored them and opened the door to enter the weather deck.

The light of the sun shining down hurt Edward's eyes when he walked out of the stern cabin, but he didn't move to block the beams. "Men!" he called out. He walked to the quarterdeck ladder, and went up halfway. As he did, the crew gathered around him, whispering and watching. "Roberts has abandoned us," he declared.

The shock of the announcement was evident on all the crew's faces. Coming after the fight Roberts and he had had, they were reasonably sceptical, and angered that they were low on fighting power. Anne was right; he wouldn't be able to spin a lie this time.

"He was a coward who couldn't finish the job he was meant to do: get revenge. He abandoned us in our hour of need because of the creed you all swore to. This ship isn't called *Queen Anne's Forgiveness*, it's called *Queen Anne's Revenge*, and revenge is what we'll have." Edward paused for a moment to search the crowd. Even in that short speech he had said enough. The men no longer looked angered, and instead looked ready for a fight. "Who's with me?"

The crew shouted their answer, and stomped their feet to make the sole of the ship shake. Edward let it continue for a moment, the raucous nature spreading to each man as the noise and the shaking rose. He looked at Anne and the others, and raised his brow, asking in his head if this was what they had wanted. Anne gave a simple, curt bow of her head in response.

Edward raised his hand to cease the noise. "I need sixty men to man the *Gallant* for the coming battle. There also needs to be a helmsman, and a senior mate to lead the crew."

"I will be your helmsman," Christina blurted out before any other could speak up.

Edward looked at Christina, and then glanced at Herbert.

"Don't look at him!" she shouted as she stepped forward. "I am the most qualified to navigate a ship, and I'm not a child who needs her brother's permission to do something. Let me do this."

Edward looked Christina in the eyes, those wide, sky-blue eyes of hers. She had a twinge of a smile on her face, and she had her fists clenched. Edward nodded. "You'll be the helmsman for the *Gallant*," he said.

William took a few steps and held his hands behind his back. "If you'll permit it, Captain, I can lead the crew on the *Gallant*."

"This will be a difficult task with what I have in mind, and I know you're the best man for it. What say you, men? Do these two have what it takes to lead you?"

The crew shouted their agreement with a mix of laughter and pats on William's and Christina's backs. The two of them accepted the praise with grace, grinning and smiling at their crewmates and friends.

"Choose amongst yourselves who wishes to serve aboard the *Gallant* while we prepare a battle plan. We will not simply survive. We will *win* this fight."

"The *Gallant* is giving the signal," a mate from the crow's nest shouted. He was periodically focussing his gaze through a long spyglass.

"Good," Edward said aloud. He looked at the position of the sun, just coming down with several hours before it fell below the horizon. "Take us into position, Herbert," he said.

"Aye, Captain," Herbert replied. He turned the wheel of the ship slightly, then ordered a change in the sails to bring them circling around the faraway *Gallant*.

"You are certain your plan will work?" Edward asked Anne while looking through his own inferior spyglass. The muddied, scratched lens could only show him the position of the *Gallant*, but he wasn't able to make out anything other than its general shape. Beyond the *Gallant* he saw a blob barely the size of a speck nearby, which he wouldn't have been able to see if not for the signal from the other crew.

"From what the crew who helped Roberts mentioned, Kenneth Locke's spy arrived before us in the morning. If my counting is correct, and provided the galleon wasn't delayed, before the few hours of light we have are gone, the galleon should arrive. Locke will be too focussed on the coming battle to look closely at the *Gallant*'s crew, or in our direction."

"Let's hope that Locke doesn't enjoy gazing directly at the sun."

"From what I knew of the man, he was not the most attentive."

"Mmm," Edward mumbled. He put his spyglass away and rubbed his eye where it had been.

"What leads you to be certain the galleon will even come this way still? We told them of the attack, it would be wiser to choose a different route."

"The captain of the galleon was a bold one. He challenged us when we met with him back in Panama, and I don't think he's one to back down from a fight. Also, if he was to take another route, why hire two sloops-of-war to assist as an escort?"

"It could have been a precaution," Anne said. "There's no guarantee that they will come, despite your assumptions."

Edward shrugged. "Well, if they don't, we still have the backup plan. We'll follow Locke back to land, and ambush them when we have the advantage."

Anne sighed. "I suppose that is an option," she said.

"Keep me informed of our situation, Quartermaster."

"Aye, Captain," she replied with a smile.

Edward went down the steps of the quarterdeck to the weather deck, which now stretched out all the way to the bow. He spoke with the crew, ensuring that the ship and their minds were prepared for the coming battle. There was a nervousness in the way the men spoke, and the perspiration dangling from their noses wasn't entirely from the heat of the day.

Edward noticed a noise coming from the bow, and when he looked over he could see Nassir there, half his body off the side as his knees held onto railings he had just fixed. He went over to see what the carpenter was working on.

When he approached and leaned over the side, he saw Nassir at it again with a hand plane, shaving off pieces of wood from the planks they had recently affixed. With each stroke of the large man's arms, bits of the Caribbean pine parted from the larger planks and fell into the ocean. Edward could see the pieces floating down the sea current with the waves like poor excuses for driftwood.

As Edward examined the bow, he noticed that Nassir was nearing the end of his work. "She looks good as new, Nassir!" Edward shouted over the sound of the waves.

Nassir jumped at Edward's voice, and almost dropped the hand plane into the sea. He gripped the tool close to his chest and then pulled himself back onto the deck. He was breathing heavily and looked startled. "Captain, you must watch what you are doing. My heart almost seized."

Edward chuckled. "Sorry, Nassir, I didn't mean to frighten you so."

Nassir took a few more breaths. "It is fine, Captain. Nothing was lost."

Edward reached down and offered his hand to help Nassir to his feet, which the carpenter accepted. "I only wanted to mention how the ship is looking well due to your skilled craftsmanship. You've done a fine job, and the ship is moving faster than she ever has because of it."

Nassir waved his hand. "You give me too much credit, sir," he said simply.

"Were there any troubles that I should be informed of?"

Nassir shook his head. "No, the work went smoothly. We were able to use the reclaimed wood, so there was little need for new pieces. The braces and the railings were simple enough, as the originals don't have nothing fancy to them. I made a new fife rail, with William's instruction," Nassir said, pointing to the fore mast. A rather large construction of wood went around the bottom of the mast with pegs at the top to hold the rigging. "They'll need some staining to match the look of the old wood though."

Edward looked at the new fife rail, and the bow railings, and there was a clear difference in the colour between the two. "Yes, I see that. The old girl is looking a bit weathered, it seems," he said, smacking the rails with a chuckle.

"She's been through much over the years," Nassir said, glancing around at the ship. He soon settled his gaze on the figurehead of Anne's likeness at the bow, an hourglass in one hand and a spear in the other.

Edward followed Nassir's gaze, looking at the flowing locks of hair and the robes covering the body of the figure. "Aye, she has," he said. "Hopefully, with your help, she'll have many more years ahead of her."

Nassir smirked. "Provided you stay out of trouble some of the time."

Edward chuckled. "I think we could manage some of the time."

Nassir returned to work, and Edward went over to starboard to gaze at the ocean. He was there only a moment before someone smacked him hard on the back. He had to take a step forward to steady himself before he could turn to see who it was. Pukuh was standing behind him, grinning.

"That bloody hurt, you bastard," Edward said as he rolled his shoulder, trying to remove the throbbing feeling.

"If the look on your face wasn't so sour I would not have to hit you. Come out of it, brother."

Edward folded his arms. "I'm doing just fine, and once this battle has concluded I'll be that much better," he replied. Edward looked over starboard, to where the *Gallant* was coming more into view. "What about you, brother? Are you well?"

"As well as ever," Pukuh said. "The phantoms of my right aches for a fight, while the left itches for it." Pukuh held up his left hand and clenched it into a fist. "It has been months since we had a proper battle."

Edward shook his head, but he had a grin on his face. "You pray for a battle? A strange thing indeed."

Pukuh wagged his finger at Edward. "Do not try to tell me you do not ask for the same. You've been wanting this for months as well."

Edward didn't want to think about it any more than he had to. He still felt a crippling dread when he thought of Kenneth Locke, and the only way to bring him out of it was the thought of crippling him. In one sense, he supposed he did want this, but in another sense he just wanted it to be over.

"Yes, it has been a long time coming," was all he could say.

Some crewmates called Pukuh over to help them with the trimming of the sails, and so Pukuh said a goodbye and headed over to work. Edward stayed behind, looking out over the ocean at the *Gallant*.

Somewhere, you're there, Edward thought. The pain gripped him again, and the throbbing wounds on his chest, his back, his legs, his arms, and his mind all cried out at once, but he silenced them. *Soon, I'm going to kill you.*

An hour after the *Queen Anne's Revenge* was in position in front of the setting sun, a call came from the crow's nest.

"Ship approaching south!" the man shouted.

Edward's ears perked and his eyes opened wide. He was on the quarterdeck with Anne and Herbert. He glanced off the starboard stern, but he couldn't see anything. "How many ships?"

The man in the crow's nest looked through his spyglass once more, moving side to side, but shook his head after a moment. "I can't tell."

Edward nodded. "Keep checking," he said. He glanced at Anne. "Do you think we should head over to the *Gallant* now, or wait?"

"I suppose the true question is, do we want to take the risk?"

Herbert looked off to port. "The sun's nearly gone now. We will have the same risk in waiting."

Edward stroked his beard as he thought over the options. "Take us in, Herbert. We need to be ready to take down one of those sloops as soon as they come into range."

Herbert gave the order to lower and trim the sails, then turned the wheel to starboard. The ship lurched forward, the wind only slightly in their favour. After a time, the speed built and the ship was under way.

As the *Queen Anne's Revenge* approached, Edward was able to see the other ships waiting for the galleon. From what he could tell at this distance, they both appeared larger than the *Gallant*, but, if he were to guess, not as large as Edward's ship.

"Three ships," the man in the crow's nest yelled. "One large, two smaller."

"That's them," Edward commented. "We need to be ready to take on one of the sloops."

Anne nodded and stepped up to the edge of the quarter-deck. "Man cannons, to arms!" she shouted.

The gunners on the weather deck went to their stations

and prepared the cannons to fire, while other men went down below to inform the crew on the main gun deck and gather weapons. Some men brought Anne, Herbert and Edward muskets, and the three loaded their weapons.

As seemed usual before battle, the feeling aboard and in the air changed. It became heavy, hard to breathe, and every task felt laborious and exhausting.

Edward could see one man hunched over, loading his musket with shaking hands. He dropped the ball and caught it before it rolled over the side of the ship, but then couldn't get the ramrod in the muzzle. He was swearing under his breath with each time his shaking moved the rod down the outside of the barrel.

Edward handed his loaded musket over to Anne and walked over to the man. When he got close, the ball fell off the top of the musket again. Edward stepped on the ball to stop it from rolling away as the crewmate reached forward. He looked up to see Edward towering over him, and immediately blanched.

"S-Sorry, sir," he said. "I'll get it next time, I promise."

Edward knelt down and retrieved the ball. "What's your name?"

"Clement, sir," he replied.

Edward placed the ball on top of the paper sitting on the muzzle. "That's a rare name for one so young in this age. Did your parents hate you?" he said with a smirk.

The young man chuckled. "Nah, it's after my grandpap." He picked up the rod, and this time he was able to get it into the musket.

Edward nodded as Clement pushed the ball into the barrel. "No need to be nervous, Clement," he said. "All you have to do is look down the barrel and pull the trigger."

Clement grinned. "That's not the trouble…" He lost his grin, and looked away. "I don't want to get hit," he said.

"I'll tell you a secret that helps me, Clement," Edward said as he leaned forward and gripped the young man's shoulder. "Most people miss."

Clement grinned at Edward's words, and then nodded.

Edward smiled back, shook the man's shoulder, and then went back to his place at the quarterdeck.

As the *Queen Anne's Revenge* drew closer to the *Gallant*, two things became clearer: the first was that the ships Kenneth Locke had were both three-masted sloops-of-war, one bigger than the others with a few more cannons from what they could tell. The second was that the galleon and its two sloops-of-war were slowing down. As they came closer, they were soon able to see that the three Spanish ships had furled their sails, and were drifting with the current.

"They mean to draw us in," Edward muttered.

The only moving ship at the moment was theirs, with three ships on either side waiting in somewhat calm seas. They each faced the other, a standoff on the high seas. Edward imagined that on the decks of the other ship it was deathly still and quiet. On his ship it was loud and frantic, with the sound of the ship crashing against the water, the wind whipping the sails, and the men shouting and grunting as they heaved to the rigging.

"Now, the question is… do we let them?" Herbert asked with a sidelong glance at Edward and Anne.

Edward and Anne looked at each other, both knowing what the other was thinking. "Take us in, Herbert," Anne said.

"Aye." Herbert relayed the order to the men, and twisted the wheel starboard once more.

The ship turned until it was almost heading back where they had come from. They headed south south-west in a beam reach, with the wind heading southeast. They wanted to keep their distance in the hopes they could draw out one of the sloops.

When they began heading towards the Spanish ships, the *Gallant* made to join them. They let loose their sails and were catching up to Edward and the rest.

After the *Gallant*, Kenneth Locke's ships followed suit, forced to join a forward attack. The bigger of the two was on the inside, next to the *Gallant*, but the both of them headed straight south towards the galleon.

Three sloops-of-war against a galleon… their plan was quite risky. Sloops may be faster, but one hit from a broadside could cripple them. Either Locke is desperate, or they had some sort of plan. What, though?

After ten minutes of sailing, the Spanish side finally began to move. The galleon stayed put, not dropping their sails an inch, but the two sloops opened theirs up. They headed west to intercept the *Queen Anne's Revenge* and the *Gallant*.

"I believe the sloops plan to hit us with a broadside, tack through the wind, and then head back to the galleon," Anne said.

"Why wouldn't they go south?" Edward asked.

"They're supposed to be protecting the galleon. If they head south, they would be hard-pressed to make it back up in time to stop all four of our ships from attacking the galleon. The wind would be against them every step of the way, and they would need to be close hauled to make any progress."

Herbert nodded. "That is sound reasoning," he said. "As far as they know, we could all be on the same side. They aren't close enough to see the name of our ship and know our allegiance. Those sloops will want to attack us and distract us from going after the galleon."

"And what should we do to counter them?"

Anne folded her arms and bit her thumb for a moment. "If they wanted to do the most damage, they would form up to hit us with both broadsides one after the other. To counter that, we need the *Gallant* to stay on their starboard so we can hit them from both ends."

Edward glanced off to port, where the *Gallant* was coming up beside them. "How will we inform the *Gallant*?"

"Not necessary," Herbert said. "My sister will know what to do when the time comes. We'll have both ships on our broadsides, I guarantee it."

Herbert was smiling from ear to ear, confidence trickling through in his movements and his tone. Edward grinned and nodded back to him, infected by Herbert's optimistic mood.

The *Queen Anne's Revenge* headed east in an arc towards the other ships, with enough leeway to ensure they would end up on the port side of the farthest sloop. The *Gallant* followed suit, but kept its distance, seeming to understand what the plan of attack was. Soon, the four ships were heading straight at each other, two heading east, and two heading west.

As the minutes passed and the ships closed in, the mood and movements aboard began to change. The places the men went to were ones that were well guarded. Their hands gripped the ropes, the linstocks, the muskets, and the railings tighter. But most noticeable of all was the silence that crept in from the edges of the ship to the centre. Soon the breezing wind, the flap of the sails, the splash of the sea, the creaking of wood, and the smack of boots was all they could hear.

One of the enemy sloops changed direction, tacking into the wind as much as possible. They were trying to get outside of where the *Gallant* would be, and escape the double broadside. With Locke's ships still heading for the galleon, they wouldn't be able to turn in time to help and trap the enemy sloop.

Edward, Anne, and Herbert all peered over to their sister ship, waiting to see what she would do. What Christina would do. After a brief moment, the sails moved, and the *Gallant* changed course to match the other sloop and keep it in the pincer.

Edward, Anne, and Herbert all grinned widely at the sight. Anne gripped Herbert's shoulder, and he looked up at her, the two beaming with pride.

Edward smacked Herbert's back. "You taught her well," he said.

"I wasn't the only one," Herbert replied, looking at Edward and Anne, the significance not lost on Edward.

The enemy sloop that tried to escape turned back and joined its brother again. The second sloop slowed itself down and closed the distance between them. The two ships matched in speed and went side to side.

"They've abandoned their initial plan," Anne commented. "Now they're trying to minimize the damage by protecting each other."

"We've caught them in a snare," Edward said with a devilish grin.

"Now all that's left is to tighten the noose!" Herbert gritted his teeth and repositioned himself before turning the wheel to port. "Moving to firing range," he shouted.

"Gunners at the ready!" Anne yelled in response.

The men manning the cannons loaded the powder into the pan. They made small adjustments here and there, using their eyes and their guts to estimate what the best angle would be to hit the oncoming ship.

Meanwhile, men in teams would be doing the same with the cannons below deck. Using their experience and expertise to aim the first volley and make it true could mean the difference between an easy victory or a protracted battle.

The *Gallant* followed with the *Queen Anne's Revenge*, coming in closer to the sloops on a broadside run. It didn't have the same number of guns the other sloops had, but with another ship aiding they could do some damage.

Mere minutes remained before the ships were all within firing range. Edward couldn't help but be stirred with excitement as the men were. It had been months since they'd had a real battle, and one where they would be the most likely victor. He had to hold himself back from smiling, despite knowing that once it started it could be far from exciting.

Anne intently watched the oncoming ships. Her eyes flitted between the enemy ships to the bow of the *Queen Anne's Revenge* and back every few seconds. After a moment she shouted "ready," and the crew tensed. Edward gripped the quarterdeck railing, waiting for the moment.

"Fire port!"

The gunners on the weather deck were first to drop the linstocks into the pan of the cannons. Some of the men turned away from the flare that erupted from the large beast they were in charge of, while others watched to ensure they hit their mark.

After the first volley, the gun deck was quick to follow suit, and fired their cannons as well. The two booms sounded distinct from one another, a smaller explosion followed by a larger blast.

Those sounds were as a dam breaking apart on the mouths of the crew. Silence died as the fight burst into life.

Before the cannonballs hit their mark, the enemy sloops fired their cannons off as well. The iron flew at them with unmatched speed, wreaking destruction on their path. The new planks and railings broke apart in the blast, sending wood everywhere.

Edward turned away from the assault, and when he looked up, what he saw made him laugh under his breath. The sloops were pitiful in comparison to the galleon they had faced not a few days before. The scene left behind was like night and day.

That was not to say that they went unscathed. Edward could hear the shouts of the injured amongst the yells of those still fighting. He looked over the side of the quarter-deck to see one man clutching a leg with an exposed bone, and another with a chunk of wood jammed in his eye, yet he was still alive. Many others were bleeding from various small wounds, but kept doing their duty.

Alexandre and Victoria were first on the scene, tending to the wounded. They were uninjured, but armed, in case they needed to switch from being healers to attackers.

As the crew reloaded their cannons, Herbert turned the ship to port. The sloop on their side could only go south if they wanted to turn back around, but the pirates could shoot another volley before then.

Herbert brought the *Queen Anne's Revenge* in close to the other ships. The men manning the sails changed the trim with each degree of movement as their brothers worked on reloading the cannons. Each man had his part to play, and because of their experience, both as individuals and together, they were playing it beautifully. This battle, compared to their first, was also as night and day.

"Form up, port-side muskets at the ready!" Anne shouted above the din.

Men holding muskets rushed to the port side of the ship and placed their weapons along the railing to keep their aim true. They pointed them at the other ship, searching down the barrel for anyone they could hit.

When the ships were close enough, Anne shouted "Fire!" once more. Blasts of powder not so loud as the cannons, and spouting lead rather than iron, shot at the enemy ship. The wave of lead shot cascaded upon the crew and felled many of them.

The sloop's crew returned fire, but they were sorely outmatched in numbers and in the size and power of their cannons. A few of Edward's men were hit, but not many, and none of them fatal shots.

Another wave of cannonballs from Edward's ship crashed into the sloop as they were passing the stern. One of its masts had snapped, and many of its crew were injured, but it was not wholly beaten.

As they came around, they were able to catch glimpse of the other sloop, and the *Gallant* coming about the stern as well. The second vessel wasn't damaged as much as the first, but Edward could see several crewmates lying bloody on the deck.

The *Gallant* was worse off, with several holes dotting the side. It was listing to the starboard side in the way that could only mean it was taking on water. Through Edward's spyglass he could see Christina and William at the helm, alive and well, though bloodied from battle. A few men were lying sprawled dead on the deck, but the damage to the crew was less than Edward had expected given the damage from the cannons.

"We can't go any farther than this, Captain," Herbert said. "Unless you wish to tack into the wind."

Edward assessed the situation, then shook his head. "No, we'll lose too much time chasing the sloops as we are. We should head back to the galleon before we lose the advantage against Locke."

"Aye, Captain," Herbert said.

The crew moved the ship east, back towards the galleon, and the *Gallant* followed behind. They soon heard the sounds of battle coming from the galleon, with much more cannon fire than in Edward's battle. He could see great plumes of smoke coming from each of the ships, most especially the galleon with its larger complement of cannons. All three ships still floated, and Edward had a mix of emotions over it.

"Slow us down, Herbert. The *Gallant* is taking on water. We need our men back onboard before the sloops come back around."

Herbert yelled to the crew to furl the sails, and the ship slowed. It took some time, and they drifted closer to the galleon as they slowed.

Edward expected to see the sloops turning about to renew their fight, but they continued heading west.

He couldn't help but burst out laughing at the sight. "They're sailing away, the cowards," he said.

Anne, who had been paying attention to where they were headed, glanced at him with a raised brow before looking back at the retreating ships. She too couldn't help but chuckle. "That's a boon for us," she said.

The sound of a powerful crash brought all eyes back to the galleon. They were still some ten minutes' sailing away from them, but it sounded as if it happened right beside them.

Edward pulled out his spyglass and peered through it towards the galleon. At first he saw nothing the matter, but as he looked more intently he saw what had happened. One of the ships under Locke's command had crashed into the galleon's stern. The crew had already abandoned ship, some swimming and others in longboats. The galleon's rudder had broken off, effectively crippling it.

"One of the ships crashed into the galleon," Edward said.

"Do you believe it by mistake or by design?" Anne asked.

"Hard to say, but the crews are heading over to climb up the side of the galleon." Edward relayed what he saw through the spectacle. "No matter," he said while putting away his spyglass. "That's one fewer ship we have to deal with."

The *Gallant* came up beside the *Queen Anne's Revenge*, and the crew helped their brothers return to the main ship. In no time the sixty crewmates who had volunteered, less their fallen mates, were back to their home.

Edward and Anne helped Christina and William back aboard. Christina was bleeding from her forehead and breathing heavily, one eye closed and covered in blood from the wound. William had grazes on his shoulder and leg from bullets, but wasn't the worse for wear.

"Good job, Christina, William," Edward said.

"Could have done better," Christina responded through ragged breaths. Tala ran over excitedly and licked Christina on the arms and cheek.

"Nonsense," Herbert protested, wheeling himself over to his sister. "You were excellent out there. I'll have to watch out if I don't want to be replaced," he said with a grin.

Christina smiled at the praise and the pride in her brother's eyes. "Thank you, brother," she said.

With the full crew aboard, Edward went to the edge of the quarterdeck. "Men, ready yourselves. The night is young, and this battle is far from over!"

20. DROWNING

"It looks as if they had a far larger crew than their ship demanded," Anne commented while looking through a spyglass towards the galleon. "They meant—at the very least—to board the galleon and take the fight to them."

Edward also looked through a spyglass at the carnage off the bow. Night had slipped in since their battle with the sloops, and it was getting darker as the minutes passed. The ship that had crashed into the galleon had slid off with the current and settled on the starboard side of the Spanish ship. It could be some time before it was moved as the crew was too occupied repelling boarders to do it themselves. It allowed Locke's other ship to attempt boarding from the starboard bow without fear of the cannons ripping them apart.

It was a desperate gamble if they had meant to do it, but Edward guessed it was half planning and half luck. *I suppose that's true of most battles,* he thought.

"Many of those men will perish on the climb," Anne said. "What are we to do? If we wait, the crew of the galleon could win, and not only would we have to face them next, but Locke will die."

"And we can't forget about Sam," Christina added, petting Tala as she rested near the helm.

"If Sam is there, he won't even know who this ship belongs to," Edward said. "Locke won't win against the galleon's crew with their numbers. We need to ensure both sides are left too wounded to continue fighting, and search for Sam."

"And how will we do that?" Herbert asked.

Edward thought on the problem for a moment. *From where we are, if we board we risk a three-fronted battle erupting if Locke sees us or his crew recognises who we are. We can't attack the galleon or we could end up at their broadside. Just because the rudder's mucked doesn't mean they're immobile. What can we do?*

"Captain," William said, interrupting Edward's thoughts.

"The galleon is taking on water."

Edward looked through his spyglass and noticed what William was looking at. On the stern of the galleon, near where the other ship had hit it, there was a hole in the wood. Judging from the size and position it would be difficult to cover, and could sink the ship given enough time.

Edward grinned, an idea forming in his head. "That's how we'll win this fight," he said. He looked at the senior officers gathered around him. "We're going to enter the galleon from that breach, and fight our way to the top." Edward pointed at Anne. "At the same time, you'll attack Locke's ships with ours. All three ships will be in the drink when we're done with them."

Those around him looked at him as if he were mad, for a moment. In the silence of shock, they pondered the plan, and each person's face changed to reflect a sceptical acceptance.

"It may actually work," Anne said finally.

"Herbert," Edward called, "bring us in as close as you can to the galleon. We're going to need the crew who remain here to keep the men aboard the galleon from attacking us."

Herbert nodded and then focussed his attention on helming the ship. They were already on an approach, so there wasn't much to be done at the moment.

Edward stepped up to the quarterdeck railing and placed both his hands on it, leaning forward to speak with the crew. "Men, we have an opportunity ahead of us to bleed all our enemies dry. We're going inside the Spanish galleon from the stern, and I need fifty strong swimmers to join me."

Fifty volunteers formed up to join Edward in this expedition. Victoria was among them, but not Alexandre.

Christina stood up. "I wish to join," she said.

Edward shook his head. "I need you here, helping your brother." Christina opened her mouth again, no doubt to object, but Edward cut her off. "That is an order," he said, his finger raised.

Christina pouted and sat back down on the sole of the deck.

William stepped forward. "I will be joining you, Captain. I believe the exercise would aid my constitution."

Edward chuckled. "Provided it doesn't kill you?"

William bowed his head a touch. "Yes, barring that," he said.

Pukuh was strangely silent during the volunteering process, though he was nearby and no doubt heard the plan. "Pukuh, will you not be joining us?"

The Mayan shook his head. "I will do better here. I am not as strong a swimmer as I was," he said, glancing at his missing arm.

Edward looked at it as well, and at the shattered pride in Pukuh's eyes. "Then you had better start practicing after this battle. I won't have you slowing the storm over something as trivial as losing one of your arms," he said with a smirk.

Pukuh looked at him, at first with light shock, and then he too grinned. "Soon I will swim better than you, and they will call me Pukuh, The Bringer of the Storm."

Edward chuckled, overjoyed by his friend's resilience in the face of every challenge.

As the *Queen Anne's Revenge* sailed closer, the men who would join Edward prepared for the journey. They would have to approach the galleon on longboats before entering the breach.

"As soon as we're away and inside the ship, give Locke's ships our broadside. We don't want them escaping if the battle doesn't turn in their favour."

"Aye, Captain," Anne said, a pensive look on her face. Edward turned around to enter a longboat, but Anne stopped him. "Don't die. Revenge isn't worth your life."

Edward smiled, trying to reassure his wife. "I don't plan on perishing anytime soon." He leaned in and gave her a kiss before entering the longboat.

The crew lowered the longboats into the sea, and they rowed towards the galleon. The moon's glow was the only source of light now that evening had set in. The flash of gunpowder from the ships in front of them was a poor substitute for a lantern, but they thought it best to hide their advance.

As they approached, the sounds of men screaming, cannons, muskets, and pistols firing, and steel clashing became louder. The sound of the wind was lost, but its bite was not. The cold of the night was just starting, and it would no doubt get worse before their battle was over.

Edward shuddered at the thought of entering the icy waters of the sea, his body preparing for the shock and suddenness of it.

The smell of burning gunpowder met Edward's nose, tingling with its acrid smell in the way that forces one to rub one's nose. The itch meant something else to Edward, and he imagined his crew felt the same—it meant a fight was on the horizon.

Twenty feet from the galleon's stern, a crossbow bolt hit one of Edward's men in the shoulder. Edward looked up to where the bolt had come from, and could see Spanish navymen on platforms halfway up the masts.

"On the masts!" he shouted before pulling his musket out and firing.

The crew joined Edward in firing upon the Spanish, while the rowers continued pulling the longboats in further. The Spanish fired bolts back at them in kind. A few fell into the sea, a few hit the boat with a thunk, and a few more hit Edward's men.

The crew aboard the *Queen Anne's Revenge* fired at the Spanish as well, providing cover for the boarders.

Edward's longboat made contact with the stern first. He pulled the boat along the behemoth to where the hole was. It had been covered over with planks now, but the outside was still open. The hole was half above and half below the water-line, and wide enough for one person to squeeze through if it was open.

Edward pulled out his golden cutlass, and jumped from the boat into the cold water. The sea stole his last shred of warmth, and he couldn't help but shiver. He focussed on the task at hand, pushed aside the thoughts of the frigid drink, and swam to the covered hole.

He jabbed his blade between the planks of wood and wiggled the blade up and down to pry apart the pieces. When that didn't seem to do any good, he pulled his blade out. It was covered in a thin film of tar used to seal the hole. He hit the wood vertically, poking holes in the planks above and below the water line to weaken the beams.

William appeared beside him, and the two kicked the planks with all their might. The water made their attacks weaker, but Edward's blade had done the priming work for them. With each kick, they could feel the nails holding them in place loosen. The two became more coordinated with each strike, and before long they were synchronized.

Two planks snapped in half with a loud crack at the end of Edward's and William's boots. Water once more flooded freely through the hole, and the pressure aided their cause. A few more kicks saw a whole plank dislodged, and more pieces of wood breaking off.

Edward could see men in the darkness beyond the breach. "Fire, fire!" he yelled while looking at his men and pointing to the new hole.

Edward and William moved aside and the men fired their muskets at the hole. Some of the shots missed entirely, but many made it through to the other side. When the firing subsided, the two in the water waded back over and looked inside. From what Edward could see in the void of the galleon's bilge, the shots had hit their marks.

Edward lifted up his legs and entered the small hole feet first, with the water guiding him in. He landed inside the bilge of the galleon and looked around, four dead men sprawled on the sole greeting him.

He went to the nearest plank and used his cutlass as a lever to pull it out. It was already loose from the kicking he and William had given it, and after a few mighty tugs it gave way and Edward was able to toss it to one side.

William entered the hole next, landing in a pool that reached halfway up his shins already. When he saw what Edward was doing, he pulled out a cutlass from his belt and did the same.

Edward was cold, wet, and his every movement laden down by the water soaked into his clothes. He couldn't even tell whether the beads dropping from his hair, forehead, and nose were salt water or sweat.

As Edward and William pulled out the planks, the crew filtered in through the hole one by one. Some of the men caught their trouser legs or arms on the exposed chips of wood from the new boards and the old breach. After Edward and William finished removing the wood, they sheathed their weapons and helped the other men through the breach.

With each new man, the water in the bilge rose another few inches. The sound of the rushing water, splashing in faster with the waves and pitch of the ship, overtook everything else in the small compartment.

Victoria jumped through the hole, landing next to Edward. Her short hair was matted to her forehead with the water, her cap lost in the sea. She held her usual buckler and short sword.

Edward grabbed her by the arm and pulled her in close. "How many more men are there?" he yelled over the din, spitting water in her direction.

"No more than ten," she yelled back.

Edward pointed towards the hatch leading to the next deck, where the crew had gathered, waiting. "Get them up there and start the fight. Stay alive and I shall join you presently."

Victoria nodded and then trudged through the chest-high—and rising—water over to the men, shouting something Edward couldn't hear. He went back over to William.

"Go join the others, I can handle the rest," Edward shouted.

William gave a quick salute, and then pulled one of the crewmates over with him towards the hatch.

Edward continued helping the others through the hole, which was now entirely covered by the sea. He counted each man down that came through until he reached eight, and then there were no more.

Edward grabbed hold of the man who had come through last, grasping through the shoulder-high water he could barely see in. "Are there any others?"

The man pointed as best he could towards the hole. "One more left, Captain."

Edward nodded and pushed the man along towards the bilge hatch. He went back to the breach, but still did not see another man come through.

Edward cursed, took a deep breath, and dove under. He moved through the murky mess towards the opening, and felt a body in front of him. He looked around but couldn't see much of anything. His hands became his eyes as he felt blindly in front of him. After a moment, another's hands grasped his own, and pulled them over towards a leg. Through his sense of touch, Edward could feel the fibers of pantaloons ripped and wrapped around the exposed wood.

Not wanting to risk losing his precious cutlass, nor accidentally cut the man he was trying to save, Edward pulled out a knife from his pocket. He traced the lines of his other arm to where the pants were caught, and sawed at the strings. The water made everything slick and the darkness didn't help Edward judge his progress. He just kept sawing as the crewmate kept pulling on his pant leg. After a moment, Edward lost all sense of resistance, and felt the strings of the pant leg slip through his fingers.

Edward planted his feet on the sole, but in the time he had been under the water it had risen above his head. He kicked his legs up, and his head poked through the water. He saw the other crewmate with him, catching his breath.

"The hatch is that way," Edward shouted over the noise. "We have to swim."

"I can't see a bloody thing," the crewmate responded, an undertone of fear in his shaky voice.

"Then die here," Edward said harshly. "Go. I'll be right at your tail."

The man nodded, took a breath, and dove into the water. Edward did the same, and he kicked his legs forward to the hatch.

The dark of the night could not hold a candle to the dark of the waters in the depths of the galleon's bilge. The moon gave some illumination to the night's activities, but the belly of a ship knew no light save by lantern, and there were no lanterns here.

Edward cleaved through the water, his muscular forearms and chest straining with each stroke. His legs paddled behind him, and the two worked together to push him in a direction he hoped was forward.

He moved up for a breath, but could no longer surface his head, and had to lean back to bring in another breath of air. He wasn't able to check for the mate he had tried to help, and even if he did it would be fruitless.

He sank down and continued moving in the direction he thought would take him to the hatch. His body was so cold it no longer felt cold to him. He felt a strange numbness in his hands and feet, not the same as when slept upon, but a strange void of feeling in his fingers and toes.

He wasn't sure how far he had gone, but if he was to take a guess he had to be getting close to the hatch. He went up for another breath of air. His fingers outstretched above him, he could feel the wood of the deck above him, but there was no gap in the water. He felt around for a few seconds, but could find nowhere to gather air.

Edward's heart beat faster as the urgency of escape hit him all at once. He needed more air, and quick.

He pumped his legs and stroked with his arms against the cold sea water, pressing forward to the hatch. No matter where he looked, it was infinite darkness in front of him, with nothing to guide his way.

He felt pain in his chest, and his body called out for more air. His thoughts shrank to nothing, and all that drove him was the instinct to find the surface. As the seconds passed, small spots of light flashed across his vision, pulsing in with each heartbeat.

The beating slowed.

Am I to drown here? Edward thought, still pushing forward. He shook his head as best he could. *No! No! This isn't where I'll die. Not today!* Edward forced the spots away.

His fingers clawed at the wood above him, desperate for the edge of the hatch he knew should be near him. His legs beat against the water, ungracefully pushing it away like the killer it was.

The spots of light returned, taking over his vision one second at a time. Each pulse came slower, but with it the pain in his chest grew as well.

Edward's arms and legs became weaker and weaker with each stroke forward. They were heavier than solid lead, and as sluggish. His hands outstretched, Edward flailed and thrashed to gain each inch forward.

His finger grazed something unfamiliar, and it renewed his vigor, if by a small margin. He combed the area where he had felt it, and his hands soon gripped someone's forearm.

The owner of the forearm pulled, and Edward broke the surface of the water with a great splash and heave of a breath.

His head whipped around, sending water flying off his slick hair as he tread water in the small opening to the bilge. William and Victoria were at the hatch, both as soaked as he.

"There—" Edward started, but had to catch his breath some more. He gulped down air as he treaded water. "There was another man ahead of me," he said, hoping the question was evident.

William and Victoria glanced at each other. "There were none before you," William answered.

Edward's eyes fell to the void below his chest, and the man whom he had tried to save. It would have been impossible for him to still be alive, and Edward couldn't even begin to think of the agony he must have felt in his last moments.

Edward pulled himself out of the bilge and onto the sole of the hold. The water was filling the ship in a rapid rise, and in a few minutes would snake its way through the cracks in the planks, up to the hold and beyond. The best part was that the Spanish galleon was a massive ship, and would take a fair amount of time to sink regardless of how quickly the water flooded it.

Around him, Edward could see the men who had volunteered to join him. They were either waiting and watching him, or keeping an eye on the open orlop deck from below. On all sides of him were barrels and boxes and bags filled to the brim with supplies of God-knows-what. The containers were stacked to fill every inch of the hold, save the bilge access port and a thin corridor to walk through.

Edward had the brief thought to search the containers for the silver, but there was no time to wait around. The water from below was already beginning to bubble up and spill out from the bilge hatch, and the sounds of battle raged above them as harsh as ever.

Edward pulled out his cutlass, the ring of the blade singing as it left its sheath. The tune it sang spoke of the promise of blood soon to be spilled on its edge, and filled each man with more courage than a dozen rousing speeches.

"Let's tear this ship apart, men!" Edward shouted.

Edward's crew had the sense to give their responses in brutish smiles rather than loud hollering, and all of them pulled out their weapons in kind if they hadn't already done so.

Edward motioned for the men to move, and they made their way up to the orlop deck carefully and quietly. As each man moved along, Edward could hear muffled screams and thunks of steel meeting flesh. After a few moments, he came to the steep steps up to the orlop deck, overlooking the ship's magazine of gunpowder.

He climbed up the steps to the orlop deck, holding fast to the sides as he did so. On the next deck, the dead bodies of two young men lay on the sole, bleeding out. They couldn't have been older than eleven.

Powder-monkeys, Edward thought. *They would have died anyway, had we not been here.* "Were there any others on this deck?" Edward whispered.

One of the men shook their head. "They all up top fighting."

Edward nodded. "Let's join them then, shall we?"

The men went up the next set of steps to the first gun deck, the one covered on the starboard side by one of Locke's sloops. When Edward emerged on the deck, he could see the Spanish running around, taking no notice of the new invaders coming up from below. They were dealing with Locke's crew who were shooting at them and entering the ship from the gun-ports.

Edward's men entered the battle, slashing at the Spanish running around the confined deck. Edward had to bend over to stop himself from hitting the top of the deck, so towering was he.

William led the charge against the dual enemies, and he was in top fighting form. He deftly dispatched half a dozen men in a row without stopping. They were powerless before his might as he manipulated them into making mistakes of which he then took ruthless advantage.

Edward turned from watching William and lunged at a man running over to the port side with a musket in hand. The man turned just before seeing the giant in front of him thrusting a blade towards his gut. Edward's blow took him off his feet, and he dropped the musket to grab the blade, but it was too late. A look of fear and confusion was plastered on his face, a permanent remnant of his last moments on earth.

When Edward and his men joined the fray, Locke's pirates initially thought them to be on their side, since they were also attacking the Spanish. With their guard lowered, Edward's men charged the other pirates, and in less than twenty minutes they had cleared the entire gun deck.

William advanced to the second gun deck, and Edward followed closely behind him. William dispatched the Spaniards with precision and wit, while taking in all his surroundings to ensure he wasn't caught unawares.

The gunpowder smoke was thick in the air on the second gun deck. With nowhere to release it, it billowed and piled up at the top. Edward's height, normally an advantage, was proving his downfall in more ways than one this day, as he couldn't breathe without taking a full whiff of smoke. After the near-drowning from before, the smoke was a welcome presence, but still not pleasant or easy on his lungs.

He fought his way to the stern of the ship, towards the captain's cabin. He could see three pirates at the door to a cabin, knocking against it with the butt of their muskets.

The deck was much more illuminated than the bilge and the sea water, and Edward was able to see everything with near-perfect clarity. He noticed a flash at his side, and he pulled his chest back, stepping on his heels as he did so. A blade stabbed in front of him, and Edward reached out to grab the arm holding it. He found purchase and pulled the arm forward, then elbowed the man in the face. He heard a snap as a nose broke. Edward moved to the side of the ship, reared back, and chopped at the man's chest, cleaving him halfway through. The man fell to the sole in an instant, dead before his body hit.

Edward was covered in the blood of his enemies, and still soaked with seawater. His hair and beard were dripping wet, and his blade coated in tar and blood. Every inch of him felt chilled to the bone, and exhausted from the effort he had had to exert until this point.

And yet, somewhere deep inside of him, he was revelling in the chaos of it all.

An explosion erupted on the gun deck, the sound shaking Edward to his core. He noticed something dart past him towards the bow of the ship. He stepped forward and looked at the bow to see a cannonball lodged against the hull. The cannonball had taken out some of the Spanish as well as one of Edward's men, and two of Locke's pirates. He looked at the stern, and saw that the three pirates knocking at the captain's door had been eviscerated by the cannonball. What was left of them was splayed out from the door, their hands clutching at air as they breathed their last breaths.

What remained of the door swung open with a loud creak, and out stepped a woman and two men. The woman wore a cloak, but the hood was down, revealing her face. She had long black hair, a tanned, angular face, and a sour glare directed at the invaders. In her hands she carried a pistol and a short sword.

That cloak, Edward thought. *It's the same as the one worn by the figure who accompanied the galleon's captain when we tried to join them.*

The woman raised her pistol and fired it at Edward. Someone grabbed his arm and pulled him to the side, out of the way of the bullet. He looked at the person who'd grabbed him to see Victoria there.

Before he could thank her, she looked to the stern and gritted her teeth. She pushed Edward back in the other direction with all her might, and pulled up her buckler where he'd stood. The clang of metal on metal told Edward that someone had attacked, and looked to see the cloaked woman wielding her sword.

Edward stepped to the side to regain his footing, and two blades were thrust at him. He jumped backwards and swiped his cutlass at the blades, knocking them to the side. He bent down as he backed up and pointed his weapon at the two Spanish guards.

"Come now, gentlemen. Two on one is a mite unfair, is it not?" he said, not expecting an answer.

One of the men glanced at his companion. "*Este hombre es más tonto de lo que él parece si él cree que él nos puede llevar tanto.*"

The second man laughed. "*Cierto.*"

Did they just call me an idiot?

After the brief interlude, the two men stepped forward and attacked Edward at the same time. Their blades came one after the other, each meant to knock him off balance and unnerve him. Edward had experience with this type of fighter, but two of them was a challenge he hadn't faced before.

Edward kept stepping backwards out of the way of the attacks until he bumped into someone else. He glanced over his shoulder to see a man he was unfamiliar with, whom he was certain was on Locke's crew. Edward twisted around, pulled the pirate to the side, and tossed him into the Spanish guards.

The pirate toppled over the Spanish, and the three of them fell to the sole. Edward stepped up to them and slashed his cutlass in a wide arc. In one swift and powerful stroke he sliced all three necks open.

Edward rushed over to where Victoria and the Spanish woman were fighting. He circled the duo as their blades clashed, looking for an opening.

"I can handle this," Victoria said through gritted teeth. "Find your mark and finish this!"

Edward paused for a moment, but decided to trust her ability and moved to the stern. Before heading up top, he entered what he supposed was the captain's cabin. He searched the room, but there was no one there.

Captain Miguel must be on the weather deck, fighting with the rest.

Edward turned around and went to the nearest ladder He climbed it up to the weather deck of the galleon.

The sounds of the battle hit Edward in full now that he was in the open air. The small pops of gunshots went off every second in erratic intervals, followed by the loud booming sound of a dozen cannons firing off nearby. The shouts of men fighting and the clash of metal rang out almost simultaneously, closely followed by death screams.

The air was filled with smoke from the constant igniting of gunpowder. The light musk of sweat and blood mixed with the smoke and the sea air and created a strange, unique aroma that spoke to Edward's animal instincts and made him grip his cutlass tighter.

Around him, Edward could see countless people fighting at every level and section of the ship. From the stern poop deck to the bow forecastle, pirates clashed with the Spanish defenders, and all the while their ships were sinking.

Edward turned around and rushed to the starboard side of the galleon, passing by men dueling and bleeding out. He looked over the side to see the two pirate sloops half-sunk into the ocean, and the *Queen Anne's Revenge* circling around. The crew on the weather deck fired at the pirates swimming their way.

The flash of the muskets and pistols and the flare of the cannons created beautiful bursts of light in the evening. The sparks flew from their containers, lighting their surroundings and reflecting off the sea for a moment as the flares dropped to the water or wood below.

The galleon had begun sinking as well, and from the look of the water, he could tell it was leaning towards starboard. With the size and instability of the galleon, Edward knew it wouldn't be long before it toppled over.

Edward scanned the galleon for the two people he was looking for. With the chaos aboard, the bullets flying, men running and dying, it was difficult to see anything with clarity.

How hard could it be to find a man with a chest attached to his arm?

Edward's eyes went from one person to the next in rapid succession, each one not the man he was looking for. *Wait a moment,* Edward thought. *Captain Miguel.*

On the bow of the ship, Captain Miguel was overseeing the battle, directing his men against the boarders and attacking them with his own musket.

Before Edward could make for the bow, a man with a feathered cap turned around after stabbing a man in the chest with a rapier. Edward recognised the man as one of Locke's trusted mates, Philip Culverson, and, judging from the up and down glance followed by widened eyes, Philip recognised Edward as well.

"You…!" Philip said, dumbfounded.

"Allow me to handle this one, Captain," William said, walking up beside Edward.

"Are you sure you'll manage?" Edward asked.

William replied with a curt nod of the head, and then positioned his blade in front of him to engage in a duel with the pirate. Edward stepped behind William and took a wide path around Philip, all the while pointing his own blade at him just in case. Philip kept one eye on Edward until he was far enough away not to be trouble.

Edward turned around and stalked over to the bow, avoiding the fights happening on all sides of him. He ran up the steps and cut down one of the Spanish along the way. The Captain's back was turned, and he was aiming down the barrel of a musket. Edward walked over to him, and one of his men rushed Edward, but he dispatched the man easily.

Edward pulled his blade back, and stabbed Captain Miguel in the back. Miguel's musket fired as the cutlass pierced his flesh.

He leaned up to Miguel's ear. "You should have joined us. You and your men would still be alive were that the case."

Edward pulled out the cutlass, and Miguel did a half-turn before his knees buckled and he fell backwards. He made a desperate attempt to hold himself up, but landed on the deck with one hand clinging to the forecastle railing and the other holding fast to the wound on his chest. His eyes were wide with shock and fear as he stared up at Edward.

"I didn't—" Miguel stopped short and coughed up blood, splattering dark red on his clothes as it seeped out his chin. "I didn't want this," he said, his words shaking like his body as his life left him. "It wasn't my say."

Edward looked down on him with all the rage he'd felt over the betrayal. "I don't care," he said.

He stabbed Miguel through the throat, ending the man's life. His eyes retained the fear and shock it had in the seconds before his death, in part from the prospect of dying, and in part from the man who'd caused it.

When Edward pulled the blade out, he turned on his heel to see if any were about to do something about what he'd done to their captain, but all the men on the bow were too busy fighting for their lives. He turned back around to view the ship once more, and he spotted the man he was looking for on the weather deck.

Kenneth Locke, Cache-Hand, was there with his crew in the thick of battle against the Spanish. He looked just as Edward remembered him: unkempt, grotesque features, sweat and blood matting his hair to his forehead, and a wicked smile showing off his crooked yellow and black teeth.

His right arm, visibly more muscular than the left, ended not with a hand, but a chest full of gold pieces—the same chest that had been there when he was a part of Edward's crew years ago. His greed caused him to fall into a trap, locking the chest on his hand with no way to remove it. A strange thing that it was a trap laid by Benjamin Hornigold, and now Locke worked for him, though under the name Calico Jack.

Edward's stomach felt empty and hollow, and his heart beat faster at the sight of Locke. His breathing turned rapid, and his feet itched to move, but in the opposite direction. His wounds all over his body screamed pain once more, screaming not to his ears but to his senses. They called for him to run away and avoid that pain again.

Edward grabbed hold of the forecastle railing and gripped it until his knuckles were white. In his other hand, he held fast to his cutlass. He couldn't tear his eyes away from Locke, but it wasn't his face he saw in his mind. He couldn't stop seeing John, his former quartermaster, the tired old man. The memory of Locke running the blade against John's neck repeated in Edward's mind over and over, and with each flash his legs weakened more and more.

The feeling was so much more intense now than it had ever been. The feeling of losing not just John, but everyone he cared for. The possibility of that happening was there, and it gripped his heart like a vice and wouldn't let go.

You are here, you are now, you are not then, Anne's voice repeated in Edward's head.

His wife's voice took the place of the visions in his head, overlapping and taking them over until it was just her there. He relaxed his grip, took long and deep breaths until the feeling passed, and he replaced it with something different.

I will not lose anyone else to him. It ends today!

Edward ran down the forecastle, straight at Locke. He leapt into the air, his cutlass high, and as he landed he brought the cutlass down like a great pendulum.

Locke noticed Edward at the last moment, and he raised his chest-hand in the air as he turned around to face him. The blade bit into the chest, creating a large cleft between the wood and iron.

Edward pulled the chest down with his cutlass, placed his foot against it, and kicked the thing off his blade. He pushed Locke back with it, and Locke had to take a few steps back to keep his balance.

His eyes widened at the sight of Edward. He looked as if he saw an apparition. "You... You're dead," he said. "I killed you." His voice shook, a different kind of fear taking hold of him.

"Aye, and I've come back to kill you," Edward said. He slashed at Locke, but the other pirate deflected it. "Where is Sam?"

Locke's brow raised in confusion. "You've gone mad," he said as he backed away, his eyes still filled with fear. "Who're ya talkin' about? I don't know no Sam."

"Enough with the games, Locke. Tell me what you did with Sam, now."

Locke's eyes changed into a frustrated squint. "I told ya I don't know who yer talkin' about."

Edward tightened his grip on his cutlass, his anger rising. He went on the offensive, slashing and jabbing at the other pirate. Locke stayed defensive, backing away and dodging or parrying the blows. With a large, powerful swing, Edward knocked Locke's cutlass out of his hand.

Edward continued pushing Locke back. He took advantage of the man's shock and tried to force Locke into a corner. When Locke stepped to his right, Edward moved with him and pushed him back to the left. He used light controlling jabs to keep Locke on his toes and stepping in the direction he wanted. After a moment, Locke's back hit the stern cabin bulkhead.

The smack on his back seemed to awaken Locke and knock him back into his senses, and he used the recoil to go on the offensive. He swung the chest on his arm in a wide arc, knocking Edward's cutlass out of the way.

Edward's hand stung from the blow, and he had to concentrate hard to keep his grip lest he too lose his blade, but it pulled his whole body to the side. His eyes followed his hand on instinct, and when he looked back at Locke it was too late to react.

Locke thrust the chest forward as if he were punching,

and hit Edward in the chest. The force of the blow sent him reeling backwards. He tumbled over and fell to the sole. The pain from the blow was excruciating across his whole rib-cage, and it felt like something had broken. The punch knocked the wind out of him, and he dropped his cutlass to his side. He reflexively curled up to cover his chest as he tried to recover his breath. It was a worse feeling than when he had been drowning earlier, as air was all around him, but his body couldn't take it in.

"No sorry sod of a ghost would be feeling that," Locke said as Edward writhed. "Yer so pathetic ya can't even die right."

Kenneth kicked Edward in the face, his head rearing back from the force. It also knocked Edward's body back to work, and he could heave air in. The pain in his chest and chin remained, and his vision blurred. He felt the taste of blood in his mouth, and possibly a loose tooth. He turned over onto his stomach and forced his weary head up to search for his foe.

Locke grabbed hold of Edward's hair and pulled him up to his knees. "I don't know where ya came from, but I'm going ta kill ya for sure this time," he said. "Remember what I did to that old fool? I'm going to find every last one of your crew and do the same to them." Locke pulled back the heavy wooden chest, the coins inside rattling, and aimed for Edward's head.

Edward grabbed hold of Locke's hand on his head and placed his other hand out against the chest. He stopped the punch mid-way with a loud thud before reaching around and gripping Locke's forearm. He then stood to his full height, forcing Locke to let go of his hair.

Edward stared down at Locke with all the malice he felt towards him in that moment. "Do you remember what I promised you that day?" he asked. "I promised you that I would live, and make sure the last thing you saw was my hands around your neck as I choked the life out of you."

The fear in Locke's eyes returned in full force.

Edward pulled Locke's arms down, forcing his upper body down as well. He kneed Locke in the face, smashing his nose.

Locke took a few steps back, clutching his broken and bloody nose. He gritted his teeth, glared at Edward, and went to uppercut him with his chest-hand.

Edward stepped to the side, dodging the blow. He levelled Locke with a punch straight to his jaw, and the man fell to the sole in a heap.

"You're too slow, Locke. My wife's punches are ten times as fast as yours." Edward backed up, keeping his eyes on Locke, until found his cutlass by the light of the moon and picked it up again.

Locke sputtered a hoarse laugh as he came to his knees. "Trouble with the missus, eh Thatch?"

Edward grinned. "Far from it," he said. "It wasn't an insult towards you, it was simply a fact. I train with her nearly every day. She could have killed you six times over by now, I'd wager."

"Captain," William called behind Edward.

Edward turned around to see William and Victoria, bloodied and soaked with sweat, on the weather deck along with his other crewmates. Victoria and the rest of the crew looked as if they had just come up from below.

"The ship's about to topple over," William said.

Before Edward could grasp the words William had said, the ship began angling down towards the sea. The shift was as sudden as it was drastic, and it didn't stop once it started tilting.

As the angle of the ship changed, Edward's legs had naturally adjusted to compensate, and only after the listing became more pronounced did he fully understand what was happening. He ran up to the port side of the ship as the deck changed to an incline, and jumped for the portside railing. He clung to the railing, wrapping his arm around the beams.

The loose equipment aboard the ship rolled and fell from one end to the other, cascading down and bouncing off the deck before being flung into the ocean below. Men lost their footing and tumbled backwards toward the starboard side. Edward could hear loud bangs and crashes within the ship as well. The large iron cannons, with nothing but their own weight to hold them in place, rolled to the other side of the ship, further speeding the ship's tilt. Just before the ship's side collided with the dark ocean below, Edward heard the sound of wood cracking open, and several small splashes preceding the larger one.

The ship hit the water with a thunderous crash. Seawater surged up the weather deck beneath Edward's feet and covered him in an icy chill all over again. The main mast and the fore sail both hit the pirate sloops, which were also sinking. The spars of the masts had broken through the decks of the sloops, joining the ships together in their destiny to sink to the bottom of the ocean. There was no possible saving the lot of them.

Edward looked down and could see his crew swimming in the ocean, trying to avoid the sinking masts and rigging. He couldn't take a count, but with the rough look he estimated most of them had survived.

Edward looked to his right, and could see Locke dangling off the port railing just as he was. They locked eyes, and Locke scrambled to pull himself up. Edward moved to do the same, and climbed over the side of the railing to the port hull of the galleon.

In the dark waters off the side, Edward could see many men swimming their way, and others standing on the sinking side of the ship. Even then, some of the men still continued to fight, whether out of anger or blindness, he could not tell.

Locke came at Edward with everything he had, wildly swinging his one weapon at him. Edward knew his every move by heart. Locke moved the same as he had those months ago in Ireland. He hadn't grown, he hadn't gotten stronger, he hadn't improved himself as Edward had. Locke was no match for the Edward of today, the Edward he let live because he couldn't finish the job the right way.

There was one problem: the galleon was still sinking. In a few moments, the ship would be under water, and their fight wouldn't be able to continue.

No, no, I still need to question him about Sam. I have to get him to the Queen Anne's Revenge *before I kill him.* The words of Edward's wife filtered into his head once again. *If you want to knock a man off balance and get behind him, use his own attacks against him.*

Locke kept swinging his chest arm like a wild man, trying

to hit Edward's head over and over. His right arm had grown strong over the years, and he had much more stamina than before, which meant he could keep fighting for some time.

Edward backed up a few steps, and baited Locke by leaning his head forward. Locke, too frustrated or foolish to care, swung at Edward all the same. Edward pulled back to avoid the blow, then placed his hands on the back of the heavy chest and pushed it with all his strength. Locke continued his arc further than expected and the weight of the chest turned him around. The man lost his balance and dropped to his knees. Edward pounced on Locke, wrapped his arms around the pirate's throat, and squeezed.

Locke tried to get up off his knees, but Edward pushed forward and placed his boot on top of the chest, effectively pinning Locke where he was. Locke pulled against Edward's arms as he pulled in stifled breaths. As the seconds passed and he began to lose himself, Locke clawed at Edward's arm, then elbowed him in the gut, but Edward never released his grip.

After a moment of the struggle, Locke's hand fell to his side, limp. Edward continued to hold the pressure for another few seconds, and then let go. Locke fell to the galleon's hull, his legs and body contorted unnaturally.

Edward stood up and caught his breath. The cold air filled his lungs, but it had never felt sweeter than in that moment. He had won the battle of three in the Caribbean Sea.

He didn't have time to celebrate, as the water touching his feet told him. He lifted Locke up and placed him over his shoulder. The man was a heavy load, but nothing Edward couldn't handle.

He searched for the *Queen Anne's Revenge* and saw it floating around where the bow of the galleon was pointing. It wasn't far, but between it and him were a few dozen people from all sides of the battle.

Edward looked behind him to see his crew there, swimming towards him, and not far towards the stern of the galleon he saw two longboats still intact. He walked over to the nearest one and tossed Locke inside.

He pointed to the second longboat and commanded his crew to fetch it. With the little surface left on the side of the galleon, he leapt from it into the longboat.

His crew swam to the boats and boarded them, while at the same time defending them from the Spanish and the pirates. For simple longboats, they were massive. The two were enough to fit the remainder of his crew inside with ease.

William and Victoria were in the longboat with Edward, and they looked worse than he'd first thought, but not on the edge of death at least.

William was bleeding from a wound on his arm and breathing heavily, which was unusual. Edward figured it was his previous injuries and being bedridden for so long.

Victoria's face and chest were covered in blood, and she too was taking in deep breaths. She didn't appear to have any visible wounds, but her fatigue was evident.

"Are you both well?" Edward asked.

The two of them nodded, but didn't answer, which was good enough for him considering the circumstances.

The crew removed oars at the sides, and paddled their way towards their ship. As they moved, Edward looked down to the dim, murky waters of the sea, and the galleon which was being swallowed by its depths. All that wealth, treasure, and history was lost to Davey Jones, and it had all been done in a matter of hours.

The crew repelled those still alive trying to steal the boat from them, killing many in the process. None of the swimmers' guns would work, and the only choice was coming in close to attempt taking the longboats from their occupants. After a few lost fingers or their lives, the rest didn't dare attempt to board.

On the decks of the *Queen Anne's Revenge*, those same pirates and Spanish were trying to board. After having spent their proper weapons, they were no match for the crew still holding muskets and pistols and manning cannons.

Edward and company rowed the boats up next to their ship, and climbed aboard with ease. All the while, muskets still cracked with their burning explosions, and cannons still boomed with their bursts of iron death.

Edward slung Locke over his shoulder once more, and climbed up to his home. He dropped his enemy onto the weather deck, and jumped over the side to join his family.

As soon as he did, Anne rushed over to embrace him and kiss his forehead.

"I knew you would be safe," she said.

Edward chuckled. "You say that, but your voice sounded worried."

Anne smiled at him and embraced him again. The two stood there for a moment, warming each other with their love, until Edward stepped back.

"It's almost over," he said. "There's just one thing left to do." Edward stepped over to the port side and made sure that his crew were aboard, then turned back around to face the helm.

He saw a man not of his crew board at the stern, only to have Christina and Tala appear out of nowhere and attack him. Christina cut the man's chest open, and Tala tore his throat out.

Edward nodded with a devilish grin on his face at the sight. "Get us out of here, Herbert," he said.

Herbert smiled. "Aye, Captain."

"Someone bring me a pistol," Edward said.

After a moment, one of the crew brought Edward a loaded pistol. Edward thanked the man, then fired it at Locke's leg. The bullet pierced the man's thigh straight through.

Locke woke with a loud scream of pain, clutching his leg. Blood pooled beneath the wound and spilled over his pantaloons and hand. Locke's face contorted in pain, changing from clenched teeth to a rapid breathing and back again, all the while accompanied by another cry of agony.

Edward bent down to get to eye level with Locke. "Where... is... Sam?"

"I already bleedin' told ya, I don't know who yer talkin' about," he replied between his stifled cries.

Edward sighed and glanced over his shoulder. "Sam had taken a false name before joining Locke's crew. Does anyone remember what it was?"

Anne folded her arms. "James, I believe."

Edward nodded and turned back around to Locke. "He may have gone by the name James while he was with your crew. Black hair, foul mouth."

Locke's expression seemed to change as he glanced from Edward to Anne and to the others in his crew who were watching. "W-why would ya want to know about that sod?" He continued looking back and forth at the people gathered, and his expression changed again, this time into a sweat-soaked, uneasy smirk. "Ah, I gets it now. He was part of yer crew. No wonder he looked so familiar." Locke convulsed into a sickening fit of laughter.

Edward rose to his full towering height. "What happened to him?"

Locke was still laughing, but he stopped just long enough to say, "I killed the bastard," with a smug look in his eyes as he stared at Edward. "I killed him just like I killed that old fool Jo—"

Edward slammed his cutlass down on Locke's shoulder, severing the arm that had the chest attached to it. Locke's laughter turned into a sharp cry of anguish. He pulled his severed arm close to his chest as blood gushed from the wound. His body shook as he tried to close the wound with his good hand, but it was no use.

Edward dropped his cutlass to the sole with a loud clang, and then jumped on top of Locke, his massive body pinning the much smaller man down. He wrapped his hands around Locke's bloody throat and pushed down as hard as he could.

"You never got it, did you?" Edward shouted. "You never had the power between us. You should have bowed to me!"

Locke struggled with his stump and his fist and his legs, but nothing could stop Edward from choking the life out of him. His mouth opened in a pathetic attempt to draw air, and all he could do was croak as his throat tried to bring him life again. His eyes bulged and his face turned a garish shade of red.

"Not laughing now, are you?" Edward seethed, but of course Locke couldn't answer him. "Laugh," he screamed as he shook Locke by his neck. "Laugh, I said!"

But the man couldn't laugh even if he'd wanted to. After a moment, Locke's arms went limp once more, and he could no longer even try to resist the force on top of him. Edward squeezed tighter and tighter and tighter still, and there was a small pop.

Blackbeard's Blood

Edward took a breath, released his grip on Locke's neck, then grabbed the man's severed arm and the chest which had been his companion for so many years. He lifted the chest above his head and smashed it down on Kenneth Locke's head. The heavy chest broke Locke's face, caving it in and sending a wave of blood out from it. Edward didn't stop there. He lifted the chest once again, the blood dripping from it on top of his head. He slammed it down on Locke's face again and again and again until there was nothing left of Locke but a red mess on the planks of the weather deck.

Edward dropped the chest in front of him, arms burning and chest heaving. He got up from his knees and to his feet once again. He was covered in blood from head to toe, and the whole business gave his own crew pause; they stared at him, wide-eyed and silent in their shock.

"This," Edward said, pointing to what was left of Locke, "is justice."

21. THE STORM

Unable to sleep, Edward leaned back in a chair in his captain's cabin and stared out the stern windows to the night sky and sea. The water below churned and spiralled away from the ship, waves dancing in its wake.

After a quick funeral for those that had died during the battle—thirteen, to be exact—the injured were patched up and the crew took some much-needed rest.

Edward held a glass of rum in his hands, watching it for a moment before he downed the contents in one great gulp. It burned as it went down, and the heat filled his cheeks and lingered for a long while.

The scenes of the battle repeated in his head over and over. The feeling of drowning, both in the bottom of the ship and when he saw Kenneth Locke, was as present as ever, and it made Edward furious. Locke's face was burned into his mind, and wouldn't go away.

Edward took another drink, and another, and another, and soon his head was light and Locke's face left his mind. The dark sky, full of bright stars, swirled like the water below, and mixed with the windows and the planks of the ship into a sea of dull colours. He had to close his eyes to stop the spinning.

Edward put down the glass and got up from his seat. His legs wobbled and his balance was precarious. He took a few steps, placed his hand on the windows, and used it to guide him around the cabin towards his bed. The rocking of the ship was no aid as he stepped forward, but he succeeded after a time.

He flopped into the bed, shaking it with his weight, and his wife stirred at his side. "Can you not sleep, Edward?"

Edward shuffled and got underneath the covers. "I was celebrating," he said, a slight slur in his words.

There was a pause, then Anne said, "Try to sleep, your

injuries need to heal."

Anne's words were lost on him in the haze of his mind. As the drink took over, he calmed and sleep soon washed over him. This time, a more welcome darkness enveloped him, and all thoughts of Locke dissipated into the ether.

Knocking at Edward's door woke him from his slumber. His eyes opened in an instant and he took in a sharp breath through his nose. Sweat covered his face, chest, and back, neither cold nor warm on his body. His head pounded with each movement, and the light of day hurt his eyes.

He looked at the bed, and Anne wasn't there. As his eyes adjusted, he turned to look at the room, but she wasn't there either.

The knocking came again. "A moment, if you please," he shouted, but he had to press on his temple afterwards.

He got up and clothed himself, making himself look a slight bit presentable, and then went to open the door. Herbert was in front of the door, and he had a wide smile on his face and a bottle of something in his lap.

"Good day to you, Captain," he said. "I thought we could share a drink to celebrate now that you've had some time to rest."

Edward's head still throbbed, and when he looked at the bottle in Herbert's lap it nearly made him sick, but he pushed aside the feeling. He stepped aside and held the door open. "Certainly. Please, enter."

Herbert wheeled himself into Edward's cabin and up to the table at the back of the room. He placed the bottle on the table in front of him as Edward acquired glasses for the both of them.

"So, what's this you have?" Edward asked, gesturing at the bottle.

Herbert grinned. "I bought this a few months back from the Bodden brothers," he said. "It's a highland scotch from their hometown. A rare vintage, from what they told me. For special occasions such as these, I believe it necessary."

Edward chuckled. "Better with us than where they are now," he said.

"Hear, hear." Herbert popped the cork and poured each of them a drink.

Edward took one of the glasses and sipped the scotch. He was pleasantly surprised by how smooth the drink was, nothing like the sharp and harsh rum he had had the night before. It had notes of toasted nuts and something almost sweet to it.

Hebert too had taken a sip of the scotch, and he smiled yet raised his brow at the same time. "Dad damn, that's good."

"You can say that again," Edward replied. "You made a good choice."

Herbert lifted his glass. "To your revenge."

Edward paused for a moment, his hand gripping the glass hard. He recovered a moment later and clinked his glass with Herbert's. "Revenge." He pulled back the glass and downed the drink in one gulp.

Herbert frowned, but smiled soon after. "Now, now, Captain. This drink is to be savoured."

Edward nodded, but didn't say anything. Herbert filled his cup once more, and Edward decided not to offend his generosity by trying to hold back.

"So, Captain... how do you feel?"

Edward stared at Herbert for a moment, not sure of what he was truly asking. "I'm well," he said.

Herbert frowned. "Come now, Captain, you must tell me more. You've just gotten revenge on Kenneth Locke. How does it feel?" There was a moment of silence as Edward contemplated the question. "You're... you're not still upset with me, are you?"

Edward shook his head. "No, no, of course not," he replied. "Truth be told, I thought you might have wanted to take Locke for yourself, given that he was one of Calico Jack's men."

Herbert looked surprised. "No, he was yours to kill. He wasn't one of Calico Jack's men when I was part of the crew."

Edward nodded and took a swig of the scotch. The smooth taste was still there, but a hint of smokiness bit the back of his tongue. "After you killed Gregory Dunn, you said you felt content. Does that still hold true?"

Herbert looked down at the glass in his hands, staring at the drink for a long while. "I don't know... It's been so long. I've grown cold to the memory. Calico Jack's officers no longer hold any appeal to me. I believe only the man himself could quell the burning inside me now."

"Then perhaps we should be more direct in our aspirations," Edward said. "We should sail straight for him... No more beating against the wind, as it were."

Herbert raised his brow and his jaw dropped. "You cannot believe that is the best course for us."

Edward set his cup down. "And why not? He wouldn't see us coming if we planned our actions right."

"The very notion is suicide, Captain," Herbert replied. "He has more men on his side than we do, more ships, more... everything. We have to do what he did to us: remove his support and then attack him head-on on even ground." Herbert took a drink and then placed his cup down as well. "This is especially the case now that we've... lost Roberts."

Edward leaned back in his chair. "You may be right."

After a moment of silence, there was a rap at the door. Edward called to enter, and a crewmate walked in.

"Captain, we was able to open Locke's chest."

Edward leaned forward, a slight twinge of a grin tugging at his cheeks. "And...?"

"The coins're fake, sir. Not real gold."

Edward shook his head as he chuckled. "Of course they are," he muttered. "You've checked all the coins?"

The crewmate nodded. "What should we do with them, Captain?"

Edward looked away in thought for a moment, and then touched the golden cutlass at his side. "Bring it here to my room. It will serve as a reminder of a battle well fought."

Herbert raised his glass as the crewmate left the room. Edward picked his up again and the two clinked them together again. Herbert drank the rest of his, and set the cup down again without refilling it.

"I should be heading back. I have to make sure Christina hasn't led us astray."

"I'm sure it's fine, but there's no harm in being diligent." Edward topped off his glass with a grin and then put the stopper back in the bottle before handing it back to Herbert.

Herbert began turning himself around, but stopped. "I suppose that reminds me. Where exactly should we be heading now?"

"Hmm," Edward said, stroking his beard. "That's a good question. The first order of business should be resupplying, so bring us to the nearest port. Perhaps you can send in Victoria on your way up? I'll ask her if she knows anyone who can tell us where our next target is."

"Aye, Captain."

As Herbert was heading towards the door of the cabin, it opened and Anne stepped inside. She held the door open for him, and the two exchanged greetings before Herbert left.

Anne walked over and sat down in front of the table across from Edward. Her long red curls bounced and swayed as she moved, but were stifled slightly by the cap she wore. She let out a sigh and removed the cap from her head.

"Difficult morning, Quartermaster?"

"Not so, husband, but without their captain present the crew are harder to control."

"You managed to bring them in line, I trust?"

Anne nodded. "After a time." She sat up and rested her arms on the chair. "So, are you feeling better after some sleep?"

"I am well now that Herbert brought me this," Edward replied with a smirk as he lifted his cup before taking another drink.

Anne frowned. "Can you talk with me, Edward?" she said, and then leaned forward and placed her hand on his. Her face shifted to a sad look of concern. "You were unable to sleep yesterday, and over-drank to the point of intoxication before returning to bed."

Edward put the glass down and held his wife's hand. "There is no need for concern. The battle was exciting, and

I needed the drink to settle my nerves."

Anne squeezed his hand. "You know you can talk with me about anything, yes?"

Anne's concern bled into her voice, and it pained Edward to the core. She was calling out to him to open up, but he couldn't bear to dwell on the thoughts in his head even for a moment. He needed to move forward and forget about the man who haunted his dreams still.

Edward forced a smile. "I know," he replied and then kissed his wife's hand. "You are too good for me."

Anne grinned. "That's correct. Should you ever need a reminder, I will be here."

Edward chuckled, but before he could respond there was another knock at the door. "Enter," he said.

The door swung open and a crewmate walked in with the chest cradled between his hands as he leaned back for extra support. "Where do ya want it, Captain?"

Edward pointed to the side of the room, near the back where he could see it from the table where he was sitting. "Over here should do," he said.

Anne was watching the crewmate over her shoulder as he brought the chest inside. "Why do you wish to keep that chest?"

"It may not have real gold coins, but it will serve as a nice trophy."

Anne nodded, still watching the crewmate as he set the chest down. "I should return to the weather deck before the ship falls apart. Will you be joining us sometime today, Captain?" she asked with a smirk.

Edward grinned along with her. "I'll join you shortly. I called for Herbert to send Victoria in so that we may set our course to find someone who may know where we can find the next of Calico Jack's men."

"Good. I know the men are eager to find their next quarry." Anne got up from her seat. "Don't be long, Captain. The men are also eager to congratulate you on your victory."

"I'll be sure not to disappoint."

Anne and the other crewmate left the cabin, and Edward was alone. With no other distractions, the noises from outside made their way into his cabin—the rush of water surging and slapping against the ship, the shouts and laughter of men working and enjoying themselves, and the subtle noise of sails moving and rope scraping against wood and iron.

Edward stared at the chest of false gold coins as the noise took over his thoughts. The chest was broken in several places, the bands of iron scraped and bent, the wood chipped and split, and had one large cut coming from the back half-way through the top. He recalled the fight, and how he had made that cut on the chest. Dried blood covered most of the chest in dark splotches, remnants of Edward's final ruining of its former master.

This is all that's left of you. You're dead and gone, and no one cares about you. You can't touch anyone where you are now. No one will remember your name or your legacy.

Edward took a deep breath in and held it for a moment before letting it out. For a moment, there was peace in his mind.

You'll remember, a voice called in Edward's head, shattering his peace.

He tightened his grip around the cup and drank the rest of its contents in one filling gulp. This time, the scotch stung as it went down his throat. The smokiness of the aged alcohol overpowered everything else and burned his insides.

The door to his cabin opened abruptly and Victoria walked in. Behind her, Alexandre followed. They both walked up to the table and sat down in the nearby chairs.

"What did you wish to speak to me about, Captain?"

"Welcome, and a good day to you as well, Victoria."

Victoria sighed, showing her distaste for Edward's jesting, and leaned her head on her hand. Alexandre carried his usual indifference in his sullen eyes, but a grin on his face.

Edward leaned back and let out a different kind of sigh. "I wanted to know if you had any more contacts who may aid us in our search Calico Jack's other allies."

Victoria sat up and looked away in thought for a moment. "There may be a man in Jamaica who could help us, although as with my acquaintance in Porto Bello, he will not provide information without something in return."

Edward waved his hand. "That shouldn't be an issue."

"Do you wish me to inform Herbert?" Victoria asked.

"No, no… Not necessary. I'll be heading up shortly. My thanks for the information."

Victoria nodded, then rose from her seat and headed to the door of the cabin. Alexandre stayed seated. Victoria seemed to have known Alexandre was going to stay, and she closed the door on her way out.

Edward raised his brow. "Something you wished to discuss with me, Alexandre?"

"*Oui.* I am concerned with your mental state. I wish to know how you are feeling now that you've killed Mr Locke."

Edward chuckled and scratched his brow. "Why does everyone insist on asking me how I'm feeling? I'm well, thank you for asking," he said, though he felt exasperated rather than appreciative.

Alexandre leaned forward in his chair, rested his elbows on his knees, and locked his fingers in front of his mouth. "Oh, is that so?" he said, long and drawn out.

Edward sat up straight at Alexandre's penetrating gaze. "Yes," he replied firmly.

"I've noticed you… what is the word… breaking down over the last year."

Edward's mouth was a line, and he clenched his jaw, annoyed by the Frenchman's oddness. "Oh, is that so?" he mimicked.

"Yes, ever since you shot your old friend, Henry."

Edward's heart skipped, and his stomach turned. His face felt hot, and a lump stuck to the back of his throat. His whole body tensed up, and his vision blurred around the edges.

"What are you talking about?" Edward forced out past the lump.

"There is no need to put on such airs. I care not what you've done, and would never tell another. That would ruin the game. I am, as I've said several times, an observer."

Edward gripped the edge of his chair's arm so hard it was in danger of breaking off. "How did you know? I've told no one."

Alexandre scoffed. "It is not so hard to know to one watching you. You leave to chase after Henry when he seeks to leave the crew, and when you return you are smelling of gunpowder and disappear into the stern cabin. The crew were too busy manning the ship in a storm to worry about you, and hours later you emerge, but without mention of why you shot your pistol... it is not *difficile* to make the connection, *mon Capitaine*."

Though there was no cause for it, Edward felt as though his privacy had been violated. His anger overwhelmed him, and his blood boiled in his veins.

"You have continued to spiral since that time, and events have not aided in your *récupération*. I can—"

"Get out," Edward seethed.

Alexandre paused for a moment, and stared at Edward with a curious expression on his face, as if he was confused by Edward's anger.

"Get out before I rip your throat open with my bare hands."

Alexandre continued to stare at Edward for a moment, and then he rose from his seat. "By your leave, *mon Capitaine*," he murmured.

Edward sat stock still in his seat as waves of anger pulsed through him on lines across his forehead. The faces of all the crew and friends dead at his hands and others' flashed in his mind, and wouldn't stop. On some level, Edward felt good that those faces were haunting him. Like the chest they would serve as reminders, both good and bad.

One hour later

Edward stepped up to the weather deck, and the crew all around greeted him warmly. They congratulated him on yesterday's battle, and the ultimate fate of Kenneth Locke. He returned the compliments and congratulations in kind to the men who'd joined him and those who'd stayed behind and protected the ship.

He noticed William, Pukuh, and Victoria all working dil-igently with the other men on the rigging of the sails or clean-ing the weather deck. Nassir was also off at the end of the bow, fixing planks which had been broken during the last battle. Alexandre was there as well, checking up on the in-jured.

He made his way up to the quarterdeck overseeing the rest of the ship. Hebert was at the helm, watching the skies and sea with his keen eyes. Anne and Christina were nearby, playing with Tala.

The day was half over, but there was plenty of sun left, and the wind was strong. The smell of the sea rejuvenated Edward and brought clarity to his thoughts.

"Captain," Herbert said, tipping his cap with one hand as he held to the wheel with the other. "Do you have our head-ing?"

"I will in a moment," he replied as he stepped up to the quarterdeck railing. "Men, hop to it. We must discuss where next to sail."

The crew stopped what they were doing and gathered close to the quarterdeck to listen to what Edward had to say. Once everyone on the main deck was present, Edward nod-ded.

"First off, I want to tell you how proud I am of all of you. It is thanks to your efforts that we made it through the last battle." The crew hooted their own thanks to him, and proudly patted each other on the backs. "We fought against five ships, and we won!" Another, louder shout from the crew. "We fought against a galleon, and won!" Again the crew yelled their approval.

"Our resident one-armed savage, Pukuh," Edward said, gesturing to his friend with a smirk on his face, "once said to me that I was the storm that other men feared." The men patted Pukuh on the back and he grinned. "But that was un-true... *You* are the storm," he said, now pointing in a wave across the crew. "You are the crew that other men fear, and will continue to fear. The crew of the *Queen Anne's Revenge* will soon be known across the Old World and the New."

The crew rallied and hollered and stomped their feet together, shaking the deck. Their faces beamed with pride as they looked at their captain.

"To make our names known, what say we continue our revenge against Calico Jack, the man who burned our town to the ground? The man who thinks we're weak. The man who thinks he can survive the storm."

The crew gave a resounding roar of approval to Edward.

"We will destroy all those who stand against us." The crew shouted another yes. "All those who think they're better than us." The crew yelled louder still. "All those who turn their backs on us," Edward said, looking at Alexandre as he did so. Edward was sure that the significance wasn't lost on him.

"We are the storm!" he roared with his fist raised. The crew repeated the saying, also raising their fists in the air. "Now get back to work, you ugly bastards."

The crew burst out laughing before they returned to their duties aboard the ship.

"Herbert," Edward called. "We're heading north-east, to Jamaica."

Herbert smiled widely. "Aye, Captain," he replied.

Anne came up beside Edward and looked up at him with a smile on her face. He returned the smile and gave her a kiss. The two of them gazed at the bow of the ship towards the bright horizon ahead of them, wondering where their next adventure would take them.

For a moment, Edward was at peace. His body and mind calmed by the sun, sea, ship, and woman he loved. But a certain red stain on the weather deck caught his eye, and, in a different way, he became the storm once again.

THE END

BOOK FOUR OF
THE VOYAGES OF QUEEN
ANNE'S REVENGE

BLACKBEARD'S
FAMILY

1. STABBED IN THE HEART THROUGH THE BACK

"We should strike now. We know where he'll be, and it's the perfect chance to kill him without a huge battle." Herbert sat forward in his wheelchair, one arm leaning on the table in the *Queen Anne's Revenge* war room. His other hand was in front of him, palm open and motioning in supplication to his pirate brethren.

"Although I defended you in the past to be fair to everyone, Herbert, you must know you're biased in this decision." Anne, the *Queen Anne's Revenge* quartermaster, sat stoically, her posture perfect, arms resting on the chair. She had a slight investment in the outcome due to her own past with their enemy, Calico Jack, but her tone and muted expression painted things otherwise.

Herbert lowered his head, more in frustration than shame, and looked up at Anne from under furrowed brows. "My emotions may be compromised, but my faculties aren't. I'm not wrong."

William, his arms crossed as he too leaned forward in his chair, stared at the wooden boards of the ship as he said, "I am inclined to side with Herbert." William gave Anne a sidelong glance, then added, "My apologies, ma'am." He couldn't help but channel his former royal guard nature when speaking with Anne.

Anne's clenched jaw betrayed her annoyance at both of William's comments. She didn't enjoy being outnumbered but also didn't enjoy being reminded of her former royal status. "And what if the information we were given is incorrect, hmm? What if we head to Tortuga and his crew is there waiting for us?"

"Impossible," Victoria said, shaking her head. "My informant doesn't make mistakes, and he wouldn't betray us.

Besides, Calico Jack frequently visits Los Huecos to check on his commander Silver Eyes before travelling to Tortuga. Then, after he's had his fill of his baser inclinations, he heads back to his base of operations in Nassau. I know this from my time on his crew."

"Also, *ma chérie*," Alexandre, the *Queen Anne's Revenge* surgeon, chimed in, "it should be noted that when on land, Calico Jack would not travel to all places with his entire crew. A covert assassination should prove effective, provided he doesn't know we are *arrivant*."

Anne sighed, her responsibility as quartermaster wavering against the mounting offensive from her crewmates. "I suppose you may be right. But," she said, turning her gaze to her husband, Edward Thatch, "what does the captain think?"

Edward's hands were clasped together in front of his face, his fingers entwined and his elbows resting on the table. He had listened to everything in silence, his eyes trained on a map in the middle of the table, but not focused on any of the shapes.

He eventually looked up at all the eyes staring back at him, suddenly aware of the entire room waiting for him to make the definitive decision. He unclasped his hands, leaned back, and stroked his long black beard.

Herbert spoke again. "If we let this opportunity slip away and do nothing, we will eventually come to regret it. This isn't like before. We'll do this together, and we'll do it right this time."

The others nodded in approval when Edward turned his gaze on them. All of them agreed with Hebert's declaration. Herbert met Edward's gaze, unwavering, letting Edward know that he wouldn't hesitate in following him into the unknown battle ahead.

"Set course for Tortuga."

"You found him?" Edward questioned the breathless crewmates. "You're sure it was Calico Jack?"

The crewmates both nodded at the same time. "No doubt, Captain. From what William told us 'bout his looks and the manner he carried himself, this was Calico Jack."

"How many were with him?" Herbert asked, wheeling himself over to the commotion.

The sky was darkening above Tortuga and the *Queen Anne's Revenge*. The crew had only just finished settling the ship at anchor a ways from the harbour. The three masts' sails had been furled, and the halyards secured to the vessel, and the crew was ready for the long night at rest.

"Far as we could tell, it was just him an' two others what came to the tavern. They entered after a time and were bein' served food and drinks just as we left."

"That means we don't have much time. How many were in the tavern?"

"Not more than twenty."

"Then we proceed as planned," Edward said as he turned towards Herbert. "Get your pistol ready, Herbert, we're ending this tonight."

Herbert couldn't help but smile, but his eyes soon misted, and he cast his eyes downward. He turned away from Edward. "Sorry, Captain," he said, his words catching in his throat.

Edward issued a few commands to the nearby crewmates to prepare the ship for departure and bring the crew up from below before coming back. Then he knelt next to Herbert.

"No need for that now," he said.

Herbert nodded as he wiped his eyes. "I know, Captain, I'm not sure what came over me. The deed's not even done yet."

Edward nodded. "True, but we both know that this is revenge years in the making. It may not bring your legs back, but if it can bring closure, it's no wonder one would be overcome by the magnitude of it."

Herbert looked up at Edward, his eyes still shining in the waning light as the wind of the sea blew against his short brown hair. "Tonight changes everything. Tomorrow will start a new life for me. You have my thanks, Edward. Without you, this wouldn't be possible."

"Not so. You made a choice to join a bunch of pirates under the condition that we help you in your vengeance." Edward placed his hand on Herbert's wheelchair. "You are the architect, I'm just the hired help."

Herbert and Edward both chuckled at that, but then Herbert shook his head in defiance. "No, you're family. And I've told you before that this family is my strength. It's the only reason I've gotten this far."

Edward's face warmed, embarrassed, but happy to have Herbert make such a declaration. "Let's kill Calico Jack then, shall we, brother?"

"Let's," Herbert said as he clasped Edward's forearm. Edward grabbed Herbert's forearm back and shook it to seal the informal bond of vengeance.

Christina, Herbert's sister, rushed up from below deck over to Herbert and Edward, with Anne trailing behind her. "We found him?" Christina asked expectantly. After a quick nod from Edward and Herbert, tears filled her widened eyes, and she fell to the deck on her knees next to Herbert. Her arms wrapped around him, and she shoved her face into his chest, her strawberry blond hair draping over him. Herbert's chest muffled her sobs.

Herbert wrapped his arms around his sister, and his tears came back at once. He consoled her, but knew that she was crying for the same reason he had; this was joy, and possibly relief.

After a moment, the other crewmates rushed up from the depths of the ship and began preparations to leave Tortuga at a moment's notice.

Christina regained her awareness with the noise of the many feet pounding against the weather deck. She got to her feet and wiped her tears away, a quick transition to the determined, anxious look of a woman ready for a fight.

The crewmates who had found Calico Jack returned with the men who were going to help with the plan. Ten men in all would help while Edward, Anne, and Herbert would carry out the other half of the plot.

"Do we all know our parts to play?" The crewmates nodded. "Then show us the way, men," Edward commanded.

"Captain," Christina said, stepping forward before they could leave. "I know that I'm supposed to stay here and prepare the ship for departure, but I wish to join you." She stood defiantly, her fingers balled into fists. "Please."

"Christina—" Herbert began, but Edward's hand on his shoulder stopped him.

"Rest assured, you will have your chance to extract your pound of flesh from Calico Jack," Edward declared. "But we need you here. Without Herbert, you are our best helmsman."

Christina's gaze fell, and her fingers dug into her palms for a moment. Nassir, the negro shipwright, came over beside Christina and wrapped his massive arm around her, pulling her in close. She looked shocked at first, but when she gazed up at him, her features softened. They shared a bond of loss over the years aboard the ship, and it carried a weight that a captain's command simply could never hope to rival. Next, her wolf companion, Tala, nudged her fist with a whine. Christina looked down at her, opened her palm and scratched her friend on the nose.

When her gaze came back to meet Edward's, she wore a false smile and misted eyes. "I'll hold you to that promise," she said.

"Understood," Edward replied.

As the departing crew began boarding a longboat for shore, Edward stopped to talk with William, the boatswain in charge of the ship while Edward and Anne were away, and Jack, the musician.

"Keep the men in line and entertained," Edward said, leaning in with a soft voice. "Tensions are high, and we can't have any mistakes. Not tonight."

William gave a stiff salute, and Jack nodded. "Understood, Captain," William replied.

"I'll bring out the fiddle tonight," Jack added with a smile. "That should lighten the mood a touch."

Edward gave the two men a few more explicit orders about when to be ready, and whom in the crew to use at which stations, before turning around to join the others still boarding the longboat. Before he could disembark, another crewmate came up behind him and gave him a forceful slap on his back.

Edward let out a grunt as the stinging on his back coursed through his spine. He glared at the Mayan prince he knew to be behind him, and the prince smirked back at his captain.

"Pukuh, I thought you to be sleeping at this hour."

"I would not miss this," he replied. Pukuh's smile faded, and he gave a stern look. "Do not underestimate this man, Calico Jack. According to my father, when he was known as Benjamin Hornigold, he was a fearsome man to his enemies, and the years seem to have hardened him." Pukuh's light accent belied the harsh tone he employed.

"Not to worry, friend, we have our best opportunity here and now, and I wouldn't let my guard down during such a crucial time."

"You would not let your guard down? How was it I hit you on the back a moment before then?" He shot Edward an impetuous grin.

Edward shook his head. "I knew you were there, but it seemed like you could use a boost of confidence after losing your arm. Perhaps if you were in good form you would have been able to sneak up on me," Edward tried his best to add a fake tone of pity to his words, but he couldn't help but grin at his own jesting.

Pukuh playfully punched Edward in his arm before he exchanged another few words of encouragement for the battle to come.

The crew watched as their captain and the shore party entered the longboat and paddled to shore. They were mostly silent, imparting strength in solidarity for the task ahead. Everyone knew who their captain was about to face, and the weight of what it meant when they would come back with the enemy in hand.

Edward noticed Alexandre and Victoria on the quarterdeck, near the helm. When deciding who would be part of the team to face Calico Jack, Victoria had chosen to stay behind. By her demeanour, though she portrayed a mask of strength, Edward believed she didn't wish to confront Calico Jack, the man who had tortured her, again.

Though the torturer had been different, Edward knew the feeling well. It was that feeling which forced him to keep a flask in his pocket at all times.

The longboat docked at Tortuga's harbour, and from the sounds that met the crew's ears, it was the beginning of a night full of drunken revelry and debauchery. For Tortuga, it was a Thursday.

Edward commanded a few of the crew to find the men who had taken leave at the shore and bring them back to the ship. Thankfully, everyone was expecting to leave on short notice and agreed to stay close to the harbour, so he didn't expect there would be any issues finding the men.

The sound of pistols, battle cries, and lamentations, coupled with the occasional cracking of breaking glass, echoed across the dingy stone walkways the crew traversed on their way to the tavern where Calico Jack was waiting for them. The smell of hard liquor, ale, body odour, and piss wafted towards them, mixed with the scent of the ocean and nearby grass and tropical trees. Years of dilapidation and neglect meant that the smells simply compounded on top of one another, and the air was forever tainted by the musk of the pirates and rebels that inhabited the lawless island.

When they were three buildings away from the tavern, the crewmates who had found Calico Jack pointed out the tavern in which he was to be found. With a quick check of readiness, Edward continued towards the tavern.

"Hold, Captain," Herbert said, stopping at the back of the group. "I cannot enter the tavern. I shall wait around back."

Edward's jaw went slack for a moment. "Why?"

"I know I was but a child when I was on his ship, but there is no mistaking my condition. My wheelchair will stand out like a sore thumb, so it would be best if I remain outside not to disrupt the plan you have in mind."

Edward looked deep into Herbert's eyes and saw no sadness in them. He could only see the same determination as before staring back at him.

"Understood," Edward said. "You stay with him," he added, pointing to one of the crewmates. The crewmate nodded, and he and Herbert went around the back of the nearby buildings to where they would take Calico Jack before bringing him back to the ship.

The rest of the crew proceeded to the tavern, and gradually entered in groups. The last group consisted of the two crewmates who had found Calico Jack initially, and Edward and Anne.

The inside of the tavern smelled another level worse than the outside of Tortuga. With little ventilation, the foul odours concentrated in the confined space and permeated the walls and air of the establishment. The twenty or so patrons, now bolstered by the ten from Edward's crew, packed the quarters and made the space uncomfortably hot. It also didn't help that, although expected given the gravity of the situation, Edward felt tense and on edge.

"Where is he?" Anne asked, staying hidden behind Edward's large body until she could get a line of sight.

"In the corner on the left," one of the crewmates answered, being sound of mind enough not to point as he did.

Edward and Anne both tentatively glanced in that direction, only briefly catching a glimpse of Calico Jack and his mates.

Edward almost felt that he could sense the man's presence, as though his reputation weighed on the hot, stuffy air. Even so, he wasn't sure if it was merely nerves, so he asked, "Is that him, Anne?"

Anne's face scrunched pensively. "I cannot tell. There are too many people here."

"At worst, we point a pistol at another pirate. Let's find somewhere to sit."

Edward, Anne, and the two crewmates found a few empty chairs and a table to sit at, and shortly afterwards a husky woman brought them all pints of ale without their asking. She let them all know they would bring them food should they have the coin to pay, though not letting them know what the food was or how much it cost.

Edward took a few coins from his purse and tossed them her way. After a check of their quality, she nodded in approval and left to the back of the establishment.

Edward looked around at the other patrons. Many of

them were men, some young and foolish, and some old griz-zled seamen, but there were also a few women of the night, as well as a few middle-aged female bruisers who seemed to be sharing stories with the seamen. He noticed that he was growing accustomed to the smell, and it, like the noise sur-rounding them, faded into the background. But, as the sounds faded, his nerves finally caught up with him, and he suddenly felt ill.

Thoughts he wanted to keep buried crept into him, gnaw-ing and itching. *Not now. Please, not now*, he begged, but he could already feel his skin go cold, and his hand trembled. His chest felt as though a cannon was sitting on top of it.

Edward swallowed and moved his hand into his breast pocket. The thick air now seemed an ocean of mud on his body. He thought all eyes were on him, and he was moving too slow, too unnaturally, to look normal. He forced against the mud, and it made his hands shake with the effort. The thought that his weakness was showing only made the trem-bling worse, and it took all his strength to twist off the cap of his flask. He brought the flask full of rum to his lips and took a long and deep drink from it.

The sharp and bitter harshness cut through his other pains like a blade through flesh, and he sighed in relief. The rum gave him no pleasure in its taste, only respite from the weight of the mud around him. This was his only way to con-trol it, but the mud was hardening as each day passed and required more to wash it away as well.

Edward could feel Anne's gaze on him, and he glanced over at her. She had a look of concern on her face. He lifted the flask up in the air and did his best to grin as he said, "Liq-uid courage," but the grin felt hollow even to him. He took another deep drink from the flask.

The woman who had served them the ale returned with a few plates full of what appeared to be some sort of stew with meat in it and old bread. She didn't say another word to them and left to serve other people.

None of the crew even entertained the thought of trying the food, and so Edward leaned forward after pushing his plate aside. The others at his table followed suit.

"The back room is a bit far from where he is. We'll need to act fast while our crewmates are doing their part."

Anne and one of the crewmates nodded, but the other leaned in further. "Captain, I know we wus supposed to wait a bit before startin' the ruckus, but I think Ca— I think our man is close to finishing his meal."

Edward's eyes widened slightly, and he glanced over to where Calico Jack was sitting. From what he could tell, the men at the table looked relaxed and took small bites of their food and infrequent drinks of ale.

"It's time," he said.

Edward rose from the table and locked gazes with one of his crewmates in another part of the tavern. The crewmate scratched his nose, showing he understood what to do next.

Edward casually walked towards the back corner where Calico Jack waited, followed closely by Anne and the two crewmates they were with. As they moved, the crewmate whom Edward had given the signal started an argument with another mate.

The other patrons hooted and hollered, cheering on the arguments and adding to the insults tossed at each other and tossing actual objects at them as well. The air in the tavern was changing swiftly as the excitement of a brewing fight riled everyone else up.

According to plan, when Edward and the others were a few feet from Calico Jack, the shouts and taunts changed to fists. Most of the patrons were all paying attention to the fight now, and none were looking at Edward and the others.

To ensure nothing went wrong, a few other crewmates started fights with other patrons in the bar, and in a matter of seconds, the entire right side of the tavern had turned into a riot.

Edward, Anne, and their companions took advantage of the commotion, pulled pistols from their coats, and pointed them at the back of Calico Jack and his mates.

"Calico Jack, I presume you wouldn't enjoy a bullet to the back, so don't move," Edward commanded.

For a moment, there was complete silence from the man in front of Edward. He glanced over to the other mates on the other end of the table, the ones whose faces he could see, and noticed that they looked wholly and utterly calm. They appeared as though they didn't care in the slightest that they had pistols trained on them, and the looks unnerved Edward even more than he had been, despite the drink hitting him at that moment.

"So, you're finally here, son," Calico Jack, the man in front of Edward, said over the commotion on the other side of the tavern.

Even above the commotion, Edward knew the voice was a familiar one. He couldn't place it, but Calico Jack raised his hands, rose from his seat, and turned around, and then he knew why the voice was familiar.

"Dad?" Edward said, his mouth going slack as he stepped back in shock.

"Ed?" Anne called.

Before Edward could recover, his father slapped the pistol away and punched Edward in the gut. Edward doubled over in pain but was pulled up by his hair and put in a chokehold.

"You disappoint me, Edward," his father whispered in his ear.

Edward felt a sharp pain shoot into his lower back and travel all through his body, and then there was a sudden empty feeling. He felt warm blood gushing out of the wound.

"Let him go!" Anne shouted, firing her pistol at Calico Jack.

Jack ducked out of the way, but Anne's shot was wide and more a warning. "I think not, little queen," he replied. He pulled a small hunting horn that appeared to be made of tarnished gold from his pocket and blew into it.

The tone from the horn was piercing and like no other sound Edward had ever heard. It shook his whole body with the noise it made, and after it went away, there was silence. Silence, not because Edward temporarily went deaf, but because the patrons in the tavern stopped fighting.

Edward couldn't move his head, but looking over, he could see all eyes on them. The men and women who had not a moment before been beating each other to a pulp were now staring at Calico Jack in a sort of religious reverence. Edward's crew had stopped as well, though from confusion rather than whatever the sound of the horn had wrought.

"By the sound of the Golden Horn!" one of the men in the crowd shouted.

"By the sound of the Golden Horn!" another continued the chant.

Edward hadn't heard the chant himself but had been informed by Anne about its significance to Benjamin Hornigold, Calico Jack's former alias. *His father's* former alias. It was a battle cry used by those pirates in league with Hornigold in a failed war years ago.

Soon most of the patrons were shouting the same battle cry as they descended upon Edward and his crew. After each chant, they took a step forward in unison, as though under a trance.

"By the sound of the Golden Horn!"

"By the sound of the Golden Horn!"

"By the sound of the Golden Horn!"

Anne's eyes were wide with terror at the sight of all those men and women walking as one towards them. She reloaded her pistol, but didn't know where to point it, whether at the man who had sounded the call, or the crowd that had answered it.

Edward's father pushed him away, and he fell into Anne's arms. His legs were weak, and he had difficulty moving. The drink and the loss of blood were taking its toll on him, and he could feel the void creeping up on him.

"You would have had me if you weren't so weak," Jack scolded. "Try again when you grow a spine."

In front of Calico Jack, his crewmates stood as an honour guard, shielding him from any harm. All the while, the crowd was still chanting and getting closer.

Edward put all his strength in his feet and pushed Anne towards the back of the tavern. The crowd didn't pounce on them, they simply forced them back with each step they took. They were letting them go, but Edward didn't know for how long that would remain so. They needed to run.

Anne kept her pistol trained on the crowd, shifting its

muzzle from one person to the next as she backed towards the tavern's kitchen. In the kitchen, the men and women who worked the tavern continued the chant in the tight corridors. Their eyes stayed trained on Edward and Anne, but it felt as though they were looking through them.

Edward and Anne stumbled out of the back exit of the tavern to the alley, where Herbert and another crewmate were waiting. Herbert's eyes looked like saucers at the sight of Edward.

"What happened?" he shouted.

"By the sound of the Golden Horn!" Behind them, the chant was getting closer.

"There's no time!" Anne yelled back. "We're getting out of here. Someone help me with Edward."

Edward tried to get to his feet to help his wife and crew escape, but he'd lost his strength long ago. His head became leaden, and his eyes closed. As his world faded to black, the image of his aged father stabbing him in the back burned in his mind.

2. RESOLVE

Edward awoke with a jump and a pounding headache. By the time he was sitting upright, the pain in his backside flooded over him. He grabbed his left side where the wound was and turned over to avoid lying on it again.

"Welcome back, *mon ami*," a familiar French voice called behind him.

Still deep in pain, Edward lowered his head and peered through the crook in his arm to see an upside-down Alexandre sitting behind him. He smiled in his hollow way and turned his head slightly to match Edward's orientation before waving to him.

Edward lifted his head and glanced around. He was back on the ship in the surgeon's own room. Various bottles filled with coloured liquids dotted secured shelves alongside every manner of medical equipment and textbooks from across the globe. The strange concoction of medicine and decay hit Edward's nose, and he remembered part of the reason he'd never liked the room.

Edward noticed his body weight shifting back and forth rhythmically. "We're sailing?" he asked.

"*Oui*," Alexandre replied. "After the run-in with your *père*, it was decided to leave before trouble follow us."

The pain left Edward in a flash as he remembered what had happened. His father had been in that tavern, and had stabbed him, his own son, in the back. Worse still, his father was Calico Jack, and Benjamin Hornigold before that.

His father had been alive all this time. His father had been alive and hadn't come home.

'Your father is in the Caribbean, Edward.' Those had been the last words of John, the former quartermaster of *Queen Anne's Revenge* and an old friend of Edward's father. *He knew,* Edward thought. He didn't like to dwell on that moment, as he had been tortured for days on end afterwards, and so he'd

forgotten its significance. *He knew where my father was, and who he was, all along.*

Edward's hand shook as the pain returned, and not just the physical.

"I need a drink," he sputtered as his eyes became hazy.

After a moment of shuffling behind him, Alexandre handed Edward a glass. Edward took it and gulped the liquid down. After finishing half, he stopped and shoved the glass back.

"Rum," he demanded.

Alexandre produced a flask in an instant as if he'd predicted the desire for hard liquor before Edward had asked. Edward cared not for the surgeon's ways and took the drink. In a matter of seconds, Edward guzzled down half the flask's contents before he had to come up for air.

Edward's hand still shook as he lowered the flask. He took in ragged deep breaths, trying to bring air back to his lungs, which felt, to him, so desperately empty. His head and heart pounded in his chest, and he couldn't make sense of the feeling of dread washing over him.

He finished the flask with abandon and lay there on his elbows for a time. He had trouble thinking and didn't know how much time passed. The drink hit him hard and fast, his loss of blood no doubt contributing to the swift onset. The haze clouding his thoughts changed to a different kind, and ever so slowly, Edward felt he could breathe once more.

Edward looked to his right to see Alexandre there, watching him. Alexandre's eyes were dull and cold, as usual, but Edward thought he could see an expectant look on the surgeon's face. Alexandre must be awaiting some sort of explanation for what just happened.

"Stop staring at me, you damn Frenchman, before I cut your eyes out." Edward cared little for his harsh words now that the drink was affecting him.

Alexandre rose from his seat and walked away without a word. Edward shuffled over and rose to his shaky feet. Turning around, he noticed Victoria, Calico Jack's—his *father's*—former plaything sitting there watching him.

"Did you know too?" he shouted before tripping over his

own feet. He grabbed onto the frame of the door nearby to steady himself.

"Know what?" she replied, clearly irked by Edward's accusation, but giving him a chance to back down.

"Hmph," Edward scoffed. "Whoring yourself out to him must have made you privy to his secrets."

Victoria crossed her arms and flashed him a vile look. "Watch what you say next unless you want to lose the chance to have your own son come to try and kill you," she said, nodding towards Edward's nether regions.

Edward laughed a chuckle at first, and then full-blown laughter as he leaned against the door frame. He covered his eyes with his hand as he laughed, rubbing them as they misted, from the humour or the sadness he knew not.

"He tried to kill me," Edward let out between breaths. "My own father tried to kill me. And not just once. He sent me for the keys to this ship, knowing I could die trying. He knew just how to prick me to make me jump the way he wanted."

Edward lowered himself to the sole of the deck, his back resting against the open frame of the door. The pain from his wound was a dull sensation now, dissipated in the haze and spinning that the drink and blood loss brought him.

Time lost meaning to Edward, and he vaguely felt as though he were floating or being carried before lying in his familiar bed. The gentle rocking of the waves and the spinning in his head lulled him to sleep.

The sun hit Edward's eyelids, waking him from his slumber. Reflex forced his eyes open and then closed again from the glare. He blinked quickly to adjust himself to the sudden brightness and rose from his bed.

His head was pounding, and his body aching. He sat doubled over on the edge of the bed, holding the sides of his skull to hold back the beating, but it was no use.

"Finally awake, then?" Anne asked near the captain's

cabin window.

Edward glanced her way, the light from the sun behind her setting alight her auburn hair. He could barely see her face because of the luminance, but he could tell she was frowning from her arms folded in front of her chest. As soon as she moved, the sun shone directly on his eyes again.

"Agh," he shouted as he looked away. "Dammit, woman, you're killing me."

"No, I'm afraid the drink is to blame from your woes," she replied. She walked over to a barrel secured in the corner of the room, lifted the top of the cask and dunked a cup inside. "Here, drink this," she said as she walked over with the cup.

Edward took the cup and drank the contents. The water, mixed with enough rum to sanitize it, felt good on his tongue.

"We've landed in Puerto Plata for a quick restock and regrouping. The sun will set soon, and we need to decide where to go from here and what to do about recent... revelations."

Edward looked up into his wife's pained eyes. They seemed on the edge of tears, mourning for his situation.

"We're quite the pair, aren't we?" Edward said, casting his gaze on his half-filled cup. "Both our parents want us dead."

Anne lifted Edward's chin up. She still had the glow of the sun surrounding her long red curls. "They aren't our family any longer." Anne stroked Edward's cheek, running her hand down his long black beard before giving it a light tug. "The men and women on this ship are your family now, and they're all that matters."

Edward nodded and forced a smile for his wife. Her sentiment made his heart swell, but it wasn't enough to quell the storm bubbling beneath.

Anne gave him a kiss on his forehead and sat down next to him, not saying another word, but holding him as he continued drinking the water.

"Could it be he just didn't approve of the beard?" Edward joked, giving Anne a sidelong glance with a grin.

Anne looked a bit shocked at first, but chuckled after a moment. "Perhaps you should cut it off and try again?"

Edward laughed with his wife and then gave her a peck on the cheek before resting his head on hers. For a moment, they sat in silence together, embracing each other in solidarity and strength.

"This doesn't change anything," Edward said eventually. "The only thing that's changed is how I must now seek out answers from him. He still abandoned me, abandoned Herbert, tried to kill all of us with foolish trials, and more directly. He's not the man I once called my father."

Anne pulled away from Edward and cocked her brow. "You can't mean that you're still going to kill him? Edward…"

Edward opened his mouth, but for a moment, the words wouldn't come. "I… I know in my mind that if I want this family to survive, and if *I* want to survive, he needs to die." He stared at his cup for a moment. "What I'll do when I face him next, I cannot say. But I need to face him."

"Then I'll stand by you when that happens. *We* will," Anne said, placing her hand on Edward's.

Edward smiled, this time more genuinely, and held his wife's hand. They once more sat in silence as Edward finished his water. After it was empty, Edward let go of Anne's hand and rose from the bed.

"Could you gather the senior officers to the quarterdeck cabin? I must tell everyone of my intent."

Anne nodded, gripped Edward's hand for another second, then rose to her feet to leave the Captain's Cabin. Edward watched her as she left, and just before she exited the room, she glanced back his way and smiled at him.

Edward let out a long sigh after Anne left the room, and he lay back in his bed. The weathered boards of Caribbean pine above him suddenly felt unfamiliar and no longer like his home of the last few years. Even the bed appeared lumpier and uncomfortable, though he admitted to himself that the stab wound could be to blame.

He had to get up. He couldn't dwell on his thoughts for long. He could feel the creeping sensation coming at the back of his head, and his legs began to itch.

Edward got up and dressed in his standard attire, save for

his tricorn hat. He left that behind, but donned his longcoat, given that night was approaching. Following a visual inspection in a mirror, he left the captain's cabin.

He headed through the gun deck to the ladder leading to the weather deck. On his way, several crewmates tipped their caps and inquired about his health. He gave a few short words telling them not to worry and that he was doing much better now.

On the weather deck, a cold salty wind hit Edward's face and hands on his ascent. The sun was just hitting the horizon, but its warmth had all but vanished.

Edward passed by many a crewmate, some lounging, some testing the myriad rigging ropes and knots, and others conversing about what had happened. Their voices grew silent as Edward approached before quickly returning with concerned tones passed along by well-worn phrases asking of his condition.

After repeating the same words he'd said to the crewmates below deck, he laughed off their concern, ensuring that all knew he was in good spirits despite the opposite being true. After wading his way through the throngs, he entered the quarterdeck cabin—the war room, as they called it.

Inside the war room, a smell of musty tomes and gunpowder wafted his way as he entered. The room had its fair share of old books and maps littering tables and cabinets, lending their essence to the ship's wooden architecture.

At the main table, a large oval table stood beneath an ornate chandelier, and on an equally lavish red velvet carpet covering most of the room. Around the table, Anne, William, and Alexandre were sitting in chairs, as Victoria read one of the books on the port side of the room. Christina, her arms folded, leaned against the starboard side of the cabin next to her brother, Herbert, who sat in his wheelchair facing parallel to the entrance to the room.

Upon hearing the door open, all eyes turned towards Edward, and Herbert turned his wheelchair around to watch Edward enter. Herbert's eyes and expression were inscrutable, a mix of confusion or pity or anger which Edward couldn't pin down. He chose to ignore it.

He walked over to his high-backed chair on the other side of the oval table as the heat of all those eyes bore down on him. After sitting down, his back as straight as he could manage with his wound, he stared down each person in the room for a few seconds before lingering a touch longer on Herbert.

"We missed our golden opportunity in Tortuga. There's no use in dwelling on my mistakes, so let's focus on correcting them," Edward said. He turned to Victoria, who still had the book she was reading in hand. "We go back to the original plan and dismantle Calico Jack's empire. Where was Silver Eyes located, Victoria?"

Victoria opened her mouth to respond, but Christina interrupted her. "We're not to talk of what happened?" she said, her hand half-raised in the air, emphasizing her incredulity. "Are we living in some fantasy where you expect us to ignore that we're talking about your father?"

Edward clenched his teeth. "What of it?" he seethed. "Does it change what he's done to us all? Does it change the undeniable fact that he wants us dead?"

"It changes you. Doesn't it?" Christina asked, her tone of anger shifting to concern. "We all know that part of the reason you went to sea was to find your father. It may not have been the focus, but it was always there. And now you find out that the person who's been pulling your strings, who abused and nearly killed everyone in this room, including your wife, and more, is your father, alive and well? Which also means he truly did abandon you as a child." The room was silent, and even the sound outside the cabin couldn't penetrate the tension left by Christina's plain levelling of the facts. "You mean to say you're still willing to kill him, despite knowing he's your father?" She glanced at the others in the cabin. "Come now," she called. "I cannot be the only one who has doubts."

After another moment of silence, Herbert looked up at Edward. His expression had changed, but Edward still couldn't read him. "I also have questions," he said first, "but, Edward, if you say you're still going to see this through, then I won't doubt you. You've taken us this far, and I'm sure that this only makes you want to confront him even more."

"You can't expect him to kill his own father, can you?" Christina shouted. "Are you mad?"

Herbert turned in his wheelchair to face his sister directly. "Christina, shut it. This is bigger than you or me now." He turned back around, considering the matter done.

Edward stared at Herbert for a moment, trying to read him, but gained nothing. "I plan on seeing this through to the end, as promised."

Herbert paused for a few seconds and then nodded. "That's good enough for me," he said.

Christina clenched her jaw tight enough to bite her tongue, and then stormed out of the room, slamming the door behind her.

Herbert's expression didn't change from before, and he didn't even glance over his shoulder when the door crashed against the frame. "Shall we move on then?"

Edward began the discussion and proposed again that they should move back to the original plan and go after either Silver Eyes or Copper Legs. The only one they had reliable information on was Silver Eyes, so they decided to go after him.

Copper Legs was always on the move, so it was hard to pinpoint her location at any given moment. From their information, she was never too far behind where Calico Jack was, but everyone agreed that it was too dangerous to go back to Tortuga.

After making the decision, they gathered the crew, and Anne proposed a vote. With a few deft words and Edward's reassuring presence, the crew seemed placated and didn't bring up the recent revelations. Edward was happy to not have to broach the subject in further detail over and over and hoped this would be the end of it.

With the vote cast, the crew slept, awaiting tomorrow when they would set sail. Edward, however, was restless.

He tossed and turned in his bed as the gentle rocking of the ship did its best to lull him to sleep, but a nagging feeling pricked the back of his mind. Warning chills travelled down his spine as though he saw a subtle grey cloud out of thousands.

Herbert had acted strange, and Edward had to check on him to alleviate at least one of his worries.

He stepped out of bed and donned some basic clothes. Anne roused with the rustling, her hand reaching out to the empty space where Edward was supposed to be, and she was instantly awake and alert. Her eyes soon found him in the dim light of the moon filtering through the windows in their cabin.

"Edward, are you well?"

Edward smiled, though he wasn't sure if she could see. "All is well, I simply feel I need some of the night air," he said, walking back to the bed and leaning over to give his wife a kiss. "I will be by your side again soon, worry not."

Anne said nothing, and Edward didn't wait for a reply. He rose again and went to open the cabin doors. Before he was through, Anne finally called to him again. "Edward?" she said in a near whisper. Edward stopped and looked her way. "You know I love you, right?"

To Edward, her wording conveyed a message of support as well as a declaration. "Of course," he replied simply. "You know that I, too, love you?"

Anne grinned, reassured by his words. "Of course," she mimicked.

Edward smiled again and closed the door behind him, heading into the gun deck.

On the gun deck, the thirty twenty-two-pound cannons remained secured in place with heavy lines attached to the back of them and to the side of the ship. Nary a crewmate was in sight, save a few men keeping watch and having a lively but quiet conversation about which mate's wife cooked the best pie.

Edward passed by them with a nod of his head when they looked his way. The lot returned his gesture with a "Captain," before returning to the debate over spices and pie preparations.

In the infirmary, Alexandre and Victoria were still awake, speaking in French while preparing what Edward thought was medicine. He steered away from the open door, not wishing to turn into a subject of whatever concoction they were making.

He headed down the ladder into the orlop deck to the crew's quarters, brig, and various other parts of the ship just above the waterline.

No matter where Edward looked, he couldn't find Herbert, nor his wheelchair. He wasn't sleeping, he wasn't conversing with the crewmates awake in the communal area, and none awake were able to give a hint of where he was either.

His worry deepened when he noticed Christina sound asleep. The two were never far apart, and even their sleep patterns often matched each other. Only in times of distress would Edward sometimes find Herbert on the weather deck, unable to sleep, as Edward often was.

Edward rushed up the ladders to the gun deck and then to the weather deck, grabbing one of his coats hanging on a hook before heading into the frigid air above.

On the weather deck, several crewmates were milling about, talking with each other and keeping their eyes open for any suspect activity around the port. They were also in charge of ensuring the ship was ready to leave at dawn before switching with the other crewmates sleeping below.

Edward couldn't see Herbert anywhere, and even a quick glance in the quarterdeck cabin proved fruitless.

"What'cha lookin' for, Cap'n?" one of the crewmates on watch asked.

"I'm looking for Herbert," he replied. "I need to talk with him about something, but he's not on the ship as far as I can tell."

"Aye. He went inta town not an hour ago, I'd wager. Said he was tryna gather some last-minute supplies. Had a big pack with him as well."

Edward's face must have contorted into a look of massive shock, as the crewmates around began to ask if he was well. Herbert was planning on leaving on his own, Edward was sure of it. Leaving the ship in the middle of the night just before he was to helm it, and with a large pack full of supplies, no less. It was so unlike his usual activities, there could be no other explanation.

"I am well, gentlemen, return to your duties," he said after a moment to regain his composure. "I think I'll find our man Herbert and bring him back. The hour is late, and he needs to be fit and fresh for tomorrow."

With a few final words to the crew on board, Edward stalked towards the town of Puerto Plata with purpose. There were only two places Herbert could be: either somewhere in the port, talking with ship's crews to seek passage, or in an inn for the same purpose. He didn't have much time before they lost Herbert, so he had to work fast.

Edward started by going ship to ship himself, asking the crew still awake if they had seen or talked with a man in a wheelchair. Many affirmed they had spoken with such a man who had been seeking passage to Tortuga, and even offered a fair bit of coin for it too, but was turned away because Tortuga was a lawless pirate haven.

Dammit, Herbert. What are you thinking?

Tracing each ship's account of where Herbert went next, Edward found a man who pointed towards town. One ship's mate said he directed Herbert to a local inn to talk with his captain about passage, as they would be sailing close to Tortuga at dawn.

Edward thanked the crew of the ship and rushed to the inn in question. Thankfully it wasn't far from the port, and he was there in a matter of minutes.

Inside, the inn was a typical, ordinary establishment with a large interior parlour in which guests could eat and drink. At this time of night, there were scant men in the room, with only a few at a table and another couple in the corner, as well as a man Edward assumed was the owner's son tending to them.

Edward quickly found the familiar back of Herbert's wheelchair, a large pack, stuffed to the brim, slung over the back. He was conversing with the sailors at the table, a jovial discussion to be sure, and one in which Edward was sure Herbert had already secured passage, going by the tone.

Edward took a breath to calm himself and take stock of just what he was going to do. He could force Herbert back to the ship, but to what end? If Edward thought about it for but a moment, it was clear Herbert was trying to save him the pain of facing his father, as well as secure revenge. However foolish the plan was, stopping him needed tact.

Wait... What exactly is his plan? Infiltrate Jack's crew to get close to him and assassinate him? Jack never saw his face in Tortuga. He could do it... and then die in the process. But everyone else would be safe...

Edward's thoughts turned to his beloved Anne and the rest of his crew. His father was the cause of many of their miseries, and by asking them to fight, they would be putting their lives on the line to solve his family problems.

Maybe Herbert has it right, Edward thought, a plan forming in his mind.

He walked towards the table, grabbing a chair along the way, and went up beside Herbert to sit down with the rest of the men.

"So," Edward said as he sat down, and all eyes turned towards him, "have you secured us passage to Tortuga, my friend?" Edward looked at Herbert directly for a moment, and after the shock left Herbert's eyes, Edward gave him a single nod, hoping to convey his plan with that subtle gesture and his open question.

After another moment, and a grin, Herbert nodded back. "Ah, yes, gentlemen, I owe you my most sincere apologies. My friend here, Edward Teach, was also seeking passage, if you would have us both. He could help in sailing as well. You will find no more skilled a sailor than he, I can assure you."

Herbert repaid Edward's hope tenfold—the years they had spent together, the talks they had had, the promises they had made to each other. They had built a relationship of trust and awareness of the other. Edward had known there was something off about Herbert's earlier words, and Herbert knew what Edward had wanted to do at that moment.

"As long as he can pay the price, then your friend is more than welcome," the captain replied. "We've no fear of where we've gone before. We hunt whales, and those beasts have nothing on those prancing rogues in Tortuga."

Edward found out the price of passage, paid it, and after some introductions, he did his best to make a good impression on his new host. Though, with the price of passage,

Edward doubted it would matter what kind of man he was.

Another hour passed, and the captain and his men finished drinking and eating and left for the ship to prepare.

"And, Captain, as discussed, and as was included in the price we paid, your crew's discretion is most appreciated," Herbert said.

"You've no need to have your boots quivering, young master Blackstad. I'll be sure to let my crew know that we've no stowaways or new crewmates aboard today. Only old mates that've been with us for years," the captain replied with a wink.

Outside the inn, the captain, his crew, and Edward and Herbert all made their way to the harbour. Herbert was slowing down in wheeling himself forward, prompting the captain to turn around and check on him.

"You and your men go on ahead, we'll catch up," Herbert said. After a moment to give them some room, Herbert shot Edward a nasty look. "I was doing this for you, you bastard. What are you doing?"

"Tch," Edward spat. "I know what you're doing, and you're getting yourself killed, that's what. I'm here to save you from yourself."

Herbert's face softened. "From what just happened, I know that means you won't be taking me back to the *Queen Anne's Revenge.*"

"No," Edward affirmed.

"So," Herbert began, then stopped wheeling himself forward for a moment. "Are you sure you can do this? I know I said I before that I wouldn't doubt you, but my sister was right. This changes things."

"It means that I need to do this more than before. My father has done so many wrongs, killed so many of my men. I can't put this burden on the crew any longer."

Herbert had a stern look on his face. "If Roberts were here, he would tell you that your father's sins are not your responsibility and share some scripture to prove his point. You are not your father's keeper."

"That is a nice sentiment, but not practical. If I allow my father to continue what he's doing unimpeded, then that would be a greater sin."

Herbert nodded. "I guess I have no more objections," he said. "We should catch up if we're going to make it. The price I paid was to leave well before dawn."

Edward and Herbert began hurrying towards the harbour. "Just as a curiosity, how do you plan on masking yourself from Calico Jack and his men? They know your face now."

Edward smiled. "I have a plan for that," he replied.

Edward stepped out of the barber-surgeon's room aboard their temporary ship as it was sailing towards Tortuga. His face no longer held the mass of black hair with which he had become known. He was clean-shaven, aside from the nicks here and there left by the barber's blade.

Herbert sized up his captain without his beard and appeared unimpressed. "I don't know if I can get used to this," he said. "You look but a boy now."

"Then that means it'll work," Edward replied.

"I suppose." Herbert stared at the blank canvas that was Edward's chin for a moment more before looking him in the eyes. "Ready?"

Edward nodded. "Ready."

3. COURSE CORRECTION

Unease forced Anne awake. The pre-dawn air and a feeling of unease chilled her to the bone, needling her with her every movement. Edward was not next to her in bed still, and some of his last words echoed in her mind.

"I will be by your side again soon, worry not."

Soon had come and gone as far as Anne was concerned, and something had felt off about the way he was acting. He was more restless these days, but a different kind of restless. Frequently it was one of cold sweats and gasps for air. This had been an inquisitive restlessness. A search for answers.

But what was the question? Anne pondered.

She sat up, cleared her mind, and let the rocking waves guide her breathing. Meditation was an early lesson in mindfulness she had been taught when learning to fight. A healthy mind and a healthy body went hand in hand, but meditation had other uses as well. She reflected on the day's events, tumultuous as they were, to find out what was plaguing her husband so she could trace his steps.

It didn't take her long to come to an answer. "Herbert," she said aloud.

Anne rose from the bed and donned her clothes, and it was then that she noticed Edward's cutlass hanging from a chair, firmly in its scabbard. Its presence wormed more worry into Anne's mind. It meant, if Anne was right, that Edward was confident he was going to be coming back and forgotten it, or that the golden blade was too conspicuous and he couldn't be seen with it.

Anne swore under her breath and rushed to the weather deck. There, the crewmates on the night watch were talking amongst themselves. Their shift would end with the earliest rays of the morning light, which were quickly approaching.

"The captain has gone ashore, has he not?" Anne asked

as she approached the men.

The men dropped what they were doing for their quartermaster. "Aye, ma'am, he went not two hours a'fore."

"And Herbert before him, I imagine?" she said, annoyance evident in her tone.

"A... Aye," the crewmate replied, fear breeding hesitation.

"Dad dammit!" she cursed. "Drop everything you're doing and search the harbour for them. Ask every ship if they took notice of a man in a wheelchair and a fearsome man with a black beard."

"Ma'am?" the crewmate asked.

Anne folded her arms. "Herbert and the captain are about to abscond to pursue Calico Jack on their own. We haven't much time if we mean to stop the fools before they leave the harbour," she explained. "Now go!"

The crewmates on deck hopped to their feet and rushed off the gangplank to the harbour. They quickly split up and began asking the men milling about preparing to leave for their captain and helmsman.

Anne gazed upon the harbour to both sides of the *Queen Anne's Revenge*. Ships dotted the angled harbour, each with crews preparing to leave, each of them a merchant or trading vessel and each, unlike a pirate ship, needing to be on the move early to ensure they met their predetermined shipping times and made the money they were promised.

Anne's faculty of memory was a work in progress. She didn't have perfect clarity that Alexandre seemed to possess or the recall that Christina had built up over time, but she was close. After a few minutes, she was confident that at least two ships had already left the harbour. She scanned the horizon but couldn't see any others. If Edward and Herbert had been on one of those ships, there was no chance of finding exactly where they were going.

Anne soon received her answer by the hand of an errand boy and in the form of a letter addressed to her.

Dearest Anne,

With the recent revelations, I can no longer in good conscience allow the crew to take part in this family matter. Herbert and I plan to end this ourselves. When you hear the news of our enemy's passing, come to his former base of operations. It will be safe then.

You'll be safe then.

I love you,

Edward

Anne crumpled the paper and tossed it in the ocean with a huff. The errand boy, waiting to see if Anne wanted to send a letter herself, looked afraid and confused. She handed him a coin and sent him on his way.

She walked over to the edge of the ship, looking over the port side and up and down the harbour. Her gaze eventually caught one of the crewmates searching for Edward, and after a moment, their eyes met, and he stopped in his tracks. She motioned a circle in the air, telling the crewmate to gather the others and return to the ship. He nodded, letting her know he understood before going about his task.

She turned around and rested on the port railing. She closed her eyes and tilted her head back, letting the sea breeze flow over her.

"What now?" she muttered aloud.

There was only one choice that didn't involve them rushing into an obvious trap—the only one that could help before heading to Nassau, and possibly to help Edward as well.

"On to Los Huecos then."

"This is foolish!" Christina shouted, accentuated by a slam of her fist on the war room's ornate table. "My brother's obviously going to Nassau to kill Edward's fa—" Christina paused, the word hanging on her tongue like a curse she dared not utter. "To kill Calico Jack," she finished.

"And what if they plan on heading to Tortuga instead?" Anne countered. "What if both of us are wrong, and we step into enemy territory no closer to recovering Edward and Herbert?" Her tone held a hint of the anger Christina was displaying openly, betraying her genuine emotions like a grey cloud on the horizon. Anne's ire was there, just as the approaching storm, but she had control over it, unlike her junior.

Christina barreled onward, not pausing to think over her words. "Then at least we can finish the job in their stead." She reeled back as soon as the words left her mouth, as though she knew it was a fool's errand, but she kept going to save face. "It's no different if we head to Los Huecos. There we face certain danger in attacking Silver Eyes, and have no clue if that's where Edward and Herbert are heading."

Anne levelled her simmering gaze on Christina, the gouging look of royalty that forces the haughty to kneel lest they wish to be impaled. "Then you are more a fool than I took you for," she said flatly, letting her eyes do the talking. "Sit down," she added softly, but the words fell with the thunder of a command in the still air of the room.

Christina locked up for but a moment, her expression souring in the face of Anne's dangerous gaze and her own foolish comment, and then sat down in her seat with a thud.

"We head to Los Huecos not just for the off chance it is one of the three spots Edward and Herbert could be going, but because it's the safest option we have. Nassau is Calico Jack's base; we have no support there, not in numbers or knowledge." Anne kept her gaze on Christina, though she was slumped in her chair. "Thanks to Victoria," she said with a wave in her direction, "we know the island's original inhabitants have been forced under Calico Jack's thumb. We can use that to our advantage. The best that could happen is we help Edward and Herbert in whatever it is they're trying to do next and join up with them there. The worst is that we keep Calico Jack's allies occupied for them."

Christina had crossed her arms as though she were protecting herself from Anne's attacks. Her face bloomed the flushed look of an embarrassed youth.

Anne let out a sigh and relaxed in the high-backed chair Edward usually sat in. "I won't lie to you," she began, her tone softening as though she'd just remembered she was talking to a young woman, not an adult, "Edward and Herbert are most likely trying to assassinate Calico Jack." She let the words hang, like a silent prayer for the plan to succeed, as she eyed those in the room—from Alexandre to Victoria, and over to William before finally resting back on Christina. "If we go to Tortuga, we die. If we go to Nassau, we die."

Christina shuffled in her seat a bit before grinding out, "I know, Dad dammit. You don't have to rake me over the coals for it." After the shuffle, she absent-mindedly grabbed the wooden rose around her neck, a sure sign to Anne, and possibly most in the room, that she was agitated.

The rose, so delicate in its craftsmanship, was a memento from Ochi, Nassir's son, who had passed in a battle years ago and caused a rift between Nassir and Edward. Anne took the remembrance of that time as a clear sign that she couldn't allow what happened then to happen now between her and Christina. The crew needed unity now more than ever.

"You're right, I don't," Anne replied. "But I do need you on my side. I can't manage this crew without a helmsman."

It took a moment for Christina to notice the unasked question. When she did, she looked up at Anne, then over at William, as though she were wondering why her and not him.

Anne shrugged. "William will be busy as quartermaster when I take on the role of captain until Edward returns. And while I know a bit of reading clouds and steering the ship, I'm no match for you or your brother." Anne spun a convincing lie with just the right amount of frustration filtering into her voice to match the audience's perceptions of her.

The truth was that Christina was still wet behind the ears and needed practice without her brother there for guidance. She was like a rider taking the reins for the first time. At first, if the horse is ill-tempered or not used to the rider's voice or touch, a familiar hand can prove useful. If the rider isn't left alone, before long, that familiar hand turns into a crutch. Christina needed to take the reins alone to gain the confidence necessary to tame the beast that was the *Queen Anne's Revenge*.

The lie worked, and Christina's face lit up with joy as a smile spread across it. "I'll do it!" she said, brimming with bravado. "I'll be your helmsman!"

4. CAPTAIN'S ORDERS

Over the few days' travel from Puerto Plata to Tortuga, Edward and Herbert ingratiated themselves with the crew of whalers and sailors on the *Hunter* through demanding work and a good share of stories.

Their tales of hollowed island puzzles, savage natives ready to sacrifice an outsider, and run-ins with a Spanish galleon and pirates took on a note of tall tales in the ears of the humble, honest men aboard their host vessel. They listened attentively as Edward and Herbert went back and forth, telling their version of events, laughing as the two men bickered over the finer details, and all the while shaking their heads at the foolishness of it all.

It made a difference that Edward and Herbert both neglected to mention they were captain and helmsman. They also didn't correct the men's thought that they had been travellers aboard a different ship in each tale.

The men laughed all the harder when one of their own snidely remarked that the two were bad luck if it were all true, and jested that if any hint of a storm showed they should be cast into the ocean to save themselves the trouble.

The laughing stopped when Edward removed his sweat-soaked shirt in the middle of travel one day, showing off his multitude of scars across his large barrel of a chest and muscular back. That night, the attentive audience was a bit quieter when Edward told of a wounded man who sniffed a mysterious poison that gave him speed and strength beyond that of an average man.

During the travel, Edward's sudden shift from being a captain of over a hundred souls to a lowly deckhand jarred him in an at first confusing but ultimately relaxing way. Not having responsibility over dozens of men at a time, juggling being a kind yet firm measure of authority, lifted a weight from his shoulders he hadn't known was there.

At the same time, he had to catch himself several times before he chastised his new crewmates and issued orders beyond his station. Each time it was minor, but he had to bite his tongue lest he sour the relationship between the men giving him passage and they did indeed throw him and Herbert overboard.

Herbert, it seemed, enjoyed the lack of responsibility even more than Edward, and for a good reason, as the crew expected exactly nothing of him. A few gave him dark looks the first day when he got in the way of more than a few men milling about tending to ship's duties, only holding back from swearing and smacking him because he'd paid his way. After warming to the duo, it turned to simply ignoring him as he stared off at nothing on the horizon.

Edward mused to himself that he wasn't the only one with a hidden weight that needed lifting.

It also took Edward a goodly amount of time to adjust to taking orders. More than a few times, the captain and first mate of the *Hunter* had to repeat orders to him, even shouting his fake name, Teach, louder for him to come to his senses.

It was a valuable lesson and one he was glad he learned now on a ship they'd paid passage for rather than when aboard an enemy ship where their only protection would be their false identities.

When they arrived in Tortuga, it was with a warm cup of whiskey and a smile and a wave from each of the ship's crew. Edward was glad for the time in many ways, as soon, he suspected, there would be no smiles to spare.

"There it is," Herbert commented delightedly.

Edward's gaze followed Herbert's outstretched hand as he pointed towards a ship stationed in the harbour. It flew the familiar flag of one of Calico Jack's crew, a white, symmetrical skull with crossed swords underneath it, but the burnished copper trim around the edges of it denoted that it was for one of his subordinates. The flag flapped towards the two men as though it were a supple young lady beckoning them closer, but Edward knew the lady to be a siren in disguise, and so he steeled his mind appropriately.

"Herbert, whatever happens next, don't question me. Understood?"

Herbert looked over to Edward with a confused, half-cocked expression. Before he could ask Edward what he meant, Edward spoke again.

"I need you to promise me first, then I'll tell you what I plan to do. I don't want to have to order you as your captain, but I will."

Herbert glanced back at the flag, then down briefly to the dock, his chin soon setting as hard as a lock. He gave Edward a nod and said, "Understood."

"From what we've seen from Calico Jack's crew, and from what you've told me, they value strength above all else."

Herbert stroked his chin. "That is true. Before Cache-Hand could become part of their crew, he had to capture a Spanish galleon. A near-impossible feat. It makes one wonder what strange acts the others had to do to prove themselves to Mad Jack."

Edward grimaced at the casual mention of his former enemy, the pain of each inflicted wound returning to him, along with memories of dead crewmates' warm blood on his hands and the sick smell of death in his nose. A thousand thoughts like silent needles stabbed his skin and mind, and his hand and heart began to shake. He reached inside his breast pocket with laboured movement, grabbing the flask held there, and hastily took a large drink from it.

Herbert was at a loss for words as he watched his captain drink. After a moment, he sputtered out a meek, "Sorry."

Edward forced a smile just as laboured as his hand's moving, then chuckled. "You have nothing to apologize for. That was for what's about to happen," Edward said before taking another drink. He then turned to face his friend and crewmate directly. "I'll be blunt," Edward began, "Calico Jack's crew doesn't like cripples. If we both want on that ship, we need to prove to them you're not going to be a burden. We can't expect them to allow you passage with some coin, and they will have a helmsman currently, so they have no need of another."

"So, what do you propose?" Herbert asked.

"We ask them what we need to do to be a part of their crew, and whatever they ask for, I'll do the work of two men." Edward pointed towards himself with his thumb, full of the confidence that comes partly from being a foolhardy young man, and partly from frequent imbibements.

Thinking the matter settled, Edward headed towards the ship. "That's not a very good plan," Herbert shouted after him.

"Have you a better one?" Edward replied over his shoulder as Herbert rolled up next to him.

"No, I suppose I don't," he replied with the sulky tone of a chided child.

Edward leaned a bit closer to Herbert, trying to talk secretly over the din of the surrounding town and harbour. "Also, I think it best if we were brothers for this. More reason for us to stay together than just being friends. We'll be the Blackstads, travelling and trying to find work as sailors but not finding luck."

Herbert touched his nose and grinned. "I see, brother. So… why are we trying to join so obvious a pirate ship?"

"Better a wolf than a sheep," he replied with a shrug.

"I suppose that's as good a reason as any."

Edward and Herbert passed by many rough-looking sailors preparing to leave in the early morning. The hour was late, and these were not merchants who lived by the hours of a well-wound clock but were pirates who struck in the midday when ships aplenty were found in the vast and plentiful trade routes along the Caribbean Sea.

However, Edward was interested to see there were more than a few men like those they had been with earlier, a few whaling ships looking for hardened men who weren't afraid to face down a beast half the size of the ship they were about to travel on. A few others were merchants Edward suspected served as middlemen to ill-gotten gains, closer to pirates than merchants, but with a foot firmly in the trade business. They had gained the respect of the pirates who frequented these parts, whether through might or connections Edward could not tell.

Upon reaching the pirate's ship, the mates bringing cargo aboard gave them wary glances. All of them were battle-hardened; the faint grey-white of faded scars and the dark lines of sliced and reformed skin protruded and poked out from behind woollen longshirts and beneath messy cleft hair. More than a few had tattoos blackening part of their necks or faces, a brand of their well-worn travels for some, and, from his dark complexion, a tribal honorific for another. Edward read the words "Hold Fast" across one man's knuckles, saw constellation across the back of another's hand, and on the dark-complexioned man were segmented lines in a stunning wave-like pattern across half his face.

Edward leaned down slightly and whispered to Herbert. "You still have those hidden implements in your chair, yes?"

Herbert nodded. "Aye, along with a few other surprises our friend Nassir made for me. I'm never too far from something with which to defend myself."

Herbert spoke of the *Queen Anne's Revenge's* shipwright, who doubled as a wheelchair expert when it came to Herbert's condition. The most recent addition was hidden compartments only he could reach with weapons at the ready should Herbert need them, and apparently that wasn't all.

"Good," Edward said. "We may have use for them."

Edward and Herbert continued their advance to the gangplank of the ship. It was a two-masted light brigantine with a single deck, and Edward estimated about thirty or so cannons aboard. It would be fast and efficient in any fight, and with a skilled commander it might even give the *Queen Anne's Revenge* a challenge. Emblazoned in large white letters on the side was the name of the ship, *Black Blood*, a singular contrast with the words written as they were neither black nor red, but it got the point across. The ship and the men aboard it were not to be trifled with.

"What d'ye want?" a gruff man asked as Edward and Herbert approached. He held his hand aloft in front of him, stopping the men.

The man wasn't tall but built like a rough sailor used to

the harsh rigours of a ship at sea with all the right callouses in all the wrong spots. He also had the marks of battle across his face, arms, and no doubt all over his body. His face looked a weathered mess of white scars, pocks from some childhood condition, and broken and healed bones. He couldn't have been that much older than Edward, perhaps in his thirties, but he looked much older.

"We're looking for work and heard you were looking for a few good men to join you on the seas," Edward replied.

The man spat on the pier. The mucous glob stayed mostly intact as it splayed on the grubby wooden planks. Edward and Herbert's gaze followed the spit and the motion of the man's head as he looked back on them. "That's a lie," he said flatly. "No one 'ere would'a told ye ta try joinin' us, less they want ye dead."

Edward noticed the man's hand lower and rest on his hip, near the hilt of his cutlass. He could feel the air around him thicken with eyes watching him more intently now.

Edward inched his own hand to his hip and felt nothing. He remembered he was unarmed, his golden cutlass left behind because he had forgotten it.

A bead of sweat formed on his forehead and rolled down the side of his cheek.

"Nigel, fuck off with that, would ye?" a gruff woman's voice called from the deck.

"But ma'am, we best be leavin' soon if'n we're gonna catch the bastard what done in Jeremiah."

The owner of the voice strode to the port side of the deck and leaned on the railing, her right arm resting lazily across it while her left held steady on her hip. The look was casual, but Edward saw a coiled snake ready to strike at a moment's notice. She could jump over the railing to the deck, or just as quickly pull a knife from behind her, and any number of things in between.

"He's not going anywhere a few minutes won't change. Bring them aboard," the woman said before eyeing Edward and Herbert up and down. "If you're able," she added before casting a sidelong glance at Herbert's chair and walking away from the railing.

Blackbeard's Blood

The man guarding the gangplank stepped aside, letting Edward and Herbert board. Herbert went first, and Edward helped push him up the steep incline and force his wheelchair over the lip of the deck. He landed on the sole with a loud snap of wood on wood, gaining the attention of the other crewmates who had been paying them no heed until then.

Now on deck, Edward was able to get a better look at the woman who appeared to be in charge—Grace 'Copper Legs' O'Malley, by Edward's estimation.

Her coal-red hair was cropped short and, if not for her attractive features, would have made her look more a boy than a woman. Her body was voluptuous and well figured, with plenty of meat on her bones and quite different from the women on his ship, but from what Edward could tell, it was all muscle.

"My, my, you are a big one, aren't ye?" she said as she eyed Edward up and down, her voice drawn out with a hint of Gaelic on the edges. Her accent was faint, as though weathered away after years away from home. The barest hint remained like single boulder on a sandy beach.

She walked around Edward, poring over him, studying his features beneath his loose clothes. Though she was far shorter than he, and shorter than most of the men aboard, her gaze made Edward feel exposed. A woman he should be wary of was measuring him against some unknown weights.

Edward clenched his jaw and returned the gaze. He needed to project strength, match her, and beat her at her own game to impress her. He needed her to need him more than how little she would feel she needed Herbert. And so, he scrutinized her in return.

She was built like the northern mothers he had heard about from other sailors telling stories—the mothers who could match the men in feats of strength and could cook you dinner after breaking your arm in an arm-wrestling match. He had thought they were jovial jesting meant as a tall tale of boasting, or a jibe when the sailor lost a match but claimed his mother could whup the other sailor handily. Edward now suspected they weren't just stories.

Most striking was her legs, or that which covered her legs. She had on solid copper greaves, which covered her feet, calves, and knees, stopping just short of her thighs. Edward could see small indents and holes in symmetrical vertical lines on either side of the front of the armour, but they didn't look like bullet holes from battle, they looked to be there by design. What design they served, Edward could not even guess.

The medieval armour seemed out of place on a wood-and rope-and canvas-laden ship, but not so out of place on her, perhaps. Her hair nearly matched the shade of the greaves, and she walked in them with no sign of hindrance.

He noticed her looking straight at him, and so he ended his inspection and returned her steely gaze.

After a moment, O'Malley nodded appreciatively. "I'll have to test you further, but for now, I think you'd make a good addition to our crew. You've obviously been hardened in battle, and you've got a sailor's calluses." She turned a sidelong look over to Herbert. "You, however, need to leave. We can't have you on our crew."

Just as Edward had predicted, but without the preamble given to him. No inquisitive inspection, no scrutinizing of his features, only a dismissal. Edward had known this would be difficult, but he hadn't thought it would be *this* difficult.

"This man is my brother. Wherever I go, he goes."

"We don't have cripples on our ship," she replied curtly. "They slow us down." She let out a sigh. "Off my ship then, the both of you. No more wasting my time."

With a wave of her hand, some of the crew moved forward, pressing Edward and Herbert back to the gangplank.

"My brother has the best eyes you've seen. He's also the best man at the helm you could ever want."

"I already have a helmsman," the captain replied as she walked away. Then she glanced over her shoulder. "Besides, I don't like the look of him. All I've seen from his eyes are hatred, he's like a cornered dog ready to strike."

Edward flashed Herbert a glance and noticed she was right. Herbert had the same look in his eyes he'd had when they'd faced off against Gregory Dunn, one of Calico Jack's other crewmates, and a crewmate Herbert had personally known.

Thinking on his feet as the crew pressed in on them further, Edward created a convenient excuse. "How can you blame him? Five of your crewmates have had their weapons at the ready from the moment we stepped onto the deck."

This stopped the captain in her tracks for a moment, and, as though they had eyes in the back of their heads, the crewmates pushing them off the ship stopped as well.

"There were six, Ed," Herbert chimed in. "You missed the one with his hand on the hilt of a cutlass hidden by the fife rail." Herbert pointed to a man standing half behind the mainmast.

Edward followed the finger to the man, and with the too-casual, too-slow movement of a man caught in the act, the crewmate moved his hand from where it had rested to the top of the fife rail.

Edward looked over at O'Malley again, and she too had followed Herbert's pointed finger to the crewmate whose hands had been hidden from their view. When she turned her gaze back to Herbert, it was with a bit more scrutiny than before. Just a bit.

This was the opening that Edward needed. If he just pushed a bit more... "If you won't accept my brother as a crewmate, then accept him as a passenger. I'll do the work of two crewmates to make up for it." The words would have come out as pleading from any other man, but coming from Edward, they were a statement of fact.

O'Malley spat. "You'd have to work as hard as three men for all the trouble it'll be worth to bring him along." There was a pause as she glanced at the floorboards of the ship for a moment. Edward let her her peace as she thought it over. The tension in the air lifted as she considered. After another moment passed, she looked straight into Edward's eyes. "If you can pass our tests, you and your brother may join. For the moment."

Edward and Herbert glanced at each other, relief in their eyes but not reflected in their faces. This was just a step back on the plank, a small step to their final goal.

"I'm ready," Edward said, despite not knowing what was

going to happen next.

O'Malley eyed Edward skeptically. "Nigel, Tiege, Grant, get yer asses over here."

The man who had first accosted them when they'd tried to board stepped closer, along with two other men of equal stature and similarly weathered faces. All established sailors, all established fighters. All three were not ones Edward wanted to be facing in a fight, especially all at once. Especially in a test he needed to pass.

"Yes, ma'am?" Nigel asked, though to Edward it felt as though they all knew what was coming next.

Edward ignored the next words from the captain of the *Black Blood* and instead chose to take that time to steady his breathing and center himself. He breathed in through his nose the full, unfettered sea air tainted with hints of the vile town and odorous men around him. The smell threatened to break the calm he was forcing onto himself, but he pressed forward, and his heartbeat steadied.

Upon opening his eyes, the three men had surrounded him, the weight of their hard, blood-hungry eyes pressing on him from all sides. Edward focussed his senses on his immediate surroundings, filtering out the noises of gulls squawking above, of the wind rustling the trees and myriad sails along the harbour, of the shouting men and clamour of boots and wood knocking about. He filtered it all out just as he had been trained until it was just him and the three men.

Edward felt a shift behind him, and he stepped aside. One of the crewmates of the *Black Blood* stumbled past him, his balance shattered with a too-confident punch. Edward spun around and punched the staggered man in the back of the neck. The force, multiplied by Edward winding up as well as punching down due to his superior height, sent the man crashing to the floor of the deck. His chin hit the wood with a loud crack, and he lay there slack and unconscious.

Edward faced the other two men, who at first were shocked, then snarled in anger at their crewmate so quickly dispatched. Before they could rush Edward, O'Malley stopped them with a shout. They backed up a pace or two; one man calmed a bit with O'Malley's order, but the other,

Nigel, kept the snarl of anger plastered on his face. The more time passed, the angrier he seemed to get.

O'Malley walked over to the unconscious crewmate, her greaves clanking slightly as she nudged the man with her foot. She frowned.

"Impressive," she commented. "I suppose we don't need to see how well you fight if you can do that with one punch." She levelled her gaze at Edward. "Now I want to know how well you follow orders." O'Malley walked back behind Nigel and the other crewmate still conscious. "You're going to let these two fight you, and you will not fight back under any circumstances. I don't even want to see you block any of their punches. Hear me?"

Nigel's snarl turned into a sneer of glee at the prospect. Edward didn't like that look, nor what it meant.

"And what is this to prove, exactly?"

"As I said, it will show that you can take orders," she replied, her Gaelic hints making the words more sinister in their intention. "If I'm to be your captain, I need to know you will do what I say. I can't tell you how many come aboard, wide-eyed and ready to please, only to balk at taking orders from a woman. If I must beat it out of you now, all the better."

O'Malley's smile was even more sinister than Nigel's, and Edward started regretting their leaving the *Queen Anne's Revenge* already. He glanced over to Herbert, who was watching the scene with a mix of horror and coiled rage blanching his face. Edward guessed he was regretting a few things as well.

But they couldn't back down now.

"I won't be much use if I'm dead or have a broken bone," Edward said flatly. He knew there was no way out of this, but he had to try.

O'Malley grinned. "Don't worry yer pretty little head on that, son. The boys'll make sure not to damage the goods. Ain't that right, boys?"

"Yes, ma'am!" the two replied without looking back at their captain.

Edward took a deep breath and prepared for the onslaught.

5. THEY DON'T BOTHER US NONE

The sun was just past high noon when they caught sight of land on the horizon. The small speck of black jutting out on the horizon was still too far off to recognize colours, but was unmistakably a piece of earth in the middle of the vast ocean—too irregular and too small to be a storm, and, should Christina's navigation prove accurate, just in line with their calculations based on their maps and Victoria's approximations of where the island was located.

Anne, through her lookout on the crow's nest, coupled with a spyglass built into the wooden apparatus, was able to see the point of land well before her companions on deck. Unless particularly well endowed with vision above that of a normal man, they wouldn't be able to tell the land was there for some time yet.

"Land spotted," she shouted to Christina below. "Half point to port."

Christina nodded and repeated the order in a carrying voice she had been practicing for days. "Half point to port, aye Captain!"

The loud boom, almost unnatural coming from Christina's mouth, half-woke the wolf, Tala, lying underneath a nearby table. Anne could just make out the coppery-furred muzzle of the creature opening in a yawn as it looked around for a moment, and then, satisfied there was nothing of note occurring, went back to sleep.

Anne watched Christina turn the giant wheel of the helm clockwise, and the unseen rudder shifted with it. Slowly and imperceptibly, the ship drifted to port for a brief few seconds before Christina turned the wheel counterclockwise, and the ship levelled out at the new heading.

Christina, one hand holding the wheel steady, pored over a few instruments to double-check the heading, but Anne already knew her movements were correct. Christina was steadily treating the helm as an extension of herself, intuitively recognizing the shifting of the ship with each bob of the waves. She only needed the instruments for more significant changes or double-checking that the movement she saw and felt was correct.

Anne recalled a time during one of the trials left by the ship's previous owner, Benjamin Hornigold—whom they now knew to be Edward's father—where Christina had been able to navigate an ever-shifting maze. She had somehow managed to find her way through and back from the labyrinth by memorizing the changes and returning the way she had come. At the time, it had seemed nearly impossible, but Christina's mind and memory were unparalleled, and any other crewmate, even Anne herself, probably wouldn't have been able to manage the task.

That memory was a part of her; working out the way the ship moved, how it pitched and rolled, and how her movements of the wheel translated to movements of the ship. As she gained confidence, and provided that the crew followed orders, Anne didn't doubt that Christina could forgo using those instruments except in the direst of circumstances. The ship would become an extension of herself, like a sword to a fighter, until without thought she could wield it as though it were her own arm.

Anne stopped staring at Christina, then took one last look at the approaching land. Their course was righted, and if Victoria's information was correct, they would make landfall on the eastern side of the island farthest from the town Silver Eyes made his base in.

"Relief," Anne called out. William looked up to Anne, then ordered a crewmate up to the crow's nest.

Anne jumped over the side of the railing keeping her secure in the nest, and with deft hands trained over the years, she climbed down the rope ladders secured in a chaotic pattern from the mast to the deck. Her fingers were no longer the dainty fingers of a cultured woman; they were the rough fingers of a sailor sanded and scoured by handling rough rope, rough work, and the occasional rough rogue.

She landed with a thump on the quarterdeck and walked

over to Christina. The noise and jolt brought Anne a glance from Christina and the cautious animal underneath the table nearby. The younger woman's strawberry blond hair fanned out in a great wave across her back despite the tie holding it in at the base of her neck. As Anne came closer, she noticed that the wooden rose Christina typically wore around her neck was what kept her hair in place now.

She touched the rose, gently caressing the beautiful carving of Caribbean pine, the same as the *Queen Anne's Revenge*'s deck. As she did, Christina glanced over her shoulder and smiled, though tinged with sadness.

Christina pivoted on her heels, and the hair fell from Anne's hand. Christina then pulled her unruly hair over her shoulder in front of her, closer to her heart. "It looks nice on you," Anne said, smiling widely.

Christina looked at the rose as best she could as she ran her fingers through the wind-swept strands of her hair. "Thank you." She returned the smile, but it was the same marred smile as before. Then, after a reflective moment, her eyes focused on Anne's hip, and she pointed to the cutlass at Anne's side. "That looks nice on you as well," she said with a more genuine grin curling up at the corners.

Anne followed the finger to the golden cutlass, Edward's cutlass, resting on her hip in its sheath. She appreciated the unique steel at her side. It became a comfort against the anxious energy creeping up from her gut.

"A shame to waste a good weapon by saving it for the fool of a man who left it behind."

The two women chuckled at the barb for a moment, and Christina seemed back to her usual self. The worry creasing her forehead relaxed a touch, and she let out a large breath. She turned away from Anne and looked back to the horizon. "What do you think we'll find there?" Christina nodded her chin towards the open ocean.

Anne stepped forward and placed one hand on the quarterdeck railing just in front of the wheel, and another on the cutlass at her side. "Victoria said that the island is a major resource for Nassau, providing crops and other supplies to the pirate haven. I can't imagine the relationship is mutually beneficial, so perhaps we can convince the people around the island to join us."

Christina nodded. "And if we can't?"

Anne gave Christina a sidelong glance for a moment and then turned back to the speck of black on the horizon. "Then we burn it and salt the earth."

Christina's jaw went slack for a moment. "Remind me not to become your enemy."

Anne chuckled. "I get it from my parents."

She let out a long sigh, turned around, and leaned against the quarterdeck railing with her arms crossed in front of her chest. "My father, though his station is mostly a formality, wanted to avoid being seen as weak, and pursued an education in war as well as fitness for combat. He doesn't generally take an active role in battles... except in that one instance..."

"Except in that one instance," Christina repeated, no doubt recalling the incident that had seen Edward eventually imprisoned so long ago.

"And," Anne continued, "he ensured that interest was passed on to his children."

Christina's brow raised. "Children? You have siblings?"

"Had," Anne corrected. "They passed from sickness. Some survived longer than others, but I outlived them all." Anne tried her best to keep her composure, but her last few words came out ragged, stilted by remembrance. Childhood images, marred by age and fear, of so many siblings taken by disease, miscarriage, and stillbirth flashed in her mind unbidden. The thought of their rictus bodies scarred by sickness or the simple act of passing the womb already broken sent a shiver down her spine even now.

"I'm sorry," Christina said after a moment of Anne's quiet contemplation. "I shouldn't have asked."

Anne raised her head, noticed tears forming in her eyes, and wiped them away before shaking her head. "No, no, it's fine. I've just not thought about them in... quite some time." Before she went into her contemplation again without thought, Anne got up from the railing and wrapped an arm around Christina. "Besides, I have a new sister right here... I hope."

Christina blushed and looked away from Anne despite leaning closer into her embrace. "You don't need to say it aloud, you know." Her voice was barely a whisper.

"And then how will I see such a cute embarrassed face?" Anne replied, a huge smirk tugging at her cheeks.

Christina pushed her hip against Anne's, forcing her away. "Back to the crow's nest with you!" she shouted angrily, but she couldn't rid herself of the smile on her face.

"All right, all right, I'll leave you alone for now... sister," Anne said over her shoulder as she went down to the weather deck.

Transitioning from the quarterdeck, meant for officers and guests, to the bustle of the main deck would have been jarring to Anne years ago. She had been on ships when she was a child but had stayed sequestered far away from the sweat-soaked, rough, sea-hardy sailors. Now she was one of them, and a pirate no less. She forced herself to acclimate, lest she fall behind.

The men around her, kept busy by William's guidance, were milling about securing rigging, cleaning the deck or weapons, and practicing drills for combat. The wind was favourable, so the work was lax, but still, the signs of labour were there.

The cleaning was hard work, and sweat slicked many a brow and cast shadows on the backs of the rough cotton shirts that stuck to the men's backs. Hot breath over hotter sea air seemed to create its own environment aboard the ship, leaving it muggy and thick, but thankfully the wind cut through it. If Anne were below deck, it would be worse, but it was never as bad as some of the land-based establishments favoured by the same sailors. With no wind to carry the filth away, it would settle until layer after layer made breathing difficult.

At the far end of the ship, around the foremast, Anne could see many crewmates practicing with weapons and some holding contests of strength. Pukuh, the one-armed Mayan warrior prince, was doing push-ups as a crowd cheered him on. Three other crewmates—and maybe a fourth; it was difficult for Anne to see against all the rigging and bundle of bodies in the way—were also doing push-ups with Pukuh, but they all had the advantage of two arms.

One by one, sweat dripping to the deck, the other crewmates collapsed to the sole with a thump and a loud gasp for air, until it was only Pukuh left. The crewmates cheering them on exclaimed loudly for the victor of the contest but cut short as Pukuh kept going. Anne could see him straining, his one arm bulging with the effort and his whole body moving as he worked his way up and down. She knew how difficult it was to do one-arm push-ups, but he was as prideful as he was fierce. As his final act of pride to the astonished onlookers, Pukuh grinned at the top of his stride, then curled four of his fingers in, leaving only one left to hold him up. Through shaking extremities, Pukuh managed that one last push-up and then slumped to the deck.

The few in the crowd, as well as some who had gathered at the last moment by the cheers and the silence, erupted in cries of compliment, congratulations, and disbelief. They picked Pukuh up off the deck, slapping him across the back and pushing him around in displays of revered brotherhood. Through the sweat and exhaustion, Pukuh smiled slyly from the praise, saying words Anne could only guess from where she was. After it was over, the men went back to their drills, while some others continued the contest, though with far fewer onlookers.

Some of the crew were sitting in groups talking with fervour and exclamations with broad gestures, and others were singing along with Jack as he played a tune on his fiddle. It was a good day when he brought out the fiddle. When the man brought out his drum, it meant a storm was approaching, or a battle was close. The fiddle meant lively jigs and jaunty tunes about a sailor and a bar wench, or a sailor and a talking fish, or a sailor and most anything one could think of. Anne didn't know where this well of music came from for Jack to draw from, or if he simply plucked the words from the air as he did the strings of the fiddle, but the man was talented. A fiddle day was a slow day, but an enjoyable one.

Jack noticed Anne watching, and he had another crewmate of less experience take his place playing music. The other crewmates feigned disappointment and the man taking over lightly smacked and kicked the naysayers with a smile on his face before he began playing.

"Mr. Christian," Anne said with a slight bow.

Jack chuckled and pointed at Anne as he approached, then stopped and did a flourish. "Miss Anne," he replied with a posh, mocking drawl so unlike his north-western.

"To what do I owe this pleasure?" she asked.

Jack walked with her over to the port, a bit away from the rest of the crew. "I merely wished to inquire about your well-being."

Anne smiled. "I am well and thank you for asking."

Jack nodded, his expression genial, but nonplussed. He leaned in and lowered his volume. "Some in the crew express concern over Edward's sudden departure. You've done well in painting Edward and Herbert as the silent assassins while we create a distraction for them, but I know there is more to this." He looked Anne straight in the eye, his face deadly serious. "The late, sleepless nights, the imbibements when he thinks none are looking, the irritability, and now this?" Jack tilted his head as he frowned. "Edward's been treading water for a spell, and now he disappears? I've been down that road before. I may have even set some of the stones down for its foundation."

Anne looked away from Jack's gaze for a moment, out to sea. She recalled Jack's story about losing his family to a jealous naval admiral, George Rooke, and his struggles with the drink, and the gambling. He had been able to overcome it somehow.

She knew what had been happening to Edward too. She tried to talk with him about it, but he wouldn't open himself to her. And now, he found his father alive and trying to kill him? It would be enough to drive anyone mad.

After a long silence, she asked, "How did you manage it?"

"Aye, there's the rub, miss. I still am." Jack joined Anne in facing the sea and leaned his arms on the railing. "Every day, at some point in the day, I want it. Most times, it's the smell, and you can't avoid that here by any means," Jack said with a dark laugh. "But, some days, it could be nothing and just like that," he said, snapping his finger, "the worm's in you and not letting go." Jack was silent for a moment as he moved around and began gripping the railing. "The only thing that keeps me going is knowing that I have a family here. That I didn't lose mine back then, I just gained a few new members now." Jack glanced at Anne, his eyes shining. "I can't tell you what Edward needs to get by in the day, but I know he needs us, and he needs you."

Anne took a long, measured breath, making sure not to let her emotion show. She wanted to tell him everything at that moment. She wanted to say to him that Edward had run off on his own with no consultation. She wanted to tell him that she's just trying to keep things held together, wanted to scream it, but she couldn't. She needed to be resilient, and they needed to present a unified front to the crew. If they knew the truth, she wasn't sure she could keep the crew together.

She looked at Jack Christian once more. He was as loyal as they came, a faithful friend of Edward's and smarter than his appearance would lead one to believe. He would understand and could provide a voice of reason to the crew where she could not.

"Mr. Christian, I will not lie to you. We may be heading into a battle soon, and we cannot have the crew worrying over Edward and his decision. I hope you can understand and help the crew to understand, for their morale. If Edward is on this island, then we will laugh about it, and you and I can have a long chat with him together." Anne placed her hand on Jack's.

"And if he's not?"

"Then our chat will have to be delayed, and in the meantime, we'll be the best damn distraction Calico Jack has ever had to deal with."

The longboat landed at the natural shore on the coast of Los Huecos, carrying with it the landing party appointed by

William, as well as a few sightseers. *Queen Anne's Revenge* bobbed with the waves just a short distance from the coast. Far enough that they wouldn't hit land, but not too far in case the landing party needed to abscond quickly.

Along with Anne, William, and six other crewmates, Alexandre, the *Queen Anne's Revenge*'s surgeon, and Victoria, his partner in medicine and possibly more, as well as former crewmate of Calico Jack, sought to join in of their own accord. When asked about their wishes for joining, the Frenchman replied with a curt "research" in his usual sly manner. Victoria refrained from answering, but her typically cold eyes were more distant than usual, a well-submerged burg rather than her typical frost.

Anne saw no benefit to leaving them on board and significantly less use to arguing with them, so she let them join. When Victoria emerged from below wearing her leathers and had her buckler strapped to her arm and her short sword at her hip, Anne became suspicious. When Alexandre brought a large satchel that jangled with the tune of the surgeon's instruments, and he too had a pistol and his immaculate rapier at his side, Anne's suspicions turned to an anxious knot in her gut.

What calculations had you come to this conclusion, mon ami?

Anne had already been expecting trouble on the island, but she was hoping they could gather some intel first. The first rule to winning any battle was knowing the other person's strengths, as well as your own; whether to strike fast and hard like a battle axe, whether to whittle the enemy down like a thousand mosquitoes sucking a man dry, or whether to retreat and seek another way all depended on the information. Without such intel, Anne would be lacking.

Anne *hated* to be lacking.

After she landed her feet on the shifting but stable ground of the sandy coast, Anne closed her eyes with her back to the other crewmates. Anxiety would do her no good here, especially when she needed to project absolute and unwavering strength. As a woman attempting to lead hardened men, she could settle for no less. She took the anxious feeling, wrapped it in a flaming hand, and with one last curse to

Alexandre for his gift, she snuffed it out with a lengthy but silent exhale.

"Eyes sharp, men. We don't know what to expect out there," she shouted over her shoulder. The men behind her yelled an "Aye" back as she walked up the incline to the rolling hills ahead.

At the top of the first small hill, the sand of the beach met the grass in stark opposition to one another. The sand appeared to be clawing its way forward as the grass and earth fought to stay aloft, causing the grass to curl down and almost touch the sand beneath an overhang. The grass clung to its former solid ground like a climber on the edge of a precipice. One slip and it would crash away, and it too would become the sand.

Across the small beach, Anne could see many such scenes of the eroding coast, exposing years of compacted earth and stone to the air. The soil here was unstable near the beach, and if it held true across the island, then they were unlikely to have any ports aside from the town that Silver Eyes occupied: one major town for trade, which the other villages supplied.

Once at the top of the hill, Anne was able to get a better view of the island, or at least what she could see of it. The rolling hills obstructed much from view, but she noticed the top of a few buildings to the north, one being a large bell tower, as well as a well-travelled dirt road nearby.

William and the other crewmates crested the hills to join Anne, and she directed their attention to the village nearby. "We'll head there first. Stick to the road and keep your weapons hidden as well as you can manage for now. We don't want to alarm the villagers and have them sending scouts to warn Silver Eyes."

Anne looked over her shoulder, and the crewmates who were watching her nodded their understanding while some took in their surroundings. They each had cloaks covering down to their ankles, and each of them adjusted the weapons on them to remain concealed under the heavy fabric.

"Hubert, Lucas, head to that hill over there and keep watch." Anne was pointing to a rather tall hill just west of the town. "You should be able to see the town and the ship from there. If you see anyone leaving town or any ships approaching, find us." The two crewmates gave an "Aye, Captain," before leaving for the hill.

Anne led the others down the dusty dirt road towards town. As they approached, the hills tapered off and turned into fields filled with rows upon rows of farmland. Anne could see wheat prominently, with some just ripening for harvest, as well as large fields of corn, and smaller fields of potatoes, tomatoes, varieties of lettuce, and other greens Anne couldn't distinguish.

Going from the salty air of the sea to the hot sand and earth on the coast, to the freshly tilled soil, manure, and vegetables felt like stepping into another world. Most of the places that Anne had been to, not just while with the *Queen Anne's Revenge*, had been towns of considerable size, large bustling machines composed of men and women working at a pace set to a particular rhythm, the rhythm of people trying to stay alive and make a living in a harsh world. Stepping into this village, which couldn't house more than fifty residents, was like stepping through the gates to a new world. A smaller world, a slower world, one removed from the harsh realities of life on the sea, or life led by the whims and fancies of others.

As they walked into the village, they passed by farmers, old grizzled men with their sons at their side, working the fields. Using hoes, they delicately removed weeds from the budding vegetables or crushed bugs threatening the harvest between rough, dirty, but skilled fingers. They waved and called pleasant hellos to Anne and her company, broad smiles on their faces as though they had no care in the world and were welcoming to any and all visitors.

The joviality forced the knot back into Anne's gut.

This was not the attitude of a village of oppressed men and women under the thumb of a tyrannical pirate regime. It wasn't even reminiscent of a remote village visited by eight strangers who, even with weapons hidden, had the appearance of fighters. No one sounded an alarm, none rushed to tell the other villagers of their arrival, and not a single person gave them a wary look of concern.

Peculiar. Anne could describe it no better than *peculiar* in her mind. If they hadn't been in the heart of enemy territory, it would have been a simple thing, an oddity she could whisk away with the thought that they were a strange group of people. Here, though, it set her mind to a razor's edge.

Without thought she settled a hand on the golden cutlass at her hip. She only came back to her senses when she felt the tip of the metal, guarded in a sheathe, pressing against the fabric of her cloak. She adjusted her weapon and forced her hands to her sides.

When they reached the village proper, where the farmland turned into houses and a few small businesses, she had to force herself to keep her hands still.

There were men working wagons, repairing wheels and feeding horses, women gossiping near the local general store while a pair of men played a game of chess on the deck near its entrance, and some just walking to another part of the village on an errand. Anne could hear the slow, methodical clang of metal striking metal in a nearby smithy, though she couldn't place the building among those she could see.

In the centre of the hamlet, Anne was able to better see the tall bell tower, and it was by far the most arresting architecture around them. The other buildings looked well worn, old, and humble. The bell tower had all the same trappings, but the bell itself glinted against the late afternoon sun with a brilliance no ordinary metal could produce. The golden light reflected off what appeared to be a pure gold bell of at least a few hundred pounds. That golden bell's metal resembled Edward's cutlass at her side, and a blade owned by his father, Calico Jack—or by his other name, Benjamin 'The Golden Horn' Hornigold.

The sight of that bell smashed away any doubts about this being an island under Calico Jack's purview. There was no chance this hamlet could afford, or even desire, a bell of such opulence. The bell had some significance on the island, perhaps some significance related to the strangeness going on with the citizens. Whatever the meaning, Anne didn't wish to stay long enough to find out, but she had the feeling that to continue, she would have to find out.

Each of the villagers in the centre of the village took note of them, nearly in unison, and each did the same simple wave and hello the farmers and their sons had done on the way in. Two flicks of the wrist, a slight bow of the head, and back to what they were doing before. If not for the consistent banging from the smithy, and the horses chomping, the village would have been silent for the few heartbeats that the wave took.

Alexandre and Victoria walked past Anne, and only then did she notice she had stopped moving. "*Intéressant...*" the Frenchman mumbled on his way past.

"Wait, Alexandre," she called sharply.

Alexandre stopped and turned on his heel. "*Oui*? Yes?"

Though he had stopped, his tone was curt and perfunctory. His eyes wandered with each movement from the villagers, and his tapping foot alluded to his impatience more than anything about his manner. It seemed his foot was the most spirited thing at that moment, a stark contrast to the people around them who seemed to be merely going about the motions of activity. If this were a play, the villagers were the atmosphere, and he the principal.

Anne leaned forward and spoke for Alexandre's ears only. "There's something... odd about all this. We need to stay together."

Alexandre smiled, though the smile was as devoid of life as the hamlet around them. "Then you may stay together. I wish to learn more of this... *étrangeté...* my own way."

As though the matter were settled, he turned back around and walked away. It was then that Anne noticed Victoria already talking with some of the citizens, a sheaf of paper in one hand and a piece of graphite in the other. She had her shield and short sword exposed, and she and the people she was talking with paid them no heed from what Anne could tell.

Anne shook her head and rubbed her temples. After a moment, she composed herself and headed towards the general store to see if she could gather some information. Before heading up the steps to enter the store, she instructed the crew, save William, to stay outside, but within sight.

Anne and William both stepped up the well-worn wooden steps and into the general store. The cracked paint on the wood and the groans and creaks as they stepped spoke to the age of the building, and if that hadn't been enough, the scuffs and indents that warped the wood over the years was a reasonable testament.

Inside the store, a small establishment that could fit no more than thirty in the room standing shoulder to shoulder, the walls were lined with an assortment of miscellaneous items. Glass display cases separating the standing area from the owner also contained all manner of trinkets for sale.

On the left, there were bags and tins of spices, dried meat and other fresh produce from the farms outside, next to what appeared to be a second-hand set of pots, a dark iron fire poker and tongs made by the local smith, and some tools Anne wasn't familiar with. At the back, Anne saw other, heftier tools for maintaining livestock and axes and pistols and muskets with ammo and cleaning instruments in the glass cases. On the right, there were homespun fabrics and clothing made in town, from what Anne could tell, and separated on its own were well-made clothes and dresses that must have been imported. In the glass cases in front of the clothes, there were glasses of assorted sizes, ladies' gloves, and toys for children.

Because of the size of the village, Anne surmised the general store was the sole source of any of the items found inside and thus probably sold liquor stored in the back as well. That made the general store the hub of information and trade, and their best chance at getting information.

That was if this were any ordinary hamlet with ordinary citizens. And, so far, this had been anything but ordinary.

The owner of the general store stepped out from the back and into the main room when he heard Anne and William enter. He gave the two the same wave and hello the others had and then walked over closer to them while still staying behind the glass cases so that he was handy to any of the items for sale.

"Hello, good sir, we're—" Anne bit her tongue.

She had been going to explain that they were sailors seeking supplies due to a storm forcing them off course when they happened upon the island, but she had doubts about her own cover story. The way these villagers were acting, however, could be part of the manner they were *supposed* to act around Silver Eyes' men. Perhaps the strangeness was synchronized through practice, and perhaps the relationship was a healthy one for both parties and explained why they were given a warm welcome. Maybe it was all in her head, and maybe not.

Anne decided to err on the side of caution and do her best to act as though she belonged there. She straightened her back, her eyes cast down with a slight air of hostility and authority.

"We're here for the next shipment," she continued. "But this is a new assignment for us, so we don't know who's in charge."

The older gentleman behind the counter smiled widely, his greying moustache curling as his plump cheeks rose. "Understood, ma'am. No trouble at all, I will see to the shipment personally. The name's Jules, and you're in the right place." His voice was upbeat and amicable, as though he were talking with a wealthy patron and trying to make a sale. Anne gave her name as Sofia Stewart, and though she loathed using that last name, it provided her protection now. "Any change to the supplies?"

"None," Anne replied. "But I will need a manifest for inspection. How long until the cargo is ready for shipment?"

Jules' face scrunched as he looked outside the window to the hamlet. Anne followed his gaze over her shoulder. She could see the crewmen milling about within view of the general store, and Victoria was talking with the women who were gossiping out front while Alexandre observed the gentlemen on the step playing their game of chess.

"Given the time, we could have it ready before nightfall. The road's a bit treacherous at night, are you sure you want to be heading back tonight?"

"No, I suppose not." Anne took a few seconds to assess the situation. If they indeed were from inland and part of the pirate's crew, they would not be arriving by ship. No roads were leading to the coast for cargo, and there had been no harbour that they could see for the stretch of land they'd been able to observe when sailing in. That meant mentioning the ship would be out of the question. "Would you have some lodging for my men and me for the night, so we may head back on the morrow?"

"Most certainly," Jules replied. "You can sleep upstairs. There are a few beds and some cots."

"Thank you," Anne said.

The interaction was pleasant enough to set Anne's mind at ease. The owner of the general store and the others in town simply thought they were part of Silver Eyes' men, and they acted accordingly, and seemingly not out of fear, either. If nothing else had happened, Anne would have thought that it must have been because the relationship between the two groups was mutually beneficial.

Then, Anne saw a fly crawling around on Jules' hand. He didn't seem to notice the fly, and because he was standing stock still, the fly was comfortable staying where it was. The fly soon moved up his arm, onto his neck, across his cheek, and settled on his nose. And he never moved, nor did he even twitch with the recognition that something unpleasant was there.

Anne glanced over to William, and by the look on William's face, cutting through the man's usual stoniness, he had noticed the oddity too. He looked as confused and disgusted as she felt.

"Jules, there's a fly… on your nose," Anne said, pointing to the insect.

Jules chuckled and waved a hand in front of his face. "So there is," he replied. Then with a shrug he said, "They don't bother us none."

"Right," Anne said, drawing the word out at the end. "I suppose they don't."

"You there," Alexandre called from outside the door of the general store, "Princess, Captain, Missus Thatch, whichever it is these days. Come."

Anne shot Alexandre a look of annoyance and was about

to lay into him about his liberal use of titles in front of people they couldn't trust, but he had already stepped away from the entrance by the time she turned.

Anne left the shop to follow Alexandre, just in front of the two men playing the game of chess on a small table between two benches at the side of the store's deck.

"What is—?" Anne began, but Alexandre held up his finger.

"Observe," he said, as his finger pointed towards the men.

Anne looked at each man sitting at the table, a young man and an older gentleman who appeared to be in his fifties. The state of the game looked typical, but suggested an amateurish nature. Anne felt that if played correctly, the younger man, playing black, could win with checkmate in ten moves, or played poorly reach check within eight. Nothing appeared out of the ordinary.

"How is the game, gentlemen?" Alexandre asked.

"Terrible, just terrible," the older man replied. "Rotten. You teach the young everything they need to know, and then they use it against you."

Alexandre lifted a piece of paper he had been holding to his chest a moment before, and Anne noticed the same words, exactly as the old man had said to them, written on the paper. And there was more.

"Now, now, George," the young man said. "You can't expect your mind to remain as sharp as it ever was. I have to win a few games here and there."

"Nonsense," the old man cut in. "Respecting your elders means letting them win, young man."

The young one laughed, and then looked up at Alexandre, Anne, and William. "We shouldn't be much longer with our game, and then you can have a go if you'd like."

"Not if I have anything to say about it," the old man said finally, and then the two went back to their game.

Each word, verbatim, was written on Alexandre's page. No variation in the words whatsoever, and unless Alexandre was psychic or a seer, the two had said the exact thing to him while Anne and William were inside the store.

Before Anne could wrap her head around the implications, or even begin to formulate a question, Alexandre pocketed the papers and stepped closer to the two men playing.

He knelt closer to the table, placed his hands on the chessboard, and glanced over his shoulder at Anne to see if she was watching. After a moment, to ensure neither of the men playing had their hands on the pieces, Alexandre pushed the chessboard to the other side of the table, away from the men, and then backed away.

The men didn't react. They both stared in the same spot on the table where the chessboard used to be, as though it were still there. After a moment, the older man made the motion of picking up a piece, a rook by Anne's estimation, and moved the imaginary piece across the non-existent board.

"How about that?" he said triumphantly.

"Not bad, old man, not bad."

The older gentleman scoffed, taken aback. "I oughta have you switched for that. Make your move. Not bad, he says."

Alexandre turned to Anne, looking at her for a moment as though what he'd showed her were enough. Anne stared at the two men for a moment longer, pondering the problem.

She spun on her heel and walked back into the general store. After she and William had exited, he had gone back to some busywork about the store. Upon hearing them enter again, he gave the same hello and wave in that practiced way the others in the hamlet had all done.

"I'm rather hungry, and I'd like to purchase some of the dried meat you have."

"Why, certainly," Jules replied.

He walked around the perimeter of the store to the left side with all the food and pulled down a glass jar filled with the dried and spiced meat within. He placed the jar down on the glass cabinet in front of him and took off the top. The long strips of what appeared to be beef wafted a gentle fragrance of pepper, cloves, and the unmistakable iron-like smell of dried blood towards Anne.

"How much?" Anne asked.

Jules scrunched his face in thought as he has done a few moments before, then pulled out his ledger from behind the counter. He rifled through the pages, his finger skimming down the lines of the ledger as he searched for his product. "Hmm, let's see... For one strip of dried beef, it would be... doo-doo-doo... Zero pieces of eight."

Anne had been fixated on the ledger and almost didn't hear what Jules had said. She was sure she had heard him wrong and looked up from the ledger, her brow cocked, and head turned slightly to hear better. "Pardon?"

Jules briefly glanced down at the ledger again, then repeated, "Zero pieces of eight."

Anne couldn't help but pause for a few seconds, incredulous, shocked, disturbed, or some combination of the three halting her natural ability to react quickly. "I'll take two," she finally said.

Jules held out his hand, waiting for the 'payment.' Anne mimicked the act of reaching into her cloak for some coins and dropped the imaginary pieces into Jules' outstretched hand. He accepted the mock coins and then tilted the jar towards Anne, allowing her to take some of the beef.

Anne, channelling the Frenchman and wishing to test things a bit further, reached inside and took all the strips of dried beef out of the jar in one bundle, leaving the container empty. "Oh! It seems you're all out."

Jules looked back into the jar, not noticing, or perhaps *unable* to notice, that Anne had taken well more than two pieces. "Oh my, terribly sorry about that, miss. I'm sure I have some more in the back, just give me a moment." Jules put the jar down and walked to the back of his store through an open doorway.

Anne turned around to Alexandre and William. "Something's not right with these people," she said, her fist clenched in a death grip on the dried strips of meat.

Alexandre smirked. "Astute observation."

Anne's anger flared, but she tempered the rage with a clench of her jaw. "Do you know what's wrong with them?" Anne gestured with the strips of beef, and after she realized she was still holding the batch, she handed some to William, some to Alexandre—despite him clearly not wanting any—and placed the rest on the counter.

Alexandre's brow raised. "My dear *princesse*, you of all people should know better." He crossed his arms in front of him, his face uncharacteristically serious. "Knowing a thing means you have an intimate awareness of the surrounding circumstances of a thing. This is no simple illness defined by a large *rouge* spot on an appendage. I have many theories, but not enough facts to say with any certainty what ails these people. They could be infected with *un parasite*, they could be acting, as unlikely as it may be, or they could be beings from the sky with no concept of our culture beyond a set of pre-described functions and phrases."

Anne's anger turned to a sour exasperation. Alexandre may be exhausting and withheld information at times, but he was proud and revelled in lording his superior intellect over others. If he didn't know a thing, and he said as much, then he didn't know it.

There was something they were missing, a crucial piece of information that would tie it all together. Anne took a bite from the beef and stared at the worn floorboards of the general store as she thought over the matter. She went deep, digging to every nugget of information Victoria, Christina, and, most importantly, Herbert had given about Silver Eyes over the years, searching for something that Alexandre didn't know that could turn one of his hypotheses into the most likely scenario.

"Three things come to mind that may narrow our focus," Anne said before looking up at Alexandre again. "One is the golden bell. It would be no coincidence were it to be the same metal as Edward's cutlass"—Anne touched the cutlass for emphasis—"and the same as Benjamin Hornigold's horn and his own cutlass. When he blew that horn the night we tried to kill him, it was as though the people around him went into a trance. Not all in the tavern, but most." Anne paused a moment, and after Alexandre nodded, she continued. "The second and third are things Herbert has said about Silver Eyes that you may not know."

"Yes, that could be valuable information," Alexandre

agreed.

"He's said before that his crew never loses their morale, and when I questioned him about this further, he meant that in the most literal sense. They don't stop fighting, even if they lose their men, even if they lose their limbs."

Alexandre stroked his chin as he looked off to the side, tabulating the additional variables. After a moment, he looked at Anne again. "And the third?"

"Herbert also mentioned once that Silver Eyes has a unique method of persuasion. Whenever there were disputes with him among the crew, he could turn them around with a few pats on the shoulder, and some whispered words. Any would-be enemies, no matter how upset they were with him, turned jovial in mere moments. I don't care how silvery his eyes or his tongue are, no one's that good at persuasion, at least not with one hundred percent effectiveness."

Alexandre nodded as he took a moment to absorb the information. Then Anne saw something she never thought she would or could ever see from the Frenchman: his eyes flew open in shock for the briefest moment, and then he was angry. No, not angry; enraged. His eyes smouldered with volcanic activity, a stark contrast with his relaxed body. That look was the look of a man ready to kill.

"These people are under a forced trance." Alexandre said the words as though he were making a comment about the weather, but Anne could tell he was disgusted.

"Are you sure?" As soon as Anne asked, she felt the fool for asking. One did not doubt Alexandre's diagnosis.

"Of course."

Alexandre was now looking at the back of the shop, in the direction of the storage room where Jules was rummaging around unseen but heard.

"Can you help them out of the trance?" William asked, his first comment in some time.

"I don't know."

Alexandre was not his usual self. Anger showed in his typically passive eyes, but it went deeper than that. During times when he was short with people, as he was now, it was with an exasperation of not wanting to be a part of a dull conversation and a desire to end it as soon as possible. Now... Now Alexandre's short replies felt as though he were holding back, like he could explode at any moment, or as though he were distracted, not by something interesting to him, but by something upsetting.

"To be this far gone... " Alexandre closed his eyes and shook his head in a mournful expression and muttered a French expletive under his breath. "They must be under several layers of their own mind. Months of work went into this."

Anne suddenly realized what that would have meant and why Alexandre was so disgusted by the event to actually show it, and it made her sick. The people were docile because they had no choice. In their fugue, they probably weren't even aware of what was happening.

"Whatever you're thinking, it is far worse than that," Alexandre said, his eyes still smouldering, but Anne could see his profound pity for these people. "Putting one in a trance is a useful tool for the willing, something that can help ease pain or strengthen the mind. The trick is that you can't be put into a trance for long unless you let yourself. And, there are tricks to bring one out of a light trance as well. To do this," Alexandre gestured to the hamlet, "one would have had to start small. Perhaps one would begin with promising to ease the mind of the ailing or exhausted, then with a sense of letting go of worries. Deeper and deeper in the mind one goes, the easier it becomes to say yes. Soon, one wants to say yes without knowing why. Then, he could have made them question everything. Why do you toil for a worthless coin? It is just a burden. Give it for free. Released from your worldly possessions, you will have no more to worry about. Why live with worry?"

The anger made Alexandre's accent thicken, but he didn't lapse back to French, his mind caught between the two in a more perfect balance. His hands were a wild flurry of gestures with each statement, the kind only seen from those raised on the impoverished streets of Paris. He was more animated than he had been in years, and Anne was beginning to understand why.

"After this, consent is meaningless. The trance is so deep and penetrating that a sense of self can be overwritten. You may think it impossible, but with enough time and a few key steps, one can break a mind. I could convince you that you were not of royal lineage, I could convince William that he committed atrocities that had never happened."

"And this is just one of several villages on this island," William said, breaking into Alexandre's abyss of atrocities.

Alexandre sighed and resigned his arms across his chest once more. "*Exactement.*"

Alexandre's explanation and William's observation sent an icy chill down Anne's spine. How many people had Silver Eyes entranced? How many were doing things against their will and being taken advantage of? Worst of it all, how many of the women were being victimized by this? Anne, though her time aboard was brief, had been on Calico Jack's ship before. His men were savage monsters that wouldn't hesitate to commit heinous acts against women, she knew that for a fact. Victoria was also living proof of it.

"This is abhorrent, and an affront to *le médecine* and *les science.*" Alexandre looked deep into Anne's eyes. "Whatever happens on this island, Silver Eyes dies by my hand."

Another wave of shivers crawled across Anne's body. She nodded, knowing it wasn't a request, but a proclamation.

"Without knowledge of the trigger, of which there could be several, I may not be able to help these people. If I knew it, I might be able to reverse it, but there is no way to know."

Anne cocked her head and brow, confused. "What about the bell? Isn't that the trigger?"

"Perhaps, and perhaps not. We do not know if it is meant to trigger a deeper state of trance, if it is some type of control should the citizens not comply, or if it serves some other purpose." Alexandre glanced over his shoulder in the direction of the bell tower, though the bell itself was shrouded by the walls of the general store. "It would be dangerous to ring the bell not knowing what it does."

Anne nodded. "Agreed. We leave the bell alone for now." She turned to William. "Send a few crewmates back to the ship and let them know we'll be staying the night here.

Perhaps with that time, we may be able to reclaim one of the citizens." Anne eyed Alexandre, then glanced over her shoulder at Jules, who was just returning from the storage room.

"Terribly sorry, miss, no more in the back. Here, your money," he said while holding out his hand.

"My thanks," Anne replied, following the act.

With her newfound knowledge, instead of the same unease she had been feeling before, she felt a profound sense of pity for the men and women of this island. Pity, and a wave of rising anger boiling up.

⚓ ⚓ ⚓

"You must have your rest, Captain," Alexandre chided. "If we are to have you leading our troops, you must be of sound mind."

Anne stifled a yawn, cursing the Frenchman for talking of rest at the late hour it was. Alexandre, Victoria, Anne, and William had huddled themselves in the storage room of the general store. Soft lamplight illuminated the windowless room, casting shifting shadows and bounding bands of light against the barrels, boxes, and bags of supplies in the crowded room.

Their charge, Jules the shopkeeper, sat slumped in a chair in the middle of the four. If an onlooker caught a glimpse of the half-shadowed face of the man between them all, they might think he was asleep, but he was not. He was under a trance, this time of Alexandre's doing.

Anne knew nothing of the practice and had thought not long ago it was superstitious nonsense, and so thought it equally odd that to remove one from a trance, they must again force them into the same experience. That lack of knowledge, and thus an inability to truly help, and the stifling yawn, made Alexandre's words sound like honey. The only thing keeping her awake now was a vague sense of duty and curiosity over the entire strange matter.

"And what of you?" she eventually asked.

Alexandre smiled in his usual, civil way, and though Anne

couldn't be sure, it seemed warmer to her somehow. "I rarely sleep, and Victoria, for entirely different circumstances, is plagued by a similar affliction as I. We will see you in the morning, and perhaps you will then be able to talk with the real Jules."

Anne didn't need much convincing, and with a dull nod and heavy eyes, she headed up the stairs in the storage room to the second floor of the general store.

There, a few crewmates who weren't out on watch were sleeping on cots, leaving two beds on the left side of the room for William and Anne. With a few words, Anne ordered William to rest as well and refused to lie down until she saw him do so first. He was reluctant, but he too had had a long and tiring day from the early morning sailing until now, and she could tell that he fell asleep soon after his head hit the pillow.

Anne laid her head down to rest, tossing and turning as she ran through the events of the day in her head once more until eventually sleep took her. Her sleep was short-lived when a sound forced her from her bed to full alertness.

It was the cutting crack of a pistol fired outside.

6. BY THESE COPPER LEGS O' MINE

Edward's whole body ached in a painful expression of his own stupidity. Bruises blotched his face, back, arms, and legs from the beating Grace's crewmates had given him. True to their captain's word, they'd managed not to break any bones, but Edward wasn't sure how much better off he was for it.

The worst was his back, as they had opened the wound given by his father, which had been only a week old at the time. Edward did his best to protect the injury without making it seem as though he were guarding it as per the rules of the engagement, but it had been unavoidable. After that point, he focussed simply on not crying out in pain over the ordeal.

And after it all, he had to man a ship that was not his own, taking orders from a captain he had to act amicably towards.

As his arms shook, he secured coarse rigging; as his legs wobbled, he ran the length of the ship to perform increasingly menial tasks, tasks meant to break him and have him regret his decision. And as he bled on the deck from his forehead and back, he kept going. Despite the pain, the weakness, and the not-so-subtle slights from the crewmates tripping him up, he did the work of three men—just as he had been told to do, just as he had agreed he would.

To Edward's dismay, this only served to infuriate several members of the crew. The more he pushed on despite his injuries, the more contempt he could feel in their gazes; the heat against the back of his neck told him those gazes were measuring him and finding him wanting no matter how well he performed.

The primary source of the contempt came from the first man they had spoken to before boarding the *Black Blood*: the pock-marked, sour crewmate named Nigel. He had an inner circle of other crewmates Edward learned about over the day's work, and they were the ones trying to trip or knock him over at each corner when the captain wasn't looking.

Despite this, some in the crew seemed to warm up to Edward after his stubborn refusal to submit to his injuries. As the day progressed and his sweat and blood poured out of him, he noticed a few go out of their way to aid him. When he fumbled with a knot his numb fingers just couldn't manage, one man finished the loop for him. When he snuck in a few laboured breaths behind the mast and away from prying eyes, another crewmate secretly handed him a tin full of water. It wasn't much, but it helped.

"I've been where you were before," the man with the cup said. "It'll get easier as soon as Grace trusts you're capable."

Edward took the cup with a shaking hand and downed the water in one enormous gulp. "If I don't die before then," he sputtered through his laboured breaths. He glanced over his shoulder and around the foremast towards where Nigel and his friends were talking amongst themselves.

The crewmate who gave him the water followed Edward's gaze. "Just ignore Nigel. He'll tire of you eventually. This is just his way." The man turned back to face Edward, and he smiled. "I'm John, by the way."

The name made Edward's eyes widen, and his pounding heart skipped a beat. John was a common name, but nonetheless, it still brought to mind the old crewmate Edward had had aboard his ship before he had become a pirate and stayed on afterwards. The same crewmate whose neck had been sliced open right in front of him by the same man who had tortured Edward for days before leaving him for dead. The thought brought with it the same unpleasant ache of a different kind.

His throat seized, and he couldn't move. He breathed deep through his nose, desperately trying to quell the raging squall in his mind. He reached for his flask, popped off the stopper, and tried to drink, but it was empty.

"Anything stronger than that swill?" Edward eked out, referring to the lightly rum-laced water he had been given. The rum kept the water from forming a scum on a long

voyage with little fresh water but did little else for one looking to ease a particular pain.

John smiled and took the cup from Edward before filling
it from a secret flask of his own. After getting it back, Edward downed it in one gulp just as he had the water before
it. Edward knew and was hoping that with all the activity, the
blood loss, and the sweat, it would hit him harder than it
usually did. He wanted the numbness of a different kind.

"My thanks," he said after a moment.

The thought of Edward's former crewmate brought old
memories of the man. The way he'd looked with his salt-and-
pepper hair, his typically nervous disposition outside of battle, and his relationship with his father. Before John had been
killed, when his tired eyes had showed Edward the look of
an old man's soul stretched thin as smoke and ready to let
the wind take it off, he had confirmed that Edward's father
was still alive. Had John been aware of what Edward's father
had become? Had he been aware of the things his father had
done to him, or would do to him, or had he merely been
trying to tighten Edward's resolve to live by telling him a
sweet lie he'd had no way of knowing was accurate?

Edward's eyes shot up as the flood of memories came
back to him. *No*, he thought, *John knew. He was given the keys
to my ship before I received it. He met Benjamin Hornigold, he said as
much himself. He met my father and kept the lie to take me to the trials
where I nearly died. How much did he know? How deep did this plot
run?*

Edward pondered the question for another moment, but
it only served to heat his cheeks and his core with fresh anger
over the lies he had been fed and embarrassment over his
falling for them. He shook his head to cast away the demons
he called the past and looked over the young man in front of
him right now.

The John in front of him had little in common with Edward's old John. He was younger than Edward by quite the
degree, in his early twenties if he wasn't in his teens still, and
it was clear that he was new to the crew, or new to battle. He
had a few small scars, one on his face and another few

Edward could see snaking their way out of his shirt towards his neck, but he was far from the battle-hardened sailors aboard the *Black Blood*. His black hair was cropped short, too short for the youth's narrow features. In his mind, it was easy to separate this John from his John, but far harder for his body to.

"Strange for one on a crew such as this to show me a kindness," Edward commented as he turned his gaze to the horizon.

Being at the front of the ship meant getting the full force of each smash against the waves. Each time the ship lurched below the line of the ocean in front of them, seawater misted Edward and John. The mist was refreshing on Edward's hot, tired, aching body.

"You know much of Calico Jack's crew, I see," John said, his mouth a line. "Perhaps if this were Calico Jack or Lance Nhil's ships, your words may ring a bit truer. Grace doesn't use fear or magic to control the crew as they do. She just follows a simple rule: her word is law. Break that law, you're off at the next port if you even make it that far."

Edward took stock of the young man's choice of words, specifically the bit about magic. Did he mean Nhil? Silver Eyes? Or was his father implicated here as well? Edward had seen inexplicable things over the years—metal unlike any other, islands that would take far too long for human hands to construct—not to mention the visions his crew had seen in the Devil's Triangle.

Edward suddenly had a sickening feeling that he and Herbert were in over their heads. If his father had some unknown magic, how could they defend against it?

He noticed John looking at him, and he remembered where he was. Now was all that mattered. He would have to worry about the future when it was on them.

"Doesn't sound much different from intimidation to me."

John shook his head and placed a hand on Edward's shoulder. "Trust me," he said, his eyes serious, "I know."

This first kind hand, after so many seeking to trip Edward up or to stab him in the back, served as a calm wind to his sails, a buoyant driftwood in a treacherous ocean on all sides.

The elation he felt turned to bile in his mouth. How many times must his father's minions betray Edward until he learned his lesson? This John may look nothing like the John that had been his crewmate and confidant for years, but Edward could trust this one no more than he should have trusted the first.

Nigel didn't strike Edward as bright, but it didn't take a bright man to recognize that a gentle hand can lure one closer to a hidden knife. It is especially so when the gentle hand comes after so many harsh ones. John might be in league with Nigel in secret.

He could no more trust John than he could Nigel, or any of the crew aboard the *Black Blood*. Edward decided he would always have to keep one hand near a blade and sleep with one eye open. Thankfully for him, Edward thought as he eyed Herbert on the quarterdeck, he had a second pair he could rely on.

"That was foolish," Herbert said from behind Edward as he did his best to close the stab wound in Edward's back.

Edward winced as the needle passed through his skin for the third time. After so much pain over so many years, the pain of the needle came to him like an old friend whispering jibes and slapping him on the back. If he were mad, he might even say he enjoyed the delicate pain the needle provided, but he wasn't mad, and he jerked as the needle pierced his skin again.

"We're here, aren't we?" Edward said, peering over his shoulder at Herbert's face buried in the task of sewing him up.

Edward was sitting on a box in the hold of the *Black Blood*, surrounded by shoulder-high stacks of watertight barrels and other boxes of pungent spices. On the side of every barrel and box, Edward noticed the label of a shipping company that operated in the West Indies. He wasn't sure exactly which company it belonged to, but he knew it was one of the larger ones. It spoke to how prolific Calico Jack and the crew aboard this ship were, given the audacity to target one of the companies able to defend against pirates.

"Sit still," Herbert ordered, his tone harsh. As soon as Edward readjusted and complied, he finished the stitch in his back and covered it with a cloth before wrapping a strip around it. "It won't be nearly as good as Alexandre would have done, but it'll hold if you keep the weight off."

"My thanks," Edward said, trying to crane his neck to see the wound and stitching.

"You're lucky it had healed a bit before that incident. It could have been worse. If I didn't know any better, I'd say your father knew what he was doing. The wound was meant to bleed you, and the cut was clean and precise."

Edward spat. "If he wanted to kill me, he could have, easily. That's the point. I think he means for me, for us, to bleed." Edward shook his head. "He had so many chances to make things so bad for us we couldn't recover. When he attacked Bodden Town, he could have stayed behind and attacked again after we anchored. In the tavern, everyone was under his control, but they let us go."

Herbert's mouth was a line, as straight as the horizon at dusk, betraying no curve of emotion. "Any ideas as to why?"

"None," Edward replied.

For a moment, the two sat in silence as Edward donned his blood-stained shirt and coat. He thought it over, recalling everything that they knew about his father.

With his recent remembrance that John had been part of the plot, it wasn't unreasonable to think that John had been sending letters to his father. He'd had the means. He had been the person in charge of selling cargo; he could easily have sent a letter here or there. From there, it was reasonable to think that his father knew his pirate name of Blackbeard and more.

It made sense now why Calico Jack had never retaliated for the killing of one of his commanders, Gregory Dunn, until Edward had finished the task of unlocking the ship. His father was the one who'd given him the ship, and had wanted him to face those trials first.

The thoughts and the rumination itched Edward to the point that he needed to move. He couldn't sit still for a moment longer. He rose to his feet but had to remain bent slightly due to the low ceiling of the hold.

Edward kept his voice low despite being in the hold farthest from where crewmates in the deck above would most likely be. "My father gave me the ship as Benjamin Hornigold with the intent to go about unlocking pieces of it. If I survive, then I become stronger as the ship itself becomes mine. Once that happens, why attack and provoke us? Would he have done it even if we hadn't killed Gregory Dunn? I don't see the purpose."

Herbert shrugged and gestured towards Edward. "Perhaps this is the final test then? Perhaps this would have happened regardless of us attacking Gregory Dunn. I loathe to take advice from *him*, but Alexandre once said to me, 'People always tell more than they wish to. You need but to listen.'" Herbert tried a French accent but butchered it in the best way possible.

Edward laughed at Herbert for a moment before addressing the quote. "And what am I to listen to, exactly?"

"What did your father say to you in that tavern?"

Edward only needed a few seconds to recall it. "'Try again when you grow a spine.'"

Herbert cocked his brow. His eyes and the crook of his neck as he stared at Edward was the look of a man who didn't want to say something out loud that should have been obvious at that point.

Edward sighed. "So, you're saying that my father planned all this from the beginning, and he wants me to kill him?"

Herbert's brow lowered, then he spread his hands as though he were unveiling a bountiful feast, a feast of evidence towards the conclusion Edward had spelled out.

Edward's earlier frustration and itch faded away and left a hole so deep it could take the very light of the sun with it.

He fell to the box he had been sitting on before, sinking into it like the light into the emptiness inside him.

"My father wants me to kill him."

Edward and Herbert headed back to the deck above the hold where the crew's quarters were. All that separated the hold from the crew's quarters were the maze of barrels and boxes on one end of the ship, thinning out near the other, and a short ladder.

The narrow space between the cargo was barely enough for Edward to walk through, let alone Herbert in his wooden wheelchair, but he managed with only a few snags. Edward had his own issues with his height in the cramped part of the ship. He had to remain bent over as they walked through the hold towards the ladder.

Edward climbed up the ladder, one hand carrying Herbert's wheelchair and the other gripping the rungs. Each step was a labour in balance and delicacy, and Edward needed to take his time. After a few heaves, and a tenuous leverage over the lip of the other deck's edge, the wheelchair was up, and Edward himself wasn't far behind.

"Next time," Edward said to Herbert over the side to the hold through a few laboured breaths, "we leave the chair."

Herbert chuckled as he began his climb. "Aye, Ca… Aye, Ed," Herbert amended quickly. This was the *Black Blood*, and Edward was not his captain.

Herbert's journey up the ladder was nearly as laborious as Edward's, as Herbert could only rely on his hands for stability, leaving his legs dangling beneath him and swinging with each advance up the rungs. Once on the other deck, Edward held Herbert's chair steady for him as he climbed into in and got comfortable again, placing a small blanket over his emaciated limbs to hide them from sight.

Edward recalled that Herbert had once said the act was meant more for others than himself, as he had already come to terms with his circumstances. Hiding his legs did nothing for him—they were a part of him—but for others, it stopped the staring and the shrinking that came after they realized they were staring.

After Herbert settled, they went the short distance to the crew's quarters, now adjusted for dining. The hammocks, usually stacked three high in rows along the hull with a mere inch or two of clearance for each row's swinging arc, had been put away. The accessible area was now filled with crew-mates in clusters sitting flush on the deck as they ate from large soup bowls.

This ship, unlike the *Queen Anne's Revenge*, had no desig-nated dining area, no tables, no benches, no segregation be-tween living and eating space. And no privacy. By the time each man had their bowls, Edward could tell that the dining space would be shoulder-to-shoulder with bodies. The thought of having to sit shoulder to bloody shoulder with these men in an already oppressively humid environment rankled Edward more than the rigorous work above deck had.

Close to the stern, near the cut-off to the hold but centred between port and starboard, was a large iron stove in the middle of a pit of sand held in by sturdy wooden planks cov-ered in more iron. The stove was an older design than in Ed-ward's ship and had far less utility. The meals it could supply were limited to the standard stews common on long voyages made in pots as big and broad as Edward was.

Near the stove, hanging from the rafters of the ship in twine, were a variety of dried spices swaying with the bob-bing of the waves. From a distance Edward couldn't recog-nize many of the spices, save basil and parsley. They still looked fresh from what Edward could see; given that they were just in port they may have been bought the day before, or they could have been stolen from a merchant ship before that for all Edward knew.

Mixed in with the heavy and thick air of sweat, shit, and salt from the sea, Edward could smell the distinct aroma of boiling potatoes, but that was about it. None of the spices hanging in the air, nor those in the stew, made it to his nose. All else was lost in the pot, but Edward surmised it was some meat salted heavily enough to dry the throat, and some other vegetables that fared well over long voyages, hearty vegetables that on their own could be tasty and healthful, if only one joined it with complementary foods. The problem was that most complementary foods were impossible to keep aboard a ship.

And after months on board, that was when the scurvy came in. Edward was fortunate enough to never have been that far from shore when he was younger, and after Alexandre joined, he claimed to have knowledge of a concoction that helped in prevention over long voyages, though Edward wasn't privy to the ingredients. It helped his crew avoid the bleeding gums, the loss of teeth, and the bone weariness and pain that came before the fever, the tremors, and the death.

Thinking about the sickness, Edward thought back to the crewmates he'd had the displeasure of meeting over the day. Many had lost teeth, but not one man had the signs of the disease, or if they had, it seemed it was long behind them. He wondered what was their secret, as they certainly couldn't have another Alexandre aboard.

As Edward took in the surroundings of the ship and how small it was, it felt as though the *Queen Anne's Revenge* were a castle in comparison. The economy of space in the *Black Blood* seemed to be taken to an extreme, and the best way to describe it would be with one word: cramped.

Edward felt cramped in the small quarters and the mass of controlled clutter around the ship. Each deck, and each section of each deck, was more compact and efficiently used. Even on Bartholomew Roberts' small ship, it felt more open, as though he could move and breathe freely. Here, the confined spaces boxed him in, the weight on his chest bending him inward like wood bowed from stress. Edward was trapped in a tinderbox with over one hundred enemies in the middle of the sea, and he was on the edge of sparking.

But not all was dire. As Edward had been taking stock of the scene before him, he noticed John, the same John with the cup of water, walking towards Edward and Herbert with three bowls cradled precariously in the crook of his arms. John carried the food, as important as a child in this exhausting work aboard a ship, with the same delicacy and mannerism of carrying his own baby.

Edward stepped forward and took two of the bowls from John's arms and handed one to Herbert. Before Edward or Herbert could give their thanks, John spoke up.

"If you men would enjoy a bit of privacy, I happen to know just such a location," he said with a genial smile bordering on a youth's naïveté.

Edward glanced at Herbert for a moment. "Lead the way."

John took them away from the crew's quarters and towards the bow of the ship. They passed by some other men late in getting below deck for their share of food, drawing long, covetous stares at the bowls in the three men's hands.

Midships Edward noticed the surgeon's room, slightly off-centre with the rest of the ship, thick walls of hard timber on all sides save for the open doorway with no door running down the middle on both ends. It looked hardly big enough for two men to lie out on a table, and as they approached, Edward could see just that: two cots side by side with two men lying in them and a third empty one happening to be poking out on the starboard side, while on the port side, Edward could just make out closed shelves and storage for a surgeon's instruments.

On the starboard side there was a small space just barely wide enough to walk through that John was leading Edward and Herbert towards. It had evidently been a design flaw in the construction of the ship, as the surgeon's room could have been centred to allow ample room on both sides for any and all types of cargo to head towards the hold. As it stood, the port side was open enough for three to walk shoulder to shoulder, but the starboard could barely fit Herbert's chair, if that.

For that reason, it seemed, the walkway had been blocked with a barrel and a makeshift curtain. John placed his bowl on top of the barrel and gently slid the wooden keg over, allowing access to the alcove beside the surgeon's room. He moved the curtain aside and motioned Edward and Herbert inside.

"I don't think I'm going to fit," Herbert said, with a slight frown quickly forced into a smile when John looked over at him. Before John was able to respond, Herbert spoke again. "I'll manage, you two go on."

Edward took the lead and entered the alcove without another word on the subject. He didn't want John to dwell and mutter useless platitudes on the subject, as he knew Herbert wouldn't want that either.

Edward and John entered the alcove and sat down, Edward on top of a barrel at the other end of the cramped space, and John leaning into the bowed shape of the ship's starboard planks. Herbert positioned himself where the barrel had been previously, side-faced to the opening with his legs touching the corner of the surgeon's room. Herbert locked himself into place and then turned in his chair to better see the other men.

"There," Herbert said, a small smile on his face, "this should do."

John handed out two cloth sacks to Edward and Herbert, holding biscuits, four each, for the day's rations. The ship's biscuits were hard as rocks and would break the teeth if eaten as they were, but they were necessary after the hard day's work.

As though on some stage cue, the three men took a biscuit each from their bags, knocked them on a plank of the ship once, and dropped them into their stew. The ritual was so common amongst sailors, none typically gave it a second thought as the biscuit soaked and softened in the thick broth.

Edward did give it a second thought, as the memory of where and when he'd learned of the ritual came to mind. It was his father who had taught him, as it was his father who had taught him most everything he knew about ships.

He was brought back to his younger years, brought on by a now tainted nostalgia, to a time when his father had brought him on a short fishing trip with his friends. The small boat had had only one sail, and a single deck to store provisions and their haul.

"Salt pork again, is it?" Edward's father said with a wry smile.

Edward remembered looking up at his father; so enormous and imposing was his frame in those days he could think of nothing but awe at the form he wished he could attain someday.

"Er'y day is salt pork," one of the shipmates said. Edward couldn't remember his face or name, but he remembered those words. "Afternoon, salt pork, evening, salt pork, 'morrow'll be salt pork, and the day affer that too. Every bloody day salt pork."

"Now, now, gents," the cook said, "that's just not true. We've got salted beef too."

The group of them laughed at the comment as ship's biscuits were handed out. The men got four each, but Edward's father only handed him two. Edward remembered wanting to object and ask for more, but he didn't want to make a fuss in front of his father's men.

Edward's father took a biscuit in hand, held it up and gave his son a glance to see if he was following along. Edward had already been mimicking his father and looked more towards him than at the bowl or biscuit, despite his hunger.

His father smacked the biscuit against the wood of the ship at his feet, then dropped it into the stew. A half step behind, Edward did the same. His father smiled at him, and Edward smiled back.

The memory was a curious but arresting look back at the father of his younger years. It was so far removed from the father he'd met just a few moons back, the one who now called himself Calico Jack, that it felt like a different person. His father had never been cold to him, had never scolded him without reason, and had only been hard when he'd needed to be. Edward had never known his father to do vile things to both women and men, let alone all the other horrible stories he had heard told about Calico Jack over the years.

Edward would be lying to himself if he thought it didn't make what they were about to do easier. Calico Jack wasn't his father now, not really, and the more he thought it over, the more Edward thought there was no way to avoid giving his father exactly what he seemed to want.

Edward pushed aside the dark thoughts and focussed on the hunger in his belly. The other two were already well into their stew, and Edward needed to catch up.

As Edward had suspected, the stew had been saturated in an ungodly amount of salt, the results of curing and storing aboard a ship. There was almost no way to rinse the salt away, and so it ended up in the stew. This was on a whole other level from what he experienced aboard the *Queen Anne's Revenge*, and it made Edward's toes curl.

Sensing another cue, John produced three cups from his own cloth holding his biscuits and filled them with the laced water from a waterskin.

The three men, so focussed on their food, neglected each other's company until they had halved their stews and thrown another biscuit into the mix. Edward was first to take pause and speak.

"How does your crew manage the scurvy? I notice few have the signs."

John smiled. "See the red bits in the stew?"

Edward took closer note of the broth, leaning to catch the light coming from grated rafters above them. Just as John had said, there were bits of some red vegetables in the stew. Edward isolated the vegetable and chewed on it. After a moment, his tongue felt as though it were on fire.

"Hoo, I think I've had this before. Some type of pepper, is it not?" Edward managed through painful breaths. He took a drink of water, but it only made the pain worse.

John chuckled. "Yes, it helps ward off the disease, and if it's properly dried, it can last quite some time. And the rats don't seem to like 'em, so we have no fear of losing them on a long voyage."

"Clever," Edward said as he held his hand over his mouth. The heat was dissipating slowly, but at that moment it was nearly unbearable.

"Interesting that it becomes so masked in the stew," Herbert commented as he stirred his spoon and peered into his bowl.

"Not much is needed, from what I'm told."

"I'll have to remember this, though I don't know if I want to," Edward sputtered, the heat now starting to simmer down.

The three men chuckled at Edward's misfortune and continued eating for a bit in their small private space on the ship.

A noise at Edward's back sent pricks down his neck and arms. He got up and turned around, some combination of his senses telling him he should be on alert.

Sure enough, a hand pulled away the curtain on Edward's side of the secluded spot. The hand belonged to Edward's chief tormentor and his reason for staying so wary despite their making it aboard the *Black Blood*. Nigel's pock-marked face came into view, a broad, wicked grin pulling at his cheeks.

"What 'ave we here?" he said. "Couple'a babes ready for the slaughter?"

Edward heard footsteps behind him, and one of Nigel's friends was on Herbert, a knife at his throat. It was the man whom Edward had knocked down during his trial to join the crew, though Edward could not recall his name.

Herbert's eyes were wide. Edward saw his hands inching to the secret compartment of weapons in his wheelchair, and it made him painfully aware of his own lack of arms.

Edward turned back when the sound of wood scraping across floorboards sounded from Nigel's direction. He'd moved the barrel aside during Edward's distraction, and held a long knife in his hands. Behind Nigel was another man, blocking any chance of escape.

"Let's finish wut we started earlier."

Edward raised his hands in a defensive position, his years of training and conditioning working without thought. He assessed the length of the knife, his distance from Nigel, and Nigel's reach. Edward generally had the advantage in height, but it meant nothing in the confined, trapped space beside the surgeon's room.

At least they can patch me up quickly, Edward mused, a soft, dark chuckle escaping under his breath.

"Nigel, stop this madness!" John shouted, but he hadn't moved from his near supine position against the starboard wall.

"I'm jus' giving the greenhorn what's coming to him."

"What should he have done? Laid down and died? The captain told him to fight you, and so he did."

Nigel gritted his teeth and glanced over at John. "He shouldn'a tried to join in the first—"

Edward sprang, his hand darting down and then up towards Nigel's wrist. Nigel's eyes—anyone's eyes, for that matter—were too slow for the smooth and efficient motion. Like a viper, Edward snapped at Nigel's wrist, striking it smartly. The swiftness took Nigel by surprise, and the knife flew from his grip and lodged itself into the wooden wall of the surgeon's room with a thunk and a twang.

Behind him, Edward heard a scuffle that he hoped Herbert was in control of. Edward couldn't afford to look away from Nigel now, even if it meant getting stabbed in the back again.

A voice broke through the small din of the fight, taking the wind out of everyone's sails. "By these copper legs o' mine, if you all don't stop yer fighting, I'll dump the lot of you overboard." The words came from behind Nigel, a simple, almost soft, declaration that carried with it a queer kind of weight.

The tension was cut at once, a sharp contrast to the still swaying blade in the plank of the surgeon's room.

"Get out here, all of ye."

Nigel gave Edward and John a harsh look before turning around and exiting the alcove. Edward gave himself a moment to glance over his shoulder at Herbert, who had gotten the better of his opponent and looked unharmed. He gestured to Edward, signalling everything was all right before he headed the long way around the surgeon's room along with

Nigel's friend. Edward and John were the last to leave the small space.

Nigel and his friends all lined up in front of Grace and the other men, while Herbert stayed off to the side away from Edward. John pulled Edward back, and the two stayed a few paces from the three who had just attacked them.

"Want ta try and explain just what you were about to do?" Grace asked.

"Jus' a little welcoming party for the new recruits, ma'am," Nigel responded, with a bit too much cockiness by Edward's estimation.

Grace grinned as though she enjoyed the joke Nigel made, then kneed him in his nether regions more swiftly than Edward had knocked the knife from his hands.

Too much cockiness by far.

Nigel doubled over in pain, grabbing his ballocks in both hands. He fell to his knees with a gasp of pain.

Grace bent down slowly to Nigel's pain-postured level. "You would'a killed him if I hadn't come along. Just admit it, for both our sakes." Her words were soft, but they carried the same measured, even, and cold words of command. This was not the kind of tone that could be taught, only the kind learned over a lifetime of experience.

Nigel, still whimpering, protested at first, before lapsing into begging. Edward understood the protesting, but not the begging. Why was he begging?

Grace rose to her feet in that same measured, even, and slow way she had moved when she'd knelt. "I don't permit liars on my ship," she said, "nor those who kill a crewmate."

In one motion, Grace pulled a pistol from her belt and fired it at the back of Nigel's head, his last supplication brought short by a lead ball through the brain. His pulpy mass exploded onto the deck below as the loud crack rang across the ship and took all other noises with it if but for a brief moment.

When the other noises returned, although stunted by the crew recognizing the sound of gunfire, Edward was able to process what had just happened.

Edward felt pressure on his sleeve and noticed John had gripped his shoulder and a part of his clothes. When Edward looked over, he let go.

"Ugh, got blood on me boots!" Grace lamented. "Get this mess off my ship," she commanded. The senior officers leapt into action and dragged the bloody body of Nigel away.

Grace looked into the eyes of the two remaining attackers, followed by Edward, John, and Herbert, one by one. "Let this be a lesson to each of you. I'm the captain here, and I don't take kindly with my crew trying to kill each other. Or being a cunt. Don't be like Nigel," she said, waving a hand at the splayed viscera on the deck and over her copper greaves.

Satisfied with the looks of shock plastered on the faces of her audience, she gave a curt nod before she turned and walked away from the scene. The slamming of her copper boots echoed down the deck, cutting through the growing crowd's animated questions about what had happened.

The whole event was so quick, the only remnant left of the fight and of Nigel was his knife still lodged in the wood beside the surgeon's room.

7. FOR WHOM THE GOLDEN BELL TOLLS

The crack of the pistol awoke not just Anne, but most of the men on the upper floor of the general store. That sharp, whip-like sound touched at the inner parts of the mind that controlled urgency like no other, and for those with the sense, it stripped away all tiredness in an instant. Those without the sense were not long for this world that Anne and company found themselves in.

Anne glanced at William, who also awoke just as she did, and then she jumped from her bed and over to the window overlooking the hamlet. William was but a half-step behind her, and the rest of the men a few steps behind him.

Anne scanned the small crossroads of the hamlet below for signs of the fight. She only allowed herself a few seconds before she began to turn around and head outside, but William stopped her with a point of his finger.

She looked back to see two of the crewmates who were out on watch retreating to the general store as they loaded pistols. Another crack sounded, and a puff of dirt shot into the air a few feet from one of the crewmates.

Anne had seen all she needed to see. "To arms," she declared.

Before the last syllable left her lips, the crew were on the move. William wasted no time in procuring his sword and slinging a musket over his shoulder. Anticipating her need, he tossed her golden cutlass and a rifle to her. Anne caught the two as she rushed to the stairs to the main level of the general store.

She jumped down the steps two at a time and passed through the storage room with a tied-up Jules sitting in the chair where she had left him earlier that night. Alexandre and Victoria were at the front of the store, observing the crewmates losing ground outside as they prepared muskets for an offensive.

Anne slowed her pace for a moment as she took the rifle off her shoulder and handed it to Alexandre in exchange for the loaded musket. With a practiced hand and a bit of black powder from Alexandre, she readied the musket with a few flicks of her thumb. Walking sideways with the musket aimed towards the unknown assailants, she exited the store, found her mark, and shot.

After the shot was away and the acrid smoke surrounded her, she ducked back into the store, confident she had hit her mark, and not wanting to risk getting shot in return.

William was next out the door with a loaded musket in hand. He fired, sending more smoke into the small space, with no wind to take it away. He moved outside the store to a nearby pillar keeping the roof of the store's deck aloft.

Alexandre handed Anne her rifle, now loaded, and took back the spent musket. She bent down below the window of the general store for a moment and closed her eyes. She counted the shots and where they were coming from.

Only two men remained by her estimation, and they were staggering their shots to keep Anne, William, and the others at bay. They were skilled in battle. Three bangs. A thud. Only one man left.

Anne counted down the seconds. She knew the approximate time the last man took to reload based on the time between previous shots. There would also be a momentary hesitation when he moved out of cover to take aim. She aimed for that hesitation.

Anne sprang from her cover like a snake from between two rocks. She flew through the smoke, forcing her eyes open despite the burn and the watering. When the smoke broke, she saw movement to her right. She aimed down the centre of her rifle at the movement and pulled the trigger. The bullet, more accurate than the musket she'd shot before, hit the target right through the neck. The man, just in the middle of aiming, reared back, firing wildly into the air. The last crack sent a wave of smoke in front of the man. Spurts of blood from his neck broke through the grey cloud and splattered on the dirt road.

Anne relaxed but remained on alert. "Any others?" She didn't look away from the direction the enemy had come from but said the words loud enough for her crewmates to hear.

"Two more, headed to the bell tower," one of the crewmates said.

The bell tower. The unknown element. The trigger for something unknown. *An alert to others?*

Anne's mind raced with questions, but a single thought rose above them all: *Stop them.*

She dropped her spent rifle and stole William's loaded musket before gliding into a sprint towards the bell tower. She caught a glimpse of the other crewmates coming out of the general store, armed to the teeth, before everything turned into a blur.

Anne was faster than the rest of the crew. Lighter in step, lithe, and catlike, she ran like the wind of a storm beating close to the ground as it swelled up a narrow street. Her feet were a flurry on the dirt road, the sound of a mad dance on the cobbles.

She passed the silent houses with the dead-still villagers resting inside. She fought the silence of that stillness with her beating feet and pounding heart in her ears. She would stomp away that silence any way she had. Until she finished the job, she would not brook any silence.

Figures in the night cut moonlight shadows onto the ground forty paces in front of her, and twenty from the bell tower entrance. The figures, cloaked in brown, ran toward the bell tower at a quick pace, but Anne was quicker.

She slowed a step to aim the musket and fired at the closest figure. Her aim was true, and it hit the man in the back. The man staggered, turned around, and drew a pistol. She ducked, and the bullet rushed over her head. She ran, pulling her cutlass from the sheathe. The man pulled out his own blade, but he was too slow. She sliced his gut open in passing. She moved forward, not looking back and not losing stride, her golden weapon outstretched and gleaming in the moonlight as she ran.

The second man busted through the door of the bell tower and tried to close it behind him. Anne leapt, her legs thrusting at the door just before it closed. The planks splintered and the door burst open, the cloaked man behind it staggering back into the bell tower.

The man fell, grasping for purchase. He found it on the bell's thick rope. His gaze shot up as he realized what his hands gripped. Anne rose from her jumping kick and thrust her blade at him before he had the chance to gain his wits. The man jumped into the air. Her cutlass pierced his chest with a soft thunk. He held tight to the rope, despite the wound, with a preternatural strength for a man soon to be dead. He pushed his full weight back down to complete the pull on the rope. Anne, holding fast to her blade in his chest, couldn't hold his weight.

The rope came down with his desperate pull, and the golden bell sounded overhead, its tone unlike anything Anne had ever heard before, and she was in the centre of it.

The chime was low and reverberating, and louder than all other sounds. It overpowered her heavy, frenzied breaths for air, and it seized the beating of her heart in her ears. She felt as though she were a sail held taut.

The low reverberation echoed in her bones, rattling her chest and legs and arms as though she had whacked a heavy stick with all her might against a metal beam. She let go of her sword, still stuck in the chest of the man who rang the bell, and staggered back from the pain of that noise.

As the bell rang, the low unnatural tone shifted and changed into a high pitch. The slow change could have been beautiful, as though she were present in the most compelling and evocative opera she had ever had the privilege of attending. Instead, the high pitch split her skull in twain with its crescendo. The noise became Anne's world. There was nothing but her and the noise.

The instinct to stop the noise subdued all other thoughts and overpowered her self-preservation. It compelled her to cover her ears, fall to her knees, and close her eyes to quell the melody of that bell.

After a moment, after an eternal, painful moment, the din

subsided, and Anne opened her eyes and unclamped her ears, the world returning to her.

Silence had fallen in her absence from the world. Silence of the dead, or the soon to be.

The man Anne had killed inside the tower held fast to the rope with his death's rigour, keeping the striker of the bell at bay. Her golden cutlass still protruded from his chest, drops of blood pattering to the wooden floor. She eased him up gently to allow the striker to stay at rest before she cut him down so the bell could not sound again.

She stepped outside to see William and some of the other crewmates scattered about on the road leading back to the general store, eyes flickering back and forth. From the looks on their faces, even William's, the bell had rattled them just as much as her.

In that confusion in the wake of the bells cresting, Anne needed to be the rock that held the crew together. She took a deep breath, held in her frustrations, anger, and questions, and snuffed them out.

Just as she was about to issue orders to scout for more of the enemy crew, she swallowed her words when a tone similar to the golden bell rang out from the interior of the island. Though far off, it was clear and just as strange and ominous. Thankfully the volume of the ringing was low and didn't have the same effect as it had earlier.

A signal then, Anne thought. Some of the tension left her shoulders as she understood the reason behind the bells. It didn't change the fact that they had been found out by the enemy, but knowing what the bell was for eased some worry in her mind.

A few more tones sounded from different places on the island, one after the other. From what Anne could tell, there were four distinct rings, which meant there were at least four other bells. After another moment, the sounds faded, and silence returned.

The second element that robbed Anne of her speech was something altogether different. A door of a nearby home opened, and one of the residents of the hamlet stepped out. His slow, shuffling feet broke through the silence once more.

Anne moved to meet him. "You should head back inside," she said, and then she remembered the strange way they had been acting earlier. She gripped her cutlass tighter. "It's late, sir, you should be in bed."

He took another shuffling step forward. His face was pale in the moonlight. The shadows of some trees overhead shaded his eyes.

Another door creaked, splitting the silence again. Anne saw motion at another home down the dirt road.

She gripped her cutlass tighter still. Something wasn't right. "Back to the general store, now!" she ordered.

The man came closer, and Anne saw his eyes. They were hollow and lifeless, and there was no recognition of a spirit within them. Anne had only seen something similar in the eyes of men and women broken in one way or another through trauma, left in the world like husks, their bodies and minds forever torn.

The crew were stuck in place, watching the man as he came closer and closer to them, as though caught in the trance of those dead eyes. They couldn't tear themselves away from the spectacle, invisible tethers holding their feet in place.

The hollow man sprang into action, sprinting towards Anne, William, and crew. He moved quicker than Anne would have thought possible. He burst through the wooden fence between his house and the road, sending wooden chunks flying away with force.

The crew were too slow to react, and before they could move, the man hit a crewmate in the chest with a punch. The sailor toppled backwards as though hit with a cannonball, and Anne heard the distinct pop of bones breaking. The crewmate rolled back onto his side, clutching his chest and gasping for breath.

Anne's mind reeled with sudden realization. The golden bell was a trigger, a trigger for an even deeper trance, one that washed away all reason in the brain, perhaps washed away even the reason that kept one from utilizing the full power of their own muscles to avoid injury. And on top of that, these people with untold strength, stamina, and speed were hostile.

"William, help James back to the store," she ordered. "Everyone, run! Run, you fools!"

The crew, back in their right minds after seeing their mate attacked, followed orders and dashed back to the store. The hollow man, drawn to the movement, ran after the first who went into action. He leapt onto another crewmate and ravaged him with blow after horrifying blow.

The crewmates ahead kept running, but those behind stopped and levelled their muskets. They each unloaded their shots at the hollow man, careful not to hit their now bloody crewmate. With each shot, the hollow man recoiled, but he didn't stop his assault. *Crackcrackcrack, crack, crack.* Fifteen shots later the man fell over, his body as dead as his mind.

Anne pulled the hollow man off the crewmate, but it was too late. His skull had been bashed in with such force, it appeared as though he were the victim of a horse trampling.

"He's dead," she said curtly. "Back to the store!"

Anne took one look back to William to see that he was making along well and then hurried back to the store herself.

Against the myriad of stomping boots, Anne heard more creaking as doors were opening across the hamlet. She didn't let up in her stride, taking note of the noises but not letting it draw her attention. She passed the crewmates who had gone ahead of her. She needed to get to the store first.

On approaching the store, Anne noticed a few crewmates who had stayed behind, as well as Alexandre and Victoria. All were on alert from the activity they had heard and stood watch with weapons drawn.

"Barricade!" Anne yelled when she saw them. "We need to barricade the store, we're under attack."

Anne's words, urgency, and the crewmates just behind her flying towards them lit a fire under the crew's feet, and they ran into the store. Alexandre and Victoria seized the table holding the chessboard and the chairs from the deck, scattering the board and pieces across the dirt.

Anne jumped up to the deck, sliding across the wooden boards as she stopped in front of the entrance. She took a moment to breathe as she entered the store, once more taking stock of the thousand items and sorting them for their usefulness in her mind.

The crew brought boxes from the storage room, dense and filled with food or other items, into the central part of the store and began stacking them haphazardly.

"Bring them to the front, cover the windows. Make sure there are no gaps. Put the barrels in front to secure them in place." The crew, with a sound mind directing the action, put more focus into their work. "And someone bring me rope."

Just as someone brought her rope to work with, the crewmates who had joined her at the bell tower were making their way into the store again. She put the new men to work at once, forming a line from the storeroom to the side windows to bring the boxes forward.

Anne put the rope over her shoulder and closed one of the store's double doors, sealing the locking latch at the top and bottom of the door. William and the injured crewmate had yet to return, so she left the other door open.

Anne exited the store and peered down the road leading to the bell tower. William and the injured crewmate were slowly coming to the store, but behind them, the awakened townsfolk were gaining ground. Further to that, down each road leading to the store came more of the hollow people.

"Hurry," she yelled to them, though she knew they understood the urgency all too well.

The injured crewmate looked over his shoulder at the people gaining on them, but it didn't seem to give him renewed purpose. Instead, in his eyes, even at that distance, Anne could tell he had resigned himself to his fate. William pushed harder, taking on more of the weight, but his strength alone wasn't enough to make it in time.

The injured crewmate pushed William away before he pulled out his pistol. "Go," he muttered. There was an absolute strength in his soft declaration. William faltered but for a moment, then thanked the man for his bravery, and ran at full speed to the store.

The crewmate fired his pistol into the crowd as he did his best to back away, drawing the attention of the hollow people towards him instead of William and the general store. He tumbled over a nearby fence, lumbered to his feet, and pulled out a cutlass. He sliced wildly at the men and women approaching, a valiant effort against the storm, but they overwhelmed him. The hollow citizens tore the crewmate apart.

William reached the store, and pulled Anne back inside, not sparing a look back to the crewmate who had sacrificed himself to buy them time. Anne snapped back to the moment, resolving, no doubt as William had, not to waste those precious moments given them.

They closed the other door and latched it shut, but Anne knew it wouldn't be enough against the incredible strength that these entranced people were capable of.

"Bring the heaviest barrels over here in front of the doors."

The crew brought over three barrels so heavy they had to roll them across the floor rather than carry them. They placed all three directly in front of the two doors, flush against them.

Anne took the rope from over her shoulder and wrapped it around the three barrels, pulling them tightly together. After the rope was secure, she tied both ends around the handles of the doors in a reef knot. The crew brought three more barrels and worked in pairs to place the new ones on top of the first, completely covering the door. With more rope, the six were secured into place as a unit and would be nearly impossible to topple.

Nearly impossible for normal humans.

"It's not enough," Anne muttered. "Is there more rope?"

"More?" one of the crewmates replied as he looked at the massive wooden fortification they had made.

"There is some left, though *le patron* is holding onto it at the moment," Alexandre said, though he trailed off as he seemed to realize something in his statement, and his gaze travelled to the doorway to the storage room.

Anne followed his gaze, and understood the problem at once. She drew her cutlass, the ringing of the foreign steel mimicking the cry of the bell in a way that made Anne wince.

As the sound of the blade waned and Anne focussed her attention on the back room, she could hear a vile frothing as if of some beast coming from the depths of the storage.

"Step away from the storage room!" she shouted.

A half a heartbeat passed before a loud snapping came from the storage room, followed by stomping boots across wooden floorboards. Jules barreled into the main room of the store, knocking against the walls.

His eyes, both aware and not, both alive and not, trained on Anne in a strange half-focus as though he were only taking in the shape of her and the cutlass in her hand.

Anne tried to act first and stepped forward, planning to strike, but Jules moved more quickly than she did. He darted forward, moving like a trained fighter, and lashed out at her as he dodged her strike. Anne pulled back her shoulder and twisted away from the blazing-fast fist, avoiding the blow and repositioning.

Though his strength and speed were extraordinary, it was no replacement for proper training. He was a simple general store owner, not a fighter, and Anne had the training and the wherewithal to react to him.

Jules was wild, but hammered with a strength unparalleled. As each blow came Anne's way, and as she dodged just out of the way, she felt the force of each one. If any one of them made contact, bones would break.

William struck in the chaos, a fierce punch to the head knocking Jules back, but only slightly. Jules snarled, beast-like and feral, and turned his attention to William. Anne reared back and thrust her cutlass into Jules' stomach, gutting the portly man.

Were he a normal man, Jules would have doubled over in pain, but he kept fighting even as his intestines spilled out in front of him.

William faltered in the face of the walking dead man. Jules shot his fist forward. William pulled back, but too late. Jules' fist caught William in the left shoulder. A successive snap of several bones cracking broke through the tense air around them. William stifled a cry of shock and sliced his sword down and across Jules' head. The blade slammed halfway through Jules' skull and caught in the man's brain.

Finally, mercifully, Jules fell to the floor of the store.

William held onto his blade as it fell with the dead man, stuck in the hard bone of the skull. He wiggled it free and backed away from the body, breathing hard. For a moment, William and Anne stared at the body together, along with several of the crewmates.

A noise outside drew their attention. The citizens of the hamlet were approaching the storefront en masse.

The din began as a small rap on the front doors but grew to a thunder of slamming bodies, breaking glass, and cracking wood. The six tall barrels at the front jolted forward with each second, teetering as though precariously perched on a precipice edge.

Instinctually, the crew rushed to reinforce the lifeless wooden barricade keeping them from the horde of hollow men and women on the other side. They pressed their large sailor's bodies against the curved planks, adding weight to them.

On the sides of the general store, the citizens attacked the glass windows and less secure wooden boxes covering them.

Anne, pushing with her might against the barrels in front of the door, could see through a small gap as they broke through the glass and grabbed at the boxes in their way.

Though the townsfolk had obviously lost their wits, there was some intelligence still working the gears in their minds. The men slamming against the doors were ramming in unison, and the others took down the ramshackle wall to access the interior. Blood stained the hands of those prying at the boxes through the broken glass, shards sticking out from long slashes running up their arms.

"Gunners forward!" she shouted through the synchronized slams. "Aim for the head or the heart!"

The brave souls who heard the call jumped up to the ledge holding the boxes and barrels against the windows. Victoria was one such soul, and she fired into the thick of the men and women coming at them. First, she aimed at those taking down their protection, and then she took aim at the men attacking the front doors.

With each shot, smoke filled the room and settled in the small space. It wasn't long before the air was thick with the remnants of the black powder. The smell was bad enough, but the worst of it was the choking and seizing it brought to the lungs, and the effect on one's vision.

Anne could manage her breathing better than some, but the thick grey mist overtook her eyes and made them water.

"Cease—" Anne coughed as the smoke entered her throat proper. It arrested her voice as her body forced it out. "Cease fire!" she managed after a laboured moment.

The gunfire stopped after a few more shots into the thick mass of bodies in front of the store, and though the crew stopped firing, it only stopped more smoke from accumulating. With no breeze, it lingered in the spaces between the crew's bodies, shifting and swirling with the small movements in a dance of air rarely seen.

A loud splintering noise split through the grunting on both sides of the store as one of the barrels burst open in the front. Its contents—potatoes buried in sand—spilled out in front of the double doors.

Suddenly, the synchronized slamming against the doors stopped, and there was a brief silence, a stillness of the air. At that moment, the silence closed in on Anne's heart and fixed it in place with an icy hand.

Just as suddenly as the silence came, it left again. The slamming didn't return, and instead, the wave of the hollow people outside the store rushed at the broken barrier. They punched and pulled at the weak spot, the chink in the armour, all hands and fingers prying and tearing at splinters and sand and potatoes. They smashed the wood to pieces inch by inch, creating an opening for the raging pile of people on the other side.

Anne knew it wouldn't be long for them if they stayed. "To the roof!" she shouted above the clamour, another cough of smoke choking the volume of her words. "Retreat!" she yelled as she led the charge up to the second floor of the store. Along the way, Anne grabbed an axe from the shelf.

The second floor of the store opened like an attic, with a hatch at the top of steep ladder stairs not unlike their ship. Anne climbed first and held the door open for the crew to climb in more quickly.

The crewmates who had made it inside the store were uninjured, aside from the smoke lingering in the lungs. A few of the men coughed and took long and laboured breaths as they entered the storage room and climbed the stairs up to the second floor.

The only one injured was William, who was last up the stairs. He couldn't move his injured shoulder, but one could hardly tell if it slowed him any as he climbed the stairs like any other.

As soon as William was on the other side of the horizontal door, Anne planted her feet square as she held the hatch open with her hip. She lifted the axe she had pilfered from the storefront in both hands and slammed it down on the top of the stairs. The axe cut through the wooden beam a quarter way, revealing it to have an old, blunted edge.

Anne cursed under her breath and wrenched the axe free before tossing it aside. She pulled out the golden cutlass, the strange, ever-sharp metal made of the same ore as the bell, and it rang into the frigid night once more with its peculiar song.

Just as she pulled it out, the first of the citizens who had made it through the front of the store ran into the back room and began climbing the stairs.

Anne sliced the blade downwards at one of the hinges bolting the stairs to the top floor, and it cracked in half. The stairs went slightly uneven but still stood.

The man who was climbing only faltered a bit when his weight shifted beneath him, but continued his ascent.

Anne had no time to rear back for another strike; if she did, the hollow man would be on her. She pulled back and threw the hatch closed. The man's hand crashed upwards through the hatch, and he clawed at the boards.

William, who had stayed by her side, locked the hatch in place before the man could push it open. It wouldn't do much against that abnormal strength, but each second counted.

Anne didn't waste a breath for thanks and ran to the second floor sleeping quarters. "To the roof!" she said as she pointed to two windows overlooking the front of the store.

Her voice was almost back to normal without the smoke choking her throat.

The crewmates used their muskets to break the glass of the windows and clear the debris before jumping through. Anne turned around to watch the doorway to the second floor, her cutlass poised in front of her.

Slam! The hatch pulsed up with a loud thud and clank of the metal lock. Anne tensed and bent her knees. *Slam!* Another crack against the wood from below. Anne backed up, feeling the crewmates behind her thinning as they went to the roof. *Slam!* The pounding came with a creak as the wood strained to stay together. She gritted her teeth and shifted to holding the cutlass in both hands.

Slam! The wood broke open in two, one plank still attached to the lock as the other side flew open. The side that opened hit the wall and came back down on the head of the man at the top of the stairs, but he climbed through unabated.

"Anne!" Victoria called out to her.

Anne turned around and jumped out the nearest window in one motion. The shards of glass still attached to the frame cut through her clothes and sliced into her skin before she landed on the small roof on top of the deck. A musket shot rang out behind her just as she fell, the crack of the black powder coinciding with the crack of her shoulder against the wood.

Alexandre helped Anne to her feet, his typically placid eyes burning with that same volcanic rage she'd seen before but mixed with a pitying expression on his face. He felt sorry for the men and women attacking them at that moment, for the reason behind their unreasonableness.

Anne gripped his arm. "If you have time for pity, you have time to think a way out for us."

Alexandre glanced at her and then doubled back as her words hit him. He smiled, but there was none of the small warmth in it she had felt before she had gone to sleep. "Is it not obvious?" he said. "We must kill them all."

"How can we kill them when we can't even hold them here?" Victoria yelled over her shoulder at Alexandre as she shot into the window again.

"We won't have to hold them for long," William said at the side of the roof.

Anne joined him at the side of the roof and looked in the direction he was pointing. In the distance, she could see the shapes of twenty people advancing in the waning moonlight towards the town. They came in the direction of where they first landed, so chances were they were crewmates from the *Queen Anne's Revenge*.

And, if that weren't enough of an indication, Anne could make out another figure ahead of the pack running at blazing speeds towards them. The figure had a spear in one hand, and he was missing an arm.

As though challenging William's assertion, one of the entranced jumped through the window at Victoria. Victoria fell backwards, her musket braced between her and the crazed man on top of her. Victoria kept rolling back and kicked the man off the roof with her momentum. Anne watched as the man fell headfirst to the ground, his neck snapping violently to the side in a deathly contortion.

Before Victoria fell off the roof with the man, Alexandre caught her hand and pulled her to safety.

"Back away from the windows," Anne commanded. "There's too many of them. Kill them as they come onto the roof."

The musketeers moved away from the open windows and stepped back as much as the small space allowed. Another citizen climbed through the windowpane a moment later, and an iron ball met his temple. With the musket spent, the crewmate moved out of the way to allow another a better vantage point.

Anne glanced back to the road and saw Pukuh nearly at the centre of the hamlet. Anne called to him, and he looked up to their perch, losing a half step. Anne pointed to the front of the store.

"Fight them one on one. Aim for the head or heart."

Pukuh motioned with his spear in her direction and slowed his gait even further as he approached the corner of the general store's front deck. He lowered his stance as he glided towards the remaining enemies.

The twenty crewmates on his tail approached, weapons drawn. Noticing Pukuh's caution, they slowed to join him. Anne repeated her message to the newcomers before turning around to the rooftop battle.

The change in vantage point proved effective at managing the numbers, and before long the sounds of raging, entranced people dissipated, and the battle with them. When no more enemies jumped through to attack them, the crew risked looking inside.

After confirming it was safe and all the villagers were dead, Anne and the rest of the crew on the roof re-entered the second floor. They went down to the first floor where the other crewmates, along with dozens of dead bodies, awaited them.

The smoke of the earlier musket fire had abated, and Anne could see and breathe more freely. Blood splattered every wall and covered much of the items in the store. Twenty to thirty bodies lay in piles in each corner and out to the deck, blood and guts and brains pooling and oozing out of their now truly lifeless bodies.

The crewmates who had come to their rescue, including Pukuh, appeared winded, wounded, and confused as they looked over the bodies of what, to them, were ordinary farmers and housewives.

Before anyone could ask, Anne spoke up. "Everything will be explained in time. For now, I want to be back on the ship to rest. Questions can wait for dawn."

Anne awoke in the middle of her sleep for the second time that night, but this time it was not with the cracking sound of a pistol ringing into the night. It was with the warning of more to come on the horizon.

"Ship approaching off the port bow. To quarters!" she heard William shouting outside her door.

Before the inevitable knock came, she was out of bed and

opening it to his startled face. Behind him, men were clamouring to ready the cannons and muskets for a ship battle.

Anne and William went to the weather deck, where Anne traced across the horizon towards the approaching ship. She pulled out a spyglass and saw a sloop heading for them. Dawn had broken, and she would have overslept if she had gotten enough sleep the first time. As it stood, she was burning the candle on both ends, twice over.

Anne wiped away the tired from her eyes, took a deep breath, and prepared herself for a battle of a different sort.

Amidst final preparations for battle, something strange happened as the sloop approached. It slowed to a full stop just out of range of the cannons, just close enough for her to see the name *Whydah Gally* on the side, and Anne could see its crew lowering a longboat into the water.

What sort of trickery is this? "Muskets to port! Hold steady," she commanded.

She watched the longboat as it slowly came closer and closer to the *Queen Anne's Revenge*. Before long, she could make out those in the boat, as well as the one at the head, standing tall and lean with a familiar pretty face and jet-black eyes.

Anne gasped and shook her head in disbelief. "Sam?"

8. PIRATES AND THIEVES

Edward went to stroke his beard absentmindedly before he remembered he had shaved it off not a few days prior. His hands shook. The haunting feeling he so desperately wanted to suppress had returned. He took another drink from his flask.

"May I?" Herbert beckoned with his hand outstretched.

Edward, Herbert, and John all sat just outside of the alcove near the surgeon's room. Edward was sitting directly on the deck, his arms resting on his bent knees and his back against the wall of the room. Herbert was in front of him, leaning forward in his wheelchair, and John was to his left sitting on a tall box of cargo.

Edward took another swig and reluctantly handed it to Herbert, who took a generous portion for himself.

The crewmates who had gathered before at the sound of the gunfire had dispersed back to their eating or work above deck. Very few crewmates seemed surprised or even upset over the news that their captain had just executed Nigel, and the few that were didn't hold the feeling for long.

"You said she didn't rule this ship through intimidation," Edward mumbled. The words blurted out without his meaning to say them, and he regretted them at once. It was a childish accusation of a lie and felt more lash than a question.

John looked at Edward, knowing the words were meant for him. His face was stone, but his youthful eyes showed the pain of that lash. "And I stand by it," he said simply. "She saved your life, probably all our lives, by doing what she did to Nigel."

"And then she threatened us," Herbert chimed in.

"She told you the rules. I already told you that her word is law, that's the difference."

"And where exactly are these laws written?" Edward levelled John with a forceful gaze he hoped had the intended effect. After John was silent for a moment, Edward continued. "She rules on whims only she can know. Had he done something else that displeased her, she could have come up with some other law of hers to justify the act. How are we to know when we step on her toes?"

John rose to his feet and balled his fists. "Nigel was told to leave you be. He disobeyed that order. Or did you forget that?" John stared daggers at Edward in defence of his captain. He seemed almost a bit too invested. "Would you have done any differently were you captain and someone nearly killed a crewmate over a petty dispute?"

Edward glanced over at Herbert, remembering how he had punished him for disobeying orders. Had Herbert been more like Nigel, would he have killed him over it? He'd left Kenneth Locke stranded on an island to die, doing everything but pull the trigger—and he'd later regretted it when Kenneth came back as Cache-Hand. He'd also admonished Bartholomew Roberts for sparing Walter Kennedy.

John seemed to hit hard at Edward's sensibilities. He hadn't been as consistent upon reflection as he had hoped he had been in practice. In some ways, he had become harsher, and in others, more lax in his responsibilities.

Edward let out a sigh as he looked away from Herbert and stared at the deck. "I don't know what I would have done had I been in her position," he said. "Perhaps you are right, and perhaps I would have done the same."

John's hand and face relaxed in tandem as Edward backtracked. "So, what does this mean?"

Edward shook his head. The rum was beginning to make him hot, or perhaps it was the slight twinge of embarrassment. "I suppose it means I owe you an apology for my outburst." John appeared taken aback at the comment but accepted the apology. "And it means we need to be more cautious around our new captain." This time Edward glanced over towards Herbert, the words meaning more for him than what he was letting on in front of John. Herbert understood the message and gave Edward a nod.

There was another moment of silence as the group reflected on what had just happened, as well as the tense conversation. Each of them seemed shaken by how close they had come to be a splatter of gore on the deck of the ship.

John looked at Edward, a small smirk on his face now that he had calmed down. "If nothing else, this will make quite the story. First day on board and you got someone killed. That must be an accomplishment somewhere."

It was Edward's turn to be taken aback this time, and he was shocked into a different kind of silence for a moment. He glanced over at Herbert, who had what felt like the same dumbfounded expression on his face as well. Then the two burst out laughing, and John joined in.

"I suppose that is true," Edward said through the laughter. "On a pirate ship perhaps less so, but I shall see it as an accomplishment nonetheless." Edward, for the first time in a long while, laughed sincerely and with genuine mirth. It forced him to rise to his feet and clap John on the shoulder.

After another moment of laughter, and a sharing of Edward's flask, the three compatriots, now in better spirits, headed back to the crew quarters.

Now that supper had officially ended for the first shift, and the evening shift had broken their fast, the crew slung hammocks in the cramped space. With the numbers they had, as well as the small size of the quarters, each row of hammocks was stacked three high. The bottom one would have one's posterior scraping the sole of the deck, the middle gave no room to move without touching the mate above, and the top ran the risk of smacking one's head on the overhead.

Herbert chose the middle as it allowed him ease of sliding into and out of his chair. John went to the top as he was smaller than Edward, and it forced Edward to the bottom. His bigger frame and heavier build meant that he was touching the floor more than the average crewmate. Instead of just a light scraping with the sway of the ship that could be ignored, his hip struck the sole hard with each swing. He tried to tighten the hammock, and it provided some relief in exchange for more rigidity, and so instead of no sleep, he was left with little sleep.

Not that his dreams would allow him much more

regardless. The rum mitigated the deeper sleep that brings with it images both pleasant or harrowing familiar to most folk, but it couldn't stop them completely.

Two times in the night, Edward awoke with a start, stopping himself just shy of hitting Herbert's backside with his face. As with most dreams, whether joyful or distressful, he lost all knowledge of it upon his waking. All he had was a fog of dread arresting his thoughts and a tremble of the fingers that wasn't from a cool breeze. He had no way to know for sure, but from the way his sleeping mind and body reacted, the dreams couldn't have been pleasant ones.

Edward had been paralyzed by similar dreams for nights on end, long enough that he couldn't remember the last time he'd had a full night's sleep.

After a few hours of fitful slumber, the beat of a drum and a young man shouting orders to wake and relieve the other crewmates forced Edward awake.

Edward's body ached more than it had before he'd tried to sleep. His tired limbs were slow to act, and pressure in his head pushed from the back, increasing the fog and exhaustion he felt. He resorted to rubbing his eyes and slapping his face to wake himself, and taking another drink from his ever-emptying flask to stave off the pain.

Herbert, though forced to journey as a passenger, also rose and entered his chair to join Edward on the weather deck. He looked a touch more refreshed than Edward did, but it was clear that he too had trouble sleeping on the foreign ship.

John jumped down to the sole of the deck, fresh and ready to go with energy only youth could muster. Even with only a few hours of sleep, he seemed to not need any more. Though if Edward could place a wager, he had a feeling that before long, John would lag behind the more experienced crewmates.

The three headed towards the ladder leading to the weather deck, and Herbert and Edward went into motion with a practiced efficiency of long years together. Herbert jumped off his chair and climbed up the ladder as swift as a snake. Edward, after a few breaths and repositioning to not reopen his wounds, and declining help from John, lifted the chair overhead. Balancing it with one hand, and with the other holding to a rope leading up the steep ladder, he climbed to the weather deck. After another moment's respite to catch his breath, he took the chair further up some steps to the quarterdeck where guests were meant to stay.

After gingerly placing the chair down, Herbert climbed in. "Are you well?" he asked Edward, keeping his voice low.

Edward nodded, though he knew his breathing would say otherwise. He also caught himself leaning on the handle of Herbert's chair for support and stopped himself.

"You haven't been sleeping well, I notice." Herbert left a second question unuttered.

Edward decided to sidestep Herbert's undertone with a retort. "Neither have you," he said, not looking at Herbert directly.

Herbert frowned. "Come now, we're in…" Herbert's gaze flitted to the other crewmates already on watch, and the closest few near the helm. He lowered his volume again. "We're alone here. We need to be together here more than ever. If you need help, you need to tell me."

Edward's everything itched at the conversation. He wanted to be away from it more than anything. He clenched his fist and levelled a steely gaze at Herbert. "And how exactly can you help me here?" he snarled. "How can you when you can't even rig a ship in that chair of yours?" Edward rose to his full height as Herbert's expression turned from brows raised to furrowed, with a side of clenched jaw.

"That was unnecessary," Herbert replied with bared teeth.

Edward knew that what he'd said was wrong, but he was too tired for remorse. "I'm sorry," he said hastily, too hastily for sincerity, "but I can handle myself, and it would behoove you not to place more of a burden on me with your incessant questions." Edward rubbed the sleep from his eyes, hoping to catch some of the frustration in between his thumb and forefinger at the same time. "I've got work to do," he said as he walked away.

Throughout the night, Edward was tasked with securing

rigging, keeping watch and relaying navigational information to the helmsman, making minor repairs to the spare sails in the quarterdeck cabin, and when that was exhausted, he had to swab the deck.

All the while, the crew were taking every opportunity to make his job harder than it had to be. From outstretched feet trying to send him tumbling to 'accidental' drops of tools to the sole of the deck, to creating the messes they forced him to clean, the crew united in a passive-aggressive battle to break him.

And, to make it just that much worse, when Edward had a chance to look up from his work and wipe the sweat from his brow, he took notice of the other crewmates on night watch lounging and not even working a third as hard as he.

If this were any other ship, he would have taken issue with the disparity, and at that moment, as irritable as he was, he felt such rage over it he could have slit someone's throat. On this ship, and with the smirks the other crewmates were giving him, his hardship was by design, the silent architects of his misfortune being the captain's declaration that he does the work of several men to make up for Herbert's presence, and upheld by the mate in charge and the crew.

At the end of several hours of that backbreaking work, and the leering crew watching, it was finally time for a change of crew on deck. Herbert told Edward he would stay on deck to observe for the rest of the night, so Edward headed towards the ladder below deck.

The mate in charge stopped him. "Hold there," he said. "You're to stay working."

Edward's hand twitched, the itch to grab the man by the throat almost overpowering his reason. He said nothing, just stared down at the man while breathing hard from the exertion.

Something about Edward's silence, his towering height above the mate, and his crazed look seemed to give the man pause, and he backed up half a step. "Captain's orders," he stammered.

Edward felt too exhausted to even speak a response. He simply grunted as he pushed past the mate and went to the quarterdeck, all the way to the stern behind some rigging and storage, to rest before the new crewmates arrived to start working again.

John was on Edward's heels just as he turned around to flop onto the deck. "What happened?"

Edward took several deep breaths before answering. "It seems," he paused for another breath, "I am to do the work of several men in the most literal of senses. Not only am I working while others gawk like some beggar freak in the street, but I cannot even rest as a normal crewmate would." John didn't know how to respond and stammered a few words, which Edward paid little attention to. The stammering reminded Edward of his dead crewmate with the same name. "Get out of here before I take out my frustration on you."

John looked like he had been slapped in the face. He took a few steps back, turned about, and was quickly out of sight.

Edward closed his eyes and draped his forearm over them to rest as much as he could, but through all the layers, he could still feel Herbert's gaze on him. "If you've some witty comment to say, just be done with it so I can rest what little amount possible."

"Hmph," Herbert scoffed. "You know you're quite skilled at pushing allies away? Does it come naturally, or is it from your father?"

Edward's hand clenched, and his breathing caught in his throat, but he didn't move his arm away nor open his eyes. After a moment, he could hear Herbert's wheelchair scraping against the wood of the ship as he turned around and let Edward be.

Edward lay there motionless as the rocking of the ship swayed him in all directions. The frigid night breeze pulled away his heat, both from exertion and anger, and when he had calmed, he opened his eyes to the pale waxing sliver of the moon.

A gift from my father? I wonder.

Edward rose to his shaky feet and gave himself another moment to muster the strength he needed to continue. After that tenuous moment, he went back to work with the new set of crewmates who looked much more full of vigour than he.

That extra vigour didn't change their attitude towards him, and the new mate in charge continued the work of the last. They conspired in pushing Edward beyond his limits while letting the other crewmates be. Since Nigel's untimely end, those meagre few who had seemed to be of a better calibre, who had helped him in the morning, were either gone or no longer sympathetic to his plight.

The thought only served to irritate Edward further, and incidentally bestowed him with a bit more wind in his sails.

Edward worked, and pushed, and pulled, and ripped every last ounce of strength he had. He had been going with practically no rest for nearly a whole day, and he felt it in his bones.

The sounds of the mate shouting orders, the wind whipping the sails, the waves lapping against the ship, and even the creaking of the vessel itself washed away. He only felt his heart beating up around his ears and the breath in his chest.

The cool sea air felt crisp and alive as he took it in and made it a part of him over and over. It made him feel strange at that moment, though. Coupled with the exhaustion, he felt as though he were floating in that wind surrounding his body. He was no longer himself, but he was the sea and the air.

Before, it had always been in battle, but now the only battle was against himself and his own body. He told himself to take stock of this feeling, whatever it may be, and hold it within. Through the fog of his mind at that moment, he knew this was important.

Edward looked around the ship with new eyes, as though seeing it for the first time. The crew around him were inconsequential, just statues atop a beautiful piece of craftsmanship.

After a moment to take in all he felt and memorize it, he noticed the statues moving on the quarterdeck in a peculiar pattern.

The crew had bunched up on the quarterdeck, several of them surrounding Herbert. They had trapped Herbert between them all, and he couldn't get away.

Edward kept hold of his state of mind, the floating feeling between the sky and sea, where he could see everything clearly. He glided over to the statues, the crewmates who were not his crew, the many faces he cared not to take stock of.

On the quarterdeck, two of the statues moved to stop him, and Edward understood better then why they reminded him of statues. Their movements looked unnaturally slow and stiff at that moment.

Using the lessons Anne, William, Pukuh, and countless battles had taught him, he grabbed the men and used their own momentum and limbs against them. With the most minimal effort on his part, Edward pushed one of the men over the side of the railing of the quarterdeck, where he fell to the deck below, and the other tripped and dashed down the ladder behind Edward.

The other men surrounding Herbert took notice of Edward approaching and said words to him, but he couldn't hear them. He was floating too far above everyone for the words to reach him. The sea air would not carry the words to him across its sweet notes.

He walked forward on legs so far beyond numb that it felt as though he were gliding across the deck. Judging by the faces of the men in front of him, he must have looked like a spectre coming towards them. They pulled back at his gaze and moved out of his way without a touch, each of them turning pale when they looked up at him.

Next to Herbert, two of the men, stouter or stupider than the others, it would be hard to say, stayed put. They made threatening gestures and appeared to shout obscenities, a possible plea for him to stop his advance.

Edward stopped, but not because of anything they said. He bore his gaze down on the first man who had the gall to take a step forward and before long, the man's threatening words caught in his throat. He coughed and stepped aside.

The other man had hands on Herbert, and though he looked confusedly back and forth from his comrades to Edward, his brow was slick with sweat, and his lips trembled.

Edward stared into the man's eyes and then recalled a

saying that the eyes were the window to the soul. He pictured himself bashing the man's head into the fife rail of the nearby mast and the man's body twitching before it went limp. As he imagined it in his own mind's eye, he slowly pulled his massive fist into a ball.

The final crewmate received the message in his core. The tremble in his lips extended to the rest of his body as he let go of Herbert and backed away. His body involuntarily hunched in deference as Edward's gaze followed him to the fife rail, where the wooden railing appearing behind him caused him to jump.

Edward took the last step towards Herbert and looked him in the eyes next. He didn't conjure any image in his mind, nor did he think he looked at him with any malice, but in Herbert's eyes, Edward could tell he looked crazed.

He felt of two minds at that moment. On one side, he was free from all his exhaustion and pain over the last hours, and it also gave him the respite from the arresting thoughts that plagued him of late. On the other, he felt a different pain from the look in Herbert's eyes: the look of fear mixed with the look one would give a stranger together told Edward he wasn't himself.

His mind split into the two thoughts broke the spell he was under, and he could once more hear the whispers and movement of the men surrounding them.

"We're done for the night," he said as he looked at Herbert, but loudly enough for those around him to hear. He turned around and faced the night crew. "Any objections?"

"So, what were they on about up there?" Edward asked when they were below deck.

Herbert paused for a moment, not looking at Edward as he pushed his chair forward towards the crew quarters. "They took issue with some notes I had taken."

"Notes?"

Herbert stopped his advance and reached into his jacket

pocket, then passed a small booklet to Edward. He didn't explain any further, and Edward expected he was to find the answer himself.

Edward flipped through the pages of the booklet, taking note of small drawn charts and numbers he was able to recognize as calculations of wind speed and orders issued by a helmsman. As he went further, he took notice of names and designs relating to the brigantine they found themselves on. At the front few pages were a list of corrections and errors on the part of the helmsman and lower-ranking officers in charge of the *Black Blood*. He also noticed a few attributed to the captain, Grace O'Malley herself.

Edward chuckled as he closed the booklet and handed it back to Herbert. "Well, pray they've learned their lesson today."

Herbert cocked his brow. "To tell it true, I didn't know what to expect, but that's not how I thought you would react."

"Just keep that thing hidden. It may prove useful." Edward leaned closer to Herbert to whisper. "And perhaps with your eyes, you can make a list of those who are loyal to Grace O'Malley and keep a tally of their faults. That, too, could prove useful should we lose favour with our dear captain even more."

Herbert nodded, and instead of returning the booklet to his pocket, he placed it in the hidden compartment in his wheelchair.

Edward and Herbert returned to the crew quarters and back to their hammocks. John was fast asleep, swaying overhead. Edward was last in his hammock, and he lumbered in as the pain began coming back to his conscious mind. He fell into the hammock and closed his eyes and mercifully fell into a deep sleep reserved for the genuinely spent.

Just as instantly as he had fallen asleep, Edward awoke from John slapping his arm. Edward looked about in a half-dazed state. He rolled out of the hammock and rose slowly to his feet.

The slight pain he'd experienced just before falling into his dead sleep hit him in full, and across every inch of his body. He was slower now, and there was little he could do about it save push past. He recalled the floating feeling he had experienced before and tried to channel it, but it was just beyond his grasp. If he had been flying on the weather deck before, now he was simply jumping a few inches off the ground. He could hold it for the briefest moment before it turned to sand between his fingers.

John, Herbert, and he all ate a hearty meal and were given a brief rest before they returned to the weather deck. John had informed Edward that he managed to sleep through another shift, and given that they had returned early due to the previous incident, Edward estimated he had gotten a full five or six hours of sleep. It was the most uninterrupted sleep he had had in some time, and though he hoped for more, he feared it would be the last for another great while.

Edward and Herbert continued taking double shifts while getting only the barest amount of sleep as the crew pushed Edward to the brink of collapse each time.

After the second full four hours, Edward's nausea from the constant work took over, and he vomited over the side of the ship. He managed to keep silent and out of sight as he tilted his head over the side by making it look as though he was on his knees swabbing the deck near the starboard rails.

He cursed himself for his weakness. His body felt hollow and leaden at the same time, and his throat and temples throbbed continuously with each beat of his pounding heart.

That momentary weakness, hidden from the crew's eyes, was the lowest point for him. After that, the situation aboard improved, and not merely because he no longer felt nauseated.

The mood aboard the ship seemed to shift with each passing hour, and with each change of the crew. Perhaps due to pity, respect, or perhaps the words of warning from the crew involved in the earlier incident—Edward could not know which—the crew of the *Black Blood* stopped their attempts to break him. The feet trying to trip him, the 'accidents' meant to make his job harder, as well as the other crewmates not working as he broke his back slowly trickled away until none in the crew seemed to go out of their way to make his life more difficult.

After three days of the routine, the crewmates were treating him with a mild indifference rather than the overt contempt they had been expressing earlier.

And, to Edward's surprise, he had gotten used to the extra labour. His body began healing and growing stronger from the effort, and after his nausea had lessened, he worked with John to acquire more foodstuff so he could maintain his energy and not run himself ragged.

Afternoon on the third day, the *Black Blood* landed at the harbour of an island unfamiliar to him and to John. Edward felt it useless to ask others in the crew where they were as they too may not know the answer or would refuse to answer.

After they secured the ship, Grace gathered a landing party and issued orders to keep the ship ready to sail. After a moment of searching, Grace's eyes met Edward's, and she motioned for him to join her, her hands rock-solid against her hips, and her straight back and stern eyes brooking no argument—not that Edward wished to arouse her ire by attempting refusal.

Edward, his body still stiff and his muscles radiating heat, casually walked over to Grace and the two senior officers making up her landing party.

"I want ya with me. Be good ta see how we do things on this crew."

"And what exactly is it we're about to do?"

Grace scrutinized Edward like she had when they first met, but this time it was less an appraisal of his worth and more a search of his person. She leaned to the side to look beyond Edward's massive body. "Did none of you bastards give him any weapons? Someone bring him a sword and pistol before I start asking more questions."

A mate nearby rushed to a reserve of weapons and brought Edward what Grace asked as he avoided her gaze. Edward put the cutlass at his side and hid the pistol under the front of his shirt, secured in the loop of his belt.

"Does that answer yer question, or do ye have any more?"

Judging Grace's tone to be annoyance, Edward didn't

reply.

"Hmph," she scoffed, to which Edward thought he had made an error in not standing up to her. "To shore, you lot."

Grace led the way, followed by her senior officers, and Edward trailed behind them, trying to match their pace.

The town they had landed in seemed an unlikely locale for brigands and pirates, being barely big enough to call for a harbour for docking ships. The most wealth it appeared to have were its farmland Edward could see off in the distance.

So, that means it's a hiding place? But for whom?

Edward placed his hand on the cutlass at his side, and he thought the answer to his question was meaningless. Whoever was hiding here wouldn't be hiding for much longer, he supposed.

As Edward, Grace, and the two crewmates strode forward, Edward could feel the air growing thick as eyes followed them. Everyone in that small town was watching them. The hair on Edward's arm prickled under the gazes of the unseen men and women behind closed curtains and shuttered windows.

"Don't mind 'em," Grace said over her shoulder. "We're about ta do this town a favour."

The excitement coming from Grace made Edward uneasy. For the first time since Edward's moment of pure exhaustion three days prior, he felt a creeping turmoil bubbling up in his gut.

Edward reached for the flask but stopped himself short. Instead, he tried to grab hold of the feeling of floating from before. He tried to still his mind and push down the hollow gravity just beneath his ribs.

For a moment, a meagre few ticks of a clock's second hand, Edward held fast to that feeling and then lost it to the ether. Edward imbibed once more to still the trembling.

The four of them entered a local tavern and inn, and to Edward's astonishment the establishment was filled to the brim with merriment, a stark contrast to the rest of the quiet town.

With each slam of Grace's copper greaves, the room fell quieter until there was a hush in which one could hear a pin drop. She took a seat out from a table and sat down with that same casual nature she'd had just before she killed Nigel.

"Bring him ta me." In that hush, Grace's voice filled the room just as boisterously as the din that had preceded it.

There was a moment of stillness where none made a move, and all eyes stared at Grace. The brigands whom Edward supposed they were here for all seemed to know who Grace was and, judging by the terror in their eyes, the knowledge momentarily locked them in place.

The townsfolk, the owner and the tavern wenches who all looked injured in some way or another, didn't seem sure what to make of the newcomers. They, too, had a look of terror in their eyes, but there was a bit of relief in their faces, as though they hoped the newcomers would soon relieve their town of the brigands occupying it.

Grace turned her gaze to one of the men and then pointed to him before snapping her fingers. The man interpreted the message, and he ran up to the second storey to one of the rooms of the inn.

"Blackstad, sit down. Those idle hands of yers are gonna get ya killed."

It took a moment for Edward to remember the name they were using aboard the *Black Blood*, and then another moment to realize he was gripping his cutlass as though he were about to unsheathe it. He relaxed his hand and took a seat on the other side of the small table, leaving enough room for whoever was about to join them.

After another moment, the door of one of the rooms upstairs burst open, and a tall, lanky man with a greasy mess of a beard and equally messy long hair came out. He was pulling up his trousers as he took note of where Grace was. A few seconds later, after the man who had gone to get his comrade exited, a half-naked woman ran out and into another room.

Edward noticed that the woman was bloody and bruised, and he thought he could see tears streaming down her face as she ran by.

The man lazily fixed his trousers and strutted down to the first floor, his casual and cocksure attitude on full display. He didn't match his comrades' moods in the slightest, and by the time he stepped to the first floor and took a chair, sitting backwards on it with his arms resting on the back, his men relaxed a bit.

For every bit that the other men relaxed, Edward tensed. It felt as though he was the only sane person of the lot and the only one who was sure of what was about to happen. He had to restrain himself from pulling out his pistol and cutlass right then to put an end to it all.

The man glanced from Grace to Edward, to her men, and then to his own men, and back. He grinned. "It's been a long while, Grace."

"Cut it, you know what we're here for."

"Aww, Grace, you wound me," the man said, his words dripping with sarcasm. "We're old friends, ain't we? What happened to civility? Is there no honour amongst us thieves?"

"We're pirates." Grace tilted her head. "*You're* the thief."

The man appeared taken aback. "Some would say we're the same, you and I."

"Enough. Save me some trouble and return what ye stole."

Though Grace was doing her best, her commanding tone had little effect on this man. Whatever relationship they had had, the man underestimated her. Or, for all Edward knew, it was plain stupidity. Whatever the case, it was not going to end well, of that Edward was sure.

The man adopted a confused, amused expression. "If a pirate claims ownership of something and a thief steals it, is it still a crime?" He held his palm open as though he were pondering the question. "I suppose a few lawyers could settle the matter, given enough time."

Grace ignored the fool's ruminations. "I've asked ye nicely, I'll not ask again."

The man cocked his brow. "Oh, threats now? You're out-gunned, Grace. And I've got a stable full of horses rested and ready to take us to the opposite shore before the men on your ship know what's happened." The man leaned forward. "So why not just pack up and leave before my men and I pump your pretty face full of lead?"

Upon the escalation of events, the thieves became emboldened once more. They joined in with their leader's declaration, and some even pulled out their weapons to bolster the intimidation.

Grace simply sat there, staring down the leader with her cold, calm expression. Her officers didn't seem intimidated by the thieves' threats either, and they stood there with arms folded, staring at the other men in the room.

Grace waited for a full minute until the thieves' words died away and there was minimal murmur of activity and threatening gestures. As soon as it was quiet enough, she spoke again. "You know what the difference between a pirate and a thief is?"

The sudden change in subject brought him and his compatriots up short. He turned to them and flashed a wry smile before gazing back at Grace. "No, what?"

Grace leaned forward, and Edward's hair stood on end for the second time that night. "Thieves are weak."

Grace slammed her boots to the floor, grabbed hold of a hidden apparatus and pulled a string. The sound of several shots of gunfire rang out. Lead shots burst into the leader of the thieves' chest. He was dead in an instant, blood pouring from several wounds.

Grace's copper greaves for which she was famous held some mechanism inside them to fire bullets. It was seemingly a well-kept secret to those not in her crew, as the thieves had no idea what had happened or from where Grace had shot their leader.

Grace's senior officers, before she had even fired her secret weapon, drew their own weapons and attacked the rest of the thieves. The other men failed to react in time, and three of their comrades were dead almost instantly.

The thieves still living reached for their weapons, and Edward pulled out his cutlass and stabbed one of them. This drew the attention of more than a few of those remaining. Edward pulled his loaded pistol from his belt and fired. The bullet hit the last enemy in the head.

The leader of the men, so bold previously, lay there bleeding out. Grace's secret attack had made a gory mess of his chest and legs.

Grace hadn't moved from her seat since her secret weapon's firing that had started the conflict. She glanced from side to side, looked Edward up and down, then got to her feet as smoke still rose from the holes in her copper greaves.

She searched the dead man's pockets and found the item they had come for, but Edward couldn't see what it was. Grace pocketed the thing as quickly as she snatched it.

"We're done here. Back to the ship."

9. SMOKE

"You thought I wus dead?" Sam Bellamy bellowed before bursting out in his old hyena's laugh that was equal parts nostalgic and unsettling.

Anne had taken Sam into the captain's quarters, partially to show him the room he had never seen before owing to his departure prior to it being opened, and also to speak with him privately.

Anne shrugged. "We had no way to confirm Cache-Hand's claim, but we hadn't heard about your recent promotions."

"Can't say I blames ye. I thought I killed ol' Ed." Sam's face grew dark as he looked to the floorboards of that once familiar ship. "Cache-Hand beat 'im bloody, then cut him to ribbons before they poisoned 'is food and tossed him in that Irish lake. I tried to keep him safe, tried to get him out, but there was no way." Sam looked up at Anne, pain in his eyes. "Ye got ta believe me, I tried."

Anne tried her best to smile back at Sam. The memory of that time, how thin and ragged and... *broken* Edward had looked made it difficult. "No one blames you, Sam," she said before reaching across the table to squeeze his hand. "You did what you had to to survive. And, besides, he survived. I'm sure you played a part in that."

Sam seemed genuinely relieved by Anne's absolution. After a moment, his eyes went down to the golden ring on Anne's hand. He pointed at it, at first bemused, and after a moment, amused.

"Yes, it was done after we opened this room, and the ship was renamed."

Sam leaned back and let out a sigh. "Too bad I missed that. Musta been an event. A bloody princess marrying a pirate? Never thought I'd see the day, though I suppose I still didn't."

"I am a princess no longer. However, perhaps when this is all over, I shall be a Pirate Queen given how most speak of Calico Jack."

"Then when we reunite," Sam began, affecting a mocking posh English accent, "I suppose I must give a toast to my new Queen." He gave a brief bow in his seat before grinning up at Anne.

She smiled and then laughed, a real moment of levity with an old friend. After that, she poured them both a drink from a nearby cabinet, and they sipped on the spirits.

"Speakin' of that. You mentioned he and Herbert went off somewhere. What's gotten into them?"

"Well, the fools went off to kill Calico Jack on their own. Some sense of duty which they alone can fix."

"What's Edward got duty in all this? Herbert I can square away, but Edward?"

Anne leaned back as she recalled. "I suppose you would-n't be privy to that bit of information," she muttered softly. "Have you *met* Calico Jack? Have you seen him in the flesh?"

Sam nodded and then looked off to the side as he took to remembering. "Aye, I met him once."

"Did he look at all... familiar to you?"

Sam looked impatient. "What're ye on about here? I never took you fer a dancin lady."

Anne paused another moment before shaking her head and falling back to her blunt nature. "Calico Jack is Edward's father, and formerly he was Benjamin Hornigold, the one who gave Edward this ship."

Sam sat stunned for a moment, his mouth slack. "You must be mad. There's no..." Sam's expression changed, and he looked away in thought once again. "The eyes..." he muttered to himself. "But that would mean..." Sam held a hand to his mouth as he ran through it all in his head. Then when he looked up at Anne, she simply nodded her head, and he took a big gulp of the drink in front of him.

"Needless to say, that is why Edward wishes to do this alone," Anne said before taking a drink herself. "So, you haven't said much about yourself. Tell me how you came to be the captain of such a fine sloop?"

Sam nodded in the direction of his ship through the window of the captain's quarters off the stern. It listed lazily behind them, as though it were aimless without their captain aboard. "Aye, she's a fine ship, you speak it true. Made some friends in Cache-Hand's crew, convinced them to take it for ourselves. Left Cache-Hand with half his crew and none of his spoils the night after capturing it."

Anne chuckled. "How long ago was that?"

"Not three quarters of a year after leaving the captain for dead."

Anne shook her head. "What poor timing. That would not have been long before we met with him, and Edward killed him." She waved her hand. "No matter. Tell me more. How did you come to be in Calico Jack's crew?"

"Ran a few ships aground in his territory and had a little fun redistributing the wealth back to the common folk. Musta caught his eye after the pups started calling me Robin Hood."

"You still breathe, so it was a positive encounter, I presume?"

Sam snorted. "Not if ye call owing him all the money spent a boon."

Anne nodded. "Yes, I see. So, it won't take much convincing to have your crew switching sides, I have it?"

Sam shook his head. "Nah, they see 'em as another Cache-Hand, just one that we can't run from. Havin' you here and Edward there changes things. Might just be able to convince 'em if we have some support." Sam fell silent for a moment, uncharacteristically contemplative.

Anne smiled. "Less than two years and already being a captain has changed you."

Sam's mouth opened, an instinct to chime back with some witty remark, but instead he leaned back in his chair. "My last captain commanded me to live. Fool captains die quick on these seas." Another moment of silence took hold as Anne and Sam let the weight of his words settle in the air. Sam broke that silence. "So, what's the plan to save our fool?" he said, smirking like the old Sam she knew.

"Perhaps you can help with that," Anne replied. "What

are the defences like for Silver Eyes' village?"

Sam's brow cocked strangely, and he shook his head as though he couldn't comprehend what he had just heard. "What are you on about? Ed ain't here. That means he's headed to Nassau. We should be going there now as soon as I convince me men."

Anne stifled a sigh and shoved away the weakness that beckoned it forward. "I would agree with you, save the circumstances we've found ourselves in. We must stay here and save this island from Silver Eyes. These people need us."

"Like hell they do!" Sam shouted, bursting from his seat. "This place can burn. *Edward* needs us. Ye can try ta convince yerself it's fer those people, but yer not so soft ta risk yer life for a bunch'a farmers."

Anne locked her fingers together and rested her elbows on the arms of the chair in a movement of practiced authority. "You're right," she said. "Edward needs to keep his plan secret. We don't know the details, but we know he needs surprise on his side. The enemy knows our ship, and being in Nassau would risk a battle at sea." She gave the briefest pause for her words to sink in. "And beyond that, these people, with your help, can provide a distraction."

"Aye? And how's that?" Sam asked, placing one hand on his chair as he looked down at Anne, trying to match her presence.

"We make a show of power, and you tell Silver Eyes they need reinforcements to fight us. You convince Silver Eyes you should be the one to head to Nassau and instead back Edward up when he arrives. You and your ship being in Nassau will not raise alarm." Anne took a long breath and a drink, her half-formed plan coming together in her mind. "If Edward's father and his subordinates are as smart as they think they are, then I imagine the main village is a fortress with battlements. A single ship, no matter the size, would pose little threat, but if we choke the food supply on land and at sea, we can starve them. And as no one will be coming to their rescue, we'll eventually take the island for ourselves."

Sam scoffed. "Ye make it sound so easy." Sam began pacing the room as he drank from his cup. After a moment he let out a frustrated grunt, pulled something from his belt wrapped in cloth, and placed it on the table. "If yer gonna stay, you'll need this."

Anne glanced at the mystery wrapped in cloth, then back at Sam. He simply nodded towards it before taking another drink. She took the object and unwrapped it to find a small golden handbell.

"That'll work on the crazed on the island, but not that bastard's men."

Anne did a double take on the small, unassuming bell in her hands as the weight of the ringer took root. "So, this will reverse the trance?"

"The what?"

"The spell that the citizens here are under."

Sam nodded. "Aye, that'll do it," he affirmed. "His men don't have the same spell, though. Whatever they got, it makes 'em tough bastards, but they still got all the goods upstairs," he said, tapping on the side of his head. "The farmers and such're just distractions."

It was Anne's turn to scoff. "We almost died to those distractions."

"That's what that's for," Sam said, pointing at the handbell. "Otherwise, they'll attack everyone."

Anne looked at the handbell with new eyes as the wheels began turning in her head. "Is that so?" she muttered.

She gave the handbell a small ring, and a sharp tone filled their room. It was so wholly unlike its larger brother she had head not a few hours before, but it struck a chord in the centre of her just the same. She felt as though the ring of that bell was pulling her soul forward, the same as when your body moves to join the swell of the wave and the inclination of a ship. Judging by the vacant stare in Sam's eyes and the bulge of his jaw, he felt it too.

After the tone fell away to nothing, Anne's and Sam's wits returned. "This may be useful to ye too." Sam pulled out a silver key from his pocket and placed it in front of Anne. "It's a tight squeeze, but there's a passage on the east of the fort near the waterline. It's there for a flanking attack should the fort be breached, and that key will let you past the gate. Don't think about bringing any cannons, the reef'll kill 'em."

Anne rose from her seat, dropping with it her all the authority and bluster she had previously mustered, and embraced Sam. "Thank you, Sam. With these, we'll surely win."

Sam's generally cool facade blew over, and he looked flushed. "I ain't done nothin' but what a man ought. Don't go givin' me a big 'ead over it."

Anne smiled. "Happy to see you alive nonetheless. After all this is over, we'll have a feast, and you can tell us all about your adventures with your merry men, Mr. Hood."

Sam chuckled. "Aye, that we will, my Queen."

After another brief embrace, Sam walked towards the door of the captain's quarters before looking over his shoulder. "Prepare yer men. After I convince me crew, we'll need to make a show of it."

It was Anne's turn to be confused. "What do you mean?" she asked as she joined him.

"Can't go on back to Silver Eyes ta convince him we need reinforcements without a bit'a damage, now can we?" he replied. "A short skirmish oughta be just the ticket. We can damage the ship ourselves, but without some live fire for 'em ta hear, it won't seem real. Jus' a little smoke, s'all."

"Just a little smoke? Happy to oblige." Anne held out her hand, and Sam shook it. "Oh, and take this with you." Anne removed the scabbard and golden cutlass from her hip and handed it to Sam.

Sam took the cutlass in hand, lifting it slightly out of its scabbard to see the golden hue of the mysterious metal before returning it to its resting place. "It'll soon be in its owner's hands."

The two left the captain's quarters and assembled the crew on the deck. It took some time for the men to settle and for Sam to talk with a few of his old friends, but eventually, they were able to explain the plan. Sam's crewmates who joined him appeared to already have his approval, and after they went back and convinced the rest to join in, they would signal the *Queen Anne's Revenge* by raising the black. Once the *Queen Anne's Revenge* was prepared, they too would raise the black, and their 'battle' would commence.

With all the details decided, Sam and his crewmates went back to their ship, and Anne and the crew waited. And waited. And waited still.

"It's taking too long," Christina said as she petted her wolf Tala. The two were leaning against the quarterdeck railing and watching the bobbing of the *Whydah* off the stern.

Anne had her spyglass trained on the other ship. Sam and the other crewmates were talking on the weather deck, but she couldn't make out the details. "They're just talking."

"Maybe some in the crew don't like the thought of betraying Calico Jack," Christina commented.

"Or Benjamin Hornigold," Pukuh added as he came up beside Anne to observe the other ship.

Anne took her attention away from the spyglass and glanced over at Pukuh. Pukuh looked gravely serious as he turned his gaze back to Sam's ship.

"You may be right," Anne replied.

An unmistakable crack met Anne's ears, sending an alert down her spine. She reached for the cutlass at her side as she looked over her shoulder. The other crewmates, the lot of them, even Tala, had their ears perked and brows furrowed from the noise.

Anne went back to the spyglass and found the source of the noise. She could just barely make out the figure of Sam with his jet-black hair and a smoking pistol in his hand. He was standing stock still, and Anne thought she could see his other hand holding a sword at his side.

"What happened?" Christina asked.

"Sam executed a crewmate." *You said you were no fool, Sam. I hope you know what you're doing.*

"Let us hope that man lacked mates," Pukuh said.

Anne didn't reply. She tensed her jaw as she watched the scene on the other ship unfolding.

Sam put his pistol away and brandished his sword, gesturing with it as he spoke. After a moment or two, the crew went into action. Some took the body of the dead crewmate and tossed him overboard, as others raised the anchor and prepared the ship for sailing.

Sam, still holding fast to his sword, walked up to his own

quarterdeck. Halfway up the steps, he turned and looked over at *Queen Anne's Revenge*. Sensing or seeing all the eyes on him, he openly shrugged his shoulders and shook his head. Anne couldn't see through the spyglass, but she felt he was grinning.

Anne chuckled despite herself. "You dammed fool," she muttered.

After a time, and a flurry of activity, the *Whydah* raised the black flag on its tallest mast. The simple skull of death with crossed bones, similar but different enough from Calico Jack's crossed cutlasses, waved in the wind at them.

Anne put away her spyglass and turned around to the crew, who had gathered around when the gunfire sounded. "Let fly the black. Load starboard, men! We've some smoke to make."

10. WARNING SIGNS

"What happened out there?" Herbert asked.

Edward had returned from the excursion onshore with Grace and was now below deck with Herbert and John. They were huddled in a corner near the ladder leading up to the weather deck, Edward sitting on the lip of a barrel and John standing next to him with Herbert in his chair holding tight to the nearby cargo.

"Grace killed a bunch of thieves who had stolen something from her, or someone else. I wasn't privy to the details."

Edward still felt tense from the encounter. Aside from the few minor altercations aboard the *Black Blood,* it had been some time since he had been involved in a real battle. He closed his eyes and took a few deep breaths. Thankfully, Herbert and John both let him alone for that moment he needed to channel that feeling of floating. It came more naturally this time, and he was able to hold it for longer than any other time save the first time when he had been near fainting from exhaustion.

"Does everyone aboard know about the captain's greaves?" Edward asked John.

John's eyes widened. "She used *them?*" He seemed shocked at the notion, but soon let out a low whistle. "Whoever it was must have irked her something fierce. She rarely uses them."

Edward laughed. "The man was irksome, that much is sure. And whatever it was that he stole, it's been returned."

John let out a sigh. "That's a relief, but it also means you two are about to meet *him.*"

Edward took a moment to register John's meaning. "Calico Jack?" he asked to be sure.

John nodded. "We were tasked with retrieving something stolen from him, but don't ask me what it was. All I know is it was important, and when Mad Jack Rackham tells you to sail, all you ask is how far." John's tone was light, but Edward could tell there was a hint of anger in his voice. That hint spoke to a feeling he dared not utter on a ship full of men in Calico Jack's employ.

Perhaps... "You've met the man?" Edward asked, his attempt to pry open that shaded window subtle.

Herbert understood the game, leaning forward to whisper. "I've heard that he's... well." He paused to flash a concerned look to Edward and John. "Well... that he's not to be trifled with."

John's mouth became a line. "Yes, well, I will say that you are right. And as you're new to the crew, you'll have to meet with him before you're truly considered a mate. If there's one piece of advice I can give you: don't question him, but don't simply bow to him either. He likes to have men he can trust, but who also have a backbone." John rolled his shoulders and glanced at his sides to ensure there were no ears nearby. "Whatever happens, if he tries to play his hunting horn, just run. Run as far as you can and escape the island by any means."

Edward knew the horn John was referring to, but the sudden nature of his dire warning took him aback. His mouth went slack as he searched for words a person who shouldn't know of the horn would say, but it didn't seem to matter, as John took it differently.

John shook his head. "No questions, not here. It's not safe. Just remember to run."

Before Edward or Herbert could say another word, John was already walking away and beckoning them to join him.

Could there be more to the horn than just a signal? Those men and women in the tavern... Anne said they seemed in a trance. Was it the horn's doing?

Before Edward could ruminate on his questions too long, Herbert was nudging him forward and out of his thoughts. Edward glanced at Herbert, who motioned with his chin towards John's backside. Edward nodded, and the two went to the crew's quarters to eat.

The meal, as it had been the time before and the time

before that, was a stew of salted beef with various vegetables and the spiced pepper that burned Edward's tongue. Edward threw all his ship's biscuits into the stew at once to soak up the spice, and it seemed to work. Either that or he had become used to the heat of that foreign pepper after so many times.

After the meal, Edward and Herbert were about to make their way above deck for the next shift of the crew, but a mate stopped them.

"Captain's orders," he said as he stopped Edward with a hand on his chest. "Get yer rest, yer useless to her if yer dead on yer feet."

Edward glanced at Herbert and John, who were both as shocked as he. "Truly?"

The mate nodded. "Aye." The mate glanced back and forth all the way over his shoulder and then leaned forward to whisper as best as he could in Edward's ear. "She's taken a shine to ye, so be sure and not refuse her… if ye catch my meanin'." The man winked before taking the crewmates above for the next watch.

"What do you suppose he meant by that?" Herbert asked.

Edward's gaze went from Herbert and fell on John, but John shrugged and seemed as dumbfounded by the exchange as the others.

It didn't take long for Edward and Herbert to stop worrying over the mystery and sleep in their hammocks. The gentle rocking of the ship and normal noises of a bustling machine of wood and men lulled Edward to sleep surprisingly quickly.

Edward awoke in what felt like an instant, the ache of his muscles and bones hitting his whole body immediate and with a fury. After a few stretches as he awoke and readied for work, the pain was mostly gone.

Edward and John's work and rest schedules were now aligned and, together with Herbert, the men went above deck to tend to the ship in the dead cold of the night.

The other crewmates working nights with them were a more amicable sort than Edward had dealt with for most of his time aboard the *Black Blood*, and so the work was lax and the conversation genial. Edward, Herbert, and John learned more about John and his time aboard the ship, but the conversation steered clear from any mention of Calico Jack's mysterious horn.

John told some fantastical stories of battles against the Spanish off the coast of Honduras, where they were secretly paid by the British for each ship sunk. They performed so well that the British couldn't pay and agreed to turn a blind eye to the pirates' other activities.

During one such battle, Grace's pistols jammed, and she was forced to use her greaves where she single-handedly killed five Spaniards at once. After that, so it was told, the Spanish began calling her *Gracia de la Muerte*, or Death's Grace.

He also told of the time where a third of the crew swore they had seen a ghostly ship on a foggy night, which they pursued despite the danger. They eventually came upon an empty vessel, full sail and cargo, drifting at sea, no crew anywhere to be seen. Even Grace, not one to be superstitious, was rattled and ordered the ship burned, cargo and all.

One thing missing from each of John's stories was the man himself. His version of events seemed to not have a place for him, save as an observer, as though he were inconsequential.

When pressed to hear a story about him, John reluctantly obliged. He told a story about when he helped an orphaned girl being accosted by bandits in a town the crew had stopped in. The girl fled with the crew aboard the ship, for fear that the bandits would just come back against her after they had left.

"What happened then?" Herbert asked.

John's mouth parted for a moment before his lips twisted into a sad smile. "Her ending was something I would not wish to revisit."

Edward and Herbert shared a look after John's comment and changed the subject.

The two shared their own stories, taking care to not let slip anything too detailed to allow John, or any eavesdroppers, to glean who they were. When those stories seemed exhausted, Herbert weaved a few tales plucked from the sea air itself that involved the Blackstad brothers in their prime. The tale he told was so full of bravado and wild fancy it beggared belief, but after the ghost ship story, it may not have mattered much.

Over three days, it was the same routine. Edward could rest and work as a normal crewmate instead of working for two as he had before, and he, Herbert, and John all shared their time together aboard. When they weren't working hard on the ship, they shared their stories, talked about life aboard a ship, tips for managing the needs of their wooden estate, and sometimes just a relaxing silence.

Edward also noticed that his sleep came easier each time he lay down, and he awoke less and less in the middle of his slumber. The feeling of overwhelming dread left him, and he often found his flask full at the end of the day.

On the third day, before Edward went to work again, he was called to the captain's quarters by one of the mates.

"Why does Grace want to speak with me?" he asked.

"That's for her to know," the mate replied. "Don't keep her waitin'."

Edward glanced over his shoulder at Herbert and John, and they both had stern looks on their faces though Edward suspected it was for different reasons. Edward steeled himself as he followed the mate past the surgeon's room, past the ladder to the weather deck, and over to a small cabin at the bow of the ship.

As he made the walk, he quickly ran through their backstory, what little they had come up with, in his head. He also checked the weapons at his side, cutlass and knife, should he need them. If it came to that, though, they were already dead. He couldn't kill everyone aboard a ship eighty strong. He was confident in his abilities, but that was impossible.

The mate knocked on Grace's door, and when she gave the word, he opened the door for Edward. "Blackstad here to see you, ma'am."

"Thanks, Richard," she said before she waved him away.

Edward watched as the mate closed the door behind him, noticing a broad grin on his face as he did so. He didn't like that grin. As tense as he was in enemy territory, if the mate were expressionless as William, he would have felt the same. The grin just made it more explicit.

"Sit," Grace commanded, pointing to a chair across from the table.

As Edward stepped forward to take a seat, he glanced around the room. It was small and spartan, as it had to be aboard a brigantine, but it was larger than it would be in a sloop. The only light in the room came from a few hanging lanterns and two windows at the back.

One corner held a bed big enough for two, and beside it, a few sets of clothes hung on hooks fastened to the wall. In the opposite corner stood a bookshelf teeming to the brim with sailing books, charts, and other instruments, and next to it a table with various tools, disassembled weapons, and copper. Some of the tools and items had fallen to the deck from the swaying of the ship. Edward saw the same scene on the table in front of them, with sailing charts, books, and weapons and tools from edge to edge.

Edward sat and locked his fingers together, mimicking Grace—a trick Anne and Alexandre had taught him when trying to endear someone to you, mimicking another person's body language to put them at ease.

However, Grace's gaze seemed immediately drawn to Edward's hands, and she instantly changed her posture. She leaned back and folded her arms in front of her and stared at him for a moment.

Edward didn't dare move. He realized Grace was too smart for such tactics, and if he folded his arms, it would be much too obvious. He decided to take the offensive. "What did you need, Captain?"

She didn't respond for a moment, staring at Edward as she waited. Then she relaxed, if only slightly, and reached into a drawer on her side of the table. She pulled out two glasses and a decanter filled with brown liquor. After filling both glasses generously, she passed one of the drinks to Edward.

"I wanted ta welcome ye to our crew," she finally said.

Edward held back his surprise with the motion of taking

the cup in hand and took a drink to think up a response. He needed another moment to let the burn of the whiskey subside. "I suppose I passed some test?"

Grace grinned and raised her glass to him after she took a drink herself. "That's right. Ye handled yerself well out there, if a bit slowly for my taste. Next time, try to keep up if ye don' want ta be shot."

"Now that I know about those legs of yours, I'll be more aware."

Grace leaned back and placed her feet up on the table. Dried mud flaked off the bottom of the copper boots onto the papers below, and Edward couldn't help but think Herbert would be appalled that the charts were being soiled. Grace ran her fingers over the copper greaves.

"They're quite a pair, thas' for sure. Pain to reload, though."

Edward nodded. He could tell that she was relaxing around him; perhaps the drink was helping, but maybe this was an advantageous direction to take the conversation. "You must have made them yourself judging by the tools you have there." Edward nodded his head towards Grace's workshop over his shoulder.

"Aye, that I did. These legs've got a few other tricks. Play yer cards right, and maybe I'll show them to you." Grace slid her hands down her legs to her thighs and looked at him with an unmistakable expression of lust.

Edward was in the middle of a drink and had to hold back a cough and sputter. *Bollocks! That's what that crewmate meant by not refusing her. I must change the subject.* "Your name," he blurted out.

"What about it?" Grace replied, annoyance clear.

"I'm not too learned when it comes to history, but was there not a famous Grace O'Malley whom some would say was also a pirate from a couple of hundred years ago?"

Edward thought he could hear Grace let out a small sigh as she moved her feet off the table. "Aye, that there was." She took another drink of her whiskey. "O'Malley ain't me last name. Had no need of me last one affer…" Grace trailed off but shook her head and moved on. "Probably good fer you to do the same if ye want to go back to yer home some-day." Grace pointed with one finger at Edward's ring, slosh-ing some of the whiskey on the table as she did so.

Edward looked down at the golden wedding ring on his left hand, and he could feel his cheeks flush. Grace took his redness as embarrassment and chuckled, but he was far from embarrassed.

Wrapped around his finger was that familiar gold that was not gold, and he hadn't spared it a second thought. He and Anne had been married for so long it had become a part of him, and it was made of the same material that his father, perhaps more so under the alias Benjamin Hornigold, was known for. He was so worried about letting something slip in what he said that he forgot about the smallest piece that could almost immediately give him away.

As it dawned on him, he became painfully aware of how quiet he had been. "I'll keep that in mind, thank you." *Keep the conversation going. Don't draw attention to the ring anymore. Names. Keep talking names.* "I had a friend who was named af-ter a rather famous pirate as well. Though I doubt his parents had known about the man when they named their son. I don't think he was aware of it either as I only learned of it recently myself."

Grace burst out laughing, the whiskey hitting her now. "Ain't that somethin'? Named after a killer and not even knowin' it."

Edward let out a sigh as he switched the whiskey to his right hand to lower his ring from sight. He would have to remove it later, but what he would do with it after that he didn't know.

It was then that he realized what he had said exactly. He talked about his friend, Henry Morgan, the one he had killed, and he didn't get the same feeling he had in the past. His hands weren't shaking, and the sense that the world narrow-ing in on him was gone as well. And, though he was thinking of it now, the flashes of those who had died because of him, including his old quartermaster John, never came unbidden to his mind's eye.

Perhaps the whisky is hitting me as well, Edward thought as he took another drink.

When he looked up, Grace was there beside him, sitting on the edge of the table with her legs spread and her back arched. She wore a smile that was unmistakable save to the simple or the blind.

"So," Edward said, drawing out the word as he did his best to lean away from her, "I'm curious as to what it was that we were there to retrieve during my test?"

She reached into her pocket and pulled out the item she'd taken from the thief's corpse and handed it to Edward.

It was an ordinary necklace made of what Edward thought was driftwood in the shape of a spiral seashell, half as big as Edward's palm. He turned the necklace over in his palm a few times as he examined the unique shape. He couldn't place it, but he felt he had seen the necklace before. Could it have been when Grace was picking it up? No, the angle was wrong. It had been somewhere else, a long time ago.

Then it hit him.

This was his mother's necklace.

"So, you figured it out, did ye?"

Cold sweat trickled down Edward's face, and his body seized. "What?" he managed to get out.

"Knew you was a smart one." She playfully stroked his hand. "Ye worked it out that that's the boss man's property, didn't ye?"

Edward couldn't say a word. All he could manage was a nod of his head as he placed his late mother's necklace on the table. This was too much for him to digest, and he felt sick to his stomach. He got up to leave, but Grace pushed him back down to the chair.

Grace leapt on top of him, straddling him and pinning him to the chair. She pulled his face up and kissed him. The surging pressure of her lips against his kept him pinned like a surging wave. The smell of gunpowder and whiskey—and, strangely enough, cinnamon—broke through his other senses as she forced her tongue into his mouth.

Edward gained his senses and pushed her off. It was then that he noticed just how petite she was compared to him. She certainly had more muscle than the average woman, including Anne, but she almost looked dainty compared to his large form. She was an attractive woman, with curves like a crested sail in the wind and a face that could belong in a painting. Though it was short, with her red hair she could be mistaken for Anne's older sister in the right light.

What am I thinking right now? Edward's better judgement came back to him, and when Grace tried to force herself back on him, he pushed her off again as he rose to his feet.

"Ah, ye like it rough, do ye?" she said, not losing her smile as she loosened one hand from Edward's grip before grabbing his groin. "Aye, seems ye do," she purred.

"No," he bellowed. The force of his single word took her aback, and she pulled herself away from him.

Before she could gain her wits about her, and before Edward could move for the door again, there was a knock from outside.

Grace regained her composure and folded her arms as she took a few steps away from Edward. "What is it? I told ye not ta disturb me."

"Aye ma'am, it's urgent. Ship off the starboard bow."

Grace cursed under her breath and stalked to the door to her cabin, her stride rushed and heavy.

Edward followed a few steps behind, and Grace left the room without looking back at him. He closed the door to her cabin as he chased her and the mate up the ladder to the weather deck, where some other crewmates were rushing up to see the commotion.

As Edward emerged to the humid brine of the sea air, he could see almost the entirety of the crew watching the seas. Many held spyglasses to their eyes, and those who had none held their hands up to their eyes to look through the pinhole of their palms, and others tried their best with their naked eye.

Herbert and John were both on the quarterdeck where Grace headed. One of her senior mates handed her a spyglass, and she peered through it. As Edward climbed the ladder up, he turned his gaze starboard. Even without aid, he could see the distinct dark shape approaching on the horizon. Whoever was aboard the ship, and whatever allegiances they held, would be unknown until they were much closer, but one thing was clear: they didn't fear to pass another ship on their route. That meant much more than a flag could ever tell them.

"Change course. Head west," Grace commanded her helmsman. "We'll take the scenic route to Nassau."

The helmsman shouted orders to the milling crew, who swiftly went to work changing the sails and rigging, and working with the helm to move the ship further to port.

Grace, feeling her job was finished, handed the spyglass back to her mate and headed to the quarterdeck ladder. Edward decided he would not join her and instead stayed put where he was.

"Wait, Captain," Herbert's voice called.

For a moment, Edward thought Herbert was talking to him, and he stifled his normal response when he remembered who he was. He looked over to see Herbert glancing through his own spyglass west, their new destination.

"What?" Grace's tone had shifted from annoyance to anger.

"I suggest we head east. We will be heading into a storm if we sail west."

Grace's brows furrowed as she glanced over her shoulder towards their destination. After a moment, she looked at her helmsman, who frantically sought his own spyglass.

"I see nothing," he said after nary a glance west. "The boy lies."

Judging the matter settled, Grace once more turned around to head back to her quarters.

"Are you daft?" Herbert shouted. "There's a halo around the sun, and the pressure of air has been decreasing as we've been heading north-west. If we go further west, it'll drop even further, and those clouds I see will be right on us if we head that direction." Herbert was pointing due west as he spoke. Edward looked to the sun, and he too could see the hazy ring around it, a visible marker of increased moisture in the air. He couldn't see anything wrong with the clouds, but Herbert's eyes were better than his. "Are your senses dulled along with your wits? Can you not smell the air? It's saltier than the stew we eat!"

If it were not for every eye being on them, hot and grim, Edward would have laughed at Herbert's comment. As it stood, the ire in the air overpowered the air pressure Herbert was trying to point out.

"Enough," Grace said, her words barely rising above the din of the ship, but still bubbling with anger. "Yer not the helmsman on this ship. I suggest ye hold yer tongue unless ye want it cut out."

"Captain," Edward interjected, "my brother has better eyes than most, and knows the sk—"

"Not another word from you either, ye pissant." If Grace had been angry with Herbert, she was spitting fire at Edward. Her glare could melt a glacier.

Edward pressed forward, not caring about the flames. "Your crew will die," he said calmly.

Grace gritted her teeth, her usual calm completely broken. "Below deck, both of you. Before I throw you overboard."

Edward held back his own frustration. This was partially his fault for drawing Grace's ire by refusing her. He took a deep breath before he motioned for Herbert to join him. The eyes of the crew followed them as they headed into the dark, but Edward was sure Grace would call them back when the storm hit. And he hoped it was sooner rather than later.

11. A BELL TO FILL THE HOLLOWS

"Why do we wait and sit around like kittens?"

Pukuh, hunched down on all fours as he peered over a ridge at a nearby hamlet, looked nothing like a kitten. Despite his native garb making him look like a large eagle, there was no mistaking the hunter beneath the outfit ready to strike.

"We're not here to kill them," Anne admonished, "we're here to help them so that they in turn may help us."

"And this bell is to fill the life into their eyes?" Pukuh said, touching the bell wrapped around Anne's waist.

"That is the hope," Anne replied.

Anne, Pukuh, William, and a handful of crewmates stood on the outskirts of a hamlet, waiting and watching for an opportunity. As they had feared, and as their old crewmate Sam Bellamy had confirmed, the sounds of the bells across the island had triggered the men and women going about their lives. They, like the ones who had attacked them, were now mindless husks wandering about without purpose save to fight any who approached.

"That hope will be as hollow as those people unless we act on it."

Anne grinned at the one-armed warrior itching for a battle. She gripped his shoulder to gain his attention. "Patience."

Pukuh let out the tense breath he seemed to be holding and nodded as he showed her a small smile. After that, he relaxed a bit.

Anne turned her attention back to the hamlet, watching the people milling about. She, like Pukuh and William, was watching and waiting for an opportunity where they could use the bell.

They had learned that the people were drawn to sounds, but only when they couldn't see what produced it. Though Sam denied it, the hollow people did seem to retain some of their faculties, and they were able to judge what was human and what wasn't.

Communicating with each other was beyond them. Despite their having worked together to ram the general store's door, they worked independently. If several had heard a noise, they all had to see the source. None told the others what it was to save labour.

That knowledge would be to Anne and the crew's advantage.

Anne noticed one man splitting off from the rest and walking down one of the side roads leading out of the square. She motioned for one of the crewmates behind her to bring her a stone as they had discussed.

She waited a bit longer before tossing the stone over the ridge where she and the crew were waiting. The stone fell with a thud down the road, kicking up a small cloud of dust with it. The man was looking the other way when it fell, and it must not have been loud enough, because there was no reaction.

Anne lobbed another, larger stone down the road, this time using a bit more force. It went a few feet farther than the last one.

The man turned towards the noise and moved closer, looking around for any sign of the source of the sound as he did.

Anne threw another stone, this time much closer, and the man took the bait. He moved faster, whatever intelligence left driving him towards the ridge where he knew the rocks were coming from.

Anne, as they had planned, slunk back further down the ridge with the other crewmates waiting in the wings. They were a bit farther from William and Pukuh, who would be in the thick of it once the hollow man approached, but not too far away should the need arise.

William and Pukuh rose from their hiding spot just enough for the approaching man to see them, and he gained even more speed when his eyes fell upon them.

Anne pulled out the handbell from around her belt and

held it ready.

The man bounded over to the other side of the ridge and lashed out wildly, striking at the two in front of him.

William kept his distance and positioned his right shoulder towards the attacker so that his injured shoulder was out of harm's way. Pukuh was behind the man, waiting to ensure the fight didn't go sour.

Anne rang the bell softly, the small ding of the golden metal striking her ears and pulling on the hairs on the back of her neck. Pukuh raised his spear in the air, a signal that he heard the sound, but the man remained unchanged.

The crewmates around her were tense at the sight of the hollow man in front of them, fighting with no regard for his own preservation. Anne couldn't escape the influence of that tense atmosphere, and she too felt stiff in her movements.

She struck the bell once more in a natural up and down stride. The ringer hit at the top of the arc closest to her ear, and she felt its strange pull once more in the deep of her chest.

The man continued his assault. Anne cursed under her breath. It meant she had to get closer for it to work, or it wasn't working at all.

Step by step, she advanced while ringing the bell in the same rhythmic motion. If they were to find an accurate distance, she would need to be consistent.

The hollow man, however, had other plans. As Anne approached, and William fended him off with precision strikes and manipulation, she caught the hollow man's eye. He changed targets and ran straight for her.

Anne gritted her teeth and held the bell out in front of her as though it were a pistol. With the flick of her wrist, she tossed the bell into the air just after it struck its tone when the man was not ten feet from her. She changed her stance, ready to jump out of the way and try the trick Alexandre had told them about, but something changed.

The man slowed gradually to a complete stop in front of her. She watched as the life and intelligence entered his eyes once more, and he suddenly looked confused.

He glanced about him, all eyes and several weapons pointed in his direction, but he didn't seem alarmed by the threat to his life, simply confused.

"My apologies, ma'am," he said after a moment. "I seem to be lost. Could you point me towards the main road?"

Anne let out a sigh, partially from the relief of tension, partly from what was two steps forward and one step back in their plans. There was only one way to make sure.

"Sir, are you well?" she asked, throwing as much sincerity into her words as she could muster. "We were just talking about the price of some of your town's produce when you suddenly went stark white, and now you appear confused."

The man now appeared shocked and recoiled. "Oh my! Perhaps I've come down with a fever. Well, no matter, I have my wits about me now." Anne couldn't help but scoff at the remark, but the man seemed not to acknowledge it. "Now let me think, for a ten-pound sack of potatoes that would be zero pieces of eight, we have some fresh zucchini you might like for zero pieces of eight, and..."

The man rattled on down a list of different vegetables and fruit, giving the same price for each as though it were a standard amount.

Anne once more cursed under her breath. "Alexandre," she called. "See what you can do."

Alexandre and Victoria came over, and Alexandre began his own hypnosis to lull the man into a waking slumber. Anne walked over to William and Pukuh nearby.

"I am at fault for not keeping the man's attention, my captain," William said as he bowed his head. Old habits from the days he was in service to the crown were hard to break even now.

"It is no one's fault save Silver Eyes and his abhorrent treatment of these people. And whatever madness drove him to create this hellish island is our misfortune. We must change our plans as we know now we cannot ask these people for help."

"So, we will leave them here, yes?" Pukuh asked.

"No, we can't risk leaving them at our backs like this

when we don't know exactly what drives them. Silver Eyes could have instilled a fail-safe whereupon if none come to take them out of the trance, they come inland." Anne looked over her shoulder at Alexandre and Victoria tending to the man as the other crewmates watched them with a mix of fascination and horror on their faces. "Perhaps with a bit more time, Alexandre will find a means for them to join us in the fight."

"So, what do you propose, my captain?"

"I'll need more time. For now, we proceed as planned in freeing the people and dismantling the bell towers. We know that there's a limited range even with the bell towers, otherwise they would only need one, so we can take the people with us at a distance."

"Aye, Captain," the two said in unison.

Throughout the next hours, they continued luring the men and women from the hamlet to them and using the bell to free them from the hollow trance they were in. Some required more than one strike of the handbell, which Alexandre thought possible, but they didn't have to use the last resort technique he had taught everyone.

As a test, Anne used it on one of the children as they were the easiest to control, but it didn't have an effect. Alexandre believed that they were too deep in a trance at that time for it to work. Anne hoped that Sam was right that Silver Eyes' crew were not in as deep a trance, as that technique could be their secret weapon.

None of the men and women seemed to revert to their original state, however. All, even the children, were still in that strange trance that robbed them of their right minds and agency. The only beneficial part of it was that they were compliant and didn't protest even when there was no good reasoning behind a request. Anne simply had to ask them to stay where they were, and they did as told.

"Is that everyone?" Anne asked. All told, they had gotten almost sixty people before the sun was at its peak.

William, peering through a spyglass over every inch of the small hamlet, replied without taking his attention away. "I cannot see any left, though this is not the best vantage point."

"Then we proceed with caution," Anne said, loudly enough for the crew to hear. "Begin by taking down that bell tower, but be sure not to let it ring. If you see anyone still in a trance, keep your distance and call out to me, understood?"

In unison, the crew responded affirmatively, then went to work. Some remained behind to secure the men and women in case the worst happened and the bell was struck again, and the rest left to secure the bell.

"One down, three to go."

12. YOU KNOW WHAT THEY SAY ABOUT DEAD MEN?

Edward refused to talk with Herbert after they were forced to go below deck. He had too much on his mind and needed time to think.

The foremost thought on his mind was that of the driftwood seashell-shaped necklace that Grace had retrieved. His mother's necklace. He had forgotten all about it, and almost all about her until that moment.

Edward had never actually known his mother—she had died during his tender years, and he only ever learned of her through rosy retellings from his father.

He couldn't picture her face; his only real memory of her was her hair, black and glossy like onyx, just as his own, rolling over her shoulders with waves like the summer sea.

Outside of that, the only memory that stuck with him was after she was gone, when it had been just Edward and his father. His father trying his best to keep it together in the aftermath, then throwing himself into his work before leaving Edward behind. Leaving him behind with the Hughes, a family that loathed him. Leaving him behind to become a pirate.

What made the memory of the necklace worse was that, according to his father, he had been the one to pick up the driftwood and give it to his mother. His father had carved it into the seashell shape, and it had been hers before it became his.

A thief stole it, and he must have known its value given it was simple driftwood, and Edward's father had sent Grace to retrieve it for him. Did his father value it as a memento of his lover, his son, or both?

As Edward ruminated, a few hours must have passed. He felt the ship beginning to sway harder and harder with the increasing swell of waves crashing against it. As Herbert had predicted, they were heading into a storm. It was only a matter of time until the rain began, and then there would be no way out but through.

"Edward, we need to talk. Enough sulking."

Edward gritted his teeth and bit his tongue lest he say something he regretted. Instead, he rose from his hammock and joined Herbert. They passed by a few other crewmates avoiding work and headed towards the cargo hold.

Herbert left his wheelchair on the gun deck, strapping it to a full barrel with a rope, and descended a ladder to the cargo hold below. Edward followed soon after, grabbing a lantern along the way, then the two went into the maze of barrels, boxes, and bags haphazardly left in the hold. When they felt certain their voices wouldn't carry to the deck above them, they made themselves comfortable.

Herbert levelled a glare at Edward. "So, what did you do?"

Edward scoffed. "What did I do? You're the one who insulted Grace's helmsman, and by extension herself as well." He did his best not to think about what had happened in Grace's cabin and to deflect blame, but he could feel the heat of shame filling his cheeks. The little stubble he had grown back did little to hide it.

Herbert folded his arms, and his mouth was a line. If Edward didn't know any better, he had been practicing to look as emotionless as William.

Edward rubbed his face before letting out an exasperated grunt. "She tried to lay with me, and I said no. What was I supposed to do?"

Herbert's mouth went agape for a moment, unable to formulate words, but he recovered after a moment. "Sleep with her, that should be obvious." His arms were still folded, but his voice rose a touch.

Now, Edward was at a loss for words. "I won't do that to Anne," he said as he looked away from Herbert's gaze.

Herbert paused for a moment, and his tone softened. "We're in enemy territory. She would understand."

"Yes, you're probably right," Edward conceded. "But it

would cause her pain nonetheless. I refuse to put her through that."

Edward looked at his left hand and the ring that adorned it. He touched the strange metal as he thought about the ceremony that had preceded his donning it. The sea air, the feeling of the sun on his neck, the grains of his ship's deck underfoot, even Jack's pleasant tune from his violin from that day felt somehow different than any time before or after. It was as though the strange pull of nostalgia had lifted that day's most mundane things and elevated them in his mind.

Anne's dress, her hair, the taste of her lips; even at that moment, in the hold of the *Black Blood*, he could picture them, feel them, as though he were in that moment.

He ached for Anne. His heart pulled at his core, begging for her embrace, for the touch of her lips pressed against his. He felt hollow without her near. How could he, even for a second, think of another woman's features as pleasing to his eyes?

"I don't mean to interrupt… whatever it is you're thinking about right now, but if you were going to refuse her, you could have let her down easy."

Edward came out of his mental anguish over his shortcomings to scoff. "I don't think easy is in Grace's vocabulary," Edward said, which Herbert laughed at and nodded. "Besides, I had a lot on my mind at the time."

"What happened?"

Edward scratched his head, debating whether to share with Herbert the most recent revelation, and the subtle implications that came with it.

"Ed, we're in this together, remember? We are brothers, after all, and I don't just mean because of our fake names."

Edward chuckled and then nodded. "You are right, brother." He readjusted himself on the box he was sitting on, thinking of how to go about telling Herbert. "The day we went on that island and fought those men, Grace was there to retrieve a necklace." Herbert looked confused but said nothing. "The necklace belonged to my mother. My father sent her there to retrieve it."

Herbert whistled low and long. "No wonder you weren't

in the mood."

Edward clenched his teeth. "This is no time for jesting."

"Sorry, sorry," he replied swiftly. "So, your mother..."

"Dead," Edward replied. "When I was just a lad. I barely remember her, but she was a light in my father's life. I do know that. Whenever he would tell stories about her, his face would glow."

Edward's gaze dropped to the bottom of the deck of the dark hold. He wished that he had been able to remember her, to know her beyond the stories, to share in her laughter he had been told could put a smile on the sourest, to hear her voice that could quell the storm in the most raging of hearts.

"What was her name?"

Edward looked up at Herbert for a moment before he returned to his gloom. "Areia. Areia Thatch."

Herbert's brow rose, and he scratched his chin. "Is that Greek? I'm not much for languages."

"I'm not sure. My father wasn't forthcoming with my mother's family line. I think the closest he ever came was when he told me that my mother was never meant for this world, whatever that means."

Herbert nodded, and after a moment said, "He must have loved her."

"More than anything else in this world," Edward replied. "Maybe that's why after she died, he... he became Calico Jack."

"Having second thoughts?"

Edward looked up at Herbert. In his eyes, he couldn't see any emotion, except maybe pity. "No, it doesn't change anything. I still want to talk to him, ask him why, but if he wants me to kill him, then I'll give him what he wants. It's the only way to end this."

A sudden noise came from behind them—a box shifting and the unmistakable thump of a boot. Someone was there, someone had snuck up on them, someone had been listening. Edward leapt from his seat and pounced on the person. He threw him over towards Herbert and into the light of the lantern.

It was John. He scrambled to right himself after Edward's

toss and held his arms up in front of him. "Please, please wait, Edward," he cried.

"What are you doing here? What did you hear?" Edward rose as high as he could above John, but the low ceiling of the hold didn't allow much vantage. Thankfully John was still on his back, so Edward was able to tower over him.

"I came to get you. The captain is calling you two back above," John sputtered, and the words came in a jumble. He was trembling with fear and backing away from Edward as much as he could in the confined space. "I heard what you were saying about Calico Jack, about him being your father, about how you're going to kill him. Edward, I'm your—"

Edward had already pulled out a knife from his belt. He thrust it into John's neck, silencing him at once. Blood poured from the wound even before Edward pulled out the knife, and afterwards, it flowed like water from a burst dam.

John clutched his neck, desperate to stop the torrent. He reached out towards Edward as he writhed in pain, tears streaking his face and mixing with the blood on the sole. He tried to call out for help, but he could only mouth the words as a limp, weak, gurgled noise escaped his lips before he sputtered blood. His movements became sluggish, his hands fell to the deck, and his eyes fell and opened to the rhythm of a fading heartbeat. Another few twitches and John's life left him.

The kind young man who had shared with Edward his cup and his bread was no more. The one person aboard the ship who had been kind to Edward and Herbert was dead. If only he hadn't snuck up on them to listen, he would have lived another day.

Whatever it was John was about to say to try and gain back their trust after spying on them, Edward couldn't take the chance of him telling Grace of their plan. Or at least that was the justification Edward used for lashing out on instinct born of fear. Instinct born of dozens of battles, a year in prison, and weeks of torture. It did little to quell his shaking hands, or from wondering if he made the right decision, or the bubbling bile in his stomach.

"We need to throw his body overboard," Herbert said

after some time.

"Through the portholes on the gun deck. The waves and the storm will cover the noise."

The two nodded and went to work. Edward took John's shirt and tied it around the open wound to limit the blood dripping before he picked up the body. Herbert did his best to soak up the blood using some nearby rags. Their only bit of fortune was the darkness of the hold, and the usual rankness of the bilge just beneath them that would cover the smell. Herbert moved some of the cargo overtop of what remained of the blood and joined Edward near the ladder.

"You head up first and check for any remaining crewmates."

Herbert nodded and climbed up to the next deck. After a moment, Herbert called Edward up. Edward flung John's body over his shoulder and climbed the ladder. He trusted Herbert, but before coming all the way up, he glanced over the deck before he finished the climb.

Herbert went over to the nearest porthole with a cannon nearby at the ready. He pulled on a rope to the side, which opened the port. The noise of the frantic crew above was able to filter in, and it sent a wave of urgency into Edward's mind. The sound could draw attention, and it wasn't what they needed right now.

Edward lifted John's body to the small hole. Water from the crashing waves and the fresh beginnings of rain flew into the ship and splashed Edward as he pushed the young man's lifeless body through the hole. Inch by inch, he shoved and twisted and moved the body through. Herbert also did his best to help while he kept a lookout.

"Hurry, Ed."

"I'm going as fast as I can. These weren't meant for bodies."

Edward felt sweat dripping from his brow, and with each shove, he glanced over his shoulder towards the bow of the ship.

"Almost there," Herbert called, forcing Edward's attention back to the task.

With one final push, the body fell out of the porthole.

Herbert tossed out the bloody rags he'd taken with him from the hold, then Edward and Herbert both craned their necks to listen for the splash of the body, but heard none. Edward poked his head out, but couldn't see the body, which meant he was gone, lost in the waves of the storm.

Edward pulled himself in, let out a sigh, and sat down with his back against the wall of the deck. Herbert closed the porthole, and he too let out a sigh as he wiped the sweat off his brow.

After a moment to catch his breath, Edward tensed up again, and he checked his surroundings.

"What?" Herbert asked, anxious.

Edward saw no one nearby, and no eyes on them. "Nothing, just checking. It's over."

"No... it's not," Herbert said, his expression serious. Edward looked at him, still catching his breath. "We need to get above deck, and we can't leave it like this. No one else is below deck anymore. If we head above deck but Grace doesn't see John with us and then he's missing after the storm what do you think Grace will believe happened? Remember what happened to Nigel when he only *attempted* to kill us?"

"What do we do about it then?" Edward asked, but he had a sinking feeling he knew the answer already.

Herbert leaned over, his head underneath the tip of the cannon. "You need to kill some of the other crewmates during the storm. Otherwise, we'll be the ones joining Davey Jones."

Edward looked away from Herbert. He'd barely had enough time to process how he'd just killed John over a presumption that the young man would tell their tale to Grace. He hadn't even thought about it before the blade had been in his hands. Now, he had to kill again.

The storm outside had already begun, but there was another storm brewing inside, and despite the warning signs, there was no changing course to avoid it.

13. STRIKING DOWN THE BELL OF DEATH

"There it is," Victoria said as she peered through the spyglass.

Anne took out her own spyglass. On the other end of that magnified view, she could see the main town where Silver Eyes waited. It was like a small fort with wooden walls stretching the length to form a stockade and battlements on the top where she could see cannons as well as soldiers manning them. The entrance was in the centre of the stockade, lining up with the main road, judging by the marks in the earth where the wooden beams would swing open.

Judging by the size of the stockade's beams, it would be no easy task for their own cannons to make a dent, let alone break through. Calico Jack's crew were no fools, and Anne guessed that behind those massive beams were slats of iron holding them together.

Beyond the battlements, Anne could see the tops of some houses and a rather large one near the back closer to the sea, which Victoria claimed would be where Lance Nhil, Silver Eyes, resided. In the centre of the town, she could see another tall bell tower with another golden bell at the top.

"It's different than I remember," Victoria said, pulling away from the spyglass to look at Anne. "More fortified. Nhil won't go down easy."

"We were prepared for this," Anne said. "Fortunately, we're in control of the food supply."

"So, it is to be a war of attrition then?" William asked.

Anne nodded. "It is the safer way."

Pukuh slammed his spear into the ground and leaned against it. "What of the secret entrance Bellamy spoke of?"

"We can investigate it later, but from his description, and with the guards keeping watch, we may not be able to get enough of our crew in to make a difference."

Pukuh flashed a devilish grin. "It would only take a few to open those gates."

Anne couldn't help but return his smile. "We shall see. For now, send word to the *Queen Anne's Revenge* to get into position and have our crew move forward."

"Aye, Captain," William said before he left to relay orders to the crew.

"Victoria, head back to Alexandre and watch over the islanders. Tell our men to keep their distance. We don't know how far the sound of that bell tower will reach."

Victoria nodded and headed away from the town and down the main road to join with Alexandre and a small contingent of the crew watching over the entranced men and women from the island. They had gathered about one hundred and twenty souls, with the majority coming from the first village they'd gone to after meeting with Sam.

After Victoria left, Anne watched as the *Queen Anne's Revenge*, helmed by Christina with a skeleton crew, let loose the sails and moved to the harbour of the town. As they had discussed, Christina was to stay far enough away not to allow the cannons facing the sea to strike, but close enough to keep any ships trying to escape at bay.

After the ship began moving, the crew on land moved as well. They went to a field in front of the town, just far enough away to avoid any cannon fire from the battlements and began setting up their own cannons from the *Queen Anne's Revenge*.

The air was still with only a light breeze rolling across the small hills behind them every so often. It brought with it a waft of fresh earth and green grass. Anne couldn't remember the last time they had been on land for so long, and it felt strange to have solid ground underfoot and the salt of the sea only an aftertaste on the back of her palate.

She missed the creak and groan of the Caribbean pine aboard the ship, the din of laughter, boots cracking against the deck, the feeling of rigging between the hands. This island had its own beauty, its own charm despite the nature of its inhabitants, but it was not home. Home to her was the captain's quarters on the *Queen Anne's Revenge*.

But if she was honest with herself, she hadn't been that long ashore. The real issue was that which made that place home, the *person* who made that place home, was not there and hadn't been for a lot longer than she'd been ashore.

She looked down at her left hand, at the golden ring on her finger. The memento of a celebration of love. A memento of her love for her husband Edward, and his love for her. A memento of her real home.

Home was Edward's heart beating in her ear as she lay her head on his chest. Home was his smile that sent her heart racing. Home was his touch that made her shudder in all the right places. Home was his voice as he whispered his love when they were alone.

Her home was gone, and she had a job to do. Anne closed her eyes, took a deep breath, held it tight, and slowly let it go.

She opened her eyes and looked over the crew as they approached the marker in the field they had designated: the stump of a large tree, no doubt one of the trees that had been used in the construction of the fort. There were many such stumps around, but the forest it had once been a part of thinned out and ended at that one. It was also far enough away from the town that they had no worry of the cannons even if the cannonballs rolled a fair distance.

She saw Nassir guiding in the wagons holding their supplies, and the pieces of their own cannons they had taken from the weather deck of the *Queen Anne's Revenge*, three twelve-pounders and twenty eight-pounders in all. It left their ship less armed, but not defenceless, as it still had the thirty twenty-two pounders on the gun deck.

"Nassir," she called, "how long will it take you and the crew to secure the cannons?"

Nassir took a moment to assess their current progress. The tall, muscular man stroked his clean-shaven face, his dark skin smooth and supple like a rock worn over the years from the waves, such that he hardly looked his age. There was a hardness there, born of the hardships, tempered from loss only a loving father could know, but a softness too.

The crew had only just begun unloading the wagons and the cannons, but they had no limbers to set the cannons onto, so they needed to improvise. Some of the cannons would stay on the wagons, and the others would need something made by Nassir to hold them in place.

"We will have them by nightfall, provided there are no distractions." Nassir glanced to his right towards the town.

Anne followed his gaze. She could see movement on the wall, but it was calm. If she hadn't known that Silver Eyes' men were in a light trance, she would have thought it eerily quiet. "Let us pray there are none then," she said. "How are the men you're training?"

"They are well along but have much to learn. Perhaps some still do not value the word of a negro, but they listen in time."

Anne nodded. "If anyone troubles you, let me know, and I'll make rights of it."

"Understood, Captain," Nassir said, a wide grin across his face.

As though someone had been listening in on their conversation, the large bell in the centre of the town rang out. The strange tone, low and unnatural, then high and hollow, was nowhere near as loud as when she'd first heard it in the centre of the bell tower, but its effect was only slightly diminished. It shook her core and inexplicably made her bones itch. She had to force herself not to cover her ears, to get used to the sinister chime. If she let it take over her senses, then what would she do if it rang in the middle of a fight?

Some others in the crew had no such concerns and covered their ears to dull the sound of that unique bell. Anne could see all eyes drawn to the bell, and the crew stopped what they were doing to listen.

The bell kept ringing, and the crew kept still, watching. Anne needed to put a stop to it. She stepped on top of a few of the crates of supplies, pulled out a pistol and fired it into the air. The crack of the igniting black powder cut through the bell like thunder shaking the timbers of a home.

The crew came to their senses and went for their weapons, turning their heads this way and that to find the source of the gunfire. Slowly they noticed Anne standing tall above them.

"Do not let that bell take hold of you, lest you become one of the hollows." She had to yell to overpower the sound of the bell, and to reach each crewmate stretched across the field.

Her words rang true to the men, and none of them covered their ears any longer. They returned to work, setting up the cannons and supplies and trying their best to ignore the sound of the bell.

Anne, still on her perch, nodded approvingly before she remembered the crewmates watching the citizens of the island further inland. She pulled out her spyglass and looked down the road. She could see the group of them, the citizens tied up and the twenty crewmates watching over them from a distance. They were quite a way away, so it was hard to tell who was who, but there appeared to be none in a panic, and none of the islanders were struggling.

She did notice one person in the thick of the men and women, and she guessed it was Alexandre given his lack of care for his own wellbeing. He was ringing the handbell as he walked amongst them, seemingly as a precaution as she saw no signs they were affected by the bell tower at that distance.

"Captain!" William called.

Anne put the spyglass away and turned around. The wooden beams in the centre of the stockade swung open slowly, and thirty men ran out. Their weapons were drawn, and they were charging directly at them.

"To arms!" Anne shouted. "Muskets at the ready," she commanded.

The crew dropped what they were doing and grabbed muskets from the nearby supplies and out of the wagons. They lined up in front of the supplies in two rows, just as they had planned and just as Anne and William had trained them to do. One row dropped to a knee, and the other stood behind, both loading the muskets and readying to fire. There was enough distance and enough warning to give them time to load and ready before Silver Eyes' men were even close.

"Steady," William shouted, taking over for Anne as Anne watched the men approach through her spyglass.

The bell kept ringing over and over, filling the air with its otherworldly tone. It made the dead-eyed men approaching seem more a nightmare borne from the mist than real people on their way to kill them. On and on it rang, the rhythmic striking of the bell drowning out the shouts from the men approaching.

Anne could no longer feel the breeze in the air, as though the bell had whisked it away, and she felt a bead of sweat travel down her cheek. It was not a humid day, but the bell and the oncoming battle tensed her muscles like no other battle had before. These were no ordinary men they were about to face, and Anne didn't know what to expect.

William watched the oncoming enemy behind the two rows of men. They had to wait until the enemy was closer than three hundred yards before firing, but the closer they were, the more accurate the shot. Still, with the wall of men and muskets they had, there was no particular need for accuracy.

"Fire!"

William called the order at around two hundred and ninety yards. The wall of iron fired from the muskets, and smoke filled the air around them. Without the breeze, the smoke lingered and shaded their view as a light mist. They were still able to see the enemy approaching and saw the iron balls had met their marks.

The men hit by the iron slowed a step, but then returned to their charge unfazed. Their eyes looked like the entranced islanders, and their faces were unnaturally calm despite some of them shouting a war cry. It made their charge and their shouts seem rehearsed and wooden as though someone directed them to act in such a way.

"Fire!" William shouted again.

Another wall of iron shot forward, catching many of the men charging towards them. A few fell this time thanks to a few lucky hits to the skull, but the rest kept advancing.

The crew dropped their muskets and pulled out cutlasses and pistols. Anne put away her spyglass, drew her own weapon, and joined the crew. "Remember what Alexandre taught you," she shouted above the din. "These men are under a similar spell, but it's not as strong. We can break it with proper timing. Find an opening and strike!"

The crew didn't respond, too focused on the surge of men coming at them, but she hoped they heard her.

The battle began with a fury. The clang of steel on steel rang out as blades clashed. The crew of *Queen Anne's Revenge* outnumbered Silver Eyes' men by three to one, and their enemies were injured. It should have been a quick skirmish, but it was not.

The men they were facing were faster and stronger and had level heads, unlike their counterparts residing in the villages around the island. They struck with purpose, and even when the crewmates overwhelmed them with numbers, the enemy was able to strike effectively and efficiently to incapacitate or kill.

Anne gritted her teeth at the sight as she jumped into the fray. She joined William; injured as he was, he was having a challenging time of it.

The man he was facing had an injury as well: a bullet wound in the chest, but he seemed unhindered by it. He poked and prodded William with his sword, testing William's defences as William danced out of the way. The man was fast, but William was the better fighter.

William and Anne worked with each other, years of training combining in a beautiful ballet of blades. As William aimed for the man's neck, Anne swung her cutlass low and up in an arc towards the torso. The enemy swiped both blades away with a single strike. Anne and William moved with the enemy's sword, twisting and tangling them together.

William stepped in and moved his sword forward. The tip of his blade caught on the man's crossguard. He flicked his wrist in a firm, practiced motion, and the man's sword moved up with his. The man had no choice but to let go of his weapon.

Anne dropped her weapon, and she too stepped in with both her hands forward. Just as Alexandre had taught them, she smacked her hands together directly in front of the man's face as hard as she could. The sound of the clap, the proximity of her hands to the middle of the man's eyes, and the confusion of the action coupled together in perfect harmony.

The man took a few steps backwards as he shook his head. The hollow calm in his eyes and on his face was gone, and it was as if he had awoken from a dream where he had been falling. Anne had broken the trance, and the man was dropped back into the tangled thoughts of someone in the middle of a life-or-death situation. His hand reached for the wound in his chest as if he only just noticed the pain from the bullet.

Before he could choose to fight or take flight, William stepped forward again in a riposte stance and struck the man in the gut with his sword. William pulled the blade out and retreated a few steps as blood poured from the wound.

No longer under the protection of the trance, the man cried out in pain. He held fast to the wound, trying to keep it closed, to stop the blood, and to keep his guts inside where they belonged.

Anne picked up her blade now that her opponent was no longer a threat and turned around to help with the rest of the crew. When she had a chance to look over the battlefield, she noticed that, despite the rough start, the crew were turning the battle around and using Alexandre's method to dispel the trance. They were lucky the trance on Silver Eyes' men wasn't as deep or as strong as the islanders. They had lost a few men, but with the secret technique their enemies weren't prepared for, as well as the superior numbers, they were winning.

"Captain, look," William called, pointing to the sea.

Anne turned her attention to the sea, to the *Queen Anne's Revenge*. The ship was not staying away from harbour as they had intended, but it wasn't landing ashore either. The ship was heading towards the town.

Please, God, don't tell me Christina thinks to take the fight into the town.

Anne watched as the ship came closer and closer to the town's harbour. The cannons on the harbour, a higher calibre than the ones pointed inland on the stockade, fired on the ship. Most missed with the erratic bobbing of the ship, but a few hit their mark and tore into their home.

The sound of battle around her brought Anne back to the

field, and she glanced at the crew once more. Her men were finishing up the fight, with most of the enemy dispatched. The uninjured carried the injured off the field to attend their wounds as best they could be without Alexandre there. There was no more threat, and the stockade gates were now closed as well, indicating no further reinforcements would be sent their way for the moment.

The sound of cannons pulled Anne's gaze back to the sea. Their ship had turned now, no longer on a collision course for the harbour. As the broadside faced the town, the cannons at the bow fired off, but only two at a time. Each new shot had a small delay between them as they fired into the town.

Anne could see clearly where the cannons were hitting, but not why. They weren't aiming for the cannons firing back at them.

What is Christina doing?

Shot after shot laid into the town, breaking apart some of the taller structures with the large iron balls. As the ship fired, they too took on more damage. Whatever Christina's intention, it was not a gamble Anne felt was worth the amount of destruction they were causing.

Then, with a thunderous clang, a cannonball hit the huge golden bell in the centre of town. The bell knocked against the top of the tower, breaking the structure apart with such force it sent the wood flying in all directions. The bell itself tumbled end over end in the air in a frenzy of movement and sound as the striker hit the sides of the bell over and over. After a dozen rotations, the bell fell to the ground, out of sight beyond the stockade, and rang out for the last time, the strange tone warped by the damage from the cannon and the fall, no longer the same haunting melody it once was.

The ship, their purpose fulfilled, turned away from the town and away from the defending cannons protecting the harbour. They let loose a few more volleys, hitting one of the cannon battlements and damaging one of the ships at anchor before the broadside was at too far an angle.

Anne shook her head, her anger replaced with mild frustration. Without the threat of the bell, either from the men and women it would trigger, or the haunting sound they had to deal with, it made the coming battle easier, especially if it was to be a war of attrition as they were thinking. If they had to stay there weeks, all the while listening to the droning of that bell, she suspected she would go mad.

Anne hoped that that was what Christina had been thinking with that attack. Otherwise, it had been a fool's errand, and merely a fool's luck. But it seemed luck was in ample supply this day.

With the bell destroyed, it lifted the cloud that had been hanging over the heads of the crew, and they burst out into cheers and hollers. The victory felt all the sweeter without that sound overpowering all thought. Now the air was filled with the noise of their making.

Anne smiled with the crew, happy at their boosted morale and with Christina's gamble. She also didn't doubt that Silver Eyes was watching them, and she suspected that he was very displeased.

14. SEASICK

Grace was furious.

Edward knew from the look on the captain's face that the arrival of the storm had incensed her core. With the storm now behind them, she overlooked the crew with disgust, battered and broken as they were, with many lying on the deck desperate for air and respite.

Edward was one of the few on his feet, but not by choice. He needed to keep that look of contempt, that anger, directed away from him, so he stood on shaking legs next to the helm, which Herbert now manned.

After Edward had killed John and he and Herbert disposed of the body, they'd gone above deck and into the storm. Grace had put Herbert in charge, and he filled the role as masterfully as he could under the circumstances. He shouted commands, held fast to the ship's wheel as wind and water tested his grip and endurance both, and guided the ship out of the worst of it.

As he did so, Edward was busy himself. He stayed as far from the quarterdeck as he could, as far from Grace's watchful eye as he could, and he did the one thing he seemed skilled at: he killed.

When the waves surged over the sides of the ship, and even the hardiest seaman's legs could have given out, he struck. It was so effortless; all he needed was a well-timed push. So easy to kill them. So easy, it was like breathing to him.

And it was there that Edward felt it again. The floating feeling of freedom. The same feeling when he was so far drowned into a bottle, he felt nothing else. The same feeling when he was so far beyond exhaustion, his body was moving on its own.

He was no longer in that storm, no longer subject to the whims of the wind and waves. He had become the storm, and the sea. And the sea called for new visitors.

Edward threw at least four overboard in the storm. He lost count at some point because he didn't care for the lives he was expending, so it could have been more.

And judging by Grace's anger and disgust now that the storm had ended, she noticed the missing men amongst the crowd on deck.

"John," he heard Grace mutter under her breath. She was gripping the railing of the quarterdeck so hard her knuckles were white. She turned her rage in Herbert and Edward's direction, and he could feel his heart skip a beat. "Where's John?"

Edward just looked at her for a moment. His throat seized, and he no longer had that feeling of floating to help him. Whatever he drank to bring it on, it had left his body long ago with sweat.

"He's not here, and you were the last ones with him," she continued. "Where is he?"

Edward cleared his throat. It was just as Herbert had predicted. "I'm not the boy's keeper. How should I know?"

From Grace's expression, that was not the right answer. She turned her eyes towards Herbert and pointed at him. "My quarters. Now!" Grace turned to leave, the sight of her back brooking no refusal.

Herbert glanced over his shoulder, giving Edward a concerned look before heading to the quarterdeck ladder. Another crewmate took over the helm as Edward helped bring Herbert's wheelchair down to the weather deck and then down to the captain's cabin. There was no opportunity to talk with Herbert, no chance to go over the story again and ensure they were consistent.

Herbert went into the cabin, and Grace closed the door behind him. Edward stayed nearby and waited for whatever was going to happen.

Edward waited and paced and waited some more. He kept a tight grip on his cutlass, though he wasn't sure what good it would do. As he'd surmised before, if he killed their captain, the crew of the *Black Blood* would still be there to get revenge. They were on the open sea; there was no escape in the wooden box they'd stepped into. But Edward refused to lie down and die if it came to that. He would fight, and he would die. He would not let another choose what would happen to him, even his death.

A thought came to Edward as he waited, a way to avoid or at the very least postpone their deaths.

Edward's father, Calico Jack, could have killed him, could have killed all of them in that tavern weeks ago. Edward and Herbert had guessed that Calico Jack wanted Edward to kill him in some kind of test, just as the unlocking of the ship was a test.

If Edward told Grace who he was, there was a chance that she would keep them alive, at least long enough to bring them to her master. He looked at the ring, still adorning his left hand, simultaneously a threat and a marker of his connection to Calico Jack. If he needed to, it could prove who he was.

The noise of Grace's cabin door opening brought Edward out of his reverie. His hand went to his cutlass, but when he saw Herbert unharmed and under no immediate threat from Grace, he lowered his hand.

Herbert's face was forlorn, wearing a strange look of guilt or regret as he looked up at Edward from his chair. Despite his life and limb being intact, something unpleasant happened during their discussion, and it set Edward on edge more than he had already been.

"You," Grace called. "Inside."

After one final look at Herbert and a deep but quiet breath, Edward entered Grace's cabin, and she closed the door behind him.

Edward sat down in the chair across from Grace's and waited for her to sit. The anger that had been there was now gone, and she was emotionless as she stared at him.

"What happened ta John?" she asked.

Edward was silent for a moment. He had foolishly thought about everything but how to answer her questions. He chose to be blunt. "We lost a few to the storm. He's probably dead."

Grace's jaw clenched. "He went down ta fetch ye and

never came back. You two did." Grace paused to let her words sink in. "What happened ta John?" she repeated.

"After he found us, we went straight above deck," Edward said. "I thought he was right behind us."

Grace tapped her finger on her desk. Her body was tense, each muscle taut and ready to snap like a snake. She didn't seem to care about any of the other crewmates who lost their lives at Edward's hands. She was only asking about John. That meant at least that she hadn't seen him throwing people overboard.

"I was watching for him. He never came back to the weather deck." Her expression changed. Her jaw softened, and she looked away from Edward.

"It was a storm. You probably just missed him." Grace didn't respond to Edward's comment. She just had the same faraway look now as she gazed at nothing. "Why are you only concerned about John? He was nice to my brother and me when no one else was, and I would be saddened to lose him as well, but from what I saw, we lost a few crewmates."

Grace turned to look at Edward again. "John's different."

She seemed content to leave it at that, but Edward needed to keep the conversation away from him and Herbert being suspect. "Different... how?"

Grace stared into Edward's eyes for a moment, and then she let out a sigh. "I told yer brother, I suppose I may'swell tell you, else ye'll hear it from him." She shifted in her chair, relaxing a bit, and her expression turning sorrowful. "John wus me son," she said.

"Your son?" Edward blurted out.

Edward's heart seized in his chest. Killing several of her crewmates was wrong enough. She killed one herself since they've been there. Killing her son was another matter entirely. He wasn't sure he could use his real name to forestall his death if she concluded that they had killed John.

"Aye," Grace said, long and drawn out.

After a moment of silence, she reached into the drawer of her desk and pulled out the liquor from before. She poured only for herself this time and downed the drink in one shot. There was no seeking pleasure in that drink, as

Edward knew all too well. She wanted the numbness that it brought.

"Pirates came to me village when I was not twelve, maybe fourteen," she said. "I remember the bodies piled up in a ditch, all they owned stripped. Even the rich family wasn't safe." Grace took another drink, this time slower, and then she looked at Edward again. "Have ye ever been near a house set afire when the people are trapped inside?" Edward shook his head. "At first smells like nothing more than a roast. Then you smell the hair. Smells like shit. Reminds you what's burning, and you never forget that smell."

Edward sat in silence. He could already tell where the story was headed, trace the inevitable path that led a young child to have a son not much younger than herself, and a life of piracy, and a hardness born of experience.

He began to feel sick at his killing John, presumably her only son. Beneath the anger and now her strange façade of calm, he could tell that she loved John. It may have been from afar, but she still loved him. And Edward had killed him.

Grace continued. "I envied the pirates. They killed everyone I cared about, but I envied them for what they did."

"What?" Edward asked, perplexed.

"They made everyone equal," she replied. "Rich, poor, everyone was thrown in tha same hole when the iron took their lives." Grace swirled her cup before downing the last bit of drink. "I wanted that control." She took another moment and seemed to regain focus. "I wasn't poor, wasn't rich neither, but I was smart. I knew what was goin' ta happen ta the girls they didn't kill. So, I figured out who the captain was and… I made sure that he wanted my exclusive attention. The other girls weren't so smart. The men took their turns before discarding 'em, but the captain kept me for himself."

Edward had guessed the story already, but Grace's mention of the captain turned something in his mind.

"Jack musta saw something in me worth keepin'. Then, after I had John, and he found out, he made me a permanent crewmate." Grace shook her head as she bit her lip. "He'll not be pleased about this. Not one bit."

Edward felt crushed under a sudden weight, and his vision went blurry.

John had been Edward's half-brother, and Edward had killed him.

'I heard what you were saying about Calico Jack, about him being your father, about how you're going to kill him. Edward, I'm your—'

John had been about to tell him. It was also not so much a secret that John held some hatred for Calico Jack. John probably would have told Edward that he was on his side, and Edward killed him before he could get the words out. If only Edward had waited, if only he had trusted the young man a bit more...

"Ya look like yer about ta wretch on me table," Grace commented, bringing Edward back to the here and now.

"Just exhausted," he sputtered out.

"Go on, then, we're done 'ere."

Edward rose from his seat and left without looking back or saying another word. He closed the door behind him, ignoring Herbert's questions and calls. He rushed up to the weather deck, where the crew were just now beginning to start repairs on the ship, and he vomited over the side.

He was shaking, his head ached, and he felt his world closing in again. The trembling of his hand returned in full force, as though it had never left him. Images of the dead, those he'd killed and those who had died because of him, flashed in his head, and there was a new face added amongst them.

He slumped down to the deck and reached for the flask in his pocket.

15. LOOK INTO MY EYES

The night was eerily still and calm. The winds over the sea had abated, and the water was quiet save for the occasional breeze creating a light chop. Thick clouds off in the distance hid the moon from view. Somewhere, far away, a storm had stolen the winds away from this island and left it in darkness.

The clouds obscured God's eye, and the earth and sea lost his protection. There were only devils in the sea this night.

These devils knew nothing of fear, or hate, or pain. The harsh cold of the seawater did not sap their strength as it might have for other men, and it did not hamper their movement. The sea they moved through showed the barest hint that they were there, only the slightest ripple extended from their heads as they waded closer and closer to their quarry.

A tremendous wooden beast loomed in the distance in front of them, stilled by the serene sea it called its home. Though the beast was not alive, those moving around on it were. The bellows of laughter and the hollow boom of boots against the beast's frame cut through the silence of the night.

The leader of the devils, with eyes touched by silver that was not silver, guided his minions to the beast's side. Those aboard the beast had not noticed the ripples in the waves. Their ears failed to hear the subtle drip of water cascading off clothes and back to the sea as the devils climbed up the sides of the beast. Without God's eye, they were blind to the enemy in front of them.

The leader had watched his minions the day before, had seen how they had been defeated. With his superior eyesight, granted him by one of the fingers of Midas, he knew how the wicked creatures of the light wrested control over his minions from him. And though he knew not a way to counteract it, he knew how it was done, and that was all he needed for his dark plan to succeed.

He and his minions boarded the beast, covered by the

dark of the night and their dark clothing. One after the other, each of his men captured those who called the beast home, locking their arms and covering their mouths to stop their cries and their means of disabling his control.

After they had secured the beast's back, he went over to each man they'd captured. They squirmed and fought, but his minions were stronger, and so there was no escape. He gripped their shoulders, staring into their eyes, whispered the secret words he had learned over time, casting his spell over their mind to make them his.

Some fought, their minds stronger than others, but even the strongest were no match for his power. He had learned the secret ways long ago, practiced on many minds, and each one fell to him in the end.

All but one. The one who had given him his eyes. The one who had given him his new name and had let him loose on this island. That one had his own power, his own eyes that the fewest of the few possessed, that allowed him to re-sist. No, that allowed him to *conquer*. His blood was the blood of kings, and no man could overcome it.

One after the other, the men fell asleep. They would awaken later and serve a higher purpose than they had be-fore.

Something unexpected stopped the leader of the devils from his work. A door opened to the beast's innards, and a young woman, two men—one holding a fiddle—and a wolf stepped out.

There was a silent moment where the three figures glanced across the ship, assessing the situation. Then, when they realized what was happening, they pulled out their weapons. The girl held twin daggers, one defensively to her side and the other up and ready to strike, while the man with the fiddle pulled out a pistol, and the other man his cutlass.

"Tala, *tuer*!" the young woman shouted.

The wolf, answering her call, ran forward and attacked one of the leader's minions. In one swift motion, it struck the neck, tearing a chunk of flesh away and letting loose a torrent of blood.

The leader ignored the wolf and raised his fist in the air.

He needed no words to command his minions, and they obeyed the silent order in unison. They all pulled knives from their belts and placed them under the necks of the subdued men.

"Stop!" the girl shouted.

The leader held his hand in the air, unwavering, and he stared at the girl. He didn't want to continue the command if he didn't have to, as that was not his plan, and so he waited for the girl to act.

After another moment, the girl realized there wasn't anything she could do and lowered her daggers. "Tala, *venir*," she said. The French verb meant 'come,' a command to the wolf, which it obeyed by stopping its attack and returning to the girl's side.

The leader opened his palm and lowered his hand, then pointed at the three, and his minions went to restrain them. The wolf growled but remained stationary.

Now that he was closer, the leader was able to take a better look at the girl in command.

Her features, lit from a lantern in the cabin they had just exited, were pleasing to the eye. She was blond with a hint of rouge, as a tranquil field of wheat in the red light of dawn. Her body was well-toned, a fighter's body, youthful and shapely as a budding rose that could one day bloom into motherhood.

All those they had captured so far looked to be good fighters, trained and ready for battle. They would make useful additions.

The leader pulled the young woman's chin up to face him. Her cheeks flushed with anger and embarrassment.

"Look into my eyes."

A new day began in their stalemate of a battle.

Anne awoke from her first rest in some time and assessed their battle preparations and provisions with new eyes.

Nassir and the other crewmates had worked hard through

the night and prepared a defensive wall of cannons. The makeshift, stationary limbers would hold the cannons and prevent them from flying away after each blast but were challenging to change the angle of. To be effective, they needed two men on each of the smaller cannons, as opposed to a single man had they still been at their home on the ship.

Their provisions, gathered from the many farms they had visited, would sustain them for quite some time if needed, and they could also collect more. If they couldn't win by force or by stealth, which Anne would find out about soon, then they could win by starvation. No matter how powerful the trance Silver Eyes' crew were under, they could not avoid the need for food indefinitely.

A few paces back from the line of cannons aimed at the town, Anne had set up a table with a few chairs for her, William, and some of the other crewmates to discuss strategy. She noticed William sitting there, and a bowl of food and a drink waiting for her. Pukuh was standing beside William, chewing on a piece of bread with meat and cheese on it.

Anne sat and quickly ate the modest food to break her fast. She didn't want to waste any time to discuss the investigation of the secret entrance Sam had provided the key for. She still found it challenging to eschew habits formed during her royal upbringing and waited until she finished swallowing before she spoke.

"What of the tunnel into the town?" Anne asked.

William glanced at Pukuh over his shoulder, then gave his report. "The tunnel, as Sam said, appears to be for the soldiers in need of a flanking attack. However, it has fallen into disrepair due to negligence and arrogance. It could collapse at any moment."

Pukuh scoffed. "No matter. We'll not be long there," he said.

William appeared exasperated, though to anyone but Anne, who had been studying his minute expressions, he looked as placid as ever. "It is as our friend says. We shan't be in the tunnel long, so we could possibly end the battle tonight under cover of darkness."

"Why must there always be waiting with you white

people? Now is the time to strike back. We kill their leader and dine in his puny castle before the sun is high."

William didn't respond; he had probably heard the same argument from Pukuh before she awoke. The two simply waited for Anne, their commander and current captain, to speak.

Anne, for her part, being well-rested and high off their recent victory, saw no purpose in rushing into doom. That Sam knew of the tunnel meant Silver Eyes knew of the tunnel.

"Pukuh, are you familiar with the phrase 'the better part of valour is discretion'?"

Pukuh took a bite from his bread, meat, and cheese. "No," he replied, his cheeks full.

"It is from one of our great playwrights, and it means that caution is better than blind bravery."

Pukuh nodded. "Ah, I see. So, the savage is not smart as you are."

Anne was taken aback at Pukuh's comment as she had only known the Mayan prince to be a kind and affable man. "My apologies, Pukuh, that was not my intent. I am merely trying to—"

Pukuh held up his hand. "Save your air for later. If Edward were here, the Silver man would have his head on my spear on the walls now."

Pukuh's raised voice brought the attention of the crewmates nearby, and many were visibly uncomfortable and glancing at the scene over their shoulders.

Anne took a moment to gather herself, then stared into Pukuh's eyes. "You may be right. Edward may have finished this by now, but Edward is not here. In his place, I am your captain, and I give the orders to the crew of this ship." She paused for a moment to let her words hang in the air. "I understand your frustration with how I am approaching this matter, and I'll take it under review. Having said that, I can assure you that sooner rather than later, that spear of yours will see its fair share of blood. Can I count on you to be there when the time comes?"

Pukuh didn't reply, he simply stared Anne down for a

long moment. She held his gaze, unwavering, as she sat stock still in her chair.

Another moment more, and Pukuh grinned. "You'll get your spear, princess," he finally said.

Anne returned the smile. She had never thought of him as a savage, as he put it, but she knew that their interactions so far had been brief at best. Perhaps this was his way of testing her, not knowing her very well. If it was, it appeared she had passed.

"Captain, look!" a crewmate called, his finger pointing to the sea.

Anne turned in her seat and followed the crewmate's gesture to the *Queen Anne's Revenge*. It was no longer circling the seas around the town as they planned. It had dropped anchor. That alone would not have caused too much alarm, as they had been able to damage the ships at harbour yesterday. There was no threat of Silver Eyes escaping now. What did cause alarm was the longboats of the ship carrying the crew to shore.

A tingle up Anne's spine forced her up from her chair. A dozen thoughts flashed through her mind as to what would cause the crew to leave the ship behind, but she was powerless to know now.

Her instinct guided her where knowledge could not. "Something's not right," she muttered. "Prepare for battle!"

Confused at first, the men drew their weapons and those not manning the cannons grouped up with Anne. Anne drew her own cutlass and headed towards shore.

William ordered the men to form up, making a line two strong. The high from yesterday's victory turned into a sour note as the crew realized what may be happening.

Anne pulled out her spyglass and watched as the longboats hit the shore, and the crew aboard them jumped off in a sprint towards the field in front of the town. Christina and Jack were there, both had weapons drawn, lips curled back in a snarl like some animal ready to kill. Tala, a real animal, was keeping pace with Christina.

It was their eyes that gave Anne another shiver. Their eyes were hollow. They had been put under a trance by their enemy sometime in the night.

"They're under a trance," Anne shouted to the crew around her. She stepped forward and turned around to face them, so all eyes were on her. "But we can break it. We know it works. Try your best not to harm them, but don't let yourself be killed either." The crew objected, confusion and denial overtaking reason. Anne held up her hand. "This is no time for debate. Prepare yourselves." She went back to her place in the line before she had to field any other objections. "Bring some of the men off the cannons, we'll need all the hands we can get," she said to William. William nodded and left to issue orders to the crew manning the cannons.

Anne turned around as she took a few deep breaths and faced down her crewmates on the way to kill them. The entranced crew's rapid pace set a cloud of dust behind them.

William and some of the other crew returned to join the battle. "Spread out! Start moving," Anne shouted. "Split them up so you don't get overwhelmed."

Anne moved forward to meet Christina, and the other crewmates did as she commanded. As the targets spread out, the entranced crewmates followed suit, slowing their pace to attack.

"Tala," Anne heard Christina say as she came closer, "*tuer!*"

The wolf quickened her pace and lunged at Anne. Anne didn't want to harm the beast and rolled out of the way. She put herself at an angle away from Christina and Tala so she could face both, though not flawlessly.

Anne could hear the battle all around her, chaotic and discordant. Blades and bodies clashed as dust from upturned earth filled the still air around them. She could see William trying to get close enough to Jack, but he and another crewmate were on the attack and keeping him at bay. Pukuh was similarly having a challenging time, not only dealing with having only one hand and not being able to break the trance but also having to hold back so as not to harm his fellow crewmates. Nassir had joined in the battle, but he was inexperienced and kept his distance to distract rather than attack.

Christina lunged at Anne, slamming down with her right-hand dagger. Anne blocked with her forearm. The force rippled through her bones. Christina was using all her strength, her mental limits gone with the veil to the subconscious pulled open. If Anne wasn't careful, Christina could break Anne's arm or her own.

Anne yanked her hand over and clutched Christina's right forearm tight. Christina swung low with her other dagger. Anne dropped her cutlass and caught her opponent's wrist. Just as Anne was about to twist and disarm her friend, Tala charged at Anne's side. Anne bent her and Christina's bodies, blocking and pushing Tala back.

Between stopping Christina from attacking and keeping Tala at bay, Anne couldn't end the trance. They were locked in a dance, and none of the crew were nearby to help her.

"Tala, *arrêter*!" Anne's command didn't work. The wolf only obeyed Christina and Edward.

Christina looked crazed and feral, nothing like the sweet girl with the mild temper she knew. Her eyes, though looking straight at Anne, didn't carry the same recognition of a sane person. Silver Eyes had somehow put his talons in her and made her think her friends were her enemies, but Anne knew they could break the trance. There simply hadn't been time to turn them into the state the islanders were in. Alexandre had said it would have taken months to get them to that state. If only Anne could find an opening to break the spell…

Movement at the town's wall drew her eye. The gate had opened, and more of Silver Eyes' men were exiting and heading towards the battle.

Dad dammit! We don't have the manpower for this right now. Anne dodged another strike from Tala and kept her hold on Christina by a hair. "William!" she called.

William, just managing to sort out Jack, turned to her call and started running.

"No!" she yelled. "The cannons, the cannons!"

William looked over at the cannons and then noticed the men approaching by foot. He began shouting orders and pointing towards the cannons as he moved that way. Several of the crew and even some newly conscious crewmates joined in to gather muskets and man the cannons.

"Christina!" Anne shouted. It was taking all her strength to hold on to the young woman. "It's me. It's Anne. I know you're in there. Wake up!"

Christina's eyes changed, coming into focus. She stopped moving, stopped resisting. She appeared confused but still distant, as though she were half-asleep.

Pain seared Anne's right leg, and a force pushed her to the side and away from Christina. Anne fell to the ground and lashed out towards her lower leg. Tala, at the moment Anne had let her guard down, had bitten down on her calf and shin. She'd ripped through her clothes, through the muscle on her calf, and to the bone on her shin. Anne punched the wolf, shouting commands and expletives at the beast in French. Tala snarled, tugging at Anne's leg and refusing to let go as it ripped her leg to shreds.

The pain overtook Anne's mind, just as the bell had when she had been right underneath it. She screamed in vain, punching and punching Tala to no avail. She needed Tala off her, or she would die, she knew it. Anne reached into her belt, pulled out her knife, and slammed the blade into Tala's skull down to the hilt, killing the wolf instantly.

Anne ripped the beast's jaws off her leg, another roaring pain surging up her right leg, through her pelvis, and up her spine. She reared back, all thoughts lost in that storm of pain.

She pulled herself back from the pieces the pain had broken her into and mustered her will. Her whole body shook with the effort to bring herself to her feet, and she nearly collapsed as soon as she stood.

Christina was looking at her and Tala's lifeless body. She was still in a daze, her mind still trapped. Some part of her seemed to know what was happening, even in that dream-like state, and tears were streaking her face as she gazed at Tala and Anne.

Anne, her right leg useless, limped her way to Christina. She leaned on the younger woman for support, then clapped right in front of her eyes.

The spell released, and Christina took a sharp breath as though waking from a nightmare. "Wha... what happe..." She looked around at the scene of the battle, over to Tala's dead body, and then burst into fresh tears. She covered her mouth and pulled back from Anne, but Anne needed to hold onto the young woman for support.

"Christina, listen to me," Anne said weakly, trying to keep a hold of her consciousness.

Christina's eyes were moving quickly over everything, shock taking over her senses. She was breathing too rapidly and becoming hysterical. She looked down and saw Anne's injury and began to cry harder. "Your leg, oh Anne!"

"Christina, Christina!" Anne called. "Look at me." She grabbed the woman's face and gently took her attention back. Christina's eyes still didn't focus on Anne. "Look into my eyes," she said. The words triggered something in Christina, and Anne finally had her attention. "This wasn't your fault. You did nothing wrong."

The young girl was a mess. She wept, with no way to stop the tears. Anne pulled her tight and held her as she cried. The battle raged on around them as Christina's tears and Anne's blood fell to the ground.

Cannons, muskets, swords, smoke, shouting, sweat, pain, blood. William's mind filtered through all the noise to focus on only the most essential things needed in the time of battle. He had been trained to do so, and he was adept at it.

He had not been trained to fight an enemy incapable of feeling pain. He had not been trained to fight his comrades. He had not been trained to hold back in battle.

And he had not been trained to suppress his emotions. That came from years of practice. And in that, he was struggling.

Anne had ordered him to act, and he acted. They were winning the battle, but only by the thinnest of margins. Their only saving grace was their surgeon's technique. On all other fronts—the number of men, morale, and even training, save for a few exceptions—they were on the losing side.

The cannons and muskets kept their enemies at bay while

they fixed more members of their crew who had fallen under the devil's spell, and with each person who was saved, it added to their numbers.

"Draw swords!" Some heard his command and drew their swords and cutlasses with him. "Charge!" William led the men into the fray just before the enemy would be too close.

William had been called The Arching Light, a name given to him by others in the royal guard for his speed and the way light shone off his blade with his perfect form. Here on the battlefield, as a pirate, he knew his sword did not shine, and he was no source of light. Outside of training, in a real battle, his sword turned red.

William needed to end this quickly and ensure Anne's safety. He slashed, stabbed, kicked, punched, and elbowed one man after the other. His dance of death was muted. There was no beauty in it, only the purest form of battle. Parry, thrust, parry, sidestep, thrust. There was no chaos, no wasted movement, and no thought. Memory carried his blade and his body as one to where it needed to be, memory from his unknowing mind built over years of experience and training.

When it was over, he had killed eight, sending their souls to whatever afterlife their actions warranted.

William assessed the situation, taking stock of their numbers. The enemy had sent a similar number to what they had the other day, but with Anne's quick reaction, they had managed to fend them off. There were still some left, but the crew could handle the rest.

William turned his attention back to Anne and Christina, and as he approached, he saw the two in an embrace. Relief washed over him, but he didn't slow his pace.

Though they had lost many men so far and had many more injured, the other crewmates were turning those put into a trance back to normal. Soon, the battle would be over.

As he drew near he noticed Tala, dead and off to the side of the two women. Her muzzle was bloodied, a sure sign she had inflicted grievous wounds on someone. He looked Anne over for injuries and quickly noticed her right leg bleeding profusely. He quickened his pace, and his heartbeat soon matched.

Christina noticed him coming, and she pulled away from Anne's embrace. "Anne's injured. It's my fault. I'm sorry, I—"

William held up a hand. "Bring Alexandre to the ship, most of his supplies are there."

Anne's face had blanched from blood loss. "I am well," she protested. "I simply need some assistance walking at present." William scooped her up, lifting her off her feet. "This wasn't what I had in mind."

Christina wiped tears from her face, took a breath, and nodded at William before running off to find Alexandre.

William took Anne to the shore where the longboats had landed. He gingerly placed Anne inside the boat, taking care not to bump her leg. Despite his diligence, he noticed her wincing and stifling a cry of pain. William thought the only thing keeping her awake was the pain.

After Anne was secure, William rowed the longboat back to the *Queen Anne's Revenge*. The two of them were silent for the ride, neither broaching the nature of the horrific injury she had received, nor the battle which was finishing inland. The noise of crossed blades, shouts, and pain had faded away to a whisper on the wind by the time they reached the side of the ship, replaced by the soft whistling across the weather deck, and the lapping of waves against the side.

William secured the boat to the side of the ship and then picked Anne up again. "Apologies, Captain," he said as he hoisted her over his shoulder.

Even at this, she didn't say a word, which told him that she knew the severity of her own injury. This made his heart race even faster.

William climbed up the side of the ship, his muscles burning with the effort. After a careful few minutes, he had her aboard, but he dared not put her down now. He took her below deck and into the surgeon's room and placed her on the long table in the centre. He helped her lie down and went to work before Alexandre arrived.

William was no surgeon, but he knew a concoction that would be useful for pain mitigation. He grabbed a bottle from the storage cabinets, one of the only bottles in the bunch clearly labelled, which William thought dangerous, and gave the liquid a sniff to be sure.

William handed the bottle to Anne. "You must drink this, Captain."

Anne cocked her brow. "What is it?" she asked, but she began drinking before he answered.

"Gin," he replied as she took a large drink and reeled back at the sharp taste.

He thought of cleaning the wound with the gin and dressing it, but he knew how particular Alexandre was. He didn't want to risk his ire, nor the possibility of making the situation worse. Instead, he wrapped a cloth just beneath her knee and tied it tight to stanch the blood loss, sat down in a nearby chair, and then they waited.

After a moment of silence, Anne spoke. "William?"

"Yes, Captain?"

"What kind of a man was my uncle-in-law?"

Anne spoke of William III, the king before her mother took the throne. The question caught him off guard, as they had not talked much of their lives before joining Edward's band of pirates.

William looked away from Anne as he reminisced. "I loved him," he said. "He was more than a king to me. He was like a father."

"He must have been a great man to have such high praise from you."

William still didn't know how to respond. He settled on a nod and "He was." It felt… insufficient.

There was another pause, then after another drink of gin, Anne said, "Why didn't you save him in the Triangle?"

It took a moment for William to understand just what she was referring to. William had been a kingsguard and had been framed for his king's murder, so he'd fled. Years ago, the *Queen Anne's Revenge* had entered the Devil's Triangle, where the crew had experienced strange events. William, along with Sam Bellamy and a woman they'd thought was their enemy at the time, were seemingly transported to the time just prior to the king's murder. It was thought to be a dream, but dream or real, William had chosen not to change what happened and let his king die again.

"How...?"

"Sam told me. He told me that you didn't want to risk changing history but never told me why. He said to ask you, but I never did because I thought it was too personal."

William rose from his seat to look into Anne's eyes. Her pallor hadn't improved much, but the gin seemed to be helping.

"I didn't stop his murder because of you," William said.

Anne arched her brows, a question unuttered but implied.

"I've never seen you happier than aboard this ship. Yes, there have been some hardships"—he cast a glance at her leg—"but you have made friends here, shared laughter here, and you were even married here on this ship."

William took his chair and pulled it closer so he could sit next to Anne. He sat a moment, staring off at nothing, then looked Anne in the eyes again.

"I remember meeting you when you were twelve," he said. "I was a new kingsguard then, just a few years before your uncle-in-law's death. You didn't scowl, but you never smiled. You smiled in the way that they trained you to, but you never truly smiled. Except once, when you were with the ladies in the kitchen, and you started a fight with the food they were preparing." William took Anne's hand in his. "If you would have stayed royalty, I have no doubts you would have made a wonderful ruler, a wonderful queen. I'll admit that that was what I had hoped would happen at first. I hoped I might bring you back to take your place in the palace, but I realized you belong here with these people. This is where you are you and not what someone else told you to be. This is where your family is."

There was another moment as William's words sank in, then Anne spoke. Then she squeezed his hand. "And your family too, I hope?"

William couldn't help but smile. He thought to say something affirming her question, but the words felt hollow in his mind. Too hollow to convey the feelings which held his hand firm to hers. By the look on her face, this was all he needed to say in answer.

The sound of boots slamming against wood above them took them away from their reminiscing. After a moment, Alexandre, Victoria, and Christina all entered the room.

Alexandre and Victoria wasted no time in preparing to treat Anne's wound. Alexandre first grabbed scissors and went to Anne's injured leg.

"And how is *le patiente*?"

Anne lifted the gin bottle in the air. "Excellent," she said before taking another drink.

"I see you've started already. How thoughtful."

Alexandre began by cutting away Anne's clothes from the wound. Using a deft hand, he cleared the area around the wound and then took away the pieces that had became stuck to the skin as the blood dried. After a few careful minutes, however, Alexandre stopped and stepped back slightly.

"What is it?" William asked.

Alexandre stayed still in thought. His face scrunched and deadly serious. "Victoria, prepare for amputation."

The words sent a wave of shock through William's system. Anne and Christina both looked just as shocked as he.

Christina, already in hysterics over being entranced, looked ready to burst into tears again. "Why?" was all she could muster.

"The damage is too severe. Bone fragments entered her muscle. It is impossible to remove them all. They will, at best, cause paralysis. At worst, rot."

Alexandre retrieved a sizeable curved knife and a thick piece of wood. He handed the wood to William. Victoria was shuffling around the small room, gathering things they would need after the amputation was complete.

There was no way around this, so William steeled himself. Alexandre was a consummate professional, unparalleled in the study of medicine. If he said they needed to amputate Anne's leg, there was no use arguing. Anne would survive this, there was no way she wouldn't.

William looked down at Anne. "Take another drink, Captain."

Anne, she too nearing tears, took a long drink of the gin,

then handed the bottle to William. William set the bottle aside and placed the piece of wood in her mouth.

"Hold her steady, all of you."

Christina and Victoria both came to the table and put all their weight down on top of Anne to hold her still during the surgery. William placed his hands on her shoulders as he stared down at her.

Deep in her eyes, he could see fear. It was rare for her to be afraid, let alone show it, and if he were honest with himself, he too was afraid. She needed strength now more than anything else.

She lifted her head up and looked at her injured leg, part of which she was about to lose. "No, Anne," he whispered softly. "Look into my eyes." She laid her head back down, and tears streaked her face. "It's going to be all right."

16. NASSAU

Edward hadn't slept properly in days. His body felt heavy, as though he were thirty feet below the sea. Moving, breathing, just existing, was gruelling and painful. He wanted it to end. And so, Edward did the one thing that helped him sleep and made him feel less pain, less leaden, less everything: he drank.

It didn't matter when; Edward drank all hours of the day, and it showed. His speech slurred from time to time, he lost his sea legs, and the cloud the booze gave him sapped his strength.

Strangely enough, his fighting ability had improved. Because of various blunders during his shifts, as well as a few misunderstandings on Edward's part, he brawled with a few of the crew. The drink helped him withstand even more punishment than he already could and made his movements unpredictable. His opponents hadn't known how to handle him under normal circumstances, and the drunkenness only made him more dangerous.

Herbert caught Edward after he had taken a rest. He was still dealing with the effects of having drunk the night before but was no longer intoxicated.

"Edward, this must stop," Herbert said.

Edward's head pounded in his ears, and his stomach lurched with each movement. "This is far too early for such talk, Herbert. Let me eat and drink, then we shall discuss whatever it is that must stop."

Herbert scowled. "It is precisely the drinking that I am referring to," he said. He glanced around him, then moved his chair closer to Edward before speaking in a whisper. "I know that you are mourning the loss of John. I know you two were... closer than you previously thought, but if you continue this, then—"

"What? I won't be in well enough shape to kill more of my family?"

Herbert's face went stark white and his eyes nearly bulged out of their sockets. "Keep your voice down, you fool!" he whispered harshly.

Edward didn't feel the same urgency as Herbert's tone called for, but he didn't say anything else. Instead, he reached into his pocket and pulled out his flask.

Herbert reached over and swiped the flask out of his hand. Edward tried to grab it back, but Herbert kept it out of reach. He put it in the secret compartment of his wheelchair.

"Give that back," Edward said.

"That's going to get us both killed."

Edward, his head still pounding, tired, body aching, was like a packed cannon, and Herbert was the linstock. It only took a touch for him to explode.

He reared back and punched Herbert square in the jaw. Herbert spilled out of his chair and tumbled to the deck.

Edward picked up the wheelchair, not bothering to check if Herbert was all right, and tried to open the secret compartment. "How do you work this thing?" he muttered to himself.

Herbert punched Edward on the side of the knee. He collapsed and fell to his knees, grimacing in pain. Herbert pounced and wrapped his arm around Edward's neck to choke him. Edward pulled against Herbert's arm, but Herbert's grip was secure.

"There's lead balls ready to fire from that thing, you idiot!" Herbert's words came out in haste from the strain, but he managed to be only loud enough for Edward to hear.

The other crewmates of the *Black Blood* noticed the fight and cheered the combatants on. The two of them rolled and tumbled on the floorboards as hoots and hollers goaded them to continue.

"You think you can beat me in a fight, you bastard?" Edward poured his all into pulling back Herbert's arm.

Herbert brought his other arm up and locked his grip. "Just because I don't handle rigging all day doesn't mean I'm weak."

Edward's neck was in a vice, and he couldn't breathe.

Pulling Herbert's arm was useless as he had superior upper body strength and a better position. So, Edward pulled his arm up, then slammed his elbow into Herbert's ribs. Herbert grunted, and his grip wavered. Edward brought his arm up repeatedly, smashing his elbow on Herbert's bones. Though each blow loosened Herbert's hold, it provided no chance to breathe or escape.

"By these copper legs o' mine, you boys better stop yer fightin' else I'll shoot the lot of ye."

Grace O'Malley stormed through the crowd that had gathered, looking down on the two she thought were brothers having a squabble.

Herbert released Edward from his hold, and Edward rolled off him, sputtering and coughing to catch his breath. Herbert went to his chair and got in it.

"We're about ta land in Nassau and you boys're about ta meet Calico Jack. If ye want ta survive the experience, I suggest ye stop fuckin' about." Her hands were on her hips, and her expression daunting. "Herbert, get ta the weather deck. The helmsman needs relief."

"Aye, Captain," he replied as he pushed himself forward to the ladder.

"As fer you," she continued, looking at Edward, who was sitting on the deck and rubbing his sore neck, "ye've been useless of late. If ye want me ta put in a good word, take stock and get ta work. Otherwise, take yer chances overboard. Ye'll 'ave better luck with the sharks than with Jack, I can tell ye that much." The other crewmates chuckled, and some muttered agreements. Then she turned her attention to them. "Did I ask any of ye ta say somethin'? Back to work!"

Grace and the other crewmates dispersed at once, leaving Edward alone on the sole of the deck in the crew's quarters.

Edward's body still ached, but now he also felt the red flush of embarrassment join with it. He gritted his teeth, slammed his fist on the floorboards, and went to the weather deck.

Herbert was already at the helm, so either he'd carried his wheelchair himself or someone else had helped him. He glanced Edward's way when he appeared, then turned his attention back to steering the ship.

Off the bow of the ship, Edward could see the dark shadow of their destination, Nassau. It wouldn't be long before they arrived. It wouldn't be long before he had to kill again; not long before he had to kill more of his family.

Edward, without the numbing effects of the rum, decided to pour himself into the work aboard the ship. He tried to distract himself from the arresting thoughts his mind wouldn't let go of—thoughts of killing his best friend, Henry Morgan, his stepbrother John, and the countless people young and old he had ended over the years.

Haunting him too were the faces of those he had let die through his own weakness. His old quartermaster, John, returned to him. If he had just killed Kenneth Locke instead of leaving him to die, then John might have lived.

John's last words came back to him again as they had the last time he'd thought about the man. *'Your father is in the Caribbean, Edward.'* As Edward thought over the words and what they had meant, something itched in his mind.

If John knew my father was alive and he knew that he took the name of Calico Jack, then he knew what my father wanted all this time. He was the one who handed me the first clue to finding the keys of the Queen Anne's Revenge. *John was trying to protect me, guide me, and push me to pass the tests. Was he also sending my father letters, telling him of my progress?*

Edward's head hurt, but now for a different reason.

No, that can't be. Calico Jack attacked Bodden Town after we got all the keys. If he was to be the final test, then he couldn't have done it any sooner, and John died before we got the last key. It was someone else. Someone else in the crew must have told him we finished. Could it have been Victoria? No, she joined in Port Royal after I acquired the ship. Unless that too was a lie. She and John could have co-ordinated together to… Edward shook his head violently and regretted it just afterwards. *It's no use thinking of that now. Focus on the work. The work, man!*

Edward returned to his duties, trying to clear his mind in the endless repetition afforded him by the menial labour. With considerable effort, he was able to clear his mind enough to relieve his need for the booze. Before he knew it, the ship had its sails furled and coasted into the harbour towards a nearby port.

The *Black Blood*, being a brigantine, loomed over the smaller sloops and even smaller ships in the harbour. There were very few that matched the *Black Blood's* size, and only one that Edward could see that surpassed it. If his ship had been there, it would have been out of place in the harbour, as it often was. The *Queen Anne's Revenge* was an anomaly amongst pirate vessels, being a three-masted light frigate.

Herbert guided the ship into port, where the crew were ready to secure it to the mooring of the wharf.

Edward took in his surroundings. The town of Nassau wasn't large, but it was bustling with activity. From the many ships in the harbour coming and going to the noise in the town itself, Edward could tell it was a hub for trade.

The buildings were centred around the main wharf they had settled into, where several larger ships were also moored. Many of the buildings close to the wharf were well built and well established, made of hardwoods and atop cleared ground. Further out, the buildings were shabbier, fashioned with inferior cuts of wood and straw roofs overhead. A few smaller piers where longboats could unload smaller cargo saw better housing or business for trade, but only a few.

The swaying palms dotted the landscape, with some poking out above the taller buildings in front of the wharf and progressively becoming denser the farther one looked. Beyond the buildings, Edward could see forested vegetation with pockets of clear-cutting for roads and the homes around them.

To his left, west of town atop a slight hill, he could see an old fort with two high walls overlooking the harbour. It could be a deterrent for attacking ships at that elevation, but beyond it was even taller hills that would make inland defence impossible. Edward noticed cracks in the foundation and holes in the walls from cannon fire. He would be surprised if it were still in use.

The crew lowered the gangplank, and a swarm of hawkers came down the pier to sell their goods. Before they even set foot on the gangplank, Grace was standing there looking down at them. Without a word, the hawkers backed away and left.

After they left, Grace spoke to her senior officers, then called Edward over. "Before I introduce ye ta Jack, I'll be headin' over ta tell him what happened ta John. Ye won't want ta be anywhere near him then. Stay aboard the ship, I'll come back ta get ye if the time is right. Otherwise, we may need ta leave in a hurry."

Edward tried to hold back his anger. Would his father be so incensed if *he* died? Considering the many times his father, either directly or indirectly, had attempted to kill him, he doubted it.

Grace took Edward's silence as affirmation he'd heard her, and she left the ship. The two senior officers, stoic and quiet as ever, both stayed aboard and blocked the gangplank access. When some of the crew approached, trying to leave for shore, they stopped them.

Edward went to the quarterdeck, where Herbert had been watching. The crew had abandoned their duties now that the ship was moored, and the two were alone.

"We need to get off the ship, but Grace ordered everyone to stay aboard."

Herbert's anger was evident, but he looked past Edward to the two men guarding the gangplank against the horde of crewmates. Though they outnumbered the two senior officers by twenty to one, with even more below deck, the crew were only making a play at trying to leave. None dared to take it as far as to attack the senior officers. So complete was Grace's intimidating force that it was there even when she was not.

Herbert let out a deep breath. "We could try to convince the crew to go ashore, but looking at them now, I don't think they have the spine in them to go against Grace."

"So, a distraction, then?"

Herbert nodded and stroked his chin. "But what kind of distraction would pull both of them away from their post?"

Edward mulled it over, he too reaching up to his chin before his lack of a giant beard made the physical act of ruminating somehow more distracting. After another moment, he shook his head and shrugged his shoulders.

"I'm just going to start a fire," Edward said finally.

"Wait, what?"

"Stay here, I'll not be long."

Edward heard Herbert stumble to say something else as he walked down to the weather deck. He didn't have time for further debate. They needed to get off the ship one way or the other, and he didn't care if he destroyed Grace's ship in the process.

Edward went below deck and found two lanterns filled with oil. He spread some of the oil in one of the corners of the ship, then over some other cargo, and lit it on fire when no one was looking. He chose a few other spots where the fire could spread but not be put out quickly. It was just enough fire to cause a panic but not enough to burn the whole ship down. Or, at least he thought it wasn't.

Before anyone could see the fires beginning to engulf the ship, Edward went above to the quarterdeck again.

"We should probably stay back so they don't see us waiting around," Edward said, pointing to the stern.

Herbert pulled his wheelchair back from the edge of the quarterdeck, and Edward followed before crouching down to be out of sight from the senior crewmates. They waited a few minutes until they head shouting below them.

The shouting, indistinct and scattered, continued for another moment longer before a few crewmates ran above deck. "Fire!" one man shouted. "Fires below deck. It's spreading."

The crewmates above deck answered the call and rushed below, but not all left to investigate. Ten crewmates, and the two senior guards, all stayed behind. Edward cursed under his breath, thinking he should have lit more fires.

Another minute more and smoke began rising through the opening to the deck below and through the grated hatch covers near the ladder. The shouting grew louder and calls for aid filtered through the noise.

Edward watched as the crewmates who'd stayed behind changed from being complacent to concerned until they went into action. The guards, too, looked at each other and rushed to help the rest of the crew below deck.

Herbert wheeled himself forward to the edge of the quarterdeck as black smoke billowed up from below. "Edward... how many fires did you set?"

"No time for that, we have to leave."

Edward picked up Herbert's chair, with Herbert still in it, and took him down the quarterdeck steps as far from the ladder and grates as he could. The effort put pressure on his head, making it pound again. He let Herbert back down on the gangplank before pushing the wheelchair at top speed. There was no point in stealth given the level of noise below deck. In no time, the two were off the *Black Blood* and onto the wharf where a crowd was gathering towards the sight of the smoke.

Edward kept pushing Herbert forward and through the crowd towards Nassau. He rushed onto the main road, a large dirt and mud track wide enough for carts, ignored the terrible odours emanating from every person and every corner, and entered the nearest tavern.

Inside, Edward finally stopped running and looked down to see Herbert breathing heavy and holding onto his wheelchair like driftwood in a storm.

"Are you well, Herbert?" he asked.

"No thanks to you. I know we needed to get away from there, but once we were in the crowd, you could have slowed down." Edward grinned and shrugged. After Herbert caught his breath, he took in his surroundings. "What are we doing here?"

Edward stepped up to the bar in the tavern and ordered two glasses of whiskey. After taking the drinks in hand, he answered Herbert's question by lifting them up into full view. He motioned for Herbert to follow him, and the two went to a corner of the bar out of view of the windows and entrance.

The two sat in silence, slowly drinking the whiskey as they calmed their nerves. Edward hoped that none had seen him lighting the fires and that the crew were able to put it out. Earlier, he didn't care, but now that it was done, he would regret it if the ship burned down. They'd managed to keep their identities hidden so it wouldn't do to have Grace and her crew looking for them because they torched her ship.

After a few moments, Herbert spoke. "This was a mistake, coming here."

The comment took Edward aback, and he didn't know how to respond. "What?" was all he managed.

"Us coming here was a mistake," Herbert said. "Because of me, you killed your brother, and who knows how things are going with our crew. How are we to even find them again? And then we're supposed to kill your father, without a plan, without help, with no way to escape."

Edward gripped his glass harder. "You mean *me* coming here was a mistake."

It was Herbert's turn to be confused. "What?"

"Look, I—" The words choked in Edward's throat. "I know I'm messed in the head, but I meant what I said. My father has done horrible things, and he wants me to kill him. Some twisted final test of his I'll never understand. So, I'm here to end it before he hurts anyone else I care about." Edward took another drink from his whiskey, letting the burn take over his mind.

"He… he wasn't all bad."

Edward looked up from his glass at Herbert, who was staring into his own glass intently. He had a small smile on his face.

"When I was young, before my accident, he was the first one to show me how to read clouds, how to man the helm, how to read a map. It was all basics, but for me, it meant a lot." Herbert took a long drink of his whiskey. "He has done horrible things, but he wasn't evil." He looked up at Edward, pain in his eyes. "Was he?"

Edward couldn't think of what to say. Calico Jack had always been Herbert's entire world. Revenge had been his reason for taking to the seas. It had once caused him to steal away the *Queen Anne's Revenge* in pursuit of Jack and leave Edward behind. For him to say the man wasn't evil felt strange.

"And you know what the worst part of it is?" Herbert's voice cracked, and he had tears in his eyes. "I don't even know if I was right this whole time."

"About what?"

"Gregory Dunn, the one you got that gold from to make your sword and rings, said that I was his favourite. And I remember that I used to get money sent regularly to me by someone, but then it suddenly stopped. Sometime after I left, Dunn became Jack's Gold Division Commander. They're the ones in charge of the money."

Edward was putting the pieces together. "You think he... stole it? Stole the money my father sent to you?"

Herbert shook his head. "I don't know. But what if he did? Then it means your father didn't really abandon me because he thought I was useless. All I've had since I lost my legs was hate, and when you came along, I had hope again. What if the reason for that hope is a lie?"

Edward gritted his teeth. "And what if it's not?" he seethed. "What if that money was from someone else? What if you don't remember things right? He still left *me* when *I* was ten; he still became Calico Jack." Edward was nearly shouting. It took everything he had to hold back his anger and keep his voice low. "Grace told you her story, the bodies piled up, the girls taken, hell, even Grace herself. You must have known about it already, you were there." Edward took the last drink and slammed the glass down. "I don't care if he wants us to do it, he needs to die."

Herbert nodded and looked defeated. Perhaps the drink was hitting him harder than he'd thought it would. "I know. We're in too deep to swim back to shore now." There was another moment of silence before Herbert took the flask out from his chair and threw it across the table to Edward. "Look at us. Pathetic, aren't we? We're about to kill your father, a man we both loved and hate, and here we are trying to find the courage to do the deed at the bottom of a bottle."

Edward let out a dark chuckle as he pocketed the flask. "Lately it seems to be the only way I can find it." He rubbed his eyes and slapped his face. "Apologies for my outburst earlier. I'll not drink anymore until the deed is done."

Herbert nodded. "I'm sorry as well. I could have handled that better. And," he added with a wide grin, "I too promise not to drink anymore until the deed is done."

Edward and Herbert both laughed together, the first time that they had in a long while.

"Well, I see ye both're gettin' along well enough without me."

A familiar voice drew the two men's attention, and when they looked up, they saw a ghost in the flesh. Edward rose half from his seat at the sight of the man in front of them.

"S—Sam!" the two of them said in unison.

"I heard ye bastards thought I was dead. Don't ye know ye can't kill a man what looks this good? Why, just think of the ladies whose hearts would break."

"Sam!" Edward said again as he ran in to embrace his long-lost crewmate, Samuel Bellamy.

"Whoa, whoa, Captain, ease yourself. Don't bring any attention this way. As I understand it, you're here to kill the big man. Wouldn't do ta ruin the surprise now."

Edward pulled away from Sam. "How do you know what we're here for?"

Sam walked over to one side of the table and sat down. Edward joined him and sat back down to hear Sam's story.

"I met yer wife nearabouts a week past. She got me up ta speed with what you ran off ta do, and I agreed to come help."

The news that Anne knew where Edward was, and that Sam had come in her stead, was almost as shocking as the revelation that Sam was alive.

"I know," Sam said. "I had the same dumb look on me face. She's facin' off against Silver Eyes ta save the island he took over and keep him distracted. If ye ask me, she made the wrong move, but the woman's got standards, that much is true."

Edward nodded. If the people on that island needed her help, Anne wasn't the type to let them die, nor leave a job half-finished. As much as he yearned to see her again, this was probably her way of telling him to finish things as well.

"So, what about you? What happened after I escaped Cache-Hand?"

Sam waved his hand. "We got no time fer that. We'll

small-talk later. Right now, we need to take care of yer pa," he said. "So, what's the plan?"

Edward and Herbert looked at each other, then back at Sam. "We don't have one. We just got here."

"I thought we might scout his villa and come up with a plan from there."

Sam chuckled. "Are... are ye boys tellin' true? Ye have no plan?" Sam shook his head and rubbed his face. "Well, there ain't no chance of ye getting ta him in his home. Too heavily guarded, so best leave that out. Ye need ta strike when he's outside. Me crew and I can help ye with an ambush, we jus have ta find the right time."

"You have a crew?" Edward asked. Sam gave him a stern look of disapproval. "Right, focus," he said. "That won't work, we don't have the time. Grace O'Malley will be looking for us soon, so it's now or never."

Sam's eyes bulged nearly out of their sockets. "Grace fuckin' O'Malley'll be lookin fer ye? The hell did you boys do?"

"We joined her crew to get here, and we're supposed to go meet Jack soon as new crew members," Herbert explained. "And could you not call us boys anymore? We're older than you."

Sam ignored Herbert's comment. "Wait, you're supposed to meet Jack?" Edward and Herbert both nodded. Sam looked at them both as though the next trail of thought were self-evident.

Edward shook his head. "No, it's too dangerous. You said yourself, his home is well guarded. As soon as he sees either of us, it's over. Our only opportunity is a surprise."

"I'll handle the guards. I'll have me crew start a small riot o' sorts, something he won't be able to ignore. You use that chance ta finish him off and get outa there, head ta me ship the *Whydah* and we'll head back to yer wife. Done and done."

Edward hunched over in his seat, thinking it over in his head. He looked at Herbert, who also seemed to be testing the plan in his mind. Herbert saw Edward looking at him, and he shrugged his shoulders.

"I suppose it will bring us directly to him, rather than us

waiting for him to come to us."

"Aye, it's the best plan we got," Sam said before standing as though it were settled. "Ye better get back to Grace's ship, she's not a woman ta be left waitin'."

"Tch," Edward spat. "You don't know the half of it." He held out his hand to Sam. "Good to have you back, Sam. We'll be counting on you."

Sam shook Edward's hand. "As it always was." Edward and Herbert both went to leave, but Sam stopped them. "Almost forgot this," he said as he took his cutlass off his belt and handed it to Edward. The hilt was covered in cloth, but once Sam pulled it out from its sheath, he saw the familiar golden gleam of his cutlass shining out.

Edward reached for his blade, the familiar gold that was not gold calling to him, but he pushed it back towards Sam. "I can't. If any saw it, they would know something was wrong. You hold onto it for me."

Sam nodded and put the cutlass back on his belt. "Don't die, Captain."

"Same to you, Sam."

Edward and Herbert headed back to the *Black Blood,* still moored to the wharf. The crowd that had been gathering before was gone, and the ship looked, at least on the outside, undamaged. As they approached, however, they saw Grace on the weather deck, and she looked quite displeased.

When they came closer, a crewmate pointed at them, and Grace turned around. She seemed surprised, but her expression changed at once, so it was hard for Edward to tell if he'd read her right.

"Ye boys have fun in town disobeying orders?"

Edward and Herbert stayed at the bottom of the gangplank. "We were thirsty, so we thought we'd grab a drink in town," Edward said.

Grace nodded, her usual calm feeling strange to Edward at that moment. "Aye, and what of the fire on my ship? Ye wouldn't know anything about that now, would ye?"

Edward glanced at Herbert. "We were above deck when it started. And the other crewmates seemed capable of handling it, so we let them take all the glory."

Edward knew he was playing a dangerous game, but it was all he could think of at the moment. He was hoping their imminent meeting with Calico Jack would be more important than them leaving the ship during a crisis.

If Grace was angry, she didn't show it outwardly. "We'll discuss this later. Now, you need to meet Jack." She marched down the gangplank and joined them on the pier. "Come," she said as she walked past them.

Edward took a few silent breaths at the narrow escape, and he and Herbert followed Grace into town once again. She led them down the main road, past the many houses, taverns, brothels, inns, and various businesses of the town before stopping in front of a gated two-storey villa.

With its wrought-iron fence, open lawn, pure whitewashed wooden exterior, and two floors, the villa looked like the home of a wealthy magistrate. It reminded Edward of the home of the Bodden Brothers in their town Edward had taken over—the town his father as Calico Jack had attacked, setting this series of events in motion.

The main difference here was the level of security. There were five guards Edward could see at the front of the property, two at the gate, two at the door, and another on a balcony on the second floor. Edward guessed there were more both outside and inside.

Is my father not supposed to be a king here? Why does he need so many guards? Is he simply paranoid?

Edward had no time to think about it, as Grace led them inside the gate. She didn't take them to the front door and instead led them to the side of the villa. There was another entrance there, with a lone guard stationed at the ready. When he noticed her, he opened the door for her, and she headed inside.

Edward and Herbert followed her, and it was then that Edward realized why Grace had been acting slightly strange. Inside the room, a half-dozen men had muskets trained on the two of them. At the back of the room, there was a cell with an open door.

Edward raised his hands in the air, and someone threw Herbert to the ground beside him before the door was closed behind. The guard from outside had his weapon out and trained on them now as well. There was no escape.

"Inside," Grace commanded, gesturing to the cell.

Edward walked forward, his hands still in the air, and entered the cell. Herbert crawled into the cell beside him, and they closed and locked the doors shut.

"Not the welcome I expected," Edward said.

"Cut the shit," Grace spat. "I know who you are, Thatch. And you, Blackwood."

Edward glanced down at Herbert, who was sitting at the bottom of the cell looking up at him. "What gave us away?"

"A six-foot-two behemoth with Jack's eyes and a cripple helmsman. It weren't that difficult to piece together, even after giving yerself a shave." Grace stepped closer to the cell. "Now tell me true. Did ye kill my John?"

Edward didn't answer. He gritted his teeth and lowered his head. "I didn't know he was your son."

Edward saw Grace's hand ball into a fist. She slammed it against the bars of the cell, and the iron rang out. She pointed a shaking finger at Edward. "He was a good boy. He was yer brother! He didn't deserve that."

"I know."

"You know what I know? I know it's gonna kill Jack that ye weren't up ta snuff, but I'll enjoy seeing you hang. That much is sure, Thatch." Grace looked on the verge of tears, from anger and from a future relief she was envisioning, Edward thought.

The sound of gunfire rang out outside of the villa's prison. Judging from the volume, it was nearby. Sam's crew were implementing the distraction as planned, unaware Edward and Herbert weren't anywhere near Calico Jack.

Grace looked daggers his way. "Is this your doing?"

"We just arrived here, how would we have had the time?" Edward said, thinking on his feet. "You have a town full of pirates, and none of them fight?" Edward sat down on a hard chair in the cell with a loud thump. "This must be a paradise if you manage that."

Grace's jaw flexed with anger, and she stormed out of the prison. One guard stayed behind to watch them, and the rest left with Grace to handle the situation outside.

Edward leaned back, resting his head against the stone wall at the back of their cell, and closed his eyes. The sounds of more gunfire and fighting filtered in through a window at the ceiling near the door.

"Now what?" Herbert asked, frustration clear in his tone.

Edward opened his eyes and folded his arms. "We're pirates, right?"

Herbert nodded but looked confused.

"We'll just have to steal this victory back from them."

17. BREAKING POINT

Anne had been in a daze of high fever, the time passing without her knowledge. She could only half-way remember the rare bits of clarity through the haze. The sun and the moon through a window. Movement at her periphery. Many muddled faces visiting her, helping her eat, changing her bandages. A young girl—Christina, Anne thought—sobbing as she held Anne's hand and apologized. For what, Anne was too delirious to remember.

When the fever broke, she woke in a cold sweat, both famished and thirsty. At her bedside waiting for her was bread and water, which she devoured. Her head still ached, and her whole body was weak. Even her jaw muscles strained to chew the bread.

She took in her surroundings as she gathered her strength. She was lying in her bed aboard the *Queen Anne's Revenge* in the captain's cabin. It was the same as it always was—table and chairs, dresser and bookshelf, Edward's clothes hanging on a rack on the wall. The only new thing was two crutches near the foot of the bed, and some of Alexandre's medical supplies on a bedside table.

Then Anne remembered why she was there lying in her bed weak from fever for God knows how long. Her leg. She didn't want to look at it, as though the longer she went without seeing it, the less real it was. As though if she never looked down, it had never happened. But real life didn't work that way. Not looking at a problem doesn't make it go away.

Anne pulled her blanket away in one swift motion to get it over with, and there it was. Covered thick with cloth tied tight was a wound just beneath her knee. There was no blood, which was both a good and bad sign. It meant that it had healed enough that it no longer needed frequent changes, but that also meant some time had passed in her delirium.

She knew that someday soon, she would feel hollow without her right foot, but for now it remained a curiosity. A painful, ugly curiosity.

But more than anything, it made her angry. Angry at her momentary lapse that had allowed the injury to happen. Angry at herself for killing Tala, Christina's poor wolf, who hadn't known any better and had died for it. Angry at Silver Eyes and his wicked skill that turned her comrades and friends into enemies. Angry that she'd chosen to stay here out of some foolish sense of duty, and what that foolish sense had brought her.

Anne pulled herself up, her hands shaking to keep her body steady. A painful minute later, and she had her upper body slumped forward. Even with that little movement, she was sweating and felt dizzy. After catching her breath and waiting for the room to stop spinning, she turned her body sideways and placed her left leg on the deck.

The cold of the wood beneath her foot felt pleasant, as her body still felt hot, especially her wound—another reminder of her loss, her weakness, her enemy. More anger arose to fuel her weakened muscles.

With care and a lot of time, Anne pulled herself over to the end of the bed and took the crutches in hand. She had little experience with crutches. She had broken a leg in her earlier years, but she had been forced to be bedridden or into a wheelchair rather than allowed to stalk the halls of the palace in crutches. She had seen them used before, though, and thought it couldn't have been that difficult.

What made it difficult wasn't her lack of knowledge, it was her lack of strength. She was able to get herself balanced, and at rest she could lean on the crutches for support, but her leg wobbled and shook as though it would give out with each step forward.

Then came the door to the cabin. There was simply no crafty way to stand to reach the handle. She planted her foot down and in a swift motion, grabbed the handle and pulled the door ajar. She backed up a bit and used one of the crutches to knock the door open enough for her to walk through.

With one obstacle out of the way, she was able to exit the captain's cabin. She already had sweat soaking her brow and the small breeze coming from the weather deck down to the gun deck was a welcome respite.

Strangely, none of the crew were in the gun deck. She could hear voices coming from the bow, and movement from Alexandre's room, but no sounds were coming from above or below.

Anne swung herself forward to the bow. With each plop of the crutches on the wooden floorboards, she found herself acclimating to her new situation. It felt strange not planting her right foot down with each step forward, strange to not feel the cold of the wood or the air on her toes, but she pushed the feeling aside. She needed to ignore the curiosity for now. Now she needed to know what had happened as she'd slept.

She entered the surgeon's room too quickly and nearly fell over when she tried to stop herself. Nassir was there to catch her.

"Careful, miss," he said.

After righting herself, she tried to thank Nassir, but her throat seized, and she began coughing. The coughing only emphasized how thin and frail and hungry she was. With each cough, her stomach heaved as though it would cave in.

Victoria came up beside her, a cup of water in hand. Anne took the cup and drank it down in great gulps. She coughed one last time, wiped her chin, and thanked both Victoria and Nassir as she handed the cup back with a shaking hand.

"How long was I asleep?" she asked as she made eye contact with Nassir, Victoria, and Alexandre.

Alexandre answered. "Eight days."

She had guessed it to have been some time, but the news floored her still. She rebalanced herself in her crutches as she absorbed Alexandre's words.

"Silver Eyes?"

"He still lives," Alexandre said. "We have been starving him and his men, as per your orders. William held back from attacking through the tunnel until you awoke. The men are eager to see this ended, but he held them back."

Anne's anger bubbled forward. "Good, I want to see him die for myself," she spat.

Her tone must have alarmed her companions, as they all became silent. She tried to soften her tone. "Worry not, Alexandre, I recall our promise. You will have the honours of the final blow; I simply wish to see it happen."

Alexandre nodded. "*Merci*."

Anne looked down at the table, and she understood why Nassir was here in the surgeon's room. On the table lay a nearly complete imitation of a leg. Though it was not within her realm of study, Anne knew of medicine and recent advancements, especially amongst the wealthy who could afford the best of care. The device on the table was of the newest design and would allow her to walk as it didn't lock into place and instead had hinges to mimic the movement of the leg.

The sight of it was enough to bring tears to her eyes. She reached out to touch the apparatus, and then she looked at the three in the room. "Thank you," she said before wiping her eyes.

"It is nearly complete, but your wound won't support it yet. You will need another week to heal before it is safe."

"Understood," Anne said as she dried her eyes.

The gesture warmed her heart, but it did little to quell her anger at the man responsible for her injury. It only served to focus her mind away from her lost limb and towards a way to finish the battle with minimal casualties.

"Where's William?"

"He's ashore, managing the crew," Victoria replied. "I'll take you."

After a few more words of thanks to Alexandre and Nassir for their craftsmanship, Anne left with Victoria to go ashore. It took quite a bit of time to get above deck, and with each minute wasted, she grew increasingly impatient, but she managed the ordeal with little incident.

On the weather deck, Anne did see a few crewmates on watch, weapons at the ready and cannons nearby loaded. William must have overseen some of the deck cannons returning to the ship after the incident with the crew.

The crew left their posts to greet her and ask after her wellbeing. Though there was evident concern in their eyes, none were insensitive about her appearance and frailty. Anne tried to rush things along, the delays irritating her despite her crew's concern. After the crew were done seeing how she was, they helped her and Victoria into a longboat to take to shore.

In the boat, it was just Victoria and Anne. Anne rested as Victoria rowed the boat to shore. It would be a short trip, and Victoria was capable enough, but Anne wished she had the strength to help just to make the trip that much quicker.

With nowhere to go, Anne's irritation stewed within her, and the sight of the town and the fortified walls off in the distance only served to incense her further. Knowing that Silver Eyes was in his villa unharmed and unburdened by what his actions had wrought made her skin itch.

Anne needed to calm herself, and so she decided to look at Victoria instead. It was the first time in a while that the two were alone, and the first time in a while that Anne actually took note of the woman.

Despite all knowing her nature as a woman, she kept her black hair short enough that most would mistake her for a boy. Her clothes, too, showed little of her femininity. Anne had an inkling of the reasons.

She had heard about what had happened to Victoria at Calico Jack's hand. She saw the way that she shirked away from most men, nay, all men save Alexandre. It was not from a lack of ability; with her lithe form, she could kill a man three distinct ways before he had his belt unbuckled. That kind of skittishness reminded Anne of Edward at times. Times when memories came unbidden into the mind. Times of turmoil, of pain, of helplessness. It seemed that even for her, the years had not healed the wounds put upon her.

"How do you deal with the anger?" Anne said. Victoria stopped rowing for a moment and looked at Anne. Anne realized that she had said what she was thinking aloud without the usual preamble. "Apologies. What I mean to say is... with all that you've been through, how do you deal with the anger from it?"

Victoria was silent for a moment, and then she began rowing again. "Anger's a shield at your front and wind at your back. It'll get the job done, but it won't last long. Once it's gone, you'll wish you had it protecting you still." Victoria tapped on her temple. "Use it while it lasts."

Anne nodded and didn't ask any further. The two women remained in silence for the rest of the short trip.

On shore, Christina, Pukuh, Jack, and William were all waiting along with a small contingent of the crew. William helped Anne disembark.

William said no words, but from the look in his eyes, Anne could tell that he was remaining strong for her sake. He probably blamed himself for not being there to help her but would not say the words in public.

Anne placed a hand on his chest as she came down from the longboat and gave him a warm smile that she hoped would tell him all that he needed to hear. He took hold of her hand and squeezed it gently as he placed it back on her crutch. To everyone else, it would look as though he were simply helping her back into her crutches. It was his way of remaining close yet respectful.

After settling herself, Christina came up to her. She was already in tears again and hugged Anne tight. Christina began whispering apologies and sobbing into Anne's shoulder, and Anne tried her best to console the young woman. "Worry not." "It's just a leg." "The one I blame is Silver Eyes."

Then, after Christina had calmed herself enough to pull away from Anne, Anne turned it around by giving her own apology. "I'm sorry… for Tala."

Christina shook her head so vigorously Anne thought it hurt the girl. "No, don't apologize. I should have trained her better."

Anne rubbed Christina's shoulder. Though she was holding it in, it was clear that the loss of Tala pained Christina. They had been inseparable since meeting near Pukuh's village. Anne remembered how the two of them had fought a bear and won, just to bring back medicine to save Anne when she was sick. If not for Tala and Christina, Anne would have died.

"You trained her well. She was a true warrior, and she will be missed by all." Anne pulled Christina in and embraced her again for a moment.

Jack also offered his apologies, lamenting his weakness. Anne gave him the same words she gave Christina, reassuring him that it was no fault of his. She leaned in and whispered to him, "Now more than ever, the crew and I need your music. Keep their spirits high until this is over."

Jack smiled. "I understand, Captain," he said before stepping back to let others have their chance to speak with her.

After pulling away, Pukuh was standing there with his arms folded. He looked her over, barely glancing at her missing leg, his face inscrutable. "You look like death."

Anne couldn't help but laugh, and it was both joyful and painful in her state. "I feel it."

"Soon, it will become a part of you. This, I know," Pukuh said, touching his right shoulder, the stump that used to be his right arm.

"I shall have to take you at your word," Anne said. "For the time being, I suppose I'll look and feel like death."

"It was praise," Pukuh said. "Death is my namesake. I mean you look ready to end this."

"I was ready eight days ago," Anne replied. "So, let's end it, shall we?"

Anne had run through the various scenarios in her head before the battle with her crew. She did the math, and if not for her injury, she would have ordered the use of the secret tunnel long ago. Doing so would have cost them several crewmates, and there was only one way around the problem. It was a cruel method, and before she had only thought of it as a last resort, but now, in the throes of her anger-fuelled mind, she didn't care about the morality.

Others did. William, Alexandre, and some of the crew objected, but their voices were few. William eventually followed her orders as he always did and carried out the first part of the plan. Alexandre realized quickly that there would be no swaying Anne, but he was visibly angry. If Anne had been in the right state of mind, she might have rethought her actions, but she was not.

After William and some of the other crewmates returned from their task, Anne gave the signal.

They removed a large cloth covering one of the golden bells they had taken with them from one of the villages on the island. It, unlike the one Christina had managed to destroy in Silver Eyes' town, was whole and intact. The sound it would produce would have its desired effect.

The crew laid the bell down, so the open bottom was facing the town, then looked at Anne for final confirmation. Anne waved her hand in a striking motion, and the crew lifted the bell's striker and slammed it down.

The sound of the bell was loud in her ears, with the same pull as it had had before. She was able to resist the numbing effect it had, but she did have to close her eyes. She wondered just what the metal was, the same ore that her ring and Edward's cutlass were made of, that could produce such a tone.

After the bell's tone died away, the crew struck it again. This time, Anne forced her eyes open to watch the town. Silver Eyes' men were stationed along the perimeter as before, and they remained unchanged, unfazed by what Anne thought would be a strange development.

Again, and again the crewmates struck the bell, but nothing changed. At least, not on this side of the town.

Soon, Anne could hear sounds of fighting within the town in between the striking of the bell. The crew didn't let up, because Anne didn't tell them to, and the sounds inside grew with each strike. Shouts, snarls, gunfire, and clashing swords, a bizarre counterpoint to the ringing of the bell.

After some time, the fighting came to the stockade. Those fighting Silver Eyes' crew were not the crew of the *Queen Anne's Revenge*. Those fighting were the crazed, entranced villagers they had previously been trying to save. Triggered by the bell, they would attack anyone, even their masters.

The cruel, immoral act that Anne had chosen to commit was to use those poor souls to do the fighting for them. They had taken the entranced villagers, unable to refuse, into the tunnel and locked the entrance behind them. Then with the bell turning them mad, there was nowhere to go but into the town. There, they fought Silver Eyes' men.

Exhausted and enraged, Anne just wanted it over with, and with the least casualties to her crew as possible. They had suffered enough; *she* had suffered enough, and she wanted it to be over.

She had considered leaving, briefly, but her anger wouldn't let her leave before she'd had her revenge.

They kept ringing the bell as the fighting continued. There was no doubt that Silver Eyes' men had access to a handbell like the one that Sam gave them, but they knew that it wasn't permanent. As they continued ringing the bell, they ensured the fighting would continue.

When the sound of the fighting died down to almost nothing, Anne ordered the crew to stop striking the bell. Then they brought the cannons forward.

In the eight days that Anne was unconscious, Nassir had built a few limbers from the wagon parts. That gave the cannons more maneuverability and stability and enabled the crew to take them in closer to the stockade. And, without their enemy manning the stockade's cannons they had no fear of retaliation.

They fired the cannons at the stockade's entrance, the large iron bouncing off the massive wooden beams. With each hit, the beams cracked increasingly until they finally gave way under the force. The entrance now open, the crew were free to enter the town and finish off Silver Eyes' men.

Anne, in no shape to fight, stayed behind as the crew entered the town to finish the job. She hated waiting, but she knew better than to be involved with their enemies who had already been stronger and faster than her *before* she was injured.

William, too, stayed behind as Christina, Pukuh, Victoria, and Alexandre all entered the battle. Jack wasn't far behind, a drum in hand, playing a rousing beat for the fight.

And so, the two waited as they listened to the sounds of the battle growing once more. William seemed content to remain in silence with Anne, but after a few minutes, Anne became restless.

"Do you think less of me for this?" she asked.

William, silent for a moment as he looked at Anne and then back at the town, replied with a simple "No." After another moment, he elaborated. "Alexandre may be upset, but he was making no progress in freeing those people. With time, perhaps he could have undone the trance put upon them, but we don't have such time. We couldn't have taken them with us either. This will ensure victory and the least casualties for us. You made the right decision."

Anne had expected him to say as much, but it disappointed her still. He had objected to the plan before; there was no way he wholeheartedly agreed with her decision. He was trying to ease her mind at that moment.

She knew deep down that she would regret the decision, she could feel it. At the moment, it was as Victoria said: her anger shielded her, protecting her from the guilt which would weigh on her later.

More time passed, and again the sounds of battle waned. Anne decided then to enter the town with William and the few crewmates who had stayed behind with her. With her still on crutches, it took some time to reach the town.

Bodies littered the roadway, the fronts of buildings, and the alleyways. It wasn't a large town by any means, and so between the hundred and twenty villagers they had gathered, and however many of Silver Eyes' men had been left, you couldn't make it five steps before encountering one of the dead.

Thankfully, it hadn't been long, and so the stench of death was light. It smelled of fresh blood and gunpowder as smoke still whirled around the town.

The only activity was from their crewmates keeping watch nearby, and the sound of shouts from farther off. Some of their enemies appeared to still be alive and making a last stand.

Anne recognized a woman, one of the villagers, reaching

a bloodied hand towards them. Her legs had been cut or torn off during the fight, and her hair was matted with blood. She was still, even in that state, entranced and trying to reach them to attack.

"I'll handle this," William said. He pulled out his sword and put the woman out of her misery.

Her eyes stayed open, staring at Anne. Those hollow eyes from the trance remained unchanged in death. Whether under Silver Eyes' spell or free from their mortal coil, their eyes were the same.

Christina ran over to them as they walked through the maze of bodies. "We have Silver Eyes surrounded. He's holed himself up in a fancy house. Come, I'll show you the way," she said.

Anne, William, and the other crewmates went through the small town, around all the dead bodies, and to a small but opulent house near the centre of town. It was located beside the bell tower, and it appeared as though the two buildings were joined.

Jack was outside the home catching his breath. He had a weapon drawn, and his fiddle slung across his back. He waved as they approached.

They entered the home, and Christina took them to the back where Alexandre, Victoria, and Pukuh were standing guard next to a door.

"Let's end this," Anne said. "Kick down the door, but be wary."

Pukuh grinned and nodded, then did as Anne ordered. In one swift kick, the door busted in, swinging wildly. Pukuh rolled off to the side, away from the entrance.

Nothing happened. No one ran outside to face them. No pistols fired off into the air. No traps sprang. Only the sound of the door swinging back from hitting against a wall.

"Enter," a voice called from inside.

The lot waiting outside the door glanced at each other, unsure of just what game Silver Eyes was playing.

"I can assure you this is not a trick. I know when I am defeated."

Anne motioned for the others to enter, and one after the

488

other they went into the room. Anne was last, taking her time to stay steady in her crutches. Each step forward sent her heart racing a mite faster, to the point that she could feel it pounding in her ears by the time she came up beside William.

Inside the simple room, a study with a large window overlooking the sea, their enemy, Lance Nhil, sat leisurely in a chair facing them. He was of a darker complexion, close to Pukuh, and looked to be from the Near East with thick and short brown hair and a full beard. He would not have looked out of place in an Ottoman palace in Constantinople, or perhaps as a refined captain of a Barbary corsair vessel.

His eyes shone from the sunlight streaming through the great window behind him and made them appear a solid silver. There was something strange about the colour that Anne couldn't place, an otherworldly quality about his eyes that made him look, for lack of a better word, inhuman. They were as beautiful as they were haunting.

"That's him," Christina seethed. "He's the one who came aboard the ship."

Lance looked at Christina, and he appeared to recognize her. "Ah, yes, the pretty girl from the ship. I am surprised you survived," he said with a smile that sent shivers down Anne's spine. "*Alqamar*," Lance said—the Arabic word for moon.

Christina's hands dropped to her sides, and her face lost all emotion.

"William, get Christina out of here!" Anne shouted.

William put away his weapon and took Christina's out of her hand before she could do anything with them. Thankfully, the trigger didn't send her into a frenzy as before. William was able to lead Christina out without fighting her, and Victoria left with them to help.

That left Pukuh, Alexandre, and Anne in the room with him. Pukuh and Alexandre both were keeping their distance, and Anne was the farthest away, as she could do little in her condition.

"Tell me, where is Edward? Where is Blackbeard?"

"I would worry about yourself right now," Anne spat back. "He's off killing your captain."

Lance shook his head. "A pity. He was supposed to come here first. The young always love to rush things." Lance sat there in silence for another moment before turning his attention back to Anne. "You pitiful thing, you've lost your leg." He rose from his chair. Anne pulled herself back instinctively and nearly fell. She caught herself at the last second, and her face flushed red hot with anger. "Do you fear me, girl?" Lance took a step forward.

Alexandre's rapier stopped Lance's advance. "Apologies, *mon ami*, but you will not be taking another step."

Lance looked down at the rapier tip at his chest. He reached one hand up to the blade and stroked it. "Such a fine blade." There was a snapping sound. "Sleep," Lance said, and Alexandre's arm went limp.

Lance had brought his other hand up in front of Alexandre's face while attention was on the blade and had done what he did best. He put Alexandre in a trance, his eyes hollow and out of focus. Alexandre kept his grip on his weapon, but the tip was now dragging on the floor.

Pukuh growled and leapt forward, striking with his spear. Lance stepped to the side, grabbed the spear and pulled it forward, bringing Pukuh closer before punching him in the gut. Pukuh doubled over in pain but kept hold of his spear. Before he could jump away, Lance grabbed Pukuh's shoulder and pulled him close. Lance whispered something in Pukuh's ears, and he froze in place.

Then Lance turned to Anne. She tried to back away, but this time she did lose her balance and fell backwards to the floor. She panicked and scrambled backwards away from Lance's advance.

Lance leaned forward, reaching towards her. "Look into my eyes," he said.

Anne, whether through defiance or fear, closed her eyes tight. Sweat and tears poured down her cheeks. She couldn't move, she couldn't even scream.

Silence. Lance's hand hadn't touched her, he hadn't whispered his spell into her ears. She opened her eyes. Lance was there, towering over her, about to touch her shoulder. Pierced through his neck was Alexandre's rapier. It was the precise kind of strike that only Alexandre in his full state of awareness could have done.

He removed the blade in one smooth motion, and blood shot out from the wound. Lance, somehow still alive, grabbed his wound as he turned around to see his killer before tumbling to the floor. When he saw Alexandre there, a small smile at the corner of his lips, Lance's eyes widened even more, which gave away his last thoughts as plain as day.

Alexandre put away his rapier, reached over, and helped Anne to her feet and back into her crutches. "Alexandre, how did you...?"

"Come now, after all this, you think I could be put under his spell?"

Anne accepted Alexandre's simple explanation, and Alexandre went to help Pukuh out of the trance. She looked at Lance in his last moments, his beautiful silver eyes marred by blood from him straining to stay in the world of the living. The look of confusion mixed with his pain pleased her, more so than she liked to admit. She was happy that he could be taken down a level before he passed. It was the least he deserved after all he had done.

Alexandre brought Pukuh out of the trance, and they both came up to her. Satisfied, she was ready to move on. "We're done here. Let's go home."

18. THE PIRATE WITH THREE NAMES

"So good to see you again, boys," Edward's father said. "Especially you, Herbert. How long has it been? Ten, eleven, twelve years? I'm sure you've kept track," he said before cackling.

Edward and Herbert were led into the study of Calico Jack's villa, a large room on the second floor with several tables filled to the brim with papers, letters, and books. On the walls hung several trophies, including a golden horn like the one his father carried at his side, and a strange hand that Edward thought must have been fake. Or at least he hoped it was.

The double doors on both sides of the study leading to balconies were open, letting in a breeze free from the smell of filth that lingered at street level in Nassau.

Edward's father, true to his third name, wore a suit made of coarse green cotton with a floral pattern around the trim. It didn't fit with his imposing figure and scarred features. One scar, running from his right eye down to his mouth, made him look a monster in human form. Edward recalled that his wife had given him that scar.

"So, what am I supposed to call you? Benjamin Hornigold, Jack Rackham, or your real name, Albert Thatch? Or would you prefer to keep it simple, and I call you *Father*?"

Edward, his hands bound in front of him, tried his best to keep calm, but it was proving difficult.

"Let's stick with Jack for now," the man said, still smiling.

"Why are we here?" Herbert said. "Why don't you just kill us and get it over with?"

Jack folded his arms. "All in due time, gentlemen. All in due time." He stared at the two of them for a moment before unfolding his arms and walking over to a cabinet, waving a finger as he talked. "You know, I was really rooting for you this time. Grace told me how you got aboard her ship and nearly had her fooled, too." Jack took out a few glasses and some dark drink. "She wouldn't admit it, but I imagine if you hadn't killed your brother, she wouldn't have figured it out. Even I can't recognize you since I last saw you with that thick beard." Jack poured the rum into the glasses in equal portions and brought two of them over to his captors. "Oh, that's right, you're a little tied up now. Just open your mouth, and I'll pour it down."

"I'll pass," Edward said. He desperately wanted to say yes, but he remembered his promise.

Jack looked at Herbert, and Herbert simply stared at him. He shrugged. "More for me," he said before downing one of the glasses in a single gulp.

This was not the father he remembered from his youth. Edward remembered a kind, gentle man who loved to play and teach him about sailing. A man who would go on walks with him, name the stars for him. A man who would tell him stories before sleep, comfort him, drop everything for him. A man who loved him.

This man was wholly and completely Calico Jack, a pirate who seemed to love himself and the sound of his own voice. His old father was dead.

"To answer your question: you're here because I thought we could talk a bit. I wanted to hear about what's happened to you over the years before it's too late. The gallows are being prepared as we speak, so we'd best get on with it, gentlemen."

"Your spy didn't give you enough information?" Edward asked.

Jack arched his brow for a second and then grinned. "A spy? Now, what makes you think I sent a spy aboard your ship?"

"John, at the very least, knew everything. Victoria is another. They could have been working together to send you information."

"I see," Jack said as he rubbed his chin. "Just those two, hmm?"

Edward's jaw went slack. There were more than just John and Victoria? Some of his most loyal crewmates had been with him from the beginning since he'd set out to be a whaler. From there, they had gone to Port Royal, and there John got them more crewmembers, many of whom were also still on the crew to this day. Edward supposed with his father's reach it could have been any port, but Port Royal was the closest to their home island. It would have been simple to have some other crewmates ready to join them there, including Victoria.

But Edward remembered that Sam was the one who had suggested they head to Port Royal, not John. Could Sam be a traitor too? How did he get involved with his father's crew after their run-in with Cache-Hand? It all seemed too coincidental.

There was no way to be sure, and right now, Sam and his crew were their last hope to escape this situation. He had to believe in Sam and not give up any information that could tip their hand.

"Tch," Edward spat. "As Herbert said, just kill us and be done with it. I'm tired of the games you've had us playing these past years."

Jack shrugged. "Well, if that's what you wish, who am I to object?" He whistled as his gaze turned to one of his guards keeping watch at the door.

Edward turned his head to look behind him. The guard pulled a pistol from his belt and aimed it at Herbert. Edward shouted and jumped at Herbert to knock him out of the way. There was a loud shot and Herbert roared as the iron ball seared into his back.

The guard began reloading his pistol. Herbert, his hands tied in front of him, couldn't grab hold of the wound to stop the bleeding. He pulled himself tighter as he stifled shouts of pain between heavy breaths.

"Stop!" Edward shouted at the guard, then looked at his father. "Stop it, you bastard!"

Jack raised his brows again and placed his hand on his chest. "Me? Isn't this what you wanted? You both begged for it." He shook his head. "Now who's playing games?"

The guard finished loading the pistol and aimed it at Herbert again. Edward pivoted, ready to tackle the guard, but he pulled the pistol back and put it away. Edward looked at his father again, and he was holding his hand up. The guard walked back to his post.

"So, speaking of John," Jack began as though nothing had happened, "could you tell me what happened to him? I know he's passed, but details were scarce in the reports."

Edward gritted his teeth, unable to hold back his anger. Herbert was bleeding out, but still holding on and conscious. "Herbert's going to die. We need to stop the bleeding." Edward pressed down on the wound, doing his best to keep the pressure on it. Herbert groaned but didn't scream.

"He'll survive long enough for the execution." Jack took another drink from the second glass of rum he had gotten. "Now, answer the question, if you please."

"Shut it. I'm not going to talk to you as if you're still the man who was comrades with John. You took on the man who killed him as a crewmate."

Jack pointed at his son. "Don't forget that he also tortured you half to death," he said. "I couldn't let that kind of talent be squandered. Locke... or what was it he called himself? Chest-Hand? Money-Mitten? Box-Fist?" Jack shook his head as he scratched his face.

"Cache-Hand," Edward said.

His father snapped his fingers and pointed at Edward. "Cache-Hand, that's the one. He made for a good, if unexpected, test for you a bit ago. Twice. He paid back his usefulness. Now you, on the other hand. What a disappointment you've been."

"Why? Because I haven't killed you yet? If you want to die so badly, do us all a favour and kill yourself."

Jack burst out laughing, a howling, cackling laugh. "That's good, I like that. Where was that anger when I stabbed you in the back? You had your wife carry you away like some useless drunk. In fact," he stroked his chin again before running a finger down the scar along his cheek, "she was the one who gave me this wound. Maybe she should be the one in your place. She seems far more capable than you. She could have been queen by now if not for being declared dead, what with her mother's passing."

"Anne's mother passed away?" The news floored Edward and broke through what had been happening up until then.

Jack stopped stroking his scar and looked at Edward. "Yes, almost a year ago," he said. "Does she not know? Where is she right now? Did you leave her behind?" He waved his hand. "No matter, perhaps after you've failed, she'll try her hand at revenge." Jack placed the empty glass on the table. "It doesn't seem you want to talk with your dear father, so let's get this over with."

Jack walked past Edward and Herbert and left the room.

Edward was still reeling over the news of Anne's mother. She had been a thorn in their side and announced Anne had died as a means to tell Anne she had been disowned, but deep down Anne still loved her mother. If he made it out of this alive, he would have to break the news to her.

The guards picked Edward up off his feet, and one of them pushed him towards the door. Edward stumbled forward as he looked over his shoulder towards Herbert who was still bleeding from his back. The other guard picked him up with no regard for his wound, and Herbert let out a yelp of pain.

The guards brought the two of them out of the room and down the stairs to the first floor. Jack was already gone, headed to the gallows ahead of them.

Herbert's wheelchair was at the foot of the steps. Edward remembered the weapons Herbert had hidden, as well as the secret weapon built into the wheelchair by Nassir. It could be crucial to getting out of this alive. He needed to get Herbert into the wheelchair, even if he was injured.

After they descended the stairs, and it became clear the guard was just going to carry Herbert the whole way to the gallows, Edward stopped.

"Let Herbert have some dignity in his last moments," he said. "Put him in his chair, for God's sake." The guards didn't listen and pushed Edward forward. What could he say for them to listen? He couldn't make it sound like he was desperate.

"Just put the boy into the wheelchair and be done with it," someone said from the front door of the villa.

Edward turned around to see Grace standing there. As usual, she looked ready for a fight wearing her copper greaves, which Edward guessed were loaded and prepared to fire.

"You'll be pushin' 'im, though," she said, pointing at Edward.

The guards put Herbert in his wheelchair, and he winced from the wound. From what Edward could see, the bullet didn't go all the way through and was still lodged inside. It would get infected if they didn't treat it soon.

The guard pushed Edward back to the wheelchair. He looked down at his locked hands and then at Grace. He opened his mouth, but Grace put up a hand.

"Don't even try it," she said, her tone as filled with annoyance as her face showed. "Ye can still push him with yer hands tied. Ye think me daft, boy?"

Edward closed his mouth and didn't say another word. He pushed Herbert's chair forward, and Grace left the door open and went ahead. Behind Edward, the guards were following on his heels.

Edward pushed Herbert over the lip of the door and down the steps towards the villa's gate. Outside, he could hear loud shouts of many voices from the centre of Nassau. From beyond the gate, some ways down the road, a crowd had begun gathering.

Edward looked up at the other buildings crowding the street, and he could see all eyes were on him and Herbert. It hadn't taken long for news about the execution to spread.

Once outside the gates, with the noise of the looming crowd providing some protection, Edward leaned down to whisper to Herbert. "Are you well?"

Herbert was sweating and visibly in pain. "Well enough," he said.

"Get it ready," Edward said.

Herbert looked up at him, looking confused. Edward motioned with his eyes to the compartments in the armrests of his chair. Herbert nodded, then went to work.

First, Herbert had to shuffle around, stifling groans of pain as he did, to get his blanket, which had ended up underneath him. He pulled it up and unfolded it to cover his legs and hide what he was doing with his arms.

Edward kept pushing Herbert forward, keeping with Grace's pace. He didn't want to risk her paying more attention to them at that moment.

As they went down the road, the crowd that had gathered became thicker, with more bodies standing in the street waiting for the hanging. As they came closer, Edward could see the podium.

The noise grew louder as people began noticing them approaching. Those in the crowd were more varied than Edward had thought they would be. Many looked to be sailors—pirates, Edward could tell—but some women and men appeared to be more respectable. Traders, business owners, some people of import, and even some children about. But pirates outnumbered the others by ten to one, so it was clear that pirates ruled the town. And Edward's father was their leader.

Herbert looked up at Edward and nodded. The weapon was ready, but if they unleashed it now, they wouldn't get far. As soon as they had been captured, their opportunities had narrowed to only one choice.

The only way out alive was to kill his father and end this. Grace and his father's words confirmed that it was what he wanted. *'I know it's gonna kill Jack that ye weren't up ta snuff.' ' Maybe she should be the one in your place.'* His father had set all this in motion as a test, that much he guessed, but they had confirmed it. *'By the sound of the Golden Horn!'* Their rallying cry. He was their leader, and he wanted Edward, his son, to kill him, and it was all a test. It wasn't much of a stretch to see that the test was whether Edward was strong enough to become his father's successor.

If Edward killed his father, there was a chance that the pirates wouldn't kill him in return, and he would become their new leader. It made a twisted kind of sense to Edward, and it was their only real chance to survive. Everything else led to death.

Grace was the only wildcard. They had killed her son, and she hated them for it. He knew from her story that she probably didn't have any real affection for his father. If it looked like he was about to escape or win, she would probably kill him afterwards. Edward had to kill Grace first.

Edward was so deep in thought that he didn't see the oncoming missile as it hit him in the face. A bystander had thrown a rock his way. He reeled back but stamped his foot down to stay upright. He stood back up to his full, towering height and looked for the aggressor. Soon he found the man, who had gathered another rock to throw, but when Edward's eyes met his, he stumbled and dropped it. He cowered at Edward's gaze. Edward noticed others in the crowd who had gathered the courage to throw something because of the first volley, and he stared each one of them down.

Whatever power Edward held in that gaze of his made the people in the crowd sink into themselves with fear despite him heading for the gallows in bonds. He didn't question it and turned his gaze to the men and women on the other side of the road for good measure. He could feel blood trickling down the side of his face where the rock had hit, but he didn't wipe it away.

The crowd parted as they came closer and closer to the gallows, giving them a straight path to the wooden structure. Edward could see his father there, waiting for him, and another man who would operate the lever. His father moved to the side and motioned behind him, beckoning Edward towards the noose hanging at the top.

When they were not thirty feet from the gallows, Edward noticed Sam there in the crowd. Sam winked and grinned at Edward, then looked down to his hip. Edward followed his gaze and Sam tapped on the cutlass at his hip, Edward's golden cutlass, and then he tapped his wrists.

It was all the confirmation Edward needed. He could count on Sam and his crew to help them through this. Relief washed over Edward, but the feeling was brief. He steeled himself for what was coming.

Grace passed Sam, staring daggers at him. Sam shrugged and laughed. The failed distraction from earlier had blown over, but not without a loss of Sam's position. Grace turned her attention back to the gallows in front of her, ignoring Sam.

Sam pulled the golden blade from his sheath. The strange golden metal sang. Edward put his hands out and held the rope tying his wrists taut. In one swing, Sam cut the rope in two. It was no match for the razor edge of Edward's blade. With another flick of Sam's wrist, he cut the bonds from Herbert's hands as well.

Then Sam tossed the cutlass to Edward. He caught it and swung around in an arc behind him. He sliced open the two guards behind him in one stroke. They fell to the ground, instantly dead.

"Now, Herbert!"

Grace had turned around just as Edward had killed the guards.

"You're not the only one with a secret weapon, you bitch!" Herbert shouted.

Herbert pulled on a cord within the arms of his wheelchair. The cord was attached to several small flintlock mechanisms inside the arms. The flintlocks fired off all at once, sending iron balls out the front of the wheelchair.

Grace jumped out of the way and to the ground. Some of the iron balls missed, but a few caught her in the stomach, and she clutched the wounded area. She gritted her teeth and rose to shaking feet. She grabbed onto the cords in her copper greaves and pulled.

Edward grabbed Herbert out of his wheelchair and jumped as Grace's weapons fired. Edward didn't feel anything hit him, but he heard Herbert groaning in pain. They tumbled to the ground together.

"Herbert, were you injured?" he asked as he got to his feet.

Herbert coughed. "I can't feel my legs."

Edward shook his head. "This is no time for jesting." Edward looked over his friend, and it appeared that he was mostly uninjured.

Edward rose to his feet to see Grace standing there, still clutching her stomach as she bled out. "Sam, protect

Herbert."

Sam came over, another weapon drawn. "You got it, Captain. Now kill yer da so we can get out of here!"

Sam's crew had surrounded the gallows and were keeping the rest of the pirates at bay. The earlier shouts of a crowd eager to see a hanging had been replaced with women screaming and the battle cries of pirates loyal to Jack. Something felt off about it all though, as though there should have been more fighting and more noise than there was. For the number of people who had gathered there, it felt subdued.

Then Edward looked up at the gallows, and he could see his father had his hand raised. When Sam's crew noticed what was happening, they stopped provoking fights but remained at the ready.

Then Jack jumped off the podium to the ground below. "Grace, are you well?"

"Well enough," she said, though the sweat on her brow and the blood from her stomach told another tale.

Jack pointed at Sam. "Kill Sam," he said.

Grace took a few deep breaths and pulled out a cutlass from her belt. "Gladly."

Jack stepped away from Grace to give her some space, and Edward followed. He held his blade forward, pointed at his father and ready to strike or defend.

Edward felt ready. His body was healed, better than it had been before he had been stabbed. The demanding work on Grace's ship had paid off. He had more stamina, more strength, and he felt more agile. The only point he felt weak on was his swordsmanship. He hadn't been in an actual fight in ages, but his golden sword with the eagle pommel, the one he'd had for several years now, felt right in his hands.

Jack unbuttoned his calico jacket and tossed it to the ground. He then took off his white undershirt, showing his toned body underneath. Though he was at least twenty to thirty years older than Edward, his body looked like someone of Edward's age. Other than the unprecedented number of scars across his body, it would be hard to tell his age just from his frame alone.

But it was his father's eyes which told the story, and the

true nature of his strength. It also gave Edward an answer to why, aside from his towering height, people cowered at his gaze. His father's eyes, more than any other part of him, conveyed an air of strength. Looking into those eyes was like looking into the eyes of Death—a swift inescapable death. It conjured the feeling you get in the seconds before waking up from a nightmare where you're falling.

He had felt the same feeling many times. The first was when he'd seen the man who called himself Plague, and since then, Edward realized he felt it along with the unbidden thoughts of those he'd killed, the torture he'd endured, and those who had died because of him. He knew that feeling well, so well that it had become a part of him.

And yet, Edward still fought on despite it. His father's gaze held no power over him because he experienced it daily.

"I find it quite interesting, the way we think alike, son," Jack said as he gently pulled out a blade from a sheath at his belt. It, too, was golden like Edward's and sang a similar, eerie song as though it were a yawning beast waking up from a long slumber. "Only *my* son would think to make a blade from this metal."

"We're nothing alike," Edward shouted back. "You use people, rape little girls, and kill innocents."

"Oh? Acting holier than thou, are we? I know of your deeds. I've heard all about them. You have a silver tongue you use to manipulate others into doing your bidding. Your crew has done horrible things to innocent people, and to get your ship back, you fired cannons at the homes of innocent people at Portsmouth. Or do you forget your own actions?"

Jack rushed in, slashing wildly at Edward. Edward ducked and dodged the blows. Jack was testing him with a flurry of strikes, and Edward managed to avoid them. His father was skilled, and Edward could tell that he was only warming up.

Edward cut through and retaliated, pushing his father back. He channelled the feeling he'd had aboard Grace's ship, the feeling of floating on air far above everything else. It wasn't a completely freeing feeling like when he was exhausted beyond all reason, but it was enough.

"I remember everything," Edward said, his tone and

mind calm. "Every face."

Jack laughed. "Do you also remember where you got the metal to make your blade?" he asked before thrusting forward.

Edward parried the strike, slid forward, and slashed down at Jack's head. Jack turned his body and took a step to the left out of the way. Edward followed through with another slash to the body. Jack jumped back and out of harm's way.

"Was it not from the body of one of my commanders? Gregory Dunn? What kind of a man takes the arm off a dead man and turns it into a sword?"

Jack leapt towards Edward and came down hard with his blade. Edward parried again, pushing his father's sword off to the side. The clash of the blades sent sparks flying with the strange harmony they produced together. Jack punched Edward in the jaw. Edward turned his chin with the punch and twisted away.

"What kind of a man turns another man's arm into gold?"

"I gave Dunn a gift from Midas. He desired wealth more than anything else, so I gave him enough to last a lifetime if he only sacrificed an arm."

"You think you're some Greek god come to earth? What kind of a trial is that for a person? What kind of a man sends his son off to die to solve a bunch of puzzles all around the world? What kind of a man tries to kill his own son?"

Edward took the offensive. He thrust forward, aiming for his father's stomach. Jack knocked Edward's blade aside. Edward spun around, using the momentum, and went to a knee as he attacked in a wide arc. Jack jumped over the blade.

"What kind of a man faces those trials? Someone willing to stand up to a challenge. You could have walked away so many times. You had so many opportunities. And look at you! You're stronger now than you ever were." Jack lowered his cutlass. "You're stronger than *I* ever was." Jack stood there for a moment, his face changing, softening. "Do you remember what I told you when you went into the Devil's Triangle?"

Edward's guard faltered. "What?"

"When you met me in the Devil's Triangle, on the

Freedom. We were in the captain's cabin, though I imagine it looked quite different from how I left it for you. For me, it was." Jack looked down at the ground in thought. "It must have been eight, no, nine years ago."

Edward remembered the moment vividly. The crew had landed on an island in the Devil's Triangle and walked into a strange mist, and he'd gotten separated from Anne. Then he'd seen a vision of his father. Many had seen strange events, some from their past, some from a loved one's past. Edward and the others had debated whether what they had seen was real, or if it had been a hallucination.

"It can't be," Edward said. He had never told anyone about what had happened to him. Not even Anne knew. There was no way that his father could have heard about it from one of his spies.

"I told you that I was proud of the man you had become. You told me about your adventures, the keys, everything. I had been Calico Jack for a time by then, and work had already begun on the trials and the keys. It was then that I knew this was the right path to take." Jack held his hands out to his side and closed his eyes. "Now, end it, Edward. End it, son."

Edward looked at his father, arms open and eyes closed, calling on Edward to kill him. Edward lifted his cutlass and pointed it at Jack Rackham, at Benjamin Hornigold, at his father, Albert Thatch, who had raised him, for good or ill, to be the man he was today. The one who had put him through so many trials, both fantastical and horrifying; trials that had made him stronger, but had also caused him so much pain; trials that had allowed him to meet his captor who made him want to die, but also his wife who gave him a reason to live on.

"I…"

"Do it, Edward!" Herbert shouted from behind him.

"Do it, Ed ya bastard!" Sam said, his voice strained.

"I… can't," Edward said. He dropped his blade to the ground, and it fell with a clang.

"What?" his father said, opening his eyes to look at his son.

"I can't do it. Despite everything you've done, I love you. I can't do this." Edward felt hollow. "Please, just stop this madness. We don't have to fight each other. This is a fool's errand."

"Pathetic," his father snarled. "How did I raise a boy so weak as you? We don't have to fight each other? Everything has been building to this moment, you snivelling little shit. I don't have... When I'm gone, someone needs to rule here, and you're supposed to be that someone." Jack took a deep breath, rubbed his temples, and let out a sigh. "Then I suppose I'll have to settle for second place. Perhaps after I kill you, your wife will try to get revenge. If she manages to kill me, she could be a queen yet. Better a queen of pirates than the alternative, I'd say."

Edward's thoughts went back to Anne, and just what his father was saying. He was going to try killing Anne next. Edward knew that Anne would seek revenge, there was no way she wouldn't. Edward, in his current state of mind, cared little for his own life, but he still cared deeply for Anne. He loved her more than he loved himself. He also loved her more than he loved his father.

The thought of Anne dying took over his mind, and a wave of great anger washed over him. It stripped away the floating feeling he had been holding onto during the fight. It ripped from his body the arresting memories that haunted him. Rage took over.

Jack stepped forward and thrust his blade at Edward's chest. Edward rolled out of the way, grabbed his blade mid-roll, and slashed his father's stomach. His father couldn't dodge out of the way, and the blade sliced through him from front to back.

Edward bounded to his feet and turned around to clash blades with his father again, but Jack had fallen over and was bleeding out from the wound on his stomach. It was a mortal wound, Edward was sure.

Edward ran over to his father and pressed on the wound.

"No, no," Albert said. "Go get Herbert." Edward, his mind in shock, going from enraged to his instinct to save his father, couldn't hear him. "Go, go," he said again. This time

Edward heard.

Edward got up and turned around to see Herbert sitting up, watching everything. Sam was nearby, wounded and breathing heavy, but alive. Grace was lying in a pool of her own blood farther away.

Herbert was listless and pale, but from the tears in his eyes, he knew what had happened. Edward picked Herbert up and brought him over to his dying father.

"He's here, Dad, Herbert's here."

Albert, his face soaked with sweat, and already paler than Herbert, was barely clinging to what little life was left in him. He reached out and touched both of them.

"I'm proud of both of you. You've become so strong," he said. "Herbert, you became a fine helmsman; better, I heard, than any I knew in my lifetime." The pool of blood beneath the three of them was growing and covered his father's whole body. "Edward, I'm sorry for what I made you do, but I wanted this. Don't blame yourself." Albert reached into his pocket and took out the driftwood seashell necklace that had once belonged to Edward's mother and handed it to him. "It's yours now. Don't lose it, it's the only thing of hers left."

Edward, his hand shaking, took the necklace and nodded. His memory of his mother was faint, but at that moment it felt stronger than it had before.

Albert's voice was fading fast, and he had trouble keeping his eyes open. "And I forgive both of you for John. He was a good boy; he wouldn't fault you for what you did." Albert couldn't keep himself up any longer, his strength waning. "I'll see him soo..." Albert's voice trailed off, and his eyes closed.

"Dad?" Edward called, but his father didn't answer.

Herbert pulled Edward in close and embraced him. Edward couldn't help but weep for his father's death. Despite everything that he had done, he still loved him, and Edward mourned.

The two sat in the middle of the road in Nassau for several minutes, the crowd around them silent. Then a chant began, starting with one person in the crowd, then another, and another, until it felt like the whole of Nassau were speaking as one.

"By the sound of the Golden Horn!"

"By the sound of the Golden Horn!"

"By the sound of the Golden Horn!"

The chant continued unabated. Edward pulled away from his tearful embrace with Herbert to see all eyes were on them. All eyes were on him.

Edward looked upon his father's body again. The familiar golden hunting horn, from his father's time as Benjamin Hornigold, was tied around his waist. Edward loosened the horn, took it in hand, and rose to his feet.

He took a deep breath and sounded the horn.

19. WATER AND BLOOD

In the week since leaving the island, Anne started to acclimate to the prosthetic Alexandre, Victoria, and Nassir had made for her. It felt altogether strange and uncomfortable and itchy where it secured to her thigh with a leather, corset-like strap, but she could walk in it, and that was what mattered most to her.

She still had a problem with her gait and putting the right amount of weight on it, but she had the rest of her life to perfect that, so it didn't bother her.

She also liked the privacy that it gave her, as she could wear a boot and cover it with her pant leg. If she were standing still, none could tell that she had lost her foot. None save her. Though she supposed for some in their profession, it could be seen as a badge of honour, she saw it as a sign of weakness.

They left Los Huecos after gathering and burning the bodies of the dead, as well as the main town that Silver Eyes had occupied. The crew agreed to break and toss the golden bells into the ocean. Whatever strange power they held was better off at the bottom of the sea with Davey Jones.

If Anne never heard them ring again for the rest of her life, it would be too soon.

They set sail for Nassau, and before setting anchor, sent out a scouting party by longboat. They came back after hearing word that Blackbeard had killed Calico Jack.

The news nearly caused Anne to collapse. She had been holding a secret weight, secret even to herself, over the thought that Edward might have perished in his attempt. The weight lifted, and her heart felt free. She was eager to land and see him again.

Only then did she take in what the news meant. Edward had killed his own father. The same father whom he, from day one, had insisted was alive and was partially the reason

508

for his being at sea in the first place. The same father for whom he'd held such complicated emotion after learning the truth about who he was.

Anne's heart broke for Edward as she thought of how hard it must have been to end his own father's life. It also made her scared. He already had a drinking problem from the nightmares that haunted his waking thoughts. What would this new trauma do to him?

"What news of my brother?" Christina asked, clutching the carved rose at her neck.

The crewmates shook their heads. "No mention of 'im. Sorry."

Christina nodded, but her face looked dire. It seemed to Anne like she too had been holding onto a secret weight of her own.

Anne went over to Christina and touched her back. "I am sure your brother is safe and well. Take us into the harbour, and we shall see for ourselves."

Christina managed a weak smile and a nod before she took the helm and issued orders to the crew. She deftly guided the ship into the harbour before ordering the anchor lowered.

Anne, Christina, William, Alexandre, and Victoria were the first party to head to shore in a longboat with some other crewmates. Jack, Pukuh, and Nassir stayed behind, choosing to go later.

As they approached the pier near the centre of town, they noticed Sam waiting for them at the dock. Sam helped moor the longboat, and the crew disembarked onto the pier.

"Sam, happy to see you well and uninjured. Our scouts tell us that Edward killed his... killed Calico Jack."

Sam nodded, his face dour despite what should be good news. "Aye," he said. "You were right ta send me off ta help. Ed woulda gotten 'imself killed if not."

"And what of my brother?" Christina asked once more, stepping forward, her eyes desperate.

Sam's face still held fast to its grim demeanour. "I'll take you to 'im," he said, but would say no more.

Christina didn't seem relieved by the news that he was

still alive, and why would she when Sam seemed reluctant to give any more information?

Sam took them through the town, full of revelling pirates as far as the eye could see, and explained what had happened. He gave a brief telling of Edward and Herbert's time aboard Grace O'Malley's ship.

Sam also explained that Edward killed Grace's son who also turned out to be Edward's brother, but they hadn't known it at the time. The news sent Anne's heart racing. Not only did Edward kill his own father, but he killed a brother he hadn't even known he had. Edward's mental state had been hanging on a razor's edge *before* all this had happened. She hoped he was coping with it well, but she felt more fear than anything.

Sam's recounting continued, explaining how they met in Nassau and hatched a plan that backfired due to Grace knowing the truth of Edward and Herbert's identities. Then Sam had regrouped and saved Edward from the gallows, allowing Edward to finally finish off his father.

After a funeral for his father—a muted affair from Sam's estimation due to what happened afterwards—they gave Edward the official title of Magistrate for Nassau and the unofficial title of King of the Caribbean among the pirates. There was a ceremony, which really was just him being named Magistrate and Edward blowing his father's golden horn again, and afterwards the pirates partied for several days and nights.

Benjamin Hornigold and Jack Rackham would live on through Edward, their names and their legacy taken over by him as if his father had never died. That was what Edward's father had wanted for him, what he had tested him for: to prove he was worthy of taking over those names by the republic his father had created. They'd learned that it was the only way Edward's father could force the other pirates to come to an agreement over their next leader.

Anne surmised that on the surface, it functioned as a democracy, but behind the scenes, it was an oligarchy. Edward needed to be savage to rule through force if needed and keep the pirates in line.

After the ceremonies, Sam continued, Edward did his

best to catch up on the administrative side of his father's business. Or, at least, that was what he told everyone. Sam knew that Edward was in mourning and spent his days and nights reading things left behind in his father's study as his new staff kept him plied with liquor. He hadn't left the study since the ceremony.

They eventually reached a large gated villa near the edge of town. There were many guards around the premises, but upon noticing Sam, they opened the gates and allowed him entry.

Upon entering the villa, Sam pointed to a room on the first floor. "Herbert's in that room, Christina."

Christina, her face still filled with worry, rushed off without another word. Sam looked at Alexandre and motioned his head towards the room, and Alexandre and Victoria both understood the message and joined Christina.

Anne's heart sank further. That Sam wanted Alexandre to see Herbert meant something terrible had happened to him in the battle. He was still alive, perhaps, but in what state of living was he?

"Come, I'll take ye two ta the captain," Sam said.

"Does he know I... we've arrived?" Anne asked.

"I sent one of me men off when I saw the *Freedom*... ah, I mean the *Queen Anne's Revenge* sailing in," Sam said, then muttered, "That's going ta take some gettin' used to."

Anne and William followed Sam to the second floor of the villa to a room at the back. The other crewmates decided to stay behind and visit Herbert first. A guard opened the door for them and let them enter a large study.

Anne saw Edward sitting in a chair at a table layered with papers, charts, and various oddities. The sight of him, alive and well, took another weight off her, and she felt she could breathe normally again.

After the relief, she noticed his beard was almost completely gone. There was hair there, just not at much as she remembered. It made him look younger and less menacing than he had previously.

Edward looked up from some papers, and when he noticed Anne, his eyes opened wide. He rose from his chair and nearly ran over to her. He scooped her up in his arms and spun her around. He had the widest smile on his face, and his eyes had misted. He pulled her close, and they kissed and wrapped their arms around each other as they let out all the built-up passion from their time apart.

After a moment, he settled himself and rested his head on top of hers. "I missed you," he said.

Anne laughed. "I can see that," she replied. She nestled her head into his chest. "I missed you too."

He smelled of booze, but it was not so pungent as to be intolerable, and Anne decided that now was not the time to broach the subject. It was a time for reunion and time for her to be there for him.

Anne lifted her head up and looked into his eyes. She placed her hand against his cheek, feeling the warmth on her palm. "Sam told us what happened. Edward, I—"

"Let's not speak of it," he said. "There will be time enough for that later." Edward looked behind her to William and Sam. "Where are the rest of the crew?"

Anne stepped back awkwardly due to her leg and answered, "Most are on the ship. Some came with us. Christina, Alexandre and Victoria are visiting with Herbert."

Edward had heard her, but he was looking at her feet. He must have noticed the awkward way she had stumbled backwards.

Anne let out a sigh, wishing that she could have held it for a time when they were alone. Perhaps if she dispensed with it sooner than later, it would be simpler.

Anne knelt and lifted her pant leg up above her knee, showing the prosthetic. "Sam told you of our battling Silver Eyes? Well, the battle did not go as planned, nor as simple as I would have desired."

Edward knelt, joining his wife, and examined the prosthetic. "How did this happen?" His words were short, and his tone a mix of concern and sadness.

Anne shrugged her shoulders. "It's a rather long story. There will be time enough for that later," she said with a grin.

Edward nodded and smiled as well, a bit of relief in his eyes. "This is a remarkable design. Did Alexandre make this?"

"Yes, he, Victoria, and Nassir all had a hand in it."

Edward continued his appraisal, and then he lifted a finger up. "I have just the thing to finish the design and make it even better." He rose to his feet and went to the back of the study and began rummaging through some things.

Anne kept her pant leg rolled up, but she stood up as well, waiting. After a moment, he came back, holding a pair of copper greaves in his hands. He showed them to Anne and handed one to her.

"These are from one of Calico Jack's commanders, Grace O'Malley. She won't be needing them anymore, given that she's with Davey Jones now. They have a secret weapon inside them which fires off bullets out the front."

Anne inspected the greaves, taking note of the weapon inside. "That is ingenious." She handed the greaves back to Edward, and he laid them on a nearby table. "Can you tell me what happened to Herbert? Sam wasn't forthcoming, I assume because Christina was with us," she said as she glanced over her shoulder at him. Sam had his arms folded and shrugged.

Edward's face soured, and he stroked his chin. "He was injured before we fought with Jack, and, well, perhaps it would be best to see him for yourself. I would wish to speak with Alexandre and Victoria soon besides."

Edward left the study and led Anne, William, and Sam to the room on the first floor where Herbert was. The crewmates who had gone to see him were waiting at the door, and they greeted Edward with joyful but muted expressions, which quickly reverted to sullen. Edward opened the door, and a distinct smell of rot mixed with chemicals and herbs met Anne's nose.

Inside, Alexandre and Victoria were standing in a corner near the door, there was an attendant at the other corner, and Christina was sitting beside a bed where Herbert lay. Christina was weeping as she held Herbert's hand.

Anne rushed over to see Herbert's eyes open and alert. He was still alive, but judging from the looks on the faces there, it was not a good prognosis.

She placed her hand on Christina's back, and Christina looked at her. Christina opened her mouth to say something, but she burst into fresh new tears. Anne leaned down and hugged the young woman as she sobbed.

After a few moments, Christina was able to compose herself, though not entirely.

"Glad to see you well, Anne," Herbert said. His voice was hoarse and weak, and with each breath, there was a guttural noise from his throat.

"I am happy to see you as well, Herbert. We sorely missed you these past weeks, but your sister makes a fine helmsman. She managed the ship well in your stead."

Herbert smiled, but then had a coughing fit. He coughed hard for a full minute before he was able to stop and then he took a few deep breaths. "That is good to hear. The *Queen Anne's Revenge* will be well cared for."

Christina's head sank, and she gripped the folds of her pants until her knuckles were white. She didn't need to hear it spoken aloud, for it was clear that Herbert was not long for this world. There was nothing Alexandre could do for him in this state. Whatever injury he suffered must have been infected, and they had failed to treat it in time.

Anne touched Christina's hands, and the young girl looked up at her. Her eyes, filled with grief, pleaded to Anne, begging her to do something.

She looked at Herbert, unable to bear Christina's gaze. "We will let you alone with your sister," she said.

Anne and the rest left the room. Outside, Anne questioned Alexandre.

"So, there is truly no hope? What of the herb from Pukuh's home that you used on me those years ago?"

Alexandre waved his hand. "No two infections are alike, you should know this," he said. "Herbert's has reached his lungs. Even should we use the medicine, it would only prolong his suffering. There is no cure for him."

Anne shook her head. "How long does he have?"

Alexandre crossed his arms in thought. "Perhaps a few days, perhaps a week. It is hard to say."

Edward appeared unfazed. He had been with Herbert

from the time the infection began and appeared to know that it was dire. Alexandre was his last hope, but not one he had been holding out for, it seemed.

"Victoria, I'd like to speak with you alone about a matter involving my father. Join me in the study," he said. "And I suppose, Alexandre, you may join, as I know trying to keep you out will be a futile matter." Edward looked at Anne. "Not to worry, my dear, this won't take long."

Edward left, and Alexandre and Victoria followed behind him, leaving Anne and William waiting. Anne wondered just what it was that he wanted to talk with them about.

Christina, alone with Herbert, couldn't hold back the tears any longer and began crying again. She felt as though she had done nothing but cry for the past week and a half. Crying over what she had done to Anne, crying over her weakness that had allowed it to happen, and now crying over her brother's inevitable demise. She hated it.

Her hands instinctively went to her rose necklace. The necklace became a totem of loss and serenity. When she touched it, she felt calmed. It brought her comfort as she ran her finger along the intricate grooves.

Ochi, her first love, Nassir's son, had given it to her as a gift—a gift expressing his affection for her. She had been wearing it ever since.

Ochi had died. She had loved him, and he had died, and a piece of her died along with him.

Everyone close to her was dead or dying. She hated it.

She ripped the necklace off her and pulled it back, ready to throw it against the wall. She gritted her teeth and looked at the wall, but she couldn't do it. She lowered her hand onto her lap and looked at the rose again. She traced the lines, the curves of the small petals made by a skilled hand, a hand cut short before his prime, and she calmed herself.

She wiped her eyes and glanced at her brother. "What am I going to do when you're gone? You are all that I have left in this world."

There was a moment of silence, then Herbert said, "Do you mock me?"

Christina's jaw dropped. "How could you say that?"

"I recall I said those exact words to you once before," Herbert said before a few weak coughs. "And you said to me 'We are—'"

"Your family," Christina finished.

Herbert nodded. "You were talking of the crew. You have so many aboard that ship who care for you, who love you, and would die for you."

"The crew doesn't share my blood; you do. The crew weren't there for me when Mother and Father died; you were. The crew didn't support me by joining a merchant ship as a powder-monkey before being captured and crippled on a pirate ship; you did. The crew didn't raise me; you did."

Herbert waved his hand. "Blood brought us together by chance. The crew chooses to be with you. And if we're getting into specifics, I would say this crew raised you just as much as I have. I think Anne could hold some stake in that claim if pressed upon it. You two are like sisters."

Christina chuckled. "I suppose you're right."

There were a few more moments of silence, and then Herbert spoke up. "So, are you getting more comfortable with sailing?"

Christina spoke with her brother about how Anne wanted her to become helmsman, and her time with the ship, as well as the details of their adventure. She recounted the entranced islanders, knocking down the bell with the cannons, getting put under the spell and what had happened to Anne because of it, and finally the sailing to Nassau.

As she recounted the story, she saw him smile, and it warmed her heart. Up until then, he had seemed to be in so much pain. By the end of her telling, they were both holding hands again, and Christina was no longer crying.

After a few moments of silence, Herbert spoke again. "Christina, I need to ask you for a favour."

"Yes? What do you need?"

There was a long pause as Herbert sought for words. He

didn't look at her, and instead out the window next to his bed. "I don't want to let this affliction ravage my body any more than it has. It will only get worse from here."

Christina pulled her hand away from her brother's. "What are you saying?" she asked, but she already knew the answer.

⚓ ⚓ ⚓

"How many spies for my father are aboard the *Queen Anne's Revenge*?

Edward, Alexandre, and Victoria stood in the study— Edward's father's former study. Edward kept a hand at his hip, ready to draw his weapon at a moment's notice. He didn't know what Victoria would do at this line of questioning.

Victoria stood silently for a moment before answering. "Half, perhaps a bit more than half. I'm not their keeper."

"And you've been sending him reports with our status, our whereabouts?"

"Yes," she replied, her face like stone.

Edward's rage reached a tipping point, and he pulled out the blade from its sheath. "Tell me why I shouldn't kill you right now."

Alexandre and Victoria both had their own weapons drawn, Victoria a short sword and round shield, and Alexandre a rapier.

"I doubt you could," she said first. Then she followed up with, "I wasn't the only one sending letters."

Edward calmed himself and dropped his stance. "No… no, you weren't." He put his cutlass away, and the other two followed suit. "Tell me why you did it. According to you, you hated my father, so why follow his orders and spy on me? Why report back to him?"

"Simple," she said. "Your father wanted to die, and I wanted him dead. It was an uncomplicated decision."

Her flippant attitude was making him angry once again, but he couldn't fault her for wanting the man dead. After all, Edward was the one who'd killed him. His father seemed to have a knack for bringing people together and setting them apart.

Like father, like son. "So, what am I to do with you then, hmm? If I cast you away, then by rights I should be casting away half my crew. By that reasoning, this whole bloody island was loyal to my father and his ends, I can't rid myself of all of them."

Alexandre stepped forward. He had the same slight smile on his face, the one that showed no genuine emotion. "Perhaps I can be of assistance. We were planning on leaving after this matter was settled, so we shall depart of our own accord."

The revelation took Edward aback and confused him. "You were planning on leaving the crew? I thank you for saving me the trouble, but why?"

"As I said when we first met, I was here for the entertainment. I enjoyed watching you over the years, but I have had my fill. Your wife may be able to illuminate you as to the breaking point that came about during her *aventure.*"

Alexandre and Victoria turned around to leave and headed towards the door to the study.

"Hmph," Edward scoffed. "And what about that question about me that was puzzling you so? Do I enjoy the smell of blood?"

"Ah, yes, I found the answer to that some time ago."

Edward's jaw dropped. "And? What's the answer?"

Alexandre grinned. "What indeed," he said, and then he headed out the door.

The crew held Herbert's funeral on the deck of the *Queen Anne's Revenge.*

Before Alexandre and Victoria left, they heard about his passing and decided to attend and use it as an opportunity to say goodbye to the rest of the crew.

Sam also joined with some of his crew to pay their respects.

It was the first time in quite a while that Edward had been

aboard his ship, but the circumstances were far from pleasant. He had already prepared mentally for Herbert's passing, but the suddenness and the manner were unexpected.

Only those who were on land in Nassau knew the truth of what had happened. They told the crew that he had died of illness from an infected wound and kept Herbert's head covered to hide his final shame. None of the crew who knew the truth blamed Christina for helping her brother end his life and end his pain, but it was a shock nonetheless.

Christina remained composed as best she could for the funeral, but her eyes were red, and she either kept one hand on her rose necklace or clutching tight to her pant leg. She told Edward that she couldn't bear to say anything given what she had done. Edward thought the poor girl wouldn't have made it through more than a few words either way.

And, so, the task fell to Edward. Edward walked up the ladder to the quarterdeck slowly. He could feel all eyes on him, and he thought it funny that some time ago, the thought of speaking in front of such a large crowd terrified him. Now, the crew, and him also, thought nothing of the act.

Edward looked at the immense helm, Herbert's domain. He touched the familiar wood, staring at it for a moment. He could almost picture Herbert holding it, his wheelchair positioned at an angle so that he could reach the massive wheel. The thought made him smile.

"You know," he began, changing what he had planned to say, "this wheel is almost as tall as I am." Edward held his hand out, gesturing to visualize the height difference. It reached his neck at its highest point. "And yet, Herbert, our helmsman sat half that height." Edward moved his hand down, below the railing of the quarterdeck. "One would wonder if Herbert was manning the helm, or if the helm was manning Herbert." Edward's comment made the crew laugh. Then he pointed at the wheel. "Day in and day out, Herbert struggled with this beast, and he won." He clenched his fist. "He won every single day in his battle to ensure that each one of you got to where you wanted to go. To make sure that each of you was safe from storms. To make sure that we won any battle we had at sea." Edward let the words hang in the air for a minute. "Each one of us, at some point or another, owed our life to Herbert. And now we won't ever get the chance to repay that debt."

Edward needed a moment. And from the looks of it, so did many in the crew. His eyes were watering. He wiped them and took a few deep breaths.

"Herbert was my brother," he said. "We may not have shared blood, but he was my brother. We fought like brothers, too, as you're well aware." The crew chuckled again, and Edward could see a few wiping tears away as well. Anne, comforting Christina, wiped her eyes. "He was our brother. We were his family." The crew shouted in agreement. "Now, with his vengeance complete, may he rest in peace." The crew roared again at Edward's declaration.

Edward nodded to Pukuh to begin the final ceremony. As he had done before for others in the crew, he placed a piece of corn and a small piece of jade in Herbert's mouth: food for the journey he was about to take, and jade to pay for passage. Then he said a prayer, which the other crewmates joined in by bowing their heads.

The crew placed Herbert in a longboat and lowered it into the sea. They tossed a torch inside before letting it loose on the swells. As his body drifted out, some in the crew fired off muskets into the air. After three shots, they stopped, and it meant the service was over, but many continued to watch as the longboat went farther and farther out to sea, the fire reaching higher as it and Herbert drifted from the earth.

"So, Silver Eyes was putting everyone in a trance?"

Anne nodded as she took a bite from some food they'd brought into their cabin. "It's a shame you weren't there to see it. It was hard to imagine that the islanders could be so far gone from a simple trance, but I suppose it's a testament to your father's crew."

Edward and Anne, as well as the rest of the crew, had decided to stay aboard the ship after the funeral. They had a feast where many drank to Herbert's honour and recounted his time at the helm. Some even lamented being against him at first but gaining respect for him due to his tenacity.

After the feast, and after Anne saw Christina to her bed where she finally slept after some mournful drinking, Edward and Anne had retreated to their cabin where they sat leaning against their bed, a plate of food in front of them and a lantern nearby. Anne told Edward about what had happened on the island, and how Silver Eyes had controlled the crew to attack them.

Edward shivered at the thought of the men and women of the island, hollow-eyed and out for blood, and stronger than one with their full senses.

"What say we take a trip to the Devil's Triangle?" Edward said with a grin. "We can switch places: you join Herbert and kill my father, I'll take the ship and go after Silver Eyes."

Anne gave Edward a dark look. "Don't jest about such things. We've already been there once, and once was too much." She shook her head. "I cannot believe that what we saw there was real. If that's true, then we cannot go back. If we were to change something in the past, then it could have untold effects on the present. Our present, at least."

"That's not how I see it," Edward said. "Think about it. We were already well into our journey for the keys when we entered that mist. My father said that my visit to him secured his doubts about what he was going to do. And, you said William did the exact same thing that he had done in the past: he left the room where his king was and didn't go back in to stop his murder. The present was the same in both situations. Going back didn't change anything because it played out exactly as it had. Even if we go again, whatever happened would have already happened in the past, and the present would remain the same."

Anne raised her brow. "But what about Sam and Miss Alston?"

Edward opened his mouth to respond and then closed it again. He looked off to the side as he thought it over. Sam and Theodosia Burr Alston, whom at the time they had thought was their enemy, had been with William in his vision of the past. They had most certainly not been there with William when he had been a royal guard, so them being there must have changed history.

"My dear, I'm far too intoxicated for this right now. You've just rattled my brain a bit too much."

"Eat something, Ed," Anne said, handing him some meat and bread.

Edward ate the food offered, and despite wanting to move on from their time in the Devil's Triangle, a thought occurred to him. "You've never told me about what you saw that day," he said.

Anne looked at Edward for a moment, her red curls draped over her shoulders as she moved her head. She looked away and at the wall. "I, like you, saw my parents. Both of them. I didn't know where I was at first, but I quickly realized it was one of my mother's houses. I hid when I heard someone coming, and it turned out to be my mother. She had just given birth to my brother George, but he died minutes after." Anne leaned her head back and looked at the ceiling above. "I would have been eight at the time, far too young to remember the details, but I do remember the fights. My father tried his best to console my mother, but she rebuffed him. My mother's friend, Sarah, came next and comforted my mother in her time of need. Then my aunt visited, and Sarah left. Instead of comforting her, my aunt berated my mother for her relationship with Sarah. They fought, shouting at each other the vilest things." Anne closed her eyes for a moment. "That was the last time they saw each other."

Edward watched as Anne told her story. Her expression was a mixed shadow of pity and anger that had simmered and evaporated over the years but still existed in the ether.

He remembered what his father had told him about Anne's mother. She had passed almost a year ago. He hadn't told Anne about it yet, but he knew he should. Before he could, Anne continued her story.

"I never did put the two together, but I realize now why my leaving was such a betrayal to her, why she chose to declare me dead as a way of disowning me and sending an assassin to make it true. Though they fought, my mother loved my aunt, but my aunt was so cruel to her. That's what made her an overbearing, overprotective and controlling woman. The cruellest irony is that that's what pushed me away." Anne glanced at Edward and let out a sheepish chuckle as she wiped the mist from her eyes. "Sorry, Ed, it's the drink talking. I didn't mean to drown you in melancholy."

Edward laid his hand on Anne's and looked deep into her eyes. "Never apologize for opening your heart to me. I am your husband, remember? We're supposed to share in the burdens too, not just the joys."

Anne leaned forward and kissed Edward, then the two embraced. Anne held him tight, and Edward could feel the slight damp of fallen tears against his back.

"I love you, Edward," she said.

"I love you too, my Anne."

They sat there for a moment in silence. Anne repositioned so that she was leaning her back into his chest, and she held Edward's arms wrapped around her body. The stars shone outside, giving a small bit of light into the cabin along with the ever-dimming lantern in front of them.

"Besides, there's no use worrying about the dead. It's a lesson we'll both have to learn, it seems," Anne said suddenly.

Anne's comment shocked Edward. "What?"

She turned a bit and looked up at Edward. "Yes, I suppose I never told you. Back when we were in Porto Bello, I learned that my mother passed away."

Edward's jaw dropped in shock. "You knew?"

Anne sat up and turned around to face Edward. "Wait, you knew about it too?"

"I just found out recently. I was trying to find the right time to tell you about it." Edward let out a sigh and ran his fingers through his hair.

"Well, I suppose I've saved you the trouble," Anne said with a laugh.

"I suppose so."

They sat in silence once again.

After a moment, Anne shook her head. "We're quite the

pair, aren't we?" she said.

Edward cocked his brow. "I recall I said the same to you once. What do you mean by it?"

"Though you weren't aware at the time, you had an overbearing, controlling father who tried to kill you, the same as my mother. Fate is the mother of all coincidences. I take that as more proof we were meant to be together."

Edward smiled at his wife. The thought that they were meant to be together, though their shared circumstances may have been the inciting incidents, warmed his heart.

"Anne, I want you to have this," Edward said as he reached into his pocket. He pulled the driftwood seashell necklace and handed it to her. "It was my mother's. My father had it with him. I think it would be better if you kept it safe."

She examined the carved necklace with care and reverence, gently touching the curves in the porous wood. After a moment, she put it around her neck.

"How does it look?" she asked.

"Better than it would on me," he replied with a grin.

Anne laughed with him. "You've never talked about your mother before. Tell me about her."

Edward told Anne about the only memory he had left of his mother: her beautiful, long black hair, as black as onyx, and wavy like the summer sea. Then he recounted the stories that his father had told him about her and finished with his father's comment about his mother not being meant for this world.

Anne gave him a warm smile, then touched the necklace. "I'll keep it safe and wear it with pride."

She turned around and laid her head in Edward's lap. She held his hand across her chest, and they sat there for a time. Edward watched the stars outside the cabin as the waves splashed against the hull, the familiar sound pulling at his core and reminding him of what he missed on his ship.

The familiar smells of the sea air and the Caribbean pine that lined the ship from stem to stern, as well as his wife's warmth in his lap, calmed his mind. For the moment, despite the loss of his father and his brother Herbert, he was at peace.

"So, have you thought about what we'll do from here?" Anne asked.

Edward looked at his wife, her eyes deep green like the ocean, her gleaming red hair shining in the light of the lantern. The small freckles around her face and her rose-coloured lips made his heart race.

"I have a few things in mind for us to do tonight," he said with a cheeky grin. Anne smacked his hand, but she couldn't hold back a smile and a blush. Edward kissed his wife, then looked out the window to the stars again. "We're free from our horrible parents, and we're pirates. We can do whatever we want."

EPILOGUE

It was a stormy day, and Edward holed himself up in his father's study reading through the mass of notes and letters, ledgers and journals left behind. He was trying to find some purpose behind the noise, trying to stay afloat in the business his father had created.

Suddenly, the doors to the study swung open on a gust of wind. Edward looked up to see an older man with salt and pepper hair and a pipe sticking out of his mouth at the entrance. The man held no weapon, but Edward drew a pistol all the same.

Edward stood up from his seat and pointed the pistol at the man. He held his finger at the ready but didn't fire. "Who are you? What are you doing here?"

The man looked Edward up and down, as though appraising him. "So yer the egg, eh?" he said in a gravelly voice. "You'd better have been worth all this. I lost my eye because o' you."

Edward, from this distance, could just barely make out the slash on the man's left eye and cheek. His eye looked clouded over.

"I'm afraid you have me mistaken for another," he said. "Now, I'll ask you to leave unless you want to die."

The man nodded and stepped forward, unfazed. The sound of a peg leg snapped against the wood of the floor. "Aye, you have some fire in you, that's good," the man said. He looked around the room, then when he eyed a cabinet nearby, he stalked over to it and opened it up to find a bottle of liquor. "You remember the man you fought, Edward Russell? What was the name that fool called himself? Ah, yes, *Plague*. What a joke. At least when people call me a foolish name, it wasn't my idea."

The mention of the assassin Edward had fought piqued his interest. He didn't lower the pistol, but he did approach the man. "What about him?"

The old man pulled the cork of the liquor out with his teeth, spat it away, and took a long drink. "I'm the reason you won that fight, little egg," he said. Then he motioned with two fingers from his left shoulder in a line to his right hip.

It took a moment to remember, but Edward recalled that Plague had had a wound in that same spot. The wound had only been hours old when they had fought, and Edward surmised that without that wound, he very well might not have won his fight. Only those who were with Plague, or on Edward's crew, knew of that wound.

Edward furrowed his brow. "Who are you?" he asked again.

"I'm William Kidd. Some fools call me The Tsunami. I'm a friend of yer father, and I'm here to help you with what comes next."

THE END

BOOK THREE OF
THE PIRATE PRIEST

BARTHOLOMEW
ROBERTS' MERCY

1. THE TRIAL

From the Journal of Bartholomew Roberts
Entry #54 Dated July 5th, No Year Given

We sail for Providencia with a brief stop in San Andrés for re-supply.

I find myself on the eve of a years- long journey to find Walter Kennedy, the Irishman who stole my ship. Though our fates are set to intertwine once more, it brings me no pleasure.

There will be a battle ahead, and a decision I must make.

We have enlisted the aid of Edward Thatch, better known as the upstart pirate Blackbeard, in the battle to come. He is presently delayed due to an unfortunate meeting with a Spanish Galleon. He bid me to continue on as he made repairs to his ship, offering spare crewmates to hasten our voyage, and promised to meet again in Providencia.

He asked me what I would do to Kennedy upon meeting with him once more, to which I said I would deliver God's justice. He stated that if he met with the one he wanted revenge on, he would kill the man. I pondered aloud whether that was a just action that God would approve of, and he said that it was a pirate's justice.

Can the two not be the same?

Fortune anchored in the harbour of San Andrés. A small English colony had been built into the northeast of the island and taken over the paradise. Many of the tropical trees and wildlife which would have spread to the edge of the island had been cut back for wooden homes and buildings across the shore. A few larger brick buildings dotted the northern side and interior of the island.

"Hank, I'm going ashore for a time. Would you handle the re-supply for us?"

Hank nodded as he placed his thumbs between his belt and trousers. "You can count on me, Captain."

"Good man," Roberts replied with a smack against Hank's back.

"What will you be doing in town?"

"There's a chance the pirates we're after stopped by here on their way to Providencia. No harm in asking around to see if any of the townsfolk saw their ships."

After Hank nodded again, Roberts turned around and headed to the quarterdeck ladder towards the longboats. "We'll get him," Hank said behind him.

Roberts looked over his shoulder at Hank. His eyes were wide and there was a smirk curling the corner of his lips. "Of course," Roberts replied. He had to force himself to return the smile, and his muscles pulled against the change in expression.

After three days of hard labour, working day and night to reach San Andrés in time, Roberts had had no time alone to think. Going ashore would be as much about information gathering as it would be to contemplate what he would do when he met Walter Kennedy again.

Roberts boarded one of the longboats bound for shore to return supplies to the *Fortune*. The men aboard were talking excitedly about the upcoming battle, and their soon-to-be revenge.

That's right, these men must also feel betrayed by Kennedy and their old crewmates.

The longboat, powered by strong rowers, was soon docked at the pier of San Andrés, and the *Fortune's* other longboats were not far behind.

The sounds of the pier overwhelmed all other noises. Men were shouting, rolling barrels, dropping boxes, and stamping their feet at the bustling though small pier. Roberts once more found no respite, and couldn't focus on his thoughts amidst the noise.

He left the longboat as his men were lashing it to the wooden pier and walked into town. He barely took notice of the sights around him, but what he did see was the same stale colony life followed by many from Britain. Dull wooden houses, horses pulling carts over cobbled stone or dirt, dainty women in dresses and men of various garb according to their station, and mud. Always mud.

Roberts soon found himself in a tavern, devoid of most patrons, and he sat himself at a table in the corner of the room. Soon, a young woman asked him what he wanted, and went to fetch him a meal and some ale.

Out a window, Roberts could see the sun descending on the town in a slow arc. It was nearing time for an evening sup, but would still be a few hours before nightfall.

Should Hank haste in re-supplying the ship, we could arrive in Providencia in the middle of the night.

The young woman returned with a mug filled to the brim with a pale ale in one hand, and a plate lined with several cured meats, soft cheeses, and biscuits in the other.

"My thanks, my dear," Roberts said. He cocked his head to the side as he gazed into the young woman's hazel eyes. "Tell me, would you happen to know if any frigates happened upon your shores of late? Tall ships outfitted for battle?" Roberts asked, gesturing with his hands.

The young woman smiled, but seemed flustered at the inquiry. She looked off to the side in thought. "Well, sir, we see several merchants in these parts... and pirates, if that's your meaning."

Roberts cocked his brow. "Pirates?" he asked, not knowing much of the colony.

The girl nodded and held her arms close to her chest, as if warmth had escaped her in that brief moment. "Yes sir, pirates," she replied. "They attack on occasion, but never in earnest. A few merchants lose their cargo before they can be chased off, nothing more."

"Have there been any recent attacks?"

"Umm, yes, actually. There was one a few weeks ago. The pirates left empty-handed though, and one of them was captured."

"Their luck left them that day, wouldn't you say?" Roberts said with a smirk before taking a long drink of his ale.

The girl smiled along with him for a moment. "Are you staying in town for the afternoon, sir?"

Roberts nodded. "I will be here until nightfall."

"Should you like it, the pirate is on trial right now at the courthouse in the centre of town."

Roberts' ears perked up. "Oh? Is that why it's so empty here?" he said, looking around at the empty chairs and stools, and clean tables.

The girl nodded. "It's not so often we have a pirate on trial," she said, dimples showing at the corners of her cheeks. "If you want to see it, it's in a large brick building, you can't miss it."

"My thanks for the ale, the food, the information, and most of all your pretty smile," Roberts said as he too smiled and placed a coin in her hand.

The girl blushed bright red and thanked Roberts before heading back to the other side of the tavern.

Roberts took a slice of the marbled meat and a piece of sharp cheddar together and placed it on the edge of one of the biscuits, then took a bite. He looked out the window to the blue-yellow sky as the three different textures and tastes mixed to create a sublime taste greater than the sum of its parts.

A pirate's trial, hmm?

Roberts ate a few more slices of meat, a few more pieces of cheese, and another biscuit before chugging the large mug of pale ale. After he finished he set the mug down with a boisterous sigh, and then rose from his seat.

Roberts tossed the girl another coin on his way to the front of the tavern before exiting the establishment. He headed towards the centre of the town, searching for the courthouse the girl mentioned.

He walked up the muddy cobblestone, slick with water from rain or lingering puddles, and when he reached his destination it was just as the girl had said: there was no missing the courthouse.

The large brick building was longer and slightly taller than any other building around, and men and women of all ages were spilling out of its confines. The double doors at the front were wide open; not that it mattered though, as people had crowded around and blocked the way inside and all the way to the bottom of the stairs leading up. On the sides of the building, children and adults alike were standing atop boxes and barrels trying to catch a glimpse inside through the windows. More people were talking in groups and hovering around the stairs and entrance, not wanting to get involved with the larger crowd and bustle, but still interested in the goings on inside.

Ah, to lead a colony life such as this, where the most excitement is the trial of a pirate. Roberts let out a short laugh at the thought, then made his way up to the entrance.

As he passed by the townsfolk, he could hear them talking of the trial and what was going on inside. Each spoke of the villainy and the unspeakable atrocities the accused committed, and each person's recollection was more sinister than the last.

Roberts pushed past the men and women crowded around the entrance. As he tried to squeeze his large frame through the throng many flashed him dirty looks followed by wary glances. Soon, the commotion his well-above-average height caused forced others to look his way and move aside before he got near. A small part in the sea of the crowd formed, and they ushered him further into the courthouse.

Inside the courthouse, the waning light of the day provided a slight amount of light. The whole building was open, with a tall ceiling, and a large gallery for people to watch in the middle and the sides.

Near the entrance was an elevated wooden platform with two armed men blocking the stairs up. A man stood atop the podium, but Roberts wasn't able to see his face. Judging from the way he was wringing the life out of the cap in his hands, Roberts knew the man was in distress. A mirror reflected the little light from the windows straight on the man, so all could watch him with ease.

On the other end of the courtroom, another, taller podium took up much of the far wall. There sat five men wearing powdered wigs and ornate outfits of black and gold. Roberts could only assume, by their position, appearance, and sour disposition, that they were a panel of judges overseeing the trial.

Throughout the ordeal of entering and finding a suitable spot from which to listen and watch, Roberts caught the gist of the trial. From what he could gather, they were nearing the end, but it seemed like it had been drawn out for some time. Witnesses had been called, and a neutral party was recapping the pirate's various murders and depravities for the court.

Roberts found a spot in the gallery where he could see both the judges and the accused with ease. Looking at the pirate, he was a sorry sight. He had been washed for the trial, but fresh wounds covered his head, neck, and hands. Dark spots from punches or kicks had turned his skin a sickly colour, and his face took on a ghostly pallor from weakness and malnourishment. Even had he been well fed, the look in his eyes did not show Roberts he was a battle-hardened pirate. Either the man was a coward, or things were not as they seemed.

"Does the accused have any final words before deliberation?" the judge in the centre asked.

There was a small pause, and then the pirate spoke up. "Sirs, I say again that I am no pirate. I am falsely accus—"

The head judge held up his hand to silence the pirate. The judges looked perturbed, and the townsfolk in the gallery shouted and booed. The head judge called for silence, and soon the crowd quieted.

"The only falsehood... is the one you have been spouting here. We have brought witnesses forth to speak of your barbarisms. Give yourself some lasting grace, and admit your crimes."

The accused was on the verge of tears, and his fingers went white against the cap in his hands. "Please, you must listen to—"

"Enough," the judge shouted. "It is clear that you do not repent your actions in the least." The judge glanced to his contemporaries, and they nodded back at him. "This court finds you guilty of piracy, indecency, and acts of violence and depravity against the citizens of this fine town. By our powers given by the grace of God, and these citizens, you are hereby sentenced to death by hanging," the judge announced to raucous cheers.

As the town threw shame upon the man, Roberts couldn't help but become angered. Looking at the sorry state he was in, the words he said, and his own experience working with the world's best liars, cheats, and killers, he could tell that the man wasn't lying. He was no pirate, and he was about to hang for a crime he didn't commit.

This is not God's justice, only man's.

"Sentence will commence at sunset," the judge said. "This court is now dismissed."

Roberts found himself heading towards the exit of the courthouse without thought. He pushed past the others trying to leave the gallery and watched as guards took the accused away in chains. The guards took him outside of the courthouse, and Roberts followed close behind.

Upon exiting, the crowd threw all manner of things at the accused, from small rocks to vegetables. Though he suspected none truly knew the man or witnessed his crimes, they were willing to part with expensive vegetables that had taken so long to cultivate. Even if the accusations had been true, it spoke of the hatred those men and women held in their hearts in that moment.

Walking over the broken and smashed vegetables, Roberts continued to follow the trio at a distance. Other citizens followed as well, continuing to throw insults and objects at the man. As they ran out of items or patience, the other people began to trickle away and stop following, but Roberts continued onward.

Roberts wasn't sure himself why he kept following the man, but an idea soon formed in his head. *When I have the chance, I'll help him escape.*

Roberts waited, watching the three for a moment of opportunity. Out of the range of the angry voices, Roberts could hear the heavy plop of footsteps splashing water from crevices in the stone, and the piercing clang of the chains dangling off the man's listless arms and dragging legs.

The guards turned in front of a building, and the accused stopped in his tracks. He pulled his head up, and Roberts could swear he heard a large crick from the wrenching of unused bones. A few seconds passed with him standing there, deathly still, a painting of what was soon to come etched into Robert's memories.

Now! It must be now!

Before Roberts could act, the accused shoved his elbow into one of the guards, toppling him over to the wet stones below. He bent down and jumped over the guard before the other one could react, and ran as best he could down an alley.

The second guard shouted at the accused and ran after him down the alley as the first guard picked himself off the ground to give chase.

The man's escape attempt shocked Roberts still for a moment, but he ran after the three when he regained his composure. Halfway down the alley, the accused was lying on the ground, huddled up as one of the guards kicked him in the stomach. The other guard, the one who was attacked, bent over and clutched his chest to catch his breath.

"He's a feisty one," Roberts commented.

The two guards looked at him for a second, taking note of his size, but the escape attempt suppressed their awe. "Aye, but we caught the bastard," the uninjured guard said before he went back to kicking the man on the ground.

Roberts walked closer to the injured guard, and just as he reared back his massive fist the man's expression twisted.

Roberts slammed his fist into the man's jaw, and his face smashed on the stone, splashing more water and mud over the surrounding rocks.

The noise drew the second guard's attention, but before he could react Roberts grabbed him by the face and lifted him off the ground. He threw the man into the wall of the building beside him, slamming his back against the brick. Roberts let go, and the man fell in a heap.

Roberts bent down and searched the guards' belongings for a key. After fumbling through pockets and belts, he found a set of keys on an iron loop, and rose to his feet.

Roberts looked over at the man accused of piracy. His mouth was agape and his breathing heavy. Sweat dripped down his cheeks and over the bruises and scars on his face.

"Wh— who are you?" he asked. "What do you want with me?"

Roberts walked over, and the man tried to back away. "It's alright, friend. I'm here to save you."

The man calmed as Roberts reached over and used the keys on his shackles. "Why are you helping me?"

Roberts tried each of the keys on the loop, none of them working. "I was at your trial, and over the years I've learned how to tell when someone is telling the truth. You are no pirate, and I could not let this injustice stand." After a moment, Roberts found the correct key and unshackled the man.

Roberts helped the man to his shaking feet, who then dusted himself off. He held his hand out to Roberts. "I am called Desmond," he said.

Roberts shook the man's hand with a firm grip. "I am Bartholomew Roberts. It is a pleasure to meet you, Desmond."

Desmond's brow raised at Roberts' name. He looked away, his focus elsewhere. "Bartholomew Roberts... where have I heard that name?"

Roberts laughed, his hefty chest heaving with each bellow. "Perhaps you've heard of the pirate, Bartholomew Roberts?" he offered.

Desmond's eyes widened. "Ah yes, that must be it..." He

stared at Roberts for a moment, and Roberts held a grin on his face as he watched his expression change. "D—Don't tell me... you're...?" he said with a shaky point of the finger.

Roberts nodded. "I am the pirate Bartholomew Roberts," he confirmed.

Desmond stepped back from Roberts, his eyes as wide as saucers and his brows upturned like the arched back of a cat. "W-what do you want with me? You know I'm not a pirate... stay back!" he said at once, his hands raised in front of him.

Roberts held his hands up. "Desmond, as I told you, I came to help you. I know you're not a pirate, but I can help you escape from here. My ship is bound for Providencia. Upon arrival you are free to leave, but any further stay here would be... unwise," he said. Desmond still looked wary, but his legs had firmed up, and his hands returned to his sides. Roberts folded his arms and let out a sigh. "You have two options: come with me if you want to live, or stay here and perish."

Desmond stared at Roberts for another moment, and his eyes slowly lost the fear they had once had. "I want to go with you."

"Good choice," Roberts said with a smirk. He walked over and pulled Desmond further down the alley. "It would be best if we avoided the main streets for now."

Roberts and Desmond went down the alley and around the bend behind another house, then headed towards the harbour where the *Fortune* waited. They were careful to check each alley for people before walking down one, and alternated between the different streets when no one was looking.

"So, what brought you such misfortune, friend?" Roberts asked as he looked around the corner of a wooden house.

"Truly, I don't know who it was I angered," he replied. "I'm a sailor, nothing more. I don't belong with any company, and so I find work on the next port. The night before the true villains attacked, I had far too much to drink, and I found myself in the tank the following morning." The two men moved down the next street. "No sooner had I awoken than I was charged with piracy."

"Tch," Roberts spat. "They meant for you to serve as

scapegoat for the attack to appease the populace."

"That looks the size of it."

"Well, no more, friend. Look, there is our longboat. We make it to that, and we are free." Roberts pointed to the longboats they had used to arrive at the pier. His men were loading them with supplies of barrels, bags, and boxes. "And we seem to have fortune on our side; my men are about to set off. Come, your freedom awaits," Roberts said, looking over his shoulder with a grin pulling at his cheeks.

Before they could make for the pier, they heard loud shouting coming from the centre of town. Both of their heads snapped to the side, towards the noise, and their expressions grew dire.

"We must move, now," Roberts said.

"Yes."

Roberts went out from the house they were hiding behind and walked at a brisk but leisurely pace towards the pier. Desmond came up beside him, kept his head down, and tried to hide behind the side of the larger man.

As they walked they passed by some villagers, but the men and women were too busy looking at the commotion towards the centre of town to take notice. Their pace quickened the closer they were to the pier, and soon their boots were slamming on the wooden planks as they ran to the longboats.

"Men, we have a new recruit, and it is imperative that he returns to *Fortune* post-haste."

Roberts pulled Desmond over to one of the longboats already filled with cargo. Desmond climbed inside, aided, or hindered, by Roberts' insistent pushing and prodding.

Every few seconds Roberts glanced from Desmond and the longboat over to the pier where they had come from. His head and eyes darted back and forth across the wooden platform as he searched for trouble.

After Desmond sat in the longboat and Roberts began entering it, trouble came. Several men from the local militia stormed out of town to the pier. One man at the head of the pack looked back and forth down the pier, then waved his hand to those with him. The men spread out down the pier and began questioning the merchants and fishermen there.

"Get down, get down!" Roberts ordered in a loud whisper as he waved his hand towards Desmond.

Desmond dropped from his seat and went under the plank, lying flat against the bottom of the longboat. "W-what should I do?" Desmond stuttered, the tremor inside escaping him as he spoke.

"Stay still, and don't make a sound," Roberts said. He looked over to his men. "Men, as you were."

Roberts glanced around the longboat, then reached over and grabbed a rolled blanket from the side. He unfurled it and threw it on top of the plank and covered Desmond. Roberts touched up the edges of the blanket to cover the man fully, then sat down in the longboat.

As soon as he sat down, one of the armed militiamen walked over to them. "Have any of you noticed a man of your build with bruises pass by here recently?" he asked.

Roberts' men shook their heads. "Should we be concerned, sir?" Roberts asked.

The militiaman looked at Roberts, taking in his height. "No, nothing a man of your stature need concern himself with." The man glanced around at the longboats Roberts' crew were filling with supplies, and the large stacks piled near the edge of the pier offshoot they were on. "What's all this?"

"Supplies for our trip. Headed north to Port Royal."

The man nodded and took a few steps around the supplies, looking them over as he held his weapon tight. Roberts flashed his men looks, and their hands rested at their hips, close to their hidden weapons. Roberts inched his hand over to the side of the longboat where a musket was fastened. He didn't pull it out, but kept his hand steady on the barrel.

The militiaman took his time looking over the cargo, glancing in the longboats for far longer than was necessary. His eyes were sharp, and his brows sharper still. They were furrowed down towards the bridge of his nose, wrinkles appearing in the gap.

"Is there a problem with our cargo, sir?"

"No, no issues here," the man replied. "What was it you were transporting again?"

Roberts forced a smile. "Didn't say, sir. We're bringing bibles to the new world." Roberts took his hand off the musket, reached in his pocket, and pulled out the bible he had. "Nothing more needed than the holy word for the heathen natives. Why not sit with us for a spell, and we can talk scripture?" Roberts asked, a bit of Hank's vocabulary creeping in.

The man shook his head. "No time for that, preacher," he said. "Carry on."

The militiaman nodded to the group of them, and then moved on down the pier to continue his search. After the sound of his boots smacking against the wood was far enough away, Roberts let out a sigh. Beneath him, he could hear Desmond mimicking him.

Roberts lifted the edge of the blanket to see Desmond there, looking up at him. "Just a bit longer and we'll be on our ship," Roberts said.

Desmond nodded. "You sure are quick-footed. If I didn't know any better, I'd believe your story too."

Roberts bowed. "My thanks," he said before laughing.

Roberts placed the blanket down, then brought out oars. His crewmates released the longboat from the dock, and Roberts rowed the boat back to the *Fortune*. Once there, Roberts and Desmond climbed up rope ladders to board as other crewmates prepared to bring up the longboat full of supplies.

Hank met with Roberts and Desmond. "Welcome back, Captain," he said. "Another stowaway for us?"

"Yes, it appears that way. Desmond, this is my first mate, Hank Abbott. Hank, this is Desmond. He was falsely accused of piracy, so I thought to help him reach safe haven in Providencia."

Hank grinned as he nodded. "I understand. So, am I to assume we should prepare to leave?"

"As soon as the supplies are aboard, yes. The sooner the better."

Hank nodded once more, then looked at Desmond. "Pleasure meeting you Desmond," he said.

Desmond returned the pleasantry, and Hank headed back to the helm to instruct the crew. "Sir, I cannot thank you enough for the kindness you have shown me this day. I—"

Roberts placed both his hands on the man's shoulders. "I will have no more talk of giving thanks. I only did what righteousness demanded."

Desmond grinned. "For a pirate to talk of righteousness... the world is surely in a sorry state," he said.

Roberts nodded and stroked his chin. "Yes, that it is. We do all that we can to simply live another day it seems."

"By your mercy, and the Lord's grace, I shall see another. I only hope that tomorrow's trial is not so difficult to overcome as this one."

"That is every man's hope," Roberts replied. He smirked. "Now, what say we have a toast to celebrate your head remaining on your shoulders?"

Desmond gave a morbid chuckle. "That sounds delightful."

2. SABOTAGE

From the Journal of Bartholomew Roberts
Entry #56 Dated July 7th, No Year Given

A young man named Desmond has temporarily joined our outfit for the short trip between San Andrés and Providencia.

He was to be hanged for supposed crimes, though he claimed innocence. Believing in that innocence, I took it upon myself to free the man from his bondage and eventual undue punishment.

Am I a fool to act thusly? Each action as a pirate brings with it a bevy of possible consequences, and any action that brings attention to us can bring no good.

And yet, to stand idly by would mean I would be as much to blame for the man's death as those who falsely convicted him.

When is it just to let someone die, or for that matter, to kill? The bible says thou shalt not kill, but also to follow the laws of man as they are there by the will of God.

But, if all men sin, how can man's laws be without sin?

Fortune arrived at Providencia well after nightfall, when the moon and the stars were all that illuminated their journey. The star's reflection danced on the waves in their path and wake.

From the little light available it was hard to see the town properly, but the ships in the harbour and the homes and businesses were lit up from lanterns. A lighthouse to the east of the harbour shone its light down their way, and helped the crew of Fortune anchor far away from the other tallships.

To avoid detection, Roberts also had the crew cover the name of their ship with loose canvas. It gave the appearance of a ramshackle ship, but protected them from the crews that knew the name.

Once anchored, Roberts made to join some crewmates ashore to look for Walter Kennedy and his crew. It was late into night, but not so late that night-time revelry was at an end. Roberts hoped that they would find Kennedy and his comrades amongst the revellers.

Roberts and Hank boarded a longboat for shore with ten other crewmates and their fugitive stowaway Desmond. The dark waters illuminated by a lantern swinging off the bow. The light bounced off the water and cast long shadows on the creases and wrinkles on his crew's cragged faces. Their expressions reflected the sombre tone of the time of day, and what they were about to do.

"Hank, I would have you and some men inspect the taverns and inns ashore. I and the rest will see if we can find Kennedy or his companions' ships aboard this longboat."

"How will you know what ships are theirs?"

"I would not be much of a captain were I to forget the faces of my former men. Should my memory fail me, luck may be on our side if Kennedy is captain of one of the ships. I have an idea of what the name of that ship may be."

Hank nodded. "Understood, Captain. If we find anything I'll send a man out to look for you on the pier."

Desmond, sitting nearby, leaned in closer to Roberts. "Searching for someone in Providencia?" he asked.

"Yes... an old crewmate who stole away with one of our vessels some time ago."

Desmond's eyes seemed to light up like a child seeing a new toy. "That so?" he said, pulling in closer still. "You going to have some battle at sea over the ship you lost? Pirate's vengeance on the high seas?"

Roberts paused for a moment, thinking over the prospect. "I should like to avoid a battle if possible." He looked off to the side of the longboat.

"Right, right..." Desmond said, trailing off as he looked at Roberts.

Is that what we're really here for? Vengeance, not justice? Roberts took in a deep breath of the cool night air and let it out.

The longboat knocked up against the pier, and the men staying behind held it steady for those leaving. With a last goodbye, Hank left towards the town, his boots echoing off the wooden planks over the moonlit waters.

Roberts stepped up to the dock and helped Desmond up to the pier. "Well, my friend, I suppose this is where we part ways."

"I suppose so..." Desmond replied. He put his hand out to shake Roberts'. "Though it was a short journey, I enjoyed the company of you and your men, Roberts. If only all pirates were as you were, perhaps the seas would be safer."

Roberts chuckled and shook Desmond's hand. "If only," he said.

After another pleasantry, Desmond went off towards town, leaving Roberts and his remaining crewmates at the longboat.

Roberts jumped back into the longboat, where his crew waited for him.

"So Captain, what's the plan? Douse the lantern and push the boat around the harbour?" one crewmate asked.

Roberts put palm to chin as he thought it over. He looked

around at the other ships with men aboard them, drinking and singing, distracted, and then scanned the water. The stars were visible against the dark water, broken only by the waves from their boat.

"We're easily spotted on a night such as this," Roberts said. "We must blend in by standing out. How much of the good stuff do we have?"

The five crewmates who remained with Roberts checked their surroundings, under their legs and behind them, searching for bottles. A few pulled out several bottles filled with dark liquid from under their seats.

"That should do. Take us out, and get your singing voices ready men. We're celebrating."

After Roberts instructed the crew to make it look as if they were drinking to intoxication rather than actually drinking to intoxication, they rowed the longboat out towards the middle of the harbour.

Roberts motioned to the crewmates rowing to move aside and he took over. "Sing, men, sing!" he said in a forceful whisper.

The crew glanced from side to side at their mates, unsure of who would answer the call first, and nervous to be the one to start. Two of the boys stuttered and started singing, and the others joined in, sipping from their drinks between beats.

> ♪ In Amsterdam there lived a maid,
> Mark well what I do say!
> In Amsterdam there lived a maid,
> And she was mistress of her trade.
> I'll go no more a-roving with you fair maid! ♪

Roberts shifted his strokes to his mate's singing beat, keeping it slow and methodical. The sound of his strokes overpowered the men's song at first, but as they sipped on their drinks they soon found their voices.

His mates' breathing carried the smell of the alcohol to his nose, tickling it with harsh bitterness. He turned his head to the side and focused on the rowing and the smell of the sea and the song they sang.

They were quick to reach the tallships anchored in the harbour, the men aboard drinking on the weather deck in the cold night. They wore thick coats and wool caps as they drank from tin cups.

> ♪ Windy weather boys, stormy weather, boys
> When the wind blows we're all together, boys
> Blow ye winds westerly, blow ye winds, blow
> Jolly sou'wester, boys, steady she goes. ♪

Roberts weaved the boat to and fro, bringing them close enough to the tallships to read the names painted on their sides. He couldn't see any ship that he was familiar with, so he kept rowing.

As the longboat passed the ships, the crews took note of Roberts and his men and their boisterousness. The jovial singing from his crew—who had perhaps taken a bit too much to drink in the spirit of things—had roused the men on the tallships to join in. Most of the ships were near to one another, and so began a great chorus on the sea. Dozens of men began singing in unison, and their voices carried across the waters and bounced off ships' hulls. It was loud enough for Roberts to feel it in his chest.

> ♪ Gather together young men and hear this tale
> Of a man of the seas you all should know well
> His name is Great Gus and of this you be sure
> He was the best mate ye could ask for in all the land ♪

Roberts was singing along as well, to keep with their ruse. Being Welsh, Roberts had a natural singing voice, given the language's melodic nature, and he often enjoyed chanting side by side with his crew. He had to force himself to stay seated, as the chorus caused an itch in his heel. He wanted to join his men in their light dance aboard the longboat, but he needed to pay attention to the names of the ships.

There was the *Black Pearl*, the *Inferno*, the *Seaswift*, and the *Surprise* to Roberts' right, closer to the town. And to his left, further to sea, he saw the *Jack and Nab*, the *Captain's Delight*, and *At The Ready*. They varied in size and class, and some didn't even have a gun deck to speak of, which eliminated them from the possibilities.

The rowing was slow and tiring, and Roberts didn't have the luxury of a reprieve as his crewmates seemed to forget their purpose after a time. They passed ship after ship at a steady pace for nearly an hour, and Roberts couldn't see any ship name that he recognized.

Then, as the longboat passed the middle of the harbour, he saw three sloops of war anchored parallel to each other. The first had two masts, and the other two ships had three each.

When Roberts noticed the name of the first ship his singing stopped in his throat, a lump gripping hold of his voice.

The name *Gallant* was written on the side of the small sloop-of-war—the same name for a ship that his old friend-turned-enemy Walter Kennedy said he would use should he become a captain.

The other men didn't take notice of Roberts' sudden pause in the middle of their shanty, and continued to sing unawares of their Captain's demeanour. The crews of the various ships also kept up the chant, though many were now off-tempo with those who started the tune.

Roberts resumed rowing, and turned the longboat around to bring it back to the pier. He couldn't tell if it was from the constant rowing, or from seeing the name of that ship, but his heart was pounding in his ears and he felt hot around the collar. The jolly chants of his brothers turned to nothing, and all he could hear was the pounding of his chest and deep breaths through his nose.

The boat smacked against the pier and bounced back, jolting the other crewmates back to awareness. They stopped their singing short and glanced around at their surroundings. Off in the distance, the ships they had left were still singing those well-travelled tunes, and they could still be heard even at the pier.

"Captain, are you well? You look a touch flush," one of the men said.

Another man held out a bottle of rum towards Roberts.

"Here, Captain, for what ails you."

Roberts glanced up at the dark bottle in front of him, then took it in hand and chugged a generous amount. He barely felt the sting as it burned his tongue and throat on the way down. He let out a loud gasp as he removed the bottle from his lips and handed it back to his crewmate.

"He's here," Roberts said. "Walter Kennedy is here, of this I have no doubt."

Some of the men's eyes widened as they glanced from Roberts back out to the many ships in the harbour. "How can you be sure? Did you see his ship?"

Roberts nodded. "Aye, the *Gallant*, the smallest in that line of ships over there," he said as he nodded towards the three sloops-of-war.

The crewmates all turned to look at the three ships Roberts motioned towards. After a quick glance, they looked at him again, this time with wide grins and devilish smiles.

"Now we jus' have to find the bastard, then we'll show him what-for, right Captain?"

Roberts looked up at the crewmate who spoke. A grin curled the corners of his lips, and his eyes betrayed a deep lust for blood and vengeance. Roberts wondered if his own eyes looked that way as well, such was his anger in that moment. He simply nodded to the crewmate, and the men turned into schoolchildren eager for a tussle.

Roberts' face was still hot, and his thoughts were on his former friend and crewmate who wronged him. He cast his gaze to the floorboards of the longboat. *Why do I feel such anger in my heart? How long has this hate been brewing in my soul?* Roberts looked up at his jovial mates in front of him. *Is it wrong to feel this way?* Roberts sat up and reached for the book in his breast pocket which he felt had the answer, but the sound of heavy footsteps stopped him.

"Captain!" Hank's voice called to Roberts.

Roberts rose to his feet, then pulled himself up to the pier as he turned around to meet with Hank. His first mate was jogging towards him down the pier and waving.

"Did you find them?" Roberts asked when Hank came close.

"Aye, we did," Hank replied. "We found Kennedy and his cohorts drinking together at an inn not far from here. I had some of Edward's men who joined him not long ago secure a table to listen in and see if they can glean some information on where they may be heading next. Were you able to find their ships?"

Roberts nodded and pointed over to the row of ships. "The smallest on the right is Kennedy's, and I have no doubt that the other two are his companions."

"Thatch isn't due to arrive for another day, weather permitting. If they plan to leave on the morrow, then we must delay one of those ship's departure. We cannot fight all three ships, even with Thatch's help."

Roberts glanced around, wondering just how they would go about delaying a ship without drawing unwanted attention. After a moment of not-so-helpful ideas floating in his head, Roberts turned back around to Hank.

"We must first find out if they plan to set out tomorrow or not, and where. If they are to leave, we'll figure out something."

Roberts motioned for the other men to join them, then they followed Hank to the inn where Kennedy and his companions were staying. Hank led them to the back entrance of a small three-storey building close to the middle of the pier.

They entered the building through the server's entrance, and though there were men and women who worked at the inn they paid the pirates no heed. They were too busy to mind them, and chose to continue their work instead.

Hank walked casually through a hallway to the main hall and held the door open as he leaned over the threshold. "Kennedy and friends are at a table over in the corner there," Hank said, his eyes pointing where his hand dare not.

Roberts stepped forward and leaned inside as well. The main hall was bustling with activity, the tables and booths filled with patrons of all sorts. Merchants, sailors, and no doubt more pirates, were dining and drinking and telling stories in that room.

He followed Hank's eyes towards the corner of the other side of the room, and first noticed Edward's men sitting in a booth with drinks in hand, having a light conversation. Then, in the next seats over, he saw men he didn't recognize huddled together.

After a moment, the men pulled away from their huddle and got out of the booth they were sitting at. Then, Roberts saw the man they had been looking for, Walter Kennedy, standing there. Though his friend's face had changed a bit over the years—his cheeks shallow and his muscles more defined—there was no doubt it was the same Irishman he had worked with before.

Once more, Roberts felt the hot flash of anger rush over him, and he found it difficult to control himself in the face of the man responsible. His feet moved of their own accord, but Hank's hand on Roberts' chest stopped him.

"They're coming this way," Hank said as he tried to push the massive Roberts back.

Roberts stepped back, and Hank pulled the door closed most of the way. Hank left a hair's breadth open so he could see through and watch their adversaries.

Roberts had to close his eyes, ball his fists, and take a few breaths to calm himself. He didn't know where this anger was coming from, and he was finding it difficult to cope with.

"They went upstairs to a room," Hank said over his shoulder. "Let's hope Edward's men were able to find something out. I'll go and fetch them."

Hank walked through the door, checked his sides, then went to retrieve the spies they had left. After a moment of talk, the men returned with Hank to the back of the inn.

"They say Kennedy and his associates got spooked and went to a room to finish discussing their plans. They were only able to find out that they do plan on leaving tomorrow, but not their heading."

Roberts was looking at the floor in silence as his companions stared at him.

"Bartholomew?" Hank called.

"I'm thinking," he replied, though in truth he was still trying to calm himself. After another moment, he looked up at Hank and the other crewmates. "We need to hear what's going on in that room... We might be able to watch them as they depart, but that doesn't mean they won't change course later. We may be after Kennedy, but Edward is after the other crews. If things go south, we'll need to know where they're heading."

"What do we do then? We can't very well listen outside the door in full view of the inn's patrons, and there aren't any open balconies we could spy from."

Roberts took another moment to look in his men's eyes. "I'll need a drill... and a loud distraction."

Hank turned to Edward's men. "You'll be able to handle the distraction, won't you gents?" The men nodded and smiled in a way that spoke of their experience and joy in such matters. "Good. We'll give you a signal when we're ready." Hank pointed to one of their crewmates. "You find us a drill. There may be one in the stable out back. If not, ask the workers for one."

The crewmate turned to leave the inn in search of the drill, but Roberts stopped him. "We'll be in the room to the right of Kennedy, so bring the drill there." The crewmate gave an "Aye, Captain" before turning around again.

"Come, Hank, let's secure us a room." Roberts exited the hallway with Hank and the other crewmates following behind.

The five men from Edward's crew walked over to a table in the middle of the inn and joined a group playing a game with cards. Roberts went up the stairs to the second floor and kept a close watch on the door leading to Kennedy's room.

When they approached, Roberts took a quick glance at the room below, taking note of the inn staff. None were looking their way, so Roberts tapped on the door to the room they wanted to enter. If luck were on their side it would be empty, but the chances of that were unlikely.

It almost seemed as if luck was on their side, as there was no answer to Roberts' call. Roberts knocked on the door again, louder this time, and then came an answer.

"Hold, hold a moment," a man shouted from beyond the door.

After a few seconds, and a few grunting noises, Roberts

heard footsteps coming to the door. The door opened, and a short and stocky man appeared before them. He wore a robe and nothing more, and his cheeks were red and his forehead slick with sweat.

"What in the Devil's name do you..." the man said, trailing off as his gaze shifted from the floor up Roberts' massive frame.

"We have need of your room for the moment, sir. If you'll excuse us," Roberts said.

Before the man could respond, Roberts placed his hand over the man's mouth and held fast to his cheeks. He pushed the man back into the room, and he and his crewmates entered.

In a bed near the back of the room, a woman was watching what was happening, and she let out a gasp as she sat up. Roberts bade her to quiet herself with a finger to his lips and a threatening look. She muffled a scream with her hands as tears formed in her eyes.

Hank closed the door behind them with a quick look towards the inn's first floor. "It doesn't appear as if we were seen," he said. "So far, so good."

Roberts pushed the man he was holding back to the bed next to the woman, and then leaned down to stare straight in his eyes. "Stay quiet, and nothing bad will happen to you. Understood?"

The man nodded as best he could, and Roberts released him with a small push causing him to fall on the bed. The woman came close to him and grabbed hold of his arm, the fear in both of their eyes telling Roberts that they would stay quiet.

Roberts looked at his crewmates. "Keep watch on them, and make sure we're not heard," he said. After his crew acknowledged the order, he went over to join Hank at the wall next to Kennedy's room.

Hank had his ear pressed up against the wall, his eyes closed, and his hands sprawled to his sides. Roberts joined his first mate in trying to listen through the wall, but he could only hear muffled voices and heavy boots smacking against the floor.

Before he could comment on the situation, there was a knock at the door. Roberts and Hank looked at each other, brows raised. Roberts removed himself from the wall and walked over to the door.

"Yes?" he called.

"Captain? I have the drill."

Roberts opened the door, glanced around the crewmate, and then pulled him in. The crewmate handed a small brace drill to Roberts.

"This will do nicely," Roberts said. He turned to Hank. "Hank, give the signal and keep watch for us."

Hank went to the door and opened it up wide. He stepped out, and then waved to give Edward's crewmates the signal. Hank came back in the room and left the door open a hair to see through.

Roberts moved to the other end of the wall, towards the back of the inn, and waited with the hand drill propped against the wood. He watched the door and Hank's back, his hands tensing on the curves of the brace handle and spindle.

After a moment's wait, Roberts could hear a rising commotion from beyond the door. It sounded as if a fight was breaking out downstairs, but it hadn't yet escalated beyond words. Another moment passed, and Roberts head a crash of glass, then shouting, and soon the whole inn erupted in noise.

Roberts had to give credit to Edward's men, as they knew how to make a ruckus. The first floor of the inn was already loud, and getting louder. Bottles and cups were thrown, chairs and tables broken, and all the while the shouts and fighting intensified. Some projectiles flew up to the second floor, knocking against the walls and doors of the inn's patrons.

Hank had to close the door shut for a moment as some of the debris was flung his way. Afterwards, he opened it up again and shifted his feet. He seemed to be looking at something. A moment passed, and Hank waved his hand in Roberts' direction without moving his focus from the opening in the door.

Roberts cranked the brace, moving the bit of the drill into

the wood of the wall. With each turn of the brace, the bit dug into the grains of the wood. The noise of the inn overtook the noise of the wood breaking.

Roberts was already sweating, though not from the hard labour. He was a man of keen fitness, having been a sailor so long, and no small amount of drilling would tire him. His sweat came from the heat of the room, and the heat of stress. He kept splitting his focus from the drill and the wooden wall to his companion at the door, waiting for a signal to stop.

Roberts' hand slipped as the bit surged through the wall. The brace knocked against the wood with a loud thump, which caused all in the room, including Hank, to turn his way.

Roberts flashed his gaze over to Hank, and his horrified expression said everything. That thump was loud enough to be heard over the noise of the inn. He turned back to the drill and yanked it out of the wall, adding a scraping sound to the mix. He shook his head as his face washed over with rage over his blunders. He set the drill down on the floor and rushed to the bed with the room's occupants still sitting atop it.

"Make some noises as if you're having relations!" he said in a haste.

The man looked him up and down as if he were mad. "I shall do no su—"

Roberts directed his best vision of anger towards the two and said "Now!"

The tone and force of Roberts' words visibly shook the man, and he flashed his companion a flustered glance before he made some strained noises. His lover also joined in, and the two began making uneasy noises one might make during copulation—or at that point they could have been imitating goats, Roberts was unsure. After a moment, the two seemed to find their rhythm and it sounded more akin to the act than acting.

Roberts waved to his men, and they took hold of the bedframe. Following Roberts' lead, they rocked the bed back and forth with the couple's noises, ensuring it smacked against the wall a few times and scraped the floor some. The whole affair gave the appearance of some enthusiastic, though peculiar, love-making, which Roberts' hoped would cover for the noise made by the drill.

Roberts looked at Hank, and after a moment he closed the door, then went over to the hole Roberts had made. Hank took a look into the room and then listened through the hole, before waving to Roberts.

Roberts guided the couple and his crew into a crescendo finale before slowing the bed and the noise to a gradual finish, and then joined Hank.

Hank periodically switched from listening to peering through the hole in the wall. After a moment, he leaned over and whispered to Roberts.

"They're none the wiser about the hole. They seem to be discussing the noise."

Hank pressed his ear up against the wall once more and closed his eyes. Minutes passed with him listening intently to the conversation beyond the wall. He gave nary a clue of the goings on beyond a few shakes of his head. After the noise outside died down, and some more waiting, Hank's eyes shot open and he held his hand up.

Roberts waited on baited breath for Hank to say something, to tell them the news they so desperately wanted to hear. Hank's mouth was half open, the words on the tip of his tongue, and clear anticipation in his eyes. He too wanted to tell of what he was hearing, but didn't want to miss a detail.

"They leave on the morrow, as Edward's men said," Hank relayed in a whisper, his ear still pressed against the wood. "They head west until out of sight of the island, where they wait for their mark, a ship they plan to attack, at sunset." Hank listened for another minute before pulling himself away from the wall. "Now we have what we need. We can attack them with Edward and finally have our vengeance."

The other men in the room uttered slight hoots and chuckles, their fists clenched and smiles all around. Roberts once more thought on the word Hank used, and just what they were here to accomplish. Before he could ponder on what he was going to do with Walter Kennedy, Hank spoke again.

"So... have you thought about how we will delay one of their ships?"

In truth, Roberts hadn't had the chance, but when he looked at the hole beyond Hank's head, and the drill now lying on the floor, an idea formed.

"I'm of the mind that Kennedy's ship could use some modifications," he said as he picked up the drill.

3. A PERSONAL DECISION

From the Journal of Bartholomew Roberts
Entry #59 Dated July 10th, No Year Given

The weight of sin is heavy on my heart as of late.

I must make a decision which I have avoided for years, and I know not what I should do.

I sensed an anger well inside me which I did not know I possessed upon seeing Walter Kennedy. That anger calls for his head, but I know in my heart, and from the scriptures, that no good can come from anger.

I am a conflicted and contradictory man in many ways, and this decision serves now as a symbol of those contradictions.

I sin, yet I think I am fit to carry out justice. I am fallible, yet I think I am fit to judge others. I have anger in my heart, yet I seek so-called righteousness.

I am reminded of Luke's words of caution when trying to remove a speck from another's eye when there is a beam in one's own.

How can I say I am doing the work of God when I cannot tell if I have a beam affixed to my own eye?

Roberts and others on the *Fortune* watched the three ships owned by their enemies through the magnifying lenses of spyglasses. They kept a close eye on them as they prepared their ships to sail by the light of the morning sun.

The clear rays of light burst forward from across the horizon, affording Roberts a clear view of the three ships. He watched as the crews prepared their ships to leave, but paid special attention to the Gallant, the ship owned by Walter Kennedy.

Roberts and crew had been watching since the Gallant's initial preparations, and they were close to setting sail with nary a notion that anything was the matter with their ship. But Roberts noticed two crewmates rush up from below deck. They went straight to Kennedy, explained something to him, and then the three went back into the bowels of the ship.

"It appears they've found the holes we left for them," Hank said as he pulled away his own spyglass and looked over at Roberts.

"Now, all that's left is for the other ships to separate from the Gallant while they are stuck with repairs."

"Just as long as Kennedy doesn't suspect foul-play, we should be well to do."

"If luck is with us, they'll mistake the holes we left for wormrot."

Hank grinned. "Well, Captain, if there's one thing I've learned about you, it's that you're the luckiest bastard to sail the seven seas."

Roberts and Hank both had a good chuckle, a rare event as of late, and it reminded him of their former captain, Howell Davis. Davis was a man of good humour but decisive action, and Roberts admired him. The thought brought with it a twinge of melancholy to the laughter, the kind only nostalgia and loss can bring.

Roberts pushed away the sad thoughts and peered through the small looking-glass once more to take in the view of the small sloop. It had two decent-sized masts, a hearty-looking crew, and planks not the worse for wear. From what Roberts could tell, the ship was fair to new, which meant Kennedy might not have been its captain for long.

"Tell me, Hank, do you recognize any aboard the Gallant?" Roberts asked.

Hank cast a brief sidelong glance at Roberts with his brow raised, then returned his attention to his spyglass. He stepped forward, closer to the ship railing, to see if he could get a better view. He moved his spyglass around, covering the Gallant from stem to stern.

"Strange," Hank muttered. "I fail to recognize any of the men working on that ship, save Kennedy from earlier of course."

"It seems our old friend has lost some company along the way," Roberts commented, leaning against the Fortune's railing.

Hank chuckled. "I reckon his leadership came into question."

"Perhaps," Roberts replied.

He stared at the planks of the sole, recalling the times when both he and Kennedy and Hank had shared the same space. Though at times exasperating, Roberts felt a kinship towards Kennedy. It was that kinship which made Roberts nostalgic in that moment, but it also helped him understand exactly why the betrayal had stung so much over time.

The sound of Hank shuffling brought Roberts' attention back, and he looked up to see Hank peering at the Gallant through his spyglass again. Roberts turned around and did the same, and he could see Kennedy back on the top deck again.

Kennedy went over to the side of the ship where his companion's ships were floating. He had one hand cupped over his mouth, and he was shouting something over the side at them. Soon, the men in the other pirate ship listened to what he was saying, and presumably their captain was conversing with him.

The conversation went on for a few moments, and the other captain appeared vexed by Kennedy. He left the conversation with a huff and a wave of his hands. Kennedy's crew stared at him as his hand dropped to his side. He turned around and seemed startled at the men gathered around him. After a moment, he too waved them away with a word, and then went back below deck.

After a few moments, the two larger sloops let loose their sails and headed off to the west, just as they had overheard. They left the Gallant behind too, just as they had hoped.

Roberts lips curled into a sly smile as he turned to look at Hank, who was also smiling. "Men!" Roberts called as he faced the crew. "I want this ship ready to sail at a moment's notice. We need to follow that sloop out to sea, where we can take the battle to her without fear of interruption from the Providencia locals. We'll have need of all our speed in the coming battle, and you'll need to keep your wits about you if we're to succeed... though I understand wits may be hard for some of you to come by," he said with a jovial chuckle, which the crew reciprocated.

As the men prepared the ship, Roberts walked off towards the bow cabin. "Hank, I'm going to take a moment of rest in the cabin. Inform me when the Gallant begins to move, would you?"

"Aye, Captain," he replied behind Roberts.

Bartholomew Roberts left the crew to their task, and entered the small cabin at the front of the ship. He almost had to bend over to walk around, but it was his most favourite spot aboard the Fortune. He found its viewing windows out to the bow pleasant for contemplation, and there was a large table on which he could dine should he choose to. And, whether he wanted company or simply a moment of reprieve, it never felt too empty or too crowded. It was the perfect size, even if it took a bend of the knee to traverse.

Roberts went to the far side of the cabin, turned a chair around, and leaned back in it as he watched the goings on in Providencia. The sun had risen above the horizon to Roberts right. Though he couldn't see the sun itself, its brilliance shone against the buildings and shadows cast away from it.

Sailors in various combinations of cotton and wool cloth greeted each other as they prepared to sell the last of their cargo before sailing off. Men and women and children all began their morning routines, walking this way and that, not aware that soon, just off their shores, pirates would be battling each other.

As Roberts watched the people going about their business, the fatigue and tiredness that had built up over his lack of sleep struck him, and he let out a great yawn. His eyes grew heavy, and he had trouble keeping them open. As it usually happens, before he could take notice, he was falling asleep.

Roberts awoke with a start as his chair slammed on the planks of the cabin. He took a deep breath in through his nose and flashed his gaze to the left and right of him to gather his bearings. He soon remembered where he was, and his senses came rushing back to him.

His gaze soon settled upon the bow of the ship once more, and he noticed that not much had changed since the time of his sleep other than the light on the pier and town.

The startling awakening had jolted him and caused a stir in his heart, which now beat loudly in his chest. As he calmed himself, he once more remembered what he was waiting for, and his thoughts turned to his decision.

He knew what the book in his pocket would say, and he felt the itch to pull it out for the guidance it always provided him, but at the same time he wanted to leave it where it was. He wanted to keep his anger for Kennedy, and work the same justice his friend, Edward Thatch, spoke of.

The door opened, startling Roberts. He rose to his feet and turned around to see Hank leaning in through the doorway. "The *Gallant* is readying their sails, Captain," he said.

Roberts nodded, and Hank nodded back before starting to leave and close the door. "Hank," Roberts called. "A moment... please?"

Hank turned back around, a strange look in his eyes, and entered the cabin, closing the door behind him. "Yes, Captain?"

Roberts turned his seat around towards the table and waited until Hank was seated. "I..." he began, but he didn't know what to say. He leaned forward and looked away from Hank's gaze for a moment, searching for the right words. "I need your help," he said finally.

Hank leaned back in his chair. "It's about Kennedy, isn't it?"

Roberts replied with a curt nod of the head, but he didn't look Hank in the eyes. "I... I know not what I should do. I fear that time and anger has clouded my judgement, and I am in need of guidance." Even Roberts could hear the pleading in his own voice. He thought himself pathetic, but when he looked up at his first mate, Hank, he had a smile on his face. "You think I am jesting?"

Hank shook his head. "No—no, of course not," he said profusely. "I know that when the time comes you'll know what to do. You always do."

Roberts couldn't help but cock his brow and sit up in his chair. "But... what of the crew? They have a say in this decision as well, and they seem to be calling for Kennedy's blood."

Hank waved his hand as though he were waving away smoke. "The crew will respect your decision on the matter. Kennedy was your friend first and foremost, and you are the captain. You have the right and authority to make this decision."

Roberts let out a sigh and leaned back in his chair. "But what if I make the wrong decision?"

Hank stared at Roberts for a moment, and then he got up from his chair. He walked over to a cabinet at the side of the cabin and pulled out a bottle of whiskey. He poured some of the drink into two glasses, then handed one to Roberts.

"Drink," he commanded. Roberts downed the alcohol in one great gulp, barely letting the taste of it touch his tongue. Hank did the same, and then placed the cup on the table.

"Trust in yourself," he said, standing tall above the sitting Roberts. "It's brought you this far, hasn't it?"

Hank didn't wait for Roberts to give him an answer, instead electing to leave the cabin and prepare the ship with the other crewmates.

Roberts waited for a moment, his empty cup still in hand, thinking on what his first mate had said. He placed the cup on the table next to Hank's, rose from his seat, and left the cabin.

The sun hit his eyes and forced his hand up to cover the blinding rays. He looked over towards the source, and saw the *Gallant* and her crew preparing to leave once more. The men on the weather deck were unlashing the sails, readying them for the orders to drop the canvas.

When Roberts turned his attention back to his own crew, he noticed several of the men looking at him. He could see the anticipation in their eyes, the tension in their clenched fists and force building in their legs. They were waiting for him to make the call. Even though they too were ready to drop the sails and head out for battle, they wanted him to direct their built-up energy from two years gone by.

"Alright men, let's capture us a sloop!" Roberts shouted.

The men responded with a loud chorus of cheers and hoots. The energy and tension surged from them in an instant, and the roar of their fervour filled the ship and spilled out like a great wave from a mighty storm. Soon, they would direct that storm at the *Gallant*, and there would be no escape for her. Of that, Roberts was sure.

After the revelry died down, they took the *Fortune* out of the harbour and into the sea. They sailed away from the island of Providencia and to the west. The *Gallant* was not long to join them in their wake.

As the *Fortune* bounced and jumped with the waves, the wind whipping against the sails and sending spray across the deck, Roberts held fast to the starboard railing at the stern. He kept an eye pressed into his spyglass and watched as the *Gallant* crept up behind them.

Roberts turned around and moved midship. "Keep the name of our ship covered. We don't want to spook Kennedy before we have the chance to strike."

Several crew members stood watch on the side of the ship already covered by spare sail canvas. They kept their feet on the loose parts, and their eyes pinned below to ensure it stayed in place.

As the minutes turned to hours, the two ships left sight of Providencia, holding steady to the western direction. The *Gallant*, being the smaller of the two, had the advantage in speed, and advanced on the *Fortune* as the time passed. The *Gallant* gave Roberts' ship a wide berth, but were they lined up they would be touching stern to stem. At around high noon they reached the edge of what the people of Providencia could see and hear from sea.

"Two points to port! Prepare broadside!" Roberts shouted. "Show them who we are."

His men returned the order with a loud "Aye!" before heading to task. The helmsman spun the wheel, and the ship shifted to the left towards the *Gallant* in a South South-West direction. At the same time, the men prepared muskets under the cover of the masts.

The men covering the name of the ship with canvas removed the loose sail to show their name, and those in the crow's nest let loose their Jolly Roger. The black flag showed Roberts holding an hourglass next to death itself, and was a fearsome warning to all who saw it that their time was running out. Roberts hoped that Kennedy could see and understand the meaning of that flag.

As if in answer to Roberts' call to battle, clouds rushed in overhead and blocked the sun from view. The warm rays no longer shone on their actions, and instead brought a cold air with it.

Though Roberts felt the chill, he paid it no heed. He was too focused on the fight to come, too focused on the enemy in front of him to notice the lost light above him.

"Fire!" Roberts called.

His men answered with the sound of cannons erupting from below deck. The wave of iron burst from their shells and cascaded upon the wooden ship to port. The sound of the iron crashing against the wood, splintering and shattering the planks to pieces, returned as music to Roberts' ears.

The unprovoked attack caught the crew of the *Gallant* wholly unawares, but they hastily turned the ship south-west as well. After a few minutes, the *Gallant* returned fire with her swivel guns at the stern before giving a lacklustre broadside off the starboard bow.

Fortune sustained only light damage on the port bow, as most of the shots ended up in the drink between the ships. The crew were unharmed, save perhaps a splinter or two from broken planks.

The crew of the *Fortune* returned fire with their own swivel guns along the bow, but the *Gallant's* speed advantage was widening the gap between the two ships.

"We should turn to port and rake their stern, otherwise they're liable to do the same to our bow, Captain," Hank said.

Roberts shook his head. "No, we can't do that. We can't risk losing that ship."

Hank looked from Roberts to the *Gallant* and back, and he clenched his teeth. He stepped forward, closer to Roberts. "Captain, if this is what you want, then I stand by it, but you have to face the fact that they're about to sail away. If Kennedy runs, we may never find him again."

Roberts glanced at Hank only briefly, but it was all he needed to see the urgency in his eyes. Roberts looked at the shrinking stern of the *Gallant* as splashes of water from cannonballs shot up in the air between the two ships.

His hand tightened into a ball. "Hard to port! Load starboard cannons for raking fire!" he shouted.

Before anyone could move to carry out Roberts' orders, a man on the weather deck shouted "Ship closing in from the south!" and pointed off the port side of the ship.

Roberts looked over at the crewmate who shouted, and followed his finger to see the ship that was approaching. They had been too preoccupied with the battle to notice the ship coming in, and it was already closing in on the two sloops.

As Roberts took note of the ship in question, he couldn't help but smile. "Belay that order!" he shouted to the helmsman. "Keep us steady and give us all the speed you can."

Hank was beside Roberts, and he too was looking at the approaching ship, but from the look on his face he didn't understand Roberts' reaction. "What do you see, Captain?"

"That's the *Queen Anne's Revenge*, I have no doubt of it."

Hank glanced at Roberts, then back at the ship coming their way. He nodded. "You may be correct. It has three masts, and by its size I reckon it is a frigate. What do you propose we do?"

Roberts thought it over a moment. "Hmm... We steady our course, head west so they can't tack north, and hope the *Queen Anne's Revenge* cuts them off from the south." Roberts glanced around at the sails and the way they flapped in the wind. "With the wind as it is, our companions have the advantage and should send the *Gallant* running."

Hank smiled and let out a brief chuckle as he shook his head.

"What?" Roberts asked, a smile tugging at the corner of his mouth as well.

"Your luck knows no bounds, Captain. That Thatch would appear now of all times; none would have taken that bet."

"Perhaps it's luck, or perhaps we have someone watching over us," Roberts replied.

"Perhaps," Hank concurred.

Roberts told the helmsman to turn them back to the west and slightly away from the *Gallant*. As the ship changed course, the mood aboard also seemed to shift, or it could have just been Roberts' perception that had changed. No longer a desperate struggle with thoughts of Kennedy escaping once more, now it was a true chase against a prey they knew they would best.

Over the next thirty minutes, the three ships stayed their courses, with the *Queen Anne's Revenge* closing in on the *Gallant*. When they were close, Edward's ship fired a few shots from their cannons, though they fell well short of the *Gallant* and served as a simple warning. The *Gallant* took the warning, and whether it was from Kennedy's bumbling or the crew's inexperience, they seemed to forget about the *Fortune*. They almost tacked into the wind towards the *Fortune*, but turned back before it was too late. The damage was done, and they lost what little advantage in speed they had from the manoeuvre.

The *Gallant* furled their sails, and a man came up to the stern to wave a white flag of surrender. They won the battle, with no major injuries or casualties either.

"Furl the sails! Bring us next to the *Gallant*!"

The crew did as commanded and raised the sails, putting them away and leaving the *Fortune* with the current. The helmsman twisted the wheel and the two ships came closer and closer.

All the while, Edward's ship was closing in not far behind them, though slower than the other two ships.

"Stay armed, men. We don't know yet if they plan to ambush us," Hank warned.

The *Fortune* glided up next to the *Gallant* and the crew were quick to lash the boats together and drop gangplanks across the side. Afterwards, Roberts and his men boarded the enemy ship with their weapons drawn and ready to fire.

Roberts' pirates pointed each musket and cutlass they had at the enemy crew, and the look in their eyes called to the itch they felt at the trigger and handle of their weapons. There was no denying that they wanted a fight, and they were just waiting for an opportunity to strike.

The *Gallant's* crew were not going to give them that opportunity, however, as they seemed eager to yield to Roberts' crew. They willingly moved to the centre of the ship, some with their hands raised in submission, and offered no resistance.

Roberts searched the crowd of people waiting in the middle of the ship. Some men were wounded from the previous attacks, with fresh or dried blood covering their faces, heads, or other extremities. There didn't seem to be any dead from what Roberts could see, but the ship had suffered minor damage from the barrage of cannons.

"Where is your captain?" Roberts questioned in an angry tone. "Where is Walter Kennedy?" he said, his melodic Welsh accent taking on a harsh tone that frightened the *Gallant's* crew. If not his accent, then his stature alone inspired the fear he saw in their eyes. Despite the fear, none answered his call. Roberts turned to a few of his crewmates. "Find him," he said.

Two crewmates left and went below deck in search of Walter Kennedy. Hank walked over to Roberts, glancing at the crew and the ship as he approached.

"The ship doesn't appear to be too badly damaged," he said.

Roberts nodded, taking another look at the ship. "Aye, it should sail nicely." He looked at the men in the centre of the ship, those who had surrendered. "It's as we thought, Kennedy's crew is his own... I see no familiar faces."

Hank folded his arms in front of his chest. "And not a one of them's got so much as a rind on them. They're all as green as a summer field."

Roberts took note of the age of those in Kennedy's crew; they couldn't be much past their teens, if that. A few were older, perhaps old enough to have worked on a ship before, but they looked to have neither the experience nor the fortitude to work as a pirate.

As Roberts was looking over the crew, the large frigate of his ally, Edward Thatch, the young Blackbeard, was setting up next to the *Gallant*. His crew dropped a gangplank across the gap, and Edward walked over.

Edward was tall, nearly as tall as Roberts, and well built. He carried himself with a fearsome countenance that had grown since the two had met years prior when Roberts was hot on Kennedy's trail. His deathly stare and great black beard were enough to make most men cower, but from their time together Roberts knew that beneath that gaze lay a man solely devoted to his crew whom he considered family.

"Roberts, I'm glad we made it in time," Edward said.

Roberts shook Edward's hand. "Well met, Edward. I too am glad you arrived when you did. It could have been a long, arduous endeavour without your assistance." Roberts glanced at the Queen Anne's Revenge. "I see you've completed your modifications to the ship. It looks like a whole new vessel."

Edward glanced over his shoulder at his ship. "Aye, she's

faster now as well. We might even be able to challenge you," he said.

Roberts flashed a slight grin, but said nothing. Before Edward could say anything else, Roberts' crewmates returned to the weather deck.

His crew carried with him Walter Kennedy, and prodded him forward with muskets at his back. Kennedy was already cowering in fear at the sight of his former crew and captain. His back was arched with a hunch, and sweat covered his face. The crew pushed him in front of Roberts and Edward, and he fell to his knees.

The sight of Kennedy once again brought anger into Roberts' heart, and his face felt flush. His hands and teeth were clenched as he forced himself to hold back from attacking the man right then and there.

Edward cocked and primed a pistol, then turned it over to Roberts. "Time for justice, Roberts."

Roberts looked at the pistol in his hands for a moment, and then pointed it at Kennedy. Kennedy's eyes were filled with fear and despair. "Please, Roberts," he said with a trembling voice. "I—"

"Shut your mouth, Walter," Roberts seethed as he took a step forward and pressed the pistol against Kennedy's forehead.

Kennedy sobbed and closed his eyes, letting out a pathetic cry like a mewling babe. His whole body shook, and it looked as if at any moment he might soil himself. His hands clasped together in front of him, tightening in preparation for what was about to happen.

Roberts' finger was on the trigger, ready to fire. His anger was intense and overwhelming as he thought back to all the times Kennedy had wronged him, or even simply annoyed him.

Then, just as Roberts was about to pull the trigger, the clouds above parted, letting the light through to shine on the three ships. Roberts hesitated, and in that hesitation the seeds of doubt spread. He remembered words that he wanted to ignore, but couldn't in that moment. Words from the bible.

'Be angry, but sin not: let not the sun go down upon your wrath.' 'The discretion of man deferreth his anger: and his glory is to pass by an offence.' 'For the wrath of man doth not accomplish the righteousness of God.'

"Roberts," Edward said, a nervous chuckle following his call, "what are you doing?"

Roberts sighed, but then smiled. "You are correct. Now is the time for justice, Edward. My justice." He looked at Walter Kennedy. "I will grant you mercy this day, old friend. You will live to see another day."

4. MATTHEW 6:14

From the Journal of Bartholomew Roberts
Entry #60 Dated July 11th, No Year Given

I have lost many friends by my actions.

Edward couldn't accept that I would grant Walter mercy, and has left our company. The young man is becoming a pirate through and through. The kind of pirate whispered about to bring fear to the hearts of man. He has become hardened by the years, and that hardness has stripped him of all kindness.

And I do not blame him for his anger.

Though I have granted Walter mercy, the contradiction remains. Though forgiveness is on my lips, it has not reached my heart.

I do not regret what I have done, and yet I do all the same. My mind is as two sides of a coin, being tossed in the air and caught just to see what side I land on in that moment.

My crew has accepted my decision, though I know some, like Edward, do not understand why I chose to do what I did.

In truth, I feel it was only that the coin landed on the side it was meant to at that time.

A knock came at Roberts' cabin door. "Enter," he beckoned.

Hank opened the door and walked inside the cabin. "Captain... a word?"

Roberts nodded and motioned for Hank to take a seat at his table. Roberts had been writing in his journal, and as Hank approached he dried and set the quill down, then placed a stopper in the ink bottle.

"What is it you wish to talk of, Hank?"

Before Hank sat down, he took another bottle of alcohol from the cabinet and filled two glasses. "I thought we could have a drink, if it pleases you?"

Roberts closed the book of his journal and chuckled. "Lord knows I need a drink after all this."

Hank wore a wide grin as he turned around, glasses in hand. "Why do you think I offered?"

Roberts chuckled once again as Hank placed the glass in front of him. He took a drink, savouring the sweet notes of citrus on the back of the brandy as he sipped.

"How is the crew taking what's happened?"

"They're upset that we've lost allies, but they accept your judgement. Just as I said."

"Just as you said..." Roberts repeated.

As Roberts and Hank sipped on the brandy, they had a silent moment together. They could hear the lap of the waves against the ship, the stomp of feet against the roof of the cabin, and the general shouting customary aboard a ship.

The two relaxed in each other's company, enjoying the momentary reprieve from battle and difficult decisions. They had been through much over the years, and though these times were few and far between, Roberts appreciated them all the same.

"You know, it's quite the bit of magic you've done with this crew," Hank blurted out.

Roberts arched his brow and grinned. "Whatever do you mean?"

Hank leaned forward in his chair and held his glass in front of him as he looked off to the side. "I've been sailing for as long as I can remember. Sailed with some of the hardest men you would have ever met, and that was even before falling in with this pirating business..." Hank trailed off for a moment, and then took another drink of his brandy. "Davis, he... he uh, he was bright, but he never really had the kind of focus you have," he said, referring to their original captain. "It was always about the next score, the next place to plunder, and there wasn't much thought beyond that. The only reason he freed slaves was because some of the crew felt strongly about it. You though..." he said, pointing at Roberts, "you gave us rules, structure. You showed us that we could be better men than simple brutes. At first, I thought the men would revolt after so many rules, like with Kennedy, but they stuck by you. They might not always agree with you, but they stood by you just the same. I don't think I've ever seen someone who could inspire such loyalty." Hank took another drink of his brandy, and then chuckled. "I mean what kind of a person could convince a pirate crew to... to free slaves, give up prostitutes, and show mercy to our enemies?"

Roberts laughed along with his friend. "You flatter me, my friend. I do not think so great of myself, especially in this." He took a drink, then looked off to the side, just as Hank did when reminiscing. "I chastised the young Edward for his anger and acting on whims, when I too acted on a whim. I felt the anger in my heart against Kennedy, and I wanted to shoot him. I cast aside our greatest allies because I could not face my reflection in his eyes. I'm just a coward who ran away."

"Tch," Hank spat. "It takes more courage to forgive than to fight. Any man can pull a trigger in the hopes it fixes all their troubles. It takes true strength to know when to pull the trigger, and when to pull back."

Roberts had to look away from Hank's fierce eyes. He didn't feel worthy of all the praise, though he knew time would settle his mind. "Perhaps you are right," he said, trying to appease his friend.

Roberts downed the rest of the drink and rose from his chair. "I believe I should pay our temporary prisoner a visit. Keep the ship running for me, would you?"

Hank nodded and raised his glass as Roberts passed him by. Roberts left the cabin, closing the door behind him, and headed below deck. First, Roberts headed to the galley and grabbed some dry biscuits, and then headed to the makeshift brig; a cargo room with some of the crew keeping watch both inside and out.

Roberts greeted his men before entering the cargo room, and searched the faces of the men sequestered there. Off in one corner he noticed Walter Kennedy sitting on a barrel with his back against the wall. Roberts went over to Kennedy, and pulled over a box to sit on next to him.

Roberts slapped Kennedy's leg and he woke with a start. When his eyes met Roberts' they widened in shock and he straightened himself. "John! I... I'm sorry, I'd not seen ye there," he said, his Irish accent breaking through, unchanged after so many years.

Roberts smiled as he broke off a piece of a biscuit and handed it to Kennedy. "It's Bartholomew now, remember?"

Kennedy nodded, embarrassment clear on his face, as he took the biscuit. "Aye, of course... From that ni—I mean... from yer former slave friend who passed."

Roberts took a bite from his half of the biscuit. "Yes, I took his name as my own," he said. "That was... quite some time ago, wasn't it?"

Kennedy grinned. "Aye, an age and a half."

The sounds of the ship were amplified in those small quarters, with the sound of the other prisoners' whispers heard above all else. Silence took over the space between the two old friends, and the air felt thick with tension.

Roberts couldn't help but feel a strangeness in the pit of his stomach. His eyes flitted between the hull of his ship and the biscuit in his hand as he thought of what to say. What does one say to someone who betrayed you, who you're still angry with, and who you're trying to forgive?

"So…" Kennedy started, cutting the tension. "What did ye end up using all them jewels ye stole fer?" he said with a grin.

Roberts looked up at Kennedy and arched his brow. "Jewels?"

"Aye, the jewels ye stole from the King o' Portugal. I heard that ye succeeded, 'less that was some other bloke with the name Bartholomew Roberts what stole some King's jewels," Kennedy said with a laugh.

Roberts joined in the laughter and nodded his head as he remembered that night. The night that Kennedy absconded with his other ship. "We lived like Kings… though modest ones, and it's brought us this far. Some of the coin made its way to parishes here and there, or others who needed it more than I or the crew."

"Sounds like your doing," Kennedy commented. He looked over Roberts' shoulder at the crewmates standing guard at the door. "I see many a familiar face 'ere. Still with all the same men?"

Roberts glanced over his shoulder to see who Kennedy was looking at. "Aye. Some men come and go, as is the case, but we're mostly unchanged."

"That's good," Kennedy said, leaning his head back against the hull while looking down at his feet as he took the last bite of his biscuit.

Roberts handed Kennedy another. "What happened to the *Royal Rover* and her crew?"

Kennedy lost his smile and kept staring at his feet. "We left that night high on the thought that we had made the right choice. We learned of yer success later, and it became a bitter victory," he said, taking another bite of the dry cracker. "We struggled ta find ships with cargo worth attacking, and with each ship we brought down we barely had enough ta feed ourselves. Before our mutiny I sold myself as captain by saying I knew how ta navigate. When the men found it to be a lie, they left me at the next port and set off on their own."

Roberts could hear the frustration and sadness in Kennedy's voice, but he bade him to continue the story. "What did you do after that?"

Kennedy looked up at Roberts for a moment, then returned his gaze to his feet. "Went from port to port, picked up a few things on navigating, and found me a part of a growing pirate crew. They gave me a ship ta command, and I named it the *Gallant* as ye saw. They gave me the worst ship, with the greenest lot you'd ever seen, but I didn't care; I had a ship to call my own. Would'a ran away from 'em eventually, but ye found me, and here we are."

"And here we are..." Roberts echoed.

There was another brief moment of silence before Kennedy once again broke it. "Did ye patch things up with yer friend?"

"Edward?" Roberts asked. Kennedy nodded. "No," Roberts replied as he shook his head. "The boy couldn't accept that I would show you mercy, and we've parted ways."

Kennedy's mouth made a line, and he said, "I'm sorry," as he looked away.

"It would have occurred regardless, I feel."

Kennedy was shaking his head as he looked off to the other side of the ship. "I've caused ye such trouble over the years... Caused so many people trouble..."

Roberts smacked Kennedy on the leg. "All is forgiven, no need to wallow any more," he said.

"I'm... I'm nothing but a coward. I don't deserve your forgiveness," he said. Before Roberts could say something else, Kennedy continued. "I need to tell you something... something I did back when Davis was still our captain."

Roberts sat up and eyed Kennedy. "Go on."

"When we were on that island, just before he died... I... I ran away," Kennedy said. There was a pause, and Kennedy looked at Roberts for a response. When he didn't receive one he continued. "I was there with 'im. I could'a fought, and, who knows, we may have survived together. But I was a coward, and I ran," Kennedy held his hands up to his head. "Oh, God... Roberts, I left 'im ta die out there," he said, his voice trembling and tears dripping from his eyes.

Roberts was stunned, not by the revelation, but by the confession. To see Kennedy reduced to tears in front of him caused him to feel pangs of sadness for his old friend. The years did not seem to have been kind to him, but he hadn't the fortitude to carry on in guilt. To be able to confess to Roberts must have been like a weight lifting off him.

Roberts placed his hand on Kennedy's shoulder. "And yet, by doing as you did, you were able to save countless lives aboard the *Royal Rover*," he said. "I forgive you, Walter, for all that you've done. Whether in secret or not, I forgive you."

Kennedy fell off his seat and to his knees on the sole of the ship. Roberts went with him, and held fast to his hands as the man wept. His tears hit the wooden floorboards and disappeared into the ether as his sins were forgiven.

Roberts said a silent prayer for his old friend and crewmate, in the hopes that he would lead a happy life from then on.

The Fortune landed in Providencia just before nightfall, where they let the former crew of the Gallant go. Thankfully, the crew were cooperative and gave Roberts' crew no issues as they left in longboats to shore.

Kennedy stood at the edge of the Fortune's starboard side, getting ready to enter the last longboat with a pack of simple supplies slung over his shoulder. Roberts was there with him, and the two looked over towards the town as men and women milled about before heading home for the night.

"Well, I suppose this is goodbye, ain't it?" Kennedy said.

"Yes, I suppose so," Roberts replied, extending his hand.

Kennedy took Roberts' hand and gave it a firm shake before returning his attention to the longboat and shore. After a moment, he leaned over to Roberts. "Ye wouldn't be looking for an extra deckhand, would ye?" he said with a chuckle.

Roberts laughed as well. "No, I should like to keep my ship this time." He smacked Kennedy on the back and pushed him forward towards the longboat. "Safe travels, Walter."

Kennedy glanced over his shoulder and said, "The same to ye, Bartholomew."

Walter Kennedy boarded the longboat, and he was taken to the shore of Providencia with the last of his crew. Afterwards, the crew of the Fortune brought the longboats back, and they were promptly secured to the ship once more.

Hank came up beside Roberts. "What now, Captain?"

Roberts gave Hank a sidelong glance. "Now? Now, we set off for our next adventure!" he said with a grin.

Hank smiled, scratched his chin, and took a few steps forward. "Alright you lazy sods, the night's not over for you yet. Get this ship under way!" he shouted, and the crew replied with a booming "Aye, Aye!" in return.

The sails were set, the ship turned around, and they headed off away from the island. As the ship began moving, Roberts went to the stern and looked at the receding island. He noticed Walter standing on the pier, watching them depart.

Roberts waved to Kennedy, and Kennedy waved back, signalling their final goodbye to one another, and the last time they would see each other alive.

Walter Kennedy settled in Ireland, giving up on his dreams of pirating and being a captain to run a brothel. He was later accused of a theft he did not commit, and outed as a pirate by a former crewmate in a bid for a reduced sentence. Walter was later tried for piracy, and hung at the gallows. His crewmate, never learning the true lesson of mercy given by Bartholomew Roberts as in Matthew 18: 21-35, was also tried and hung for piracy.

THE END

BOOK FOUR OF
THE PIRATE PRIEST

BARTHOLOMEW
ROBERTS' SPIRIT

1. PROVERBS 28:1

"Hard to port! Don't let them escape!" Hank shouted, his hand outstretched over the quarterdeck railing.

The helmsman gritted his teeth and flung the great wheel of the *Fortune* to the right. Mates relayed Hank's orders down the line on the bustling ship. Though their voices were hoarse from the constant shouting and the salt air, they hollered above the din of the crashing waves and booming cannon fire and cracking black powder.

A surge of brine from the deep shot up over the starboard side of the ship, making the sole slick. As the men ran to change the rigging and adjust the sails, they slid and reached for the handholds, but never fell on that wet surface that was their home.

The mist of that salty swell brushed against Bartholomew Roberts' face as he watched their prey change course. His concentration did not allow him to enjoy that refreshing caress, but it would not be the last time he would feel it, so all was not lost.

"Ready starboard!" Roberts bellowed. His voice too was hoarse from the hours of chasing and the salt that seemed to cling to the throat, but he had no trouble making his voice carry across the whole ship. He stood tall, a modern-day Goliath some might say, and he had the tone to match.

The men not in charge of the rigging readied small cannons on the starboard side of the ship as a mate took the order below to the main gun deck. They would not have a clear shot, but it would be enough to punch a few holes at their enemies stern.

The ship, French by the flags it flew and the name *Maîtresse* emblazoned on the side, was being commanded well enough, but Bartholomew could tell the one in command was an inexperienced coward. They flew at the first sight of the *Fortune*, well before they had even dropped the black, and despite being chased for half a day and having the guns, they never fought back. If they had, they might have stood a chance. As it was, they were full of holes and taking on water.

The wind chopped against *Fortune's* sails, making them crack as the billowing mass snapped against the yards. *Fortune* tacked into the wind, so there was no avoiding the sails luffing lazily as they momentarily lost their power.

They were mimicking the *Maîtresse* and trying to keep close. The *Fortune* was a smaller, faster, and more manoeuvrable ship, but they had been beating North-West against the wind for hours and only now made some headway to fire the cannons.

Now that they'd come about, *Fortune* was just about ready to fire starboard, and the crew were just waiting, itching for the order.

Roberts raised his hand in the air then brought it down in a fierce chopping motion. "Fi—" Roberts stopped before finishing the command as a flurry of movement took his attention.

On the *Maîtresse* the sails were being trimmed. Roberts thought they were attempting to somehow turn the ship around and give *Fortune* their broadside, but the manoeuver would be impossible with such a tight curve. After waiting, his hand still transfixed in the air as though stuck along with the half-uttered command, he saw them strike their colours. The proud French flag of blue and gold was taken down as the ship moved forward on inertia alone.

Their pride stripped away willingly, the crew of the French ship furled their sails fully and let their ship slow until only the force of the waves beneath were moving them. Roberts ordered his crew to follow suit, but at a distance.

"You think it some deception?" Hank asked through a laboured breath.

Roberts shook his head. "Have you ever known a Frenchman to throw down his pride for deception?" he said with a deep chuckle, expecting no true answer from his first mate. "Given our chase, I think these men are simple cowards who've given up, but there's no need to give them our broadside."

Hank nodded. "Agreed. I'll have the crew remain at the ready and have us circle around with a wide berth." After a moment's pause to see if Roberts would object, Hank went back to his post and shouted orders to the crew.

Roberts kept a close eye, both naked and through a spyglass, on the surrendered French ship. A merchant ship, and by the look of it a new one, it had nary a nick or a scratch on the hull save what damage the *Fortune* had dealt. No signs of discolouration on the wood from weather, no blackened blotches near the gunports from gunpowder, and even the crew looked as green as newborn babes. Roberts could practically see them shaking in their boots as their eyes followed him and the pirates circling the waters.

Despite all the signs pointing to their cowardice and co-operation, it was only after Roberts saw the crew coming up to the weather deck that he felt safe in bringing his ship in close to the other. The gunports were shielded, their cannons reined in and not at the ready, but it would be a simple thing to open them and fire if they had the crew to do so. Looking at the numbers on the weather deck, it would be strange for them to have many more hiding below.

Roberts took his gaze out of the spyglass and looked over at Hank standing nearby at the helm. With a nod, Hank issued new orders to the crew to bring them up next to the French ship. Once the two were close, the crew lashed the ships together before setting down a gangplank.

The rest of the crew of *Fortune* waited for their captain to cross first, all eyes resting on him, all eyes filled to bursting with pride. It was as though the removal of the French merchants' pride became their own; as though that was the first thing they had stolen, the first act of piracy they committed against the enemy before they took more tangible prizes.

Roberts felt that pride too, but he was not one to be swept up in such emotion, and so he took a slow, measured jaunt to the other ship.

The crew of the *Maîtresse* also had their eyes fixed on

Roberts, looking up at him as he strode across the gangplank. Tense brows, dark eyes, and twitches at each creak of wood plastered across each of the men on the merchant ship. Those were dangerous eyes. Roberts knew that the fight wasn't over, even now, and he needed to act quickly before the fear seeped into their legs, before the fact that they were cornered and near to the grave sunk in.

Roberts waved his crew over, and they went to the other ship immediately, all armed and pointing those arms at the French crew.

"Good afternoon, gentlemen," he said loud and long. His Welsh accent gave the saying a merry tone like a song, and his wide smile added to the mirth. "I notice this is a French ship, though I'm afraid I do not speak your beautiful language. Is there any among you who can translate?"

After questioning once more, a young man stepped forward, and Roberts beckoned him closer before addressing the crew again.

"Today is a pleasant day, so let us keep our business pleasant as well, shall we?" The young man, after a brief pause and a frightened jump, translated for Roberts. Roberts' gaze travelled across the crewmates as he said this, but he wasn't expecting an answer. "Your cowardice today put you here. Perhaps with a little more courage, you could have escaped, but that is not possible now. If you act against us now, you will die. If you stay as you are, you will live another day. Am I understood?"

The young man passing along Roberts' message glanced up at him as he wrung his hands, then back to the crew several times as they both waited for a response.

"Speak, men!" Roberts bellowed, causing several of the French crew to jump, including the young man beside him.

The crew understood without the need for another translation, and they finally answered Roberts. Though Roberts didn't know the language, he at least understood knew the general affirmative responses he was given.

In a lower tone, he turned to the young man and asked, "Now, where is your Captain that I may speak with him?"

The young man pulled his hands in close and looked away. "Captain is gone. No captain now."

Roberts shook his head solemnly. However their captain met their end, he doubted it was from any of the cannon fire during their chase. Roberts said a prayer for the man who had died, then gave the young man a warm smile before giving him a light push and pointing him back to the rest of the crew.

"Keep watch over the men. No laxing in your duties," Roberts shouted to his crew. They replied with nods and "ayes" and lifting their weapons up to show they were alert. Now that the battle was over, and a nice rest just over the horizon, they were eager to have the business over without complications.

Roberts issued a few more orders to those who would not be on guard duty, having them search the ship for all the valuables they could find. After the search was delegated properly, Roberts did his own exploring. He found the captain's cabin below deck and began looking through the ledger book, the captain's journal, and the manifest for anything of note. The captain seemed to be working for English debtors and so it was mostly written in English. The rest he was able to surmise through context.

Through Roberts' reading, he came to truly know the extent to which this ship's former captain, and its entire crew, were like newborn babes. The captain made a series of blunders trading from port to port, not taking stock of the local region's needs and necessities.

He had tried to sell a shipment of tobacco he received from one of the northern Thirteen Colonies in the Caribbean, a short route which could have been profitable if not for it being a location already ripe with tobacco. He only managed to sell a tenth of what he had bought, and at a loss mind you, and didn't have the supplies or funds necessary to sail to Europe where he might have been able to make a profit.

From there, he made the smart decision to trade the tobacco for some sugar rather than try to sell it, but he was swindled judging by the amounts traded. Then, to make matters worse, the crew weren't attentive with the storage of the sugar, and a third of it took on water. He managed to sell the rest to one of the colonies north, then purchased various textiles, which would have come from Britain, for too much by Roberts' estimation. His final note mentioned heading to Trepassey, Newfoundland to sell the textiles.

This too would have been a disastrous move, as the French hadn't been in control of Trepassey for some years. He would have had made a better time of rolling a rock up a hill than dickering with the British colonists for textiles they probably already had.

And to top it all he was attacked by pirates. Little wonder the young captain made the choice he did after all that.

Hank entered through the open door of the cabin, his heavy boots announcing his presence. Roberts looked up from the journal and waved to him before continuing to look through the other ledgers strewn about on the table in front of him.

"Anything of interest?" Hank asked.

"Just the sad tale of a suicidal fool," Roberts replied harshly, then let out a sigh at his rashness.

Hank ignored Roberts' comment, or also didn't think much of the captain who'd left his crew and life behind. "The boys're near finished loading the ship. Wasn't much to take from this lot, but they had fresh food and good clothes."

"And boxes filled with wool blankets and rugs?" Roberts leaned back in his chair as Hank took a seat across from him.

Hank nodded. "You want us to take them?"

Roberts shook his head. "We've nowhere to safely unload them here. I believe we could make better gains farther north."

Hank raised a curious brow. "You've an idea for our next destination?"

Roberts grinned. "Aye, that I do. Trepassey. It's recently switched hands from the French to the British, so there's bound to be much trade going on in its shores."

Hank chuckled. "We colonists are useless without our

luxuries from the motherland." Hank began to rise from his seat. "I'll let the crew know we're to depart."

Roberts waved the comment away. "Sit and have a drink with me. The crew will be busy for a bit longer yet."

Hank sat back down as Roberts went into the drawers of the captain's table, and sure enough, there was a bottle of some alcohol and glasses. He poured some for the two of them and passed a glass to Hank. The two drank. It looked, smelled, and tasted cheap, with a harsh, bitter note alongside the burning of a drink meant more for the effects than for recreation, but it was still enjoyable in the right company.

The two sat in amicable silence for a few moments as Roberts reflected. Over Hank's shoulder, Roberts could see the crew bustling about, comparing their finds and talking. The chatter was overpowered by the sounds of boots against wood and the lapping of the waves on all sides of the ship.

Roberts' thoughts turned to what had led the merchant captain to his untimely end, and on what steps led Roberts to be here as well. He thought on his friend Talib, who he was powerless to help, but was freed by a pirate, Howell Davis. Even after all that Talib had been through—the loss of his wife, the enslavement—he never lost his hope.

Roberts felt it odd that Talib would keep his slave name, Bartholomew. He said it was because he wasn't truly free and kept it as some sort of penance, but Roberts still didn't understand. *The penance was not being strong enough to save your people, your wife, wasn't it, Talib?* Roberts thought. *And now, I'm Bartholomew.* Roberts smiled despite himself, thinking that he had drunk perhaps a bit too much.

After a few more minutes, and half of the drink gone, Roberts leaned forward and broke the silence. "What do you think was going through the captain's head?"

Hank looked at Roberts for a moment, then off to the side as he pondered the question. "Probably thought we were the bad sort of pirates. The red flags, the murderous bunch that they tell stories of to scare children. Might have thought it was a better way to go."

Roberts nodded at the soundness of this line of thought,

but in his mind, it didn't seem to match with the contents of the man's journal. The way he talked of his own failures, and how little recourse he would have if his debt collectors came to task for him, it seemed as though this was one failure too many.

"This may be… in poor taste," Hank began.

"No, please, continue. I should hope at this point there would be no barriers between us."

Hank nodded, his face solemn and sombre. "Have you ever… had the inclination?"

It took a moment for Roberts to understand Hank's meaning, and when he did, he leaned back in his chair again. "I think any man alive who would say 'no' to that question is a liar or a simpleton." Roberts finished his drink and rose to his feet. He walked over to his first mate and laid a hand on his shoulder briefly as he tried his best to express something that words could not to his longtime friend. After a moment, he spoke. "Let us leave this business behind us and move on to Trepassey."

Hank nodded again, and this time he wore a small smile. "Aye, Captain."

Roberts had commanded his crew to leave enough food and supplies aboard the *Maîtresse* so they may reach safe harbour alive and well, then set sail north for Trepassey. He also lifted the normal restriction of drinking on deck and on duty, in moderation, and so the men were full of good spirits in more ways than one as they sailed.

After their lengthy chase and the paltry goods seized from their quarry, it was pleasureful for the crew to have a break on their voyage. The weather cooperated with them along the way, giving them wind in their sails for most of the journey, save one peculiar day when the wind simply stopped.

On that day it was clear on all sides, and they could see no approaching ships, and so Roberts decided that would be a day of rest. Roberts looked at his journal and noticed that the day itself was also a Sunday and he chuckled to himself.

The crew rested to the full extent of their ability, drinking, playing games of cards, singing, and eating a proper meal. With no wind, there was no fear of any ship reaching them where they were, and so even Roberts had a few more drinks than typical. Before long, his booming voice was singing the loudest.

After their day of rest, they continued onward to Trepassey with all haste. The winds were once more in their favour, and they reached the harbour without incident. What awaited them was the perfect harbour for merchants, with a natural cove-like shape, it gave just enough room for ships coming and going. This resulted in almost two hundred ships within the harbour, the majority being fishing vessels, but over twenty were larger merchant ships.

This cove shape also meant it was the perfect harbour for pirates. With a bit of work, a single pirate ship could hold the harbour, and none could escape without risking a wave of cannon fire—unless the ships worked together, which is difficult in the best of times, let alone with crews who hardly know each other. There was no escape against a properly outfitted and experienced crew.

And Roberts had such a crew in spades.

"General quarters! Raise the black!" Roberts shouted. "Load port and starboard! Bring to the sails. Show them our colours men, and let's see who answers the call!"

At the end of each order, the crew shouted back an, "Aye, Captain!" and the last left a devilish grin on each man's face.

The black flag of the *Fortune*, a new one depicting Roberts standing on two skulls, was raised to the topmast where all could see. Then the sails were taken in, and their momentum stopped, but the crew held the lines at the ready, waiting for the order to take to the wind.

"Fire a warning shot," Roberts commanded Hank.

"Single fire, starboard!" Hank shouted, and a mate relayed the order below deck.

After only the briefest of moments, one of the cannons

off the right side of the ship fired. The heavy sound knocked against Roberts' chest, and he moved to the balls of his feet to stay stock still with his hands behind his back. Smoke rose from the front starboard, lingering and twisting in the air around the ship, clouding the view of Trepassy and the many ships in the harbour for a small, fleeting breath.

After the sound of the cannon fire was gone, there was silence. The only sound heard was the gentle breeze whistling its discordant sound across the deck and the off-beat accompaniment of the lapping waves.

Then the small chirps of chaos swelling to a cacophony met Roberts' ears. Alarm bells rang out soon after, drowning out most other noise in its wake. The bells were loud and piercing, meant to hit the part of the ear that you simply couldn't ignore, and the irregular clanging made it all the harder to disregard.

As Roberts watched and waited with his crew, he grew more and more disgusted by what he saw. The crews of the other ships were abandoning their posts, some jumping into longboats, others fleeing to the sea and swimming to shore. One after the other, they each abandoned their ships to get away from the *Fortune* and the mere thought of danger.

"What cowardly fools," Roberts whispered to himself.

Then, to the eastern side of the harbour, a cannon shot boomed into the air. Roberts' heart thundered in his ear, the shot of energy one feels before the beginning of a fight surging through him, and the hairs on his neck prickled. He took out his spyglass and aimed it to where the cannon fire came from.

On the eastern side of the harbour, close to where the *Fortune* made its stand, was a two-masted brigantine that was bigger and longer than the *Fortune*. Looking it over, it also had more guns than them and could prove a worthy opponent.

Alas, Roberts' hopes for some courage were misplaced, as he could see the crew of this other ship dragging one of their mates from below deck off and away. The mate looked angry and tried to fight against the other men, but they overpowered him.

That young man must have gone against orders to flee, Roberts thought.

After that single act of brave defiance, there were no others. The rest of the one-hundred and seventy-two ships in the harbour were emptied of their crew, who fled to shore to hide with the citizens of Trepassey.

And then it was as quiet as the moment just prior to the panic. The streets were clear, the doors and windows of the town shut, shuttered, and secured. The only sound was the friendly wind at Roberts' back, and the waves jostling the ship.

Roberts was stunned into silence by what he had witnessed. In all his days, he never thought this would happen. Judging by the looks on his men's faces, he wasn't the only one shocked. If the merchant crews had attacked together, even just two of them, they may have overwhelmed the *Fortune*. Many could have escaped, had they simply set off in the chaos, had they simply attempted it. It wouldn't have been worth the trouble of a chase; Roberts probably would have let some go.

After Roberts' shock and anger at the men's cowardice fizzled out, the absurdity crept in as he took stock of the number of empty ships in the harbour. Then excitement bubbled up from his gut into his chest. It swelled until he couldn't contain it any longer, and he burst out laughing. Roberts laughed in heaps, arching his back and resting his hands on his stomach as though trying to contain the good humour he suddenly felt in himself.

At first, the crew were stunned at Roberts' laughter, and then after a few tepid glances to their neighbours, the men caught the same excited feeling as their captain. In an instant, the crew were in hysterics.

Roberts shuffled over to Hank as he reached out and grabbed the man's shoulder for support and his attention. "Did... did you see the one that tripped... and tumbled over the side?" Roberts made a circling motion with his hands, and then he and Hank both burst into fresh laughter.

Blackbeard's Blood

The unexpected humour continued for a full minute before the crew tried in earnest to gather their wits about them and contain themselves.

Roberts wiped tears from his eyes as he chuckled in small fits before he finally came back to himself and addressed the crew. His voice, though composed, still held the elation and laughter now confined in his chest. "Men, let us not waste this golden opportunity we have been given. So, let us be bold like lions and take what the Lord has provided us," Roberts said with a flourish and a wave of his hand towards the ships in the harbour waiting for them.

2. APPLES

Hank stepped up from the longboat onto the pier of Trepassey and took stock of his surroundings as the twenty men who joined him came onto solid ground.

On the pier, it was slightly harder to see the total number of ships abandoned in the harbour, but there was almost no break in the line they made. Hank could barely see the line of the horizon through the dense clustering of ships both large and small drifting in the waves. The wind and the sea were pushing all of them to and fro, and those not anchored down slowly drifted towards each other at a slow pace.

The town itself was large enough to warrant the number of ships in the harbour, but it appeared to still be growing. There also seemed to be signs of battle, worn cobbles, new planks of wood in the middle of the dock at shore, and new buildings mixed with the old. Hank didn't pay much attention to current events, but his captain mentioned the town recently changed hands from the French to the English. Before that, it must have been a contested area.

With the crew ashore, Hank led the group to the market just off the dock. The small stands the minor merchants and locals used were abandoned. Fresh fruit, fish, meat, animal hides, and other small oddities any sailor couldn't do without were left in their haste.

"Go fetch me an apple, would you kindly?" Hank asked one of the crewmates as he nodded his head towards a nearby cartful.

The crewmate took a moment to follow Hank's gaze, then smiled as he jogged over to the cart of fresh ruby red apples. He scratched his chin as he searched for the best, gathering an armful of them to bring back.

Hank had first pick, thanked the crewmate, and took a hearty bite. The bite was sweet and tart with an explosion of juice which fell down his chin. Though simple, it was delicious and a welcome retreat from the salty meat they had to endure for months on end aboard their ship.

Judging from the looks on the other crewmates' faces, they were getting just as much, if not more, enjoyment from the apples than he was.

"We should bring some back for the men. Grab us the cart and load the longboat."

With wide smiles, a few of the crew went to task, taking the whole cart back to the pier where they had secured their longboat. Apples spilled off the sides as they rolled down the small mound above the cart, leaving a trail behind the laughing, giddy crewmates.

Returning his attention to the town, Hank looked at the windows of the shops and homes that faced the harbour. He could see the telltale signs of onlookers trying to remain inconspicuous. Slight bends in the blinds, the smallest crack to let in just enough sound, and even a child here and there full-faced looking at them before a swift hand pulled them away.

Hank nodded to himself, thinking it was good that they were listening. It made what was coming next easier.

"Alright boys, we're about to get started," Hank said over his shoulder before pulling out a pistol. Hank loaded the gun with black powder, but not with a lead ball, aimed off into the distance, and fired. The sharp crack bounced and echoed off the walls of the houses as it travelled across town.

After the sound dissipated and Hank was sure he had even more of the town's attention than before, he spoke into the silence. "Attention, citizens of Trepassey," he said in a booming voice for all to hear. "We are not here for you. We only lay claim to the ships and the cargo the cowardly merchants who stalk your shores left behind. If you leave us to our business, you will be left alone, and alive." Hank let the words hang in the air as he searched the windows and doors for any activity. "Now, for the captains of the twenty-two merchant ships, I would have words with you. Come out now if you want a chance to save your ships."

After Hank finished, there was silence in the town once again. He knew there would be a delay as the captains debated whether to follow the words of a pirate and risk their lives. They were without spine, but Hank was sure that the threat to their ships would move their feet eventually.

"Someone bring me something to sit on, would you? And relax, we might be here for a spell," Hank said as he readied his pistol once again, this time with a lead shot loaded.

One of the crewmates rolled over a nearby barrel and stood it up for Hank to sit on. Hank grabbed another apple off the ground from those that had fallen off the cart, wiped it off, and sat down on the barrel.

Hank took his time eating his second apple, savouring the flavour he so rarely got to enjoy, as he and the other crewmates waited for the captains to come out of hiding. The crew decided to relax as well, some sitting on the ground nearby, others taking their pick of the abandoned wares the vendors had left behind, and a few others polished their weapons or made sure their rifles were loaded and ready.

Slowly, people exited various nearby businesses into the street leading to where Hank and company were gathered. Around fifty people in total came out to meet with Hank, far more than the number of merchant ships, and many of them had weapons in hand. Hank thought it might have been an attempt to intimidate the twenty men he had brought with him, but it would be a foolhardy one.

"I suppose I'm going to have to teach these boys a lesson," Hank whispered to himself. He whistled, and the crew who had been lounging about came back to join him where he sat. He didn't rise from his seat, nor did he stop eating his apple, as the fifty men approached.

Before Hank could say anything, a few of the men holding weapons charged in unison, one of them headed straight for him. The crew of the *Fortune*, battle-hardened as they were, knew it was going to happen and struck back. One crewmate blocked the man coming for Hank and stabbed him through the stomach, and the others were dispatched just as easily. As swiftly as it began, it was over. Four were dead, none of them pirates.

The ease with which the merchants' men died soured the thought of attacking from the remaining forty-some. Hank too hadn't moved from his spot, and his casual attitude no doubt sealed it.

Hank took another bite from his apple and began speaking after signalling to one of the crew. "Thank you for joining us gentlemen," he said with a mouthful of apple. "My name is Hank Abbot, first mate of the *Fortune* captained by Bartholomew Roberts. Perhaps you've heard of him?" Hank gazed into the eyes of those thronged about him and saw some knowing looks of fear, and a few he thought might be admiration. "I trust you all understand why we're here. If you want to keep your ships intact, you'll do as we say." He waited a moment to see if there were any objections, but none came. "First, you're going to give us each of your names and which ship you belonged to."

The crewmate Hank had signalled rolled another barrel nearby along with a small crate he placed overtop, and then set down an inkwell and a piece of paper. After weighing the paper down with rocks, he looked expectantly towards the gathered crowd.

"W-why?" one of the men asked.

It wasn't a defiant question, but one borne of confusion. Hank simply looked down towards the four dead men, then back up to the man who asked 'why'.

There were no further questions.

Each captain lined up in a row as the others, their mates or villagers, stood off to the side. Most of the men looked afraid and jumpy, but Hank noticed one young man who appeared to be angry. His face held a deep contempt and shame, and it wasn't always directed at Hank or the other pirates.

The whole process was smooth and efficient, with each captain being more than amicable given the circumstances. After they were finished, the captains returned to the other crowd of people and waited.

Hank nodded, satisfied with the outcome. "I thank you for your cooperation, gentlemen. Now, down to business. If you wish to save your ships, then you are to report to our ship, the *Fortune*, after you hear the sound of a rifle. Those who fail to do so will have their ship burned at once."

At the end of Hank's declaration, there was a small

clamour from the captains and others in the crowd. Their greed took over their wits, making them forget the four that had died so easily not moments before. It seemed to be momentary, but then one of the captains stepped forward.

"This is outrageous!" the captain blared. "Just take the cargo and leave these—"

The crack of Hank's pistol cut through the noise of the captain and the men behind him. The captain who had objected stepped forward once, fell to his knees, and slumped to the ground dead.

Hank waited for a moment, letting the silence permeate the air once more as the smoke from his pistol wafted around him like a shroud before disappearing on the breeze.

"Who was his second in command?" Hank asked as he pointed at the dead captain. A young man stepped forward and raised his hand. "Congratulations," Hank said, "you're captain now. Give your name to my man here." The young man nodded and rushed over to update the list, nearly tripping over himself as he did so. Hank looked over the rest in the crowd. "Any other objections?" There were none. "Good. After the sound of a rifle, report to the ship the *Fortune*. Do not keep my captain waiting. Understood?"

Earlier

Roberts and Hank both set foot on the largest ship in the harbour. It had minimal guns, but it was even larger than the brigantine that had fired upon them. At first, Roberts thought it could make for a nice replacement ship for the *Fortune*, but upon seeing it more closely, he knew what kind of ship it was.

"Prepare food and water, and lots of it!" Roberts commanded. "And bring over some prybars."

Roberts and Hank went below deck to the small area divvied up for the crew and captain at the stern near the ladders. The next level down went below the water line for bilge access. There was enough room for a crew of around fifty to one hundred, just barely enough to run a ship of this size, and then the rest of the ship was blocked by thick timbers and a heavy locked door with no airflow to speak of.

Despite there being no way for air to escape, Roberts could smell the rank stench of disease, filth, and death beyond that door. It was a smell he had been familiar with at one time, a smell he had grown accustomed to, a smell he learned to forget until he could forget it no longer.

The wooden door had a large iron lock keeping it closed. Hank pulled out a pistol and began aiming it at the lock, but Roberts stopped him.

"Too dangerous," Roberts said, trying to limit the words and the amount of time he had to intake the smell. "Might injure someone."

Hank nodded, and the two waited for a crewmate to bring a prybar. Roberts took it in hand, set it against the lock, and using his giant form, he snapped the lock with one mighty blow.

With the door open, there was nothing to stop the smell from inside, and it nearly knocked Roberts over. The crewmate who had brought the prybar wretched and had to leave.

Inside, dozens of eyes, fearful like fawns, looked at Roberts and Hank. There couldn't have been less than two hundred and fifty men and women in that part of the ship, huddled so close together there was barely enough room to breathe.

And of all the things that Roberts thought in that moment, he was thankful that this was one of the ships where the slaves were allowed to stand. The ship he had been on in the past kept them on wooden bunks two feet apart up to the overhead, and some were worse than that. Two feet was a luxury.

The men and women were all halfway, or closer, to death. Frail from malnourishment, sickly, and with scars or lesions covering their bodies from fresh injuries.

Roberts tried his best to adopt a warm and reassuring face. "Come, come out. You're free now," he said.

At first, no one moved. Then one woman, naked save for

a cloth covering her genitals, reached for his hand. Roberts took it gently and led the woman out, pointing her to the ladder leading above deck.

After the woman, the rest of those aboard came more quickly, but still with caution and fear in their eyes. After some time, they had all those who were able on the weather deck where Roberts' crew fed and gave them water to drink. Afterwards, Roberts had his surgeon help the sick and wounded as best he could, and brought food and drink to those below who couldn't stand.

Of those there, he found eighty long dead from the voyage, rotting near the corner where the slaves were meant to relieve themselves. The sight disgusted Roberts. As many times as he had seen it, as many times he had freed those enslaved, he lost no anger over time. His righteous fury was everlasting in the face of these atrocities.

After a moment to calm himself, he joined the abled on the weather deck. The slaves were drinking and eating, some helping those weakened even from the short trip above deck. They were eying Roberts' crew warily.

"Do any here speak English?" Roberts asked. He had a dozen or so former slaves aboard his ship who he could call on if needed, but he knew from experience his message would be better received if it came from one they trusted. He waited a moment before repeating the question, then one of the men raised a hand cautiously. Roberts bade the man join him. "Do any here know how to sail a ship? Are there enough to escape on your own?"

The man, though thinning, looked a fair bit healthier than many of those who survived. He looked over the other former slaves, then shook his head. "No enough to sail. No enough for big ship."

"How many?" Roberts asked, raising his hands and motioning with his fingers. The man motioned back twenty, then waved his hand as if to say it wasn't a firm number. Roberts thanked the man and motioned for him to go back to having his fill before he turned around to Hank. "Thoughts?"

"Our ship isn't big enough to bring them all with us, and

even if we took this ship as well, it would mean putting them back in the hold again."

Roberts shook his head. "And then we would have a slaver and be worse off than before in terms of battle power."

Hank leaned back and scratched the back of his head. "If we wanted to take them comfortably, even the brigantine wouldn't do. We'd need to split to two ships. Even with the twenty who can sail helping us, it wouldn't be enough."

"They're too weak as it is at the moment. We need to train some, and we need them to regain their strength back."

Hank scoffed as he looked off towards Trepassy. "We need time is what we need. Time we don't have."

Roberts closed his eyes and stroked his chin for a few moments as he mulled over the problem. After a while, he opened his eyes again. "I have an idea to buy us some time," he said. Hank arched an eyebrow. "We're going to have a little fun with these cowardly captains."

"What are we going to do?"

The captains who had abandoned their ships were meeting together after the pirates' first mate and crew left. They had brought along many of their most trusted crewmates as well, some of whom were now dead.

"What can we do? You saw what they are capable of." Some in the crowd nodded and shared some words of agreement. "These men are cold-blooded murderers, and they're far more capable than any of us."

The debate went on for a time, with each of the captains going back and forth about whether they should follow along with the pirates to try and save their ships, questioning whether it was a trap, and wondering just what the reason behind wanting to meet with them was.

Eventually, a young man in the crowd had enough and stepped forward. "You bunch of cowards could have ended this immediately if you'd had any spine," he said.

The captains all stopped and went silent as they turned their attention to the young man. One of the captains stepped forward, bowing his head slightly in deference. "Apologies for my crewmate's remarks, gentlemen," he began, before turning and uttering, "James, now is not—"

The young man pointed at his captain sternly. "Don't you even start. You're the worst of the lot. We have the biggest ship and more guns than that puny sloop. We could have taken those pirates ourselves if you hadn't ordered everyone to abandon ship."

The captain was caught off guard by his crewmate's rebuke and couldn't think of a response. The young man pushed his captain aside and addressed the others again.

"And all of you are the same. Most of your ships have guns, and not a one fired. You didn't even try to escape with your ship. Sheep to the slaughter, all of you." With each remark, the anger and volume of James' voice grew.

After he finished, there were a few with shameful faces looking down at the ground, but many returned the anger back.

"And what would you have us do?" one of the gentlemen said in a proper British accent.

"Go meet with the pirate if you want to save your ship. Throw down your heads in shame and beg for his mercy. Or don't," James said with a shrug. "Just don't go on about it like a bunch of children told off by their teacher. Be men about it."

Before the captains could argue with James any longer, there was the distinct sound of a rifle from the harbour. All eyes shifted to the harbour, where the pirate ship *Fortune* stayed drifting.

James walked off in that direction, not looking back at his or the other captains, to prepare a longboat. With determined resignation, the forty-some in the crowd joined him, and they were soon off to the pirates' ship to meet with its captain, Bartholomew Roberts.

Once aboard the ship, the captains and mates were surrounded on all sides by pirates. One of the pirates was on the opposite side of the ship to them, sitting in a chair next to a table with what could only be described as a genteel set of teapot and cups.

The pirate himself was a giant. Even sitting down, he was an imposing figure that struck fear into the hearts of those in attendance. He delicately picked up one of the teacups in his massive hand, raised it to the gathered captains and mates, and said, "Welcome gentlemen!" with a wide smile. "Would you care for a cup of tea?"

3. AFTERNOON TEA

Bartholomew Roberts poured himself a fresh cup, paying those around him no mind as he carefully measured out the smallest bit of sugar to his liking. The sugar was taken from one of the merchants' ships, whose captain would be standing somewhere in that crowd.

Roberts took the cup up to his nose, took a deep inhale as he sampled the notes of spice and black tea leaves and then took a sip. He let out a drawn sigh of satisfaction as he peered over the crowd. "Many thanks to the captain of the *Heaven's Tackle*, you've brought in some exquisite tea." He took another sip. "Or perhaps I should say *heavenly*?" he said with a deep laugh.

Looking over the expressions of those in the crowd, it was difficult to say which of them was the *Heaven's Tackle* captain as several baulked at his jesting. He had hoped for as much. Though he knew with his stature he was an imposing figure, he hoped his demeanour would keep them off guard.

One in the crowd, however, seemed unfazed. A young man stepped forward and crossed his arms. "So are you going to tell us why we're here, or not?"

Roberts looked over at the young man and recognised him as the only one who had dared to fire a cannon at their ship while the others were escaping. Of all those in attendance, that youngster was the only one who held a shred of courage, and so Roberts held a small bit of respect for him.

"Straight to business. I like it," Roberts said as he grinned. "You are all here for a test. You will tell me of your business dealings, where you come from, what you have done to get to where you are, and why you fled your ships today. If I like what I hear, then your ships will be spared."

Before Roberts could call his first captain for questioning, the crowd of them rose up in a clamour. Their voices blended together in their rush to speak with him, all of them trying to figure out what it was they had to say to save their ships. If not for Roberts' men having their rifles trained on the group, they would have probably dared to clamber around him in their eagerness.

Roberts waited until their questions died away, sipping his tea and ignoring them as he did so. Once there was silence again, he turned his attention back to the men. "I will not be able to say just what answers I am looking for to forestall the destruction of your ships; all I will say is to answer truthfully."

"Who do you think you are? God?" The young man from before asked. His arms were folded, and he had a contentious look on his face.

Roberts let out a hearty laugh. "I'm not judging their souls, boy. I'll leave that to Him." He got up and walked over to the young man, and despite Roberts standing a head and a half above him, he didn't cower. "What's your name, boy?"

"James Skyrme," he replied.

"A good name," Roberts said. "I have been pirating for several years, and I haven't met a merchant yet who hadn't deserved what was coming to him."

"You're just a thief. Exodus 20:15, 'Thou shall not steal'."

Roberts raised an eyebrow, not expecting to be the one on the receiving end of a bible quote. Roberts shrugged and shook his head. "If what I'm doing is unjust, then I too will be judged accordingly, after I take my last breath." Roberts pointed to one of the men on the ship, the frail former slave who could speak a little English. "You see that man there? He only speaks a bit of this language, but he was able to tell me how the people who brought him here stole him and many of his family away in the night. That was after they raped his wife, who died of illness on the trip here." Roberts took a breath as he felt his anger rising. That was not the way he wanted to present himself to these men. "'The thief cometh not but for to steal, and to kill, and to destroy: I am come that they might have life, and have it in abundance.'" Roberts made a flourish as he quoted John 10:10, raising his arms towards the slaves aboard that they had just freed.

James gritted his teeth. "So, you don't think yourself God,

but instead a saviour?"

Roberts shook his head. "No, my boy. I don't *think* of myself as anything. I *am* a pirate." He leaned forward and spoke in a whisper that only James and a few close by could hear. "Some time ago, I decided to take on the spirit of a departed friend of mine and vowed to free any slaves I could in his name. If God considers me a thief for stealing back that which was stolen, then so be it. I will hope that the good that I am doing will serve to absolve me of my sins."

Roberts turned away from James and motioned to one of the crewmates. The crewmate nodded and made a signal towards the harbour. Afterwards, he looked through a spyglass, and then said, "It's done."

"Good," Roberts replied. "To the captain of *Brooken*, you have already failed, and so your ship is no more. You may remain ashore the next time I call on the other captains."

The captains looked amongst themselves, trying to identify the captain of *Brooken*, when one of them rushed to the side of the *Fortune*. They all followed the man with their eyes, then they too were looking off towards the harbour where the largest ship was already burning. The fire was growing rapidly, taking over the ship until the light from it was too bright to look at.

The captain of *Brooken* fell to his knees in tears, shock stealing the words from his mouth. Not only had his slaves been freed, but his ship destroyed in front of his eyes.

Roberts thought that this must have been how the captain of *Maîtresse* must have felt, but he shrugged it off and went back to the table where his tea waited for him.

Roberts took a sip of his tea and waited for the captains to turn their attention back to him. After a few moments, after the peripheral shock had worn thin, they turned around to face their captor once again, and this time with a fresh, new type of fear in their eyes.

"Would the captain of *Resolute* please join me?" he said, motioning his hand towards the seat in front of him.

After the interrogation with the pirate captain, the merchant captains and mates went back to a pub in Trepassey to discuss what to do next. They were all given some basic introductory questions from Roberts, but most of what they did for business was left out, which meant that would come later.

"We need a plan," one of the captains suggested.

"What kind of plan?"

"One where we all get out of this with our ships intact, and maybe more." The captain had a sleazy grin on his face as he sat down in the middle of the throng of captains. "This pirate is a godly man, so I say we appeal to his godly nature. Tell him about what good we've done. Tell him about all the charity we do, the sort of sob story he's sure to eat up."

James' captain spoke up next. "I don't know about this," he said. "He doesn't seem like the type that should be lied to. What if he finds out?"

The first captain raised his brow. "Well, that's why we're here making sure we have our stories straight, innit? 'Sides, that negro-lover ain't got his head on straight, so he won't know the difference. Now, here's the plan."

The captains all came close together, listening to the first strong voice that spoke up rather than thinking for themselves. It made James sick, and so he spat and left the tavern to find his crewmates. He knew what to do about the pirate problem, and he knew his mates would have his back when the time came.

4. *GOOD FORTUNE*

Over the course of three days, Roberts continued his interrogation of the merchant captains. Each morning they fired a rifle, and each morning like clockwork they arrived on his ship. Roberts' goal was to stall for time until the slaves were fit to sail, and so he only asked the captains a few questions each as he drank tea. Some questions had to do with their trade, some with their background, and others about the crewmates aboard their ships.

Though Roberts was at times talkative, a trait his crew could attest to, talking with these merchants was tiring. Each one of them was too eager to please him: calling him 'sir', wringing their hands and bowing their heads, giving more information than he had asked for and being extra polite. It was sickening how false they were in front of him. In some it was fear, in others he could tell they had an open disdain for those he'd freed but were trying to hide it to appease him.

After the captains had left on the third day, Roberts let out a long sigh and stretched his hands into the air, arching his sore back. He looked out to the harbour with all the empty ships still floating about. Most of the fishing ships and those who were not anchored down had clustered together on one side of the harbour from the drifting waves, leaving the harbour looking barren and deserted.

Hank came over next to Roberts and leaned forward on the starboard railing. "The crew just finished stripping the merchant ships. We can leave a hefty amount of cargo for the men we freed, and still have a goodly amount for us to sell ourselves. There's almost too much to choose from."

"Aye," Roberts said. "I thought as much. I don't expect us to have such good fortune as this again. Our enemies have done half the work for us."

Hank turned around, and half sat on the railing as he looked at Roberts. "Speaking of the cowards, how is your tea time?" Hank had a small grin on the corners of his lips.

"Exhausting. How much longer until the men are trained and well enough to sail?"

Hank shrugged and shook his head. "They're learning quickly enough, and teaching select people specific tasks is more effective, but it's no small feat to sail a ship. I would want another week, maybe two for them to be fit enough to sail on their own."

Roberts felt a sour taste in his mouth at the prospect of having to entertain talking with the merchants for another seven-to-fourteen days. With that much time on their hands, however, they could do some much-needed repairs on the ship or...

"Perhaps we should use this time to procure ourselves a better ship," Roberts said. He pointed to the largest ship in the harbour, second largest prior to them burning the slaver. It was a two-masted brigantine with ten more guns than the *Fortune* had, a total of twenty-six.

Still half sitting on the railing, Hank looked over his shoulder at the ship Roberts was pointing at. "Aye, that ship would do us well. The extra cannons could provide us better protection. Lord knows we can't expect this to happen again," Hank said with a smirk on his face as he motioned around him.

"Luck comes but once to the unexpectant, and not at all to those who desire it." Roberts stroked his chin for a moment. "I think our new ship deserves a fitting name to match the circumstances around us taking it."

"What were you thinking?"

"How about *Good Fortune*?"

"One—no, two ships approaching from the South-East, Captain!" one of Roberts' men shouted from the port side of their new ship.

Roberts and Hank both looked at the crewmate, then each other, before they dropped what they were doing to look over the side of the ship. Some of the other crewmates joined in as well.

The two ships on approach were still a few hours out from Trepassey, but there was no denying that they were headed their way. The crew was halfway through bringing their belongings over to the *Good Fortune*, having yet to secure the cargo and supplies they had taken from the other ships in the harbour. If they hadn't been so focussed on switching to their new ship, they may have spotted the approaching ships sooner and had more time to prepare.

Roberts took out his spyglass and looked through it. He couldn't make out the flags or the size, but he could tell they were both loaded with cannons. One was a shade bigger, probably an escort for the smaller ship.

"What should we do?" Hank asked. "If we beat to, we could have the ship loaded and ready before they arrive and be on our way."

Roberts gritted his teeth at the thought of running, but it was the safest course of action. Without knowing the size and number of guns the ships had, it was difficult to know how they would fare in a battle.

He looked over his shoulder at the men and women they had set free, watching the sea with fearful eyes. They could take them all on their new ship, but they wouldn't get very far laden down with that many bodies, and that's before taking into account the amount of food they would need and didn't have, or how crowded it would be with over four hundred aboard a brigantine.

"No, we'll take a gamble and fight. I want the guns loaded and at the ready on both the *Fortune* and *Good Fortune*. We might need them both."

Hank nodded and said, "Aye, Captain," before he turned to issue orders to the crew aboard their new ship. He sent runners off on one of the longboats to inform the crew on *Fortune* to ready for battle.

"Now the question is, how do we fight them?" Roberts said out loud.

Roberts pondered the question. Now that the men they had freed were slightly trained, they could help on *Fortune* to do some small manoeuvers, while the bulk of the crew in *Good Fortune* took the fight to the ships. But if they did that it wouldn't be long before they realised the smaller *Fortune* was an easy target and sink it.

If they could get just one of the ships in close enough, the two could fire broadsides at them and might be able to take out the larger escort ship. But how would they lure them in that close? They would of course need to take down their black flags, but the rest of the ships in the harbour were empty of crew. If they saw two ships with a full complement then…

The idea struck Roberts at once. He called for a runner to pass along new orders, and then they prepared for battle.

As the two ships approached, the cannons were loaded and ready, but the two ships under Roberts' command kept the sails lashed and the anchor lowered. When they needed to, it would be a simple thing to cut and run, loose the sails to enter battle.

As the ships approached, most of the crewmates aboard both pirate ships went below deck, with only a scarce few staying atop to watch their approach. Those above hid behind the corners of the ship or the cargo lying about so as not to be seen by the enemy ships.

Roberts stayed above deck, watching as the two ships rose and sunk, their bows crashed against the waves as they approached. When they came closer to harbour and the sails were taken in, the crashing turned into a small chop. The crewmates of both ships were too busy gawking at the myriad empty ships in the harbour to man the sails, and they let the ship go forward on the tide.

The air was still and thick with anticipation. Sweat soaked Roberts' brow as he peered at the approaching ships. He could feel his heart beating sharp and swift in his chest, a thunderous drum that sounded so loud but was only his to hear. He couldn't help but lift his hand up, wooden and stiff, and place it just beneath his throat.

He took a few deep breaths as he watched the larger escort ship inch forward, closer and closer to where they could give them broadsides. It felt as though they should have been close enough already, but they needed to be closer.

Then Roberts locked eyes with one of the enemy crewmates. Roberts' heart stopped, and he clamped his teeth down hard. There was no way the man on the other ship could see him. Was there? He was looking at the ship with eyes unaided by any instrument. But if Roberts could see him, then the opposite was true.

Roberts pried his eyes away from the enemy crewmate and noticed the ship was in position. For a split second, he looked back at the man who spotted him and he noticed a hand outstretched pointing at Roberts—but it was too late.

"Fire starboard!" Roberts shouted so loudly he felt that his other ship, the *Fortune*, could hear as well.

A frantic few heartbeats later and cannon fire thundered from below deck. The noise echoed across the harbour, bouncing off the houses and back before the iron had even smashed into the other ship. The asynchronous snapping of a dozen dozen wooden planks exploding into bits all at once came next as smoke crept up from starboard and billowed on the weather deck. There was a short lull during which Roberts could hear the screams of the panicked and injured before another wave of thunder from the other side of the harbour sounded off.

Roberts ducked down to safety behind the quarterdeck ladder, but nothing happened. Then he realised the second wave of cannon fire had been from the *Fortune*, not the enemy ships. Roberts came out from behind cover as his crew returned above deck, and he saw the larger ship was taking on water, and before long would sink. The two broadsides had crippled it to the point there was no saving it.

Before he could let himself relish in the plan working, he looked south to the smaller ship that the larger one had been escorting. Without protection, it would be easy to take, provided they didn't let it escape.

"Loose the sails! Cut and run!" Roberts shouted before pointing at the small merchant ship. "Don't let that ship leave the harbour!"

The crew went to work, letting the sails down for the wind to take them. Hank ran to port, raised his cutlass above his head, and slammed it down against the anchor's rope. He severed it in two with such force that his cutlass embedded itself in the port railing. The rope tethering the ship in place fell into the drink, and they were free to move.

The small merchant ship had only dropped their sails again by the time *Good Fortune* had begun turning around and into the wind, the suddenness of the attack on their escort no doubt slowing their reaction. *Good Fortune* was beside them before they could turn themselves around. The pirates threw grapples across, and the two ships were secured together.

Gunfire erupted across both ships; the pirates shooting at the merchants trying to cut the lines holding the ships together, and the merchants returning defensive fire.

Black powder, the smell of it burning the nostril, the sound of it piercing the ears, the feel of it kicking the musket against the shoulder. It was all at once old and familiar and exhilarating, and at the same time new and strange and terrifying to Roberts. He was both accustomed to the feeling of battle, and yet it was like sailing into the chaos of a typhoon. There was no telling what would happen, and it was both thrilling and frightening in equal degrees.

The ships were pulled together, partially by the tidal forces, and partially by the grapples. Once close enough, the pirates aboard *Good Fortune* braved the hail of lead to cross the gap and take the fight to the other ship's deck.

Roberts joined his crewmates in leaping across, not looking to the small bit of sea jumping up at them between the ships, and landed on the enemy ship. He drew his cutlass, and from the looks of those aboard, looking up at him and his towering frame, they were afraid. This too, this fear in the eyes of his enemies, was a familiar, exhilarating, and terrifying feeling.

Once Roberts began cutting down the defenders two at a time, it became clear to the rest that continuing the fight was futile. The rest of the crew surrendered and dropped their weapons on the deck of their ship.

Roberts wiped his brow of sweat as he took a few deep breaths and watched the crew of the merchant ship herded to one side. He also noticed some of the men of his own crew were injured and being tended to. Hank was bandaging his arm as blood trailed down it, and his chestnut hair was matted to his forehead. Hank looked up and saw Roberts there, and flashed a devilish grin before going back to his work.

"Men, I want this ship's valuables stripped and moved to *Good Fortune*. She's a touch bare at the moment and needs some new cargo, wouldn't you agree?"

The pirates chuckled and said, "Aye," as they went to work.

In little time they took all the valuables from the merchant ship, leaving a scant few things for those left. The haul they got was better than most of what they were able to salvage from the merchants who'd abandoned ship. Roberts thought it might have been because this ship only just arrived to Trepassey, unlike the others.

As the pirates moved the cargo over, the remaining men from the escort ship had made their way to the merchant ship on longboats. A few of them were armed but threw their weapons away when commanded by Roberts' crew.

The escort ship was still sinking, so there was no way to salvage any of its cargo in time, but Roberts wasn't concerned. With the limited space aboard *Good Fortune* and the other ships they had already pillaged, it wasn't much of a loss.

As the crew were finishing bringing the supplies from the merchant ship over, one of Roberts' crewmates came to get him. "Captain, that kid from before is here. Says he wants to speak with you."

Roberts arched his brow, not remembering who it was his crewmate was referring to. He walked over to the side of the ship, where the young man named James Skyrme was waiting in a longboat with his hands in the air.

Roberts grinned. "Bring him aboard. Let's see what he has to say."

Blackbeard's Blood

"Fire! Fire in the harbour!"

Shouts from the street awoke the merchant captains and crew in Trepassey, and they all left their temporary lodgings to see what the commotion was about. A cursory look at the houses nearby showed no signs of fire or smoke, but the townsfolk rushing to the harbour told the story at once.

In the harbour, the remaining twenty merchant ships were burning. The fires raged so intense that one could feel the heat of the blaze even on land. The only thing stopping it from spreading to the other abandoned ships and threatening the houses were the anchors pinning the ships together, but the ropes wouldn't last long.

The captains of the merchant ships watched as their entire livelihoods went up in a plume of black smoke in front of them. They stared for silent minutes as the citizens shouted and ran to work, taking precautions to save their houses should the fiery cluster of ships move closer inland.

A runner came to them after a time with a letter, and the captains gathered to read it.

To the captains of the merchant ships in Trepassey,

> *You will no doubt find your ships already burning at the arrival of this correspondence and wrongfully come to the conclusion our agreement was broken. This is not so, as I shall explain.*
>
> *Throughout our acquaintances you have all of you lied in one form or another. Whether about your business dealings, or otherwise. You attempted to deceive in an effort to save yourselves, but instead, all of you together assured your ships' destruction.*
>
> *I shall leave you with these parting words from Revelation 21:8:*
>
> *"But the fearful and unbelieving, and the abominable and murderers, and whoremongers, and sorcerers, and idolaters, and all liars shall have their part in the lake which burneth with fire and brimstone, which is the second death."*

Bartholomew Roberts

"I must thank you, young lad," Roberts said as he raised his cup of tea in the air. "Without your help, not only would we still be stuck in Trepassy biding our time to train the former slaves, but I may have missed out on teaching some of those merchants a lesson."

James Skyrme raised his cup as well, and then the two took a few sips. "I couldn't stand by as those bunch of cowards slipped by, lying and cheating again. I thought I'd rather be a pirate than work for any of them again, and some of my mates agreed."

Roberts smiled. "Well, I am certainly glad for the change of heart. If I had to talk with them for another week longer, I'd have needed some stiffer tea." The two men laughed together for a moment and sipped at their not-so-stiff tea once again. "So, have you considered my offer?"

Skyrme lowered his cup onto the saucer nearby. "I have, and I'll accept it. But won't some of your crew be angry?"

Roberts shook his head. "I've already consulted them on the matter, and they agreed to it. All that was left was to see if you wanted the same."

Skyrme raised an eyebrow. "I suppose it's settled then."

Roberts took the last sip from his teacup and rose from his seat. "Are you ready?"

Skyrme nodded and joined Roberts. The two of them headed towards the exit of the *Good Fortune's* cabin, but Skyrme stopped short.

"There was one matter I forgot to ask you about. Would I be able to rename the *Fortune* to the *Ranger?*"

Roberts grinned. "Why, of course," he said as he slapped the young man on his back. "You're her captain now. Just treat her well, that's all I ask."

Skyrme smiled back at Roberts. "Aye, Captain."

Roberts and Skyrme headed out of the cabin and up to the weather deck where some of the crew had gathered. Skyrme was sworn in on the Pirate Commandments under oath with Roberts' bible and then announced to be the new captain of the ship formerly known as *Fortune*. After the ceremony, and a small celebration, Skyrme and his mates headed back to the newly named *Ranger* in a longboat.

Hank joined Roberts in his new cabin after the festivities and the two shared a drink.

"After all this interesting business you'd think you'd be sick of tea," Hank commented.

Roberts laughed. "One would think." Roberts took a sip and admired the flavour. "You are right in that this has been an interesting few weeks."

Hank nodded. "Mayhaps this was our best haul yet, if we don't include your raid of the Portuguese ships."

Roberts grinned and nodded as well. "Yes, that one would be difficult to topple. I suppose I'll simply have to try harder next time." The two had a small chuckle and raised their cups at the prospect. "I know the crew had a discussion already about it, but I do hope you're not angered that I made that young man captain. I feel your daily council is something I cannot do without."

"No need to trouble yourself on it. I don't want to be captain. Too much responsibility, if you ask me," Hank said, and waved his hand as though waving away smoke.

"You sound like someone I once knew."

Hank leaned forward. "Aye, I knew that man too," he said. "I think his name used to be John, as I recall. And that same man became the best damn captain there was. I'd have it no other way."

The two smiled and raised their cups once again before enjoying a few minutes of congenial silence as the ship bobbed up and down against the waves.

Once more, Roberts' thoughts turned to his old friend Talib, and he wondered if he was doing right by him. Whether it was righteous to steal from the wicked he knew not, but he would continue on regardless. *Once I take on my old name and meet with you again, Talib, I'll know then whether what I've done is righteous. Until then, this shall be my penance.*

When the tea was finished, Hank rose from his chair. "Suppose I'll have a bit of a rest," he said. "Where are we headed to next, you figure?"

Roberts leaned back in his chair and looked off into space. "I suppose we should unload our cargo somewhere south. Once our guests are fully trained, we can secure them their own ship elsewhere to head back to their homeland in."

Hank raised his brow. "South? Back to the Caribbean?"

Roberts nodded, and he couldn't hold back a grin. "It's been some time since we've been there. I'm interested to see what's happened since we've been gone."

Hank grinned as well, the both of them knowing that the true purpose was to check in on an old, estranged friend. Roberts hoped beyond hope that that old friend might be a different man than when he last left, and if so, he hoped beyond hope that they might rekindle that friendship once again.

Proverbs 10:28: "The patient abiding of the righteous shall be gladness…"

THE END

OTHER BOOKS
BY THE AUTHOR

The Voyages of Queen Anne's Revenge Series:

BLACKBEARD'S FREEDOM

BLACKBEARD'S REVENGE

BLACKBEARD'S JUSTICE

BLACKBEARD'S FAMILY

The Pirate Priest Series:

BARTHOLOMEW ROBERTS' FAITH

BARTHOLOMEW ROBERTS' JUSTICE

BARTHOLOMEW ROBERTS' MERCY

BARTHOLOMEW ROBERTS' SPIRIT

The Collection Series:

BLACKBEARD'S SHIP (Includes Books 1&2 of The Voyages of Queen Anne's Revenge & The Pirate Priest)

BLACKBEARD'S BLOOD (Includes Books 3&4 of The Voyages of Queen Anne's Revenge & The Pirate Priest)

ABOUT THE AUTHOR

JEREMY IS CURRENTLY LIVING IN NEW BRUNSWICK, CANADA WITH HIS WIFE HEATHER, AND THEIR TWO CATS, NAVI AND THOR.

Jeremy's first foray into the writing world was during a writing competition called NaNoWriMo, where the goal is to write a certain number of words in the month of November.

After completing the novel he started, and some extensive rewrites, he felt it was worthy of publishing and self-published his first novel, Blackbeard's Freedom in September, 2012.

After writing over ten books under two names, his passion for writing hasn't wavered over the years, and hopes to one day make it his primary career.

Let everyone know what you thought of his novels by leaving a review. He loves getting feedback on his books, and loves to hear from fans of his work.

Want to pirate one of Jeremy's novels? Visit http://www.mcleansnovels.com/free-book-link for a free copy of one of his books.